REMAKING HISTORY AND OTHER STORIES

By Kim Stanley Robinson from Tom Doherty Associates

The Blind Geometer
Escape from Kathmandu
Future Primitive: The New Ecotopias
The Gold Coast
Green Mars
Icehenge
The Memory of Whiteness
Pacific Edge
The Planet on the Table
Remaking History
A Short, Sharp Shock

Remaking History

and Other Stories

Kim Stanley Robinson

TOM DOHERTY ASSOCIATES, INC.
NEW YORK, N.Y.

REMAKING HISTORY AND OTHER STORIES

This book is an omnibus edition, consisting of the short fiction collections *The Planet on the Table*, copyright © 1986 by Kim Stanley Robinson, first Tor edition July 1986, and *Remaking History*, copyright © 1991 by Kim Stanley Robinson, first Tor edition December 1991.

An Orb Edition
Published by Tom Doherty Associates, Inc.
175 Fifth Avenue
New York, N.Y. 10010

ISBN 0-312-89012-5

First Orb edition: October 1994

Printed in the United States of America

0 9 8 7 6 5 4 3 2 1

Acknowledgments

"Venice Drowned" © 1981 by Terry Carr. *Universe 11*

"Mercurial" © 1985 by Terry Carr. *Universe 15*

"Ridge Running" © 1984 by The Mercury Press. *The Magazine of Fantasy and Science Fiction*

"The Disguise" © 1977 by Damon Knight. *Orbit 19*

"The Lucky Strike" © 1984 by Terry Carr. *Universe 14*

"Coming Back to Dixieland" © 1976 by Damon Knight. *Orbit 18*

"Stone Eggs" © 1983 by Terry Carr. *Universe 13*

"Black Air" © 1983 by The Mercury Press. *The Magazine of Fantasy and Science Fiction*

"The Part of Us That Loves" was originally published in *Full Spectrum II*, edited by Lou Aronica and Shawna McCarthy, copyright © 1989. The story has been revised for this edition.

"The Translator" was originally published in *Universe I*, edited by Robert Silverberg and Karen Haber, copyright © 1990.

"Before I Wake" was originally published in *Interzone*, © 1989.

"A History of the Twentieth Century, with Illustrations" was originally published in *Isaac Asimov's Science Fiction Magazine*, copyright © 1991. The story has been revised for this edition.

Contents

The
Planet
on the
Table

Venice Drowned

By the time Carlo Tafur struggled out of sleep, the baby was squalling, the teapot whistled, the smell of stove smoke filled the air. Wavelets slapped the walls of the floor below. It was just dawn. Reluctantly he untangled himself from the bedsheets and got up. He padded through the other room of his home, ignoring his wife and child, and walked out the door onto the roof.

Venice looked best at dawn, Carlo thought as he pissed into the canal. In the dim mauve light it was possible to imagine that the city was just as it always had been, that hordes of visitors would come flooding down the Grand Canal on this fine summer morning. . . . Of course, one had to ignore the patchwork constructions built on the roofs of the neighborhood to indulge the fancy. Around the church—San Giacomo du Rialto—all the buildings had even their top floors awash, and so it had been necessary to break up the tile roofs, and erect shacks on the roofbeams made of materials fished up from below: wood, brick, lath, stone, metal, glass. Carlo's home was one of these shacks, made of a crazy combination of wood beams, stained glass from San Giacometta, and drainpipes beaten flat. He looked back at it and sighed. It was best to look off over the Rialto, where the red sun blazed over the bulbous domes of San Marco.

"You have to meet those Japanese today," Carlo's wife, Luisa, said from inside.

"I know." Visitors still came to Venice, that was certain.

"And don't go insulting them and rowing off without your pay," she went on, her voice sounding clearly out of the doorway, "like you did with those Hungarians. It really doesn't matter what they take from under the water, you know. That's the past. That old stuff isn't doing anyone any good under there, anyway."

"Shut up," he said wearily. "I know."

"I have to buy stovewood and vegetables and toilet paper and socks for the baby," she said. "The Japanese are the best customers you've got; you'd better treat them well."

Carlo reentered the shack and walked into the bedroom to dress. Between putting on one boot and the next he stopped to smoke a cigarette, the last one in the house. While smoking he stared at his pile of books on the floor, his library as Luisa sardonically called the collection: all books about Venice. They were tattered, dog-eared, mildewed, so warped by the damp that none of them would close properly, and each moldy page was as wavy as the Lagoon on a windy day. They were a miserable sight, and Carlo gave the closest stack a kick with his cold boot as he returned to the other room.

"I'm off," he said, giving his baby and then Luisa a kiss. "I'll be back late—they want to go to Torcello."

"What could they want up there?"

He shrugged. "Maybe just to see it." He ducked out the door.

Below the roof was a small square where the boats of the neighborhood were moored. Carlo slipped off the tile onto the narrow floating dock he and the neighbors had built, and crossed to his boat, a wide-beamed sailboat with a canvas deck. He stepped in, unmoored it, and rowed out of the square onto the Grand Canal.

Once on the Grand Canal he tipped the oars out of the water and let the boat drift downstream. The big canal had always been the natural course of the channel through the mud flats of the Lagoon; for a while it had been tamed, but now it was a river again, its banks made of tile rooftops and stone palaces, with hundreds of tributaries flowing into it. Men were working on roof-houses in the early morning light. Those who knew Carlo waved, hammers or rope in hand, and shouted hello. Carlo wiggled an oar perfunctorily before he was swept past. It was foolish to build so close to the Grand Canal, which now had the strength to knock the old structures down, and often did. But that was their business. In Venice they were all fools, if one thought about it.

Then he was in the Basin of San Marco, and he rowed through the Piazetta beside the Doges' Palace, which was still imposing at two stories high, to the Piazza. Traffic was heavy as usual. It was the only place in Venice that still had the crowds of old, and Carlo enjoyed it for that reason, though he shouted curses as loudly as anyone when gondolas streaked in front of him. He jockeyed his way to the basilica window and rowed in.

Under the brilliant blue and gold of the domes it was noisy. Most of the water in the rooms had been covered with a floating dock. Carlo moored his boat to it, heaved his four scuba tanks on, and clambered up after them. Carrying two tanks in each hand he crossed the dock, on which the fish market was in full swing. Displayed for sale were flats of mullet, lagoon sharks, tunny, skates, and flatfish. Clams were piled in trays, their shells gleaming in the shaft of sunlight from the stained-glass east window; men and women pulled live crabs out of holes in the dock, risking fingers in the crab-jammed traps; fishermen bawled out prices, and insulted the freshness of their neighbors' product.

In the middle of the fish market, Ludovico Salerno, one of Carlo's best friends, had his stalls of scuba gear. Carlo's two Japanese customers were there. He greeted them and handed his tanks to Salerno, who began refilling them from his machine. They conversed in quick, slangy Italian while the tanks filled. When they were done, Carlo paid him and led the Japanese back to his boat. They got in and stowed their backpacks under the canvas decking while Carlo pulled the scuba tanks on board.

"We are ready to voyage at Torcello?" one asked, and the other smiled and repeated the question. Their names were Hamada and Taku. They had made a few jokes concerning the latter name's similarity to Carlo's own, but Taku was the one with less Italian, so the sallies hadn't gone on for long. They had hired him four days before, at Salerno's stall.

"Yes," Carlo said. He rowed out of the Piazza and up back canals past Campo San Maria Formosa, which was nearly as crowded as the Piazza. Beyond that the canals were empty, and only an occasional roof-house marred the look of flooded tranquility.

"That part of city Venice here not many people live," Hamada observed. "Not houses on houses."

"That's true," Carlo replied. As he rowed past San Zanipolo and the hospital, he explained, "It's too close to the hospital here, where many diseases were contained. Sicknesses, you know."

"Ah, the hospital!" Hamada nodded, as did Taku. "We have swam hospital in our Venice voyage previous to that one here. Salvage many fine statues from lowest rooms."

"Stone lions," Taku added. "Many stone lions with wings in room below Twenty-forty waterline."

"Is that right," Carlo said. Stone lions, he thought, set up in the entryway of some Japanese businessman's expensive

home around the world. . . . He tried to divert his thoughts
by watching the brilliantly healthy, masklike faces of his two
passengers as they laughed over their reminiscences.

Then they were over the Fondamente Nuova, the northern
limit of the city, and on the Lagoon. There was a small swell
from the north. Carlo rowed out a way and then stepped
forward to raise the boat's single sail. The wind was from the
east, so they would make good time north to Torcello. Behind them Venice looked beautiful in the morning light, as if
they were miles away, and a watery horizon blocked their
full view of it.

The two Japanese had stopped talking and were looking
over the side. They were over the cemetery of San Michele,
Carlo realized. Below them lay the island that had been the
city's chief cemetery for centuries; they sailed over a field of
tombs, mausoleums, gravestones, obelisks that at low tide
could be a navigational hazard. . . . Just enough of the bizarre white blocks could be seen to convince one that they
were indeed the result of the architectural thinking of fishes.
Carlo crossed himself quickly to impress his customers, and
sat back down at the tiller. He pulled the sail tight and they
heeled over slightly, slapped into the waves.

In no more than twenty minutes they were east of Murano,
skirting its edge. Murano, like Venice an island city crossed
with canals, had been a quaint little town before the flood.
But it didn't have as many tall buildings as Venice, and it
was said that an underwater river had undercut its islands.
In any case, it was a wreck. The two Japanese chattered with
excitement.

"Can we visit to that city here, Carlo?" asked Hamada.

"It's too dangerous," Carlo answered. "Buildings have
fallen into the canal."

They nodded, smiling. "Are people live here?" Taku
asked.

"A few, yes. They live in the highest buildings on the

floors still above water, and work in Venice. That way they avoid having to build a roof-house in the city.''

The two faces of his companions expressed incomprehension. ''They avoid the housing shortage in Venice,'' Carlo said. ''There's a certain housing shortage in Venice, as you may have noticed.'' His listeners caught the joke this time and laughed.

''Could live on floors below if owning scuba such as that here,'' Hamada said, gesturing at Carlo's equipment.

''Yes,'' he replied. ''Or we could grow gills.'' He bugged his eyes out and wiggled his fingers at his neck to indicate gills. The Japanese loved it.

Past Murano the Lagoon was clear for a few miles, a sunbeaten blue covered with choppy waves. The boat tipped up and down, the wind tugged at the sail cord in Carlo's hand. He began to enjoy himself. ''Storm coming,'' he volunteered to the others, and pointed at the black line over the horizon to the north. It was a common sight; short, violent storms swept over Brenner Pass from the Austrian Alps, dumping on the Po Valley and the Lagoon before dissipating in the Adriatic . . . once a week, or more, even in the summer. That was one reason the fish market was held under the domes of San Marco; everyone had gotten sick of trading in the rain.

Even the Japanese recognized the clouds. ''Many rain fall soon here,'' Taku said.

Hamada grinned and said, ''Taku and Tafur, weather prophets no doubt, make big company!''

They laughed. ''Does he do this in Japan, too?'' Carlo asked.

''Yes, indeed, surely. In Japan rains every day—Taku says, 'It rains tomorrow for surely.' Weather prophet!''

After the laughter receded, Carlo said, ''Hasn't all the rain drowned some of your cities too?''

''What's that here?''

"Don't you have some Venices in Japan?"

But they didn't want to talk about that. "I don't understand . . . No, no Venice in Japan," Hamada said easily, but neither laughed as they had before. They sailed on. Venice was out of sight under the horizon, as was Murano. Soon they would reach Burano. Carlo guided the boat over the waves and listened to his companions converse in their improbable language, or mangle Italian in a way that alternately made him want to burst with hilarity or bite the gunwale with frustration.

Gradually Burano bounced over the horizon, the campanile first, followed by the few buildings still above water. Murano still had inhabitants, a tiny market, even a midsummer festival; Burano was empty. Its campanile stood at a distinct angle, like the mast of a foundered ship. It had been an island town, before 2040; now it had "canals" between every rooftop. Carlo disliked the town intensely and gave it a wide berth. His companions discussed it quietly in Japanese.

Just beyond it was Torcello, another island ghost town. The campanile could be seen from Burano, tall and white against the black clouds to the north. They approached in silence. Carlo took down the sail, set Taku in the bow to look for snags, and rowed cautiously to the edge of town. They moved between rooftops and walls that stuck up like reefs or like old foundations out of the earth. Many of the roof tiles and beams had been taken for use in construction back in Venice. This had happened to Torcello before. During the Renaissance it had been a little rival of Venice, boasting a population of twenty thousand, but during the sixteenth and seventeenth centuries it had been entirely deserted. Builders from Venice had come looking in the ruins for good marble or a staircase of the right dimensions. . . . Briefly a tiny population had returned, to make lace and host those tourists who wanted to be melancholy; but the waters rose, and Torcello died for good. Carlo pushed off a wall with his oar, and a big section of it tilted over and sank. He tried not to notice.

He rowed them to the open patch of water that had been the Piazza. Around them stood a few intact rooftops, no taller than the mast of their boat; broken walls of stone or rounded brick; the shadowy suggestion of walls just underwater. It was hard to tell what the street plan of the town would have been. On one side of the Piazza was the cathedral of Santa Maria Assunta, however, still supporting the white campanile that stood square and solid, as if over a living community.

"That here is the church we desire to dive," Hamada said.

Carlo nodded. The amusement he had felt during the sail was entirely gone. He rowed around the Piazza looking for a flat spot where they could stand and put on the scuba gear. The church outbuildings—it had been an extensive structure—were all underwater. At one point the boat's keel scraped the ridge of a roof. They rowed down the length of the barnlike nave, looked in the high windows: floored with water. No surprise. One of the small windows in the side of the campanile had been widened with sledgehammers. Directly inside it was the stone staircase and, a few steps up, a stone floor. They hooked the boat to the wall and moved their gear up to the floor. In the dim midday light the stone of the interior was pocked with shadows. It had a rough-hewn look. The citizens of Torcello had built the campanile in a hurry, thinking that the world would end at the millennium, the year 1000. Carlo smiled to think how much longer they had had than that. They climbed the steps of the staircase, up to the sudden sunlight of the bell chamber, to look around; viewed Burano, Venice in the distance . . . to the north, the shallows of the Lagoon, and the coast of Italy. Beyond that, the black line of clouds was like a wall nearly submerged under the horizon, but it was rising; the storm would come.

They descended, put on the scuba gear, and flopped into the water beside the campanile. They were above the complex of church buildings, and it was dark. Carlo slowly led the two Japanese back into the Piazza and swam down. The ground was silted, and Carlo was careful not to step on it. His charges saw the great stone chair in the center of the Piazza (it had been called the Throne of Attila, Carlo remembered from one of his moldy books, and no one had known why), and waving to each other they swam to it. One of them made ludicrous attempts to stand on the bottom and walk around in his fins; he threw up clouds of silt. The other joined him. They each sat in the stone chair, columns of bubbles rising from them, and snapped pictures of each other with their underwater cameras. The silt would ruin the shots, Carlo thought. While they cavorted, he wondered sourly what they wanted in the church.

Eventually, Hamada swam up to him and gestured at the church. Behind the mask his eyes were excited. Carlo pumped his fins up and down slowly and led them around to the big entrance at the front. The doors were gone. They swam into the church.

Inside it was dark, and all three of them unhooked their big flashlights and turned them on. Cones of murky water turned to crystal as the beams swept about. The interior of the church was undistinguished, the floor thick with mud. Carlo watched his two customers swim about and let his flashlight beam rove the walls. Some of the underwater windows were still intact, an odd sight. Occasionally the beam caught a column of bubbles, transmuting them to silver.

Quickly enough the Japanese went to the picture at the west end of the nave, a tile mosaic. Taku (Carlo guessed) rubbed the slime off the tiles, vastly improving their color. They had gone to the big one first, the one portraying the Crucifixion, the Resurrection of the Dead, and the Day of Judgement. A busy mural. Carlo swam over to have a better look. But no sooner had the Japanese wiped the wall clean than they were off to the other end of the church, where above the stalls of the apse was another mosaic. Carlo followed.

It didn't take long to rub this one clean; and when the water had cleared, the three of them floated there, their flashlight beams converged on the picture revealed.

It was the Teotaca Madonna, the God-bearer. She stood against a dull gold background, holding the Child in her arms, staring out at the world with a sad and knowing gaze. Carlo pumped his legs to get above the Japanese, holding his light steady on the Madonna's face. She looked as though she could see all time: all her child's short life, all the terror and calamity after that. . . . There were mosaic tears on her cheeks. At the sight of them, Carlo could barely check tears of his own from joining the general wetness on his face. He felt that he had suddenly been transposed to a church on the deepest floor of the ocean, the pressure of his feelings threatened to implode him, he could scarcely hold them off. The water was freezing, he was shivering, sending up a thick, nearly continuous stream of bubbles . . . and the Madonna watched. With a kick he turned and swam away. Like startled fish his two companions followed him. Carlo led them out of the church into murky light, then up to the surface, to the boat and the window casement.

Fins off, Carlo sat on the staircase and dripped. Taku and Hamada scrambled through the window and joined him. They conversed for a moment in Japanese, clearly excited. Carlo stared at them blackly.

Hamada turned to him. "That here is the picture we desire," he said. "The Madonna with Child."

"What?" Carlo cried.

Hamada raised his eyebrows. "We desire taking home that here picture to Japan."

"But it's impossible! The picture is made of little tiles stuck to the wall—there's no way to get them off!"

"Italy government permits," Taku said, but Hamada silenced him with a gesture.

"Mosaic, yes. We use instruments we take here—water torch. Archaeology method, you understand. Cut blocks out of wall, bricks, number them—construct on new place in Japan. Above water." He flashed his pearly smile.

"You can't do that," Carlo stated, deeply affronted.

"I don't understand." Hamada said. But he did. "Italian government permits us that."

"This isn't Italy," Carlo said savagely, and in his anger stood. What good would a Madonna do in Japan, anyway? They weren't even Christian. "Italy is over there," he said, in his excitement mistakenly waving to the southeast, no doubt confusing his listeners even more. "This has never been Italy! This is Venice! The Republic!"

"I don't understand." He had that phrase down pat. "Italian government has giving permit us."

"Christ," Carlo said. After a disgusted pause: "Just how long will this take?"

"Time? We work that afternoon, tomorrow; place the bricks here, go hire Venice barge to carry bricks to Venice—"

"Stay here overnight? I'm not going to stay here overnight, God damn it!"

"We bring sleeping bag for you—"

"No!" Carlo was furious. "I'm not staying, you miserable heathen hyenas—" He pulled off his scuba gear.

"I don't understand."

Carlo dried off, got dressed. "I'll let you keep your scuba tanks, and I'll be back for you tomorrow afternoon, late. *Understand?*"

"Yes," Hamada said, staring at him steadily, without expression. "Bring barge?"

"What?—yes, yes, I'll bring your barge, you miserable slime-eating catfish. Vultures . . ." He went on for a while, getting the boat out of the window.

"Storm coming!" Taku said brightly, pointing to the north.
"To hell with you!" Carlo said, pushing off and beginning
to row. "Understand?"

He rowed out of Torcello and back onto the Lagoon.
Indeed, a storm was coming. He would have to hurry. He put
up the sail and pulled the canvas decking back until it covered everything but the seat he was sitting on. The wind was
from the north now, strong but fitful. It pulled the sail taut,
and the boat bucked over the choppy waves, leaving behind a
wake that was bright white against the black of the sky. The
clouds were drawing over the sky like a curtain, covering
half of it: half black, half colorless blue, and the line of the
edge was solid. It resembled that first great storm of 2040,
Carlo guessed, that had pulled over Venice like a black wool
blanket and dumped water for forty days. And it had never
been the same again, not anywhere in the world. . . .

Now he was beside the wreck of Burano. Against the black
sky he could see only the drunken campanile, and suddenly
he realized why he hated the sight of this abandoned town: it
was a vision of the Venice to come, a cruel model of the
future. If the water level rose even three meters, Venice
would become nothing but a big Burano. Even if the water
didn't rise, more people were leaving Venice every year. . . .
One day it would be empty. Once again the sadness he had
felt looking at the Teotaca filled him, a sadness become a
bottomless despair. "God damn it," he said, staring at the
crippled campanile; but that wasn't enough. He didn't know
words that were enough. "God *damn* it."

Just beyond Burano the squall hit. It almost blew the sail
out of his hand; he had to hold on with a fierce clench, tie it
to the stern, tie the tiller in place, and scramble over the
pitching canvas deck to lower the sail, cursing all the while.
He brought the sail down to its last reefing, which left a
handkerchief-sized patch exposed to the wind. Even so, the
boat yanked over the waves and the mast creaked as if it

would tear loose. . . . The choppy waves had become white-caps, in the screaming wind their tops were tearing loose and flying through the air, white foam in the blackness. . . .

Best to head for Murano for refuge, Carlo thought. Then the rain started. It was colder than the Lagoon water and fell almost horizontally. The wind was still picking up. His hand-kerchief sail was going to pull the mast out. "Madonna," he said. He got onto the decking again, slid up to the mast, took down the sail with cold and disobedient fingers. He crawled back to his hole in the deck, hanging on desperately as the boat yawed. It was almost broadside to the waves and hastily he grabbed the tiller and pulled it around, just in time to meet a large wave stern-on. He shuddered with relief. Each wave seemed bigger than the last; they picked up quickly on the Lagoon. Well, he thought, what now? Get out the oars? No, that wouldn't do; he had to keep stern-on to the waves, and besides, he couldn't row effectively in this chop. He had to go where the waves were going, he realized; and if they missed Murano and Venice, that meant the Adriatic.

As the waves lifted and dropped him, he grimly contem-plated the thought. His mast alone acted like a sail in a wind of this force; and the wind seemed to be blowing from a bit to the west of north. The waves—the biggest he had ever seen on the Lagoon, perhaps the biggest *ever* on the Lagoon—pushed in about the same direction as the wind, naturally. Well, that meant he would miss Venice, which was directly south, maybe even a touch west of south. Damn, he thought. And all because he had been angered by those two Japanese and the Teotaca. What did he care what happened to a sunken mosaic from Torcello? He had helped foreigners find and cart off the one bronze horse of San Marco that had fallen . . . more than one of the stone lions of Venice, symbol of the city . . . the entire Bridge of Sighs, for Christ's sake! What had come over him? Why should he have cared about a forgotten mosaic?

Well, he had done it; and here he was. No altering it. Each wave lifted his boat stern first and slid under it until he could look down in the trough, if he cared to, and see his mast nearly horizontal, until he rose over the broken, foaming crest, each one of which seemed to want to break down his little hole in the decking and swamp him—for a second he was in midair, the tiller free and useless until he crashed into the next trough. Every time at the top he thought, this wave will catch us, and so even though he was wet and the wind and rain were cold, the repeated spurts of fear adrenaline and his thick wool coat kept him warm. A hundred waves or so served to convince him that the next one would probably slide under him as safely as the last, and he relaxed a bit. Nothing to do but wait it out, keep the boat exactly stern-on to the swell . . . and he would be all right. Sure, he thought, he would just ride these waves across the Adriatic to Trieste or Rijeka, one of those two tawdry towns that had replaced Venice as Queen of the Adriatic . . . the princesses of the Adriatic, so to speak, and two little sluts they were, too. . . . Or ride the storm out, turn around, and sail back in, better yet. . . .

On the other hand, the Lido had become a sort of reef, in most places, and waves of this size would break over it, capsizing him for sure. And, to be realistic, the top of the Adriatic was wide. Just one mistake on the top of these waves (and he couldn't go on forever) and he would be broached, capsized, and rolled down to join all the other Venetians who had ended up on the bottom of the Adriatic. And all because of that damn Madonna. Carlo sat crouched in the stern, adjusting the tiller for the particulars of each wave, ignoring all else in the howling, black, horizonless chaos of water and air around him, pleased in a grim way that he was sailing to his death with such perfect seamanship. But he kept the Lido out of mind.

And so he sailed on, losing track of time as one does when

there is no spatial referent. Wave after wave after wave. A little water collected at the bottom of his boat, and his spirits sank. That was no way to go, to have the boat sink by degrees under him. . . .

Then the high-pitched, airy howl of the wind was joined by a low booming, a bass roar. He looked over his shoulder in the direction he was being driven and saw a white line, stretching from left to right; his heart jumped, fear exploded through him. This was it. The Lido, now a barrier reef tripping the waves. They were smashing down on it, he could see white sheets bouncing skyward and blowing to nothing. He was terrifically frightened. It would have been so much easier to founder at sea.

But there—among the white breakers, off to the right—a gray finger pointing up at the black—

A campanile. Carlo was forced to look back at the wave he was under, to straighten the boat, but when he looked back it was still there. A campanile, standing there like a dead lighthouse. "Jesus!" he said aloud. It looked as if the waves were pushing him a couple hundred meters to the north of it. As each wave lifted him he had a moment when the boat was sliding down the face of the wave as fast as it was moving under him; during these moments he shifted the tiller a bit and the boat turned and surfed across the face, to the south, until the wave rose up under him to the crest, and he had to straighten it out. He repeated the delicate operation time after time, sometimes nearly broaching the boat in his impatience. But that wouldn't do—just take as much from each wave as it will give you, he thought. And pray it will add up to enough.

The Lido got closer, and it looked as if he was directly upwind of the campanile. It was the one at the Lido channel entrance, or perhaps the one at Pellestrina, farther south; he had no way of knowing, and at the moment didn't care. He was just happy that his ancestors had seen fit to construct such solid bell towers. In between waves he reached under the decking and by touch found his boat hook and the length of rope he carried. It was going to be a problem, actually, when he got to the campanile—it would not do to pass it helplessly by a few meters. On the other hand he couldn't smash into it and expect to survive either, not in these waves. In fact the more he considered it, the more exact and difficult he realized the approach would have to be, and fearfully he stopped thinking about it and concentrated on the waves.

The last one was the biggest. As the boat slid down its face, the face got steeper, until it seemed they would be swept on by this wave forever. The campanile loomed ahead, big and black. Around it waves pitched over and broke with sharp, deadly booms; from behind Carlo could see the water sucked over the breaks, as if over short but infinitely broad waterfalls. The noise was tremendous. At the top of the wave it appeared he could jump in the campanile's top windows—he got out the boat hook, shifted the tiller a touch, took a deep breath. Amid the roaring, the wave swept him just past the stone tower, smacking against it and splashing him; he pulled the tiller over hard, the boat shot into the wake of the campanile—he stood and swung the boat hook over a window casement above him. It caught, and he held on hard.

He was in the lee of the tower. Broken water rose and dropped under the boat, hissing, but without violence, and he held. One-handed, he wrapped the end of his rope around the sail-cord bolt in the stern, tied the other end to the boat hook. The hook held pretty well. He took a risk and reached down to tie the rope firmly to the bolt. Then another risk: when the boiling soupy water of another broken wave raised the boat, he leaped off his seat, grabbed the stone windowsill, which was too thick to get his fingers over—for a moment he hung by his fingertips. With desperate strength he pulled himself up, reached in with one hand and got a grasp on the inside of the sill, and pulled himself in and over. The stone floor was about four feet below the window. Quickly he pulled the boat hook in, put it on the floor, and took up the slack in the rope. He looked out the window. His boat rose and fell, rose and fell. Well, it would sink or it wouldn't. Meanwhile, he was safe. Realizing this, he breathed deeply, let out a shout. He remembered shooting past the side of the tower, face no more than two meters from it—getting drenched by the wave slapping the front of it—why, he had done it perfectly! He couldn't do it again like that in a million tries. Triumphant laughs burst out of him, short and sharp: "Ha! Ha! Ha! Jesus Christ! Wow!"

"Whoooo's theeeerre?" called a high scratchy voice, floating down the staircase from the floor above. "Whooooooooo's there? . . ."

Carlo froze. He stepped lightly to the base of the stone staircase and peered up. Through the hole to the next floor flickered a faint light. To put it better, it was less dark up there than anywhere else. More surprised than fearful (though he was afraid), Carlo opened his eyes as wide as he could—

"Whoooooo's theeeeeerrrrrre? . . ."

Quickly he went to the boat hook, untied the rope, felt around on the wet floor until he found a block of stone that would serve as anchor for his boat. He looked out the window: boat still there; on both sides, white breakers crashing over the Lido. Taking up the boat hook, Carlo stepped slowly up the stairs, feeling that after what he had been through he could slash any ghost in the ether to ribbons.

It was a candle lantern, flickering in the disturbed air—a room filled with junk—

"Eeek! Eeek!"

"Jesus!"

"Devil! Death, away!" A small black shape rushed at him, brandishing sharp metal points.

"Jesus!" Carlo repeated, holding the boat hook out to defend himself. The figure stopped.

"Death comes for me at last," it said. It was an old woman, he saw, holding lace needles in each hand.

"Not at all," Carlo said, feeling his pulse slow back down. "Swear to God, Grandmother, I'm just a sailor, blown here by the storm."

The woman pulled back the hood of her black cape, revealing braided white hair, and squinted at him.

"You've got the scythe," she said suspiciously. A few wrinkles left her face as she unfocused her gaze.

"A boat hook only," Carlo said, holding it out for her inspection. She stepped back and raised the lace needles threateningly. "Just a boat hook, I swear to God. To God and Mary and Jesus and all the saints, Grandmother. I'm just a sailor, blown here by the storm from Venice." Part of him felt like laughing.

"Aye?" she said. "Aye, well then, you've found shelter. I don't see so well anymore, you know. Come in, sit down, then." She turned around and led him into the room. "I was just doing some lace for penance, you see . . . though there's scarcely enough light." She lifted a tomboli with the lace pinned to it. Carlo noticed big gaps in the pattern, as in the webs of an injured spider. "A little more light," she said and, picking up a candle, held it to the lit one. When it was fired, she carried it around the chamber and lit three more candles in lanterns that stood on tables, boxes, a wardrobe. She motioned for him to sit in a heavy chair by her table, and he did so.

As she sat down across from him, he looked around the chamber. A bed piled high with blankets, boxes and tables covered with objects . . . the stone walls around, and another staircase leading up to the next floor of the campanile. There was a draft. "Take off your coat," the woman said. She arranged the little pillow on the arm of her chair and began to poke a needle in and out of it, pulling the thread slowly.

Carlo sat back and watched her. "Do you live here alone?"

"Always alone," she replied. "I don't want it otherwise." With the candle before her face, she resembled Carlo's mother or someone else he knew. It seemed very peaceful in the room after the storm. The old woman bent in her chair until her face was just above her tomboli; still, Carlo couldn't help noticing that her needle hit far outside the apparent pattern of lace, striking here and there randomly. She might as well have been blind. At regular intervals Carlo shuddered with excitement and tension. It was hard to believe he was out of danger. More infrequently they broke the silence with a short burst of conversation, then sat in the candlelight absorbed in their own thoughts, as if they were old friends.

"How do you get food?" Carlo asked, after one of these silences had stretched out. "Or candles?"

"I trap lobsters down below. And fishermen come by and trade food for lace. They get a good bargain, never fear. I've never given less, despite what he said—" Anguish twisted her face as the squinting had, and she stopped. She needled furiously, and Carlo looked away. Despite the draft, he was warming up (he hadn't removed his coat, which was wool, after all), and he was beginning to feel drowsy. . . .

"He was my spirit's mate, do you comprehend me?"

Carlo jerked upright. The old woman still looked at her tomboli.

"And—and he left me here, here in this desolation when the floods began, with words that I'll remember forever and ever and ever. Until death comes . . . I wish you *had* been death!" she cried. "I wish you had."

Carlo remembered her brandishing the needles. "What is this place?" he asked gently.

"What?"

"Is this Pellestrina? San Servolo?"

"This is Venice," she said.

Carlo shivered convulsively, stood up.

"I'm the last one of them," the woman said. "The waters

rise, the heavens howl, love's pledges crack and lead to misery. I—I live to show what a person can bear and not die. I'll live till the deluge drowns the world as Venice is drowned; I'll live till all else living is dead; I'll live . . ." Her voice trailed off; she looked up at Carlo curiously. "Who are you, really? Oh, I know. I know. A sailor."

"Are there floors above?" he asked, to change the subject. She squinted at him. Finally she spoke. "Words are vain. I thought I'd never speak again, not even to my own heart, and here I am, doing it again. Yes, there's a floor above intact; but above that, ruins. Lightning blasted the bell chamber apart, while I lay in that very bed." She stood up. "Come on, I'll show you." Under her cape she was tiny.

She picked up the candle lantern beside her, and Carlo followed her up the stairs, stepping carefully in the shifting shadows.

On the floor above, the wind swirled, and through the stairway to the floor above that, he could distinguish black clouds. The woman put the lantern on the floor, started up the stairs. "Come."

Once through the hole they were in the wind, out under the sky. The rain had stopped. Great blocks of stone lay about the floor, and the walls broke off unevenly.

"I thought the whole campanile would fall," she shouted at him over the whistle of the wind. He nodded, and walked over to the west wall, which stood chest high. Looking over it, he could see the waves approaching, rising up, smashing against the stone below, spraying back and up at him. He could feel the blows in his feet. Their force frightened him; it was hard to believe he had survived them and was now out of danger. He shook his head violently. To his right and left the white lines of crumbled waves marked the Lido, a broad swath of them against the black. The old woman was speaking, he saw; he walked back to her side and listened.

"The waters yet rise," she shouted. "See? And the lightning . . . you can see the lightning breaking the Alps to dust. It's the end, child. Every island fled away, and the mountains were not found . . . the second angel poured out his vial upon the sea, and it became as the blood of a dead man: and every living thing died in the sea.'' On and on she spoke, her voice mingling with the sound of the gale and the boom of the waves, just carrying over it all . . . until Carlo, cold and tired, filled with pity and a black anguish like the clouds rolling over them, put his arm around her thin shoulders and turned her around. They descended to the floor below, picked up the extinguished lantern, and descended to her chamber, which was still lit. It seemed warm, a refuge. He could hear her still speaking. He was shivering without pause.

"You must be cold," she said in a practical tone. She pulled a few blankets from her bed. "Here, take these." He sat down in the big heavy chair, put the blankets around his legs, put his head back. He was tired. The old woman sat in her chair and wound thread onto a spool. After a few minutes of silence she began talking again, and as Carlo dozed and shifted position and nodded off again, she talked and talked, of storms, and drownings, and the world's end, and lost love. . . .

In the morning when he woke up, she was gone. Her room stood revealed in the dim morning light: shabby, the furniture battered, the blankets worn, the knickknacks of Venetian glass ugly, as Venetian glass always was . . . but it was clean. Carlo got up and stretched his stiff muscles. He went up to the roof; she wasn't there. It was a sunny morning. Over the east wall he saw that his boat was still there, still floating. He grinned—the first one in a few days; he could feel that in his face.

The woman was not on the floors below, either. The lowest one served as her boathouse, he could see. In it were a pair of decrepit rowboats and some lobster pots. The biggest "boatslip" was empty. She was probably out checking pots.

Or perhaps she hadn't wanted to talk with him in the light of day.

From the boathouse he could walk around to his craft, through water only knee-deep. He sat in the stern, reliving the previous afternoon, and grinned again at being alive. He took off the decking and bailed out the water on the keel with his bailing can, keeping an eye out for the old woman. Then he remembered the boat hook and went back upstairs for it. When he returned there was still no sight of her. He shrugged. He'd come back and say good-bye another time. He rowed around the campanile and off the Lido, pulled up the sail, and headed northwest, where he presumed Venice was.

The Lagoon was as flat as a pond this morning, the sky cloudless, like the blue dome of a great basilica. It was amazing, but Carlo was not surprised. The weather was like that these days. Last night's storm, however, had been something else. That was the mother of all squalls, those were the biggest waves in the Lagoon ever, without a doubt. He began rehearsing his tale in his mind, for wife and friends.

Venice appeared over the horizon right off his bow, just where he thought it would be: first the great campanile, then San Marco and the other spires. The campanile . . . Thank God his ancestors had wanted to get up there so close to God—or so far off the water—the urge had saved his life. In the rain-washed air, the sea approach to the city was more beautiful than ever, and it didn't even bother him as it usually did that no matter how close you got to it, it still seemed to be over the horizon. That was just the way it was, now. The Serenissima. He was happy to see it.

He was hungry, and still very tired. When he pulled into the Grand Canal and took down the sail, he found he could barely row. The rain was pouring off the land into the Lagoon, and the Grand Canal was running like a mountain river. It was tough going. At the fire station where the canal bent back, some of his friends working on a new roof-house waved at him, looking surprised to see him going upstream so early in the day. "You're going the wrong way!" one shouted.

Carlo waved an oar weakly before plopping it back in. "Don't I know it!" he replied.

Over the Rialto, back into the little courtyard of San Giacometta. Onto the sturdy dock he and his neighbors had built, staggering a bit—careful there, Carlo.

"Carlo!" his wife shrieked from above. "Carlo, Carlo, Carlo!" She flew down the ladder from the roof.

He stood on the dock. He was home.

"Carlo, Carlo, Carlo!" his wife cried as she ran onto the dock.

"Jesus," he pleaded, "shut up." And pulled her into a rough hug.

"Where have you been, I was so worried about you because of the storm, you said you'd be back yesterday, oh, Carlo, I'm so glad to see you. . . ." She tried to help him up the ladder. The baby was crying. Carlo sat down in the kitchen chair and looked around the little makeshift room with satisfaction. In between chewing down bites of a loaf of bread he told Luisa of his adventure: the two Japanese and their vandalism, the wild ride across the Lagoon, the madwoman on the campanile. When he had finished the story and the loaf of bread, he began to fall alseep.

"But Carlo, you have to go back and pick up those Japanese."

"To hell with them," he said slurrily. "Creepy little bastards. . . . They're tearing the Madonna apart, didn't I tell you? They'll take everything in Venice, every last painting and statue and carving and mosaic and all . . . I can't stand it."

"Oh, Carlo. It's all right. They take those things all over

the world and put them up and say this is from Venice, the greatest city in the world."

"They should be here."

"Here, here, come in and lie down for a few hours. I'll go see if Giuseppe will go to Torcello with you to bring back those bricks." She arranged him on their bed. "Let them have what's under the water, Carlo. Let them have it." He slept.

He sat up struggling, his arm shaken by his wife.

"Wake up, it's late. You've got to go to Torcello to get those men. Besides, they've got your scuba gear."

Carlo groaned.

"Maria says Giuseppe will go with you. He'll meet you with his boat on the Fondamente."

"Damn."

"Come on, Carlo, we need that money."

"All right, all right." The baby was squalling. He collapsed back on the bed. "I'll do it. Don't pester me."

He got up and drank her soup. Stiffly he descended the ladder, ignoring Luisa's instructions and warnings, and got back in his boat. He untied it, pushed off, let it float out of the courtyard to the wall of San Giacometta. He stared at the wall.

Once, he remembered, he had put on his scuba gear and swum down into the church. He had kneeled behind one of the stone pews in front of the altar, adjusting his weightbelts and tank to do so, and had tried to pray through his mouthpiece and the facemask. The silver bubbles of his breath had floated up through the water toward heaven; whether his prayers had gone with them, he had no idea. After a while, feeling somewhat foolish—but not entirely—he had swum out the door. Over it he had noticed an inscription and stopped to read it, facemask centimeters from the stone. *Around This Temple Let the Merchant's Law Be Just, His*

Weight True, and His Covenants Faithful. It was an admonition to the old usurers of the Rialto, but he could make it his, he thought; the true weight could refer to the diving belts, not to overload his clients and sink them to the bottom. . . .

The memory passed and he was on the surface again, with a job to do. He took in a deep breath and let it out, put the oars in the oarlocks and started to row.

Let them have what was under the water. What lived in Venice was still afloat.

—1980

Mercurial

"She rules all of Oz," said Dorothy, "and so she rules your city and you, because you are in the Winkie Country, which is part of the Land of Oz."

"It may be," returned the High Coco-Lorum, "for we do not study geography and have never inquired whether we live in the Land of Oz or not. And any Ruler who rules us from a distance, and unknown to us, is welcome to the job."

—L. Frank Baum, *The Lost Princess of Oz*

I am not, despite the appearances, fond of crime detection. In the past, it is true, I occasionally accompanied my friend Freya Grindavik as she solved her cases, and admittedly this watsoning gave me some good material for the little tales I have written for the not-very-discriminating markets on Mars and Titan. But after The Case of the Golden Sphere of the Lion of Mercury, in which I ended up hung by the feet from the clear dome of Terminator, two hundred meters above the rooftops of the city, my native lack of enthusiasm rose to the fore. And following the unfortunate Adventure of the Vulcan Accelerator, when Freya's arch-foe Jan Johannsen tied us to a pile of hay under a large magnifying glass in a survival tent, there to await Mercury's fierce dawn, I put my foot down: no more detecting. That, so to speak, was the last straw.

So when I agreed to accompany Freya to the Solday party of Heidi Van Seegeren, it was against my better judgement. But Freya assured me there would be no business involved; and despite the obvious excesses, I enjoy a Solday party as much as the next aesthete. So when she came by my villa, I was ready.

"Make haste," she said. "We're late, and I must be before Heidi's Monet when the Great Gates are opened. I adore that painting."

"Your infatuation is no secret," I said, panting as I trailed her through the crowded streets of the city. Freya, as those of you who have read my earlier tales know, is two and a half meters tall, and broad-shouldered; she barged through the shoals of Solday celebrants rather like a whale, and I, pilot-fishlike, dodged in her wake. She led me through a group of Greys, who with carpetbeaters were busy pounding rugs saturated with yellow dust. As I coughed and brushed off my fine burgundy suit, I said, "My feeling is that you have taken me to view that antique canvas once or twice too often."

She looked at me sternly. "As you will see, on Solday it transcends even its usual beauty. You look like a bee drowning in pollen, Nathaniel."

"Whose fault is that?" I demanded, brushing my suit fastidiously.

We came to the gate in the wall surrounding Van Seegeren's town villa, and Freya banged on it loudly. The gate was opened by a scowling man. He was nearly a meter shorter than Freya, and had a balding head that bulged rather like the dome of the city. In a mincing voice he said, "Invitations?"

"What's this?" said Freya. "We have permanent invitations from Heidi."

"I'm sorry," the man said coolly. "Ms. Van Seegeren has decided her Solday parties have gotten overcrowded, and this time she sent out invitations and instructed me to let in only those who have them."

"Then there has been a mistake," Freya declared. "Get Heidi on the intercom, and she will instruct you to let me in. I am Freya Grindavik, and this is Nathaniel Sebastian."

"I'm sorry," the man said, quite unapologetically. "Every person turned away says the same thing, and Ms. Van Seegeren prefers not to be disturbed so frequently."

"She'll be more disturbed to hear we've been held up." Freya shifted toward the man. "Who are you, anyway?"

"I am Sandor Musgrave, Ms. Van Seegeren's private secretary."

"How come I've never met you?"

"Ms. Van Seegeren hired me two months ago," Musgrave said, and stepped back so he could look Freya in the eye without straining his neck. "That is immaterial, however—"

"I've been Heidi's friend for over forty years," Freya said slowly, once again shifting forward to lean over the man. "And I would wager she values her friends more than her secretaries. . . ."

Musgrave stepped back indignantly. "I'm sorry!" he snapped. "I have my orders! Good day!"

But alas for him, Freya was now standing well in the gateway, and she seemed uninclined to move; she merely cocked her head at him. Musgrave comprehended his problem, and his mouth twitched uncertainly.

The impasse was broken when Van Seegeren's maid Lucinda arrived from the street. "Oh, hello Freya, Nathaniel. What are you doing out here?"

"This new Malvolio of yours is barring our entrance," Freya said.

"Oh, Musgrave," said Lucinda. "Let these two in, or the boss will be mad."

Musgrave retreated with a deep scowl. "I've studied the ancients, Ms. Grindavik," he said sullenly. "You need not insult me."

"Malvolio was a tragic character," Freya assured him. "Read Charles Lamb's essay concerning the matter."

"I certainly will," Musgrave said stiffly, and hurried to the villa, giving us a last poisonous look.

"Of course Lamb's father," Freya said absently, staring after the man, "was a house servant. Lucinda, who is that?"

Lucinda rolled her eyes. "The boss hired him to restore some of her paintings, and get the records in order. I wish she hadn't."

The bell in the gate sounded. "I've got it, Musgrave," Lucinda shouted at the villa. She opened the gate, revealing the artist Harvey Washburn.

"So you do," said Harvey, blinking. He was high again; a bottle of the White Brother hung from his hand. "Freya! Nathaniel! Happy Solday to you—have a drink?"

We refused the offer, and then followed Harvey around the side of the villa, exchanging a glance. I felt sorry for Harvey. Most of Mercury's great collectors came to Harvey's showings, but they dissected his every brushstroke for influences, and told him what he *should* be painting, and then among themselves they called his work amateurish and unoriginal, and never bought a single canvas. I was never surprised to see him drinking.

We rounded the side of the big villa and stepped onto the white stone patio, which was made of a giant slab of England's Dover cliffs, cut out and transported to Mercury entire. Malvolio Musgrave had spoken the truth about Heidi reducing the size of her Solday party: where often the patio had been jammed, there were now less than a dozen people. I spotted George Butler, Heidi's friend and rival art collector, and Arnold Ohman, the art dealer who obtained for many of Mercury's collectors their ancient masterpieces from Earth. As I greeted them Freya led us all across the patio to the back wall of the villa, which was also fronted with white slabs of the Dover cliffs. There, all alone, hung Claude Monet's *Rouen Cathedral—Sun Effect.* "Look at it, Nathaniel!" Freya commanded me. "Isn't it beautiful?"

I looked at it. Now you must understand that, as owner of the Gallery Orientale, and by deepest personal aesthetic conviction, I am a connoisseur of Chinese art, a style in which a dozen artfully spontaneous brushstrokes can serve to delineate a mountain or two, several trees, a small village and its inhabitants, and perhaps some birds. Given my predilection, you will not be surprised to learn that merely to look at the antique rectangle of color that Freya so admired was to risk damaging my eyes. Thick scumbled layers of grainy paint scarcely revealed the cathedral of the title, which wavered under a blast of light so intense that I doubted Mercury's midday could compete with it. Small blobs of every color served to represent both the indistinct stone and a pebbly sky; both were composed of combinations principally of white, yellow, and purple, though as I say, every other color made an appearance.

"Stunning," I said, with a severe squint. "Are you sure this Monet wasn't a bit nearsighted?"

Freya glared at me, ignoring Butler's chuckles. "I suppose your comment might have been funny the first time you made it. To children, anyway."

"But I heard it was actually *true,*" I said, shielding my eyes with one hand. "Monet *was* nearsighted, and so like Goya his vision affected his painting—"

"I should hope so," Harvey said solemnly.

"—so all he could see were those blobs of color, isn't that sad?"

Freya shook her head. "You won't get a rise out of me

today, Nathaniel. You'll have to think up your dinner conversation by yourself.''

Momentarily stopped by this riposte, I retired with Arnold Ohman to Heidi's patio bar. After dialing drinks from the bartender we sat on the blocks of Dover cliffs that made up the patio's low outer wall. We toasted Solday, and contemplated the clouds of yellow talc that swirled over the orange tile rooftops below us. For those of you who have never visited it, Terminator is an oval city. The forward half of the city is flat, and projects out under the clear dome. The rear half of the oval is terraced, and rises to the tall Dawn Wall, which supports the upper rim of the dome, and shields the city from the perpetually rising sun. The Great Gates of Terminator are near the top of the Dawn Wall, and when they are opened, shafts of Sol's overwhelming light spear through the city's air, illuminating everything in a yellow brilliance. Heidi Van Seegeren's villa was about halfway up the terraced slope; we looked upon gray stone walls, orange tile roofs, and the dusty vines and lemon trees of the terrace gardens that dotted the city; outside the dome the twelve big tracks over which the city slid extended off to the horizon, circling the planet like a slender silver wedding band. It was a fine view, and I lifted my glass to the idea that Claude Monet wasn't there to paint it. For sometimes, if you ask me, reality is enough.

Ohman downed his drink in one swallow. Rumor had it that he was borrowing heavily to finance one of his big terran purchases; it was whispered he was planning to buy the closed portion of the Louvre—or the Renaissance room of the Vatican museum—or Amsterdam's Van Gogh collection. But rumors like that circulated around Arnold continuously. He was that kind of dealer. It was unlikely any of them were true; still, his silence seemed to reveal a certain tension.

"Look at the way Freya is soaking in that painting you got for Heidi,'' I said, to lift his spirits. Freya's face was within centimeters of the canvas, where she could examine it blob by blob; the people behind her could see nothing but her white-blond hair. Ohman smiled at the sight. He had brought the Monet back from his most recent terran expedition, and apparently it had been a great struggle to obtain it. Both the English family that owned it and the British government had had to be paid enormous sums to secure its release, and only the fact that Mercury was universally considered humanity's greatest art museum had cleared the matter with the courts. It had been one of Arnold's finest hours. Now he said, "Maybe we should pull her away a bit, so that others can see."

"If both of us tug on her it may work," I said. We stood and went to her side. Harvey Washburn, looking flushed and frazzled, joined us, and we convinced Freya to share the glory. Ohman and Butler conferred over something, and entered the villa through the big French doors that led into the concert room. Inside, Heidi's orchestra rolled up and down the scales of Mussorgsky's *Hut of Baba Yaga*. That meant it was close to the time when the Great Gates would open (Heidi always gets inside information about this). Sure enough, as Mussorgsky's composition burst from the *Hut of Baba Yaga* into the *Great Gates of Kiev*, two splinters of white light split the air under the dome. Shouts and fanfares rose everywhere, nearly drowning the amplified sound of our orchestra. Slowly the Great Gates opened, and as they did the shafts of light grew to thick buttery gold bars of air. By their rich, nearly blinding glare, Heidi Van Seegeren made her first entrance from her villa, timing her steps to the exaggerated Maazel ritard that her conductor Hiu employed every Solday when *Pictures at an Exhibition* was performed. This ritard shifted the music from the merely grandiose to the utterly bombastical, and it took Heidi over a minute to cross her own narrow patio; but I suppose it was not entirely silly, given the ritual nature of the moment, and the flood of light that was making the air appear a thick, quite tangible gel.

What with the light, and the uproar created by the keening Greys and the many orchestras in the neighborhood, each playing their own overture or fanfare (the *Coriolan* came from one side of us, the *1812* from the other), it was a complex and I might even say *noisy* aesthetic moment, and the last thing I needed was to take another look at the Monet monstrosity, but Freya would not have it otherwise.

"You've never seen it when the Great Gates are opened," she said. "That was the whole point in bringing you here today."

"I see." Actually I barely saw anything; as Freya had guided me by the arm to the painting I had accidentally looked directly at the incandescent yellow bars of sunlight, and brilliant blue afterimages bounced in my sight. I heard rather than saw Harvey Washburn join us. Many blinks later I was able to join the others in devoting my attention to the big canvas.

Well. The Monet positively *glowed* in the dense, lambent air; it gave off light like a lamp, vibrating with a palpable energy of its own. At the sight of it even I was impressed.

"Yes," I admitted to Freya and Harvey, "I can see how precisely he placed all those little chunks of color, and I can see how sharp and solid the cathedral is under all that goo, but it's like Solday, you know, it's a heightened effect. The result is garish, really, it's too much."

"But this is a painting of midday," Harvey said. "And as you can see, midday can get pretty garish."

"But this is Terminator! The Greys have put a lot of talc in the air to make it look this way!"

"So what?" Freya demanded impatiently. "Stop thinking so much, Nathaniel. Just *look* at it. *See* it. Isn't it beautiful? Haven't you felt things look that way sometimes, seeing stone in sunlight?"

"Well . . ." And, since I am a strictly honest person, if I had said anything at all I would have had to admit that it did have a power about it. It drew the eye; it poured light onto us as surely as the beams of sunlight extending from the gates in the Dawn Wall to the curved side of the clear dome.

"Well?" Freya demanded.

"Well yes," I said, "yes I see that cathedral front—I feel it. But there must have been quite a heat wave in old Rouen. It's as if Monet had seen Terminator on Solday, the painting fits so well with this light."

"No," Freya said, but her left eye was squinted, a sign she is thinking.

Harvey said, "We make the conditions of light in Terminator, and so it is an act of the imagination, like this painting. You shouldn't be surprised if there are similarities. We value this light because the old masters created it on their canvases."

I shook my head, and indicated the brassy bedlam around us. "No. I believe we made this one up ourselves."

Freya and Harvey laughed, with the giddiness that Solday inspires.

Suddenly a loud screech came from inside the villa. Freya hurried across the patio into the music room, and I followed her. Both of us, however, had forgotten the arrangements that Heidi made on Soldays to cast the brilliant light throughout her home, and as we ran past the silenced orchestra into a hallway we were blasted by light from a big mirror carefully placed in the villa's central atrium. Screams still echoed from somewhere inside, but we could only stumble blindly through bright pulsing afterimages, retinal Monets if you will, while unidentified persons bowled into us, and mirrors crashed to the floor. And the atrium was raised, so that occasional steps up in the hallway tripped us. "Murder!" someone cried. "Murder! There he goes!" And with that a whole group of us were off down the halls like hounds—blind hounds—baying after unknown prey. A figure leaped from behind a mirror glaring white, and Freya and I tackled it just inside the atrium.

When my vision swam back I saw it was George Butler. "What's going on?" he asked, very politely for a man who had just been jumped on by Freya Grindavik.

"Don't ask us," Freya said irritably.

"Murder!" shrieked Lucinda from the hallway that led from the atrium directly back to the patio. We jumped up and crowded into the hallway. Just beyond a mirror shattered into many pieces lay a man's body; apparently he had been crawling toward the patio when he collapsed, and one arm and finger extended ahead of him, pointing to the patio still.

Freya approached, gingerly turned the body's head. "It's that Musgrave fellow," she said, blinking to clear her sight. "He's dead all right. Struck on the head with the mirror there, no doubt."

Heidi Van Seegeren joined us. "What's going on?"

"That was my question," George Butler said.

Freya explained the situation to her.

"Call the police," Heidi said to Lucinda. "And I suppose no one should leave."

I sighed.

And so crime detection ensnared me once again. I helped Freya by circulating on the patio, calming the shocked and nervous guests. "Um, excuse me, very sorry to inform you, yes, sorry—hard to believe, yes—somebody had it in for the secretary Musgrave, it appears," all the while watching to see if anyone would jump, or turn pale, or start to run when I told them. Then, of course, I had to lead gently to the idea that everyone had gone from guest to suspect, soon to be questioned by Freya and the police. "No, no, of *course* you're not suspected of anything, furthest thing from our minds, it's just that Freya wants to know if there's anything you saw that would help," and so on. Then I had to do the difficult scheduling of Freya's interviews, at the same time I was supposed to keep an eye out for anything suspicious. Oh, the watson does the dirty work, all right. No wonder we always look dense when the detective unveils the solutions; we never have the time even to get the facts straight, much less meditate on their meaning. All I got that day were fragments: Lucinda whispered to me that Musgrave had worked for George Butler before Heidi hired him. Harvey Washburn told me that Musgrave had once been an artist, and that he had only recently moved to Mercury from Earth; this was his first Solday. That didn't give him much time to be hired by Butler, fired, and then hired by Van Seegeren. But was that of significance?

Late in the day I spoke with one of the police officers handling the case. She was relieved to have the help of Freya Grindavik; Terminator's police force is small, and often relies on the help of the city's famous detective for the more difficult cases. The officer gave me a general outline of what they had learned: Lucinda had heard a shout for help, had stepped into the atrium and seen a bloodied figure crawling down the hallway toward the patio. She had screamed and run for help, but only in the hallway was clear vision possible, and she had quickly gotten lost. After that, chaos; everyone at the party had a different tale of confusion.

After that conversation I had nothing more to do, so I got all the sequestered guests coffee and helped pick up some of the broken hall mirrors and passed some time prowling Heidi's villa, getting down on my hands and knees with the police robots to inspect a stain or two.

When Freya was finished with her interrogations, she promised Heidi and the police that she would see the case to its end—at least provisionally: "I only do this for entertainment," she told them irritably. "I'll stay with it as long as it entertains me. And I shall entertain myself with it."

"That's all right," said the police, who had heard this

before. "Just so long as you'll take the case." Freya nodded, and we left.

The Solday celebration was long since over; the Great Gates were closed, and once again through the dome shone the black sky. I said to Freya, "Did you hear about Musgrave working for Butler? And how he came from Earth just recently?" For you see, once on the scent I am committed to seeing a case solved.

"Please, Nathaniel," Freya said. "I heard all that and more. Musgrave stole the concept of Harvey Washburn's first series of paintings; he blackmailed both Butler and our host Heidi to obtain his jobs from them—or so I deduce from their protestations and certain facts concerning their recent questionable merger that I am privy to. And he tried to assault Lucinda, who is engaged to the cook Delaurence—" She let out a long sigh. "Motives are everywhere."

"It seems this Musgrave was a thoroughly despicable sort," I said.

"Yes. An habitual blackmailer."

"Nothing *suggests* itself to you?"

"No. I don't know why I agree to solve these things. Here I am committed to this headbashing, and my best clue is something that *you* suggested."

"I wasn't aware that I had suggested anything!"

"There is a fresh perspective to ignorance that can be very helpful."

"So it *is* important that Musgrave just arrived from Earth?"

She laughed. "Let's stop in the Plaza Dubrovnik and get something to eat. I'm starving."

Almost three weeks passed without a word from Freya, and I began to suspect that she was ignoring the case. Freya has no real sense of right and wrong, you see; she regards her cases as games, to be tossed aside if they prove too taxing. More than once she has cheerfully admitted defeat, and blithely forgotten any promises she may have made. She is *not* a moral person.

So I dropped by her home near Plaza Dubrovnik one evening, to rouse her from her irresponsible indifference. When she answered the door there were paint smudges on her face and hands.

"Freya," I scolded her. "How could you take up an entirely new hobby when there is a *case* to be solved?"

"Generously I allow you entrance after such a false accusation," she said. "But you will have to eat your words."

She led me downstairs to her basement laboratory, which extended the entire length and breadth of her villa. There on a big white-topped table lay Heidi Van Seegeren's Monet, looking like the three-dimensional geologic map of some minerally blessed country.

"What's this?" I exclaimed. "Why is this here?"

"I believe it is a fake," she said shortly, returning to a computer console.

"Wait a moment!" I cried. On the table around the painting were rolls of recording chart paper, lab notebooks, and what looked like black-and-white photos of the painting. "What do you mean?"

After tapping at the console she turned to me. "I mean, I believe it's a fake!"

"But I thought art forgery was extinct. It is too easy to discover a fake."

"Ha!" She waved a finger at me angrily. "You pick a bad time to say so. It is a common opinion, of course, but not necessarily true."

I regarded the canvas more closely. "What makes you think this a fake? I thought it was judged a masterpiece of its period."

"Something you said first caused me to question it," she said. "You mentioned that the painting seemed to have been created by an artist familiar with the light of Terminator. This seemed true to me, and it caused me to reflect that one of the classic signs of a fake was anachronistic sensibility—that is to say, the forger injects into his vision of the past some element of his time that is so much a part of his sensibility that he cannot perceive it. Thus the Victorians faked Renaissance faces with a sentimentality that only they could not immediately see."

"I see." I nodded sagely. "It did seem that cathedral had been struck with Solday light, didn't it."

"Yes. The trouble is, I have been able to find no sign of forgery in the physical properties of the painting." She shook her head. "And after three weeks of uninterrupted chemical analysis, that is beginning to worry me."

"But Freya," I said, as something occurred to me. "Does all this have a bearing on the Musgrave murder?"

"I think so," she replied. "And if not, it is certainly more interesting. But I believe it does."

I nodded. "So what, exactly, have you found?"

She smiled ironically. "You truly want to know? Well. The best test for anachronisms is the polonium 210, radium 226 equilibrium—"

"Please, Freya. No jargon."

"Jargon!" She raised an eyebrow to scorn me. "There is no such thing. Intelligence is like mold in a petri dish—as it eats ever deeper into the agar of reality, language has to expand with it to describe what has been digested. Each specialty provides the new vocabulary for its area of feeding and gets accused of fabricating jargon by those who know no better. I'm surprised to hear such nonsense from you. Or perhaps not."

"Very well," I said, hands up. "Still, you must communicate your meaning to me."

"I shall. First I analyzed the canvas. The material and its weave match the characteristics of the canvas made by the factory outside Paris that provided Monet throughout the painting of the Rouen cathedral series. Both the fabric and the glue appear very old, though there is no precise dating technique for them. And there was no trace of solvents that might have been used to strip paint off a genuine canvas of the period.

"I then turned to the paint. Follow so far?" she asked sharply. "Paint?"

"You may proceed without further sarcasm, unless unable to control yourself."

"The palette of an artist as famous as Monet has been studied in detail, so that we know he preferred cadmium yellow to chromium yellow or Naples yellow, that he tended to use Prussian blue rather than cobalt blue, and so on." She tapped the flecks of blue at the base of the cathedral. "Prussian blue."

"You've taken paint off the canvas?"

"How else test it? But I took very small samples, I assure you. Whatever the truth concerning the work, it remains a masterpiece, and I would not mar it. Besides, most of my tests were on the white paint, of which there is a great quantity, as you can see."

"Why the white paint?" I leaned over to stare more closely at the canvas.

"Because lead white is one of the best dating tools we have. The manufacturing methods used to make it changed frequently around Monet's time, and each change in method altered the chemical composition of the paint. After 1870, for instance, the cheaper zinc white was used to adulterate lead white, so there should be over one percent zinc in Monet's lead white."

"And is that what you found?"

"Yes. The atomic absorption spectrum showed—" She dug around in the pile of chart paper on the table— "Well, take my word for it—"

"I will."

"Nearly twelve percent. And the silver content for late nineteenth century lead white should be around four parts per million, the copper content about sixty parts per million. So it is with this paint. There is no insoluble antimony component, as there would be if the paint had been manufactured after 1940. The X-ray diffraction pattern"—she unrolled a length of chart paper and showed me where three sharp peaks in a row had been penned by the machine—"is exactly right, and there is the proper balance of polonium 210 and radium 226. That's very important, by the way, because when lead white is manufactured the radioactive balance of some of its elements is upset, and it takes a good three hundred years for them to decay back to equilibrium. And this paint is indeed back to that equilibrium."

"So the paints are Monet's," I concluded. "Doesn't that prove the work authentic?"

"Perhaps," Freya admitted. "But as I was doing all this analysis, it occurred to me that a modern forger has just as much information concerning Monet's palette as I do. With a modern laboratory it would be possible to use such information as a recipe, so to speak, and then to synthesize paints that would match the recipe exactly. Even the radioactively decayed lead white could be arranged, by avoiding the procedures that disrupt the radioactive balance in the first place!"

"Wouldn't that be terrifically complicated?"

Freya stared at me. "*Obviously*, Nathaniel, we are dealing with a very very meticulous faker here. But how else could it be done, in this day and age? Why else do it at all? The complete faker must take care to anticipate every test available, and then in a modern laboratory create the appropriate results for every one of them. It's admirable!"

"Assuming there ever was such a forger," I said dubiously. "It seems to me that what you have actually done here is prove the painting genuine."

"I don't think so."

"But even with these paints made by recipe, as you call them, the faker would still have to paint the painting!"

"Exactly. Conceive the painting, and execute it. It becomes very impressive, I confess." She walked around the table to look at the work from the correct angle. "I do believe this is one of the *best* of the Rouen cathedral series—astonishing, that a forger would be capable of it."

"That brings up another matter," I said. "Doesn't this work have a five-hundred-year-old pedigree? How could a whole history have been provided for it?"

"Good question. But I believe I have discovered the way. Let's go upstairs—you interrupted my preparations for lunch, and I'm hungry."

I followed her to her extensive kitchen, and sat in the window nook that overlooked the tile rooftops of the lower city while she finished chopping up the vegetables for a large salad.

"Do you know this painting's history?" Freya asked, looking up from a dissected head of lettuce.

I shook my head. "Up until now the thing has not been of overwhelming interest to me."

"A confession of faulty aesthetics. The work was photographed at the original exhibit in 1895; Durand-Ruel photo 5828 L8451. All of the information appended to the photo fits our painting—same name, size, signature location. Then for a century it disappeared. Odd. But it turned out to have been in the estate of an Evans family, in Aylesbury, England. When the family had some conservation work done on one corner it returned to public knowledge, and was photographed for a dozen books of the twenty-first and twenty-second centuries. After that it slipped back into obscurity, but it is as well documented as any of the series belonging to private estates."

"Exactly my point," I said. "How could such a history be forged?"

As Freya mixed the salad she smiled. "I sat and thought about that for quite some time myself. But consider it freshly, Nathaniel. How do we know what we know of the past?"

"Well," I said, somewhat at a loss. "From data banks, I suppose. And books—documents—historians—"

"From historians!" She laughed. She provided us both with bowls and sat across from me. As I filled mine she said, "So we want to know something of the past. We go to our library and sit at its terminal. We call up general reference works, or a bibliographic index, and we choose, if we want, books that we would like to have in our hands. We type in the appropriate code, our printer prints up the appropriate book, and the volume slides out of the computer into our waiting grasp." She paused to fork down several mouthfuls of salad. "So we learn about the past using computer programs. And a clever programmer, you see, can change a program. It would be possible to *insert* extra pages into these old books on Monet, and thus add the forged painting to the record of the past."

I paused, a cherry tomato hovering before my mouth. "But—"

"I searched for an original of *any* of these books containing photos of our painting," Freya said. "I called all over Mercury, and to several incunabulists in libraries on Earth—you wouldn't believe the phone bill I've run up. But the initial printings of these art volumes were very small, and although first editions probably remain *somewhere,* they are not to be found. Certainly there are no first editions of these books on Mercury, and none immediately locatable on Earth. It began to seem a very unlikely coincidence, as if these volumes contained pictures of our painting precisely because they existed only in the data banks, and thus could be altered without discovery."

She attended to her salad, and we finished eating in silence. All the while my mind was spinning furiously, and when we were done I said, "What about the original exhibit photo?"

She nodded, pleased with me. "That, apparently, is genuine. But the Durand-Ruel photos include four or five of paintings that have never been seen since. In that sense the Rouen cathedral series is a good one for a faker; from the first it has never been clear how many cathedrals Monet painted. The usual number given is thirty-two, but there are more in the Durand-Ruel list, and a faker could examine the list and use one of the lost items as a prescription for his fake. Providing a later history with the aid of these obscure art books would result in a fairly complete pedigree."

"But could such an addition to the data banks be made?"

"It would be easiest done on Earth," Freya said. "But there is no close security guarding the banks containing old art books. No one expects them to be tampered with."

"It's astonishing," I said with a wave of my fork, "it is baroque, it is *byzantine* in its ingenuity!"

"Yes," she said. "Beautiful, in a way."

"However," I pointed out to her, "you have no proof—only this perhaps over-complex theory. You have found no first edition of a book to confirm that the computer-generated volumes add Heidi's painting, and you have found no physical anachronism in the painting itself."

Gloomily she clicked her fork against her empty salad bowl, then rose to refill it. "It is a problem," she admitted. "Also, I have been working on the assumption that Sandor Musgrave discovered evidence of the forgery. But *I* can't find it."

Never let it be said that Nathaniel Sebastian has not performed a vital role in Freya Grindavik's great feats of detection. I was the first to notice the anachronism of sensibility in Heidi's painting; and now I had a truly inspired idea. "He was pointing to the patio!" I exclaimed. "Musgrave, in his last moment, struggled to point to the patio!"

"I had observed that," Freya said, unimpressed.

"But Heidi's patio—you know—it is formed out of blocks of the Dover cliffs! And thus Musgrave indicated *England!* Is it not possible? The Monet was owned by Englishmen until Heidi purchased it—perhaps Musgrave meant to convey that the original owners were the forgers!"

Freya's mouth hung open in surprise, and her left eye was squinted shut. I leaped from the window nook in triumph. "I've solved it! I've solved a mystery at last!"

Freya looked up at me and laughed.

"Come now, Freya, you must admit I have given you the vital clue."

She stood up, suddenly all business. "Yes, yes, indeed you have. Now out with you Nathaniel, I have work to do."

"So I did give you the vital clue?" I asked. "Musgrave was indicating the English owners?"

As she ushered me to her door Freya laughed. "As a detective your intuition is matched only by your confidence. Now leave me to work, and I will be in contact with you soon, I assure you." And with that she urged me into the street, and I was left to consider the case alone.

Freya was true to her word, and only two days after our crucial luncheon she knocked on the door of my town villa. "Come along," she said. "I've asked Arnold Ohman for an appointment; I want to ask him some questions about the Evans family. The city is passing the Monet museum, however, and he asked us to meet him out there."

I readied myself quickly, and we proceeded to North Station. We arrived just in time to step across the gap between the two platforms, and then we were on the motionless deck of one of the outlying stations that Terminator is always passing. There we rented a car and sped west, paralleling the dozen massive cylindrical rails along which the city slides. Soon we had left Terminator behind, and when we were seventy or eighty kilometers onto the nightside of Mercury we turned to the north, to Monet Crater.

Terminator's tracks lie very close to the thirtieth degree of latitude, in the Northern hemisphere, and Monet Crater is not far from them. We crossed Shakespeare Planitia rapidly, passing between craters named after the great artists, writers, and composers of Earth's glorious past: traversing a low pass between Brahms and Verdi, looking down at where Degas had crashed into the Brontës. "I think I understand why a modern artist on Mercury might turn to forgery," Freya said. "We are dwarfed by the past as we are by this landscape."

"But it is still a crime," I insisted. "If it were done often, we would not be able to distinguish the authentic from the fake."

Freya did not reply.

I drove our car up a short rise, and we entered the submercurial garage of the Monet museum, which is set deep in the southern rim of the immense crater named after the artist. One long wall of the museum is a window facing out over the crater floor, so that the central knot of peaks is visible, and the curving inner wall of the crater defines the horizon in the murky distance. Shutters slid down to protect these windows from the heat of Mercury's long day, but now they were open and the black wasteland of the planet formed a strange backdrop to the colorful paintings that filled the long rooms of the museum.

There were many Monet originals there, but the canvases of the Rouen cathedral series were almost all reproductions, set in one long gallery. As Freya and I searched for Arnold we also viewed them.

"You see, they're not just various moments of a single day," Freya said.

"Not unless it was a very strange day for weather." The three reproductions before us all depicted foggy days: two bluish and underwater-looking, the third a bright burning-off of yellow noontime fog. Obviously these were from a different day than the ones across the room, where a cool clear morning gave way to a midday that looked as if the sun was just a few feet above the cathedral. The museum had classified the series in color groups: "Blue Group," "White Group," "Yellow Group," and so on. To my mind that system was stupid—it told you nothing you couldn't immediately see. I myself classified them according to weather. There was a clear day that got very hot; a clear winter day, the air chill and pure; a foggy day; and a day when a rainstorm had grown and then broken. When I told Freya of my system she applauded it. "So Heidi's painting goes from the king of the White Group to the hottest moment of the hot day."

"Exactly. It's the most extreme as far as sunlight blasting the stone into motes of color."

"And thus the forger extends Monet's own thinking, you see," she said, a bit absently. "But I *don't* see Arnold, and I think we have visited every room."

"Could he be late?"

"We are already quite late ourselves. I wonder if he has gone back?"

"It seems unlikely," I said.

Purposefully we toured the museum one more time, and I ignored the color-splashed canvases standing before the dark crater, to search closely in all the various turns of the galleries. No Arnold.

"Come along," Freya said. "I suspect he stayed in Terminator, and now I want to speak with him more than ever."

So we returned to the garage, got back in our car, and drove out onto Mercury's bare, baked surface once again. Half an hour later we had Terminator's tracks in sight. They stretched before us from horizon to horizon, twelve fat silvery cylinders set five meters above the ground on narrow pylons. To the east, rolling over the flank of Wang Wei Crater so slowly that we could not perceive its movement without close attention, came the city itself, a giant clear half-egg filled with the colors of rooftops, gardens, and the gray stone of the buildings crowding the terraced Dawn Wall.

"We'll have to go west to the next station," I said. Then I saw something, up on the city track nearest us: spread-eagled over the top of the big cylinder was a human form in a light green daysuit. I stopped the car. "Look!"

Freya peered out her window. "We'd better go investigate."

We struggled quickly into the car's emergency daysuits, clamped on the helmets, and slipped through the car's lock onto the ground. A ladder led us up the nearest cylinder pylon and through a tunnel in the cylinder itself. Once on top we could stand safely on the broad hump of the rail.

The figure we had seen was only ten meters away from us, and we hurried to it.

It was Arnold, spread in cruciform fashion over the cylinder's top, secured in place by three large suction plates that had been cuffed to his wrists and ankles, and then stuck to the cylinder. Arnold turned from his contemplation of the slowly approaching city, and looked at us wide-eyed through his faceplate. Freya reached down and turned on his helmet intercom.

"—am I glad to see you!" Arnold cried, voice harsh. "These plates won't move!"

"Tied to the tracks, eh?" Freya said.

"Yes!"

"Who put you here?"

"I don't know! I went out to meet you at the Monet museum, and the last thing I remember I was in the garage there. When I came to, I was here."

"Does your head hurt?" I inquired.

"Yes. Like I was gassed, though, not hit. But—the city—it just came over the horizon a short time ago. Perhaps we could dispense with discussion until I am freed?"

"Relax," Freya said, nudging one of the plates with her boot. "Are you sure you don't know who did this, Arnold?"

"Of course! That's what I just said! Please, Freya, can't we talk after I get loose?"

"In a hurry, Arnold?" Freya asked.

"But *of course*."

"No need to be too worried," I assured him. "If we cannot free you, the cowcatchers will be out to pry you loose." I tried lifting a plate, but could not move it. "Surely they will find a way—it's their job, after all."

"True," Arnold said.

"Usually true," said Freya. "Arnold is probably not aware that the cowcatchers have become rather unreliable recently. Some weeks ago a murderer tied his victim to a track just as you have been, Arnold, and then somehow disengaged the cowcatchers' sensors. The unfortunate victim was shaved into molecules by one of the sleeves of the city. It was kept quiet to avoid any attempted repetitions, but since then the cowcatchers' sensors have continued to function erratically, and two or three suicides have been entirely too successful."

"Perhaps this isn't the best moment to tell us about this," I suggested to Freya.

Arnold choked over what I took to be his agreement.

"Well," Freya said, "I thought I should make the situation clear. Now listen, Arnold. We need to talk."

"*Please*," Arnold said. "Free me first, *then* talk."

"No, no—"

"But Terminator is only a kilometer away!"

"Your perspective from that angle is deceptive," Freya told him. "The city is at least three kilometers away."

"More like two," I said, as I could now make out individual rooftops under the Dawn Wall. In fact the city glowed like a big glass lamp and illuminated the entire landscape with a faint green radiance.

"And at three point four kilometers an hour," Freya said,

"that gives us almost an hour, doesn't it. So listen to me, Arnold. The Monet cathedral that you sold to Heidi is a fake."

"What?" Arnold cried. "It certainly is not! And I insist this isn't the time—"

"It is a fake. Now I want you to tell me the truth, or I will leave you here to test the cowcatchers." She leaned over to stare down at Arnold face to face. "I know who painted the fake, as well."

Helplessly Arnold stared up at her.

"He put you on the track here, didn't he?"

Arnold squeezed his eyes shut, nodded slowly. "I think so."

"So if you want to be let up, you must swear to me that you will abide by my plan for dealing with this forger. You *will* follow my instructions, understand?"

"I understand."

"Do you agree?"

"I agree," Arnold said, forcing the words out. "Now let me up!"

"All right." Freya straightened.

"How are we going to do it?" I asked.

Freya shrugged. "I don't know."

At this Arnold howled, he shouted recriminations, he began to wax hysterical—

"Shut up!" Freya exclaimed. "You're beginning to sound like a man who has made too many brightside crossings. These suction plates are little different from children's darts." She leaned down, grasped a plate, pulled up with all of her considerable strength. No movement. "Hmm," she said thoughtfully.

"Freya," Arnold said.

"One moment," she replied, and walked back down the hump of the cylinder to the ladder tunnel, there to disappear down it.

"She's left me," Arnold groaned. "Left me to be crushed."

"I don't think so," I said. "No doubt she has gone to the car to retrieve some useful implement." I kicked heartily at the plate holding Arnold's feet to the cylinder, and even managed to slide it a few centimeters down the curve, which had the effect of making Arnold suddenly taller. But other than that I made no progress.

When Freya returned she carried a bar, bent at one end. "Crowbar," she explained to us.

"But where did you get it?"

"From the car's tool chest, naturally. Here." She stepped over Arnold. "If we just insinuate this end of it under your cuffs, I believe we'll have enough leverage to do the trick. The cylinder being curved, the plate's grasp should be weakened—about here." She jammed the short end of the bar under the edge of the footplate's cuff, and pulled on the upper end of it. Over the intercom, breathless silence; her fair cheeks reddened; then suddenly Arnold's legs flew up and over his head, leaving his arms twisted and his neck at an awkward angle. At the same time Freya staggered off the cylinder, performed a neat somersault, and landed on her feet on the ground below us. While she made her way back up to us I tried to ease the weight on Arnold's neck, but by his squeaks of distress I judged he was still uncomfortable. Freya rejoined us, and quickly wedged her crowbar under Arnold's right wrist cuff, and freed it. That left Arnold hanging down the side of the cylinder by his left wrist; but with one hard crank Freya popped that plate free as well, and Arnold disappeared. By leaning over we could just see him, collapsed in a heap on the ground. "Are you all right?" Freya asked. He groaned for an answer.

I looked up and saw that Terminator was nearly upon us. Almost involuntarily I proceeded to the ladder tunnel; Freya followed me, and we descended to the ground. "Disturbing not to be able to trust the cowcatchers,'' I remarked as my heartbeat slowed.

"Nathaniel,'' Freya said, looking exasperated. "I made all that up, you know that.''

"Ah. Yes, of course.''

As we joined Arnold he was just struggling to a seated position. "My ankle,'' he said. Then the green wash of light from Terminator disappeared, as did the night sky; the city slid over us, and we were encased in a gloom interrupted by an occasional running light. All twelve of the city's big tracks had disappeared, swallowed by the sleeves in the city's broad metallic foundation. Only the open slots that allowed passage over the pylons showed where the sleeves were; for a moment in the darkness it seemed we stood between two worlds held apart by a field of pylons.

Meanwhile the city slid over us soundlessly, propelled by the expansion of the tracks themselves. You see, the alloy composing the tracks is capable of withstanding the 425 degree centigrade heat of the Mercurial day, but the cylinders do expand just a bit in this heat. Here in the terminator is the forward edge of the cylinders' expansion, and the smooth-sided sleeves above us at that moment fit so snugly over the cylinders that as the cylinders expand, the city is pushed forward toward the cooler, thinner railing to the west; and so the city is propelled by the sun, while never being fully exposed to it. The motive force is so strong, in fact, that resistance to it arranged in the sleeves generates the enormous reserves of energy that Terminator has sold so successfully to the rest of civilization.

Though I had understood this mechanism for decades, I had never before observed it from this angle, and despite the fact that I was somewhat uneasy to be standing under our fair city, I was also fascinated to see its broad, knobby silver underside, gliding majestically westward. For a long time I did nothing but stare at it.

"We'd better get to the car," Freya said. "The sun will be up very soon after the city passes, and then we'll be in trouble."

Since Arnold was still cuffed to the plates, and had at least a sprained ankle, walking with him slung between us was a slow process. While we were at it the Dawn Wall passed over us, and suddenly the twelve tracks and the stars between them were visible again. "Now we'd better hurry," said Freya. Above us the very top of the Dawn Wall flared a brilliant white; sunlight was striking that surface, only two hundred meters above us. Dawn was not far away. In the glare of reflected light we could see the heavily tire-printed ground under the cylinders perfectly, and for a while our eyes were nearly overwhelmed. "Look!" Freya cried, shielding her eyes with one hand and pointing up at the sun-washed slope of the city wall with the other. "It's the inspiration for our Monet, don't you think?"

Despite our haste, the great Rouen cathedral of Mercury pulled away from us. "This won't do," Freya said. "Only a bit more to the car, but we have to hurry. Here, Arnold, let me carry you—" and she ran, carrying Arnold piggyback, the rest of the way to the car. As we maneuvered him through the lock, a tongue of the sun's corona licked briefly over the horizon, blinding us. I felt scorched; my throat was dry. We were now at the dawn edge of the terminator zone, and east-facing slopes burned white while west-facing slopes were still a perfect black, creating a chaotic patchwork that was utterly disorienting. We rolled into the car after Arnold, and quickly drove west, passing the city, returning to the night zone, and arriving at a station where we could make the transfer into the city again. Freya laughed at my expression as we crossed the gap. "Well, Nathaniel," she said, "home again."

* * *

The very next day Freya arranged for those concerned with the case to assemble on Heidi's patio again. Four police officials were there, and one took notes. The painting of the cathedral of Rouen was back in its place on the villa wall; George Butler and Harvey Washburn stood before it, while Arnold Ohman and Heidi paced by the patio's edge. Lucinda and Delaurence, the cook, watched from behind the patio bar.

Freya called us to order. She was wearing a severe blue dress, and her white-blond hair was drawn into a tight braid that fell down her back. Sternly she said, "I will suggest to you an explanation for the death of Sandor Musgrave. All of you except for the police and Mr. Sebastian were to one extent or another suspected of killing him, so I know this will be of great interest to you."

Naturally there was an uneasy stir among those listening.

"Several of you had reason to hate Musgrave, or to fear him. The man was a blackmailer by profession, and on Earth he had obtained evidence of illegalities in the merger Heidi and George made five years ago, that gave him leverage over both of you. This and motives for the rest of you were well established during the initial investigation, and we need not recapitulate the details.

"It is also true, however, that subsequent investigations have revealed that all of you had alibis for the moment when Musgrave was struck down. Lucinda and Delaurence were together in the kitchen until Lucinda left to investigate the shout she heard; this was confirmed by caterers hired for the Solday party. Heidi left the patio shortly before Musgrave was found, but she was consulting with Hiu and the orchestra during the time in question. George Butler went into the house with Arnold Ohman, but they were together for most of the time they were inside. Eventually George left to go to the bathroom, but luckily for him the orchestra's first clarinetist was there to confirm his presence. And fortunately for

Mr. Ohman, I myself could see him from the patio, standing in the hallway until the very moment when Lucinda screamed.

"So you see"—Freya paused, eyed us one by one, ran a finger along the frame of the big painting—"the problem took on a new aspect. It became clear that, while many had a motive to kill Musgrave, no one had the opportunity. This caused me to reconsider. How, exactly, had Musgrave been killed? He was struck on the head by the frame of one of Heidi's hall mirrors. Though several mirrors were broken in the melee following Lucinda's screams, we know the one that Musgrave was struck with; it was at the bend in the hallway leading from the atrium to the patio. And it was only a couple of meters away from a step down in the hallway."

Freya took a large house plan from a table and set it before the policemen. "Sandor Musgrave, you will recall, was new to Mercury. He had never seen a Solday celebration. When the Great Gates opened and the reflected light filled this villa, my suggestion is that he was overwhelmed by fright. Lucinda heard him cry for help—perhaps he thought the house was burning down. He panicked, rushed out of the study, and blindly began to run for the patio. Unable to see the step down or the mirror, he must have pitched forward, and his left temple struck the frame a fatal blow. He crawled a few steps farther, then collapsed and died."

Heidi stepped forward. "So Musgrave died by accident?"

"This is my theory. And it explains how it was that no one had the opportunity to kill him. In fact, no one did kill him." She turned to the police. "I trust you will follow up on this suggestion?"

"Yes," said the one taking notes. "Death declared accidental by consulting investigator. Proceed from there." He exchanged glances with his colleagues. "We are satisfied this explains the facts of the case."

Heidi surveyed the silent group. "To tell you the truth, I am very relieved." She turned to Delaurence. "Let's open the bar. It would be morbid to celebrate an accidental death, but here we can say we are celebrating the absence of a murder.''

The others gave a small cheer of relief, and we surrounded the bartender.

A few days later Freya asked me to accompany her to North Station. "I need your assistance."

"Very well," I said. "Are you leaving Terminator?''

"Seeing someone off."

When we entered the station's big waiting room, she inspected the crowd, then cried, "Arnold!" and crossed the room to him. Arnold saw her and grimaced. "Oh, Arnold,'' she said, and leaned over to kiss him on each cheek. "I'm very proud of you.''

Arnold shook his head, and greeted me mournfully. "You're a hard woman, Freya," he told her. "Stop behaving so cheerfully, you make me sick. You know perfectly well this is exile of the worst sort.''

"But Arnold," Freya said, "Mercury is not the whole of civilization. In fact it could be considered culturally dead, an immense museum to the past that has no real life at all.''

"Which is why you choose to live here, I'm sure," he said bitterly.

"Well of course it does have some pleasures. But the really vital centers of any civilization are on the frontier, Arnold, and that's where you're going.''

Arnold looked completely disgusted.

"But Arnold," I said. "Where are you going?''

"Pluto," he said curtly.

"*Pluto?*" I exclaimed. "But whatever for? What will you do there?''

He shrugged. "Dig ditches, I suppose.''

Freya laughed. "You certainly will not." She addressed me: "Arnold has decided, very boldly I might add, to aban-

don his safe career as a dealer here on Mercury, to become a
real artist on the frontier.''

"But *why?*"

Freya wagged a finger at Arnold. "You must write us
often.''

Arnold made a strangled growl. "Damn you, Freya. I
refuse. I refuse to go.''

"You don't have that option," Freya said. "Remember
the chalk, Arnold. The chalk was your signature.''

Arnold hung his head, defeated. The city interfaced with
the spaceport station. "It isn't fair," Arnold said. "What am
I going to do out on those barbaric outworlds?''

"You're going to live," Freya said sternly. "You're going
to live and you're going to paint. No more hiding. Understand?''

I, at any rate, was beginning to.

"You should be thanking me profusely," Freya went on,
"but I'll concede you're upset and wait for gratitude by
mail.'' She put a hand on Arnold's shoulder and pushed him
affectionately toward the crossing line. "Remember to write.''

"But," Arnold said, a panicked expression on his face.
"But—''

"Enough!" Freya said. "Be gone! Or else.''

Arnold sagged, and stepped across the divide between the
stations. Soon the city left the spaceport station behind.

"Well," Freya said. "That's done.''

I stared at her. "You just helped a murderer to escape!''

She lifted an eyebrow. "Exile is a very severe punishment;
in fact in my cultural tradition it was the usual punishment
for murder committed in anger or self-defense.''

I waved a hand dismissively. "This isn't the Iceland of
Eric the Red. And it wasn't self-defense—Sandor Musgrave
was outright murdered.''

"Well," she said, "*I* never liked him.''

I told you before: she has no sense of right and wrong. It is a serious defect in a detective. I could only wave my arms in incoherent outrage; and my protests have never carried much weight with Freya, who claims not even to believe them.

We left the station. "What's that you were saying to Arnold about chalk?" I said, curiosity getting the better of me.

"That's the clue you provided, Nathaniel—somewhat transformed. As you reminded me, Musgrave was pointing at the patio, and Heidi's patio is made of a block of the Dover cliffs. Dover cliffs, as you know, are composed of *chalk*. So I returned to the painting, and cut through the back to retrieve samples of the chalk used in the underdrawing, which had been revealed to me by infrared photography." She turned a corner and led me uptown. "Chalk, you see, has its own history of change. In Monet's time, chalk was made from natural sources, not from synthetics. Sure enough, the chalk I took from the canvas was a natural chalk. But natural chalk, being composed of marine ooze, is littered with the fossil remains of unicellular algae called cocoliths. These cocoliths are different depending upon the source of the chalk. Monet used Rouen chalk, appropriately enough, which was filled with the cocoliths *Maslovella barnesae* and *Cricolithus pemmatoidens*. The cocoliths in our painting, however, are *Neococcolithes dubius*. Very dubious indeed—for this is a North American chalk, first mined in Utah in 1924."

"So Monet couldn't have used this chalk! And there you had your proof that the painting is a fake."

"Exactly."

I said doubtfully, "It seems a subtle clue for the dying Musgrave to conceive of."

"Perhaps," Freya said cheerfully. "Perhaps he was only pointing in the direction of the patio by the accident of his final movements. But it was sufficient that the coincidence gave me the idea. The solution of a crime often depends upon imaginary clues."

"But how did you know Arnold was the forger?" I asked. "And why, after taking the trouble to concoct all those paints, did he use the wrong chalk?"

"The two matters are related. It could be that Arnold only knew he needed a natural chalk, and used the first convenient supply without knowing there are differences between them. In that case it was a mistake—his only mistake. But it seems unlike Arnold to me, and I think rather that it was the forger's signature. In effect, the forger said, if you take a slide of the chalk trapped underneath the paint, and magnify it five thousand times with an electron microscope, you will find me. This chalk never used by Monet is my sign. —For on some level every forger hopes to be discovered, if only in the distant future—to receive credit for the work.

"So I knew we had a forger on Mercury, and I was already suspicious of Arnold, since he was the dealer who brought the painting to Mercury, and since he was the only guest at Heidi's party with the opportunity to kill Musgrave; he was missing during the crucial moments—"

"You *are* a liar."

"And it seems Arnold was getting desperate; I searched among his recent bills, and found one for three suction plates. So when we found him on the track I was quite sure."

"He stuck himself to the track?"

"Yes. The one on his right wrist was electronically controlled, so after setting the other two he tripped the third between his teeth. He hoped that we would discover him there after missing him at the museum, and think that there was someone else who wished him harm. And if not, the cowcatchers would pull him free. It was a silly plan, but he was desperate after I set up that appointment with him. When I confronted him with all this, after we rescued him from the tracks, he broke down and confessed. Sandor Musgrave had discovered that the Monet was a fake while blackmailing the Evans family in England, and after forcing Heidi to give him a job, he worked on the painting in secret until he found proof. Then he blackmailed Arnold into bankruptcy, and when on Solday he pressed Arnold for more money, Arnold lost his composure and took advantage of the confusion caused by the opening of the Great Gates to smack Musgrave on the head with one of Heidi's mirrors.''

I wagged a finger under her nose. "And you set him free. You've gone too far this time, Freya Grindavik.''

She shook her head. "If you consider Arnold's case a bit longer, you might change your mind. Arnold Ohman has been the most important art dealer on Mercury for over sixty years. He sold the Vermeer collection to George Butler, and the Goyas to Terminator West Gallery, and the Pissarros to the museum in Homer Crater, and those Chinese landscapes you love so much to the city park, and the Kandinskys to the Lion of the Greys. Most of the finest paintings on Mercury were brought here by Arnold Ohman.''

"So?''

"So how many of those, do you think, were painted by Arnold himself?''

I stopped dead in the street, stunned at the very idea. "But—but that only makes it worse! Inestimably worse! It means there are fakes all over the planet!''

"Probably so. And no one wants to hear that. But it also means Arnold Ohman is a very great artist. And in our age that is no easy feat. Can you imagine the withering reception his work would have received if he had done original work? He would have ended up like Harvey Washburn and all the rest of them who wander around the galleries like dogs. The great art of the past crashes down on our artists like meteors, so that their minds resemble the blasted landscape we roll over. Now Arnold has escaped that fate, and his work is universally admired, even loved. That Monet, for instance—it isn't just that it passes for one of the cathedral series—it could be argued that it is the *best* of them. Now is this a level of greatness that Arnold could have achieved—would have been *allowed* to achieve—if he had done original work on this museum planet? Impossible. He was forced to forge old masters to be able to fully express his genius.''

"All this is no excuse, for forgery or murder.''

But Freya wasn't listening. "Now that I've exiled him, he may go on forging old paintings, but he may begin painting something new. That possibility surely justifies ameliorating his punishment for killing such a parasite as Musgrave. And there is Mercury's reputation as art museum of the system to consider. . . .''

I refused to honor her opinions with a reply, and looking around I saw that during our conversation she had led me far up the terraces. "Where are we going?''

"To Heidi's," she said. And she had the grace to look a little shamefaced—for a moment, anyway. "I need your help moving something.''

"Oh, no.''

"Well," Freya explained, "when I told Heidi some of the facts of the case, she insisted on giving me a token of her gratitude, and she overrode all my refusals, so . . . I was forced to accept.'' She rang the wall bell.

"You're joking," I said.

"Not at all. Actually, I think Heidi preferred not to own a painting she knew to be a fake, you see. So I did her a favor by taking it off her hands.''

When Delaurence let us in, we found he had almost finished securing *Rouen Cathedral—Sun Effect* in a big plastic box. "We'll finish this," Freya told him.

While we completed the boxing I told Freya what I thought of her conduct. "You've taken liberties with the *law*—you lied right and left—''

"Well boxed," she said. "Let's go before Heidi changes her mind.''

"And I suppose you're proud of yourself."

"Of course. A lot of lab work went into this."

We maneuvered the big box through the gate and into the street, and carried it upright between us, like a short flat coffin. We reached Freya's villa, and immediately she set to work unboxing the painting. When she had freed it she set it on top of a couch, resting against the wall.

Shaking with righteous indignation, I cried, "That *thing* isn't a product of the past! It isn't *authentic*. It is only a *fake*. Claude Monet *didn't paint it*."

Freya looked at me with a mild frown, as if confronting a slightly dense and very stubborn child. "So what?"

After I had lectured her on her immorality a good deal more, and heard all of her patient agreement, I ran out of steam. "Well," I muttered, "you may have destroyed all my faith in you, and damaged Mercury's art heritage forever, but at least I'll get a good story out of it." This was some small comfort. "I believe I'll call it 'The Case of the Thirty-third Cathedral of Rouen.' "

"What's this?" she exclaimed. "No, of course not!" And then she insisted that I keep everything she had told me that day a secret.

I couldn't believe it. Bitterly I said, "You're like those forgers. You want *somebody* to witness your cleverness, and I'm the one who is stuck with it."

She immediately agreed, but went on to list all the reasons no one else could ever learn of the affair—how so many people would be hurt—including her, I added acerbically—how so many valuable collections would be ruined, how her plan to transform Arnold into a respectable honest Plutonian artist would collapse, and so on and so forth, for nearly an hour. Finally I gave up and conceded to her wishes, so that the upshot of it was, I promised not to write down a single word concerning this particular adventure of ours, and I promised furthermore to say nothing of the entire affair, and to keep it a complete secret, forever and ever.

But I don't suppose it will do any harm to tell you.

—1983

Ridge Running

Three men sit on a rock. The rock is wet granite, a bouldertop surrounded by snow that has melted just enough to reveal it. Snow extends away from the rock in every direction. To the east it drops to treeline, to the west it rises to a rock wall that points up and ends at sky. The boulder the three men are on is the only break in the snow from the treeline to rock wall. Snowshoe tracks lead to the rock, coming from the north on a traverse across the slope. The men sit sunning like marmots.

One man chews snow. He is short and broad-chested, with thick arms and legs. He adjusts blue nylon gaiters that cover his boots and lower legs. His thighs are bare, he wears gray gym shorts. He leans over to strap a boot into an orange plastic snowshoe.

The man sitting beside him says, "Brian, I thought we were going to eat lunch." This second man is big, and he wears sunglasses that clip onto prescription wire-rims.

"Pe-ter," Brian drawls. "We can't eat here comfortably, there's barely room to sit. As soon as we get around that

14

shoulder''—he points south—"the traverse will be done and we'll be at the pass.''

Peter takes in a deep breath, lets it out. "I need to rest.''

"O.K.,'' Brian says, "do it. I'm just going to go around to the pass, I'm tired of sitting.'' He picks up the other orange snowshoe, sticks his boot in the binding.

The third man, who is medium height and very thin, has been staring at the snow granules on his boot. Now he picks up a yellow snowshoe and kicks into it. Peter sees him do it, sighs, bends over to yank his aluminum-and-cord snowshoes out of the snow they are stuck in.

"Look at that hummingbird,'' the third man says with pleasure and points.

He is pointing at blank snow. His two companions look where he is pointing, then glance at each other uncomfortably. Peter shakes his head, looks at his boots.

"I didn't know there were hummingbirds in the Sierras,'' the third man says. "What a beauty!'' He looks at Brian uncertainly. "*Are* there hummingbirds in the Sierras?''

"Well,'' Brian says, "actually, I think there are. But . . .''

"But not this time, Joe,'' Peter finishes.

"Ah,'' Joe says, and stares at the spot in the snow. "I could have sworn . . .'' Peter looks at Brian, his face squinched up in distress. "Maybe the light breaking on that clump of snow,'' Joe says, mystified. "Oh, well.''

Brian stands and hoists a compact blue pack onto his shoulders, and steps off the boulder onto the snow. He leans over to adjust a binding. "Let's get going, Joe,'' he says. "Don't worry about it.'' And to Peter: "This spring snow is great.''

"If you're a goddamn polar bear,'' Peter says.

Brian shakes his head, and his silvered sunglasses flash reflections of snow and Peter. "This is the best time to be up here. If you would ever come with us in January or February you'd know that.''

"Summer!" Peter says as he picks up his long frame pack. "Summer's what I like—catch the rays, see the flowers, walk around without these damn flippers on—" He swings his pack onto his back, steps back quickly (clatter of aluminum on granite) to keep his balance. He buckles his waistbelt awkwardly, looks at the sun. It is near midday. He wipes his forehead.

"You don't even come up with us in the summer anymore," Brian points out. "What has it been, four years?"

"Time," Peter says. "I don't have any time, and that's a fact."

"Just all your life," Brian scoffs. Peter shakes off the remark with an irritated scowl, and steps onto the snow.

They turn to look at Joe, who is still inspecting the snow with a fierce squint.

"Hey, Joe!" Brian says.

Joe starts and looks up.

"Time to hike, remember?"

"Oh, yeah, just a second." Joe readies himself.

Three men snowshoeing.

Brian leads. He sinks about a foot into the snow with every step. Joe follows, placing his yellow snowshoes carefully in the prints of Brian's, so that he sinks hardly at all. Peter pays no attention to prints, and his snowshoes crash into and across the holes. His snowshoes slide left, downhill, and he slips frequently.

The slope steepens. The three men sweat. Brian slips left one time too often and stops to remove his snowshoes. They can no longer see the rock wall above them, the slope is so steep. Brian ties his snowshoes to his pack, puts the pack back on. He puts a glove on his right hand and walks canted over so he can punch into the slope with his fist.

Joe and Peter stop where Brian stops, to make the same

changes. Joe points ahead to Brian, who is now crossing a section of slope steeper than forty-five degrees.

"Strange three-legged hill animal," says Joe, and laughs. "Snoweater."

Peter looks in his pack for his glove. "Why don't we go down into the trees and avoid this damn traverse?"

"The view isn't as good."

Peter sighs. Joe waits, scuffs snow, looks at Peter curiously. Pete has put suntan oil on his face, and the sweat has poured from his forehead, so that his stubbled cheeks shine with reflected light.

He says, "Am I imagining this, or are we working really hard?"

"We're working very hard," Joe says. "Traverses are difficult."

They watch Brian, who is near the middle of the steepest section. "You guys do this snow stuff for *fun?*" Peter says.

After a moment Joe starts. "I'm sorry," he says. "What were we talking about?"

Peter shrugs, examines Joe closely. "You O.K.?" he asks, putting his gloved hand to Joe's arm.

"Yeah, yeah. I just . . . *forgot*. Again!"

"Everyone forgets sometimes."

"I know, I know." With a discouraged sigh Joe steps off into Brian's prints. Peter follows.

From above they appear little dots, the only moving objects in a sea of white and black. Snow blazes white and prisms flash from sunglasses. They wipe their foreheads, stop now and then to catch their breath. Brian pulls ahead, Pete falls behind. Joe steps out the traverse with care, talking to himself in undertones. Their gloves get wet, there are ice bracelets around their wrists. Below them solitary trees at treeline wave in a breeze, but on the slope it is windless and hot.

* * *

The slope lessens, and they are past the shoulder. Brian pulls off his pack and gets out his groundpad, sits on it. He roots in the pack. After a while Joe joins him. "Whew!" Joe says. "That was a hard traverse."

"Not really hard," Brian replies. "Just boring." He eats some M and M's, waves a handful up at the ridge above. "I'm tired of traversing, though, that's for sure. I'm going up to the ridge so I can walk down it to the pass."

Joe looks at the wall of snow leading up to the ridge. "Yeah, well, I think Pete and I will continue around the corner here and go past Lake Doris to the pass. It's almost level from here on."

"True. I'm going to go up there anyway."

"All right. We'll see you in the pass in a while."

Brian looks at Joe. "You'll be all right?"

"Sure."

Brian gets his pack on, turns and begins walking up the slope, bending forward to take big slow strides. Watching him, Joe says to himself, "Humped splayfoot pack beast, yes. House-backed creature. Giant snow snail. Yo ho for the mountains. Rum de dum. Rum de dum de dum."

Peter appears around the shoulder, walking slowly and carelessly. He spreads his groundpad, sits beside Joe. After a time his breathing slows. "Where's Brian?"

"He went up there."

"Is that where we're going?"

"I thought we might go around to the pass the way the trail goes."

"Thank God."

"We'll get to go by Lake Doris."

"The renowned Lake Doris," Peter scoffs.

Joe waves a finger to scold. "It is nice, you know."

* * *

Joe and Peter walk. Soon their breathing hits a regular rhythm. They cross a meadow tucked into the side of the range like a terrace. It is covered with suncones, small melt depressions in the snow, and the walking is uneven.

"My feet are freezing," Pete says from several yards behind Joe.

Joe looks back to reply. "It's a cooling system. Most of my blood is hot—so hot I can hold snow in my hand and my hand won't get cold. But my feet are chilled. It cools the blood. I figure there's a spot around my knees that's perfect. My knees feel great. I live there and everything's comfortable."

"My knees hurt."

"Hmm," Joe says. "Now that is a problem."

After a silence filled by the squeak of snow and the crick of boot against snowshoe, Pete says, "I don't understand why I'm getting so tired. I've been playing full-court basketball all winter."

"Mountains aren't as flat as basketball courts."

Joe's pace is a bit faster than Pete's, and slowly he pulls ahead. He looks left, to the tree-filled valley, but slips a few times and turns his gaze back to the snow in front of him. His breaths rasp in his throat. He wipes sweat from an eyebrow. He hums unmusically, then starts a breath-chant, muttering a word for each step: *animal, animal, animal, animal, animal.* He watches his snowshoes crush patterns onto the points and ridges of the pocked, glaring snow. White light blasts around the sides of his sunglasses. He stops to tighten a binding, looks up when he is done. There is a tree a few score yards ahead—he adjusts his course for it, and walks again.

After a while he reaches the tree. He looks at it; a gnarled old Sierra juniper, thick and not very tall. Around it hundreds of black pine needles are scattered, each sunk in its own tiny pocket in the snow. Joe opens his mouth several times, says "Lugwump?" He shakes his head, walks up to the tree, puts a hand on it. "I don't know who you are?" He leans in, his nose is inches from bark. The bark peels away from the tree like papery sheets of filo dough. He puts his arms out, hugs the trunk. "Tr-eeeee," he says. "Tr-eeeeeeee."

He is still saying it when Peter, puffing hard, joins him. Joe steps around the tree, gestures at a drop beyond the tree, a small bowl notched high in the side of the range.

"That's Lake Doris," he says, and laughs.

Blankly Peter looks at the small circle of flat snow in the center of the bowl. "Mostly a summer phenomenon," Joe says. Peter purses his lips and nods. "But not the pass," Joe adds, and points west.

West of the lake bowl the range—a row of black peaks emerging from the snow—drops a bit, in a deep, symmetrical U, an almost perfect semicircle, a glacier road filled with blue sky. Joe smiles. "That's Rockbound Pass. There's no way you could forget a sight like that. I think I see Brian up there. I'm going to go up and join him."

He takes off west, walking around the side of the lake until he can go straight up the slope rising from the lake to the pass. The snow thins on the slope, and his plastic snowshoes grate on stretches of exposed granite. He moves quickly, takes big steps and deep breaths. The slope levels and he can see the spine of the pass. Wind blows in his face, growing stronger with every stride. When he reaches the flat of the saddle in mid-pass it is a full gale. His shirt is blown cold against him, his eyes water. He can feel sweat drying on his face. Brian is higher in the pass, descending the north spine. His high shouts are blown past Joe. Joe takes off his pack and swings his arms around, stretches them out to the west. He is in the pass.

Below him to the west is the curving bowl of a cirque, one dug by the glacier that carved the pass. The cirque's walls are nearly free of snow, and great tiers of granite gleam in the sun. A string of lakes—flat white spots—mark the valley that extends westward out of the cirque. Lower ranges lie in rows out to the haze-fuzzed horizon.

Behind him Lake Doris's bowl blocks the view of the deep valley they have left behind. Joe looks back to the west; wind slams his face again. Brian hops down the saddle to him, and Joe whoops. "It's windy again," he calls.

"It's always windy in this pass," Brian says. He strips off his pack, whoops himself. He approaches Joe, looks around. "Man, for a while there about a year ago I thought we'd never be here again." He claps Joe on the back. "I'm sure glad you're here," he says, voice full.

Joe nods. "Me, too. Me, too."

Peter joins them. "Look at this," calls Brian, waving west. "Isn't this amazing?" Peter looks at the cirque for a moment and nods. He takes off his pack and sits behind a rock, out of the wind.

"It's cold," he says. His hands quiver as he opens his pack.

"Put on a sweatshirt," Brian says sharply. "Eat some food."

Joe removes his snowshoes, wanders around the pass away from Brian and Peter. The exposed rock is shattered tan granite, covered with splotches of lichen, red and black and green. Joe squats to inspect a crack, picks up a triangular plate of rock. He tosses it west. It falls in a long arc.

Brian and Peter eat lunch, leaning against a boulder that protects them from the wind. Where they are sitting it is fairly warm. Brian eats slices of cheese cut from a big block of it. Peter puts a tortilla in his lap, squeezes peanut butter out of a plastic tube onto it. He picks up a bottle of liquid butter and squirts a stream of it over the peanut butter.

Brian looks at the concoction and squints. "That looks like shit."

"Hey," Peter says. "Food is food. I thought you were the big pragmatist."

"Yeah, but . . ."

Pete wolfs down the tortilla, Brian works on the block of cheese.

"So how did you like the morning's hike?" Brian asks.

Pete says, "I read that snowshoes were invented by Plains Indians, for level places. In the mountains, those traverses"—he takes a bite—"those traverses were terrible."

"You used to love it up here."

"That was in the summers."

"It's better now, there's no one else up here. And you can go anywhere you want over snow."

"I've noticed you think so. But I don't like the snow. Too much work."

"Work," Brian scoffs. "The old law office is warping your conception of work, Peter."

Peter chomps irritably, looking offended. They continue to eat. One of Joe's nonsense songs floats by.

"Speaking of warped brains," Peter says.

"Yeah. You keeping an eye on him?"

"I guess so. I don't know what to do when he loses it, though."

Brian arches back and turns to look over the boulder. "Hey, Joe!" he shouts. "Come eat some lunch!" They both watch Joe jerk at the sound of Brian's voice. But after a moment's glance around, Joe returns to playing with the rocks.

"He's out again," says Brian.

"That," Peter says, "is one sick boy. Those doctors really did it to him."

"That *crash* did it to him. The doctors saved his life. You didn't see him at the hospital like I did. Man, ten or twenty years ago an injury like that would have left him a vegetable for sure. When I saw him I thought he was a goner."

"Yeah, I know, I know. The man who flew through his windshield."

"But you don't know what they *did* to him."

"So what did they do to him?"

"Well, they stimulated what they call axonal sprouting in the areas where neuronal connections were busted up—which means, basically, that they grew his brain back!"

"*Grew* it?"

"Yeah! Well some parts of it—the broken connections, you know. Like the arm of a starfish. You know?"

"No. But I'll take your word for it." Peter looks over the boulder at Joe. "I hope they grew back everything, yuk yuk. He might have one of his forgetting spells and walk over the edge there."

"Nah. He just forgets how to talk, as far as I can tell. Part of the reorganization, I think. It doesn't matter much up here." Brian arches up. "Hey, JOE! FOOD!"

"It does too matter," Peter says. "Say he forgets the word *cliff*. He forgets the concept, he says to himself I'm just going to step down to that lake there, and whoops, over the edge he goes."

"Nah," Brian says. "It doesn't work that way. Concepts don't need language."

"What?" Peter cries. "Concepts don't need language? Are you kidding? Man I thought Joe was the crazy one around here."

"No seriously," Brian says, shifting rapidly from his usual reserve to interested animation. "Sensory input is already a thought, and the way we field it is conceptual. Enough to keep you from walking off cliffs anyway." Despite this assertion he looks over his shoulder again. There stands Joe nodding as if in agreement with him.

"Yes, language is a contact lens," Joe says.

Peter and Brian look at each other.

"A contact lens at the back of the eyeball. Color filters into this lens, which is made of nameglass, and its reflected to the correct corner of the brain, tree corner or rock corner."

Peter and Brian chew that one over.

"So you lose your contact lenses?" Brian ventures.

"Yeah!" Joe looks at him with an appreciative glance. "Sort of."

"So what's in your mind then?"

Joe shrugs. "I wish I knew." After a while, struggling for expression: "I feel things. I feel that something's not right. Maybe I have another language then, but I'm not sure. Nothing looks right, it's all just . . . color. The names are gone. You know?"

Brian shakes his head, involuntarily grinning.

"Hmm," Peter says. "It sounds like you might have some trouble getting your driver's license renewed." All three of them laugh.

Brian stands, stuffs plastic bags into his pack. "Ready for some ridge runnning?" he says to the other two.

"Wait a second," Peter says, "we just got here. Why don't you kick back for a while? This pass is supposed to be the high point of the trip, and we've only been here half an hour."

"Longer than that," says Brian.

"Not long enough. I'm tired!"

"We've only hiked about four miles today," Brian replies impatiently. "All of us worked equally hard. Now we can walk down a ridge all afternoon, it'll be great!"

Peter sucks air between his teeth, holds it in, decides not to speak. He begins jamming bags into his pack.

They stand ready to leave the pass, packs and snowshoes on their backs. Brian makes a final adjustment to hipbelt—

Pete looks up the spine they are about to ascend—Joe stares down at the huge bowl of rock and snow to the west. Afternoon sun glares. The shadow of a cloud hurries across the cirque toward them, jumps up the west side of the pass and they are in it, for a moment.

"Look!" Joe cries. He points at the south wall of the pass. Brian and Pete look—

A flash of brown. A pair of horns, blur of legs, the distant *clacks* of rock falling.

"Mountain goat!" says Brian. "Wow!" He hurries across the saddle of the pass to the south spine, looking up frequently. "There it is again! Come on!"

Joe and Pete hurry after him. "You guys will never catch that thing," says Peter.

The south wall is faulted and boulderish, and they zig and zag from one small shelf of snow to the next. They grab outcroppings and stick fists in cracks, and strain to push themselves up steps that are waist-high. The wind peels across the spine of the wall and keeps them cool. They breathe in gasps, stop frequently. Brian pulls ahead, Peter falls behind. Brian and Joe call to each other about the goat.

Brian and Joe top the spine, scramble up the decreasing slope. The ridge edge—a hump of shattered rock, twenty or twenty-five feet wide, like a high road—is nearly level, but still rises enough to block their view south. They hurry up to the point where the ridge levels, and suddenly they can see south for miles.

They stop to look. The range rises and falls in even swoops to a tall peak. Beyond the peak it drops abruptly and rises again, up and down and up, culminating in a huge knot of black peaks. To the east the steep snowy slope drops to the valley paralleling the range. To the west a series of spurs and cirques alternate, making a broken desert of rock and snow.

The range cuts down the middle of it all, high above every-thing else that can be seen. Joe taps his boot on solid rock. "Fossil backbone, primeval earth being," he says.

"I think I still see that goat," says Brian, pointing. "Where's Peter?"

Peter appears, face haggard. He stumbles on a rock, steps quickly to keep his balance. When he reaches Brian and Joe he lets his pack thump to the ground.

"This is ridiculous," he says. "I have to rest."

"We can't exactly camp here," Brian says sarcastically, and gestures at the jumble of rock they are sitting on.

"I don't care," Peter says, and sits down.

"We've only been hiking an hour since lunch," Brian objects, "and we're trying to close in on that goat!"

"Tired," Peter says. "I have to rest."

"You get tired pretty fast these days!"

An angry silence.

Joe says in a mild voice. "You guys sure are bitching at each other a lot."

A long silence. Brian and Peter look in different directions.

Joe points down at the first dip in the ridge, where there is a small flat of granite slabs and corners filled with sand. "Why don't we camp there? Brian and I can drop our packs and go on up the ridge for a walk. Pete can rest and maybe start a fire later. If you can find wood."

Brian and Pete both agree to the plan, and they descend to the saddle campsite.

Two men ridge running. They make swift progress up the smooth rise, along the jumbled road at the top of the range. The bare rock they cross is smashed into fragments, splin-tered by ice and lightning. Breaking out of the blackish granite are knobs of tan rock, crushed into concentric rings of shards. They marvel at boulders which look like they have sat on the range since it began to rise. They jump from rock to rock, flexing freed shoulders. Brian points ahead and calls out when he sees the goat. "Do you see it?"

"Sure do," Joe says, but without looking up. Brian notices this and snorts disgustedly.

Shadows of the range darken the valley to the east. Joe hops from foothold to foothold, babbling at Brian all the while from several yards behind him. "Name it, name it. You name it. Naammme. What an idea. I've got three blisters on my feet. I named the one on the left heel Amos." Pause to climb a shoulder-high slab of granite. "I named the one on the right heel Crouch. Then I've got one on the front of my right ankle, and I named that one Achilles. That way when I feel it it's not like pain, it's like a little joke. Twinges in my heel"—panting so he can talk—"are little hellos, hellos with every step. Amos here, hi, Joe; Crouch here, hi, Joe. It's amazing. The way I feel I probably don't need boots at all. I should take them off!"

"You'd probably better keep them on," Brian says seriously.

Joe grins.

The incline becomes steeper and the edge of the ridge narrows. They slow down, step more carefully. The shattered rock gives way to great faulted blocks of solid mountain. They find themselves straddling the ridge on all fours, left feet on the east slope and right feet on the west. Both sides drop sharply away, especially the west. Sun gilds this steeper slope. Joe runs his hand down the edge of the range.

The ridge widens out, and they can walk again. The rock is shattered, all brittle plated angular splinters, covered with lichen. "Great granite," Joe says.

"This is actually diorite," Brian says. "Diorite or gabbro. Made of feldspar and darker stuff."

"Oh, don't give me that," Joe says. "I'm doing well just to remember granite. Besides, this stuff has been granite for a lot longer than geologists have been naming things. They can't go messing with a name like that." Still, he looks more closely at the rock. "Gabbro, gabbro . . . sounds like one of my words."

They wind between boulders, spring up escarpments. They come upon a knob of quartz that rises out of the black granite. The knob is infinitely cracked, as if struck on top by a giant sledgehammer. "Rose quartz," says Brian, and moves on. Joe stares at the knob, mouth open. He kneels to pick up chunks of the quartz, peers at them. He sees that Brian is moving on. Rising, he says to himself, "I wish I knew everything."

Suddenly they are at the top. Everything is below them. Beside Brian, Joe stops short. They stand silently, inches apart. Wind whips around them. To the south the range drops and rises yet again, to the giant knob of peaks they saw when they first topped the ridge. At every point of the compass mountains drop away, white folds crumpling to every horizon. Nothing moves but the wind. Brian says, "I wonder where that goat went to."

Two men sitting on a mountaintop. Brian digs into a pile of rocks, pulls out a rusty tin box. "Aha," he says. "The goat left us a clue." He takes a piece of paper from the box. "Here's its name—Diane Hunter."

"Oh, bullshit!" cries Joe. "That's no name. Let me see that." He grabs the box out of Brian's hand and the top falls off. A shower of paper, ten or twenty pieces of it, pops out of the box and floats down to the east, spun by the wind. Joe pulls out a piece still wedged in the box. He reads, "Robert Spencer, July 20th, 2014. It's a name box. It's for people who want to leave a record of their climb."

Brian laughs. "How could anyone get into something like

that? Especially on a peak you can just walk right up to." He laughs again.

"I suppose I should try to recover as many as I can," Joe says dubiously, looking down the steep side of the peak.

"What for? It's not going to erase their experience."

"You never know," says Joe, laughing to himself. "It very well might. Just think, all over the United States the memory of this peak has popped right out of twenty people's heads." He waves to the east. "Bye-bye . . ."

They sit in silence. Wind blows. Clouds pass by. The sun closes on the horizon. Joe talks in short bursts, waves his arms. Brian listens, watches the clouds. At one point he says, "You're a new being, Joseph." Joe cocks his head at this.

Then they just sit and watch. It gets cold.

"Hawk," says Brian in a quiet voice. They watch the black dot soar on the updraft of the range.

"It's the goat," says Joe. "It's a shapechanger."

"Nah. Doesn't even move the same."

"I say it is."

The dot turns in the wind and rises, circling higher and higher above the world, coasting along the updraft with minute wing adjustments, until it hovers over the giant, angular knotpeak. Suddenly it plummets toward the peaks, stooping faster than objects fall. It disappears behind the jagged black teeth. "Hawk," Joe breathes. "Hawuck divvve."

They look at each other.

Brian says, "That's where we'll go tomorrow."

Glissading down the snow expanse, skidding five or ten feet with each stiff-legged step, the two of them make rapid progress back to camp. The walking is dreamlike as they pump left . . . right . . . left . . . right down the slope.

"So what about that goat?" says Joe. "I never did see any prints."

"Maybe we shared a hallucination," says Brian. "What do they call that?"

"A folie à deux."

"I don't like the sound of that." A pause while they skid down a steep bank of snow, straight-legged as if they are skiing. "I hope Pete got a fire going. Damn cold up here."

"A feature of the psychic landscape," Joe says, talking to himself again. "Sure, why not? It looks about like what I'd expect, I'll tell you that. No wonder I'm getting things confused. What you saw was probably a fugitive thought of mine, escaping off across the waste. Bighorn sheep, sure."

After a while they can see the saddle where they left Peter, far below them in the rocky expanse. There is a spark of yellow. They howl and shout. "Fire! FIRE!"

In the sandy camp, situated in a dip between slabs of granite, they greet Pete and root through their packs with the speed of hungry men. Joe takes his pot, jams it with snow, puts it on the fire. He sits down beside Peter.

"You guys were gone a long time," Peter says. "Did you find that goat?"

Joe shakes his head. "It turned into a hawk." He moves his pot to a bigger flame. "Sure am glad you got this fire going," he says. "It must have been a bitch to start in this wind." He starts to pull off his boots.

"There wasn't much wood, either," Pete says. "But I found a dead tree down there a ways."

Joe prods a burning branch, frowns. "Juniper," he says with satisfaction. "Good wood."

Brian appears, dressed in down jacket, down pants, and down booties. Pete falls silent. Glancing at Pete, Joe notices this, and frowns again. He gets up stiffly to go to his pack and get his own down booties. He returns to the fire, finishes taking off his boots. His feet are white and wrinkled, with red blisters.

"Those look sore," says Pete.

"Nah." Joe gulps down the melted snow in his pot, starts melting more. He puts his booties on.

They watch the fire in silence.

Joe says, "Remember that time you guys wrestled in the living room of our apartment?"

"Yeah, we got all those carpet burns."

"And broke the lamp that never worked anyway—"

"And then you went berserk!" Brian laughs. "You went berserk and tried to bite my ear off!" They all laugh, and Pete nods, grinning with embarrassed pride.

"Pete won that one," Joe says.

"That's right," says Brian. "Put my shoulders to the mat, or to the carpet in that case. A victory for maniacs everywhere."

Ponderously Peter nods, imitating official approval. "But I couldn't beat you tonight," he admits. "I'm exhausted. I guess I'm not up to this snow camping."

"You were strong in those days," Brian tells him. "But you hiked a radical trail with us today, I'll tell you. I don't know too many people who would have come with us, actually."

"What about Joe here? He was on his back most of last year."

"Yeah, but he's crazy now."

"I was crazy before!" Joe protests, and they laugh.

Brian pours macaroni into his pot, shifts to a rock seat beside Peter so he can tend the pot better. They begin to talk about the days when they all lived together as students. Joe grins to hear them. He nearly overturns his pot, and they call out at him. Pete says, "The black thing is the pot, Joseph, the yellow stuff is fire—try to remember that." Joe grins. Steam rises from the pots and is whipped east by the evening breeze.

*   *   *

Three men sitting round a fire. Joe gets up, very slowly, and steps carefully to his pack. He unrolls his groundcloth, pulls out his sleeping bag. He straightens up. The evening star hangs in the west. It's getting darker. Behind him his old friends laugh at something Pete has said.

In the east there are stars. Part of the sky is still a light velvet blue. The wind whistles softly. Joe picks up a rock, looks at it closely. "Rock," he says. He clenches the rock in his fist, shakes it at the evening star, lofts it skyward. "Rock!" A tear gleams in his eyes. He looks down the range: *black dragon back breaking out of blue-white*, like consciousness from chaos, an unbroken range of peaks—

"Hey, Joseph! You lamebrain!"

"Space case!"

"—come take care of your pot before it puts the fire out."

Joe walks to the woodpile grinning, puts more wood on the fire, until it blazes up yellow in the dusk.

-—1975/1977/1983

The Disguise

I pulled open the theater door and stuck my foot against it to keep the wind that swirled in the street from slamming it shut. I swung my duffel bag through the doorway and followed it inside. The door closed with a forced hiss and the bright lights of the street were replaced by dim greys. The air was still.

My eyes adjusted, and slowly, as if candles were being lit, I perceived the narrow high room which was the foyer of the Rose Theatre. I crossed the room and peered in the ticket window. A thin young man, with eye sockets blacked, and white hair cropped close to his head, looked up at me. I dropped my bag, pulled my card from my pocket and handed it to him.

"Pallio," I said.

"Very good," he said, and looked at the card. "Now when Velasquo arrives we'll have everyone." He picked up a cast list and put a check beside my name. After slotting my card into the register, he touched some keys, and the square of plastic disappeared. "The charge is twelve percent higher now," he murmured. "They're trying to tax us to death." The card reappeared and he handed it back to me. "Let me take you to your room."

I picked up my bag. The cashier appeared through a doorway beside the window and led me down the hall, looking back over his shoulder to talk: "I don't trust this *Guise* play, I think that whole Aylesbury Collection is a Collier forgery. . . ." I ignored him and watched the footprints he left in the thick blue-black carpet. Dull bronze-flake wallpaper shattered the light from a half-dozen gas jets. The Rose was in its full Regency splendor, for the first time in months. The halls felt as subterranean as before, however; the Rose occupied only a few bottom floors in the Barnard Tower, an eighty-story complex.

The cashier stopped at one of a series of doors and opened it for me. Light flooded over us. We went in and were on a different set; snapping Jacob's ladders and colored liquids bubbling up tubes made me look for a mad scientist. But it was only a white-coated technician, at the computer terminal. He turned around, revealing a scrubbed, precisely shaved face. "Whom have you brought us?" he said.

"Pallio," replied the cashier. I dropped my bag.

"We're ready to give you your part," the technician said.

The chair was dressed up like a chrome-and-glass version of the table Frankenstein's monster was born on. "Does Bloomsman have to do this," I said.

"You know our director."

"Last time I was here it was a dentist's chair."

"Not many liked that one, as I recall."

I got into the chair while he tapped keys at the terminal, calling up from the artificial mind a detailed description of my brain's structure. When he was done he wrapped the pharmaceutical band around my neck. "Ready?" he asked. He tapped a key on the chair's console and I felt the odd sensation, like flexing a stiff muscle, of the injection—a tiny witch's brew of L-dopa, bufotenine, and norepinephrine. As always my heart began hammering immediately: not because of the introduced chemicals, but because of my own adrenaline, flooding through me to combat the imagined danger of a primal violation.

We waited. The room enlarged and flattened out into a painted cylinder. "Now for the hood," said the technician, his voice like tin. The hood descended and it was dark. The goggles were cold against my face, and my scalp prickled as filaments touched it.

"Time for the implant," the technician said. "Let's have alpha waves if you please." I started the stillness behind my nose. "Fine. Here we go."

In my vision a blue field flickered at around ten cycles per second, and voices chattered in both ears, creating counterpoints of blank verse. In those connected clumps known as the limbic system, scattered across the bottom of my cerebral cortex, new neural activity began. Electrical charges skipped through the precise network of neurons until they reached the edge of the familiar; synapses fired in new directions, and were forever changed. I was growing. I felt none of it.

Memories came before me in confusing abundance, passing before I could fix on them. An afternoon by the window in an Essex library, watching green hills become invisible in the grey rain. In the colony off Jamaica just after the earthquake, when everyone was silent, feeling the pressure of the hundred fathoms of water above. The run of basses in the scherzo of Beethoven's Fifth. A strong smell of disinfectant—hospital smell—and the voice of Carlos, droning quietly: "It was in the fourth act of *Hamlet*, when I as Claudius was on my knees, attempting to pray. Hamlet was above and to one side, on the balcony, and in my peripheral vision his face distorted into a mask of fang and snout. As he finished his soliloquy he turned away from the balustrade, but his head stayed fixed, twisted entirely over one shoulder, and he continued to glare down at me. My memory flooded. The moment I understood he was the Hieronomo, he jumped the balustrade, and I leaped to my feet only to meet the falling épée blade directly in the chest. I heard the cries of shock, but nothing more. . . .''

Blackness. Then the suction pulling at my eyes as the eyepieces withdrew. The hood rose and the white room reappeared. I twisted my head back and forth.

"Got it?" asked the technician. I paused and thought. Pallio . . . yes. A series of exclamations marked his entrance in the first scene, a conference with Velasquo. I knew only my first few lines, plus cue lines, and Bloomsman's laconic blocking, appropriate to the improvisational nature of the art: "Confront Velasquo center stage." The rest of my part would come to me throughout the course of the play, irregularly, recalled by unknown cues. This was the minimum script that Bloomsman allowed one to receive; it was the preferred preparation among seasoned actors.

"Backstage is that way," the technician said. He helped me up. I swayed unsteadily. "Break a leg," he said brightly, and returned to his terminal. I picked up my costume bag and left the room.

The hall expanded near the gas jets and contracted in the dimmer sections. I stopped and leaned against the wall, concentrating to recover from the dissociation of the implant. The wallpaper was not actually flake—it had once been a smooth sheen, but had cracked and peeled away into thousands of bronze shavings. Chips broke off under me and floated to the carpet. I strode down the hall, uncertain how long I had stopped. My sense of estrangement was stronger than usual, as if I had learned more than a play.

The hall ended in a T and I could not remember which way to go. Acting on a dim intuition I turned right and found myself in a veritable maze of T-connections. I alternated turns, going first right, then left. One hall I followed dropped several steps, then turned and became a flight of stairs, which I descended. At the bottom of this stairway were three long, dim halls, all furnished (like the stairway) with the same dark carpet, bronze wallpaper, and gas jets. I chose the right-hand one and ventured on. Just as I began to think myself inextricably lost there was a door, recessed into the right wall. I opened it and was at the back of the theater, looking across the audience to the curtain.

The audience was large, about forty or fifty people. Many times I had acted in plays which no one had come to see; in those the imaginary fourth wall had become real, and we had played for ourselves, aware only of the internal universe of the play. Most actors preferred it that way. But I liked the idea of an audience watching. And it was not surprising, with this play. It wasn't often that one got to see the first performance of a play four hundred years old.

An usher appeared and propped the door open for me. Behind him a fully-armed security guard looked me over. He was there, I supposed, because of Hieronomo. The usher offered me a program and I took it. "I need to get backstage," I whispered.

He smiled. "Just go through the door by the stage," he said. "It's easier."

Backstage I stopped and looked at the program in my hand. The first page listed the dramatis personae:

THE GUISE

Pallio, Duke of Naples
Velasquo, his younger brother
Donado, a Cardinal
Sanguinetto, a Sicilian count
Orcanes ⎱ gentlemen: followers of Donado
Hamond ⎰
Mura, a priest: attendant to Donado
Ursini ⎱ friends to Sanguinetto
Ferrando ⎰
Elazar, a supposed doctor

Caropia, sister to Pallio and Velasquo
Leontia, wife to Donado, and sister to Orcanes
Carmen, servant to Caropia

Courtiers, Masquers, Officers and Guards, Pages, Seer.

Director: Eunice Bloomsman

The opposite page was almost filled by one of Bloomsman's learned program notes:

> *The Guise* is one of the four previously lost plays in the Aylesbury Collection, twenty-four plays and hundreds of miscellaneous papers discovered in 2052. The invaluable books and manuscripts, found at Aylesbury Manor near Oxford, had been locked in a storage trunk for over three hundred years.
>
> The copy of *The Guise* in the Collection is a quarto volume, published in 1628 "by N.O. for Thomas Archer." Stage directions have been added by an unknown 17th century hand.
>
> The text is anonymous. It was presumed that the play was by John Webster, who mentioned a work of his by the same title in the dedication to *The*

Devil's Law Case (1623). But this has been questioned. Earlier references to a *Guise* play—variously spelled *The Gwuisse,* or *The Guesse*—indicate that there was probably more than one play so named. Most of these presumably concern the de Guise family, but the plot of our play was taken from an Italian novella, *Il Travestimento di Pallio.*

Critics have made cases for the authorship of Middleton, Tourneur, and Massinger. The debates continue—even the authenticity of the entire Collection has been questioned recently. While this state of uncertainty remains, we at the Rose have thought it best not to attribute authorship.

This is the first Vancouver performance of *The Guise.*

It was less than I already knew from talking to Bloomsman. I had been one of many requesting a part; it had been worse than trying to get reservations to play Hamlet. Everyone who performed Jacobean drama had inquired, fascinated by the prospect of a new and unknown play. It had been a surprise when Bloomsman called and said, "You'll be Pallio."

I made my way through backstage corridors to the dressing room, found the cubicle with my name on it. My first costume—grey britches, white ruffled shirt-front, long blue coat—felt as familiar to me as my street clothes. The other costumes went on hooks. I sat down before the mirror, turned on its lights, and pulled my makeup kit from the bottom of the bag. My face was damp; the white powder stuck to it. I darkened my eyelids, exaggerated the curve of my upper lip. The sight of the stranger in the mirror, face white as a mask, quickened my pulse. I considered the many layers of his character, and played over his archaic language.

A small crystal perfume bottle rolled against my foot. I reached down, picked it up; still seated, I stuck my head around the partition separating me from the next cubicle. There was no one there. Dresses, white and scarlet and black, hung from the walls, making the cubicle seem smaller. Crystal bottles like the one in my hand reflected the blue light from the makeup mirror behind them.

Within the mirror there was movement. I turned my head and looked up at an auburn-haired actress, one I had never seen before. Her face was a narrow oval. Her eyes, grey as slate and flecked with black, surveyed me calmly. She looked into her cubicle and back, clearly framing her question. I lifted the bottle in explanation, and her mouth, which curved down sharply in repose, lifted as if propelled by the same motion, into a warm smile.

"Caropia?" I asked.

Her head turned aside. She walked past me into her cubicle without responding. A strand of her hair spiraled down; her slim back was splashed with tiny streaks of the powder that whitened her shoulders. I noticed that the grey eyes were still observing me from the mirror, and I quickly withdrew. Pallio's face mocked me in my own glass. Remember where you are, he said. . . . By and large, acting was as congenial an art form as any other; friends often performed plays together. But those of us who gravitated to the world of Jacobean tragedy were not a very communicative bunch. Strangers came in, played their parts, and went their separate ways into the city, remaining strangers to each other. The Hieronomo was one of us.

The stage set was large and uncluttered. The bedroom at the rear had wide black staircases bracketing it, and a narrow balcony above, so that it was deeply recessed, like a cave. I experienced the familiar wash of *déjà vu* as I viewed it; a false one, in that I had truly *already seen* the set, as part of the implanting. Real *déjà vu* would have been an uncanny feeling, I was sure; but in a world of memory implants it was as common as recollection itself. (Still, there were people addicted to the sensation. They would implant in their memory the remembrance of a world tour and then take that very tour, in a continuous state of *déjà vu*, pulse high, adrenaline running in their arteries. . . .)

In the large prop room directly behind the stage the director, Eunice Bloomsman, was holding the first and final cast meeting. Bloomsman was quite short, and very calm. Many of the players were ignoring her, expressing the common belief among them that directors were powerless lackeys, no more than the stage managers of old. But they were mistaken—directors programmed the information to be implanted in the players, and that gave them the chance to exert much subtle influence.

Bloomsman looked up at me, then continued. "All of you but one chose minimum text, so you'll have to stay alert to keep up. I've made the cues two and sometimes three lines long, so you'll have plenty of warning. In case you get lost there will be prompters in the usual places.

"This play has an extraordinary history, as you know, and there's a large audience here to see us, so let's try to do a good job. That means an absolute ban on interpolations—agreed?" There were nods from several. "Good. Now introduce yourselves so you'll know who's who."

A tall man stood, dressed in the rich red robes of stage clergy. "I'm Cardinal Donado," he said.

Two men then rose and introduced themselves as Hamond and Orcanes, followers of Donado. I had played with them before; they always performed together.

The actor next to them tugged at his black waistcoat and looked about the chamber. "Sanguinetto," he said in a harsh, low voice. I had played with him before also. He always took the part of the most deranged villain the work had to offer, which in revenge tragedy was saying a great deal. I had watched him play Iago with the most chilling bitterness; and in *Edward II* he had laughed his way through the ugly part of the murderer Lightborn. This actor took the backstage convention of silence to its limit, and never said anything but his lines. Between scenes he stood wordlessly near his next entrance. This was too much for some. Once a young actor had drawn me aside and asked me if I thought he was the Hieronomo—I had laughed. No, I told him, the Hieronomo always takes the part of the hero. Besides, he always returns with a different face, and I've seen this man before.

The others rose and identified themselves. I didn't recognize any of them. Latecomers from the dressing room arrived, and the diverse mix of costumes now included every color, creating a confusion much more plausible than any coordinated costuming could be. This was Bloomsman's idea, another of her innovations that seemed to give the players more freedom.

When the auburn-haired actress stood, she looked directly at me. Behind the mask of cosmetics (her mouth was a dangerous sickle of dark red) her grey eyes seemed colorless. "Caropia," she said. I remained expressionless, and she smiled.

Then there was a rustle and a man stepped out of a dim back corner of the room. He was dressed in black, and his short hair was a light, dull blond. He had thin lips, and a wide jaw that made his face look square.

My heart was thumping rapidly. Bloomsman turned to him. "And you are?" she inquired.

"I am Velasquo," the man said, and at that moment I felt extreme cold, as if suddenly probability had relaxed and all the air had left my side of the room. Something about the man—the turn of his nose—told me I should know him, and in my brain thoughtless energy ran through neural corridors, struggling in vain for recognition.

"That's very good," Bloomsman was saying. Everyone else was attending to their appearance, each of them preparing for his or her five thousandth, ten thousandth entrance. . . .

I felt isolated. "The whole cast is here. Is everyone familiar with the stage?" The question was ignored. Bloomsman pursed her lips into an expression of contempt. "Let's begin."

The curtain rose. Lights dimmed, and the audience was nothing but rows of white faces, which slowly became indistinct, like blobs of dough, then faded away in the deeper gloom. Small rustlings ended, and the little room was perfectly silent, perfectly dark.

A shaft of blue light, so faint that it first appeared to be only a seam in the blackness, gained strength and defined center stage. Into this conjuration of blue walked Velasquo, who stopped as if snared by it. He turned to face the audience, and from my vantage point at stage right I could see his sharp profile, and the light hair, now glazed blue, and a suddenly raised hand, in which a sheet of paper fluttered. He spoke, in a nasal tenor:

"This note commands me: I must have revenge!"

He read the note aloud. It was a garbled, nearly incoherent document, which informed him that his father the old Duke had been murdered, "poison'd by a spider in his bed," and exhorted him to vengeance. It made only obscure references to the identity of the killer—"What now seems finest is most ill"—and Velasquo threw it down in disgust.

He explained to the audience that his father's death had been unexpected and mysterious; it had been attributed to overeating by Elazar, a doctor of doubtful reputation. He saw now that the foul play had been obvious. Bitterly he described the corrupt court of Naples, which, under the "dull and amiable" hand of his elder brother Pallio, now the Duke, had become the plaything of riotous sycophants. Pallio was too stupid to want to search for a murderer. (I listened with great interest.) The rest of the court was too evil, and probably somehow implicated in the deed. Only his sister Caropia remained untainted. As he described the rest of us, one by one, my mind reverberated with the memory of the play, which hovered just on the edge of consciousness. Suddenly I knew the end of the play; the tangled plots that led to it were still a blank, but there were tendrils of association that linked each character with his final fate, and I saw the culmination, the vivid murders, my own death, the bloody, corpse-littered stage.

Shaken, I watched Velasquo walk toward me. I had never divined the end of the play so soon before— Velasquo raised his voice, and my attention was drawn back to him. He vowed to look for the note's author, who clearly knew more than he had written, and then search for the killer:

> "I'll seek him out—to do it I'll dissemble:
> And if there be a murderer, let him tremble."

That was my cue.

I walked on stage and an aura of blue light surrounded me. Velasquo greeted me and I replied, a bit too loudly, I thought, for the size of the room. I began concentrating, working to express naturally lines I had never spoken, doing that improvisation of stance and gesture which makes ours so much different from the acting in any previous tradition.

His eyes never leaving me, Velasquo suddenly told me of the contents of the note— "Our poor father has been most foully murdered!"

My mouth fell open. "But nay," I objected, "he's dead." Velasquo ignored me and proceeded to describe the deed, in much more elaborate detail than the mysterious letter had, as if the bald mention of the crime had brought the scene up full-bloom in his imagination. At the end of the gruesome tale I said, "That's not so well done, brother!" and contin-

ued to make stupid exclamations of shock as Velasquo listed
the rest of the potential assassins at court. Finally he exhorted
me to vengeance, and I eagerly agreed to help him. "I'll be
your constant aid. But now, what shall we tell our holy
sister?"

"Nothing."

With an audible snap the stage was flooded in white and
yellow light, and nearly the entire cast paraded on. Velasquo
moved away from me and drifted off through the colorful
throng. The Cardinal led his retinue on, and I performed my
function as Duke by calling, in a clear falsetto, for order
amongst the revellers. One of the Cardinal's men proposed a
masque, to be held two days hence, and I gave the idea my
ducal approval. At the other side of the stage Sanguinetto
voiced caustic, railing asides, which were making the audience laugh; in my peripheral vision I could see their mouths
opening, faint in the wash of light from the stage. The
Cardinal lost several lines by speaking too soon. I had no
idea what he had said, and wondered if I had been cued. It
was always at this point, in the first crowd scene, that
confusions were most likely to occur. . . .

Caropia entered in a white gown, holding a cross at her
breast. By the obsequious gestures of the others it was clear
she was revered by all. Even Sanguinetto was silent. I went
to her and she held out the cross; I kissed it. Velasquo did the
same, and the Cardinal bowed deeply. She went to him and
they began a quick exchange that the rest of us were supposed to ignore. I remembered my blocking, voiced in
Bloomsman's dry tones—"Mime dialogue with Velasquo,
far stage left."

Velasquo grabbed my arm and pulled me there. I mouthed
words and he stared at my forehead. His mustard-brown eyes
were nearly crossed in their intensity. Again I had the over-
powering sensation of *presque vu* which told me I *almost*

knew him. He mouthed words and as my memory supplied his high, rasplike voice, the sensation of recognition grew to something like panic. Abruptly he turned and began his exit, yet he looked back at me, as if in response to my inner turmoil; his head swiveled almost completely over his right shoulder. At once I knew him.

I stepped back. He squinted slightly, surprised by the move. I turned and crossed the stage, unable to face him, and halted only when I was alone in the narrow corridor between the wings and the prop room.

He was the Hieronomo, I was certain of it. Was he?

Hieronomo is the hero of Thomas Kyd's *The Spanish Tragedie*, the first and most influential of English revenge dramas. In it Hieronomo's son is killed by noblemen of the Spanish court. Hieronomo feigns insanity to facilitate his revenge, but despair pushes the imitation into reality, and by the time he completes his vengeance he is mad.

Someone playing this role had apparently experienced a similar breakdown: the previous December, in a performance at the Kean Theatre, the actor playing Hieronomo's foe, the old Duke, had actually died, killed by a knife with a loose button-tip. By the time this was discovered, the Hieronomo had disappeared.

In the months following he had appeared six more times, perhaps ten, depending on how many rumors you believed; each time with a different face, and a different name, but the same deadly blade. In *Women Beware Women*, and *Antonio's Revenge*, and in three different *Hamlet*s, the end had been disrupted by the villain's death. It was said that once he had stayed to finish *Hamlet*, and had taken a round of applause before slipping away. Others reported that another Claudius had been killed at his prayers, in act four, providing a surprise ending; I knew that one to be true; I had known the actor. The rest was hearsay and rumor, spreading at differing speeds through the strange community, so that undoubtedly each of us had heard a different selection of stories, whispered to us in dressing room or lavatory.

I was sure Velasquo was he. I scoffed at the notion, aware of the power the new legend had gained among those who played in these dramas. But once the suspicion had appeared, it was impossible to expel—it was more *certainty* than suspicion, yet I resisted it. It was as likely as not that he was just another actor, doing an excellent job. In such company, how could I tell otherwise? How could I tell anything in this theater? I knew each player only as his part. It was impossible to know anything for sure—or if not, it would have to be cleverly learned.

Someone tapped my arm and I jumped. It was one of the prompters. "You're on," he said. I hurried to the stage, afraid I would have to ask him where we were, but the sight of Caropia, standing alone by the bed in the inner chamber, brought the scene to me. It was late in the act. I composed myself and walked on.

Her slim face was a shadowed mask of contemplation, and in the weak blue light she was nothing but modulations of grey. We stood frozen for long moments, until white light splashed across center stage. Then Caropia looked up. "Who's there?" she asked. "Your brother Pallio," I said, in a lower voice than I had used before, and then we rushed at each other and crashed together, to embrace and kiss with abandon. She bit at me, and I pulled my head back and laughed directly at the audience, aware of their collective gasp, which marked the pleasure of suspicions confirmed.

We desisted and I told Caropia, with suitable contempt, how Velasquo had come to me to confide that he suspected foul play in our father's death. At this her mouth set in its sharp downward curve. "You play the fool," she said, "he *is* one. Make your Sanguinetto kill him, as you had him kill

our odious father. . . ." I explained that this was impracti-
cal, since clearly someone at the court already knew what
had happened. We had to dissemble and find that person out,
before we could deal with Velasquo. Caropia shrugged; it
was my problem, I was to solve it as I would. I reminded her
that I had had the old Duke killed at her instigation—she
alone had feared his discovery of our incest—but the re-
minder was a mistake. In harsh and dangerous tones she
asked me not to mention the matter again. I agreed, but
begged her to help me find the informer, and as she walked
offstage she replied that she would if it pleased her. Out of
the audience's sight she turned and the faintest trace of a
smile lifted her mouth. She nodded at me with approval. But
I still had a short soliloquy:

"Damned bitch!" I said, "I'd kill you too did I not lust
for you." Then I looked to the audience.

"I love her as a man holds a wolf by the ears," I said, and
launched myself with vigor into the soliloquy of the villain,
the stage-Machiavel: glorying in my crimes, gleefully listing
my subterfuges, basking in my own cleverness, wittily seduc-
ing the audience to my side. "To lie upon my sister I have
laid my father under earth—grave crimes," I informed them,
and their laughter was an approval of sorts. I voiced the final
couplet as a close confidence:

> ". . . there's no one knows me.
> An honest simpleton still be my guise—
> Who does not seem a fool cannot be wise."

The theater blacked out and I made my way to the staccato
roll of applause. The first act was over.

I sat down on a stool just offstage and watched the second
act begin. Caropia stood before the bed. She was dressed in
red, a muted crimson with gold thread in it. In the sharp

white-yellow light it seemed the same color as her hair, and her mouth.

Sanguinetto entered from above. He stepped down soundlessly, choosing the stairs to the right. His black doublet complemented black hair and beard; his face was powder-white. He greeted her and told her of the arrival of the seer. "Does he read dreams?" she asked, and looked pleased when Sanguinetto answered that he did.

Sanguinetto reached the stage and crossed in front of Caropia. When he came between her and the audience it was like an eclipse; the light shifted to blue, and when she reappeared it seemed she was dressed in grey. Offstage in the wings opposite me, Velasquo leaned against a wall and watched.

With contemptuous amusement, Sanguinetto was blackmailing her. His references were vague to me; apparently he referred to something I had missed in the first act. Something that Caropia had done, or was doing, had been discovered by Sanguinetto. Now he was using the information as a lever to extract sexual favors. "Thy painted visage will be naught but candied flesh," he told her, "if you lie not with me." He circled her briskly and balked her attempts to turn her back on him. She tried to forestall him by denying his accusation, but he ran his hand over her hair and mocked her; and slowly, bitterly, she acquiesced.

As they moved back to the bed, continuing the macabre dance of thrust and parry, I marveled at their skill, at the absolute verisimilitude of their every movement and intonation. This was acting of the highest order; it was impossible for me to imagine them as anyone but Caropia and Sanguinetto.

Velasquo watched the scene without expression.

With Sanguinetto's hand at her throat, Caropia sank back on the bed. The lights dimmed with her descent and the theater was black before Sanguinetto joined her.

I sat in the dark, and considered tests.

*   *   *

I was startled to attention by my cue lines. The next scene had already begun. I strode on stage and spoke to the audience:

"O excellent! By that he'll conquer Rome!"

The audience roared. I had no idea what I had referred to, having forgotten the cue. I retreated to the left staircase, in my confusion aware only of my blocking.

More characters arrived and the scene became complex. Everyone was involved in the central event (which I had not yet deciphered), but many were making covert conversation, or uttering malicious asides. The Cardinal spoke, and suddenly I understood the import of the scene: he was asking Caropia to take holy orders, to become a nun. He persisted with an icy calm that I couldn't interpret, and her refusals became increasingly strident. Sanguinetto, Hamond and Orcanes, Ferrando and Ursini, all publicly encouraged her while privately vilifying her. Only Velasquo actually meant his praise. I could see the dim white faces of the audience breaking into laughter, and I felt Caropia's humiliation keenly. We could make her comic for the rest of the play, if we wanted to (I recalled once playing in a *Revenger's Tragedy* in which the cast had nearly killed themselves with mirth). Finally my cue lines arrived and it was easy for me to feign Pallio's anger:

"They that mock her soon will lie in heaps
    Of rotting flesh, all broken open to
    The sun and flies and maggots,
    And their half-empty eye sockets will stare
    At naught but Pallio, astonish'd still by his
    Abrupt revenge . . ."

The scene continued, but the laughter was greatly diminished. Velasquo grasped me by the arm. "Brother, I must speak to you anon," he said, staring at me curiously. I agreed, averting my gaze, and he slipped offstage behind me, leaving me with my heart knocking. He would have to be tested. . . .

Now Caropia approached me, ostensibly to consult in private about the question of holy orders. She drew me out on the apron just above the audience, and in a voice tight with rage demanded that I kill Sanguinetto. I asked why, and she told me a near-truth, the best sort of lie; Sanguinetto was blackmailing her, demanding sexual favors in exchange for silence concerning *my* guilt in the old Duke's death. I reacted with a lover's anger, and as I railed against Sanguinetto she stroked my arm, the softness of her hands belying the absolute implacability of her intentions.

She left with a last velvet command, and I found myself alone—the rest had exited during our dialogue. Blue light surrounded me, as tangible as if the gel covering the bulb had poured down into the cone of light. I collected myself and tried to project an assured, amused control:

> "The brother that I hate, and the sister
> That I hate and love (for there's
> Two feelings closer to each other than
> The minds of any pair of us) both press
> Me now like halves of a garotte,
> Yet I'll slip out and let them gnash together;
> I have a plot—yet soft—Velasquo—"

He entered. My back to him, and face to the audience, I let my features slacken into those of the Pallio he knew. There was laughter, and with a sudden leer I encouraged it, for it was directed at Velasquo. I turned and greeted him. He began by complaining that he had found no clue to the murderer's identity. I informed him that I had some news that might help him, then answered his questions so foolishly that it took him some time to deduce that if Sanguinetto kept spiders, and was blackmailing Caropia, he must indeed be the villain we were searching for. I expressed amazement at his intelligence.

While the audience laughed at my duplicity, Velasquo's face darkened, his jaw muscles bunched. The laughter died away completely before he spoke: "I'd have this be vengeance all will remember," he said, in a voice so harsh that it enforced belief, made one wonder, with squeamish anticipation, what forms revenge might take. . . . He spoke no more of it, however, which made me suspect he was omitting lines; he sent me on my way, then stalked aimlessly around the stage. Suddenly he stopped and laughed, first quietly, then in a sharp howl. In the midst of this nerve-shattering mirth the blackout snapped down and terminated both light and sound.

I was conscious of a plan that had formulated itself sometime during Velasquo's ominous drunkard's walk. I had a test, one that would leave me concealed; he would know he had been tested, of course—it was an unusual test that did not reveal that—but he would not know by whom.

In the prop room Ferrando and Ursini were running over an exchange of dialogue in double-time. A prompter at the rear entrance raised a hand; they filed on, allowing two brief bursts of yellow into the dark, grainy green of the room. I went to the prop table and casually scanned the small pile of stage-notes.

The top one was the one that would betray Pallio. I picked it up, and, holding it against me, went into the lavatory. Inside a stall I took a pencil stub from my vest pocket (my ribs were sticky with sweat), and flattened the vellum against the wall with my other hand. In a clumsy, rounded imitation of Bloomsman's Italianate lettering, I listed all the plays I had ever heard connected with the Hieronomo:

The Spanish Tragedie
Hamlet
Hamlet, Act Four
Antonio's Revenge
Women Beware Women
The Atheist's Tragedy

I couldn't think of a fully appropriate tag, and so finally added *manet alta mente repostum;* it remains deep in my mind. That would do.

I had just quietly replaced the note, and was turning from the prop table, when Sanguinetto appeared from the left hallway. He watched me as he picked up the sheet of vellum and put it inside his black doublet; I couldn't tell if he had seen me return it or not. His beard, rising almost to his eyes, hid all expression, and his steady stare revealed nothing but interest. He went to the curtained opening and paused for a moment. He pushed the curtain aside, allowing blue light to wash over him, and made his final entrance.

From the rear I could see only a portion of center stage, and I feared Velasquo would be out of my sight at the crucial moment, aborting the test and leaving me with my uncertainties. Hastily I made my way through the dark to stage right, to the vantage point where I had observed most of the play.

Caropia was there; noticing my appearance, she gestured me to her and with a lift of her head directed my attention to the stage. I stood beside her and looked out, feeling her hand's pressure against my arm.

Velasquo was in disguise, wearing a black hooded cape. He was establishing his credentials—he was, he said to Sanguinetto, Pinon d'Alsquove, a fellow Sicilian, who had been forced to flee their native island because he had unfortunately murdered a gentleman of importance. Sanguinetto accepted this, exhibiting the usual Jacobean inability to see through even the simplest of disguises. They seated themselves at a dining table set out on the apron, and proceeded to drink and regale each other with tales. Strange revelers they were, both dressed in black, presented in a brilliant white-violet light that illuminated every face in the audience. They traded bloody stories, and it became clear that Pinon d'Alsquove had much in common with his fellow countryman. (There was a certain logic to this Jacobean thinking: since all Italians were depraved, it made sense that the farther south one went, the worse they became.) The crime that caused Pinon's exile had been the last in a long and gruesome series. Sanguinetto became unnaturally gay as Pinon described the various methods he had used to dispatch his enemies back in Sicily, and they quickly finished a tall, slim bottle of wine. As Sanguinetto uncorked another one Pinon spoke to the audience, in Velasquo's high voice: "In midst of all his mirth he will meet death." Then they were roaring with laughter again, at the champagne cascading from the bottle Sanguinetto held in his lap. As he drank and bit huge chunks from a turkey leg, Pinon described one of his weapons:

> ". . . a most ingenious toy,
> A tiny spring with rapier-pointed ends,
> Held tight by threads of lightest leather; which
> Then hidden in the victim's food, and ate,
> The threads are quick digested, and the spring
> Jumps to its fullest length, ripping great holes
> Within thy rival's guts. Thus do Moors
> Kill dogs . . ."

Sanguinetto chewed on obliviously, and everyone in the theater watched him eat. "Aye," Pinon concluded,

> "Methinks I know all of the finest ways
> To end th' existence of a foe—"

Sanguinetto swallowed and struggled to his feet. He leaned over Pinon:

> "Thou missed a way that should be known
> To all Sicilians—I will show thee."

He hurried to the rear exit in long strides, knocked the curtain aside and disappeared. Pinon spoke in Velasquo's voice:

> "Now I suspect I've drawn him out like snail
> From shell, into the light where I may crush him."

Sanguinetto reappeared, holding at arm's length a tall glass box, like a candle lantern. Within it a thick-bodied, long-legged spider—a cane spider, I guessed—scrabbled up the walls and slid down again. Pinon leaped up, knocking his chair over. Sanguinetto pointed at the spider and leered proudly.

> "This spider's of a kind known but in Sicily.
> 'Tis said they come out of the sides
> Of fiery Aetna, as if escaped from hell.
> They live in fumes, feed on the fruit that's killed
> By ash, and are most poisonous."

"Tell me," Pinon said, his voice rising uncontrollably up to Velasquo's high tenor,

> "... might I buy that beauty
> From thee? I have a murder would be done
> Most fitting thus, most artful ..."

Sanguinetto considered it, cocking his head drunkenly to one side.

"I've more of these, they breed by hundreds—aye.
Done, if you pay me well enough."

Pinon: "I'll pay you."

They made the exchange, Sanguinetto accepting a small
pouch. He looked in it and grinned. Pinon was staring with
an intense frown at the spider within the glass. Sanguinetto
returned to the table and sat down, his back to Velasquo.

Sanguin: "We'll celebrate this sale with more revelry."
Pinon: "Indeed it is a glad occasion."
Sanguin: "I give you my assurance, who
           You set that tiny demon on will die
           Most painful—"

Pinon: "You'd know best, I'm certain . . ."

Now Pinon was standing right behind Sanguinetto, caped
arms high so that he appeared a huge shadow, holding the
glass box directly over the seated man's head. (Caropia's
fingers were digging into my arm.) The spider's legs struck
at the glass soundlessly. Sanguinetto reached forward and
grabbed the foam-streaked bottle, raised it to his lips, tilted
his head back; they froze:
Pinon pulled the floor of the box away and the spider
dropped onto Sanguinetto's face. He struck at it with his free
hand and it jumped to the table. As it skittered across, he
smashed the bottle on it, scattering green glass everywhere.
He staggered to his feet and arched back; his scream and
Velasquo's high staccato laugh began simultaneously. The
laughter continued longer.
On the table three or four spindly legs flailed at the air,
their fine articulation destroyed. With stiff, awkward movements, Sanguinetto pulled his dagger from his belt and stabbed
at the legs of the beast until they were still. He left the dagger

in the table and collapsed over his chair. His voice, guttural as a rasp over metal, rose from near the floor.

"Stranger, I would thy heart were that black corse
Upon the table: surely it resembles nothing closer.
You had no cause to murder me . . ."

Velasquo pushed the hood from his head, and his face, gleaming with sweat, suffused with exhilaration, shifted as he looked about the room. He circled the table, leaning over Sanguinetto to shout at him, interspersing his lines with bursts of strained laughter:

"I did have cause; I am Velasquo, see?
My father's murder made me seek revenge!
You murdered him, 'gainst you I had revenge!
Now all that's sweet is nothing to revenge!"

"Wrong," croaked Sanguinetto.

". . . As well might I commend myself
For vengeance 'gainst you, having killed that spider,
As you to gloat o'er me, who was no more
Than insect used to slay your father—"

Vel: "What's this?"
Sanguin: "I was hired, hired by Pallio—here's my
commission—"

He pulled the note from his doublet and tossed it on the floor, then twisted as spasms racked him.

"A cauldron churns and bubbles within my skull—
I see hell waiting; Death will have its fill—"

After a while he moved no more.

Velasquo kneeled at the sheet of vellum, smoothed it on his leg, read. I could feel my heart knocking at the back of my throat—

His head snapped up, his eyes, ablaze with a vicious, yellow intensity, searched from exit to exit, *looking at actors:* his expression was absolutely murderous. I wanted to flatten myself against the wall, to hide; it was difficult indeed to stand beside Caropia and feign unconcerned interest. For *his* was no acting, he had understood, he was the Hieronomo! I felt a surge of relief at the certainty of it, replaced by fear when I recalled what I was certain of. I was in mortal danger. But I *knew*.

Finally he broke the silence, in a voice that filled the room like cold air.

> "Pallio. Pallio, the simpleton, the fool.
> That mask conceal'd a parricide most cruel.
> Though first deceiv'd by his quick cloak of lies—"

He paused then, so that the next line would contain his private reference, unaware how accurate it already was:

> "I'll use his blood to wash away *his* guise."

The blackout allowed me to flee to my cubicle.

Act four began, and with it the gradual acceleration and disintegration typical of revenge tragedy. Plots skipped and jumped and ran afoul of each other, twisting without evident logic to their conclusion; characters died. . . . From my cubicle I listened to the first scenes emerging tinnily from a speaker placed in the partition. Leontia, the Cardinal's wife, whom I hadn't seen since before the play began, was being strangled by the Cardinal's men. The Cardinal entreated Caropia to leave Naples, and, perfectly aware of the danger at the court, she agreed. I felt pained at that; foolishly, I had hoped we would remain lovers until the end. Caropia was then confronted by Carmen, her maid, who had been eavesdropping. Carmen demanded payment to keep her from informing me of the Cardinal's plan—I laughed at that—it was a strange world we existed in, where some plotted against others, who listened as they did it. Caropia agreed, and then promptly poisoned her. The maid's screams brought guards, and the doctor Elazar, who declared it a natural death. He too had blackmail in mind, and after the guards left, Caropia was forced to stab him and hide his body under the bed.

I stopped listening, and attempted to decide what I should do next. Nothing occurred to me. *Nothing,* I thought, remembering with disgust the century or two of experience I had to draw on: I recalled canoeing down the Amazon, fighting in the streets of New York, a thousand other like events . . .

But what I actually had done was difficult to distinguish from all the things I remembered doing. All I was sure of was that I had spent a lot of time in a chair, living in words; and on stages. It was as if I were driving a vehicle, and the rearview mirror had expanded to fill the windshield. Or as if I were the Angel of Time, flying backward into the future! Metaphors came up to me like bowling balls out of an automatic return; but no plans, nothing like a decision. Who was I to decide? Who was I?

"Pallio," said the speaker loudly. It was a prompter, calling for me. I returned to the prop room, reluctant to take to the stage again. I could no longer remember what attraction I had ever had to it.

Bloomsman herself waved at me: I was on. I stepped out upon a dark stage. There was just enough grainy, purple light leaking down to enable me to perceive the silhouettes of three men, pulling something from beneath the bed. Something about the scene—the lithe, long-limbed black figures, crouching—lacked all familiarity—*jamais vu* swept over me like nausea. I no longer understood what I saw. The dark room was a dimensionless field, and the black figures were nameless objects, ominous because they moved. Meaningless sounds rang in my ears.

I came to and found myself confronted by Ferrando and Ursini, on a brightly lit apron. Their blades were out and pointed at my throat. My first thought was that I'd left my épée in my costume bag, and was defenseless; then synapses fired, for what reason I knew not, and my lines came to me. I was safe from them.

They accused me of Sanguinetto's murder, and in a rather weak imitation of the ingenuous public Pallio I informed them that Velasquo had been the last person seen with their late master. With trembling voice I quickly shifted their suspicions to Velasquo, feeling thankful that it made sense to play Pallio as a distracted man. I left the stage, and then had to watch while Velasquo surprised them and knifed them both in the back. He did it with a verve and accuracy that left me chilled; surely their improvised blocking couldn't be so well-done: had he begun already? But in the darkness between scenes Ferrando and Ursini brushed by me, muttering and giggling together. I shook my head in hopes of clearing it, inhaled sharply, and moved back onstage.

Again the light was deep crevasse-blue. Caropia was already there: we embraced. This was to be one of our last scenes together, I knew. Surely everyone knew. I moved to the apron and saw below me, in the front row, Ferrando, Ursini, Elazar, Carmen, Leontia, and Sanguinetto. It was the custom for actors whose work was done to join the audience, but it made me uncomfortable. Given the traditions of the genre it always seemed to me that they were still in the play as ghosts, who might speak at any time. I resisted the impulse to move to the other side of the apron.

My attention shifted back to Caropia. In her slim face the

pebble-grey eyes were large, and filled with pain. I had so
many disparate images of her to link . . . and yet, within the
play and without, I knew nothing real about her. Our backstage silence augmented the Jacobean notion that the other
sex was unknowable, a different species, an alien intelligence. Still, watching her bowed head, her slender arms
moving nervously, I felt Pallio's emotions as my own, and I
wanted to break into the play and experience that incestuous
closeness. I spoke, infusing my lines with all these illusory
feelings, to the invisible actress inside her, the one who made
them both a mystery. I spoke tenderly of our love, and
lamented our situation: "We are so far in blood . . ." " 'Tis
payment," Caropia cried, and railed against the sequence of
unchangeable events she found herself trapped in. Bitterly
she blamed our incest: "Our sin of lust has webbed these plots
around us, so I've dreamt—" I interrupted:

> "Why shouldst thou not love best the one known best?
> It is no crime, and were it, it has gain'd
> Us more than lost . . ."

She spoke of the church and we argued religion. Finally I
interrupted again:

> "In this world all are quite alone,
> All efforts grasp for union. Who's succeeded
> More than thou and I? We shar'd the womb,
> The universe of childhood; lov'd
> As lovers in the lust of youth—"

And Caropia, thinking no doubt of her pact with the
Cardinal, replied:

> "Thou know'st me well as one can know another."

I smiled, a tremendous effort, and continued:

> "Thus be calm—thy dreams are naught but visions
> Of thine other self, beheld while in
> The timeless void of sleep. We've fears enough
> In this world."

I turned from her and the tone of reassurance left me. I voiced my real concern:

> ". . . I fear Velasquo's
> Found me out; his eyes shout 'murderer'
> With all the brutal energy of horror.
> He greets me mornings, dines with me at noon,
> And stalks the palace grounds at night,
> As if he were a hungry wolf, and I
> A man alone on the trackless waste—"

Velasquo entered, several lines too early. Unable to finish in his presence, I moved to the other side of the apron and returned his baleful glare. Below me Sanguinetto was smiling.

There was silence. It was the first time the three of us had been onstage by ourselves, and the triangle we formed was the focus of all the tension we had managed to create. Beneath our polite exchange (Velasquo was inquiring if Caropia would accompany him to the masque) were layers: the reality of the play, the reality of the players . . . Velasquo's crafted jests probed at me with an intensity I alone could understand, although all that he did made perfect sense in the context of the play; indeed it must have appeared that he was doing a superb job. Only small stresses in his intonation revealed the danger, like swirls in a river, indicating swift undercurrents. I replied with a brittle hostility that had little acting in it, and we snapped at each other like the two poles of a Jacob's ladder:

Pallio: "She goes with me, keep you away from her—"

Vel: "Would you be kicked?"

Pallio: "Would you have your neck broke?"

The audience's silence was a measure of their absorption. Despite my earlier revulsion, and the blank nausea of the *jamais vu*, I felt growing within me, insidiously, the pleasure of acting, the chill tingling one feels when a scene is going very well.

This pleasure in the scene's success was soon overwhelmed by the fear which was making it succeed; Velasquo's thinly veiled attack was strengthening. His pale eyes glared at me intently, looking for some involuntary movement or expression that would show me to be the one who had recognized him. I struggled to keep only Pallio's wariness on my face, but it was a delicate distinction, one becoming more and more difficult to make. . . . I exited to the sound of his high laughter

Once off, I hurried around toward the dressing room. Caropia's was the only voice emerging from the wall-speakers in the narrow corridor, and footsteps were padding behind me. I almost ran, remembering the early death in *Hamlet*. But it was only the Cardinal, completing errands of his own.

The dressing room was momentarily empty. I took my épée from my costume bag and once again locked myself in a lavatory stall. The steel of the blade gleamed as I pulled away the leather scabbard.

It was an old épée, once used in competitive electric fencing. I had polished the half-sphere bell and removed the plug socket from inside it to convert it to a theater sword. The wire running down a slot in the blade was still there, as was the tip, a small spring-loaded cylinder. The blade was stiff, and curved down slightly. At the bell it was triangular in cross-section, a short, wide-based triangle, with the base uppermost. It narrowed to a short cylindrical section at the end, which screwed into the tip.

I tried to unscrew the tip, certain that what I was doing was not real, that I was acting for myself. Surely the thing to do was to stop the play (I winced) and proclaim Velasquo's identity to all. Or to slip away, out the back, and escape him entirely.

Yet naming him before all would not do—where was my proof? Even my own conviction was shaken by the question of evidence. There wasn't any. The first real *proof* I would get would be a sudden hard lunge for my throat, with a sharp blade. . . .

The tip wouldn't unscrew. I twisted until my fingers and hands were imprinted with red bars and semicircles, but it felt as if tip and blade were a solid piece. I clamped the tip between two molars and turned, but succeeded only in hurting my teeth. I needed pliers. I stared at the tip.

And if I were to escape, the Hieronomo would also. Surgery would change his face and voice, and he would return. I knew that in that case I would never be able to perform again without wondering if it were him again, playing opposite me. . . .

I put the tip on the floor under my boot sole. Holding it flat against the floor, I pulled up on the blade. When I lifted my foot, the tip stuck out at right angles from the blade. I put it back on the floor, and carefully stepped on the new bend until it was straight again. I repeated the operation delicately; I knew, from years of fencing, how easily the blades would snap. Presently there appeared behind the tip a ripple, a weak spot that would break when struck hard enough. I slipped the scabbard back on, satisfied that the épée could be swiftly transformed into a weapon that would kill.

At some level unknown to me I had decided. I left the stall and stared at the white face in the mirror, feeling a stranger to myself.

Back in the dressing room, Caropia and Velasquo were in earnest conference. When they saw me, Caropia returned to her cubicle and Velasquo, looking angry, crossed to the other side of the room.

I sat down beside Caropia and listened to the speaker above us. The Cardinal was arranging, with whom I could not tell, to have Hamond and Orcanes poisoned at the masque. Apparently the masque was to take place very soon. As I changed my coat I could feel my pulse throbbing in my arms.

"Disguise," said a voice in my ear. I jumped and turned to see Velasquo, his square face set close to mine.

"It's an odd word," he continued. "Shouldn't it be enguise, or beguise? Doesn't *dis*guise imply the opposite of what you want it to mean?"

I stared at him, in an agony of apprehension that he might go on, that he might reveal (disguise?) himself openly, and dare me to act—"*Dis* can also be used to intensify a verb," I finally stammered.

"You are disguised," he said, and scrutinized me closely. Then he walked away.

In my brain a chemical typhoon whirled. The exchange had been so—dramatic . . . suddenly I was stunned by the horrible suspicion that all our words were lines, all the events backstage part of a larger play . . . Bloomsman, Bloomsman . . . By coincidence (or perhaps not) Caropia appeared to sense this thought. She stuck her head around the partition and said, with a sardonic smile, "You learnt it of no fencer to shake thus," a line from a play that I myself had once spoken. I picked up my épée and strode away in agitation, all my certainties shattered.

Caropia caught up with me just outside the prop room, and touched my hand. I watched her and tried to conceal the fact that I was still trembling. She smiled and slipped her arm under mine. The archaic gesture seemed fraught with emotion. For the first time I understood that it was not just another dominant/submissive signal from the past, that it had been able to express one human's support for another. My confusion lessened. One way or other I would know, soon enough.

The prop room was filled with actors getting ready for the masque. Bloomsman had done her usual meticulous prop work; the masks were bright animal heads that covered one to the shoulders. A menagerie composed chiefly of pigs, tigers, and horses, we stared at each other and whispered with excitement. Bloomsman handed us our masks and smiled—a smile that now seemed to be filled with ominous possibility. "It's going fine," she said. "Let's do this last scene right." She put on a mask herself, a remorselessly grinning gargoyle.

I looked at my mask: a red fox. I could guess what Velasquo's would be. Caropia's was an exact model of her own head, with holes cut out for her eyes and mouth. The result, once on, was grotesque. She looked in a wall-mirror and laughed. "I'm animal enough already," she said. The gargoyle shrugged and said, in Bloomsman's calm voice, "I thought it the right thing."

Velasquo was already on stage, announcing his plans to the audience. Somehow he had learned of the relationship between Caropia and me. Long after everyone else in the theater, he had seen through her guise. His desire for vengeance now focused as much on her as me. She was to die of poison placed in her drinking cup. Beside me, she watched the cup, still on the prop table, and shivered. I felt fear for her then, and great affection, and heedlessly I whispered to her, "Don't drink from it."

She stared at me, and began to laugh. But I did not and she stopped. Her grey eyes surveyed me and slowly widened, as if in fear of me. "I won't," she whispered in a soothing voice. She disengaged her arm and moved away, glancing back once with an expression I could not read, but which could have been one of . . . terror.

The stage was divided by two long tables, both laden with silver and gold, fruits and meat, candles and flasks of liqueurs. As the stage filled with masquers, servants—in masks

that were faceless white blanks—continued to load the tables. The fantastic menagerie milled about slowly and randomly seating themselves. Lines were shouted simultaneously,
creating a cacophony that could only have been Bloomsman's
doing.

I stood behind Caropia, at one end of the front table,
peering through the eyeholes of my fox-face in search of
Velasquo. My black, shiny nose protruded far before me. I
saw that the Cardinal was not masked—he was still in his red
robes, but a papal coronet was tilted back on his head. He
viewed the uproar with an indulgent smile. Around him goats
in formal dress drank wine.

My eye was caught by a movement above. A tall figure
dressed in black leaned over the balcony and observed the
activity; his mask was a skull. I glanced into the audience,
and the backwash from the multicolored glare was enough
illumination to confirm my suspicion. Sanguinetto was gone.
It was he on the balcony, playing the medieval death-figure.
He began to descend the stairs, pausing for several seconds
after each step.

The masque gained energy. A plate piled high with meat
was tipped over; people rose from their seats, shouting
witticisms. A long body of glittering red liquid flashed through
the air and drenched one of the Cardinal's goats. There was
still no sign of Velasquo. An orange fight started between
tables, and the noise reached a frantic pitch, timed by the
metronome of Sanguinetto's steps. Two women, both with
tiger masks, began to claw at each other.

At the height of the cacophony a long scream cut through
the sound, making its ragged descant. When it ended there
was silence and the company was still, forming a bizarre tableau. A man with a pig's head and red doublet staggered to
the apron. He tore at his snout and pulled the mask off, to
reveal Orcanes. His face was bloated and purple. He clutched
his throat, sank to his knees. As he collapsed another scream

ripped the air. Another player, also in pig mask, fell to the floor and drummed out his death. Sanguinetto, now on the stage, paced between tables.

The Cardinal stood, his face grim. "Who can account for these untimely deaths?" he demanded.

"*Pallio,*" a voice behind me called. I spun around and saw the wolf's face, fangs protruding, yellow eyes agleam. I tore off my mask and stepped back to increase the distance between us.

"Who is this man?" I asked, my voice preternaturally calm. "He must be mad."

"Your brother I," he said, and pulled off his mask. "Velasquo."

"Velasquo!" I cried, and spoke to the Cardinal:

> "Why, he kill'd Sanguinetto, Ferrando
> And Ursini; yea, perhaps the old Duke too.
> These new deaths without doubt are also his devise—"

> Vel: "He's false; he is the murd'rer of our father.
> Here's proof—"

Velasquo threw Sanguinetto's note down. I picked it up and looked at it. Penciled beneath my Latin tag, in a fine imitation of Bloomsman's hand, was another title: *The Guise.* Proof indeed.

I crumpled the sheet and tossed it to the floor. "A forgery," I said, voice still calm. "He tries usurping me."

I pulled my épée from my scabbard. Velasquo did the same. The company drew back, pulling the front table with them to make room. The Cardinal made his way forward. Sanguinetto stood beside him. The two of them linked arms, and the Cardinal spoke:

> "The truth is in Fate's hands. Let them fence."

And in my mind I heard the blocking instruction, in Bloomsman's dry voice: "Fence."

Finally, finally the light became red, a bright crimson glare that bathed us both in blood. We circled each other warily. I watched his wrist, his stance, and in my concentration the world contracted to the two of us. Adrenaline flooded through me and my pulse was trip-hammer fast.

His blade had a tip on it, but that meant nothing; I knew it would slide back on contact, releasing the sharp point. The Hieronomo had used it before.

We began tentatively. He lunged, I parried, and we established a simple parry-riposte pattern, often used in practice, at very high speed. The flashing blades and the rapid clicking of clean parries were highly dramatic, but meant little.

After a short pause to regain balance, Velasquo lunged again, more fully this time, and we bouted with increased speed, using the full variety of tactics. The scrape and ring of steel against steel, the wooden thumping of our footwork, our hoarse breathing were the only sounds in the theater.

The exchange ended and we stared at each other, breathing heavily. A wrinkle of concentration appeared between his eyes. I was sure he now realized that my knowledge of fencing was not implanted, that it was learned from actual experience. Implanted fencing was adequate for theatrics, but it consisted entirely of conscious moves and strategies, it was a verbal memory. Fencing learned by experience was remembered to a large extent in the cerebellum, where movement and balance are controlled, and thus reactions were nearly reflex-fast. Velasquo was certainly aware of this, and now he knew that he had been discovered by someone capable of besting him.

Suddenly he lunged with great violence. The thrust avoided my parry and I had to leap back to dodge his blade. The real fight had begun. He lunged in straightforward attacks that were easy enough to parry, but when I did so he remised, continued to attack. He was ignoring my tipped weapon, which was clearly harmless. When I understood this, I jumped back and slapped my épée against the floor. The tip stayed on. I had to retreat and parry for my life, watching nothing but his blade, and striking it aside desperately each time it thrust at me.

My heel hit the bottom of the left stairway and I nearly stumbled. I stepped up backward, and Velasquo followed, negating my height advantage with the energy of his attack. I turned and ran up to the balcony, swinging my épée against the bannister all the way. The tip stayed on. I turned and lunged fiercely at my pursuer. He halted, lead foot three steps above his hind foot, and we engaged in a grim slashing battle, as if we were fighting with sabers. I didn't want him to reach the balcony. It was hopeless; still unafraid of my épée, he drove me back by degrees and managed, step by step, to make his way up to my level. When he reached the balcony I turned and sprinted down the other staircase four steps at a time, spinning and slashing once to impede his pursuit, and slamming my blade viciously against the side wall all the way down.

When I got to the stage, I saw that my tip had snapped off and disappeared. Exultantly I turned, parried Velasquo's running attack, and riposted straight at his chest. He leaped to one side to avoid the thrust. Several feet separated us; we stood panting.

He saw the change in my blade, invisible from more than a few feet away, and his expression became one of alarm—the idea struck him, perhaps, that tonight we had reversed roles; tonight I had become the Hieronomo. He looked up to my face, and I smiled.

Instinctively he lunged and in a fury of desperate motion drove me back across the stage. But now we were armed evenly, he had to respect my blade, and I wasn't forced to retreat for long. We battled with a sweaty, intense, total concentration.

He stopped and our blades circled each other: mine jagged and blunt, but slender; his still tipped by the treacherous false button. He started a complicated, deceptive attack. I stole the offensive from him with a stop thrust, lunged for his chest and hit just below the sternum. Amazingly, the blade did not bend and push my hand back, as it always had before: *it slid right in.*

Velasquo dropped his épée, stumbled back and fell, tugging free of my blade. I lifted it; the steel was streaked with blood, unnaturally red in the light. It dripped like water. Velasquo rolled onto his belly.

I looked up and surveyed the stage. Most of the cast had moved into the wings, which were blocked.

Caropia stepped forward, her tall cup still in her hands. Her eyes and mouth were black holes in a face as white as the mask she had long since removed. She appeared confused, but spoke her lines nevertheless, in a dry, airy voice:

"There lies he, chok'd in his own blood,
A ravenous wolf whom all the world thought good."

Velasquo rolled over. Caropia's cup toppled to the floor. Sanguinetto, his mask still on, stepped toward me. I swung my épée in his direction and he stopped. I walked toward the rear exit, keeping the blade pointed at him.

Above me on the balcony, the gargoyle waved an arm, and the curtain jerked downward. The audience leaped to their feet, and I thought *They're after me, I'm caught;* but they were clapping, cheering, it was an ovation—the gargoyle bowed—I fled.

An unfamiliar door in the dressing room gave me access to a dark storage room. I crossed it, entered another hallway. It turned and almost immediately I was lost, running without plan down hallways and through dark rooms. Muffled shouts of pursuit reverberated through the walls from time to time, spurring me on. I tried to work my way in a single direction. A short set of stairs led me up to a little closet theater, stage no bigger than a sitting room. Hearing voices backstage, I crouched down between two rows of seats. I looked through the slot between two seat backs and watched a red-coated guard, one of the extras from our play, run on stage and halt. I held my breath. He surveyed the room quickly, then left as quickly as he had entered. The voices receded like echoes and I got up and ran again, out the back of the theater.

I was in a long white hallway with a very high ceiling. Green light poured from long strips in the wall. To my left, at the end of the hall, was a door. I ran for it. As I approached I saw words printed on the door, above the horizontal bar that opened it: EMERGENCY EXIT—ALARM WILL SOUND.

The moment I comprehended the words, the dry, ineffable presence of *déjà vu* filled me: *this had happened before*. In a flash I knew everything, I understood all that had occurred in the theater, it stood before me in my mind like a crystalline sphere. But just as quickly the entire matrix of thought collapsed, leaving no trace except the memory of its existence: *presque vu, almost seen.*

I slammed into the bar crossing the door, and it flew open. To the sharp blast of a siren I leaped out into the chill air, and back into the world.

—1976

The Lucky Strike

War breeds strange pastimes. In July of 1945 on Tinian Island in the North Pacific, Captain Frank January had taken to piling pebble cairns on the crown of Mount Lasso—one pebble for each B-29 takeoff, one cairn for each mission. The largest cairn had four hundred stones in it. It was a mindless pastime, but so was poker. The men of the 509th had played a million hands of poker, sitting in the shade of a palm around an upturned crate sweating in their skivvies, swearing and betting all their pay and cigarettes, playing hand after hand after hand, until the cards got so soft and dog-eared you could have used them for toilet paper. Captain January had gotten sick of it, and after he lit out for the hilltop a few times some of his crewmates started trailing him. When their pilot Jim Fitch joined them it became an official pastime, like throwing flares into the compound or going hunting for stray Japs. What Captain January thought of the development he didn't say. The others grouped near Captain Fitch, who passed around his battered flask. "Hey, January," Fitch called. "Come have a shot."

January wandered over and took the flask. Fitch laughed at

his pebble. "Practicing your bombing up here, eh, Professor?"

"Yah," January said sullenly. Anyone who read more than the funnies was Professor to Fitch. Thirstily January knocked back some rum. He could drink it any way he pleased up here, out from under the eye of the group psychiatrist. He passed the flask on to Lieutenant Matthews, their navigator.

"That's why he's the best," Matthews joked. "Always practicing."

Fitch laughed. "He's best because I make him be best, right, Professor?"

January frowned. Fitch was a bulky youth, thick-featured, pig-eyed—a thug, in January's opinion. The rest of the crew were all in their mid-twenties like Fitch, and they liked the captain's bossy roughhouse style. January, who was thirty-seven, didn't go for it. He wandered away, back to the cairn he had been building. From Mount Lasso they had an overview of the whole island, from the harbor at Wall Street to the north field in Harlem. January had observed hundreds of B-29s roar off the four parallel runways of the north field and head for Japan. The last quartet of this particular mission buzzed across the width of the island, and January dropped four more pebbles, aiming for crevices in the pile. One of them stuck nicely.

"There they are!" said Matthews. "They're on the taxiing strip."

January located the 509th's first plane. Today, the first of August, there was something more interesting to watch than the usual Superfortress parade. Word was out that General Le May wanted to take the 509th's mission away from it. Their commander Colonel Tibbets had gone and bitched to Le May in person, and the general had agreed the mission was theirs, but on one condition: one of the general's men was to make a test flight with the 509th, to make sure they were fit for combat over Japan. The general's man had arrived, and now he was down there in the strike plane, with Tibbets and the whole first team. January sidled back to his mates to view the takeoff with them.

"Why don't the strike plane have a name, though?" Haddock was saying.

Fitch said, "Lewis won't give it a name because it's not his plane, and he knows it." The others laughed. Lewis and his crew were naturally unpopular, being Tibbets' favorites.

"What do you think he'll do to the general's man?" Matthews asked.

The others laughed at the very idea. "He'll kill an engine at takeoff, I bet you anything," Fitch said. He pointed at the wrecked B-29s that marked the end of every runway, planes whose engines had given out on takeoff. "He'll want to show that he wouldn't go down if it happened to him."

" 'Course he wouldn't!" Matthews said.

"You hope," January said under his breath.

"They let those Wright engines out too soon," Haddock said seriously. "They keep busting under the takeoff load."

"Won't matter to the old bull," Matthews said. Then they all started in about Tibbets' flying ability, even Fitch. They all thought Tibbets was the greatest. January, on the other hand, liked Tibbets even less than he liked Fitch. That had started right after he was assigned to the 509th. He had been told he was part of the most important group in the war, and then given a leave. In Vicksburg a couple of fliers just back from England had bought him a lot of whiskies, and since January had spent several months stationed near London they had talked for a good long time and gotten pretty drunk. The two were really curious about what January was up to now, but he had stayed vague on it and kept returning the talk to the blitz. He had been seeing an English nurse, for instance, whose flat had been bombed, family and neighbors killed. . . . But they had really wanted to know. So he had told them he was onto something special, and they had flipped out their badges and told him they were Army Intelligence, and that if he ever broke security like that again he'd be transferred to Alaska. It was a dirty trick. January had gone back to Wendover and told Tibbets so to his face, and Tibbets had turned red and threatened him some more. January despised him for that. The upshot was that January was effectively out of the war, because Tibbets really played his favorites. January wasn't sure he really minded, but during their year's training he had bombed better than ever, as a way of showing the old bull he was wrong to write January off. Every time their eyes had met it was clear what was going on. But Tibbets never backed off no matter how precise January's bombing got. Just thinking about it was enough to cause January to line up a pebble over an ant and drop it.

"Will you cut that out?" Fitch complained. "I swear you must hang from the ceiling when you take a shit so you can practice aiming for the toilet." The men laughed.

"Don't I bunk over you?" January asked. Then he pointed. "They're going."

Tibbets' plane had taxied to runway Baker. Fitch passed the flask around again. The tropical sun beat on them, and the ocean surrounding the island blazed white. January put up a sweaty hand to aid the bill of his baseball cap.

The four props cut in hard, and the sleek Superfortress quickly trundled up to speed and roared down Baker. Three-quarters of the way down the strip the outside right prop feathered.

"Yow!" Fitch crowed. "I told you he'd do it!"

The plane nosed off the ground and slewed right, then pulled back on course to cheers from the four young men around January. January pointed again. "He's cut number three, too."

The inside right prop feathered, and now the plane was pulled up by the left wing only, while the two right props windmilled uselessly. "Holy smoke!" Haddock cried. "Ain't the old bull something?"

They whooped to see the plane's power, and Tibbets' nervy arrogance.

"By God, Le May's man will remember this flight," Fitch hooted. "Why, look at that! He's banking!"

Apparently taking off on two engines wasn't enough for Tibbets; he banked the plane right until it was standing on its dead wing, and it curved back toward Tinian.

Then the inside left engine feathered.

War tears at the imagination. For three years Frank January had kept his imagination trapped, refusing to give it any play whatsoever. The dangers threatening him, the effects of the bombs, the fate of the other participants in the war, he had refused to think about any of it. But the war tore at his control. That English nurse's flat. The missions over the Ruhr. The bomber just below him blown apart by flak. And then there had been a year in Utah, and the viselike grip that he had once kept on his imagination had slipped away.

So when he saw the number two prop feather, his heart gave a little jump against his sternum and helplessly he was up there with Ferebee, the first team bombardier. He would be looking over the pilots' shoulders. . . .

"Only one engine?" Fitch said.

"That one's for real," January said harshly. Despite himself he *saw* the panic in the cockpit, the frantic rush to power the two right engines. The plane was dropping fast and Tibbets leveled it off, leaving them on a course back toward the island. The two right props spun, blurred to a shimmer. January held his breath. They needed more lift; Tibbets was trying to pull it over the island. Maybe he was trying for the short runway on the south half of the island.

But Tinian was too tall, the plane too heavy. It roared right into the jungle above the beach, where 42nd Street met their East River. It exploded in a bloom of fire. By the time the sound of the explosion struck them they knew no one in the plane had survived.

Black smoke towered into white sky. In the shocked silence on Mount Lasso insects buzzed and creaked. The air left January's lungs with a gulp. He had been with Ferebee there at the end, he had heard the desperate shouts, seen the last green rush, been stunned by the dentist-drill-all-over pain of the impact.

"Oh my God," Fitch was saying. "Oh my God." Matthews was sitting. January picked up the flask, tossed it at Fitch.

"C-come on," he stuttered. He hadn't stuttered since he was sixteen. He led the others in a rush down the hill. When they got to Broadway a jeep careened toward them and skidded to a halt. It was Colonel Scholes, the old bull's exec. "What happened?"

Fitch told him.

"Those damned Wrights," Scholes said as the men piled in. This time one had failed at just the wrong moment; some welder stateside had kept flame to metal a second less than usual—or something equally minor, equally trivial—and that had made all the difference.

They left the jeep at 42nd and Broadway and hiked east over a narrow track to the shore. A fairly large circle of trees was burning. The fire trucks were already there.

Scholes stood beside January, his expression bleak. "That was the whole first team," he said.

"I know," said January. He was still in shock, in imagination crushed, incinerated, destroyed. Once as a kid he had tied sheets to his arms and waist, jumped off the roof and landed right on his chest; this felt like that had. He had no way of knowing what would come of this crash, but he had a suspicion that he had indeed smacked into something hard.

Scholes shook his head. A half hour had passed, the fire was nearly out. January's four mates were over chattering with the Seabees. "He was going to name the plane after his mother," Scholes said to the ground. "He told me that just this morning. He was going to call it *Enola Gay*."

At night the jungle breathed, and its hot wet breath washed over the 509th's compound. January stood in the doorway of his Quonset barracks hoping for a real breeze. No poker tonight. Voices were hushed, faces solemn. Some of the men had helped box up the dead crew's gear. Now most lay on their bunks. January gave up on the breeze, climbed onto his top bunk to stare at the ceiling.

He observed the corrugated arch over him. Cricketsong sawed through his thoughts. Below him a rapid conversation was being carried on in guilty undertones, Fitch at its center.

"January is the best bombardier left," he said. "And I'm as good as Lewis was."

"But so is Sweeney," Matthews said. "And he's in with Scholes."

They were figuring out who would take over the strike. January scowled. Tibbets and the rest were less than twelve hours dead, and they were squabbling over who would replace them.

January grabbed a shirt, rolled off his bunk, put the shirt on.

"Hey, Professor," Fitch said. "Where you going?"

"Out."

Though midnight was near it was still sweltering. Crickets shut up as he walked by, started again behind him. He lit a cigarette. In the dark the MPs patrolling their fenced-in compound were like pairs of walking armbands. The 509th, prisoners in their own army. Fliers from other groups had taken to throwing rocks over the fence. Forcefully January expelled smoke, as if he could expel his disgust with it. They were only kids, he told himself. Their minds had been shaped in the war, by the war, and for the war. They knew you couldn't mourn the dead for long; carry around a load like that and your own engines might fail. That was all right with January. It was an attitude that Tibbets had helped to form, so it was what he deserved. Tibbets would *want* to be forgotten in favor of the mission, all he had lived for was to drop the gimmick on the Japs, he was oblivious to anything else, men, wife, family, anything.

So it wasn't the lack of feeling in his mates that bothered January. And it was natural of them to want to fly the strike they had been training a year for. Natural, that is, if you were a kid with a mind shaped by fanatics like Tibbets, shaped to take orders and never imagine consequences. But January was not a kid, and he wasn't going to let men like Tibbets do a thing to his mind. And the gimmick . . . the gimmick was not natural. A chemical bomb of some sort, he guessed. Against the Geneva Convention. He stubbed his cigarette against the sole of his sneaker, tossed the butt over the fence. The tropical night breathed over him. He had a headache.

For months now he had been sure he would never fly a strike. The dislike Tibbets and he had exchanged in their looks (January was acutely aware of looks) had been real and strong. Tibbets had understood that January's record of pinpoint accuracy in the runs over the Salton Sea had been a way of showing contempt, a way of saying *you can't get rid of me even though you hate me and I hate you.* The record had forced Tibbets to keep January on one of the four second-string teams, but with the fuss they were making over the gimmick January had figured that would be far enough down the ladder to keep him out of things.

Now he wasn't so sure. Tibbets was dead. He lit another cigarette, found his hand shaking. The Camel tasted bitter. He threw it over the fence at a receding armband, and regretted it instantly. A waste. He went back inside.

Before climbing onto his bunk he got a paperback out of

his footlocker. "Hey, Professor, what you reading now?" Fitch said, grinning.

January showed him the blue cover. *Winter's Tales*, by an Isak Dinesen. Fitch examined the little wartime edition. "Pretty racy, eh?"

"You bet," January said heavily. "This guy puts sex on every page." He climbed onto his bunk, opened the book. The stories were strange, hard to follow. The voices below bothered him. He concentrated harder.

As a boy on the farm in Arkansas, January had read everything he could lay his hands on. On Saturday afternoons he would race his father down the muddy lane to the mailbox (his father was a reader too), grab *The Saturday Evening Post* and run off to devour every word of it. That meant he had another week with nothing new to read, but he couldn't help it. His favorites were the Hornblower stories, but anything would do. It was a way off the farm, a way into the world. He had become a man who could slip between the covers of a book whenever he chose.

But not on this night.

The next day the chaplain gave a memorial service, and on the morning after that Colonel Scholes looked in the door of their hut right after mess. "Briefing at eleven," he announced. His face was haggard. "Be there early." He looked at Fitch with bloodshot eyes, crooked a finger. "Fitch, January, Matthews—come with me."

January put on his shoes. The rest of the men sat on their bunks and watched them wordlessly. January followed Fitch and Matthews out of the hut.

"I've spent most of the night on the radio with General Le May," Scholes said. He looked them each in the eye. "We've decided you're to be the first crew to make a strike."

Fitch was nodding, as if he had expected it.

"Think you can do it?" Scholes said.

"Of course," Fitch replied. Watching him January understood why they had chosen him to replace Tibbets: Fitch was like the old bull, he had that same ruthlessness. The young bull.

"Yes, sir," Matthews said.

Scholes was looking at him. "Sure," January said, not wanting to think about it. "Sure." His heart was pounding directly on his sternum. But Fitch and Matthews looked serious as owls, so he wasn't going to stick out by looking odd. It was big news, after all; anyone would be taken aback by it. Nevertheless, January made an effort to nod.

"Okay," Scholes said. "McDonald will be flying with you as copilot." Fitch frowned. "I've got to go tell those British officers that Le May doesn't want them on the strike with you. See you at the briefing."

"Yes, sir."

As soon as Scholes was around the corner Fitch swung a fist at the sky. "Yow!" Matthews cried. He and Fitch shook hands. "We did it!" Matthews took January's hand and wrung it, his face plastered with a goofy grin. "We did it!"

"Somebody did it, anyway," January said.

"Ah, Frank," Matthews said. "Show some spunk. You're always so cool."

"Old Professor Stoneface," Fitch said, glancing at January with a trace of amused contempt. "Come on, let's get to the briefing."

The briefing hut, one of the longer Quonsets, was completely surrounded by MPs holding carbines. "Gosh," Matthews said, subdued by the sight. Inside it was already smoky. The walls were covered by the usual maps of Japan. Two blackboards at the front were draped with sheets. Captain Shepard, the naval officer who worked with the scientists on the gimmick, was in back with his assistant Lieutenant Stone, winding a reel of film onto a projector. Dr. Nelson, the group psychiatrist, was already seated on a front bench near the wall. Tibbets had recently sicced the psychiatrist on the group—another one of his great ideas, like the spies in the bar. The man's questions had struck January as stupid. He hadn't even been able to figure out that Easterly was a flake, something that was clear to anybody who flew with him, or even played him in a single round of poker. January slid onto a bench beside his mates.

The two Brits entered, looking furious in their stiff-upper-lip way. They sat on the bench behind January. Sweeney's and Easterly's crews filed in, followed by the other men, and soon the room was full. Fitch and the rest pulled out Lucky Strikes and lit up; since they had named the plane only January had stuck with Camels.

Scholes came in with several men January didn't recognize, and went to the front. The chatter died, and all the smoke plumes ribboned steadily into the air.

Scholes nodded, and two intelligence officers took the sheets off the blackboards, revealing aerial reconnaissance photos.

"Men," Scholes said, "these are the target cities."

Someone cleared his throat.

"In order of priority they are Hiroshima, Kokura, and Nagasaki. There will be three weather scouts: *Straight Flush* to Hiroshima, *Strange Cargo* to Kokura, and *Full House* to Nagasaki. *The Great Artiste* and *Number 91* will be accompanying the mission to take photos. And *Lucky Strike* will fly the bomb."

There were rustles, coughs. Men turned to look at January and his mates, and they all sat up straight. Sweeney stretched back to shake Fitch's hand, and there were some quick laughs. Fitch grinned.

"Now listen up," Scholes went on. "The weapon we are going to deliver was successfully tested stateside a couple of weeks ago. And now we've got orders to drop it on the enemy." He paused to let that sink in. "I'll let Captain Shepard tell you more."

Shepard walked to the blackboard slowly, savoring his entrance. His forehead was shiny with sweat, and January realized he was excited or nervous. He wondered what the psychiatrist would make of that.

"I'm going to come right to the point," Shepard said. "The bomb you are going to drop is something new in history. We think it will knock out everything within four miles."

Now the room was completely still. January noticed that he could see a great deal of his nose, eyebrows, and cheeks; it was as if he were receding back into his body, like a fox into its hole. He kept his gaze rigidly on Shepard, steadfastly ignoring the feeling. Shepard pulled a sheet back over a blackboard while someone else turned down the lights.

"This is a film of the only test we have made," Shepard said. The film started, caught, started again. A wavery cone of bright cigarette smoke speared the length of the room, and on the sheet sprang a dead gray landscape: a lot of sky, a smooth desert floor, hills in the distance. The projector went click-click-click-click, click-click-click-click. "The bomb is on top of the tower," Shepard said, and January focused on the pinlike object sticking out of the desert floor, off against the hills. It was between eight and ten miles from the camera, he judged; he had gotten good at calculating distances. He was still distracted by his face.

Click-click-click-click, click—then the screen went white for a second, filling even their room with light. When the picture returned the desert floor was filled with a white bloom of fire. The fireball coalesced and then quite suddenly it leaped off the earth all the way into the stratosphere, by God, like a tracer bullet leaving a machine gun, trailing a whitish pillar of smoke behind it. The pillar gushed up and a growing ball of smoke billowed outward, capping the pillar.

January calculated the size of the cloud, but was sure he got it wrong. There it stood. The picture flickered, and then the screen went white again, as if the camera had melted or that part of the world had come apart. But the flapping from the projector told them it was the end of the film.

January felt the air suck in and out of his open mouth. The lights came on in the smoky room and for a second he panicked, he struggled to shove his features into an accepted pattern, the psychiatrist would be looking around at them all—and then he glanced around and realized he needn't have worried, that he wasn't alone. Faces were bloodless, eyes were blinky or bug-eyed with shock, mouths hung open or were clamped whitely shut. For a few moments they all had to acknowledge what they were doing. January, scaring himself, felt an urge to say, "Play it again, will you?" Fitch was pulling his curled black hair off his thug's forehead uneasily. Beyond him January saw that one of the Limeys had already reconsidered how mad he was about missing the flight. Now he looked sick. Someone let out a long *whew*, another whistled. January looked to the front again, where the psychiatrist watched them, undisturbed.

Shepard said, "It's big, all right. And no one knows what will happen when it's dropped from the air. But the mushroom cloud you saw will go to at least thirty thousand feet, probably sixty. And the flash you saw at the beginning was hotter than the sun."

Hotter than the sun. More licked lips, hard swallows, readjusted baseball caps. One of the intelligence officers passed out tinted goggles like welder's glasses. January took his and twiddled the opacity dial.

Scholes said, "You're the hottest thing in the armed forces, now. So no talking, even among yourselves." He took a deep breath. "Let's do it the way Colonel Tibbets would have wanted us to. He picked every one of you because you were the best, and now's the time to show he was right. So—so let's make the old man proud.''

The briefing was over. Men filed out into the sudden sunlight. Into the heat and glare. Captain Shepard approached Fitch. ''Stone and I will be flying with you to take care of the bomb,'' he said.

Fitch nodded. ''Do you know how many strikes we'll fly?''

''As many as it takes to make them quit.'' Shepard stared hard at all of them. ''But it will only take one.''

War breeds strange dreams. That night January writhed over his sheets in the hot wet vegetable darkness, in that frightening half sleep when you sometimes know you are dreaming but can do nothing about it, and he dreamed he was walking . . .

. . . walking through the streets when suddenly the sun swoops down, the sun touches down and everything is instantly darkness and smoke and silence, a deaf roaring. Walls of fire. His head hurts and in the middle of his vision is a bluewhite blur as if God's camera went off in his face. Ah—the sun fell, he thinks. His arm is burned. Blinking is painful. People stumbling by, mouths open, horribly burned—

He is a priest, he can feel the clerical collar, and the wounded ask him for help. He points to his ears, tries to touch them but can't. Pall of black smoke over everything, the city has fallen into the streets. Ah, it's the end of the world. In a park he finds shade and cleared ground. People crouch under bushes like frightened animals. Where the park meets the river red and black figures crowd into steaming water. A figure gestures from a copse of bamboo. He enters it, finds five or six faceless soldiers huddling. Their eyes have melted, their mouths are holes. Deafness spares him their words. The sighted soldier mimes drinking. The soldiers are thirsty. He nods and goes to the river in search of a container. Bodies float downstream.

Hours pass as he hunts fruitlessly for a bucket. He pulls people from the rubble. He hears a bird screeching and he realizes that his deafness is the roar of the city burning, a roar like the blood in his ears but he is not deaf, he only thought he was deaf because there are no human cries. The people are suffering in silence. Through the dusky night he stumbles back to the river, pain crashing through his head. In a field men are pulling potatoes out of the ground that have been baked well enough to eat. He shares one with them. At the river everyone is dead—

—and he struggled out of the nightmare drenched in rank sweat, the taste of dirt in his mouth, his stomach knotted with horror. He sat up and the wet rough sheet clung to his skin. His heart felt crushed between lungs desperate for air. The flowery rotting jungle smell filled him and images from the dream flashed before him so vividly that in the dim hut he saw nothing else. He grabbed his cigarettes and jumped off the bunk, hurried out into the compound. Trembling he lit up, started pacing around. For a moment he worried that the idiot psychiatrist might see him, but then he dismissed the idea. Nelson would be asleep. They were all asleep. He shook his head, looked down at his right arm and almost dropped his cigarette—but it was just his stove scar, an old scar, he'd had it most of his life, since the day he'd pulled the frypan off the stove and onto his arm, burning it with oil. He could still remember the round O of fear that his mother's mouth had made as she rushed in to see what was wrong. Just an old burn scar, he thought, let's not go overboard here. He pulled his sleeve down.

For the rest of the night he tried to walk it off, cigarette after cigarette. The dome of the sky lightened until all the compound and the jungle beyond it was visible. He was forced by the light of day to walk back into his hut and lie down as if nothing had happened.

Two days later Scholes ordered them to take one of Le May's men over Rota for a test run. This new lieutenant colonel ordered Fitch not to play with the engines on takeoff. They flew a perfect run. January put the dummy gimmick right on the aiming point just as he had so often in the Salton Sea, and Fitch powered the plane down into the violent bank that started their 150-degree turn and flight for safety. Back on Tinian the lieutenant colonel congratulated them and shook each of their hands. January smiled with the rest, palms cool, heart steady. It was as if his body were a shell, something he could manipulate from without, like a bombsight. He ate well, he chatted as much as he ever had, and when the psychiatrist ran him to earth for some questions he was friendly and seemed open.

"Hello, doc."

"How do you feel about all this, Frank?"

"Just like I always have, sir. Fine."

"Eating well?"

"Better than ever."

"Sleeping well?"

"As well as I can in this humidity. I got used to Utah, I'm afraid." Dr. Nelson laughed. Actually January had hardly slept since his dream. He was afraid of sleep. Couldn't the man see that?

"And how do you feel about being part of the crew chosen to make the first strike?"

"Well, it was the right choice, I reckon. We're the b—the best crew left."

"Do you feel sorry about Tibbets' crew's accident?"

"Yes, sir, I do." You better believe it.

After the jokes and firm handshakes that ended the interview January walked out into the blaze of the tropical noon and lit a cigarette. He allowed himself to feel how much he despised the psychiatrist and his blind profession at the same time he was waving good-bye to the man. Ounce brain. Why couldn't he have seen? Whatever happened it would be his fault. . . . With a rush of smoke out of him January realized how painfully easy it was to fool someone if you wanted to. All action was no more than a mask that could be perfectly manipulated from somewhere else. And all the while in that somewhere else January lived in a *click-click-click* of film, in the silent roaring of a dream, struggling against images he couldn't dispel. The heat of the tropical sun—ninety-three million miles away, wasn't it?—pulsed painfully on the back of his neck.

As he watched the psychiatrist collar their tail-gunner Kochenski, he thought of walking up to the man and saying *I quit*. I don't want to do this. In imagination he saw the look that would form in the man's eye, in Fitch's eye, in Tibbets' eye, and his mind recoiled from the idea. He felt too much contempt for them. He wouldn't for anything give them a means to despise him, a reason to call him coward. Stubbornly he banished the whole complex of thought. Easier to go along with it.

And so a couple of disjointed days later, just after midnight of August 9th, he found himself preparing for the strike. Around him Fitch and Matthews and Haddock were doing the same. How odd were the everyday motions of getting dressed when you were off to demolish a city, to end a hundred thousand lives! January found himself examining his hands, his boots, the cracks in the linoleum. He put on his survival vest, checked the pockets abstractedly for fishhooks, water kit, first aid package, emergency rations. Then the parachute harness, and his coveralls over it all. Tying his bootlaces took minutes; he couldn't do it when watching his fingers so closely.

"Come on, Professor!" Fitch's voice was tight. "The big day is here."

He followed the others into the night. A cool wind was blowing. The chaplain said a prayer for them. They took jeeps down Broadway to runway Able. *Lucky Strike* stood in a circle of spotlights and men, half of them with cameras, the rest with reporter's pads. They surrounded the crew; it reminded January of a Hollywood premiere. Eventually he escaped up the hatch and into the plane. Others followed. Half an hour passed before Fitch joined them, grinning like a movie star. They started the engines, and January was thankful for their vibrating, thought-smothering roar. They taxied away from the Hollywood scene and January felt relief for a moment until he remembered where they were going. On runway Able the engines pitched up to their twenty-three hundred rpm whine, and looking out the clear windscreen he saw the runway paint-marks move by ever faster. Fitch kept them on the runway till Tinian had run out from under them, then quickly pulled up. They were on their way.

When they got to altitude January climbed past Fitch and McDonald to the bombardier's seat and placed his parachute on it. He leaned back. The roar of the four engines packed around him like cotton batting. He was on the flight, nothing to be done about it now. The heavy vibration was a comfort, he liked the feel of it there in the nose of the plane. A drowsy, sad acceptance hummed through him.

Against his closed eyelids flashed a black eyeless face and he jerked awake, heart racing. He was on the flight, no way out. Now he realized how easy it would have been to get out of it. He could have just said he didn't want to. The simplicity of it appalled him. Who gave a damn what the psychiatrist or Tibbets or anyone else thought, compared to this? Now there was no way out. It was a comfort, in a way. Now he could stop worrying, stop thinking he had any choice.

Sitting there with his knees bracketing the bombsight January dozed, and as he dozed he daydreamed his way out. He could climb the step to Fitch and McDonald and declare he had been secretly promoted to major and ordered to redirect the mission. They were to go to Tokyo and drop the bomb in the bay. The Jap War Cabinet had been told to watch this demonstration of the new weapon, and when they saw that fireball boil the bay and bounce into heaven they'd run and sign surrender papers as fast as they could write, kamikazes or not. They weren't crazy, after all. No need to murder a whole city. It was such a good plan that the generals back home were no doubt changing the mission at this very minute, desperately radioing their instructions to Tinian, only to find out it was too late . . . so that when they returned to Tinian January would become a hero for guessing what the generals really wanted, and for risking all to do it. It would be like one of the Hornblower stories in *The Saturday Evening Post*.

Once again January jerked awake. The drowsy pleasure of the fantasy was replaced with desperate scorn. There wasn't a chance in hell that he could convince Fitch and the rest that he had secret orders superseding theirs. And he couldn't go up there and wave his pistol around and *order* them to drop the bomb in Tokyo Bay, because he was the one who had to actually drop it, and he couldn't be down in front dropping the bomb and up ordering the others around at the same time. Pipe dreams.

Time swept on, slow as a second hand. January's thoughts, however, matched the spin of the props; desperately they cast about, now this way now that, like an animal caught by the leg in a trap. The crew was silent. The clouds below were a white scree on the black ocean. January's knee vibrated against the squat stand of the bombsight. He was the one who had to drop the bomb. No matter where his thoughts lunged they were brought up short by that. He was the one, not Fitch or the crew, not Le May, not the generals and scientists back home, not Truman and his advisors. Truman—suddenly January hated him. Roosevelt would have done it differently. If only Roosevelt had lived! The grief that had filled January when he learned of Roosevelt's death reverberated through him again, more strongly than ever. It was unfair to have worked so hard and then not see the war's end. And FDR would have ended it differently. Back at the start of it all he had declared that civilian centers were never to be bombed, and if he had lived, if, if, if. But he hadn't. And now it was smiling bastard Harry Truman, ordering *him*, Frank January, to drop the sun on two hundred thousand women and children. Once his father had taken him to see the Browns play before twenty thousand, a giant crowd— "I never voted for you," January whispered viciously, and jerked to realize he had spoken aloud. Luckily his microphone was off. But Roosevelt would have done it differently, he *would have*.

The bombsight rose before him, spearing the black sky and blocking some of the hundreds of little cruciform stars. *Lucky Strike* ground on toward Iwo Jima, minute by minute flying four miles closer to their target. January leaned forward and put his face in the cool headrest of the bombsight, hoping that its grasp might hold his thoughts as well as his forehead. It worked surprisingly well.

His earphones crackled and he sat up. "Captain January." It was Shepard. "We're going to arm the bomb now, want to watch?"

"Sure thing." He shook his head, surprised at his own duplicity. Stepping up between the pilots, he moved stiffly to the roomy cabin behind the cockpit. Matthews was at his desk taking a navigational fix on the radio signals from Iwo Jima and Okinawa, and Haddock stood beside him. At the back of the compartment was a small circular hatch, below the larger tunnel leading to the rear of the plane. January opened it, sat down and swung himself feet first through the hole.

The bomb bay was unheated, and the cold air felt good. He stood facing the bomb. Stone was sitting on the floor of the bay; Shepard was laid out under the bomb, reaching into it. On a rubber pad next to Stone were tools, plates, several cylindrical blocks. Shepard pulled back, sat up, sucked a scraped knuckle. He shook his head ruefully: "I don't dare wear gloves with this one."

"I'd be just as happy myself if you didn't let something slip," January joked nervously. The two men laughed.

"Nothing can blow till I change those green wires to the red ones," Stone said.

"Give me the wrench," Shepard said. Stone handed it to him, and he stretched under the bomb again. After some awkward wrenching inside it he lifted out a cylindrical plug. "Breech plug," he said, and set it on the mat.

January found his skin goose-pimpling in the cold air. Stone handed Shepard one of the blocks. Shepard extended under the bomb again. "Red ends toward the breech." "I know." Watching them January was reminded of auto mechanics on the oily floor of a garage, working under a car. He had spent a few years doing that himself, after his family moved to Vicksburg. Hiroshima was a river town. One time a flatbed truck carrying bags of cement powder down Fourth Street hill had lost its brakes and careened into the intersection with River Road, where despite the driver's efforts to turn it smashed into a passing car. Frank had been out in the yard playing, had heard the crash and saw the cement dust rising. He had been one of the first there. The woman and child in the passenger seat of the Model T had been killed. The woman driving was okay. They were from Chicago. A group of folks subdued the driver of the truck, who kept trying to help at the Model T, though he had a bad cut on his head and was covered with white dust.

"Okay, let's tighten the breech plug." Stone gave Shepard the wrench. "Sixteen turns exactly," Shepard said. He was sweating even in the bay's chill, and he paused to wipe his forehead. "Let's hope we don't get hit by lightning." He put the wrench down and shifted onto his knees, picked up a circular plate. Hubcap, January thought. Stone connected wires, then helped Shepard install two more plates. Good old American know-how, January thought, goose pimples rippling across his skin like cat's paws over water. There was Shepard, a scientist, putting together a bomb like he was an auto mechanic changing oil and plugs. January felt a tight rush of rage at the scientists who had designed the bomb. They had worked on it for over a year down there in New Mexico, had none of them in all that time ever stopped to think what they were doing?

But none of them had to drop it. January turned to hide his face from Shepard, stepped down the bay. The bomb looked like a big long trash can, with fins at one end and little antennae at the other. Just a bomb, he thought, damn it, it's just another bomb.

Shepard stood and patted the bomb gently. "We've got a live one now." Never a thought about what it would do. January hurried by the man, afraid that hatred would crack his shell and give him away. The pistol strapped to his belt caught on the hatchway and he imagined shooting Shepard—shooting Fitch and McDonald and plunging the controls forward so that *Lucky Strike* tilted and spun down into the sea like a spent tracer bullet, like a plane broken by flak, following the arc of all human ambition. Nobody would ever know what had happened to them, and their trash can would be dumped at the bottom of the Pacific where it belonged. He could even shoot everyone and parachute out, and perhaps be rescued by one of the Superdumbos following them. . . .

The thought passed and remembering it January squinted with disgust. But another part of him agreed that it was a possibility. It could be done. It would solve his problem. His fingers explored his holster snap.

"Want some coffee?" Matthews asked.

"Sure," January said, and took his hand from the gun to reach for the cup. He sipped: hot. He watched Matthews and Benton tune the loran equipment. As the beeps came in Matthews took a straightedge and drew lines from Okinawa and Iwo Jima on his map table. He tapped a finger on the intersection. "They've taken the art out of navigation," he said to January. "They might as well stop making the navigator's dome," thumbing up at the little Plexiglas bubble over them.

"Good old American know-how," January said.

Matthews nodded. With two fingers he measured the distance between their position and Iwo Jima. Benton measured with a ruler.

"Rendezvous at five thirty-five, eh?" Matthews said. They were to rendezvous with the two trailing planes over Iwo.

Benton disagreed: "I'd say five-fifty."

"What? Check again, guy, we're not in no tugboat here."

"The wind—"

"Yah, the wind. Frank, you want to add a bet to the pool?"

"Five thirty-six," January said promptly.

They laughed. "See, he's got more confidence in me," Matthews said with a dopey grin.

January recalled his plan to shoot the crew and tip the plane into the sea, and he pursed his lips, repelled. Not for anything would he be able to shoot these men, who, if not friends, were at least companions. They passed for friends. They meant no harm.

Shepard and Stone climbed into the cabin. Matthews offered them coffee. "The gimmick's ready to kick their ass, eh?" Shepard nodded and drank.

January moved forward, past Haddock's console. Another

plan that wouldn't work. What to do? All the flight engineer's dials and gauges showed conditions were normal. Maybe he could sabotage something? Cut a line somewhere?

Fitch looked back at him and said, "When are we due over Iwo?"

"Five-forty, Matthews says."

"He better be right."

A thug. In peacetime Fitch would be hanging around a pool table giving the cops trouble. He was perfect for war. Tibbets had chosen his men well—most of them, anyway. Moving back past Haddock, January stopped to stare at the group of men in the navigation cabin. They joked, drank coffee. They were all a bit like Fitch: young toughs, capable and thoughtless. They were having a good time, an adventure. That was January's dominant impression of his companions in the 509th; despite all the bitching and the occasional moments of overmastering fear, they were having a good time. His mind spun forward and he saw what these young men would grow up to be like as clearly as if they stood before him in businessmen's suits, prosperous and balding. They would be tough and capable and thoughtless, and as the years passed and the great war receded in time they would look back on it with ever-increasing nostalgia, for they would be the survivors and not the dead. Every year of this war would feel like ten in their memories, so that the war would always remain the central experience of their lives—a time when history lay palpable in their hands, when each of their daily acts affected it, when moral issues were simple, and others told them what to do—so that as more years passed and the survivors aged, bodies falling apart, lives in one rut or another, they would unconsciously push harder and harder to thrust the world into war again, thinking somewhere inside themselves that if they could only return to world war then they would magically be again as they were in the last one—young, and free, and happy. And by that time they would hold the positions of power, they would be capable of doing it.

So there would be more wars, January saw. He heard it in Matthews' laughter, saw it in their excited eyes. "There's Iwo, and it's five thirty-one. Pay up! I win!" And in future wars they'd have more bombs like the gimmick, hundreds of them no doubt. He saw more planes, more young crews like this one, flying to Moscow no doubt or to wherever, fireballs in every capital, why not? And to what end? To what end? So that the old men could hope to become magically young again. Nothing more sane than that.

They were over Iwo Jima. Three more hours to Japan. Voices from *The Great Artiste* and *Number 91* crackled on the radio. Rendezvous accomplished, the three planes flew northwest, toward Shikoku, the first Japanese island in their path. January went aft to use the toilet. "You okay, Frank?" Matthews asked. "Sure. Terrible coffee, though." "Ain't it always." January tugged at his baseball cap and hurried away. Kochenski and the other gunners were playing poker. When he was done he returned forward. Matthews sat on the stool before his maps, readying his equipment for the constant monitoring of drift that would now be required. Haddock and Benton were also busy at their stations. January maneuvered between the pilots down into the nose. "Good shooting," Matthews called after him.

Forward it seemed quieter. January got settled, put his headphones on and leaned forward to look out the ribbed Plexiglas.

Dawn had turned the whole vault of the sky pink. Slowly the radiant shade shifted through lavender to blue, pulse by pulse a different color. The ocean below was a glittering blue plane, marbled by a pattern of puffy pink cloud. The sky above was a vast dome, darker above than on the horizon. January had always thought that dawn was the time when you could see most clearly how big the earth was, and how high above it they flew. It seemed they flew at the very upper edge of the atmosphere, and January saw how thin it was, how it was just a skin of air really, so that even if you flew up to its top the earth still extended away infinitely in every direction. The coffee had warmed January, he was sweating. Sunlight blinked off the Plexiglas. His watch said six. Plane and hemisphere of blue were split down the middle by the bombsight. His earphones crackled and he listened in to the reports from the lead planes flying over the target cities. Kokura, Nagasaki, Hiroshima, all of them had six-tenths cloud cover. Maybe they would have to cancel the whole mission because of weather. "We'll look at Hiroshima first," Fitch said. January peered down at the fields of miniature clouds with renewed interest. His parachute slipped under him. Readjusting it he imagined putting it on, sneaking back to the central escape hatch under the navigator's cabin, opening the hatch . . . he could be out of the plane and gone before anyone noticed. Leave it up to them. They could bomb or not but it wouldn't be January's doing. He could float down onto the world like a puff of dandelion, feel cool air rush around him, watch the silk canopy dome hang over him like a miniature sky, a private world.

An eyeless black face. January shuddered; it was as though the nightmare could return any time. If he jumped nothing would change, the bomb would still fall—would he feel any better, floating on his Inland Sea? Sure, one part of him shouted; maybe, another conceded; the rest of him saw that face. . . .

Earphones crackled. Shepard said, "Lieutenant Stone has now armed the bomb, and I can tell you all what we are carrying. Aboard with us is the world's first atomic bomb."

Not exactly, January thought. Whistles squeaked in his earphones. The first one went off in New Mexico. Splitting atoms: January had heard the term before. Tremendous energy in every atom, Einstein had said. Break one, and—he had seen the result on film. Shepard was talking about radiation, which brought back more to January. Energy released in the form of X rays. Killed by X rays! It would be against the Geneva Convention if they had thought of it.

Fitch cut in. "When the bomb is dropped Lieutenant Benton will record our reaction to what we see. This recording is being made for history, so watch your language." Watch your language! January choked back a laugh. Don't curse or blaspheme God at the sight of the first atomic bomb incinerating a city and all its inhabitants with X rays!

Six-twenty. January found his hands clenched together on the headrest of the bombsight. He felt as if he had a fever. In the harsh wash of morning light the skin on the backs of his hands appeared slightly translucent. The whorls in the skin looked like the delicate patterning of waves on the sea's surface. His hands were made of atoms. Atoms were the smallest building block of matter, it took billions of them to make those tense, trembling hands. Split one atom and you had the fireball. That meant that the energy contained in even one hand . . . he turned up a palm to look at the lines and the mottled flesh under the transparent skin. A person was a bomb that could blow up the world. January felt that latent power stir in him, pulsing with every hard heart-knock. What beings they were, and in what a blue expanse of a world! —And here they spun on to drop a bomb and kill a hundred thousand of these astonishing beings.

When a fox or raccoon is caught by the leg in a trap, it lunges until the leg is frayed, twisted, perhaps broken, and only then does the animal's pain and exhaustion force it to quit. Now in the same way January wanted to quit. His mind hurt. His plans to escape were so much crap—stupid, useless. Better to quit. He tried to stop thinking, but it was hopeless. How could he stop? As long as he was conscious he would be thinking. The mind struggles longer in its traps than any fox.

Lucky Strike tilted up and began the long climb to bombing altitude. On the horizon the clouds lay over a green island. Japan. Surely it had gotten hotter, the heater must be broken, he thought. Don't think. Every few minutes Matthews gave Fitch small course adjustments. "Two seventy-five, now. That's it." To escape the moment January recalled his child-hood. Following a mule and plow. Moving to Vicksburg (rivers). For a while there in Vicksburg, since his stutter made it hard to gain friends, he had played a game with himself. He had passed the time by imagining that everything he did was vitally important and determined the fate of the world. If he crossed a road in front of a certain car, for instance, then the car wouldn't make it through the next intersection before a truck hit it, and so the man driving would be killed and wouldn't be able to invent the flying boat that would save President Wilson from kidnappers—so he had to wait for that car because everything afterward depended on it. Oh damn it, he thought, damn it, think of something *different*. The last Hornblower story he had read—how would *he* get out of this? The round O of his mother's face as she ran in and saw his arm— The Mississippi, mud-brown behind its levees— Abruptly he shook his head, face twisted in frustration and despair, aware at last that no possible avenue of memory would serve as an escape for him now, for now there was no part of his life that did not apply to the situation he was in, and no matter where he cast his mind it was going to shore up against the hour facing him.

Less than an hour. They were at thirty thousand feet, bombing altitude. Fitch gave him altimeter readings to dial into the bombsight. Matthews gave him windspeeds. Sweat got in his eye and he blinked furiously. The sun rose behind them like an atomic bomb, glinting off every corner and edge of the Plexiglas, illuminating his bubble compartment with a fierce glare. Broken plans jumbled together in his mind, his breath was short, his throat dry. Uselessly and repeatedly he damned the scientists, damned Truman. Damned the Japanese for causing the whole mess in the first place, damned yellow killers, they had brought this on themselves. Remember Pearl. American men had died under bombs when no war had been declared; they had started it and now it was coming back to them with a vengeance. And they deserved it. And an invasion of Japan would take years, cost millions of lives—end it now, end it, they deserved it, they deserved it steaming river full of charcoal people silently dying damned stubborn race of maniacs!

"There's Honshu," Fitch said, and January returned to the world of the plane. They were over the Inland Sea. Soon they would pass the secondary target, Kokura, a bit to the south. Seven-thirty. The island was draped more heavily than the sea by clouds, and again January's heart leaped with the idea that weather would cancel the mission. But they did deserve it. It was a mission like any other mission. He had dropped bombs on Africa, Sicily, Italy, all Germany. . . . He leaned forward to take a look through the sight. Under the X of the crosshairs was the sea, but at the lead edge of the sight was land. Honshu. At two hundred and thirty miles an hour that gave them about a half hour to Hiroshima. Maybe less. He wondered if his heart could beat so hard for that long.

Fitch said, "Matthews, I'm giving over guidance to you. Just tell us what to do."

"Bear south two degrees," was all Matthews said. At last their voices had taken on a touch of awareness, even fear.

"January, are you ready?" Fitch asked.

"I'm just waiting," January said. He sat up, so Fitch could see the back of his head. The bombsight stood between his legs. A switch on its side would start the bombing sequence; the bomb would not leave the plane immediately upon the flick of the switch, but would drop after a fifteen-second radio tone warned the following planes. The sight was adjusted accordingly.

"Adjust to a heading of two sixty-five," Matthews said. "We're coming in directly upwind." This was to make any side-drift adjustments for the bomb unnecessary. "January, dial it down to two hundred and thirty-one miles per hour."

"Two thirty-one."

Fitch said, "Everyone but January and Matthews, get your goggles on."

January took the darkened goggles from the floor. One needed to protect one's eyes or they might melt. He put them on, put his forehead on the headrest. They were in the way. He took them off. When he looked through the sight again there was land under the crosshairs. He checked his watch. Eight o'clock. Up and reading the papers, drinking tea.

"Ten minutes to AP," Matthews said. The aiming point was Aioi Bridge, a T-shaped bridge in the middle of the delta-straddling city. Easy to recognize.

"There's a lot of cloud down there," Fitch nodded. "Are you going to be able to see?"

"I won't be sure until we try it," January said.

"We can make another pass and use radar if we need to," Matthews said.

Fitch said. "Don't drop it unless you're sure, January."

"Yes, sir."

Through the sight a grouping of rooftops and gray roads was just visible between broken clouds. Around it green forest. "All right," Matthews exclaimed, "here we go! Keep it right on this heading, Captain! January, we'll stay at two thirty-one."

"And same heading," Fitch said. "January, she's all yours. Everyone make sure your goggles are on. And be ready for the turn."

January's world contracted to the view through the bomb-sight. A stippled field of cloud and forest. Over a small range of hills and into Hiroshima's watershed. The broad river was mud brown, the land pale hazy green, the growing network of roads flat gray. Now the tiny rectangular shapes of buildings covered almost all the land, and swimming into the sight came the city proper, narrow islands thrusting into a dark blue bay. Under the crosshairs the city moved island by island, cloud by cloud. January had stopped breathing, his fingers were rigid as stone on the switch. And there was Aioi Bridge. It slid right under the crosshairs, a tiny T right in a gap in the clouds. January's fingers crushed the switch. Deliberately he took a breath, held it. Clouds swam under the crosshairs, then the next island. "Almost there," he said calmly into his microphone. "Steady." Now that he was committed his heart was humming like the Wrights. He counted to ten. Now flowing under the crosshairs were clouds alternating with green forest, leaden roads. "I've turned the switch, but I'm not getting a tone!" he croaked into the mike. His right hand held the switch firmly in place. Fitch was shouting something—Matthews' voice cracked across it— "Flipping it b-back and forth," January shouted, shielding the bombsight with his body from the eyes of the pilots. "But *still*—wait a second—"

He pushed the switch down. A low hum filled his ears. "That's it! It started!"

"But where will it land?" Matthews cried.

"Hold steady!" January shouted.

Lucky Strike shuddered and lofted up ten or twenty feet. January twisted to look down and there was the bomb, flying just below the plane. Then with a wobble it fell away.

The plane banked right and dove so hard that the centrifugal force threw January against the Plexiglas. Several thousand feet lower Fitch leveled it out and they hurtled north.

"Do you see anything?" Fitch cried.

From the tailgun Kochenski gasped "Nothing." January struggled upright. He reached for the welder's goggles, but they were no longer on his head. He couldn't find them. "How long has it been?" he said.

"Thirty seconds," Matthews replied.

January clamped his eyes shut.

The blood in his eyelids lit up red, then white.

On the earphones a clutter of voices: "Oh my God. Oh my God." The plane bounced and tumbled, metallically shrieking. January pressed himself off the Plexiglas. "Nother shockwave!" Kochenski yelled. The plane rocked again, bounced out of control, this is it, January thought, end of the world, I guess that solves my problem.

He opened his eyes and found he could still see. The engines still roared, the props spun. "Those were the shockwaves from the bomb," Fitch called. "We're okay now. Look at that! Will you look at that sonofabitch go!"

January looked. The cloud layer below had burst apart, and a black column of smoke billowed up from a core of red fire. Already the top of the column was at their height. Exclamations of shock clattered painfully in January's ears. He stared at the fiery base of the cloud, at the scores of fires feeding into it. Suddenly he could see past the cloud, and his fingernails cut into his palms. Through a gap in the clouds he saw it clearly, the delta, the six rivers, there off to the left of the tower of smoke: the city of Hiroshima, untouched.

"We missed!" Kochenski yelled. "We missed it!"

January turned to hide his face from the pilots; on it was a grin like a rictus. He sat back in his seat and let the relief fill him.

Then it was back to it. "God damn it!" Fitch shouted down at him. McDonald was trying to restrain him. "January, get up here!"

"Yes, sir." Now there was a new set of problems.

January stood and turned, legs weak. His right fingertips throbbed painfully. The men were crowded forward to look out the Plexiglas. January looked with them.

The mushroom cloud was forming. It roiled out as if it might continue to extend forever, fed by the inferno and the black stalk below it. It looked about two miles wide, and a half mile tall, and it extended well above the height they flew at, dwarfing their plane entirely. "Do you think we'll all be sterile?" Matthews said.

"I can taste the radiation," McDonald declared. "Can you? It tastes like lead."

Bursts of flame shot up into the cloud from below, giving a purplish tint to the stalk. There it stood: lifelike, malignant, sixty thousand feet tall. One bomb. January shoved past the pilots into the navigation cabin, overwhelmed.

"Should I start recording everyone's reactions, Captain?" asked Benton.

"To hell with that," Fitch said, following January back. But Shepard got there first, descending quickly from the navigation dome. He rushed across the cabin, caught January on the shoulder, "You bastard!" he screamed as January stumbled back. "You lost your nerve, coward!"

January went for Shepard, happy to have a target at last, but Fitch cut in and grabbed him by the collar, pulled him around until they were face to face—

"Is that right?" Fitch cried, as angry as Shepard. "Did you screw up on purpose?"

"No," January grunted, and knocked Fitch's hands away from his neck. He swung and smacked Fitch on the mouth, caught him solid. Fitch staggered back, recovered, and no doubt would have beaten January up, but Matthews and Benton and Stone leaped in and held him back, shouting for order. "Shut up! Shut up!" McDonald screamed from the cockpit, and for a moment it was bedlam, but Fitch let himself be restrained, and soon only McDonald's shouts for quiet were heard. January retreated to between the pilot seats, right hand on his pistol holster.

"The city was in the crosshairs when I flipped the switch," he said. "But the first couple of times I flipped it nothing happened—"

"That's a lie!" Shepard shouted. "There was nothing wrong with the switch, I checked it myself. Besides, the bomb exploded *miles* beyond Hiroshima, look for yourself! That's *minutes*." He wiped spit from his chin and pointed at January. "You did it."

"You don't know that," January said. But he could see the men had been convinced by Shepard, and he took a step back. "You just get me to a board of inquiry, quick. And leave me alone till then. If you touch me again," glaring venomously at Fitch and then Shepard, "I'll shoot you." He turned and hopped down to his seat, feeling exposed and vulnerable, like a treed raccoon.

"They'll shoot *you* for this," Shepard screamed after him. "Disobeying orders—treason—" Matthews and Stone were shutting him up.

"Let's get out of here," he heard McDonald say. "I can taste the lead, can't you?"

January looked out the Plexiglas. The giant cloud still burned and roiled. One atom . . . Well, they had really done it to that forest. He almost laughed but stopped himself, afraid of hysteria. Through a break in the clouds he got a clear view of Hiroshima for the first time. It lay spread over its islands like a map, unharmed. Well, that was that. The inferno at the base of the mushroom cloud was eight or ten miles around the shore of the bay and a mile or two inland. A certain patch of forest would be gone, destroyed—utterly blasted from the face of the earth. The Japs would be able to go out and investigate the damage. And if they were told it was a demonstration, a warning—and if they acted fast—well, they had their chance. Maybe it would work.

The release of tension made January feel sick. Then he recalled Shepard's words and he knew that whether his plan worked or not he was still in trouble. In trouble! It was worse than that. Bitterly he cursed the Japanese, he even wished for a moment that he *had* dropped it on them. Wearily he let his despair empty him.

A long while later he sat up straight. Once again he was a trapped animal. He began lunging for escape, casting about for plans. One alternative after another. All during the long grim flight home he considered it, mind spinning at the speed of the props and beyond. And when they came down on Tinian he had a plan. It was a long shot, he reckoned, but it was the best he could do.

The briefing hut was surrounded by MPs again. January stumbled from the truck with the rest and walked inside. He was more than ever aware of the looks given him, and they were hard, accusatory. He was too tired to care. He hadn't slept in more than thirty-six hours, and had slept very little since the last time he had been in the hut, a week before. Now the room quivered with the lack of engine vibration to stabilize it, and the silence roared. It was all he could do to hold on to the bare essentials of his plan. The glares of Fitch and Shepard, the hurt incomprehension of Matthews, they had to be thrust out of his focus. Thankfully he lit a cigarette.

In a clamor of question and argument the others described the strike. Then the haggard Scholes and an intelligence officer led them through the bombing run. January's plan made it necessary to hold to his story: ". . . and when the AP was under the crosshairs I pushed down the switch, but got no signal. I flipped it up and down repeatedly until the tone kicked in. At that point there was still fifteen seconds to the release."

"Was there anything that may have caused the tone to start when it did?"

"Not that I noticed immediately, but—"

"It's impossible," Shepard interrupted, face red. "I checked the switch before we flew and there was nothing wrong with it. Besides, the drop occurred over a minute—"

"Captain Shepard," Scholes said. "We'll hear from you presently."

"But he's obviously lying—"

"Captain Shepard! It's not at all obvious. Don't speak unless questioned."

"Anyway," January said, hoping to shift the questions away from the issue of the long delay, "I noticed something about the bomb when it was falling that could explain why it stuck. I need to discuss it with one of the scientists familiar with the bomb's design."

"What was that?" Scholes asked suspiciously.

January hesitated. "There's going to be an inquiry, right?"

Scholes frowned. "This is the inquiry, Captain January. Tell us what you saw."

"But there will be some proceeding beyond this one?"

"It looks like there's going to be a court-martial, yes, Captain."

"That's what I thought. I don't want to talk to anyone but my counsel, and some scientist familiar with the bomb."

"*I'm* a scientist familiar with the bomb," Shepard burst out. "You could tell me if you really had anything, you—"

"I said I need a scientist!" January exclaimed, rising to face the scarlet Shepard across the table. "Not a G-God damned mechanic." Shepard started to shout, others joined in and the room rang with argument. While Scholes restored order January sat down, and he refused to be drawn out again.

"I'll see you're assigned counsel, and initiate the court-martial," Scholes said, clearly at a loss. "Meanwhile you are under arrest, on suspicion of disobeying orders in combat." January nodded, and Scholes gave him over to the MPs.

"One last thing," January said, fighting exhaustion. "Tell General Le May that if the Japs are told this drop was a warning, it might have the same effect as—"

"I told you!" Shepard shouted. "I told you he did it on purpose!"

Men around Shepard restrained him. But he had convinced most of them, and even Matthews stared at him with surprised anger.

January shook his head wearily. He had the dull feeling that his plan, while it had succeeded so far, was ultimately not a good one. "Just trying to make the best of it." It took all of his remaining will to force his legs to carry him in a dignified manner out of the hut.

His cell was an empty NCO's office. MPs brought his meals. For the first couple of days he did little but sleep. On the third day he glanced out the office's barred window, and saw a tractor pulling a tarpaulin-draped trolley out of the compound, followed by jeeps filled with MPs. It looked like a military funeral. January rushed to the door and banged on it until one of the young MPs came.

"What's that they're doing out there?" January demanded.

Eyes cold and mouth twisted, the MP said, "They're making another strike. They're going to do it right this time."

"No!" January cried. "No!" He rushed the MP, who knocked him back and locked the door. *"No!"* He beat the door until his hands hurt, cursing wildly. "You don't *need* to do it, it isn't *necessary*." Shell shattered at last, he collapsed on the bed and wept. Now everything he had done would be rendered meaningless. He had sacrificed himself for nothing.

A day or two after that the MPs led in a colonel, an iron-haired man who stood stiffly and crushed January's hand when he shook it. His eyes were a pale, icy blue.

"I am Colonel Dray," he said. "I have been ordered to defend you in court-martial." January could feel the dislike pouring from the man. "To do that I'm going to need every fact you have, so let's get started."

"I'm not talking to anybody until I've seen an atomic scientist."

"I am your *defense* counsel—"

"I don't care who you are," January said. "Your defense of me depends on you getting one of the scientists *here*. The higher up he is, the better. And I want to speak to him alone."

"I will have to be present."

So he would do it. But now January's lawyer, too, was an enemy.

"Naturally," January said. "You're my lawyer. But no one else. Our atomic secrecy may depend on it."

"You saw evidence of sabotage?"

"Not one word more until that scientist is here."

Angrily the colonel nodded and left.

Late the next day the colonel returned with another man. "This is Dr. Forest."

"I helped develop the bomb," Forest said. He had a crew cut and dressed in fatigues, and to January he looked more Army than the colonel. Suspiciously he stared back and forth at the two men.

"You'll vouch for this man's identity on your word as an officer?" he asked Dray.

"Of course," the colonel said stiffly, offended.

"So," Dr. Forest said. "You had some trouble getting it off when you wanted to. Tell me what you saw."

"I saw nothing," January said harshly. He took a deep breath; it was time to commit himself. "I want you to take a message back to the scientists. You folks have been working on this thing for years, and you must have had time to consider how the bomb should have been used. You know we could have convinced the Japs to surrender by showing them a demonstration—"

"Wait a minute," Forest said. "You're saying you didn't see anything? There wasn't a malfunction?"

"That's right," January said, and cleared his throat. "It wasn't *necessary*, do you understand?"

Forest was looking at Colonel Dray. Dray gave him a disgusted shrug. "He told me he saw evidence of sabotage."

"I want you to go back and ask the scientists to intercede for me," January said, raising his voice to get the man's attention. "I haven't got a chance in that court-martial. But if the scientists defend me then maybe they'll let me live, see? I don't want to get shot for doing something every one of you scientists would have done."

Dr. Forest had backed away. Color rising, he said, "What makes you think that's what we would have done? Don't you think we considered it? Don't you think men better qualified than you made the decision?" He waved a hand— "God damn it—what made you think you were competent to decide something as important as that!"

January was appalled at the man's reaction; in his plan it had gone differently. Angrily he jabbed a finger at Forest. "Because *I* was the man doing it, *Doctor* Forest. You take even one step back from that and suddenly you can pretend it's not your doing. Fine for you, but *I was there*."

At every word the man's color was rising. It looked like he might pop a vein in his neck. January tried once more. "Have you ever tried to imagine what one of your bombs would do to a city full of people?"

"I've had enough!" the man exploded. He turned to Dray. "I'm under no obligation to keep what I've heard here confidential. You can be sure it will be used as evidence in Captain January's court-martial." He turned and gave January a look of such blazing hatred that January understood it. For these men to admit he was right would mean admitting that they were wrong—that every one of them was responsible for his part in the construction of the weapon January had refused to use. Understanding that, January knew he was doomed.

The bang of Dr. Forest's departure still shook the little office. January sat on his cot, got out a smoke. Under Colonel Dray's cold gaze he lit one shakily, took a drag. He looked up at the colonel, shrugged. "It was my best chance," he explained. That did something—for the first and only time the cold disdain in the colonel's eyes shifted to a little, hard, lawyerly gleam of respect.

The court-martial lasted two days. The verdict was guilty of disobeying orders in combat and of giving aid and comfort to the enemy. The sentence was death by firing squad.

For most of his remaining days January rarely spoke, drawing ever further behind the mask that had hidden him for so long. A clergyman came to see him, but it was the 509th's chaplain, the one who had said the prayer blessing the *Lucky Strike*'s mission before they took off. Angrily January sent him packing.

Later, however, a young Catholic priest dropped by. His name was Patrick Getty. He was a little pudgy man, bespectacled and, it seemed, somewhat afraid of January. January let the man talk to him. When he returned the next day January talked back a bit, and on the day after that he talked some more. It became a habit.

Usually January talked about his childhood. He talked of plowing mucky black bottom land behind a mule. Of running down the lane to the mailbox. Of reading books by the light of the moon after he had been ordered to sleep, and of being beaten by his mother for it with a high-heeled shoe. He told the priest the story of the time his arm had been burnt, and about the car crash at the bottom of Fourth Street. "It's the truck driver's face I remember, do you see, Father?"

"Yes," the young priest said. "Yes."

And he told him about the game he had played in which every action he took tipped the balance of world affairs. "When I remembered that game I thought it was dumb. Step on a sidewalk crack and cause an earthquake—you know, it's stupid. Kids are like that." The priest nodded. "But now I've been thinking that if everybody were to live their whole lives like that, thinking that every move they made really was important, then . . . it might make a difference." He waved a hand vaguely, expelled cigarette smoke. "You're accountable for what you do."

"Yes," the priest said. "Yes, you are."

"And if you're given orders to do something wrong, you're still accountable, right? The orders don't change it."

"That's right."

"Hmph." January smoked a while. "So they say, anyway. But look what happens." He waved at the office. "I'm like the guy in a story I read—he thought everything in books was true, and after reading a bunch of westerns he tried to rob a train. They tossed him in jail." He laughed shortly. "Books are full of crap."

"Not all of them," the priest said. "Besides, you weren't trying to rob a train."

They laughed at the notion. "Did you read that story?"

"No."

"It was the strangest book—there were two stories in it, and they alternated chapter by chapter, but they didn't have a thing to do with each other! I didn't get it."

". . . Maybe the writer was trying to say that everything connects to everything else."

"Maybe. But it's a funny way to say it."

"I like it."

And so they passed the time, talking.

* * *

So it was the priest who was the one to come by and tell January that his request for a Presidential pardon had been refused. Getty said awkwardly, "It seems the President approves the sentence."

"That bastard," January said weakly. He sat on his cot.

Time passed. It was another hot, humid day.

"Well," the priest said. "Let me give you some better news. Given your situation I don't think telling you matters, though I've been told not to. The second mission—you know there was a second strike?"

"Yes."

"Well, they missed too."

"What?" January cried, and bounced to his feet. "You're kidding!"

"No. They flew to Kokura, but found it covered by clouds. It was the same over Nagasaki and Hiroshima, so they flew back to Kokura and tried to drop the bomb using radar to guide it, but apparently there was a—a genuine equipment failure this time, and the bomb fell on an island."

January was hopping up and down, mouth hanging open, "So we n-never—"

"We never dropped an atom bomb on a Japanese city. That's right." Getty grinned. "And get this—I heard this from my superior—they sent a message to the Japanese government tellng them that the two explosions were warnings, and that if they didn't surrender by September first we would drop bombs on Kyoto and Tokyo, and then wherever else we had to. Word is that the Emperor went to Hiroshima to survey the damage, and when he saw it he ordered the Cabinet to surrender. So . . ."

"So it worked," January said. He hopped around, "It worked, it worked!"

"Yes."

"Just like I said it would!" he cried, and hopping before the priest he laughed.

Getty was jumping around a little too, and the sight of the priest bouncing was too much for January. He sat on his cot and laughed till the tears ran down his cheeks.

"So—" he sobered quickly. "So Truman's going to shoot me anyway, eh?"

"Yes," the priest said unhappily. "I guess that's right."

This time January's laugh was bitter. "He's a bastard, all right. And proud of being a bastard, which makes it worse." He shook his head. "If Roosevelt had lived . . ."

"It would have been different," Getty finished. "Yes. Maybe so. But he didn't." He sat beside January. "Cigarette?" He held out a pack, and January noticed the white wartime wrapper. He frowned.

"You haven't got a Camel?"

"Oh. Sorry."

"Oh well. That's all right." January took one of the Lucky Strikes, lit up. "That's awfully good news." He breathed out. "I never believed Truman would pardon me anyway, so mostly you've brought good news. Ha. They *missed*. You have no idea how much better that makes me feel."

"I think I do."

January smoked the cigarette.

". . . So I'm a good American after all. I *am* a good American," he insisted, "no matter what Truman says."

"Yes," Getty replied, and coughed. "You're better than Truman any day."

"Better watch what you say, Father." He looked into the eyes behind the glasses, and the expression he saw there gave him pause. Since the drop every look directed at him had been filled with contempt. He'd seen it so often during the court-martial that he'd learned to stop looking; and now he had to teach himself to see again. The priest looked at him as if he were . . . as if he were some kind of hero. That wasn't exactly right. But seeing it . . .

January would not live to see the years that followed, so he would never know what came of his action. He had given up casting his mind forward and imagining possibilities, because there was no point to it. His planning was ended. In any case he would not have been able to imagine the course of the post-war years. That the world would quickly become an armed camp pitched on the edge of atomic war, he might have predicted. But he never would have guessed that so many people would join a January Society. He would never know of the effect the Society had on Dewey during the Korean crisis, never know of the Society's successful campaign for the test ban treaty, and never learn that thanks in part to the Society and its allies, a treaty would be signed by the great powers that would reduce the number of atomic bombs year by year, until there were none left.

Frank January would never know any of that. But in that moment on his cot looking into the eyes of young Patrick Getty, he guessed an inkling of it—he felt, just for an instant, the impact on history.

And with that he relaxed. In his last week everyone who met him carried away the same impression, that of a calm, quiet man, angry at Truman and others, but in a withdrawn, matter-of-fact way. Patrick Getty, a strong force in the January Society ever after, said January was talkative for some time after he learned of the missed attack on Kokura. Then he became quieter and quieter, as the day approached. On the morning that they woke him at dawn to march him out to a hastily constructed execution shed, his MPs shook his hand. The priest was with him as he smoked a final cigarette, and they prepared to put the hood over his head. January looked at him calmly. "They load one of the guns with a blank cartridge, right?"

"Yes," Getty said.

"So each man in the squad can imagine he may not have shot me?"

"Yes. That's right."

A tight, unhumorous smile was January's last expression. He threw down the cigarette, ground it out, poked the priest in the arm. "But I *know*." Then the mask slipped back into place for good, making the hood redundant, and with a firm step January went to the wall. One might have said he was at peace.

—1983

Coming Back to Dixieland

It figures, just as sure as shift-start, that on our big day there'd be trouble. It's a law of physics, the one miners know best: things tend to fuck up.

I woke first out of the last of several nervous catnaps, and wandered down to the hotel bar to get something a little less heavyweight than the White Brother for my nerves. On one level I was calm as could be, but on another I was feeling a bit shaky (Shaky Barnes, that's me). Now, we drank the Brother during performances back on the rocks, of course, between sets sitting at the tables, or during the last songs when someone offered it; and Hook would make his announcement, "We never know if this'll make us play better or worse, but it sure is fun finding out," and then pass it around. Which was the point; we *had* to play good this day, so I wanted something soothing, with a little less pop to it than the White Brother we'd brought with us, which amplifies your every feeling, including fear.

So when I threaded my way through the hotel (which was as big as the whole operation on Hebe or Iris) back to our rooms, I expected the band to still be there sleeping. But when I'd finished stepping over all the scattered chairs, tables, mattresses and such (the remains of the previous shift's practice session) I could find only three of them, all tangled up in the fancy sheets: Fingers, Crazy, and Washboard. I wasn't surprised that my brother Hook was gone—he often was—but Sidney shouldn't have been missing; he hadn't gone off by himself since we left Ceres Central.

"Hey!" I said, still not too worried. "Where'd they go, you slag-eaters!" They mumbled and grunted and tried to ignore me. I gave Washboard a shove with my foot. "Where's Hook? Where's Sidney?" I said a little louder.

"Quit shouting," Washboard said fuzzily. "Hook's probably gone back to the Tower of Bible to visit the Jezebels again." He buried his head in the pillow, like a snoutbit diving into bubblerock; suddenly it popped back out. "*Sidney's* gone?"

"You see him?"

Fingers propped himself up on his elbow. "You better find Hook," he said in his slow way. "Hook, he'll know where Sidney gone to."

"Well, did Hook *say* he was going to the Tower of Bible?" No one spoke. Crazy crawled over to a bed and sat up. He reached behind the bed and pulled out a tall thin bottle, still half filled with cloudy white liquid. He put it to his mouth and tilted it up; the level dropped abruptly a couple of times.

"Crazy, I never seen you hit the White Brother so early in the dayshift before," I said.

"Shaky," he replied, "you never seen me get the chance."

"You going to get us in trouble," I said, remembering certain misadventures of the past.

"No, I'm not," Crazy said. "Now why don't you run down Hook, I'm pretty sure he's in Sodom and Gomorrah, he liked that place"—he took another swallow—"and we'll hold down the fort and wait for Sidney to come back."

"He better come back," I said. "Shit. Here it is the biggest day in our lives and you guys don't even have the sense to stay in one spot."

"Don't worry," Crazy said. "Things'll go fine, I'll see to it."

I took one of the slow cars through the track-webbed space between our hotel and the Tower of Bible. The Tower is one of Titania's biggest experiments in Neo-Archeo-Ritualism, sometimes called Participatory Art. Within the huge structure, set right against the wall of the Titania Gap, the setting for every chapter in the Bible is contained, which means you can participate in a wide variety of activities. The lobby of the Tower was unusually crowded for the early hours of the dayshift, but it was Performance Day, I remembered, and people were starting early. I worked from ramp to ramp, trying to make my way through the oddly assorted crowd to the elevator that would take me to Sodom and Gomorrah. Finally I slid through the closing doors and took my place in the mass of future Sodomites.

"What I want to know," one of them said happily, "is do they periodically sulfurize everyone in the room?"

"Every two hours," a woman with round eyes replied, "and does it feel real! But then they unfreeze you and you get to begin again!" She laughed.

"Oh," said the man, blinking.

The elevator opened and the group surged past me toward Costumes. I stood and looked down some of the smoky streets of Gomorrah, hoping to see my brother in the crowd. Just as I decided to get one of the costumes and start searching, I saw him coming out of the door marked JEZEBELS, one arm wrapped around a veiled woman.

"Why, he must have just got here," I said aloud, and took off after him. "Hook!" I called. "Hook!"

He heard me and quickly steered the woman into a side street. I started running. Sure enough, when I rounded the corner they had disappeared; I made a lucky guess and opened the door to a house made of sediments, and caught up with them moving up the narrow stairs. "Hook, God damn it," I said.

"Later," he mumbled back at me, face buried in the Jezebel's neck.

"Hook, it's important."

He waved his right arm back at me in a brush-away motion, and the metal rods of his hand flashed in my face. "Not important!" he bellowed. I grabbed his arm and pulled on it.

"How can you say that?" I cried. "Today's the day! The six bands those judges pick today get to go to Earth and everywhere—"

He finally stopped dragging us all up the stairs. "I know all that, Shaky, but that don't happen for a few hours yet, so why don't you go down to Psalms or Proverbs and calm down some? No reason for you to be so anxious."

"Yes, there is," I said, "a real good reason. Sidney's gone."

Hook tucked his chin into his neck. "Sidney's gone?" he repeated.

"Nobody's seen him all shift."

His three metal fingers waved up and down, scissoring the air; it was the same nervous sign of thought he'd made when he had his hand, and played the trumpet. "Did you search the hotel good?" he said after a bit. "I don't think he'd leave the hotel."

I shook my head. "I came here, I thought you'd know where he is."

"Well, he's probably in the hotel somewhere, take a look why don't you?"

"What if he's not there? Come on, Hook, if we don't find him we're sunk."

"All right," he said. "Shit. You're as bad as Sidney. I've been playing with that man near twenty years, and I never seen him so scared."

"You think he's scared?" That had never occurred to me. Sidney was quiet, not too forward, but I'd never seen him scared of playing music.

"Sure he's scared." He looked at the Jezebel, who hadn't made a sound so far. "I got to find Sidney," he explained. "I'll be back to celebrate tomorrow."

Her veiled head nodded, and I could see the flash of teeth. "We better hurry," Hook said. "We're due to be turned into a pillar of salt any minute now." We ran back and dived into the elevator, just behind the man who had been asking questions on the way up. Down in the lobby we dodged through a group of wide-eyed Venusian monks and then through a stumbling crowd of wet people from one of the aquatic scenes. Then we made it to the exit, jumped in a car, and popped out into the Gap.

"That Participatory Art," Hook said, "is really something."

"Sidney's probably hiding in the hotel somewhere, the bar or maybe the baggage rooms," Hook said as we neared our hotel.

I could see that he was as worried as I was. Despite his easygoing speculations, his nervous trumpet fingering gave him away. Sidney's absence was a serious matter, partly because it was so unexpected; Sidney was never gone, never sick, never hurt; there was nothing that could keep Sidney from playing. And how he could play that clarinet! It was more than notes, it had to do with what was inside the man, the strength and the feeling; there's no way I can describe it to you but by telling a story here; a little blues:

After the long shift's ending, when I was just a kid and still working the sheds, I'd go down to the Heel Bar to sip beer and listen to Sidney play his clarinet. At this time he was playing with just Washboard and a piano man, Christy Morton, who later got killed in the big tunnel collapse on Troilus; and they were working out all the old tunes he'd discovered in the Benson Curtis tapes.

Sidney was as quiet and unassuming then as always. It didn't matter how much stomping and shouting he stirred up, or how much Washboard and Christy sang into the tune; old Sidney would stand there, head bowed, horn cradled in his arm when he wasn't playing, as silent and bashful as a child. Then he'd raise that horn to his mouth, and when he played it was clear he had found his way of talking to the world. All the clamoring in the room channeled into him, he was transformed, and, sweat-bright with the effort, he'd wrench those songs into a sound as clean and live as a welding arc. Listening to him my cheeks would flush with blood, my heart would pound like Washboard's cowbell.

One time, late in the graveyard shift, I was joined at my front table by a Metis mute, one of the miners whose vocal cords had been ruined by the zinc blowout on Metis. Between sets Sidney sat with us, asked me how Hook was doing (this was right after his accident), and talked about Earth. He told us about New Orleans in the old times, when the jazz bands played in the streets. Telling it, he got so excited I didn't need to prod him with questions; he spoke on his own, even told us his one childhood memory of Earth: "That ocean, it was like a flat blue plate, big as Jupiter from Io, speckled with shadows from clouds; and the horizon was straight as a rail, edge to edge cutting off a sky that was a blue I can't describe." When he went back to play I was under the spell of Dixieland; and by the gleam in the mute's eye I could tell he felt it too. When Sidney played a good break the mute would put back his head and laugh, mouth split wide open, silent as space.

So when Sidney was done we decided to take the mute along to Sidney's place, to give the mute some floor to sleep on; he didn't have any money or anywhere to go. Now at this time (this was on Achilles) Sidney lived in a cubbyhole behind one of the Supervisor's big homes. When we got there Sidney wanted us to hold back while he went to check if his sister-in-law was awake—she didn't like him bringing folks home. Sidney explained this, but the mute didn't appear to understand; he must have thought he was being left, because every time Sidney walked a few steps and turned around, he found the mute right behind him, grinning and dragging me along. So there was a lot of waving and explaining going on when the JM police suddenly appeared; we didn't even have time to run.

"Where you going?" one of them asked.

"Home," Sidney said.

"I suppose you live here?" the cop said, pointing at the Supervisor's place.

"Yeah," Sidney said, and before he had time to explain, they were taking us off to jail.

We were hardly inside the jail door when they went to work on the Metis mute. Kicked him and beat him till he couldn't stand. His face was so bloody. Sidney and I stood shaking against the wall, expecting we'd be next, but they let us alone. Turned out one of the cops' wives had been killed on Metis, and he'd been after the mutes ever since. So when they were done with him they slammed us all into the bullpen.

There's not much JM can do to make its jails any worse than its mines, but what they can do they have done. The cell we were in was cold and dark, like a tunnel in a power breakdown, except for the gravity, which felt like it was over 1.00. I crawled over the rock floor, unable to see, and quietly called Sidney's name.

"Steve?" his voice said. "Where you gone to?" His hand caught my arm, and he set me down beside him.

"Quit that snuffling," he said to me. "This is your first time in jail? Is that right? Well, it won't be your last, no, not a miner kid like you. They'll put you here many times before you're done." He paused. "Look at all these folks."

A dim light gleamed through the door grating, and when my eyes adjusted I saw shapes huddled on the floor. They were gathered in knots, feet on each other's stomachs, using the survival techniques JM had taught them.

"They going to let us die?" I asked fearfully; the only times I had seen men curled together like that was when they carried the bodies, two by two, out of breakdowns.

"No, no," he said. "They just like us, just put in here for nothing, to be cold and hungry and heavy for a shift or two, to remind them who's boss on these rocks." He sounded old and tired; and yet when I looked up at him, I saw that he was pulling the parts of his clarinet out of his big old coat and putting them together. He was sitting against the rock wall of the cell, with the mute propped up beside him. When his horn was together he put it to his mouth, gave the reed a lick, commenced to play.

He started soft, barely sounding the notes, and played "Burgundy Street Blues" all the way through without raising his voice. As he played "What Did I Do" some of the huddled figures slowly sat up and listened, backs and heads to the wall, looking up at the ceiling or the yellow squares of the grate.

Then he played the new songs, written by miners' bands and only heard in the bars scattered through their asteroids. He played "Ceres," and "Hidalgo," and "Vesta Joys"; he played his "Shaft Bucket Blues" and "I Got Me a Feeling."

Then he played "Don't God Live Out This Far," one of the first of the miner blues, which made it about twenty years old; and people began to join him. These were miners, men who seldom sang in the bars, seldom did more than stomp their boots or shout something between phrases; and at first their singing was an awkward sort of growl, barely in tune or time with Sidney. But he picked them up and more joined in, hesitantly, till you could make out the words of the refrain:

"Up at the shift-start,
Down in the mine shaft,
Spend my life throwing dirt on a car—
Ain't got nothing to do
But sing me the blues—
Hey don't God live out this far."

There were about thirty verses to the song. It was about a miner who keeps getting in trouble, till JM decides to finish him: "Super comes at shift-start for me to be hung, on account of something that I hadn't done." The Supervisor believes he's innocent, but there's no proof. It was the same old, old thing.

When the singing got loud enough Sidney took off from the melody and floated up above it. And they sang! There was something in it that seemed to take my lungs away, so I could only breathe quick and shallow; it was what they had of the music inside themselves. Just hearing someone's voice in the dark, and knowing his life has a long way to go . . .

The light from the door just caught the plumes of breath frosting out from the men singing. I looked over at the mute. His eyes were open, staring out somewhere in space. As I watched he lifted up his hands and started a little syncopated clap, very soft, giving as much to the music as he could. When Sidney heard it he looked down at him, then looked back up; he played louder, filling the room with his sound, till the clarinet was all we heard or needed to hear, and the last verse came to its end.

"Oh yeah," said a quiet voice.

Sidney looked at the mute, smiled, shook his head. "A little blues for us, eh, brother?" he said. "A little slave music."

The mute nodded and grinned, which made his lip crack open again and spill blood down his chin.

Sidney laughed at him and wiped some of the blood from the mute's face. "Oh yeah," he said softly, "a little miner music."

We found Sidney just where Hook guessed he might be, huddled in the room where our baggage and instruments were stored. He was perched up on the box that Crazy's tuba traveled in, with his shoulders hunched and his legs crossed. When we burst into the room he jumped and then settled back, head down, staring sullenly across at us. His clarinet lay fitted in his arms. We all stood still, barred and hidden in the shadows thrown by the single bulb behind us, waiting for somebody to say something. The wisps of hair Sidney combed across his head looked thicker because of the shadows they cast on his bald pate. He looked like one of the tunnel-gnomes men claim to see on Pallas; creatures who were once men maybe, who escaped JM by living in the old shafts. I had never noticed how small he was.

"You scared?" Hook asked.

Sidney raised his head to stare at Hook better. "Yeah, I am," he said suddenly, loud in the dim room, "shouldn't I be?"

"Hey, Sidney." I said, "you don't got no reason to be scared—"

"Don't got no reason!" He pointed at me, clarinet still in hand. "Don't you say that shit to me, Shaky. I got the best reason possible to be scared." He jumped down from the box. "The best reason possible. This is a contest, boy, we ain't playing to please these folks, we playing to show them that we better musicianers than all them others! And if we don't show them that, if we don't win one of them grants, we gone. We back to the mines, boy, and we'll work in those shafts until JM has broke us so we can't work no more, and we'll never get to see the Earth. So don't tell me I got no reason to be scared."

"Come on, Sidney, you can't think like that," I said, searching for something I could say to him. "It ain't so bad as—"

"Sidney," Hook said, like I hadn't been talking at all (suddenly I see a picture in my head, of Sidney crouched down and shifting through a four-foot-high tunnel, Hook straddled senseless across his back, one of his hands clamped white around Hook's wrist, which ended in a tangle of bloody filaments; shouting instructions in furious fearful high voice to the men trying to get the airlock opened); I stepped back and let Hook talk to him.

"Sidney," he said, "you ain't thought this out. They been putting one over on you. You're talking like this contest is a big vital thing, like we got some chance of going out there and *winning* one of them grants. Sidney, we got *no* chance, don't you realize that?"

"Hook—" I objected.

"No, you listen to me, we *got no chance*. You seen all those other musicianers here—those folks been doing nothing but play music all their *lives*, they playing all those fancy machines and doing things with music we don't even know about! And we just a bunch of miners playing some old Earth-type of music that just showed up a few years back, and only 'cause JM salvaged a ship full of band instruments and give them to us so we'd stay out of fights! And you still think we got a *chance*?"

Sidney and I stared at him.

"No way," he continued grimly, "no more'n there's a chance that JM will retire us at forty and send us to Mars. They got us here just so they can say they got folks from everywhere, even the rocks, and they going to give the grants to those fancy-ass musicianers, not us. So just exactly what you said is going to happen, Sidney, when this thing is over they going to send us back to the rocks to work and work, every third shift, till some equipment catches you or some tunnel collapses"—waving his hooks so they flashed silver in front of us—"and then, if you're still alive, they'll dump you on Vesta rock and wait for you to die.

"And the only way you got to show how you feel about that, Sidney, is through that horn, through that skinny black horn of yours. When you get out there they going to be looking down on you, just like they always have, and all you can do about it is to *play* that thing! play it so hard they *got* to see you! play it and show them what kind of music a man plays when he works all his life digging in those fucking rocks!"

He stopped, gulped in some air. Sidney and I didn't make a sound. Suddenly he turned and walked over to the baggage, rummaged around a bit, then found the trunk he wanted and pulled it around so he could unstrap it and fling it open. He reached in and pulled out a long white bottle, held it high in the dim light while he unscrewed it. He turned it upside down to his mouth and took a long pull.

"*Eeeow!*" he whooped. He held it out toward Sidney. "So what say we have a drink of the White Brother, brother, and then go play us some music."

I looked at Sidney. I don't think I'd ever seen him indulge in the White Brother; he hardly even drank beer.

"I believe I will," Sidney said, and swallowed near half the bottle.

*   *   *

Back up in our rooms Crazy was leading Fingers and Washboard in the "Emperor Norton Stomp," running up the walls as high as he could and then diving off onto the unmade and trampled beds. He saw us standing in the doorway and from his position high on the wall he dived straight for us and bounced on the floor.

"Crazy," Hook said cheerfully, "you are crazy." He stepped over him and made his way through the stuff heaped on the floor. He pulled his trombone out of the pile beside his bed.

"Let's roll," he said.

"Wait!" Crazy cried. He poured some White Brother into cups and passed them around. When Sidney took one he didn't say a word, just grinned and pointed. Sidney paid him no attention.

We raised our cups in the air. "To the Hot Six," I said. "Play that thing!" We downed the Brother; I could feel him slide into my stomach and explode there, making my blood pound and my vision jump.

We got our instruments and made our way to the lobby. When we got there we headed for the clerk's desk, bumping together and shushing each other, trying to calm down some while Hook spoke to the clerk.

"We are the Hot Six," Hook shouted at the clerk, who stepped back quickly. "And we playing at the Outer Planets Center for the Performing Arts' W. H. Blakely Memorial Traveling Grant Competition" (we all threw in some "oh yeahs!" for such virtuosity) "and we need your fastest car right now."

"Well sir," the clerk said, "all the cars have the same speed capability."

"Oh come now, *come* now," Hook said, "are you telling me that you don't know of a single car that's set to go a mite faster than normal?"

"No sir, none except the cars reserved for emergencies—"

"Emergencies! Why, don't you know that's exactly what this is? An emergency!"

"An emergency," we all echoed, and Crazy began to climb over the desk, muttering in a low voice, "Emergency, emergency."

"If you don't give us one of them emergency cars," Hook continued in a lowered voice, "then we've come over fifteen hundred million miles for no reason at all."

The clerk looked past Hook and saw us staring at him with the intensity that the White Brother can give you; looked at Crazy, who was clawing at the buttons on top of the counter. He shrugged. "One of the special cars will be waiting for you at the departure gate."

"Make it a big one," Hook said, "we got a lot of stuff to carry."

We went to the departure gate and found a sixteen-person car, painted bright red, waiting for us. We threw all the instruments in the back and clambered in; Hook set the controls and fired us out into the Titania Gap.

The Gap is a long, straight canyon whose origins are unknown. It looks like it was carved into Titania some eons back by a good-sized rock (say about the size of Demeter) that nearly missed it. It's about two hundred miles long, four to ten miles wide, and nearly that deep, and almost the entire colony on Titania is set down in the skinny end of it. So when we popped out the wall of our hotel and shot down our track, we were greeted with the sight of the whole colony, covering the floor and climbing the walls of a canyon that would have swallowed most of the rocks we had lived on. There was only the fine lacing of car tracks looping through space to keep us from dropping two or three miles. Above us the swirling greens of Uranus blocked off most of the sky we could see.

"Shit, this thing *is* fast," Hook said, after the car had taken a long drop and thrown us back in our seats. Crazy whooped and climbed over the seats back to his tuba case, from which he pulled another milky-white bottle. Fingers cheered and started singing, half-tempo like he always starts, "I Don't Know Where I'm Going But I'm On My Way," and Hook joined him.

"I feel pretty good," Sidney said from his window seat.

I sat back and watched the other cars slide along their strands, listening to the band keep loose. The front line, I thought, would be okay. I had been playing with Hook and Sidney since I was twelve years old—twelve years now—and Hook and Sidney had been playing together longer than that; we were the best front line there was, without a doubt, maybe the best there had ever been. And our back line was almost as good. Washboard never stopped hitting; even now he was clicking out rhythms on the side of the car, metal studs already taped to his fingers. Crazy was unreliable, we'd had to play many times without him because of his wild drinking; he didn't have the virtuoso command of the tuba that old Clarence Miles, our first tuba man, had had before he was paralyzed; but nobody could pump as much air through a tuba as Crazy could, and his mad stomping and blowing was one of the trademarks of the Hot Six. Fingers—he was probably our weakest spot. He's a bit slow to understand things, and he only has eight fingers now; maybe the best thing about his playing is that all eight of those fingers hit the keys a good part of the time. That's the only way a piano man gets heard in a jazz band, especially a fine loud one like ours.

Hook slammed us into one of the track intersections without slowing down, and we dropped through it with a sickening jolt. I had visions of the whole band plummeting down the Gap like a puny imitation of the rock that had carved it.

"Goddammit Hook, what's the rush?" I asked. "We're not that late."

"Don't worry," he said. "This is just a fancy ore car here, I got it in hand."

"Yeah, don't worry, Shaky," Crazy chipped in. "Why you worrying? You ain't going to get shaky again, are you Shaky?" They all laughed, Hook hardest of all; he had named me that because I was so scared when I first played with the band that my tone had a vibrato in it.

"I feel *real* good," said Sidney.

Then we turned a curve and were pointed right at the Performing Arts Center. It stuck up from the canyon floor like one of the natural spires, a huge stack right at the end of the colony, the last structure before the black U of the Gap stretched out, lightless and empty. The car hit the final swoop of track up to it, and scarcely slowed down. Nobody said anything; Fingers stopped singing. As we drew closer, and the side of the building blocked out our view of the Gap, Hook finished the verse:

"And I got no place to go to
And I got no place to stay
And I don't know where I'm going
But I'm on my way."

The waiting room backstage was crowded with a menagerie of about forty brightly dressed performers, all wandering in and out of practice rooms and talking loud, trying to work off tension. As soon as we walked in the door I could feel a heat on my cheeks, on account of all the eyes focusing on us. Everyone was happy to have something to think about besides the upcoming few hours, and as I looked at us all, standing in the doorway gawking, I could see we were good for that. Even in our best clothes (supplied by JM) we looked like exactly what we were: bulky, roughshod, unkempt, maimed, oh, we were miners, clear enough; and under the stares of that rainbow of costumes I suppose we should have quailed. But the energy we got from adrenaline and the White Brother and our wild flight down the Gap gave us a sort of momentum; and when Hook and Crazy looked at each other and burst out laughing, it was them that quailed. Glances turned away from us, and we strode into the room feeling on top of things.

I walked over to a circle of chairs that was empty and sat down. I got my trumpet out of its case and stuck my very shallowest mouthpiece into it; hit 'em high and hard, I thought. The rest of the band was doing the same around me, talking in mutters and laughing every time their eyes met. I looked around and saw that now our fellow performers were trying to watch us without looking. As my gaze swept the room it pushed eyes down and away like magic. When Washboard pulled his washboard out of his box and compulsively rippled his studded fingers down the slats to pop the cowbell, there was an attentive, amazed silence—very undeserved, I thought, considering how strange some of the other instruments in the room appeared—if that was really what they were. I walked over to the piano in a corner of the room, and nearly fell at an unexpected step down. I hit B-flat. My C was in tune with it. Hook, Sidney, and Crazy hit a variety of thirds and fifths, intending to sound as haphazard and out of tune as possible. Sidney made a series of small adjustments to his clarinet, but Hook and Crazy laid their brass down, the better to observe the show going on around them. Washboard was already moving around the room, stepping from level to level and politely asking questions about the weird machinery.

"Hey, look at this!" Hook called across to me. He was waving a square of paper. I crossed back to him.

"It's a program," he explained, and began to read out loud, " 'Number Eighteen, the Hot Six Jazz Band, from Jupiter Metals, Pallas—an instrumental group specializing in traditional jazz, a twentieth-century style of composition and performance characterized by vigorous improvisation.' Ha!

Vigorous improvisation!'' He laughed again. ''I'll vigorously improvise those—''

''Who's that up there?'' Fingers asked, pointing with his good hand at the video screen they had up on one wall. The performer on stage at the moment was a red-robed singer, warbling out some polytonal stuff that many of the people in the room looked like they wanted to hear, judging by the way they stared at Hook. The harmonies and counterpoints the performer was singing with himself were pretty complex, but he had a box surgically implanted in one side of his neck that was clearly helping his vocal cords, so even though he was sliding from Crazy's tuning note up to the A above high C while holding a C-major chord, I wasn't much impressed.

'' 'Number Sixteen,' '' Hook read (and my heart sledged in my chest all of a sudden; only two to go), '' 'Singer Roderick Flen-Jones, from Rhea, a vocalist utilizing the Sturmond Larynx-Synthesizer in four fugues of his own composition.''

''Shit,'' Crazy remarked at a particularly high turn, ''he sounds like a dog whistle.''

''Pretty lightweight,'' Washboard agreed.

''Lightweight? Man, he's *featherweight!*'' Crazy shouted, and laughed loudly at his own joke; he was feeling pretty good. I noticed we were causing a general exodus from the main waiting room. People were drifting into the practice chambers to get away from us, and there was a growing empty space surrounding our group of chairs. I caught Hook's eye and he seemed to get my meaning. He shrugged a ''Fuck them,'' but he got Crazy to pick up his tuba and go over some turns with him, which calmed things down somewhat.

I sat down beside a guy near our chairs who was dressed up in one of the simpler costumes in the room, a brown-and-gold robe. He had been watching us with what seemed like friendly interest the whole time we'd been there.

"You look like you're having fun," he said.

"Sure," I agreed. "How about you?"

"I'm a little scared to be enjoying myself fully."

"I know the feeling. What's that?" I asked, pointing to the instrument in his lap.

"Tone-bar," he said, running his fingers over it; without amplification it made only the ghost of a rippling glissando.

"Is that a new thing?" I asked.

"Not this time. Last time it was."

"You've tried this before?"

"Yes," he said, "I won, too."

"You won!" I exclaimed. "You got one of the grants?" He nodded. "So what are you doing back here?"

"That grant only gets you from place to place. It doesn't guarantee you're going to make enough to keep traveling once you're done with it."

"Well, will these folks give a grant twice?"

"They've never done it before," he said, and looked up from his tone-bar to smile lopsidedly at me. "So I've got quite a job today, don't I."

"I guess," I said.

We watched the video for a while. As the singer juggled the three parts of his fugue Tone-bar shook his head. "Amazing, isn't he," he said.

"Oh yeah," I said. "The question is, do you listen to music to be amazed."

He laughed. "I don't know, but the audience thinks so."

"I bet they don't," I said.

This time he didn't laugh. "So did I."

Number Sixteen was leaving the stage and being replaced by Number Seventeen. That meant we wouldn't be on for an hour or so. I wished we were going on sooner; all the excitement I had felt was slowly collecting into a tense knot below my diaphragm. And I could see signs of the same thing happening to the others. Not Crazy; he was still rowdy as ever; he was marching about the room with his tuba, blasting it in the technicians' ears and annoying as many people as possible. But I had seen Fingers wandering toward the piano, undoubtedly planning to join Hook and Crazy in the phrases they were working on; some character wrapped in purple-and-blue sheets sat down just ahead of him and began to play some fast complicated stuff, classical probably, with big dramatic hand-over-hands all up and down the keys. Fingers turned around and sat back down, hands hidden in his lap, and watched the guy play; and when the guy got up Fingers just sat there, looking down at his lap like he hadn't noticed.

And Sidney got quieter and quieter. He stared up at the video and watched a quartet of people fidget around a big box that they all played together, and as he stared he sank into his chair and closed around his clarinet. He was getting scared again. All the excitement and energy the band had generated on the trip over had disappeared, leaving only Washboard's insistent tapping and Crazy's crazy antics, which were gaining us more and more enemies among the other performers.

While I was still wondering what to do about this (because I felt like I was at least as scared as Sidney) Crazy made his way back to our corner of the room, did a quick side shuffle, and slammed into another musician.

"Hey!" Crazy yelled. "Watch it!"

I groaned. The guy he had knocked over was dressed in some material that shifted color when he moved; he had been making loud comments about us from the practice rooms ever since we had arrived. Now he got his footing and carefully lifted his instrument (a long many-keyed brass box that turned one arm back into itself) from the floor.

"You stupid, clumsy, drunken oaf," he said evenly.

"Hey," Crazy said, ignoring the description, "what's that you got there?"

"Ignorant fool," the musician said. "It's a Klein synthesizer, an instrument beyond your feeble understanding."

"Oh yeah?" Crazy said. "Sounds a little one-sided to me." He burst out laughing.

"It is unfortunate," the other replied, "that the Blakely Foundation finds it necessary to exhibit even the most *atavistic* forms of music at this circus." He turned and stalked over to the piano.

"Atavistic!" Crazy repeated, looking at us. "What's that mean?"

I shrugged. "It means primitive," said Tone-bar. Hook started to laugh.

"Primitive!" Crazy bellowed. "I'm going to go hit that guy and let him think it over." He turned to follow the musician, tuba still in his arms; and before anyone could move, he missed the step down and crashed to the floor, as loud as fifty cymbals all hit at once.

We leaped over and pulled the tuba off him. It was hardly dented; somehow he had twisted so it fell mostly on him.

"You okay?" Hook said anxiously, pushing back the rest of us. From somewhere in the room there was a laugh.

Crazy didn't move. We stood around him. "God damn it," Hook said, "the bastard is out cold." He looked like he wanted to kick him.

"And look!" Sidney said, lifting Crazy's left arm carefully. Right behind his hand (his fingering hand) was a bluish lump that stretched his skin tight. "He's hurt that wrist bad," Sidney said. "He's out of it."

"Fuck," Hook said quietly. I sat down beside him, stunned by our bad luck. There was a crowd gathered around us but I didn't pay them any attention. I watched Crazy's wrist swell out to the same width as his hand; that was our whole story, right there. We'd put him on stage in a lot of strange conditions before, but a man can't play without his fingering hand. . . .

"Hey, Wright is here today," Tone-bar said. He was frowning with what looked like real concern. "Doesn't he know some old jazz?" None of us answered him. "No, seriously," he said. "This kid Wright is an absolute genius, he'll probably be able to fill in for you." Still none of us spoke. "Well, I know where his box is," he finally continued. "I'll try to find him." He worked his way through the crowd and hurried out the door.

I sat there, feeling the knot in my stomach become a solid bar, and watched a few of the stagehands lift Crazy up and carry him out. We were beat before we began. You can play jazz without a tuba player—we had often had to—but the trombone has to take a lot of the bass line, nobody can be as free with the rhythm, the sound is tinny, there's no power to it, there's no *bottom!* Sidney looked over at Hook and said, with a sort of furtive relief, "Well, you said we didn't have a chance," but Hook just shook his head, eyes glistening, and said quietly, "I wanted to show 'em."

I sat and wondered if I was going to be sick. Crazy had crazied us right back to the rocks, and on top of my knotted stomach my heart pounded loud and slow as if saying "ka-Doom, ka-Doom, ka-DOOM." I thought of all the stories I'd heard of Vesta, the barren graveyard of the asteroids, and hoped I didn't live long enough to be sent there.

There was a long silence. None of us moved. The other performers circled about as quietly, making sure not to look at us. Slowly, very slowly, Sidney began to pull apart his clarinet.

"I got him!" came a wild voice. "He can do it!" Tone-bar came flying in the door, pulling a skinny kid by the arm. He halted and the kid slammed into his back. With a grin Tone-bar stepped aside and waved an arm.

"Perhaps the finest musician of our—" he began, but the kid interrupted him:

"I hear you need a tuba man," he said and stepped

forward. He was a few years younger than me even, and the grin on his adolescent face looked like it was clamped over a burst of laughter. When he pushed all his long black tangles of hair back I saw that the pupils of his eyes were flinching wildly just inside the line of the irises; he was clearly spaced, probably had never seen a tuba before.

"Come on, man," I said. "Where did you learn to play jazz tuba?"

"Pluto," he said, and laughed.

I stared at him. I couldn't believe it. As far as I knew, Dixieland jazz was only played in the bars on Jupiter Metals' rocks; I would have bet I knew, or knew of, every Dixieland musician alive. And this kid didn't come from the mines. He was too skinny, too sharp-edged, he didn't have the look.

"I didn't even know anyone played traditional jazz anymore," he said. "I thought I was the only one."

"I don't believe it," I said.

"We don't got a whole lot of choice, Shaky, we're running out of time," said Hook. "Hey kid—you know 'Panama'?"

"Sure," he said, and sang the opening bars. "Bum-bum, da da da-da, da da-da-da da."

"Son of a bitch," I said.

"I can do it," the kid said. "I *want* to do it."

"All right," Hook said. "Might as well take him." I looked at Hook in surprise and saw that he was grinning again; clearly there was something about the kid, the intensity of those black-hole eyes perhaps, that had him convinced. He slapped the kid on the shoulder and nearly knocked him down. "Come on!" he shouted. "Time to go!"

"Time to go!" I cried. "What the hell happened to Number seventeen?"

"They getting off! Let's go play!"

And the stagehands were already carrying stuff for us, watching the kid and gabbling excitedly.

"Shit," I exclaimed, and stuck my hand out to the kid. We shook. "Welcome to the Hot Six. Solos all sixteen bars, including yours if you want, choruses and refrains all repeated, don't worry about the tags; we'll have to stick to the old songs, do you know 'St. Louis Blues'? 'That's a Plenty'? 'Didn't He Ramble'? 'Milenburg Joys'? 'Mahogany Hall Stomp'? 'Want a Big Butter-and-Egg Man'? 'Ain't You Coming Back to Dixieland'?'' and, miraculously, he kept yelling "Yes! Yes! Yes!" as he struggled with the tuba, still almost laughing, and then we were in the hall and didn't have time for any more—

We got out on stage and it was hot as a smelting chamber. The audience was just a blue-black blur outside the lights, which were glaring down exactly like the arc lamps set around a tunnel end. I could tell seats went way up above us (*they going to be looking down on you*) and then we were all standing there set to go and a big amplified voice said, *"From Jupiter Metals, Pallas, the Hot Six,"* and suddenly we all had our horns to our mouths. I put mine down and said, " 'In the Alley Blues,' " which, amplified, sounded like a single word, then put the horn up and commenced playing.

We sounded horrible. They had indirect mikes on all of us, and just playing normal mezzo forte we were *booming* out into the huge cavern of the auditorium, so we could hear very clearly how bad we sounded. Hook was solid, and so was the kid, which was a relief; but my tone was quivering with just the slightest vibrato, and sometimes I couldn't hear Sidney at all. And his fear was spreading to the rest of us. We knew he had to be petrified to even miss a note.

We brought "In the Alley" to a quick finish, and the applause was *loud*. That made me realize how big the audience was (twenty thousand, Tone-bar said) and I was more scared than ever. I could feel their eyes pressing on me, just like I can sometimes feel the vacuum when I look out a view window. I figured we'd better play one of the best songs next, so we'd get as much help from the material as possible. " 'Weary Blues,' " I said, meaning to say it to the band, since we had planned to play "Ganymede." But the mikes picked me up anyway and I heard "Weary Blues" bounce back out of the cavern, so I just raised my horn to my lips and started; and it was probably two bars before everyone caught on and joined in. That didn't help any.

And I myself was having trouble. The more I could hear the vibrato wavering down the middle of my tone, the worse it got, and the more I could hear it . . . it began to sound like an oscilloscopic saw, and I hoped it wouldn't get out of control and break the tone completely. We got to the refrain, where "Weary" usually starts rolling. I could tell that everyone was so scared they couldn't think about what they were playing, so the notes were coming out right by instinct, but there was no feel in them, it was like they were being played by a music box, every note made by a piece of metal springing loose.

"Weary Blues" ended and again the applause was triple forte. I stepped over to Hook and shouted, under my breath, "Let's do 'I Guess I'll Have to Change My Plans.' " He couldn't hear me, so I said it louder and the mikes caught me, " 'I Guess I'll Have to Change My Plans,' " I announced. There was a long flurry of laughter from the audience. Hook started the intro to "Plans," as calm as though he were playing to a crowded bar. We slid into the song and I realized how much easier it is to play fast when you're nervous. Hook was doing fine, but his backup was trembling, barely hitting the chords. With the leisure of playing accompaniment I could look up and see the silver line of boxes that held our judges, hanging high above us; and that didn't help either.

We moved quickly into "That's a Plenty," and I could tell

we'd calmed down enough to think about the music; after your body pumps full of adrenaline, soaks you in sweat, and shakes you like the ague, there's not much more it can do, you've *got* to calm down some; but that maybe wasn't helping us, since now we had to make the music ourselves, rather than leave it to instinct. I was still shaky enough that when I got to the triple-tonguing in the trumpet break, it actually seemed slow to me, and next time around I fitted in another note, hammering them with two double-tongues. This seemed to perk up the band ("Put chills down my spine," the kid said later), but we still sounded ragged; I knew if we continued like this we were in trouble. And Sidney was still *missing phrases.* I don't think I'd ever heard him miss more than a note or two in my whole life, and here he was squeaking through bars at a time, playing like he had a crimp on his throat.

When we finished the kid waved me over to him. He raised a hand in the air and lowered it, which was apparently the signal needed to get the mike men off us. The kid was completely relaxed. He looked like he was having a good time.

"Your clarinet player is dying," he said. "Does he know 'Burgundy Street Blues'?"

"Sure," I said.

"Maybe you should have him play that. If he had to play a song by himself he'd be sure to calm down some."

I turned around. "Sidney, you ready to play 'Burgundy Street'?"

He shook his head vehemently.

"Come on, Sidney," Hook said from beside him. "That's your song." He turned to the audience, and the kid quickly lifted a hand. " 'The Burgundy Street Blues,' " Hook announced.

Now "Burgundy Street," like "Just a Closer Walk With Thee" or "Bucket's Got a Hole in It," is a single-strain tune, just an eight-bar melody; and it's the variations that a clarinet player works in as he repeats it, again and again, that make the song something special. The first couple of times Sidney went through it, I could barely hear him. He was playing the melody, as simple as possible, and the sound he was making was more breath than tone. I didn't think he'd finish. He shifted toward us as if he wanted to turn his back on the audience, but Hook threw in a couple bars of harmony to bolster him, and when he started the strain a third time he took hold of himself and bore down; and that time, though the notes quivered and never got over pianissimo, he could be heard.

The kid was hopping up and down beside me as if he couldn't wait to start playing again. "Damn that man plays fine clarinet," he whispered to me. Suddenly I realized that if you didn't know Sidney you might think he was playing warbly on purpose, in which case it sounded all right. Apparently this occurred to Sidney too. Each time around he played a little louder, tried a few more variations, gathered a little more confidence. The fifth time around he usually played a variation filled with chromatic runs; he went ahead and tried them, and they came out sharp and well articulated. Amplified like he was, he could hear as clearly as anyone how good he sounded—he was learning what I'd already discovered, that even though you're scared, the notes come out. He began to take advantage of the new acoustics, building up till he filled the auditorium with sound, then dropping back so fast the mike men were lost, and he was as silent as piano keys pushed down.

And as he went on, I could see him begin to forget his surroundings and become what he was, a musician working on the song, putting together phrases, playing with the sounds he could make. His forehead wrinkled and smoothed as he carved an especially difficult passage; he closed his eyes, and the notes took on a life that hadn't been there before. He was lost in it now, completely lost in it, and the last time around he bent the notes like only a fine clarinet player can bend them, soaring them out into the cavern; a sound human and inhuman, music.

When he was done everyone was clapping, even me, and I realized that I had only thought the earlier applause was loud because I'd never heard that many people clap at once before. Now it was louder than when a ship takes off over a tunnel you're in. . . .

We played "Panama" next, and the difference was hard to believe. Sidney was back in form, winding about the upper registers with quick-fingered ingenuity, and as he pulled together so did the band. And the kid, as if he'd only been waiting for Sidney, began to let loose. He'd abandoned his steady *oomph-oomph-oomph-oomph* and was sliding up and down the bass clef, playing like a fourth member of the front line, and *leading* the tempo. Normally I set the tempo, and Crazy and Washboard listen to me and pick it up. But the kid wasn't paying any attention to me; his notes were hitting just a touch ahead of mine, and if there's anyone who can take the tempo away from the trumpet it's the tuba. I tried to play as fast as him but he kept ahead; by the time he let Washboard and me catch up with him we were playing "Panama" faster than we'd *ever* played it, and excited as we were, we were equal to it. When we finished, the applause seemed to push us to the back of the stage.

We played the "St. Louis Blues," and then the "Milenburg Joys," and then "Sweet Georgia Brown," and each time the kid took over, pumping wildly away at the tuba, and pushed us to our limit. Sidney responded like that was the way he'd always wanted to play, arching high wails between phrases and helping the kid to drive us on. And the audience was with us! Maybe the earlier groups had been too modern, maybe too many of them had been playing to the judges; whatever the reason, the audience was with us now. An hour ago none of them had even heard of Dixieland jazz, and now they were cheering after the solos and clapping in the choruses; and we had to start "Sweet Georgia Brown" by playing through the applause.

Then we were set for the finale. *"For all of you music lovers in the house,"* I said, knowing they wouldn't get the reference to Satchmo but saying it anyway, *"we going to beat out* 'The Muskrat Ramble.' "

"The Muskrat Ramble." Our best song, maybe *the* best song. We started up the "Ramble" and the band fell together and meshed like parts of a beautiful machine. All those years of playing in those bars: all the years of getting off work and going down and playing tired, playing with nobody listening but us, playing with nothing to keep us going but the music; all that came from inside us now, in a magic combination of fear, and anger, and the wild exhilaration of knowing we were the best there was at what we were doing. Hook was looping his part below me, Sidney leaping about above, the kid pushing us every note; and to keep up with the weave we were making I had to play hard and fast right down the middle of the song, lifting and growling and breaking my notes off, showing them all that there was a man *working* behind that horn, blowing as clear and sharp and excited as old Dipper-mouth Satchel-mouth Satchmo Louie Louis Daniel Armstrong himself. When we played the final round of the refrain everyone played their solo at once, only Fingers and Washboard held us down at all, and the old "Muskrat Ramble" lifted up and played itself, carrying us along as if it made us and not the other way around. Hook played the trombone coda and we tagged it; then the kid surprised us and repeated the coda, and we barely got our horns back up to tag it again; then we all played the coda and popped it solid, the end.

I motioned the band off. We were done; there was no way we could top that. We started for the wings and the roar of the audience soared up to a gooseflesh howl. We hurried off, waving our arms and shouting as loud as anyone there, jumping up and down and slapping each other on the back, chased by a wall of sound that shook the building.

We waited; tired, happy, tense, we waited:

And God damn me if we didn't win one of those grants, a four-year tour of the Solar System; oh, we leaped about that waiting room and shouted and hit each other; Fingers and Washboard marched about singing and smashing out rhythms on the walls and furniture; Hook stood on a table and sprayed champagne on us; the kid rolled on the floor and laughed and laughed, "Now you're in for it," he choked out, "you're in for it now!" but we didn't know what he meant then, we just poured champagne on his head and laughed at him, even old Sidney was jumping up and down, wisps of hair flying over his ears, singing (I'd never heard him sing) a scat solo he was making up as he went along, shouting it out while tears and champagne ran down his face:

> *"bo bo de zed,*
> *we leaving the tunnels!*
> *woppity bip,*
> *we going to see Earth!*
> *yes we (la da de dip)*
> *going (ze be de be dop)*
> *home!"*

—1975

Stone Eggs

Tom Finn got on the Greyhound bus intending never to get off. He had purchased a month pass in Chicago and gotten on bus 782. He planned to take the southern route to California, go up the Pacific coast, back to the Great Lakes, and on to New England. Or wherever. When he bought the next pass he would think about it.

In the bus it was cool. The air from the vent played on his arm. All the windows except the windshield were tinted dark green, polarizing the light and reducing the outside world to a wash of grays. Tom liked it that way.

They stopped in the run-down parts of towns where the bus depots were, to change passengers and eat meals. Joplin, Missouri; Tulsa, Oklahoma; Amarillo, Texas. Half an hour for lunch, an hour for dinner. He fell into the routine with relief.

He got on a New York-to-Los Angeles bus, and a group of passengers stayed on it for two or three days. He watched them as they lived their lives on the bus, talking and getting to know each other. Finn never introduced himself to anyone, or talked. At night people slumped in their seats, unselfconsciously sleeping. Some kept on their little overhead lights and talked all night long. Tom Finn could not sleep in a sitting position, so at night he unobtrusively crawled under his seat and slept curled on the floor, using his tennis shoes for a pillow. It was comfortable enough. In the mornings he scrambled up onto his seat and stared back at the few bleary-eyed strangers who were awake at dawn. A thin-faced young black man. A girl with stringy hair and dirty clothes. An old couple. The poor, in all their variety. . . . Then back to the little toilet room, which grew more fetid by the hour.

As they crossed New Mexico he looked out at the parched gray land, dozed, observed the occupants of the seat ahead of him. A fat young woman struggled vainly to control her four sons, slapping them and threatening them with worse. The boys—aged eight, seven, four, and one, Finn guessed—ignored her, except for the infant, who cried or slept or sucked a bottle. The mother had scarcely slept in the three days Finn had sat behind her. He watched the oldest son, who tormented the four-year-old incessantly, and wondered if the boy was naturally evil or if his meanness was the result of his upbringing. Naturally evil? . . . The boy would grow up to be a runaway, he thought. Finn was a runaway.

That evening the bus pulled off Highway 8, in the south Arizona desert, for a dinner stop. The offramp circled down to a road that stretched off into the desert to the north and extended to the south no farther than a small group of buildings just off the freeway. Approaching the group of buildings, Tom read a sign: DATELAND RESTAURANT, POST OFFICE, AND CURIO SHOP.

He joined the file of people getting off the bus. "One hour, now," the bus driver said. Although it was nearly dusk the air was still hot and dry. Finn walked across the gravel parking lot to the door of the café. There were two middle-aged men sitting at the counter. All the booths were empty. The waitresses were talking to each other. Tom saw that it was yet another restaurant that could not survive without its Greyhound concession. He sat in one of the booths, and a waitress took his order. He ordered a hamburger, fries, and a Coke. While he waited he flipped through the selections listed in his table jukebox console. Country-western, old rock and roll, songs in Spanish. Behind him sat the mother and her four boys. "Stop that. Stop that or I'll hit you in front of everybody." When his food came he ate quickly, paid his bill and left.

The main building was in the shape of an L; the long side was the café, the short side was the curio shop. Finn walked over to the curio shop, thinking to get out of the heat. Beside the door was a thermometer in an old tin Coca-Cola sign. It read 104 degrees. He went into the shop.

Quite a few people from the bus were already there, wandering about. Tom did the same. The curio shop offered for sale string ties with clasps made of clear plastic that held embalmed scorpions; cactus-growing kits; postcards with pictures of donkeys and cactus flowers and Jackalopes; turquoise rings, the turquoise white and cracked; candy in yellowed cellophane; and stone eggs. Everything in the shop had obviously been there for years and years; all those chill air-conditioned days and long hot nights had desiccated every item. No one from the bus was buying anything. The cashier stared out the window. It reminded Finn of things he could not afford to think of, and feeling that he might scream, or start to cry, he left the shop.

The heat outside relaxed him. The sun was about to set. Behind Dateland there was an old road leading off over a hill to the east. Finn began to walk on it. He was fascinated by the thin roads, asphalt or gravel or dirt, that crisscrossed the great American desert. He had seen a lot of them from the bus. Who had built them, and when? It was easy to imagine Interstate 8 being built: hundreds of men, huge yellow bulldozers and earthmovers, a whole community, moving along through the desert and excreting the highway behind it. But what about these little roads, stretching from nowhere to nowhere under the broiling sun? Finn couldn't imagine their construction. He stared down at the faded, cracked asphalt as he walked. Sand silted over the edges of the road. It could have been built a thousand years ago. These are the ruins of the twentieth century, he thought. Already here.

The road ended in a settlement of foundations. Rectangles of cement, half covered by sand, with fixture pipes rusting through at one corner of each foundation. The sun was below the hill now, and the settlement was in shadow. It was still very hot. Finn walked around the area, looking at the cement and the dry grass that had overgrown it and died. Wind gusted through the shadows, rustling the grass. In the east the sky was a deep blue.

Eventually he sat down on a concrete block and let the desert fill him. Occasionally the faint diesel roar of a truck wafted over from the interstate to the north. In the western sky the evening star appeared. This was his life, Tom Finn thought, this desert, this community in ruins before it had ever been occupied. . . . Through his tears it seemed the homes that somebody had planned to put there did indeed stand, as clear glass houses that revealed everything about their owners, brittle things that could be shattered with a blink of the eye. And each blink brought the houses crashing to the ground, and the faint stars with them so that they should have been great pyres burning around him on the desert floor.

Then the evening star dropped like a stone over the western horizon, and it didn't come back no matter how hard Finn blinked. As if it had been a meteor. Just a shooting star, Finn thought. But fear rustled through him like the wind, and he got up and walked quickly back over the old abandoned road. Something had happened. . . .

From the hill he could see the back of Dateland. The

parking lot was empty. Finn cursed out loud. He had missed the bus! Sitting out there thinking about his mess of a life he had missed his bus. He hurried down the hill, cursing still. He would have to wait in that café for the next bus, and call ahead to get the Greyhound people to recover his suitcase. Damn it! Hadn't the bus driver counted his passengers? Had no one noticed his absence?

But when he got to the building, he forgot his anger.

Dateland was empty. Boarded up, faded, sand-drifted, empty.

The sun had been down for a while now, and Finn found himself shivering. Absently he walked over to look at the thermometer by the curio-shop door; it was broken. He turned the doorknob and pushed the door in; a gust of wind pulled it out of his hand, and it hit the counter inside with a wooden *thwack*. Finn stuck his head in the door and looked around, afraid to enter. Everything in the curio shop was the same, except dustier. A handful of Jackalope postcards tumbled to the floor, caught by the wind, and Finn jumped back with his heart racing.

It took all his courage to open the door to the café. It too was deserted. Parts of it had been removed: the jukeboxes, the kitchen fixtures, the drink machines. The vinyl booth seats were cracked like dried mud. Overcome by sudden terror, Finn rushed out of the café to the safety of the gravel parking lot. But it was getting dark; the vast network of stars revealed itself; Dateland stood behind him dark and empty, like a house in a child's nightmare. He shivered uncontrollably. The dry wind made little noises against the building. A loose plank somewhere slapped woodenly a few times. He was afraid. "What's going on here?" he cried out miserably. No answer but wind.

He ran up the road to the freeway onramp. The spare concrete of Interstate 8 was tremendously reassuring. Nothing there had changed. The highway was empty in both directions, but that was not unusual. He walked up the onramp until he was out on the westbound lanes, ready to stop the next car that came by. He could just see Dateland over the shoulder of the eastbound lanes, a dark mass in the starlit desert sand.

Hours passed, and no cars drove by. He was frightened again. It got colder, and he sat on the blacktop edging the white concrete of the lanes, where it was still warm with the day's heat.

Then to the east he saw headlights approaching, and he jumped up stiffly, adrenaline pumping up his heartbeat. "Now stop," he muttered, "please stop, please stop, please stop. . . ."

Just before they would have reached him the lights slowed, turned on the big circular offramp leading down to Dateland. It was a Greyhound bus.

He ran down the onramp and along the road back to Dateland. Another bus! His pass was still in his pocket. . . .

The bus was pulling back out of the parking lot when he ran up. *"Wait,"* he screamed, the word torn out of him like no other had ever been in his life. The headlights caught him for a moment, the bus stopped, the door at the front *whooshed* open.

He jumped onto the first step, grabbed the chrome handrail and pulled himself up the steps to the main aisle. There was only one passenger on the bus, an old woman sitting in the seat behind the driver. The driver looked up at him. "Sit down," he said. "Can't go until you sit down."

Finn sat in the front seat, across from the old woman and the driver. He felt his bus pass in his pocket; but the driver was turning onto the onramp, oblivious to him. He sat back, happy to be leaving Dateland. Yet he was afraid to ask the two people across from him what they knew of it.

"So you found a new doctor, eh?" the driver said when they were on the freeway and up to speed. He was looking in his mirror at the old woman.

"Yes, I did," she replied. "The best you can find, these days anyway. A Jack Mathewson, from Gila Bend. Trained by Westinghouse. He says he'll replace the pivot in my lower back with a new part made by G.E."

"That might work," the driver said. "Got a G.E. pivot myself."

Tom Finn, pressed back against his window, stared at the two people across from him. The old woman . . . her eyes were glass. The bus passed under a light over the freeway, and he saw that her skin was some kind of plastic. He tried to control his breathing. . . .

"The plain fact is," the old woman-thing said, "it's hell to grow old. Nothing to be done about it."

"Nope," the driver agreed.

"Forty-seven years as a librarian, and me with a bad back. Sometimes you wonder why we were designed to feel pain at all."

"Keeps us alive."

"*I* think it was because people didn't want us to have any advantages," she said, looking for an instant at Finn. "Ah, well. All of my typemates dead and gone for years now. And Westinghouse has no more parts for my type, they say."

"G.E. parts are just as good. But I know what you mean. All my typemates are gone too. Last century was the good one for simulacra."

"Don't you know it!"

Tom Finn got up unsteadily and walked down the aisle to the back of the bus, thinking that he might throw up in the toilet. But when he got to the door, he couldn't bring himself to open it; he imagined looking into the coppery mirror and seeing his reflection grin at him with steel teeth—imagined unzipping, and finding only smooth metal. Had he always been a machine, and only dreamed, out there in the desert, of being something else? For a long time he stood there swaying with the bus. A part of his mind noticed that the bus's engine didn't sound like the old piston-driven ones used to. The *old* piston-driven ones? Furtively he looked up the bus at the two figures, still talking in low tones. Something had happened, back there at Dateland . . . he couldn't bear to look down at himself. After a while he forced himself (for the sake of appearances! he thought) to return to the front of the bus. He watched the simulacra talking to each other, and listened to their words for a long time, wondering how to ask what year it was. Finally exhaustion overcame him and he was lulled to sleep by their voices and the hum of the bus.

He was awakened by the sound of the bus downshifting. They were on the curve of another offramp. He jerked up and looked around. They were still in the desert; it was light, just before sunrise. Just off the freeway was their destination, another little isolated café. Finn saw the sign on the building and felt faint; DATELAND RESTAURANT, POST OFFICE, AND CURIO SHOP.

"Isn't this where I got on?" he croaked, his mouth dry with sleep and fear. They were the first words he had spoken since getting on the bus.

The driver turned his plastic head (it was obvious in the dawn) to glance at him, and laugh. "You think I drive this bus in circles? We're west of Yuma now. There's lots of places that look like that in this desert."

The old woman was asleep, or turned off, still upright in her seat across from Finn. Finn felt his own pump hammering the fluids through him, and all of a sudden it was too much. He gave in to it.

Without thinking he got off the bus when it stopped. Walked over to the door of the curio shop. Without surprise he registered the fact that the bus was driving off, back to the freeway. The thermometer by the door was still broken, the paint on the tin almost gone. It still read 104. He opened the door and walked inside the curio shop. All the goods were still there, safe and untouched, covered with dust. Finn swallowed hard. There was something about the place, something he had sensed when he first entered it so many years ago. . . .

The sun broke over the horizon, flooding the shop with dusty white light. Behind the cashier's booth there was a closet. In it he found a broom and a feather duster, and he went to work cleaning up. All of the arrowheads, the turquoise and onyx and malachite rings, the cactus-growing kits, the postcards, the stone eggs. All as clean as new.

A couple of hours later he stood, sweaty and grimy, in a clean and orderly curio shop. White dust motes like talcum swirled in the air, made bright and palpable by the low morning sun. He walked outside into the fresh air, which was still cool. Glancing in the café door, he shook his head; he'd have to attend to that later.

Another Greyhound swooped down the circular offramp. He hurried back to the curio-shop door. Maybe somebody would buy something. Nervously he watched as people stepped down from the bus. Some of them walked toward cars that Finn had assumed were wrecks, on the other side of the gravel lot; they drove away to the north, under the freeway and out of sight. But several more, observing him standing in the shop doorway, approached the shop. Finn stepped back inside, to clear the entrance.

One by one they filed past. "Opening the old place up again, eh?" a man said.

"Yes," Finn replied, and cleared his throat. "I'm going to give it a try." He stared at the man. In the klieg-light glare of the horizontal sun the man's blue eyes were quite clearly glass. But that look on his face, that curiosity . . . Finn blinked and the man blinked too, and Finn saw the film of tears and the tiny red veins. An iris could look like crystal from some angles, he knew that. . . . Eventually Finn shook himself and followed the man in. He couldn't tell. He didn't care.

"Oh, look," a young woman said to her companion, an older woman.

"That would look nice in your room," the older woman said. Finn could hear the years in her voice, and he was reminded of the old woman on his bus.

"I want this," the young woman said to Finn. "How much is it?"

She held out one of the stone eggs. He took it from her cool hand. It was smooth and brown, mottled by black cracking deep in the stone. Finn looked around: no cash register.

"Um," he said, feeling in his pockets for change. "A dollar."

"Sold," she said, and laughed. The old woman smiled. While the young woman fumbled in her pocketbook, Finn cleaned the egg one last time with a rag he had found under a counter.

"You have to be careful with these," he warned her. "They're lighter than they look. And fragile? They'd break like glass if you dropped one."

"I'll remember." She handed him a dollar. George Washington still on the front, he saw. "Where are you living?"

"Well . . ." The men examining the postcards swiveled their heads to hear his answer. "There's some old foundations over the hill to the east. I'm going to set up out there."

"We live on the other side of the freeway; you should come visit."

"I will."

Then they trailed out of the shop, talking and leaving great swirls in the mote-coned morning air. Finn watched them from the doorway; they all balanced with unnatural carefulness across the gravel. He shrugged. When they were all gone, out of sight under the freeway, he went back inside. He would have to find a cash register, and start the air conditioner up again. He straightened up the postcards. Rearranged the stone eggs. After breakfast he would walk up the narrow road to the north.

—1979

Black Air

They sailed out of Lisbon harbor with the flags snapping and the brass culverins gleaming under a high white sun, priests proclaiming in sonorous Latin the blessing of the Pope, soldiers in armor jammed on the castles fore and aft, and sailors spiderlike in the rigging, waving at the citizens of the town who had left their work to come out on the hills and watch the ships crowd out the sunbeaten roads, for this was the Armada, the Most Fortunate Invincible Armada, off to subjugate the heretic English to the will of God. There would never be another departure like it.

Unfortunately, the wind blew out of the northeast for a month after they left without shifting even a point on the compass, and at the end of that month the Armada was no closer to England than Iberia itself. Not only that, but the hard-pressed coopers of Portugal had made many of the Armada's casks of green wood, and when the ship's cooks opened them the meat was rotten and the water stank. So they trailed into the port of Corunna, where several hundred soldiers and sailors swam to the shores of Spain and were never seen again. A few hundred more had already died of disease, so from his sickbed on the flagship Don Alonso Perez de Guzman el Bueno, seventh Duke of Medina Sidonia and Admiral of the Armada, interrupted the composition of his daily complaint to Philip the Second, and instructed his soldiers to go out into the countryside and collect peasants to help man the ships.

One squad of these soldiers stopped at a Franciscan monastery on the outskirts of Corunna, to impress all the boys who lived there and helped the monks, waiting to join the order themselves. Although they did not like it the monks could not object to the proposal, and off the boys went to join the fleet.

Among these boys, who were each taken to a different ship, was Manuel Carlos Agadir Tetuan. He was seventeen years old; he had been born in Morocco, the son of West Africans who had been captured and enslaved by Arabs. In his short life he had already lived in the Moroccan coastal town of Tetuan, in Gibraltar, the Balearics, Sicily, and Lisbon. He had worked in fields and cleaned stables, he had helped make rope and later cloth, and he had served food in inns. After his mother died of the pox and his father drowned, he had begged in the streets and alleys of Corunna, the last port his father had sailed out of, until in his fifteenth year a Franciscan had tripped over him sleeping in an alley, inquired after him, and taken him to the refuge of the monastery.

Manuel was still weeping when the soldiers took him aboard *La Lavia*, a Levantine galleon of nearly a thousand tons. The sailing master of the ship, one Laeghr, took him in charge and led him below decks. Laeghr was an Irishman, who had left his country principally to practice his trade, but also out of hatred of the English who ruled Ireland. He was a huge man with a torso like a boar's, and arms as thick as the yardarms of the ship. When he saw Manuel's distress he showed that he was not without kindness; clapping a callused hand to the back of Manuel's neck he said, in accented but fluent Spanish, ''Stop your snivelling, boy, we're off to con-

quer the damned English, and when we do your fathers at the
monastery will make you their abbot. And before that happens a dozen English girls will fall at your feet and ask for the
touch of those black hands, no doubt. Come on, stop it. I'll
show you your berth first, and wait till we're at sea to show
you your station. I'm going to put you in the main top, all
our blacks are good topmen.''

Laeghr slipped through a door half his height with the ease
of a weasel ducking into one of its tiny holes in the earth. A
hand half as wide as the doorway reemerged and pulled
Manuel into the gloom. The terrified boy nearly fell down a
broad-stepped ladder, but caught himself before falling onto
Laeghr. Far below several soldiers laughed at him. Manuel
had never been on anything larger than a Sicilian pataches,
and most of his fairly extensive seagoing experience was of
coastal carracks, so the broad deck under him, cut by bands
of yellow sunlight that flowed in at open ports big as church
windows, crowded with barrels and bales of hay and tubs of
rope, and a hundred busy men, was a marvel. ''Saint Anna
save me,'' he said, scarcely able to believe he was on a ship.
Why, the monastery itself had no room as large as the one he
descended into now. ''Get down here,'' Laeghr said in an
encouraging way.

Once on the deck of that giant room they descended again,
to a stuffy chamber a quarter the size, illuminated by narrow
fans of sunlight that were let in by ports that were mere slits
in the hull. ''Here's where you sleep,'' Laeghr said, pointing
at a dark corner of the deck, against one massive oak wall of
the ship. Forms there shifted, eyes appeared as lids lifted, a
dull voice said, ''Another one you'll never find again in this
dark, eh master?''

''Shut up, Juan. See boy, there are beams dividing your
berth from the rest, that will keep you from rolling around
when we get to sea.''

''Just like a coffin, with the lid up there.''

"Shut up, Juan."

After the sailing master had made clear which slot in particular was Manuel's, Manuel collapsed in it and began to cry again. The slot was shorter than he was, and the dividing boards set in the deck were cracked and splintered. The men around him slept, or talked among themselves, ignoring Manuel's presence. His medallion cord choked him, and he shifted it on his neck and remembered to pray.

His guardian saint, the monks had decided, was Anne, mother of the Virgin Mary and grandmother of Jesus. He owned a small wooden medallion with her face painted on it, which Abbot Alonso had given to him. Now he took the medallion between his fingers, and looked in the tiny brown dots that were the face's eyes. "Please, Mother Anna," he prayed silently, "take me from this ship to my home. Take me home." He clenched the tag in his fist so tightly that the back of it, carved so that a cross of wood stood out from its surface, left an imprinted red cross in his palm. Many hours passed before he fell asleep.

Two days later the Most Fortunate Invincible Armada left Corunna, this time without the flags, or the crowds of spectators, or the clouds of priestly incense trailing downwind. This time God favored them with a westerly wind, and they sailed north at good speed. The ships were arranged in a formation devised by the soldiers, orderly phalanxes rising and falling on the swells: the galleasses in front, the supply hulks in the center, and the big galleons on either flank. The thousands of sails stacked on hundreds of masts made a grand and startling sight, like a copse of white trees on a broad blue plain.

Manuel was as impressed by the sight as the rest of the men. There were four hundred men on *La Lavia*, and only thirty were needed at any one time to sail the ship, so all of the three hundred soldiers stood on the sterncastle observing the fleet, and the sailors who were not on duty or sleeping did the same on the slightly lower forecastle.

Manuel's duties as a sailor were simple. He was stationed at the port midships taffrail, to which were tied the sheets for the port side of the mainmast's sails, and the sheets for the big lateen-rigged sail of the foremast. Manuel helped five other men pull these ropes in or let them out, following Laeghr's instructions; the other men took care of the belaying knots, so Manuel's job came down to pulling on a rope when told to. It could have been more difficult, but Laeghr's plan to make him a topman like the other Africans aboard had come to grief. Not that Leaghr hadn't tried. "God made you Africans with a better head for heights, so you can climb trees to keep from being eaten by lions, isn't that right?" But when Manuel had followed a Moroccan named Habedeen up the halyard ladder to the main top, he found himself plunging about space, nearly scraping low foggy clouds, and the sea, embroidered with the wakes of the ships ahead, was more often than not *directly below him*. He had clamped, arms and legs, around a stanchion of the main top, and it had taken five men, laughing and cursing, to pry him loose and pull him down. With rich disgust, but no real physical force, Laeghr had pounded him with his cane and shoved him to the port taffrail. "You must be a Sicilian with a sunburn." And so he had been assigned his station.

Despite this incident he got on well with the rest of the crew. Not with the soldiers; they were rude and arrogant to the sailors, who stayed out of their way to avoid a curse or a blow. So three-quarters of the men aboard were of a different class, and remained strangers. The sailors therefore hung together. They were a mongrel lot, drawn from all over the Mediterranean, and Manuel was not unusual because of his recent arrival. They were united only in their dislike and resentment of the soldiers. "Those heroes wouldn't be able to conquer the Isle of Wight if we didn't sail them there,'' Juan said.

Manuel became acquainted first with the men at his post, and then with the men in his berth. As he spoke Spanish and Portuguese, and fair amounts of Arabic, Sicilian, Latin, and a Moroccan dialect, he could converse with everyone in his corner of the lower foredeck. Occasionally he was asked to translate for the Moroccans; more than once this meant he was the arbiter of a dispute, and he thought fast and mistranslated whenever it would help make peace. Juan, the one who had made the bitter comments to Laeghr on Manuel's arrival, was the only pure Spaniard in the berth. He loved to talk, and complained to Manuel and the others continuously. "I've fought *El Draco* before, in the Indies," he boasted. "We'll be lucky to get past that devil. You mark my words, we'll never do it."

Manuel's mates at the main taffrail were more cheerful, and he enjoyed his watches with them and the drills under Laeghr's demanding instruction. These men called him Topman or Climber, and made jokes about his knots around the belaying pins, which defied quick untying. This inability earned Manuel quite a few swats from Laeghr's cane, but there were worse sailors aboard, and the sailing master seemed to bear him no ill will.

A life of perpetual change had made Manuel adaptable, and shipboard routine became for him the natural course of existence. Laeghr or Pietro, the leader at Manuel's station, would wake him with a shout. Up to the gundeck, which was the domain of the soldiers, and from there up the big ladder that led to fresh air. Only then could Manuel be sure of the time of day. For the first week it was an inexpressible delight to get out of the gloom of the lower decks and under the sky, in the wind and clean salt air; but as they proceeded north, it began to get too cold for comfort. After their watches were over, Manuel and his mates would retire to the

galley and be given their biscuits, water and wine. Sometimes the cooks killed some of the goats and chickens and
made soup. Usually, though, it was just biscuits, biscuits
that had not yet hardened in their barrels. The men complained grievously about this.

"The biscuits are best when they're hard as wood, and
bored through by worms," Habedeen told Manuel.

"How do you eat it then?" Manuel asked.

"You bang pieces of biscuit against the table until the
worms fall out. You eat the worms if you want." The men
laughed, and Manuel assumed Habedeen was joking, but he
wasn't certain.

"I despise this doughy shit," Pietro said in Portuguese.
Manuel translated into Moroccan Arabic for the two silent
Africans, and agreed in Spanish that it was hard to stomach.
"The worst part," he offered, "is that some parts are stale
while others are still fresh."

"The fresh part was never cooked."

"No, that's the worms."

As the voyage progressed, Manuel's berthmates became
more intimate. Farther north the Moroccans suffered terribly
from the cold. They came belowdecks after a watch with
their dark skins completely goose-pimpled, like little fields of
stubble after a harvest. Their lips and fingernails were blue,
and they shivered an hour before falling asleep, teeth chattering like the castanets in a fiesta band. Not only that, but the
swells of the Atlantic were getting bigger, and the men, since
they were forced to wear every scrap of clothing they owned,
rolled in their wooden berths unpadded and unprotected. So
the Moroccans, and then everyone in the lower foredeck,
slept three to a berth, taking turns in the middle, huddling
together like spoons. Crowded together like that the pitching
of the ship could press them against the beams, but it
couldn't roll them around. Manuel's willingness to join these

bundlings, and to lie against the beams, made him well-liked. Everyone agreed he made a good cushion.

Perhaps it was because of his hands that he fell ill. Though his spirit had been reconciled to the crusade north, his flesh was slower. Hauling on the coarse hemp ropes every day had ripped the skin from his palms, and salt, splinters, belaying pins and the odd boot had all left their marks as well, so that after the first week he had wrapped his hands in strips of cloth torn from the bottom of his shirt. When he became feverish, his hands pulsed painfully at every nudge from his heart, and he assumed that the fever had entered him through the wounds in his palms.

Then his stomach rebelled, and he could keep nothing down. The sight of biscuits or soup revolted him; his fever worsened, and he became parched and weak; he spent a lot of time in the head, wracked by dysentery. "You've been poisoned by the biscuits," Juan told him. "Just like I was in the Indies. That's what comes of boxing fresh biscuits. They might as well have put fresh dough in those barrels."

Manuel's berthmates told Laeghr of his condition, and Laeghr had him moved to the hospital, which was at the stern of the ship on a lower deck, in a wide room that the sick shared with the rudder post, a large smoothed tree trunk thrusting through floor and ceiling. All of the other men were gravely ill. Manuel was miserable as they laid him down on his pallet, wretched with nausea and in great fear of the hospital, which smelled of putrefaction. The man on the pallet next to him was insensible, and rolled with the sway of the ship. Three candle lanterns lit the low chamber and filled it with shadows. One of the Dominican friars, a Friar Lucien, gave him hot water and wiped his face. They talked for a while, and the friar heard Manuel's confession, which only a proper priest should have done. Neither of them cared. The priests on board avoided the hospital, and tended to serve only the officers and the soldiers. Friar Lucien was known to be willing to minister to the sailors, and he was popular among them.

Manuel's fever got worse, and he could not eat. Days passed, and when he woke up the men around him were not the same men who had been there when he fell asleep. He became convinced he was going to die, and once again he felt despair that he had been made a member of the Most Fortunate Invincible Armada. "Why are we here?" he demanded of the friar in a cracked voice. "Why shouldn't we let the English go to hell if they please?"

"The purpose of the Armada is not only to smite the heretic English," said Lucien. He held a candle closer to his book, which was not a Bible, but a slender little thing which he kept hidden in his robes. Shadows leaped on the blackened beams and planks over them, and the rudder post squeaked as it turned against the leather collar in the floor. "God also sent us as a test. Listen:

" 'I assume the appearance of a refiner's fire, purging the dross of forms outworn. This is mine aspect of severity; I am as one who testeth gold in a furnace. Yet when thou hast been tried as by fire, the gold of thy soul shall be cleansed, and visible as fire: then the vision of thy Lord shall be granted unto thee, and seeing Him shall thou behold the shining one, who is thine own true self.'

"Remember that, and be strong. Drink this water here— come on, do you want to fail your God? This is part of the test."

Manuel drank, threw up. His body was no more than a tongue of flame contained by his skin, except where it burst out of his palms. He lost track of the days, and forgot the existence of anyone beyond himself and Friar Lucien. "I never wanted to leave the monastery," he told the friar, "yet I never thought I would stay there long. I've never stayed long any place yet. It was my home but I knew it wasn't. I haven't found my home yet. They say there is ice in England—I saw the snow in the Catalonian mountains, once, Father, will we go home? I only want to return to the monastery and be a father like you.''

"We will go home. What you will become, only God knows. He has a place for you. Sleep now. Sleep, now.''

By the time his fever broke his ribs stood out from his chest as clearly as the fingers of a fist. He could barely walk. Lucien's narrow face appeared out of the gloom clear as a memory. "Try this soup. Apparently God has seen fit to keep you here.''

"Thank you Saint Anna for your intercession,'' Manuel croaked. He drank the soup eagerly. "I want to return to my berth.''

"Soon.''

They took him up to the deck. Walking was like floating, as long as he held on to railings and stanchions. Laeghr greeted him with pleasure, as did his stationmates. The world was a riot of blues; waves hissed past, low clouds jostled together in their rush east, tumbling between them shafts of sunlight that spilled onto the water. He was excused from active duty, but he spent as many hours as he could at his station. He found it hard to believe that he had survived his illness. Of course, he was not entirely recovered; he could not yet eat any solids, particularly biscuit, so that his diet consisted of soup and wine. He felt weak, and perpetually light-headed. But when he was on deck in the wind he was sure that he was getting better, so he stayed there as much as possible. He was on deck, in fact, when they first caught sight of England. The soldiers pointed and shouted in great excitement, as the point Laeghr called The Lizard bounced over the horizon. Manuel had grown so used to the sea that the low headland rising off their port bow seemed unnatural, an intrusion into a marine world, as if the deluge was just now receding and these

drowned hillsides were just now shouldering up out of the
waves, soaking wet and covered by green seaweed that had
not yet died. And that was England.

A few days after that they met the first English ships—
faster than the Spanish galleons, but much smaller. They
could no more impede the progress of the Armada than flies
could slow a herd of cows. The swells became steeper and
followed each other more closely, and the changed pitching
of *La Lavia* made it difficult for Manuel to stand. He banged
his head once, and another time ripped away a palmful of
scabs, trying to keep his balance in the violent yawing caused
by the chop. Unable to stand one morning, he lay in the
dark of his berth, and his mates brought him cups of soup.
That went on for a long time. Again he worried that he was
going to die. Finally Laeghr and Lucien came below together.

"You must get up now," Laeghr declared. "We fight
within the hour, and you're needed. We've arranged easy
work for you."

"You have only to provide the gunners with slow match,"
said Friar Lucien as he helped Manuel to his feet. "God will
help you."

"God will have to help me," Manuel said. He could see
the two men's souls flickering above their heads: little triple
knots of transparent flame that flew up out of their hair and
lit the features of their faces. "The gold of thy soul shall be
cleansed, and visible as fire," Manuel recalled. "Hush,"
said Lucien with a frown, and Manuel realized that what
Lucien had read to him was a secret.

Amidships Manuel noticed that now he was also able to
see the air, which was tinged red. They were on the bottom
of an ocean of red air, just as they were on top of an ocean of
blue water. When they breathed they turned the air a darker
red; men expelled plumes of air like horses breathing out
clouds of steam on a frosty morning, only the steam was red.

Manuel stared and stared, marveling at the new abilities God had given his sight.

"Here," Laeghr said, roughly directing him across the deck. "This tub of punk is yours. This is slow match, understand?" Against the bulkhead was a tub full of coils of closely braided cord. One end of the cord was hanging over the edge of the tub burning, fizzing the air around it to deep crimson. Manuel nodded: "Slow match."

"Here's your knife. Cut sections about this long, and light them with a piece of it that you keep beside you. Then give sections of it to the gunners who come by, or take it to them if they call for it. But don't give away all your lit pieces. Understand?"

Manuel nodded that he understood and sat down dizzily beside the tub. One of the largest cannon poked through a port in the bulkhead just a few feet from him. Its crew greeted him. Across the deck his stationmates stood at their taffrail. The soldiers were ranked on the fore- and sterncastles, shouting with excitement, gleaming like shellfish in the sun. Through the port Manuel could see some of the English coast.

Laeghr came over to see how he was doing. "Hey, don't you lop your fingers off there, boy. See out there? That's the Isle of Wight. We're going to circle and conquer it, I've no doubt, and use it as our base for our attack on the mainland. With these soldiers and ships they'll *never* get us off that island. It's a good plan."

But things did not progress according to Laeghr's plan. The Armada swung around the east shore of the Isle of Wight, in a large crescent made of five distinct phalanxes of ships. Rounding the island, however, the forward galleasses encountered the stiffest English resistance they had met so far. White puffs of smoke appeared out of the ships and were quickly stained red, and the noise was tremendous.

Then the ships of *El Draco* swept around the southern

point of the island onto their flank, and suddenly *La Lavia* was in the action. The soldiers roared and shot off their arquebuses, and the big cannon beside Manuel leaped back in its truck with a bang that knocked him into the bulkhead. After that he could barely hear. His slow match was suddenly in demand; he cut the cord and held the lit tip to unlit tips, igniting them with his red breath. Cannonballs passing overhead left rippling wakes in the blood air. Grimy men snatched the slow match and dashed to their guns, dodging tackle blocks that thumped to the deck. Manuel could see the cannonballs, big as grapefruit, flying at them from the English ships and passing with a whistle. And he could see the transparent knots of flame, swirling higher than ever about the men's heads.

Then a cannonball burst through the porthole and knocked the cannon off its truck, the men to the deck. Manuel rose to his feet and noticed with horror that the knots of flame on the scattered gunners were gone; he could see their heads clearly now, and they were just men, just broken flesh draped over the plowed surface of the deck. He tried, sobbing, to lift a gunner who was bleeding only from the ears. Laeghr's cane lashed across his shoulders: "Keep cutting match! There's others to attend to these men!" So Manuel cut lengths of cord and lit them with desperate puffs and shaking hands, while the guns roared, and the exposed soldiers on the castles shrieked under a hail of iron, and the red air was ripped by passing shot.

The next few days saw several battles like that as the Armada was forced past the Isle of Wight and up the Channel. His fever kept him from sleeping, and at night Manuel helped the wounded on his deck, holding them down and wiping the sweat from their faces, nearly as delirious as they were. At dawn he ate biscuits and drank his cup of wine and went to his tub of slow match to await the next engagement.

La Lavia, being the largest ship on the left flank, always took the brunt of the English attack. It was on the third day that *La Lavia*'s mainmast topgallant yard fell on his old taffrail crew, crushing Hanan and Pietro. Manuel rushed across the deck to help them, shouting his anguish. He got a dazed Juan down to their berth and returned amidships. Around him men were being dashed to the deck, but he didn't care. He hopped through the red mist that nearly obscured his sight, carrying lengths of match to the gun crews, who were now so depleted that they couldn't afford to send men to him. He helped the wounded below to the hospital, which had truly become an antechamber of hell; he helped toss the dead over the side, croaking a short prayer in every case; he ministered to the soldiers hiding behind the bulwarks of the bulkheads, waiting vainly for the English to get within range of their arquebuses. Now the cry amidships was "Manuel, match here! Manuel, some water! Help, Manuel!" In a dry fever of energy Manuel hurried to their aid.

He was in such perpetual haste that in the middle of a furious engagement he nearly ran into his patroness, Saint Anna, who was suddenly standing there in the corner of his tub. He was startled to see her.

"Grandmother!" he cried. "You shouldn't be here, it's dangerous."

"As you have helped others, I am here to help you," she replied. She pointed across the purplish chop to one of the English ships. Manuel saw a puff of smoke appear from its side, and out of the puff came a cannonball, floating in an arc over the water. He could see it as clearly as he could have seen an olive tossed at him from across a room: a round black ball, spinning lazily, growing bigger as it got closer. Now Manuel could tell that it was coming at him, *directly* at him, so that its trajectory would intersect his heart. "Um, blessed Anna," he said, hoping to bring this to his saint's attention. But she had already seen it, and with a brief touch to his forehead she floated up into the maintop, among the unseeing soldiers. Manuel watched her, eyeing the approaching cannonball at the same time. At the touch of her hand a rigging block fell away from the end of the main yard; it intercepted the cannonball's flight, knocking the ball downward into the hull where it stuck, half embedded in the thick wood. Manuel stared at the black half sphere, mouth open. He waved up at Saint Anna, who waved back and flew up into the red clouds toward heaven. Manuel kneeled and said a prayer of thanks to her and to Jesus for sending her and went back to cutting match.

A night or two later—Manuel himself was not sure, as the passage of time had become for him something plastic and elusive and, more than anything else, meaningless—the Armada anchored at Calais Roads, just off the Flemish coast. For the first time since they had left Corunna *La Lavia* lay still, and listening at night Manuel realized how much the constant chorus of wooden squeaks and groans was the voice of the crew, and not of the ship. He drank his ration of wine and water quickly, and walked the length of the lower deck, talking with the wounded and helping when he could to remove splinters. Many of the men wanted him to touch them, for his safe passage through some of the worst scenes of carnage had not gone unnoticed. He touched them, and when they wanted, said a prayer. Afterwards he went up on deck. There was a fair breeze from the southwest, and the ship rocked ever so gently on the tide. For the first time in a week the air was not suffused red: Manuel could see stars, and distant bonfires on the Flemish shore, like stars that had fallen and now burnt out their life on the land.

Laeghr was limping up and down amidships, detouring from his usual path to avoid a bit of shattered decking.

"Are you hurt, Laeghr?" Manuel inquired.

For answer Laeghr growled. Manuel walked beside him.

After a bit Laeghr stopped and said, "They're saying you're a holy man now because you were running all over the deck these last few days, acting like the shot we were taking was hail and never getting hit for it. But I say you're just too foolish to know any better. Fools dance where angels would hide. It's part of the curse laid on us. Those who learn the rules and play things right end up getting hurt—sometimes from doing just the things that will protect them the most. While the blind fools who wander right into the thick of things are never touched."

Manuel watched Laeghr's stride. "Your foot?"

Laeghr shrugged. "I don't know what will happen to it."

Under a lantern Manuel stopped and looked Laeghr in the eye. "Saint Anna appeared and plucked a cannonball that was heading for me right out of the sky. She saved my life for a purpose."

"No." Laeghr thumped his cane on the deck. "Your fever has made you mad, boy."

"I can show you the shot!" Manuel said. "It stuck in the hull!" Laeghr stumped away.

Manuel looked across the water at Flanders, distressed by Laeghr's words, and by his hobbled walk. He saw something he didn't comprehend.

"Laeghr?"

"What?" came Laeghr's voice from across midships.

"Something bright . . . the souls of all the English at once, maybe. . . ." His voice shook.

"What?"

"Something coming at us. Come here, master."

Thump, thump, thump. Manuel heard the hiss of Laeghr's indrawn breath, the muttered curse.

"Fireships," Laeghr bellowed at the top of his lungs. "Fireships! Awake!"

In a minute the ship was bedlam, soldiers running everywhere. "Come with me," Laeghr told Manuel, who fol-

lowed the sailing master to the forecastle, where the anchor
hawser descended into the water. Somewhere along the way
Laeghr had gotten a halberd, and he gave it to Manuel. "Cut
the line."

"But master, we'll lose the anchor."

"Those fireships are too big to stop, and if they're
hellburners they'll explode and kill us all. Cut it."

Manuel began chopping at the thick hawser, which was
very like the trunk of a small tree. He chopped and chopped,
but only one strand of the huge rope was cut when Laeghr
seized the halberd and began chopping himself, awkwardly to
avoid putting his weight on his bad foot. They heard the
voice of the ship's captain— "Cut the anchor cable!" And
Laeghr laughed.

The rope snapped, and they were floating free. But the
fireships were right behind them. In the hellish light Manuel
could see English sailors walking about on their burning
decks, passing through the flames like salamanders or de-
mons. No doubt they were devils. The fires towering above
the eight fireships shared the demonic life of the English;
each tongue of yellow flame contained an English demon eye
looking for the Armada, and some of these leaped free of the
blaze that twisted above the fireships, in vain attempts to
float onto *La Lavia* and incinerate it. Manuel held off these
embers with his wooden medallion, and the gesture that in
his boyhood in Sicily had warded off the evil eye. Meanwhile, the ships of the fleet were cut loose and drifting on the
tide, colliding in the rush to avoid the fireships. Captains and
officers screamed furiously at their colleagues on other ships,
but to no avail. In the dark and without anchors the ships
could not be regathered, and as the night progressed most
were blown out into the North Sea. For the first time the neat
phalanxes of the Armada were broken, and they were never
to be reformed again.

*   *   *

When it was all over *La Lavia* held its position in the North Sea by sail, while the officers attempted to identify the ships around them, and find out what Medina Sidonia's orders were. Manuel and Juan stood amidships with the rest of their berthmates. Juan shook his head. "I used to make corks in Portugal. We were like a cork back there in the Channel, being pushed into the neck of a bottle. As long as we were stuck in the neck we were all right—the neck got narrower and narrower, and they might never have gotten us out. Now the English have pushed us right down into the bottle itself. We're floating about in our own dregs. And we'll never get out of the bottle again."

"Not through the neck, anyway," one of the others agreed. "Not any way."

"God will see us home," Manuel said.

Juan shook his head.

Rather than try to force the Channel, Admiral Medina Sidonia decided that the Armada should sail around Scotland, and then home. Laeghr was taken to the flagship for a day to help chart a course, for he was familiar with the north as none of the Spanish pilots were.

The battered fleet headed away from the sun, ever higher into the cold North Sea. After the night of the fireships Medina Sidonia had restored discipline with a vengeance. One day the survivors of the many Channel battles were witness to the hanging from the yardarm of a captain who had let his ship get ahead of the Admiral's flagship, a position which was now forbidden. A carrack sailed through the fleet again and again so every crew could see the corpse of the disobedient captain, swinging freely from its spar.

Manuel observed the sight with distaste. Once dead, a man was only a bag of bones; nowhere in the clouds overhead could he spot the captain's soul. Perhaps it had plummeted into the sea, on its way to hell. It was an odd transition, death. Curious that God did not make more explicit the aftermath.

So *La Lavia* faithfully trailed the Admiral's flagship, as did the rest of the fleet. They were led farther and farther north, into the domain of cold. Some mornings when they came on deck in the raw yellow of the dawn the riggings would be rimed with icicles, so that they seemed strings of diamonds. Some days it seemed they sailed across a sea of milk, under a silver sky. Other days the ocean was the color of a bruise, and the sky a fresh pale blue so clear that Manuel gasped with the desire to survive this voyage and live. Yet he was as cold as death. He remembered the burning nights of his fever as fondly as if he were remembering his first home on the coast of North Africa.

All the men were suffering from the cold. The livestock was dead, so the galley closed down: no hot soup. The Admiral imposed rationing on everyone, including himself; the deprivation kept him in his bed for the rest of the voyage. For the sailors, who had to haul wet or frozen rope, it was worse. Manuel watched the grim faces, in line for their two biscuits and one large cup of wine and water—their daily ration—and concluded that they would continue sailing north until the sun was under the horizon and they were in the icy realm of death, the north pole where God's dominion was weak, and there they would give up and die all at once. Indeed, the winds drove them nearly to Norway, and it was with great difficulty that they brought the shot-peppered hulks around to a westerly heading.

When they did, they discovered a score of new leaks in *La Lavia*'s hull, and the men, already exhausted by the effort of bringing the ship about, were forced to man the pumps around the clock. A pint of wine and a pint of water a day were not enough. Men died. Dysentery, colds, the slightest injury; all were quickly fatal.

Once again Manuel could see the air. Now it was a thick

blue, distinctly darker where men breathed it out, so that they all were shrouded in dark blue air that obscured the burning crowns of their souls. All of the wounded men in the hospital had died. Many of them had called for Manuel in their last moments; he had held their hands or touched their foreheads, and as their souls had flickered away from their heads like the last pops of flame out of the coals of a dying fire, he had prayed for them. Now other men too weak to leave their berths called for him, and he went and stood by them in their distress. Two of these men recovered from dysentery, so his presence was requested even more frequently. The captain himself asked for Manuel's touch when he fell sick; but he died anyway, like most of the rest.

One morning Manuel was standing with Laeghr at the midships bulkhead. It was chill and cloudy, the sea was the color of flint. The soldiers were bringing their horses up and forcing them over the side, to save water.

"That should have been done as soon as we were forced out of the Sleeve," Laeghr said. "Waste of water."

"I didn't even know we had horses aboard," Manuel said.

Laeghr laughed briefly. "Boy, you are a prize of a fool. One surprise after another."

They watched the horses' awkward falls, their rolling eyes, their flared nostrils expelling clouds of blue air. Their brief attempts to swim.

"On the other hand, we should probably be eating some of those," Laeghr said.

"Horse meat?"

"It can't be that bad."

The horses all disappeared, exchanging blue air for flint water. "It's cruel," Manuel said.

"In the horse latitudes they swim for an hour," Laeghr said. "This is better." He pointed to the west. "See those tall clouds?"

"Yes."

"They stand over the Orkneys. The Orkneys or the Shet-
lands, I can't be sure anymore. It will be interesting to see if
these fools can get this wreck through the islands safely."
Looking around, Manuel could only spot a dozen or so ships;
presumably the rest of the Armada lay over the horizon ahead
of them. He stopped to wonder about what Laeghr had just
said, for it would naturally be Laeghr's task to navigate them
through the northernmost of the British Isles; at that very
moment Laeghr's eyes rolled like the horses' had, and he
collapsed on the deck. Manuel and some other sailors carried
him down to the hospital.

"It's his foot," said Friar Lucien. "His foot is crushed
and his leg has putrefied. He should have let me amputate."

Around noon Laeghr regained consciousness. Manuel, who
had not left his side, held his hand, but Laeghr frowned and
pulled it away.

"Listen," Laeghr said with difficulty. His soul was no
more than a blue cap covering his tangled salt-and-pepper
hair. "I'm going to teach you some words that may be useful
to you later." Slowly he said, *"Tor conaloc an dhia,"* and
Manuel repeated it. "Say it again." Manuel repeated the
syllables over and over, like a Latin prayer. Laeghr nodded.
"Tor conaloc an naom dhia. Good. Remember the words
always." After that he stared at the deckbeams above, and
would answer none of Manuel's questions. Emotions played
over his face like shadows, one after another. Finally he took
his gaze from the infinite and looked at Manuel. "Touch me,
boy."

Manuel touched his forehead, and with a sardonic smile
Laeghr closed his eyes: his blue crown of flame flickered up
through the deck above and disappeared.

They buried him that evening, in a smoky, hellish brown
sunset. Friar Lucien said the shortened Mass, mumbling in a
voice that no one could hear, and Manuel pressed the back of

his medallion against the cold flesh of Laeghr's arm, until the impression of the cross remained. Then they tossed him overboard. Manuel watched with a serenity that surprised him. Just weeks ago he had shouted with rage and pain as his companions had been torn apart; now he watched with a peace he did not understand as the man who had taught him and protected him sank into the iron water and disappeared.

A couple of nights after that Manuel sat apart from his remaining berthmates, who slept in one pile like a litter of kittens. He watched the blue flames wandering over the exhausted flesh, watched without reason or feeling. He was tired.

Friar Lucien looked in the narrow doorway and hissed. "Manuel! Are you there?"

"I'm here."

"Come with me."

Manuel got up and followed him. "Where are we going?"

Friar Lucien shook his head. "It's time." Everything else he said was in Greek. He had a little candle lantern with three sides shuttered, and by its illumination they made their way to the hatch that led to the lower decks.

Manuel's berth, though it was below the gun deck, was not on the lowest deck of the ship. *La Lavia* was very much bigger than that. Below the berth deck were three more decks that had no ports, as they were beneath the waterline. Here in perpetual gloom were stored the barrels of water and biscuit, the cannonballs and rope and other supplies. They passed by the powder room, where the armorer wore felt slippers so that a spark from his boots might not blow up the ship. They found a hatchway that held a ladder leading to an even lower deck. At each level the passages became narrower, and they were forced to stoop. Manuel was astounded when they descended yet again, for he would have imagined them already on the keel, or in some strange chamber suspended beneath it; but Lucien knew better. Down they went, through a labyrinth of dank black wooden passageways. Manuel was long lost, and held Lucien's arm for fear of being separated from him, and becoming hopelessly trapped in the bowels of the ship. Finally they came to a door that made their narrow hallway a dead end. Lucien rapped on the door and hissed something, and the door opened, letting out enough light to dazzle Manuel.

After the passageways, the chamber they entered seemed very large. It was the cable tier, located in the bow of the ship just over the keel. Since the encounter with the fireships, *La Lavia* had little cable, and what was left lay in the corners of the room. Now it was lit by candles set in small iron candelabra that had been nailed to the side beams. The floor was covered by an inch of water, which reflected each of the candle flames as a small spot of white light. The curving walls dripped and gleamed. In the center of the room a box had been set on end, and covered with a bit of cloth. Around the box stood several men: a soldier, one of the petty officers, and some sailors Manuel knew only by sight. The transparent knots of cobalt flame on their heads added a bluish cast to the light in the room.

"We're ready, Father," one of the men said to Lucien. The friar led Manuel to a spot near the upturned box, and the others arranged themselves in a circle around him. Against the aft wall, near gaps where floor met wall imperfectly, Manuel spotted two big rats with shiny brown fur, all ablink and twitch-whiskered at the unusual activity. Manuel frowned and one of the rats plopped into the water covering the floor and swam under the wall, its tail swishing back and forth like a small snake, revealing to Manuel its true nature. The other rat stood its ground and blinked its bright little round eyes as it brazenly returned Manuel's unwelcoming gaze.

From behind the box Lucien looked at each man in turn, and read in Latin. Manuel understood the first part: "I believe in God the Father Almighty, maker of heaven and earth, and of all things visible and invisible . . .'' From there Lucien read on, in a voice powerful yet soothing, entreatful yet proud. After finishing the creed he took up another book, the little one he always carried with him, and read in Spanish:

'' 'Know ye, O Israel, that what men call life and death are as beads of white and black strung upon a thread; and this thread of perpetual change is mine own changeless life, which bindeth together the unending string of little lives and little deaths.

'' 'The wind turns a ship from its course upon the deep: the wandering winds of the senses cast man's mind adrift on the deep.

'' 'But lo! That day shall come when the light that *is* shall still all winds, and bind every hideous liquid darkness; and all thy habitations shall be blest by the white brilliance which descendeth from the crown.' ''

While Lucien read this, the soldier moved slowly about the chamber. First he set on the top of the box a plate of sliced biscuit; the bread was hard, as it became after months at sea, and someone had taken the trouble to cut slices, and then polish them into wafers so thin that they were translucent, and the color of honey. Occasional wormholes gave them the look of old coins, that had been beaten flat and holed for use as jewelry.

Next the soldier brought forth from behind the box an empty glass bottle with its top cut off so that it was a sort of bowl. Taking a flask in his other hand, he filled the bowl to the midway point with *La Lavia*'s awful wine. Putting the flask down, he circled the group while the friar finished reading. Every man there had cuts on his hands that more or less continuously leaked blood, and each man pulled a cut open over the bottle held to him, allowing a drop to splash in, until the wine was so dark that to Manuel, aware of the blue light, it was a deep violet.

The soldier replaced the bottle beside the plate of wafers on the box. Friar Lucien finished his reading, looked at the box, and recited one final sentence: "O lamps of fire! Make bright the deep caverns of sense; with strange brightness give heat and light together to your beloved, that we may be one with you." Taking the plate in hand, he circled the chamber, putting a wafer in the mouths of the men. "The body of Christ, given for you. The body of Christ, given for you."

Manuel snapped the wafer of biscuit between his teeth and chewed it. At last he understood what they were doing. This was a communion for the dead: a service for Laeghr, a service for all of them, for they were all doomed. Beyond the damp curved wall of their chamber was the deep sea, pressing against the timbers, pressing in on them. Eventually they would all be swallowed, and would sink down to become food for the fishes, after which their bones would decorate the floor of the ocean, where God seldom visited. Manuel could scarcely get the chewed biscuit past the lump in his throat. When Friar Lucien lifted the half bottle and put it to his lips, saying first, "The blood of Christ, shed for you," Manuel stopped him. He took the bottle from the friar's hand. The soldier stepped forward, but Lucien waved him away. Then the friar knelt before Manuel and crossed himself, but backwards as Greeks did, left to right rather than the proper way. Manuel said, "You are the blood of Christ," and held the half bottle to Lucien's lips, tilting it so he could drink.

He did the same for each of the men, the soldier included. "You are the Christ." This was the first time any of them had partaken of this part of the communion, and some of them could barely swallow. When they had all drunk, Manuel put the bottle to his lips and drained it to the dregs. "Friar Lucien's book says, all thy habitations shall be blest by the white brilliance that is the crown of fire, and we shall all be made the Christ. And so it is. We drank, and now we are the Christ. See''—he pointed at the remaining rat, which was now on its hind legs, washing its forepaws so that it appeared to pray, its bright round eyes fixed on Manuel— "even the beasts know it." He broke off a piece of biscuit wafer, and leaned down to offer it to the rat. The rat accepted the fragment in its paws, and ate it. It submitted to Manuel's touch. Standing back up, Manuel felt the blood rush to his head. The crowns of fire blazed on every head, reaching far above them to lick the beams of the ceiling, filling the room with light— "He is here!" Manuel cried, "He has touched us with light, see it!" He touched each of their foreheads in turn, and saw their eyes widen as they perceived the others' burning souls in wonder, pointing at each other's heads; then they were all embracing in the clear white light, hugging one another with the tears running down their cheeks and giant grins splitting their beards. Reflected candlelight danced in a thousand parts on the watery floor. The rat, startled, splashed under the gap in the wall, and they laughed and laughed and laughed.

Manuel put his arm around the friar, whose eyes shone with joy. "It is good," Manuel said when they were all quiet again. "God will see us home."

They made their way back to the upper decks like boys playing in a cave they know very well.

The Armada made it through the Orkneys without Laeghr, though it was a close thing for some ships. Then they were out in the North Atlantic, where the swells were broader, their troughs deeper, and their tops as high as the castles of *La Lavia*, and then higher than that.

Winds came out of the southwest, bitter gales that never ceased, and three weeks later they were no closer to Spain than they had been when they slipped through the Orkneys. The situation on *La Lavia* was desperate, as it was all through the fleet. Men on *La Lavia* died every day, and were thrown overboard with no ceremony except the impression of Manuel's medallion into their arms. The deaths made the food and water shortage less acute, but it was still serious. *La Lavia* was now manned by a ghost crew, composed mostly of soldiers. There weren't enough of them to properly man the pumps, and the Atlantic was springing new leaks every day in the already broken hull. The ship began taking on water in such quantities that the acting captain of the ship—who had started the voyage as third mate—decided that they must make straight for Spain, making no spare leeway for the imperfectly known west coast of Ireland. This decision was shared by the captains of several other damaged ships, and they conveyed their decision to the main body of the fleet, which was reaching farther west before turning south to Spain. From his sickbed Medina Sidonia gave his consent, and *La Lavia* sailed due south.

Unfortunately, a storm struck from just north of west soon after they had turned homeward. They were helpless before it. *La Lavia* wallowed in the troughs and was slammed by crest after crest, until the poor hulk lay just off the lee shore, Ireland.

It was the end, and everyone knew it. Manuel knew it because the air had turned black. The clouds were like thousands of black English cannonballs, rolling ten deep over a clear floor set just above the masts, and spitting lightning into the sea whenever two of them banged together hard enough. The air beneath them was black as well, just less thick: the wind as tangible as the waves, and swirling around the masts with smoky fury. Other men caught glimpses of the lee shore, but Manuel couldn't see it for the blackness. These men called out in fear; apparently the western coast of Ireland was sheer cliff. It was the end.

Manuel had nothing but admiration for the third-mate-now-captain, who took the helm and shouted to the lookout in the top to find a bay in the cliffs they were drifting toward. But Manuel, like many of the men, ignored the mate's commands to stay at post, as they were clearly pointless. Men embraced each other on the castles, saying their farewells; others cowered in fear against the bulkheads. Many of them approached Manuel and asked for a touch, and Manuel brushed their foreheads as he angrily marched about the forecastle. As soon as Manuel touched them, some of the men flew directly up toward heaven while others dove over the side of the ship and became porpoises the moment they struck the water, but Manuel scarcely noticed these occurrences, as he was busy praying, praying at the top of his lungs.

"*Why* this storm, Lord, *why?* First there were winds from the north holding us back, which is the only reason I'm here in the first place. So you wanted me here, but why why why? Juan is dead and Laeghr is dead and Pietro is dead and Habedeen is dead and soon we will all be dead, and why? It isn't just. You promised you would take us home." In a fury he took his slow match knife, climbed down to the swamped midships, and went to the mainmast. He thrust the knife deep into the wood, stabbing with the grain. "There! I say *that* to your storm!"

"Now, that's blasphemy," Laeghr said as he pulled the knife from the mast and threw it over the side. "You know what stabbing the mast means. To do it in a storm like this—you'll offend gods a lot older than Jesus, and more powerful, too."

"Talk about blasphemy," Manuel replied. "And you wonder why you're still wandering the seas a ghost, when you say things like that. You should take more care." He looked up and saw Saint Anna, in the maintop giving directions to the third mate. "Did you hear what Laeghr said?" he shouted up to her. She didn't hear him.

"Do you remember the words I taught you?" Laeghr inquired.

"Of course. Don't bother me now, Laeghr, I'll be a ghost with you soon enough." Laeghr stepped back, but Manuel changed his mind, and said, "Laeghr, why are we being punished like this? We were on a crusade for God, weren't we? I don't understand."

Laeghr smiled and turned around, and Manuel saw then that he had wings, wings with feathers intensely white in the black murk of the air. He clasped Manuel's arm. "You know all that I know." With some hard flaps he was off, tumbling east swiftly in the black air, like a gull.

With the help of Saint Anna the third mate had actually found a break in the cliffs, a quite considerable bay. Other ships of the Armada had found it as well, and they were already breaking up on a wide beach as *La Lavia* limped nearer shore. The keel grounded and immediately things began breaking. Soupy waves crashed over the canted midships, and Manuel leaped up the ladder to the forecastle, which was now under a tangle of rigging from the broken foremast. The mainmast went over the side, and the lee flank of the ship splintered like a match tub and flooded, right before their eyes. Among the floating timbers Manuel saw one that held a black cannonball embedded in it, undoubtedly the very one that Saint Anna had deflected from its course toward him. Reminded that she had saved his life before, Manuel grew calmer and waited for her to appear. The beach was only a few shiplengths away, scarcely visible in the thick air; like most of the men, Manuel could not swim, and he was searching with some urgency for a sight of Saint Anna when Friar Lucien appeared at his side, in his black robes. Over the shriek of the dark wind Lucien shouted, "If we hold on to a plank we'll float ashore."

"You go ahead," Manuel shouted back. "I'm waiting for Saint Anna." The friar shrugged. The wind caught his robes and Manuel saw that Lucien was attempting to save the ship's liturgical gold, which was in the form of chains that were now wrapped around the friar's middle. Lucien made his way to the rail and jumped over it, onto a spar that a wave was carrying away from the ship. He missed his hold on the rounded spar, however, and sank instantly.

The forecastle was now awash, and soon the foaming breakers would tear it loose from the keel. Most of the men had already left the wreck, trusting to one bit of flotsam or other. But Manuel still waited. Just as he was beginning to worry he saw the blessed grandmother of God, standing among figures on the beach that he perceived but dimly, gesturing to him. She walked out onto the white water, and he understood. "We are the Christ, of course! I will walk to shore as He once did." He tested the surface with one shoe; it seemed a little, well, infirm, but surely it would serve—it would be like the floor of their now-demolished chapel, a sheet of water covering one of God's good solids. So Manuel walked out onto the next wave that passed at the level of the forecastle, and plunged deep into the brine.

"Hey!" he spluttered as he struggled back to the surface. "Hey!" No answer from Saint Anna this time; just cold salt water. He began the laborious process of drowning, remembering as he struggled a time when he was a child, and his father had taken him down to the beach in Morocco, to see the galley of the pilgrims to Mecca rowing away. Nothing could have been less like the Irish coast than that serene, hot, tawny beach, and he and his father had gone out into the shallows to splash around in the warm water, chasing lemons. His father would toss the lemons out into the deeper water, where they bobbed just under the surface, and then Manuel would paddle out to retrieve them, laughing and choking on water.

Manuel could picture those lemons perfectly, as he snorted and coughed and thrashed to get his head back above the freezing soup one more time. Lemons bobbing in the green sea, lemons oblong and bumpy, the color of the sun when the sun is its own width above the horizon at dawn . . . bobbing gently just under the surface, with a knob showing here or there. Manuel pretended he was a lemon, at the same time that he tried to remember the primitive dog paddle that had gotten him around in the shallows. Arms, pushing downward. It wasn't working. Waves tumbled him, lemonlike, in toward the strand. He bumped on the bottom and stood up. The water was only waist deep. Another wave smashed him from behind and he couldn't find the bottom again. Not fair! he thought. His elbow ran into sand, and he twisted around and stood. Knee deep, this time. He kept an eye on the treacherous waves as they came out of the black, and trudged through them up to a beach made of coarse sand, covered by a mat of loose seaweed.

Down on the beach a distance were sailors, companions, survivors of the wrecks offshore. But there among them— soldiers on horses. English soldiers, on horses and on foot— Manuel groaned to see it—wielding swords and clubs on the exhausted men strewn across the seaweed. "No!" Manuel cried, "No!" But it was true. "Ah, God," he said, and sank till he was sitting. Down the strand soldiers clubbed his brothers, splitting their fragile eggshell skulls so that the yolk of their brains ran into the kelp. Manuel beat his insensible fists against the sand. Filled with horror at the sight, he watched horses rear in the murk, giant and shadowy. They were coming down the beach toward him. "I'll make myself invisible," he decided. "Saint Anna will make me invisible." But remembering his plan to walk on the water, he determined to help the miracle by staggering up the beach and burrowing under a particularly tall pile of seaweed. He was invisible without it, of course, but the cover of kelp would help keep him warm. Thinking such thoughts, he shivered and shivered and on the still land fell insensible as his hands.

*   *   *

When he woke up, the soldiers were gone. His fellows lay up and down the beach like white driftwood; ravens and wolves already converged on them. He couldn't move very well. It took him half an hour to move his head to survey the beach, and another half hour to free himself from his pile of seaweed. And then he had to lie down again.

When he regained consciousness, he found himself behind a large log, an old piece of driftwood that had been polished silver by its years of rolling in sand. The air was clear again. He could feel it filling him and leaving him, but he could no longer see it. The sun was out; it was morning, and the storm was over. Each movement of Manuel's body was a complete effort, a complete experience. He could see quite deeply into his skin, which appeared pickled. He had lost all of his clothes, except for a tattered shred of trousers around his middle. With all his will he made his arm move his hand, and with his stiff forefinger he touched the driftwood. He could feel it. He was still alive.

His hand fell away in the sand. The wood touched by his finger was changing, becoming a bright green spot in the surrounding silver. A thin green sprig bulged from the spot, and grew up toward the sun; leaves unfolded from this sprout as it thickened, and beneath Manuel's fascinated gaze a bud appeared and burst open: a white rose, gleaming wetly in the white morning light.

He had managed to stand, and cover himself with kelp, and walk a full quarter of a mile inland, when he came upon people. Three of them to be exact, two men and a woman. Wilder looking people Manuel couldn't imagine: the men had beards that had never been cut, and arms like Laeghr's. The woman looked exactly like his miniature portrait of Saint Anna, until she got closer and he saw that she was dirty and her teeth were broken and her skin was brindled like a dog's belly. He had never seen such freckling before, and he stared at it, and her, every bit as much as she and her companions stared at him. He was afraid of them.

"Hide me from the English, please," he said. At the word *English* the men frowned and cocked their heads. They jabbered at him in a tongue he did not know. "Help me," he said. "I don't know what you're saying. Help me." He tried Spanish and Portuguese and Sicilian and Arabic. The men were looking angry. He tried Latin, and they stepped back. "I believe in God the Father Almighty, Maker of Heaven and Earth, and in all things visible and invisible." He laughed, a bit hysterically. "Especially invisible." He grabbed his medallion and showed them the cross. They studied him, clearly at a loss.

"*Tor conaloc an dhia,*" he said without thinking. All four of them jumped. Then the two men moved to his sides to hold him steady. They chattered at him, waving their free arms. The woman smiled, and Manuel saw that she was young. He said the syllables again, and they chattered at him some more. "Thank you, Laeghr," he said. "Thank you, Anna. Anna," he said to the girl, and reached for her. She squealed and stepped back. He said the phrase again. The men lifted him, for he could no longer walk, and carried him across the heather. He smiled and kissed both men on the cheek, which made them laugh, and he said the magic phrase again and started to fall asleep and smiled and said the phrase. *Tor conaloc an dhia.* The girl brushed his wet hair out of his eyes; Manuel recognized the touch, and he could feel the flowering begin inside him.

—give mercy for God's sake—

—1982

Remaking History

The Part of Us that Loves

When they came and told him of John's death he crumpled onto the packed earth of the marketplace and rocked back and forth in a fetal ball, howling. He was a small wiry man, dressed in a caftan the color of sand. His feet and hands and head were big for his size, long feet dirty in old sandals, hands immense and strange looking, head a mass of tangled unkempt black hair. Face thin under the wild hair, dominated by intent brown eyes which now stared off at nothing, or at his own death, so much like John's and now so much closer.

The autistic rocking ceased and in a staccato voice he asked how it had happened. Peter told him what they had heard and with a fierce roar he beat the ground, leaped to his feet and shouted furiously. Cheap, disgusting, meaningless, foul! His band drew back, afraid of him as they so often were. He darted through the growing crowd and ran out of the miserable fishing village to the hills, to deal alone with his fury and grief.

His little crew straggled after him, looking confused, appalled, sick. No telling what he might do next. He might disappear never to be seen again, he might return and lash them all with his fierce tongue or with an actual flail, who could say? Or at the first sight of him they might be re-immersed in the flood of his exuberant love. So they followed.

And the inhabitants of the village hurried out after them, carrying their sick and paralyzed, careless of their homes and possessions, fearful that if they waited even an instant they might lose him forever, and life return to the agony it had been before he came. No one could stand the thought of it. An hour after he had run away the entire population of the village was on foot and after him, straggling into the baked brown hills.

Naomi woke as the bus hissed to a halt. She put her pocket Bible into her daypack, grabbed her clarinet case and hopped out the door just as it was closing. Some boys were laughing at her, and haughtily she tossed her short hair and took off across Shiloh Park, skirting the long pond on her way to the church.

She remembered what she had read on the bus and forgot the boys, feeling disturbed. The Bible was so strange. People outside the church acted like reading it made you an innocent, completely out of it, and yet here it was filled with blood and gore and sex and perversion—all the world's evil, wrestling the good with devilish vigor. Chopping John's head off like that! And all because he had told Herod to stop messing around with Herod's brother's wife. And that wife, and her disgusting daughter who did the dance! It made Naomi shiver. She couldn't help trying to imagine just what sort of dancing could inspire a man to such evil. Naked, no doubt. Like the strippers in Las Vegas or *Penthouse,* or like Jeanette Thompson in the showers after workout, arms overhead and spinning under the spray. Except in this case under the eye of a dirty old man. Who went along with a slut like that even when she wanted a saint's head chopped off. And to bring the head in on a platter with her still walking around the room naked, no doubt! Oh, it was perverted all right; it made her feel queasy just to imagine it. No wonder Jesus had gotten so upset and run off into the mountains. Naomi had visited Colorado Springs, she knew what a comfort the mountains could be, how they lifted you above it all and made you feel the world was holy. Jesus needed such places; after all, he knew all along what was going to happen to him. At this time he had only a couple years left. Horrible to know like that. No wonder he led the disciples on such a rollercoaster of feeling. Every day must have seemed like a year, especially the long days, like this one beginning with the news of John's death. Filled with wonder and pain. Days all four of the Gospel writers remembered, years later when they were writing it all down.

Green park on a muggy summer morning. She came to the church complex and walked into the band room. All the band members not at work—mostly younger ones—were arriving for an early rehearsal. Putting together instruments, warming up, talking. Naomi sat next to Penny and put her clarinet together. A whole gang of boys barged in together, including Tom Osborn. Surreptitiously Naomi watched Tom go to his seat, four down from hers. She was first clarinet and he was the first and only oboe, but the band was arranged with the other first clarinets between them. Tom put his oboe together and talked to the boys in the trumpet section behind him. He looked down the row and saw Naomi, waved and said hi, went back to talking with his friends. His movements were abrupt and uncontrolled; he had grown about four inches in the last year, on the way to becoming a tall, lanky redhead. He stumbled a lot. And his laugh was a kind of boisterous honk that burst out of him before he even knew he was amused. Only his long fingers showed any sort of coordination, and that only when he was playing. Of course it took a lot of coordination to play the oboe's double reed, but that was in the mouth and no one could see it. The other girls thought he was weird for choosing the oboe in the first place. But he was interesting.

Their conductor shuffled slowly into the room. Several people greeted him. "Morning, Dave." He looked up briefly, smiled, stepped carefully onto his podium, each foot placed securely before he moved the next.

The bandmaster was old. Conductor of the Zion Band for many decades now, he was in his eighties, and suffered from a disease of the nerves that made him shake. Probably Parkinson's although one couldn't say for sure, as he and his wife still followed the teaching of the town founder, Dr. Alexander Dowie, who had held that doctors were unnecessary and that the only true healing was accomplished by Christ, through the word of God. In any case Dave had trouble moving, and his hands and mouth shook. Sometimes Naomi was amazed that he could still conduct the band. But obviously the act itself was a restorative. Like this morning; first he talked to them softly about this evening's concert. They were playing in the park's

band shell for the residents of several local nursing homes, to celebrate the hundredth birthdays of two of the old folks. Also for
whoever else came to listen. Quietly Dave named the tunes they
would play, listing them with a weak smile. He seemed hesitant,
drained, incapable of lifting his arms. But then it was time to rehearse,
and he stepped forward to his music stand, and it was as if (as she
had heard Tom say) he had a socket in the bottom of one shoe and
had just stepped onto a plug, connecting him to some powerful
electric source. He conducted clearly and vigorously, with a strong
four-four beat, head tilted up and to one side as he listened. If you
made a mistake a wrinkle would form between his eyebrows; if you
played a hard part with accuracy and expression he would look your
way and smile—just a glance, but you knew he heard everything. He
smiled at Tom's playing frequently; Tom and Andrew on the baritone
were the real musicians in the current band, Naomi thought, and she
could tell Dave agreed. How he enjoyed listening to them!

That's why we're here, she thought, here on a sunny summer
morning: because Dave was a man who loved what he did. He would
say, I've been lucky my play has been my work and not many can say
that, and all his life he had been ready at any moment to sit down and
make music, to speak through it, which speaking filled him with joy.
And seeing that people were drawn to it. It's like that with some
bands, some choirs; the conductor has a presence, spreads a joy, and
the band or choir gets larger and larger, prospers even in times when
fewer people know how to play or sing. Because of Dave it had been
like that in Zion for almost fifty years.

Then rehearsal was over, and it was time to get to the other side
of the complex for the weekly Bible class. Dave was teaching that as
well this year, so there was no need for Naomi to hurry; he would be
a while.

As she left the room Tom Osborn rushed up, banged into the
closing door, said brightly, "Hey Naomi, are you on your way to
class?" She nodded. "Good, I'll walk over there with you!"

"Sure," she said, pulse quickening.

So when he came out of the hills and down the broad sandy wash,
winding between shrubs and humming a random tune, he came on
them all at once. The whole mangy lot of them. For a moment anger

drove its iron spike through him—never to be left alone! Then he saw the looks on their faces: fear, hope, sudden release at the sight of him, deep relief. They wore all the clothes they owned: a caftan, a shirt, a tunic, wrapped skirts, threadbare with a thousand washings, sewn up, dusty, torn. Under that, ribs, scars, open sores. Distended bellies of malnourished children, gaunt musculature of malnourished adults. This was his constituency—he would never have any other—people so poor that the slightest drought might kill them, every day spent thinking about the next meal—where it would come from, how they might ration it—going without so their children could eat, falling asleep at night feeling that pinch in the gut, that pain. With disease permanent, unexplainable, unavoidable. Like a curse. And he understood suddenly that he was their only chance to escape lives that were like the lives of their beasts, grinding in poverty and pain, sudden death touching down among them like soundless heat lightning on a black summer night. Their only chance. Except you have souls it is no more than this, he said to himself, looking at the desperation in their faces, the desperation that had brought, my God, the whole village after him.

So he sat them down, using his little band as messengers, spokesmen scurrying anxiously around saying He'll be here in just a moment, sit down and he'll come. And all the while thinking of John's fierce pure devotion, he walked among them. And they watched him and waited for his approach. An ordinary little man with a tangle of hair and a dancer's step—how he drew the eye! They felt the compulsion to watch him, they felt the awful contradiction of a man who seemed relaxed, calm, soft-spoken, and yet at the same time stuffed with energy, a violent internal spin revealed in every gesture he made. Squatting elbows on knees, talking to each of them in turn with that direct gaze pinning them, brown eyes under the stray lock of hair steady and searching right to the bottom of their selves, understanding all he saw and loving them nevertheless. While he talked his strange oversized hands were always moving, fingers pointing, shaping ideas, touching his listeners—making a cap for a boy's head, wrapping around a twig-like leg, rimming an open sore or laid flat on a patch of leprosy that no one else would dare touch, and as he did so there was an almost audible tension in the air, a tension such that his low musical voice could be clearly heard all the way across the wash, humorous tones bouncing like his visible image in the heat-waves rising from their alluvial ampitheater, sounding as if spoken right into the ear, clear in the palpable silence of their ensemble breathing. And here a paralyzed arm would quiver and clench at him, a skeletal woman would swell like a wineskin and rise and ask for water, and everyone would sigh under the burning sun and sleeping children smile with contentment. And always the voice floating through the baking air, saying you are more than animals, you are human beings, God's own children, God's mirror and message, with spirits that transcend the flesh and all the flesh's meager explanations. Spirits that never die. And we prove this by the way we behave toward each other, by our compassion and love given not just to family, which after all even animals do, but to all creation and espe-cially to other human beings, your brothers and sisters all over the world. And they could feel in their marrow it was true, because of this little man spinning among them with his big hands and his quick laugh (head thrown back to the sun, teeth white in his black beard) and his quick brown eyes and his quick musical voice—because of his *presence.*

Naomi jerked and sat up. Bible class again. A bit dull. Even with Tom sitting next to her. There were only eight students there, all of them in the summer before their junior year of high school, most known to each other since childhood, and many of them restive at this class, which was mostly taken because parents commanded it. Jeanette glancing into her makeup mirror, the boys on the other side of Tom fidgeting, Martha nearly asleep, and Dave sometimes seem-ing not much more awake himself. Teaching this class did not trans-form him as conducting did, and mostly he just asked them in turn to read aloud from the Gospels, reading different versions of the same events from the four books, then reading a companion study guide, or a modern language version, to clarify any obscurities. And to the nearly infinite host of questions plaguing Naomi, all the whys and wherefores and what exactly does this *mean,* he had only his slight inward smile and a manner like that she had heard psychotherapists used. Well, what do you think it means? he would answer her. Why do you ask? What troubles you about that? And so on, until he would ask someone else to read on, and listen with a very faint, abstracted look of pleasure, enjoying it as if it were some quiet form of his beloved music. Leaving Naomi to her own devices, all the questions still snapping away inside her. Her puzzle to solve, without the help of anything on earth.

By the time he had finished wandering through the crowd the sun was low in the sky, it was cooling down marginally and they could finally feel the sweat on their skin. His band gathered around him and Philip said You'd better send them home now, they've got nothing to eat and they've been here all day. He looked at his men with the exuberant spin still clear in his gaze and laughed. How will we feed all these people, Philip? Where will we get the bread? Feeling the urge that so often struck him, to tease or even taunt these brothers of his, the men he knew best in all the world, who despite all still followed him around gnawing one worry or another, as frail and lovable as simpletons, which some of them in fact were. Philip, who was constantly trying to keep them from going broke, spluttered about how much it would cost to buy that much bread—a couple hundred pennies' worth at least—only he could make such a quick estimate of something like that—meanwhile the women of the village were walking up from a spring with the water jugs full on their heads, still in balance over their graceful swaying. They were expecting a supper of water, it wouldn't be the first time or the last. He laughed again and, returning Thomas's truculent gaze, said You feed them. Feeling mischievousness like a fountain in him, a response to the women's beauty. Who could stem it? Serious Andrew went to their bags and said slowly, We've got five loaves of bread. Oh, and two fish. Dense big loaves of brown barley bread, each would feed several men. Two smoked lake trout, bony and short, staring up with a round-eyed expression just like Peter's. He laughed again. Fine, he said. Have them move into groups of about fifty.

And they went off to do it, Thomas rolling his eyes, the rest looking puzzled and frightened almost to tears. As they arranged things he emptied out their baskets and moved onto a pebbly rise at the upper end of the wash, where everyone could see him. Certainly their eyes were all on him. He put the five loaves and the two fishes into one basket, and for a long time he stared into the setting sun, becoming still as the rock under him. He could feel the world breathing, the movement of the stars, the gaze of the people sitting in the sand around him. His long fingers twisted the first loaf of barley and tore off a chunk. He dropped pieces of bread into an empty basket, then used a fingernail to tear flesh from the fish, careful not to include bones. Thank you, lake trout. By the time his men had regathered around him he had filled two baskets. He was still just beginning on the first loaf. Peter did his fish imitation. He laughed as they scurried off with the baskets.

Watching him frightened them. His hands moved like a tailor's, quick and precise, tearing away mouthfuls of bread from loaves that never seemed to get smaller, so that it seemed barley bread and chunks of smoked fish were pouring out of his palms. It was enough to make them run away with their full baskets, running to the hungry eyes that watched it all intently, people silent as boulders scattered on the wash, focusing their concentration on the little man at their center. They ate without taking their eyes from him. And it went on like that until the red oblate sun touched the hills to the west, and the air was thick with apricot light and the smell of sweat and smoked fish. Every visit to him was more confounding; same thing happening, hands tearing quickly, his gaze direct and sardonic, challenging, a laugh playing under his moustache. So that it was actually a relief to stumble away from him with yet another full basket. This was the central fact of the experience, every time they stepped out into the luminous realm of the miraculous: it was frightening to see it! There was a lot of terror in awe.

When he was done producing food out of the five loaves and the two fishes he stood and stretched like a cat. He took up a handful of the bread, regarded it curiously, ate it piece by piece, chewing slowly. When he was done he said to the twelve Take your baskets out and collect the scraps they haven't eaten. They did it wearily, and came back humping full baskets, every one of them. Staring openmouthed. He laughed. We can have leftovers tomorrow, he said, and looking out at his people he felt the surge of affection coming from them; he turned it back out on them, the mirror of their capacity for love.

Tom tapped Naomi on the knee, startling her. He leaned over so he could whisper in her ear. "Matter replicator," he said softly; she could hear that he was smiling as he spoke. "Alien visitor from a planet with a higher technology. It's obvious, don't you think?"

Blushing, and fearful that Dave had heard him, Naomi shook her head. And Dave cocked his. "Tom?"

"Oh, uh—nothing, Dave." Tom straightened in his seat, buried his nose studiously in his Bible.

Dave looked at him dubiously. "Jeanette, would you continue?"

Naomi groaned inside. Jeanette read in a smarmy, over-expressive voice, relentlessly marking each sentence by emphasizing words or phrases chosen at random. That to her was drama. And apparently Dave liked it, or at least had no objection. Tom shifted restlessly, rolling his eyes at Jeanette's melodramatics and surreptitiously flipping through his Bible, looking for who knew what. Jeanette was reading from John, while Tom was looking through Mark. Naomi, at first pleased to sit next to Tom after their walk around the complex, now began to get annoyed. He definitely made it harder to concentrate.

"Then those men, when they had seen the *miracle* that Jesus did, said, This is of a *truth* that prophet that *should* come into the world. When Jesus *therefore* perceived that they would come and *take him by force*, to make him a *king*, he departed again *into a mountain* himself alone."

How disappointing, how terrible it must have been, to have had a day like that, filled with wonder and the tight sense of community that participation in one of his miracles always brought with it—and then suddenly to have them rise up and rush toward him shouting Be king! with their faces transfigured. Lead us! Be king! With his twelve men going right along with it as usual, jumping up and down in the front row.

To come out of that state of still spinning in which such things happened: shock, confusion, incomprehension. Then he understood; if he could make food from nothing, and if he became their king, then maybe it would happen every day. Free food, no work, security—return to infancy and sweet mother's breast. Or, to be more charitable, an end to the threat of starvation. Steep plummet of disappointment, empty despair, followed immediately as he was jostled by that old spike of anger. Shout wordlessly at them, strike at his doggy disciples and blast through them like Moses parting the sea, so he could run stumbling up the wash, to spend the night in the hills alone.

Leaving the twelve and the five thousand standing there confused, staring at baskets of bread and fish scraps. The twelve looked at each other and sighed. Done it again. They couldn't predict him; they didn't understand him, and they knew it.

John and Mark took charge and sent the villagers back, with the contents of the twelve baskets. After that they were left on the caked shore of the Sea of Galilee, with no shelter and no food, only a plan to go next to Capernaum, across the sea. And no sign of him. Doubtless gone for the night.

Irritably John suggested they precede him over the sea to have a roof for the night, and the others agreed; they convinced a fisherman who had witnessed the day to lend them a boat, and they got in and started rowing.

Night fell, the wind picked up and came right in over the bow. Low dark clouds, steep short waves falling over in white lines, in a roar of wind and water mixed, until they had to shift toward the stern so the bow would clear the waves, and they were tossed about, elbows bashing ribs and heads in the dark, the rowers crying for room and everyone getting scared; it would be difficult if not impossible to turn back without swamping the boat.

Then Matthew cried out, and when they saw what caused his shout they were terrified: there was a figure in white walking on the sea, gliding smoothly in a little pocket of stillness—

"Ah ha HA!" Boisterous horselaugh, from Tom of course. Startled, Naomi drew back and stared at him. He had a hand clapped over his mouth, but was still laughing; obviously he had been helpless to stem the outburst. Those gangly awkward arms. Everyone was staring at him. Embarrassed for him, Naomi looked down at her lap. The red lines of Christ's speech jumped off the page of black print.

"Well, Tom?" Dave said with his wrong-note frown.

"I'm sorry," Tom said, "I really am. It's just that in Mark it says, wait, here—'he cometh unto them, walking upon the sea, and would have passed by them.' I mean"—he stopped, suppressed another laugh with difficulty—"it sort of sounds like he went out there to help them, and then just forgot about it on the way—spaced out and would have strolled right on by, if they hadn't yelled for him!"

Several members of the class tittered at this interpretation, and Tom grinned widely. Dave frowned, but didn't offer a counter-explanation. He looked around at the others. "What do you think?"

"It was pitch black and storming!" Naomi said, surprising herself. She looked at Tom. "He went out there to save them, but once out there it would have been really hard to see anything." Her conception of the night on the sea was altering as she spoke. "He just lost sight of them is all."

Dave was nodding. "Jeanette, would you please continue?" Even though she'd already read most of the chapter. "Yes, let's stay with the Book of John for the moment."

Jeanette recommenced her mangling of the text, but Tom, still tensed, on the edge of a new guffaw, scribbled something on his Pee-Chee folder and slid it over onto Naomi's leg. Curious despite herself, she read it: *Walking on water—Anti-Gravity Device! See what I mean?*

She took out her ballpoint and quickly penned under his message: *Don't forget Peter did it too, then fell in when scared. It took BELIEF.*

Tom scowled, grinned, wrote: *Unless he stepped outside the field.*

Then Dave cleared his throat, and they were both nose-deep in Bibles.

It was, to put it simply, a scramble. The ferocity of concentration necessary to stay on the surface of the water was challenged by the steep tumbling waves, and eventually he was reduced to every kind of acrobatic maneuver: hopping over broken whitecaps, skidding down the backsides and sinking ankle-deep as he bottomed out in the troughs, occasionally going to hands and knees, or jumping from crest to crest and treading deep in the mush—sweeping wet hair out of eyes, pausing legs spread wide to look for the foundering boat . . . So that by the time he neared them he was sopping wet, glissading down the backsides of waves, broadjumping up the frontsides, surfing on his feet to close the cross-distance, crawling in places, slipping around like a drunk on greased glass, up and down, up and down.

Then they saw him and shrieked in fear, so that he relocated them off to one side. A ghost, a ghost! He had to laugh. They never learned. Be of good cheer! he shouted, laughing crazily as he sideslipped down a swell, balancing perfectly. It's me! Be not afraid!

And Peter, bold as the child he was, said if it's you, Lord, bid me come to you on the water!

Come then, he said, riding up and down and concentrating on Peter's bulk, his low center of gravity, his childlike mind. It made him smile with affection to see Peter step right over the transom onto the water, which held him like thick mud. Peter took five or six steps before a wave jostled him; he went to hands and knees and looked at what was under him—black water right under his nose—and yelped. Help, Lord! Save me! And then it was a real struggle, he had to skid over the waves and reach down under the surface and grab him by the arms and lift him up bodily, balanced on the swells all the while. He threw Peter over an oarlock and followed him with a neat step onto the mid-bench. They were both soaked, they couldn't have gotten any wetter. He cleared hair from his eyes and laughed. Oh man of little faith he said to Peter, why did you doubt? But then again, to take that first step out of the boat . . . He gave the bedraggled and shamefaced child a hug, then threw his mind against the wind. Spirit versus spirit. Father help me. The wind calmed, the whitecaps disappeared.

"Then they *willingly* received him into the ship: and *immediately* the ship was at the land whither they went."

Tom's eyes bugged out and with a jerk he scribbled on his Pee-Chee, poked it so that Naomi would look. *TELEPORTATION!!!!!*

Naomi pressed her lips together to keep from smiling, rolled her eyes, poked him hard in the ribs.

When class was over they put their things in their daypacks without looking at each other. Then as they walked out into the humid sunshine he rushed up to her side and almost tripped. "Hey, are you going to eat lunch now?"

Naomi nodded.

"Me too. You want to—I mean . . ."

"I've got a sack lunch, I'm going to eat in the park."

"Me too! Want to eat together?"

"Sure."

A laugh burst out of him. "Ha! And so they broke bread together. What a class!"

She snorted. "Just call you Doubting Thomas."

"Well, I can see his point. I mean, a little proof—I wouldn't mind some of that myself."

She shook her head. "You have to have more faith."

"Faith," he said, testing the word, weighing the sound of it. He shrugged. "Maybe I do."

They sat on the grassy rise at the north end of the park, and got out their lunches. Tom's was just three peanut butter and jelly sandwiches, and a Snickers bar; his family didn't have much money. He worked several nights a week at the Jack in the Box, which no doubt didn't help his complexion any. Too bad he wasn't on the swim team. Or working at Sears, like she did.

She traded a baloney and cheese sandwich for one of his, and they ate. As they ate Tom gestured at the town around them. "We live in a strange place, you know? One of a kind."

Naomi swallowed. "I know." Zion, Illinois. Founded by the Australian faith healer Dr. J. Alexander Dowie, who set up a tent outside the Chicago World's Fair at the turn of the century, and urged visitors to avoid the iniquity of the fair and live a pure life. Many people responded. His plan had been to set up Zions outside all the major cities of the world, but the town fronting Lake Michigan on marshy land north of Chicago was the only one they succeeded in building. Even that had been a close thing, at first. Now it stood there like any other Midwestern town—only different. The north-south streets were named after characters in the Bible, in alphabetical order starting at the lake and moving inland, with a peculiar emphasis on the letter E: Edina, Elizabeth, Elam, Emmaus, Enoch, Eschel, Ezekiel, Ezra . . . They must have had plans for a big town. Bethel and Shiloh Boulevards crossed at the central church complex, and there were diagonal streets crossing there as well, and a circular street around it. The park to one side. A city dedicated to God, the way they were all supposed to be.

"It was a kind of utopia," Tom said thoughtfully, blinking as he looked across the park in the direction of Dr. Dowie's big house, now a museum. "One of the last of the religious utopias started in America in the 1800s. One of the last started and one of the last still going. At least within the confines of the Christian Catholic Church of Zion, Illinois."

"Don't make fun."

"I'm not! It was a real accomplishment! In fact they had to break the laws separating church and state to do it. No drinking, no smoking, no gambling or card-playing . . . I even read a book that said they passed a law against jazz in the Twenties. But when I asked Dave about that, he got mad and said there had never been any such thing."

"I'm sure Dave knows more about music in Zion than any book."

"Me too. In the band for over seventy years!" He laughed with delight at the thought, spitting out white bits of chewed bread. "Incredible. I think"—he stopped, swallowed, looked serious—"I think Dave's the real heart of Zion. Not old Dowie." He waved a skinny arm at the museum.

"I don't see why you're so down on Dr. Dowie. He was a famous man, he did a lot to spread the word of God."

"Famous, anyway. The reincarnation of Elijah, as he decided—he certainly should be famous! He's even in Joyce's *Ulysses,* did you know that? I was looking through that book trying to read it when I came across him. I couldn't believe it!"

"So why don't you like him?"

"Well, have you seen those pictures of his church in Chicago? The walls are covered with the crutches of people he healed. Covered with them."

"So? He was a faith healer."

Tom shook his head violently. "Come on, Naomi. You know that faith healing is just what it says—a matter of faith. It's like Peter walking on the water. During the actual ceremony everyone's excited and crippled people really want to be healed, they believe it's happening and they're all pumped up and other people are standing, and so they channel every bit of strength into it, and everyone's encouraging them and so they stand and walk around a little, and everyone says they're healed. But the next day!" He blew out his cheeks. "Then it's like when Peter begins to doubt, and sinks like a stone. I'll bet you a whole bunch of those cripples woke up the next day and found they needed their crutches again, and where were they? Decorating the walls of Dr. Dowie's church! Trophies nailed up to show what a great healer he was! Pah!" He waved the big house away with both hands. "I don't like it."

"But Tom," Naomi said, troubled by this vision of the town founder. "Some people are healed by faith. I mean, Jesus did it all the time."

"Yes, I know. Healed the sick and everything else."

"But Tom! Don't you believe in Jesus?"

"Well . . . I don't know." He looked uncomfortable, troubled by the question, which Naomi could tell he had asked himself before.

"What do you believe in?" she asked, shocked.

"Well . . ." His left hand gathered up twigs, tossed them aside as if throwing coins in a toll booth hopper. "I guess what I think is . . ." He bogged down, looked at her tentatively. "I guess what I think now is, that when we talk about God, we're talking about a part of ourselves. God is inside us, right? We say that. And what I think is, there's a part of us that is better than our usual self—the animal selfishness and cruelty and all the rest. And we recognize that part in us, we know it's different, and we call it God. So that when we talk about Christ, what we mean is the part of us that loves, the part of us that helps to feed the poor and heal the sick and all like that, even if they're strangers. The part that says everyone on the planet is family."

Nodding, Naomi said, "But there's more to it than that. I mean Christ was a man who lived in Israel. He really did all those things."

Tom waggled a hand.

"You don't think so?"

"Well, he certainly did some things, sure. But which ones, exactly? You know how the commentaries Dave had us read said that the first three gospels were written about the same time, and then John wrote his a long time later. Now look at the differences in John's version! All the other three say that Christ walked over the water to the boat, and when he got in the winds died and they went on their way. But John! In John, Christ gets in the boat and they're instantaneously in the other town! I mean, am I supposed to believe that? It's teleportation! If it happened, why didn't the others mention it?"

"Maybe they forgot," Naomi said, wanting time to think.

"It sure isn't something I'd forget if it happened to me! It would've blown my mind! No, it's the kind of thing you write down forty years later, after a lifetime's remembering has heightened things a little. And then you read the rest of John and you see he was a real mystic, a space cadet in fact. I mean, have you read *Revelation?*"

"Yes I have."

Another uncontrollable horselaugh, apparently at the expression on her face. "It's crazy, you know it is! I mean the man was spaced! So how much am I supposed to believe? How much was embellished later?"

Naomi shook her head, bore down on the main point. "Dave says we should believe it all, and chalk up discrepancies to the problems people have in seeing and remembering complex and unusual events. It's true, you know—one time Mr. Delany arranged for some people to jump into class and tussle with him and run out, and afterwards when people told what they had seen, it was all different! He said that's why the police have such trouble with eyewitnesses. Everyone sees something slightly different, especially when something incongruous happens. Besides"—she poked the grass next to his restless hand—"all four of them reported a lot of the miracles, like feeding the five thousand or walking on water. They all reported it the same! How do you explain that?"

Tom shrugged, sighed. Naomi felt herself trembling, and she could see by Tom's hands that he was excited too, color high, thinking fast, really into it, and with a little quiver she thought, without articulating it to herself, finally someone as smart as me, finally someone to really talk to!

Tom said, "Maybe he was an alien, like I said. Member of an advanced race, come to teach us to live better. Impressing us with high tech."

Naomi shook her head decisively. "It's more than high tech. We're talking basic laws of physics here—time, gravity, matter coming from nothing—what kind of aliens are you talking about?"

"God-like aliens," he said, and laughed a little.

Naomi shook her head. "Either those men were walking around for three years hallucinating frequently, or else there was a being there outside the laws of nature—able to bend them at will! That's why

John was so spacy, Tom, I mean think about it—he spent three years of his life following a guy around who was constantly performing miracles, healing the sick, feeding people, raising the dead! Why, one time John went out to talk to him at night in the garden and he and his clothes and everything around him were a pure glowing white! Three years of that kind of thing is bound to make you a little mystical, you have to be fair to him. I mean he saw Jesus come back from the dead, talked to him after the crucifixion! And all those miracles—"

"Yes I know."

"Well? They were one of the main reasons people were so impressed by Jesus. He was a supernatural being. God, in fact. He said so all the time. Jesus Christ was God, the creator of the universe."

Tom frowned, shifted uncomfortably.

"Who else, if not God?"

The question stopped him; it seemed to fill the air, reverberating around the park. She could see that he was really thinking about it, and not just shunting it aside the way people did, to avoid the radical problem it presented. She liked that.

But he was troubled. Eventually he said, as if to push the whole thing away again, "Look, to be alien is to be *alien*. It might very well look supernatural to us, it might very well *be* supernatural, how can we say if our four dimensions are all there are? Time, space, gravity— there's no way to be sure these things can't be manipulated."

Naomi pinned him with a look. "Manipulated by God, sure! It's God you're talking about! You just use all that sci-fi stuff to skip the crux of the thing, the real question of do you believe or don't you. Come on, get serious!"

He was looking upset. "Well," he said querulously, "he disappeared from age eighteen to age thirty—maybe he went to India like they say and learned a bunch of yogi tricks."

"Yogis can't do what he did."

"They can walk on fire, that's kind of like—"

"They can do that because when you step on the coals you crush down a little layer that's nowhere near as hot as their middles, and then they hurry fast as they can."

"Maybe it's the same with water, you know, hotfoot to wetfoot."

"Stop joking!"

"I'm not joking," he cried, distressed. "I'm serious, I never joke!" Hoping to slide out of it with yet another one.

"I believe it," Naomi said sharply. "But it still comes out sounding like jokes. Which I find very sad indeed."

His mouth twisted, and suddenly, awkwardly, he grabbed his day-pack and lurched to his feet, then stalked away.

Speechlessly Naomi watched him leave. Oh shoot, she thought, I've hurt his feelings. She found she was trembling hard, and her lunch felt heavy and lumpy in her stomach.

She was furious at herself for hurting his feelings; but she was excited as well. To have a real conversation with someone, to really go all out and argue about important things without holding back as she always had to do with her teachers who would think her insolent, her parents who would think her rebellious, her friends who would think her conceited—it was exciting! Oh, if only she could make it up with him, and go on talking! Argue him back into belief, even. Or just be friends. Close friends. Close friends. Oh, she would have to make it up! She felt like she could. Like anything was possible.

She packed her things and walked downtown to the shops on Shoreline Drive, to do some desultory shopping for her father's birthday. Gang of mothers in Rooks's for coffee and gossip. Zion was still alive all right. Little nineteenth-century religious experiment . . . But not entirely, not any more. Zion was being inundated by greater Chicago, and signs of it were everywhere: crowds thick downtown, graffiti scrawled on the walls, more police, locked bicycles, evidence of vandalism, tales of theft, drug dealing, all the rest. A lot of cheap apartments had been thrown up in the last ten years, filled by the tide of people from the big city, many of them black, most of them poor, and Zion was changing. The little utopia, such as it was, retaken by the real world. Dikes broken. Islet in the flood. She walked on, looking in the windows. Could be just an ordinary American town now, Anywhere U.S.A. With all the emptiness that implied.

Then it was time for workout. Miz Hollins, their high school coach, ran summer workouts three afternoons a week, and everyone serious about being on the team had to come. Besides, it was fun. To clip the clear blue water and glide through that first lap without any effort at all, in a smooth rhythmic freestyle; it was one of the best moments of the day, and certainly one of the coolest.

Naomi's speciality was long-distance freestyle, mostly the 1,000 meters and the 1,500, unless they visited a twenty-five yard pool in which case she did the 1,650. So after a warm-up of sprints and IM work, she and Martha and Sandy were given pull buoys and put in the wall lane to grind out 2,500 meters, timing themselves every 500. Miz Hollins, a short, compact woman who had won a bronze medal in the breaststroke two Olympics before, gave them their instructions quickly and then went over to work with her real love, the sprinters. Barb, Simone, Jeanette: a loud lane. Jeanette was fast all right, but had no endurance at all. Anything over two hundred meters and Naomi had her beat. Tortoise and the hare.

As she swam the five hundreds she fell into the thoughtless trance-like state that was one of the reasons she enjoyed swimming. Glide along watching the bottom thinking slow, lazy thoughts. Thinking nothing. The fifty-meter pool was perfect for that; she stroked insulated in her own water world for so long that the appearance of the wall was a perpetual surprise, she had to remember how to do flip turns. Then it was off again. Remembering the day. The talk with Tom. Crutches on a wall. Hands with a rapid, neat movement (like the catch at the beginning of the pull), tearing brown bread. And the loaf never got smaller. Moving from group to group, stuffed to buzzing stillness with energy, atoms of his hands barely held together by the skin. Flip turn. The eye had to follow him. She imagined the process: God the Father and the Holy Ghost, trying to stuff Christ's spirit into a little human body, like fitting a water balloon into a small shoe. Push, heave, grunt, catch that spurt back out, finally the Ghost holds the child and the Father is jumping up and down to compress that last bit into his mouth, strain, heave, get all the pressures right and Pop! it's in there at last. And ever after he walks around fit to burst with it! A compression of everything: love, compassion, calm, indignation, anger, amusement, pride, energy. All human qualities intensified, concentrated in the red sentences among the black. Except the really bad ones. Evil not a natural part of us. If you read just the red sentences, Tom joked. Different book?

In the last 500 she was tired, arms like wood, and as her hands caught and pulled slowly down the midline she felt the water like butter or Jell-O about to set, something so thick and tangible that it was hard to believe it was clear. Such resistance—*of course* it might be possible to walk on it! Water was solid stuff; just increase the surface tension the slightest bit and crawl on up. . . . Feeling the thickness of the water and the lightness of her body, she felt she could almost do it herself. Belief. Or some sort of device. Magnetic fields. The nuclear power station down by the lake.

Afterwards Miz Hollins said, "Good pacing, Naomi—that last one was your fastest."

That's why they call it the crawl, coach.

Then in the changing room the IMers were talking about the latest Michael the Fox movie, and Jeanette and her clique were talking about a hot party in Waukegan, big deal, when Martha said to her, "Hey Nome, I think Tom Osborn is about to make his move on you."

Jeanette heard her and laughed. "Tom Osborn! He's such a nerd."

"He's not a nerd," Naomi said sharply. "He's just smart."

They all laughed at this, at the weakness of the defense, and what it said about how Naomi felt. Jeanette began to comb out her hair.

"Anyone smart in this town gets called a nerd," Naomi said bitterly.

Jeanette just laughed again, and the others joined her.

Simone said, "In that case Jeanette in no danger of her boys being called nerds, hey Jeannie?"

The other girls laughed, but this time at Jeanette; her latest was Frank Martin, the high school team's quarterback, who was a cutie and could throw a football a mile, but was notoriously stupid. It was said he could only remember four plays. Jeanette gave Simone a poisonous look and said, "True no matter how you define it. At least I only have one boyfriend at a time." But Simone walked off to the showers with a laugh, impervious, saying over her shoulder, "The more fool you." She was a cheerleader the same as Jeanette, and had more natural authority, being black and a little bit scary. The rest of the girls followed her lead and abandoned support for Jeanette's taunting.

In the showers Naomi gave Simone a grateful look and Simone

smiled, scrubbed soap into her wirebrush hair. No one could be prejudiced against Simone, she was too confident, too direct, too accomplished. We're prejudiced against black people, Naomi thought suddenly, because they are more beautiful than us. They have more presence. Black skin gleaming like some sort of fantastic wood . . . Naomi and Simone had almost the same figure, but inside black skin it looked a lot better—more muscular, fuller. Seeing Simone made Naomi feel better about herself.

After that (busy day), it was back to the band room for the dress rehearsal with the whole band, the adults coming from work in office suits and dresses, or construction site overalls, chattering and filling up the seats. A hundred members, Dave always told reporters, from twelve to eighty-six years old. Actually there were about seventy playing at any one time.

Naomi sat down and saw Tom walk in. He avoided looking in her direction and once in his seat he twisted to start up a conversation with the guys behind him, making them laugh. Naomi sighed, worried. This might turn out to be more difficult that she had thought.

Stragglers were still arriving, and the room was loud. Naomi put together her clarinet, thinking hard. She looked up and was surprised to see Dave, shuffling between music stands to her. He smiled briefly. "I want you to be sitting next to the oboe instead of the first flute tonight," he said, "so you and Tom can hear each other on the duet in 'American Eagle.' Here, just flip-flop the first clarinets."

So Naomi stood and awkwardly shifted between the row of cheap folding chairs and black metal stands, trading places with Bob Caspar. Penny and Doris switched the two inner seats, giggling as they bumped into each other. It occurred to Naomi that she had a duet with the first flute in "Holy, Holy, Holy" as well. She sat next to Tom. The room was quieting down, but Dave was discussing something with the percussion section, so they weren't going to start immediately. She turned to Tom and put a hand briefly on his thigh.

"I'm sorry about what I said at lunch," she said in a quick low voice. "It was stupid."

Tom looked surprised, pleased. You could read his face like a billboard.

She said, "I was . . ." and squinched up her mouth.

"That's okay," Tom said. "I was being stupid myself."

"I mean, I believe. . . ."

He nodded. "Sometimes I just talk, you know? Whatever occurs to me—"

"I like that," Naomi interjected.

"I shouldn't have walked off, that was dumb."

Naomi shook her head.

Tom grinned, obviously pleased by the turn of events. He flipped open the music to "American Eagle." "Shall we go over our part? It looks like Dave'll be a while yet."

They played the passage pianissimo, instruments slanted in together. Well, Naomi was thinking. What do you know. And all because of Dave moving me. Could he have known? She missed a sharp, concentrated. Have to play a bit louder than Tom in concert, to compensate for the oboe's penetrating timbre. Fun to play together. Music was . . . like swimming.

After rehearsal the whole band went to Rooks's to have dinner together. Naomi and Tom sat in a group of friends at one of the long tables, and joined in the chatter and horseplay. They said little to each other, but Naomi was constantly aware of his presence beside her. Occasionally their elbows or knees would bump; Tom was a gawky eater, and restless in his seat, shifting to find a more comfortable position or jerking back to splutter with sudden mirth, often at a joke that only he perceived. When they bumped he paid no attention to it, as if this were ordinary and not to be noted. Naomi talked to Martha and Doris and Penny about the swim team and Martha's upcoming trip to Door County and the Upper Peninsula, feeling a general glow. She saw Dave drifting between tables and talking to people. He didn't like to eat in public anymore, as he had trouble controlling his mouth. Besides it would have taken time away from the socializing. Naomi waved when he was looking their way, and ten minutes later he stopped behind them and talked for a bit. He smiled as he surveyed the crowded tables, and he seemed to glow with the contentment he always exhibited when the band was together. This was his life, right here, extending all through the town and back through the years—a four-dimensional creature, as Tom would say. The past alive in him like a lamp. All those bands, players, concerts.

The way he talked about tonight's concert was cute: "The old folks really love these things, the nurses say it's their best medicine." As if many of the people they would entertain tonight weren't actually younger than he was. But they had lost something he was still suffused with. He really did seem to glow, his old skin was spotted and sort of waxy and no doubt caught the light in a peculiar way, but she was sure she could see it. "A hundredth birthday, can you imagine! I'll bet they're proud tonight, those two. It's quite an accomplishment."

They talked of the two centenarians, both of whom had been born on exactly this day a hundred years before. All the papers had written up such a coincidence. "That means when they were your age it was still the 1800s," Dave said. "Horse and buggy to spaceships and moon landings, all in one life." He smiled at the thought. "We'll send them into their second century with a good concert."

They walked back across the park in a large straggling group. It was cooling off at last, and the late evening sun buttered the leaves on the tall trees. "Zion's only skyscrapers," Dave muttered as he shuffled beside Naomi, looking up at them with a pleased expression. Across the pond a crowd was gathering before the bandshell. It looked like a lot of them were in the middle of picnic dinners. The crickets were starting up in force, and frogs by the pond and mosquitoes around their ears added to the song of the Illinois summer evening.

When the front of the band reached the bandroom door there was a small commotion. "Hey!" someone said loudly. Then there was a rush inside and more cries. Dave tilted his head to the side curiously, and without discussing it he put a hand onto Naomi's offered forearm so he could walk faster.

By the time they entered the room the cries of alarm and outrage had mostly died away, and the members of the band were standing around in shock, looking fearfully at Dave. The room was a shambles, the floor covered with torn sheet music and tipped-over music stands, the drums punched through, the Sousaphones dented by kicks; and all the cubbyholes on the far wall were empty. Their instruments were gone.

Dave shuffled into the room, looking befuddled. He stopped to lay a trembling hand on the rim of the bass drum, his mouth turned down, his eyes searching the floor. Mr. Stevens the band manager approached him, face scarlet. "They've stolen all the smaller instruments," he said in a tight, angry voice. "And wrecked these."

Somebody was crying. Hands clenched at mouth. People stood stunned, staring at Dave sick with worry at how he might react.

"What will we do?" Mrs. Jackson said.

Dave stepped over to his podium. "Everyone sit down and start sorting out the sheet music," he said absently.

"All the music stores in Waukegan will be closed by now," Mr. Stevens said. Dave himself had owned a music store once—it would have come in handy now, but he had closed it years ago. "Besides, we don't have time. We'll have to postpone—"

"We won't postpone!" Dave said sharply. He was a gentle man these days, but oldtime members of the band said that when he was younger he had had quite a temper—you didn't want to make him angry with you. Now Naomi saw what they were talking about, just in the sound of his voice, the expression on his face. "It's those folks' one hundredth birthday today, you can't postpone that. We'll just have to make do. Sit down and get the music sorted out. Come on." A single imperious gesture.

So they sorted as he shuffled through the wreckage, inspecting the Sousaphones, poking his head in cubbyholes, pausing in corners, looking distant, pensive. People watched him anxiously. Everything suddenly seemed disorganized, pointless. When the sheet music was all picked up and sorted Mrs. Saunders, the pastor's wife, suggested they pray. Dave nodded impatiently and bowed his head, and they all did the same. "Dear Lord," he muttered, "hear us in an hour of need. Forgive the foolish vandals who did this, and help us find a way. For Jesus' sake amen." He raised his head, opened his eyes slowly, looked around. "Okay, what have we got left?"

They added it up: three of the five Sousaphones were still playable. Jack had had his trumpet with him. A piccolo in its tiny case had been overlooked, at the back of a cubbyhole. And two clarinets had been left in one of the practice rooms.

At the end of this wan reckoning Naomi saw Tom slowly straighten from a crouch on the far side of the room. He looked around the room for her, and when their gazes met he smiled sardonically. She shrugged, uncomfortable with the joke he was making. Dave was nodding in an absent-minded way. He fumbled in his pocket, got out his keys. "Alan, would you go in my office? The Christmas instruments are in there."

Tom caught Naomi's gaze again, rolled his eyes at the ceiling. But she noticed his hand was clenched hard over a music stand; and it seemed to her the air was becoming chill.

Dave said, "First let's change one of the Sousaphones into something more like a baritone, for Andrew." Keeping his best musicians equipped. "Here, everyone sit down in their proper places. We only have a little time. Jack, have you got two mouthpieces for your trumpet?"

"Four," Jack said.

"Good. Some of you check the practice rooms again, will you? Mouthpieces, parts, anything. And some of you should start moving the piano out to the bandshell, we're going to need it. I'll get Gloria out of the audience to play."

They brought him the least damaged Sousaphone, and he directed them to take off the last part of the bell, and replace the mouthpiece with a trumpet mouthpiece. "It fits if you tighten these here. I learned this down at the Orange Parade when we lost the baritones. Try that, Andrew. No, you have to blow hard to get it up an octave. Really hard. There you go."

Alan and Terry came out of Dave's office carrying the Christmas instruments: a tambourine, maracas, a big heavy set of jingle bells, a grinder that spun on a stick, polished coconut shells to make the sound of horses' hooves, a small glockenspiel, and some plastic slide whistles. Also some New Year's Eve instruments, in the form of a dozen kazoos and noisemakers.

Dave inspected these, handed back his keys. "Out in the trunk of my car is a case of instruments I use when I visit the elementary schools. Mostly toys, I'm afraid, but that's okay." It was amazing he was still allowed to drive, Naomi thought. He went fast, too. Frowning with concentration, he said, "Kathy, Linda, Jerry, get scissors and rubber bands out of my desk drawer and cut pieces from the bass drumheads. You should be able to re-head a snare drum at least, and you can rubber-band other pieces around the end of valve tubes, they'll be like bass kazoos."

There were worried faces everywhere now, a kind of basic confusion, as people contemplated the bizarre instruments Dave was proposing; they were afraid of making fools of themselves. Naomi and Tom worked side by side, feeling an entirely different sort of fear, afraid to look at each other, afraid to look up at Dave. The air was cold. . . .

Dave wandered, threading the bustle slowly. He sat at his podium and showed them how pieces of the drumheads could be wrapped over valve tubes from the Sousaphones, and when the extra mouthpieces were stuck in them, they could indeed be played like big kazoos. They laughed shakily as he demonstrated. "Dave, how do you know how to make these?"

"All kinds of things will make music. Here, try that."

And then the trombone players came in from the church in a rush, waving long thick plastic tubes they had found in a back room. No one had ever seen these tubes before, nor was it clear what they were for. Blowing in them made a deep hoot. Dave nodded. "Blow some into the drums, it'll make them louder." It did; they sounded like foghorns.

Dave stood again, wandered around as they figured out what sounded like what, and who would play what, and worked on the drums. Then he stopped suddenly and said "Alan, Terry, did you look in my bottom drawer?"

"They're still out at your car, Dave."

"Oh yes." He shuffled into his office, came back out with an armful of wooden recorders of all sizes, nodding to himself. "Naomi, you and Penny take the clarinets, and the rest of the clarinets and saxes take these. Tom, you take this one." He gave Tom the shortest recorder.

Naomi and Tom's eyes met again, very briefly. Tom was shaking; he took the recorder reluctantly, and then held it between two fingers at arm's length, as if it might burn him like dry ice. Where in the world. . . . Naomi could feel herself quiver, it seemed to her the light in the room had changed and was coming from all directions at once, somehow. Those recorders . . . it was cold! Did only Tom and she notice? People went a section at a time into the uniform rooms to suit up. She couldn't swallow well, couldn't move the corners of her mouth. She had to bite down on her mouthpiece to feel it. Honks, thumps, the tinkling of the glockenspiel. "Jack," Dave said, "you'll have to mute your trumpet or we won't be able to hear anyone else." Then blinked, looked confused, smiled. "We used to say that to my brother Bob, years ago, as a joke." He and four of his brothers had formed a saxaphone quintet, one each for bass, baritone, tenor, alto and soprano; Bob had played alto until killed in a car accident, decades ago. "His sax is still around here somewhere. . . ." He searched stiffly through the cupboards under the cubbyholes, helped by the whole sax section. They found it deep in the back of a cupboard. Helplessly Naomi looked to Tom, saw him looking for her, saw his wild eye and a scared grin fixed on his face. *Where?* Seriously frightened now, she thought *No more, please.* She and Tom sat down together and tried the duet from "American Eagle," shaking in the cold so that they could hardly play. "I've never played a recorder in my life," Tom babbled, staring at the small wooden thing in his hands, turning it around to inspect it. "Simple fingering, I'll say that." He put it to his mouth gingerly and ran up and down a scale.

"Let's try to tune," Dave said. "One at a time. We'll use the glockenspiel's C. Come on, sit down, we don't have much time. First the regular instruments."

They tuned themselves to the *bing* of the glockenspiel, with difficulty, alternating between fits of laughter and anxiety. Alan and Terry returned with the case of children's instruments. The drummers pounded happily at a repaired drum, improvised cymbals and a triangle. Finally Dave had them all play their tuning note. Weird blatting *Huhmmmmm* . . . He shook his head, frowned, smiled his slight inward smile. "Well," he said, "it'll be different."

They trailed out to the bandshell in the silence of collective fright, clutching their new instruments and staying close to each other. Not a peep. Dave led them, glowing in his white conductor's uniform with the flat-topped cap, stepping high as he did in the Labor Day parade every year. Surge of adrenaline temporarily shoring up those damaged old nerves. Up the back steps and into the bandshell. A Midwestern bandshell in the summer dusk, the park around them a furry crickety black, fireflies scoring the distant trees, the stars all smeary, the faces of the audience lit by the light of the shell, pale blobs uplifted and attentive. The old folks in the front row looked unaware that anything was wrong, all clustered around the two wheel-chaired centenarians whose laps were heaped with bouquets, all looking happy and expectant. Behind them the rest of the audience had pressed in closer; no doubt they had heard somehow, the word spreading quickly through them as they sat on the cooling grass waiting. Now their faces had the look you see on people listening to a young performer in a first recital, encouraging and anxious. Naomi looked up at the white half-dome overhead. They would need the shell's amplification tonight. Half near and white, half distant and black. Naomi shut her eyes. Calm spinning in a restless crowd, the touch of a hand. Dave ticked his baton on the music stand.

Inevitably the first march, "Atlantic Seaboard," was ragged and out of tune, their sound weaker and rougher than usual, and just plain strange. Naomi felt her cheeks burn and her heart pump and she thought We can't keep on like this! But then Dave raised his other hand and began conducting two-handed, as if drawing attention to himself. He had a stern expression on his face, and his eyes darted from player to player, commanding them to watch him. He gestured for more volume from each of the players who still had a real instrument, including Naomi; he looked her eye-to-eye for a moment and she felt a little jerk, and played on at double-forte even though her music said mezzo-forte. And over to the side Dave's daughter Gloria was pounding away with all ten fingers on the piano, she had backed up all kinds of lame church ensembles in her time and knew what to do to fill in gaps. Lot of experience between those two, hundreds of concerts played and little could shake them anymore. Naomi played louder still. Then it was over and the band sat back in their seats with a collective gulp. The applause from out in the dark was loud, warm, supportive. Dave gave them no time to think, but went immediately into "Onward Christian Soldiers," smiling his little inward smile, hand bobbing in the clear vigorous 1-2-3-4 motion. The people playing the slide whistles began to get a gauge on the little plungers. Dave gestured for the row of trombone players, trou-blemakers to a man, to blow louder into their bizarre assortment of plastic tubes and valve slides; they thumped in behind Andrew on his alto Sousaphone, and Naomi could see their eyes grinning as they heard themselves provide the bass line. Fear shifting into something akin to it, but different.

After that they did "Semper Fidelis" and Dave had Jack uncork his trumpet for the solo, and then Naomi and Penney led the piccolo and penny-whistles through the high addition, and lastly the trombone boys joined in and powered through the bass addition, and they all marched through the last chorus and the coda in fine spirits, and they were off at last. All of them focused on Dave, which was only normal with a band and its conductor, but now it was his pleasure they needed to see, that they relied on. The way he enjoyed it, the way it was his whole life! After all there were his trembling hands suddenly as steady as a magician's, and if he could do that why should these new strange instruments be any obstruction to them? Most only took singing or humming the tune anyway, and as for the rest, a kind of heightened ability to concentrate flowed from the look on Dave's face: watching him Naomi thought she could feel what a redemption music was from ordinary existence, how much singing was like praying. And then they were in "American Eagle," and playing the duet with Tom she noticed that he was not playing the written music at all, but a higher improvised part of his own, his tone penetrating with a nerve-racked vibrato. He continued to improvise after the duet was over, and in "Holy, Holy, Holy" he kept doing it, exploring the upper limits of his new recorder. Dave smiled to hear it, and then suddenly in the last great chorus of the hymn Tom was off and floating above the rest of them, in a pure clear descant. It was the reverse of the band's normal sound—usually the group as a whole had a clear sound, and the oboe cut through that with its double-reeded buzz— but now with half of them playing kazoos or honking into plastic tubes, it was the band that had a furry, buzzing, bagpipey timbre, and Tom with his little recorder who had the clear tone, a pure sweet sound that he was discovering as he played above them. Dave had them do "Amazing Grace" out of order because it too had a high floating harmony for oboe, and he shushed them all and looked to Tom to play up a bit, and Tom took off in a flying clear peaceful melody, and Naomi glanced sideways at Tom's face and saw he was staring amazed at Dave, as round-eyed as if he had his fingers knuckle-deep in Christ's palms.

And then they played "The Yellow Rose of Texas" and "When Johnnie Comes Marching Home Again," and "The Stars and Stripes Forever," in which Sheila Matthews played the piccolo solo perfectly for the first time in her life, without a trace of the fright that usually incapacitated her; and they played "Washington Post," and "Columbia, the Gem of the Ocean," and "The New Colonial," and "The Battle Hymn of the Republic," and lastly "America the Beautiful," which Dave always declared should be the national anthem, and over the sound of the band Naomi could just hear some members of the audience singing along like ghosts; her cheeks flushed at the sound.

And then the concert was over and the band was standing and walking around hugging each other and hugging Dave, and shaking Tom's hand and Sheila's too, and the trombone section was doing their part from "Semper Fidelis" as an impromptu encore, laughing and swinging their tubes back and forth in unison. Then off the stage and out of the shell, to mingle with the crowd, which was mostly friends, family, acquaintances. Part of a community. Dave walked around overlooking the scene with the same small smile of contentment he always wore after a concert. The trombone section marched through the crowd in Preservation Hall style, playing "Hold That Tiger."

After a while Naomi and Tom returned to the stage and sat in their chairs, leaned back exhausted. Under her stiff uniform jacket Naomi could feel the sweat running over her ribs. "You see?" she said to him under the din. "A miracle." She poked him hard in the leg to show she was serious. Her hands were still shaking.

"True," he said, nodding easily. Then: "That was my kind of miracle, though—we made happen it ourselves, you see?"

"Dave made it happen."

"Sure," he said, nodding again. She had never seen him look so relaxed and happy, it was as if he would agree to anything she said. "Dave made us believe we could do it. Faith, like you say."

"Faith in God, too."

He assented easily. "Faith in God. But, you know—nothing really . . . supernatural."

"Oh come on! Instruments were showing up none of us had ever seen! What about those recorders?"

He frowned, stared at the instrument still held loosely in his right hand. "Well . . . they must have come from somewhere, surely."

"Have you ever seen them before tonight?" she demanded.

"No, can't say I have." He grinned broadly, stared cross-eyed at the recorder. "Maybe I better keep this!"

She had to laugh. And he threw back his head and honked like the trombone players. "Whatever!" he said. "Whatever happened, it's ours."

And later they walked down to the shore of the pond together, still in their band uniforms. In the close warm dark summer night, crickettsong creaking underfoot. And in one pause, very awkwardly, Tom leaned down to give her a kiss, and she was quick enough to meet him halfway. Brief touch of the lips, the warmth of the other. After that they held hands, and walked the pond's edge away from the darkened bandstand.

Tom laughed softly. "That was so great. I mean, we really sounded good."

"After the first couple, anyway."

"Oh yeah. That first one—" They laughed. "Horrible!"

"I didn't think we were going to be able to get through."

"But later!" Tom disengaged his hand to wave it around, jerking with excitement. "I couldn't even believe it."

"It was a miracle," Naomi said, mostly to herself. She gave herself a shivery hug.

They stopped at the pond's end and looked back down the length of the park. Over black trees rose a sickle moon. For a second she felt a cold touch of premonition; she knew this too would end, time would pass, and she saw snatches in her mind's eye—of saying good-bye as they left for different colleges—of the trembling stilled at last, struggling against darkness on the afternoon of a Christmas concert until hearing a voice saying It's all right, Dave, the band's all right. . . . These things would come. But at that moment, standing side by side in the close summer night, the memory of the music fresh in their bodies, still *felt*—she knew that it was all worth it, that music and community and love redeemed all the trembling and pain and grief there were. To lift off and soar like that! A miracle in Zion. Big hands moving quickly, neatly, tearing away chunks of brown bread, filling a basket with a frayed upper rim and a hole in one side, the laughing eyes meeting yours in the baking sun, the loaf getting smaller but not getting smaller, still there, still spongy and brown under those deft hands that moved so deliberately despite their speed, no trick possible, nothing to it: but the hungry were fed, the sick were healed, the lame could walk and the blind see. Ah God, yes, please! If it happened once. . . .

God's grace. Or a dream we once had, a shared dream, to help those who need it. To heal the sick. The best part of our selves. Naomi looked up at Tom's horsey face, took his hand; she didn't have to decide tonight. Hands breaking bread, moving quickly, neatly. Giving. A miracle in Zion. Go you and do likewise.

"And when they were come out of the ship, straightaway they knew *him*, and ran through that whole *region* round about, and began to carry about *in beds* those that were sick, where they heard he was.

"And whithersoever he entered, into villages, or cities, or country, they laid the sick in the streets, and besought him that they might touch if it were but the border of his garment: and as many as touched him were made whole."

The Translator

Owen Rumford had a breakfast of postage stamp glue and mineral water. Combination of a rather strict diet and the fact that it was time again to send the bills to all the citizens of Rannoch Station. Rumford himself had had the stamps printed, and now he carefully counted out payment for them and shifted the money from the tavern's register to the postmaster strongbox, kept under the bar. A bit silly using stamps at all, since Rumford was the mailman as well as the postmaster—also the town's banker, tavern and hotel keeper, judge, and mayor. So he would be delivering the bills himself. But he liked stamps. These had a nice picture of Rannoch seen from space, all gray ocean with a chunk of onyx in it. Besides, in a town as small and isolated as Rannoch Station it was important to keep up the proprieties. Good for morale. Must, however, consider upgrading the quality of the stamp glue.

A quiet morning in the empty tavern. Hotel above empty as well; nothing had come in to the spaceport in the last few days. Unusual. Rumford decided to take advantage of the rare lull and go for a walk. On with his heavy orange overcoat. Tentlike. Rumford was a big man, tall and stout. Big fleshy face, cropped black hair, big walrus moustache that he tugged at frequently, as he did now while bidding a brief farewell to his daughters. Out into the stiff cold onshore wind. Felt good.

Down the black cobblestones of Rannoch Station's steep main street. Hellos to Simon the butcher, chopping away at a flank of mutton; then to the McEvoys, who helped administer the mines. Pleasant sound of construction behind the general store, tinsmiths and stonemasons banging and clacking away. Then left at the bottom of the street where it crossed the stream, up the track of hard black mud until he was out of the town and on the low hills overlooking the sea.

All views on the planet Rannoch were a bit dark. Its sun, G104938, known locally as the Candle, cast a pale and watery light. And the hills of Rannoch Island—the planet's only continent, located in subarctic latitudes—were composed mostly of black rock, mottled with black lichen and a bit of black bracken, all overlooking a dark sea. The dirt between stones had a high component of carbon ash, and even the perpetual frost on the bracken had gray algae growing in it. In short, only the white wrack thrown onto the black sand by the black waves gave any relief to the general gloom. It was a landscape you had to learn to be fond of.

Rumford had. Sniffing at the cold wind he observed with satisfaction the waves mushing onto the beach below the town. All the dories out fishing except the spavined ones, drawn up above the high tide mark. Town sitting above them nice and cozy, tucked into the crease made by the stream's last approach to the sea, to get out of the perpetual wind. Houses and public buildings all made of round black stones, some cracked open to reveal white quartz marbling. Materials at hand. Roofs were tin, glinting nicely in the low rays of the late morning sun. Tin mined here for local use, not for export. They had found deposits of the ore next to the big manganese mines. Easy to work it. Slag heaps inland of the town just looked like more hills, fit in very nicely in fact. Helped block the wind. Bracken already growing on them.

Altogether satisfactory. "A wild and unearthly place," as the song said. Rumford remembered trees from his childhood on a faraway planet, name forgotten. Only thing he missed. Trees, wonderful things. Would be nice for the girls. He'd told them tales till they'd cried for trees, for picnics in a grove, even though they hadn't the slightest. Flowering ones, perhaps. Grow in the ravines the streams cut, perhaps. Out of the wind. Worth thinking about. Damned difficult to get hold of, though; none native to this star cluster, and they were something traders out here didn't usually deal in. A shame.

Rumford was still thinking of trees when the steep black waves sweeping onto the town beach burst apart, revealing a submarine craft apparently made to roll over the sea floor. Big, dull green metal, lot of wheels, a few small windows. Some of the Ba'arni again, making a visit. Rumford frowned. Bizarre creatures, the Ba'arni. Inscrutable. It was obvious to Rumford that they were as alien to Rannoch as humans were, though he'd never gotten a Ba'ar to admit it. Good traders, though. Fishing rights for plastics, metal nodules gathered off seafloor for refined product, deep sea oddities for machine parts and miscellaneous utensils. Still, what they got from Rannoch Station wasn't enough to sustain an undersea colony. And how start it?

Aliens were strange.

The sea tank rolled above the high water mark and stopped. Door on one side clanked open, becoming a ramp. Three Ba'arni trotted out, one spotted him and they veered, trundled toward him. He walked down to meet them.

Strange looking, of course. The fishermen called them sea hippos, talked about them as if they were intelligent ocean-going hippopotami, nothing more. Ludicrous. The usual fallacy when dealing with aliens: think of them as the terran species they most resemble. Let it go at that. Rumford snorted at the idea. Really only the heads looked like hippos. Bodies too of course, to a limited extent. Massive, foursquare, rounded, etc. But the analogy held up poorly when you examined the fine bluish fur, the squat dextrous fingers on all four feet, and of course the row of walnut-sized excrescences that protruded from their spines. Purpose unknown. Like mushrooms growing out of their backs. Not a pleasant sight.

Then again the pictures of hippos Rumford had seen were none too beautiful. Still, in hippos' eyes, even in pictures, you could see something you could understand. Expression maybe hostile, but perfectly comprehensible. Not so with a Ba'ar. Faces quite hippo-like, sure. Giant faces, butt ugly as the fishermen said. The eyes did it—round and big as plates, and almost as flat. And with a look in them you just couldn't read. Curious, that. The fishermen claimed to see them swimming free in the depths, above seafloor mansions of great size. That was after they'd had a few, but still. Obviously alien to Rannoch, nothing more advanced than bracken here. At least on the land. Different in the planet-wide ocean, perhaps; evolutionary advances all submarine, perhaps down in tropics? Impossible to say. But probably visitors, like the humans. Urge to travel fairly widespread among intelligent species. Spaceships filled with seawater. Funny thought.

The three Ba'arni stopped before Rumford. The one on the left opened his voluminous mouth and made a short sequence of whistles and clicks. From experience Rumford knew this was the usual greeting given him, meaning something like "Hello, trading coordinator." Unfortunately, he usually relied on his translation box to make the actual sound of his response, and though he knew what it sounded like he didn't find it easy making the sounds himself. And the box was back at the tavern.

He gave it a try and made the first few clicks that the box emitted when he typed in his usual hello. Then he added another click-combination, meaning, he thought, "Trade, interrogative?"

The Ba'ar on the left replied swiftly. Trade negative, he appeared to say. Something else, well, Rumford had relied too often on the box to do the exact listening, but it seemed to him they were referring to the box itself.

Rumford shrugged. Only one course. He tried the whistle for translation, added the English words "Rannoch Station," and pointed to the town.

Agreement clicks from the spokesBa'ar.

Sonic booms rolled over the hills. They all looked up; Rannoch's gray sky was split by white contrails. Landing craft, coming down in a very steep descent from orbit, toward the town's spaceport a couple miles inland. Rumford identified the craft by their extreme trajectory. Iggglas.

Then an extraordinary thing happened; all three of the Ba'arni rose up on their hind legs and took swipes at the sky, roaring louder than the sonic booms.

A bad sign. One time it had taken a shotgun blast to get a pack of Iggglas off a lone Ba'ar outside the tavern. Never understood the motive; only time he had ever seen the two species together. Not a good omen. And if the Ba'arni needed translation help—

The three of them returned to all fours with a distinct thump, then more or less herded Rumford down the track to the town. Not much chance of disagreement with them; they were remarkably fast on their feet, and must have weighed a couple of tons each. Drafted.

Rumford entered his tavern and got the translation box from the shelf behind the bar. It was an old bulky thing, in many ways obsolete; you had to type in the English half of things, and it would only translate between English and the alien languages in its program—no chance of any alien-to-alien direct contact. Made for some trouble in the tavern.

Without explanation to his daughters he was out the door. Again the Ba'arni herded him up the street. Quickly they were out of town in the other direction, onto the stony windswept road leading to the spaceport and the mines beyond.

They were still hurrying up this road, the Ba'arni moving at a brisk trot and Rumford loping, when they came round a hill and ran into a party of Iggglas. A dozen or so of them, flapping about the road and squawking loudly. The Ba'arni froze in their tracks and Rumford stumbled to a halt out in front of them.

He shuddered as he always did on first sight of an Igggla. They were beyond ugly; they were . . . well, beyond words. Languages, human languages at any rate, depend a great deal on analogies. Most abstract ideas are expressed by sometimes hidden analogies to physical things and processes, and most new things are described by analogies to older things. Naturally all these analogies are to things within human ken. But analogies to the human realm largely broke down when dealing with the Iggglas, for there was simply nothing to compare them to.

Still, Rumford thought. Analogies all we have, after all. Especially for things alien. So the Iggglas were inevitably compared to vultures, because of body configuration. Fine except that their skins were covered by a white mucous substance instead of feathers. And their wings were not so much for flying as for hitting things. And their heads were distinctly fishlike, with long underslung jaws that made them resemble gars. Vultures with gars' heads, covered in whitish mucus: fair enough, only the analogy didn't really do justice to their sickening quality. Because above all they were *alien,* weird and hideous beyond appearance alone. Not even sure they occupied the same reality as other creatures; they seemed to *flicker* a little, as if disturbing the membrane between their physical realm and ordinary spacetime. Yes; disgusting. Next to them the Ba'arni seemed handsome beasts. Almost family one might say.

Rumford stepped forward to offer some kind of greeting to the Iggglas, make sure the Ba'arni didn't have to. Touchy situation. He had dealt with Iggglas before; they came from the next planet in, and used Rannoch Station as a trade center. Trade again. Remarkable what kind of thing it put you in contact with, out in this stellar group. Certainly had to get used to these creatures. Language of theirs very loud and squawky. Every once in a while they'd spit in each other's mouths for emphasis. Some kind of chemical transfer of information. Box wasn't equipped to deal with that, luckily. Their speech was enough, although it appeared to be an odd grammar. Lacked tenses, or even verbs for that matter. Another indication of different reality.

The Iggglas liked to stick out a claw and shake humans by the hand, maybe to see if they would vomit. But Rumford could do it with hardly a quiver. No worse than a cockroach in the hand, certainly. So he shook hands with the wet claw of the biggest Igggla. Hot bodies, high metabolism. It turned its head to the side to inspect him with its left eye. Foul smell, like asafoetida.

Two of the other Iggglas led a long string of little furball creatures, a bit like rabbits without legs, up to the one Rumford had shaken hands with. Rumford sighed. Probably the high metabolisms, but still. Note the others weren't doing it—

Abruptly the biggest one snapped that gar's head down and devoured the first rabbit-thing in line, swallowing it whole so that it disappeared instantly, as in a conjuring trick. The Igggla would interrupt itself to do the same throughout the rest of the interview. It made Rumford nervous.

The Igggla squawked loudly and at length. "Croownekkksee-trun-p!" it sounded like. Rumford turned on the translator, switched it to *Iggglas* and typed in the message, *"Again, please."*

After a short interval the box made a short screech. With a loud honk and a quick drumming of its talon-like feet, the big Igggla squawked its initial message again.

A moment later a message appeared in print on the small screen of the translator box. *"Hunger interrogative."*

The Igggla batted one of the worried-looking rabbit-things forward.

"No thank you," Rumford typed steadily, and waited for the box to speak. Then: *"Why do you come to Rannoch interrogative."*

The head Igggla listened to the box's hooting, did a quick hopping dance, struck one of the other Iggglas in the head, and replied.

The box's screen eventually produced a sentence. *"Warlike viciously now descendant death fat food flame death."*

A typical grammatical artifact produced by the box when dealing with the Iggglas. Rumford pondered it, switched the box to *Ba'arni*, and typed in *"The Iggglas express a certain hostility toward the Ba'arni."*

The box whistled and clicked in the oddly high-pitched Ba'arni language. The Ba'ar on the left, which was not the same one that had spoken to Rumford at first, whistled and clicked in reply. The box's screen printed out, *"Tell them we are ready to (x-click B-flat to C-sharp click sequence; see dictionary) and the hateful poison birds will die in traditional manner."*

Hmm. Problems everywhere. With the Iggglas you got grammatic hash. With Ba'arni, too many trips to the dictionary. Which was a problem in itself. The box was not entirely satisfactory, and that was the truth.

Needed to be seated to type on the keyboard properly, too. So, despite the fact that it might seem undignified, Rumford sat on the ground between the two parties of aliens, called up the Ba'arni dictionary function of the box, and typed in an inquiry. The definition appeared quickly:

"X-click B-flat to C-sharp click sequence: 1. Fish market. 2. Fish harvest. 3. Sunspots visible from a depth of 10 meters below the surface of the ocean on a calm day. 4. Traditional festival. 5. Astrological configuration in galactic core."

Rumford sighed. The Ba'arni dictionary could be nearly useless. Never sure if it was really serious. No idea who actually wrote the thing. Basic programming provided by linguists working for the company that made the box, of course, but in the years since then (and it was a very old box), its various owners had entered new information of their own. In fact this one was jammed with languages that factory-new boxes didn't have. No other box Rumford had seen had a Ba'arni program; that was why Rumford had bought this one when it was offered by a passing spacecraft pilot. But who in fact had added the Ba'arni program? Rather puckish individual, from the look of it. Or perhaps the Ba'arni relied more than most on context. Some languages like that. Impossible to be sure. The box had worked to this point, and that was all Rumford could say about it. Trade a different matter, however. Not quite as delicate as this.

After thinking it over, Rumford typed in another question to the Ba'arni. *"Clarification please. What do you mean by x-click B-flat to C-sharp click sequence, in context of previous sentence interrogative."*

The Ba'arni listened and the one on the left replied.

"Ba'arni and poison birds fight war in (z-click double sequence; see dictionary) cycle that now returns. Time for this ritual war."

Very good. Clear as a bell. Unfortunate message, of course, but at least he understood it. Must have meant definition four, perhaps tied to the timing of three, or five. Add new definition later.

Before he could convey the Ba'arni sentiments to the Iggglas, the chief Igggla ate another rabbit-thing, danced in a circle and screeched for quite some time. The box hummed a bit, and the screen flickered.

"Fine fiery wonderful this land always again war's heat slag battlefield dead fat food flame death yes now."

Rumford squinted at the screen.

Finally he typed in, *"Clarification please: where is location of ritual war interrogative,"* and sent it to the Iggglas.

The chief Igggla replied at length, howling shrilly.

On the screen: *"Fine fiery wonderful this land always again war's heat slag battlefield dead fat food flame death yes now yes."*

The Iggglas were not much on clarification.

Rumford decided to ask the same of the Ba'arni, and switched the box over. *"Clarification please: where is location of ritual war interrogative."*

The box whistled, the Ba'ar on the left clicked. The screen flickered and printed out: *"Clarification unnecessary as poison birds know every twelve squared years for twelve cubed years ritual dodecimation has taken place on same ritual ground. Tell them to stop wasting time. We are ready for conflict."*
A small vertical line appeared between Rumford's eyebrows.

He switched back and forth from Iggglas to Ba'arni, asking questions concerning this ritual war, explaining that the questions were essential for proper translation. Every Iggglas answer a long string of violent nouns, adjectives, and so forth, with never a verb. Every Ba'arni answer a hunt through the dictionary. Slowly Rumford put together a picture of Ba'arni and Iggglas contingents battling each other. Ritual phrases from the Ba'arni concerned *Air people opposition water people destruction land,* and so on. The Iggglas concentrated on *fat food,* although obviously it was a ritual for them as well—a sort of game, from the sounds of it. The origins of such a curious conflict remained completely obscure to Rumford; some things the Ba'arni said seemed to indicate that they may have had a religious ceremony of coming out onto land in great numbers during maximum sunspot activity, and that for many cycles now the Iggglas had been there to transform this ceremony into a bloody battle. Possibly indicating that the Ba'arni were in fact not native to Rannoch, as Rumford has speculated earlier. But he couldn't be sure. No way of knowing, really. Accident, misunderstanding; no doubt they themselves didn't have the faintest anymore.

In any case ritual war well established, this was clear. And either during or after the battle—sequentiality was difficult to determine, given the lack of tenses in the Iggglas—the two belligerent forces apparently torched, in a kind of sacrifice, the profane land they fought on.

Hmm. Rumford sat cross-legged on the ground between the two groups, thinking. Rannoch Station had only been there for the past thirty years or so. All that carbon in their dirt, sign of great fires in the past. But mining geologists said no vulcanism. Tremendous heat, one said. Solar flares? Or weapons. Tremendous heat. Tin would melt. It was possible. And after all, here they were.

Rumford cleared his throat. Sticky. He hesitated for a bit, and would have hesitated more, but some thirty sets of alien eyes (counting the rabbit-things) stared fixedly at him, and impelled him to action. He tugged his moustache. Sunspots underwater, astrology . . . really a shame he didn't know more about these creatures. Now where was he? Ah yes— Ba'arni had indicated readiness for conflict. We are ready for conflict. The line between his eyebrows deepened, and finally he shrugged. He clicked the box over to *Iggglas* and typed away.

"Ba'arni explain that their priest-caste have performed submarine astrology which contra-indicates ritual war this time. Request war be postponed until next scheduled time twelve squared Rannoch years from now in order to achieve proper equilibrium with the stars."

The box honked that out in a series of Iggglasian words. All the Iggglas listeners snapped their big gar jaws as they heard it, then leaped in circles thrashing the dust. Several of the rabbit-things disappeared. The chief Igggla hopped toward Rumford and shrieked for a long while.

On the screen: *"War heat slag death fat food exclamation. Delay impossible war as scheduled astrology stupid exclamation."*

Rumford tugged his moustache. Not gone over so well. The three Ba'arni were staring at him curiously, waiting for him to translate what the Iggglas had just so vehemently squawked. The line between his eyebrows deepened even more. Ba'arni had visited him more frequently in last year. Now what had they been trading for?

He switched the box to Ba'arni, typed *"Iggglas state that they do not want ritual war to take place this time. They note the Ba'arni are suffering famine and therefore population difficulties. Thus ritual dodecimation could lead to extinction of Ba'arni and end of beloved war for Iggglas. They suggest skipping this time and returning to war next twelve squared years."*

A lot of clicks and whistles to convey that. The Ba'arni retreated and conferred among themselves, while the Iggglas squawked derisively at them. Rumford watched anxiously. Ba'arni had been trading rather actively for foodstuffs. Brow needed wiping. He tugged on his moustache. The Ba'arni returned in a new line-up and the one on the left clicked.

On screen: *"Ba'arni completely capable of sustaining their part in (x-click B-flat to C-sharp click sequence; see dictionary). Ba'arni (z-click z-click; see dictionary) insist ritual be carried out as always. Poison birds will die."*

Rumford let out a deep breath, switched the box to dictionary function and inquired about z-click z-click.

"*Z-click z-click: 1. (double n-1 click sequence, B-flat; see dictionary). 2. Magnetic sense located in supra-spinal nerve nodules. 3. Eggs. 4. Large bearings. 5. Sense of place or of location. 6. Money.*"

Nothing there seemed completely appropriate, so he tried looking up double n-1 click sequence, B-flat.

"*Double n-1 click sequence, B-flat: 1. (q-click A-flat; see dictionary). 2. Honor. 3. Pride. 4. Shame. 5. Face. 6. Molar teeth.*"

Bit of an infinite regress there, could have you jumping around the dictionary forever. Definitely a prankster, whoever had entered this language in the box. But assume the Ba'arni meant some kind of pride, saving face, that kind of thing. Made sense. Every species must have a version of the concept. Fine. Assume clarification on that front. Now, where was he with the Iggglas? Looking fairly ready for an answer, they were. Rumford pursed his lips so hard that his moustache tips almost met under his chin. Astrologer bit not gone over very far. Iggglas pretty aggressive types. He clicked over to Iggglas and typed away.

"*Ba'arni live by submarine astrologer's divine words and intend to decline ritual war. Iggglas insistence will make no difference. Ba'arni have assured this by placement of heat bombs on floor of all seas on Iggglas. Twelve squared heat of weapons used in ritual war. If Iggglas insist on ritual war Ba'arni have no choice but to escalate to total war and annihilate Iggglas seas. Apologies but astrologers insist.*"

While the box spoke this message in Iggglas (and how was it doing it without verbs?), Rumford pulled a handkerchief from his coat pocket and wiped his brow. Uncommonly warm. Hunger made him feel a bit weak. Have to start eating breakfasts.

The Iggglas began to squawk among themselves very vigorously, and Rumford took a quick glance down at the screen to see if the box was translating their squabble. It was, although apparently it was having problems with the fact that two or three of the Iggglas were always speaking at the same time: "*Lying fat food no meteor shower maybe total war then purpose ambiguous no exclamation one miss translator liar idiot meteor shower no explanation maybe box direct Iggglas fat food why not meteor shower maybe,*" and so on. Rumford tried to direct one eye to the screen and the other to the hopping Iggglas. Looked like the second-largest one might be making the comments about the translator and the box. Yes, even pointing at him as he spat in leader's mouth. Problem.

The Ba'arni were whistling among themselves, so Rumford quickly typed in another message to the Iggglas:

"*Ba'arni wish to deal with senior Igggla, suggest that perhaps second-biggest Igggla is one qualified to speak for Iggglas in this matter.*"

The box squawked this out and Rumford helpfully pointed to the Igggla he had in mind. The chief Iggglas took in the import of the message and shrieked, leaped in the air, jumped at his lieutenant and beat him with a flurry of quick wing blows. Knocked the squealing creature flat and faster than Rumford could see had the lieutenant's skinny vulture-neck between his long toothy jaws. The lieutenant squeaked something dismal and was allowed to live; it crawled to the back of the group of Iggglas. The leader then strode forward and spoke to Rumford and the Ba'arni.

On the screen: "*Astrology stupid war heat fat food death always compact between Iggglas and fat food change never good annihilation of home planet outside compact realm of total war insistence on ritual war heat fat food death.*"

Rumford's brow wrinkled as he read this. Getting nowhere with the garheads. After a moment's thought he switched the box to Ba'arni, and typed in, very carefully, the following:

"*Iggglas understand Ba'arni capable of sustaining ritual war and intend no slur on Ba'arni (double n-1 sequence, B-flat).*" Possibly it was a mistake to try directly for Ba'arni terms to add power to the message. Box could mess it up entirely, in context of sentence. He typed on: "*Iggglas too have sense of honor and save face by suggestion that Ba'arni weakness is only source of problem in ritual war, but Iggglas also have famine trouble, and demand ritual war be postponed twelve squared years to keep both Iggglas and Ba'arni in sufficient numbers to sustain ritual war in perpetuity. Suggest mutual expression of honor (exclamation) by recognition of ritual promise for next time.*"

Clicks and whistles, the Ba'arni listening with their big hippo ears tilted down toward the box. Rumford felt the sweat trickling down the inside of his shirt. Extraordinarily hot for Rannoch. The Ba'arni were discussing the matter among themselves, and again Rumford put one eye to the box to see what it could tell him.

"We must not give (z-click z-click; see dictionary) exclamation. Necessary to (middle C to high C; see dictionary)."

Surreptitiously he switched over to the dictionary function and looked up middle C to high C.

"Middle C to high C: 1. Stand still. 2. Run. 3. Show interest. 4. Lose. 5. Alternate. 6. Repair. 7. Replace. 8. Subtend. 9. (high C to middle C; see dictionary). 10. Glance through turbid water."

Useful word. Rumford gave up on it.

Finally the Ba'ar on the left, the third one to speak from that position, raised its head and spoke. *"Ba'arni (z-click z-click; see dictionary) satisfied by expression of (n-1 click sequence, B-flat; see dictionary) by poison birds toward Ba'arni and sacred dodecimation ground, if agreed that ritual war should be resumed in twelve squared years at prescribed time."*

Rumford could not prevent his eyebrows from lifting a bit. One down, apparently. Now where was he with the others? Ah yes. Tricky still, the stubborn buzzards. Entirely possible they might take up his threat of total war and act on it, which would leave the Ba'arni considerably confused. And Rannoch torched. Hmm. A problem.

He thought hard and fast. Each side a different understanding of war. Ba'arni thought of it as religious event and perhaps population control, but couldn't sustain it when population already low from famine. Thus agreeable to postponement, if face saved, and quick to arrange talk when Iggglas seen approaching. Fine, clear. And Iggglas? Food source, population control, game, who could tell? Certainly didn't care what Ba'arni astrologers thought of things. Not big on religion, the Iggglas.

Need to give reasons convincing to receiver of message, not sender. Rumford blinked at this sudden realization. Senders not hearing message, after all—not even sending it in fact. Receiver all that mattered.

He switched the box to Iggglas. *"Ba'arni suffer from famine and fear war would reduce them to extinction, in which case no more ritual wars, no more fat food. Want postponement only."* The Iggglas shrieked at this in derision, but the box's screen included among the printed hash the word *understanding.* Perhaps they now had a reason they could comprehend. Best to press the point. He typed another message to the Iggglas:

"Dodecimation and fat food rely on population existence, as you say. If there

is no population there is no dodecimation or fat food and ritual war is ended forever. Ba'arni therefore insist on postponement of ritual war and if Iggglas attempt to wage it regardless of traditional cooperation of the Ba'arni then Ba'arni have no choice but total war and mass suicide for all parties. Suggest therefore postponement. Astrologer's decision necessary given population of Ba'arni."

The box hooted and squawked, the Iggglas leader cocked his head to one side and listened, watching Rumford carefully. When the message was completed the leader did a little dance of its own, all on one spot. Then suddenly it approached the Ba'arni directly. Rumford held his breath. The Iggglas leader shrieked at the Ba'arni, sweeping one wing at them in a ferocious gesture.

All three Ba'arni opened their immense mouths, which appeared to split their immense heads in half, and whistled loud and high. Rumford had to hold his hands over his ears, and the Iggglas leader stepped back. Impressive sight, those three open mouths. The Iggglae opened his long mouth as if to mock them; lot of teeth in there. Impressive as well. Battle of mouths. All right if it didn't lead to anything. Tense. Need to get a response in squawks from old gar face. Couldn't seem to intrude too much, however.

A long minute's wait as the two parties stared each other down. The Iggglas leader suddenly turned and squawked.

On screen: *"Heat death fat food postponement replacement cannibalism for Iggglas assurance renewal of slag heat war fat food in twelve squared years."*

Rumford let out a long breath.

He switched to Ba'arni, typed.

"Iggglas agree to acknowledge Ba'arni honor, promise renewal of honorable battle next time in twelve squared years."

Whistle, click, whistle. The Ba'ar on the left spoke quickly.

"The Ba'arni accept postponement and acknowledgement of their honor."

When Rumford conveyed the news to the Iggglas leader, it too was agreeable. Appeared to like the promise that the conflict would be renewed. But then it squawked on at length:

"Iggglas negative continuance until next ritual war with heat death bombs in Iggglas seas, insistence removal immediate."

Hmm. Bit of a problem, to tell the Ba'arni to remove bombs they didn't know existed. Meanwhile they were looking at Rumford to see what had been said, and to gain time Rumford switched to Ba'arni and typed, *"Iggglas agree to honor Ba'arni and agree to return to ritual war next time."*

A repeat of the previous message to them, but Rumford was too busy to think of anything else, and happily the Ba'arni didn't seem to notice. They agreed again, and Rumford returned to Iggglas.

"Ba'arni state weapons on Iggglas seafloor will be de-activated. All they can do as weapons cannot be relocated."

The Iggglas leader shrieked, pummelled the dust. *"War war war total annihilation war fat food heat death unless sea bombs removal exclamation."*

Hmm. Wouldn't do to stop a small ritual war by starting a total war even more likely to destroy Rannoch Island. Rumford quickly got the Ba'arni's assurances that they would return in twelve squared years, then returned to Iggglas:

"Ba'arni state detonator will be given to Iggglas. Detonation wavelength determined by detonator and Iggglas can change this and render bombs inoperative. Demonstration of this on small scale can be arranged in Rannoch ocean. Translator agrees to convey detonator and run demonstration as ritual forbids Ba'arni speaking to Iggglas in between ritual wars."

Could get a good long-distance detonator from the manganese mines, set up an offshore explosion. Hopefully convince them.

After a long and apparently thoughtful dance, the Iggglas leader ate two of the rabbit-things, and indicated his acceptance of this plan. The Iggglas abruptly turned and hopped back down the road to the spaceport. The meeting was over.

Owen Rumford stood up unsteadily, and feeling drained he accompanied the three Ba'arni back to the beach. As they got into their seacraft, the one on the left said something; but Rumford had his box in his coat pocket. After the Ba'arni craft rolled under the black waves, he took the box out, turned it on and tried to imitate the last set of whistles. The box printed it as, *"(y-click x-click; see dictionary.)"* He switched to the dictionary function and looked it up.

"Y-click x-click: 1. Ebb tide. 2. Twisted, knotted, complex. 3. The ten forefingers. 4. Elegance. 5. The part of the moon visible in a partial eclipse. 6. Tree."

"Hmm," Rumford said.

He walked slowly up toward the town. Y-click x-click. Those big plate eyes, staring at him. Their half of the conversation had gone pretty smoothly. Very smoothly. And all his assumptions, about the famine, the rituals. Could they be . . . just a little. . . . But no. Language barrier as troublesome in telepathy as in speech, after all. Maybe.

Y-click x-click. If he had gotten the whistle right. But he thought he had. Why have word for something they'd never seen? But Ba'arni had traded with earlier passers-by, witness box. Curious.

Tin roofs glinting in the light. Black stone walls, veined with white quartz. Black cobblestones. Very neat. Fine little town. In a hundred and forty-four years, they would have to figure something out. Well, that was their problem. More warning next time. Nothing to be done about it now.

He walked into the tavern and sat down heavily. His daughters had just finished preparing the tables for lunch. "Papa, you look exhausted," Isabel said. "Have you been trying to exercise again?"

"No, no." He looked around with a satisfied expression, heaved out a long breath. "Just a spot of translation." He got up and went behind the bar, started drawing a beer from the tap. Suddenly the corners of his moustache lifted a little. "Might get a bit of payment for it," he told her. "If so—still care for a picnic?"

Before I Wake

In his dream Abernathy stood on a steep rock ridge. A talus slope dropped from the ridge to a glacial basin containing a small lake. The lake was cobalt in the middle, aquamarine around the edges. Here and there in the rock expanse patches of meadow grass gleamed, like the lawns of marmot estates. There were no trees. The cold air felt thin in his throat. He could see ranges many miles away, and though everything was perfectly still there was also an immense sweep in things, as if a gust of wind had caught the very fabric of being.

"Wake up, damn you," a voice said. He was shoved in the back, and he tumbled down the rockfall, starting a small avalanche.

He stood in a large white room. Glass boxes of various size were stacked everywhere, four and five to a pile, and in every box was a sleeping animal: monkey, rat, dog, cat, pig, dolphin, turtle. "No," he said, backing up. "Please, no."

A bearded man entered the room. "Come on, wake up," he said brusquely. "Time to get back to it, Fred. Our only hope is to work as hard as we can. You have to resist when you start slipping away!" He seized Abernathy by the arms and sat him down on a box of squirrels. "Now listen!" he cried. "We're asleep! We're dreaming!"

"Thank God," Abernathy said.

"Not so fast! We're awake as well."

"I don't believe you."

"Yes you do!" He slapped Abernathy in the chest with a large roll of graph paper, and it spilled loose and unrolled over the floor. Black squiggles smeared the graphs.

"It looks like a musical score," Abernathy said absently.

The bearded man shouted "Yes! Yes! This is the symphony our brains play, very apt! Violins yammering away—that's what used to be ours, Fred; that was consciousness." He yanked hard on his beard with both hands, looking anguished. "Sudden drop to the basses, bowing and bowing, blessed sleep, yes, yes! And in the night the ghost instruments, horn and oboe and viola, spinning their little improvs over the ground bass, longer and longer till the violins start blasting again, yes, Fred, it's perfectly apt!"

"Thank you," Abernathy said. "But you don't have to yell. I'm right here."

"Then *wake up,*" the man said viciously. "Can't, can you! Trapped, aren't you! Playing the new song like all the rest of us. Look at it there—REM sleep mixed indiscriminately with consciousness and deep sleep, turning us all into dreamwalkers. Into waking nightmares."

Looking into the depths of the man's beard, Abernathy saw that all his teeth were incisors. Abernathy edged toward the door, then broke for it and ran. The man leaped forward and tackled him, and they tumbled to the floor.

Abernathy woke up.

"Ah ha," the man said. It was Winston, administrator of the lab. "So now you believe me," he said sourly, rubbing an elbow. "I suppose we should write that down on the walls. If we all start slipping away we won't even remember what things used to be like. It'll all be over then."

"Where are we?" Abernathy asked.

"In the lab," Winston replied, voice filled with heavy patience. "We live here now, Fred. Remember?"

Abernathy looked around. The lab was large and well-lit. Sheets of graph paper recording EEGs were scattered over the floor. Black countertops protruded from the walls, which were cluttered with machinery. In one corner were two rats in a cage.

Abernathy shook his head violently. It was all coming back. He was awake now, but the dream had been true. He groaned, walked to the room's little window, saw the smoke rising from the city below. "Where's Jill?"

Winston shrugged. They hurried through a door at the end of the lab, into a small room containing cots and blankets. No one there.

"She's probably gone back to the house again," Abernathy said.

Winston hissed with irritation and worry. "I'll check the grounds," he said. "You'd better go to the house. Be careful!"

Fred was already out the door.

In many places the streets were almost blocked by smashed cars, but little had changed since Abernathy's last venture home, and he made good time. The suburbs were choking in haze that smelled like incinerator smoke. A gas station attendant holding a pump handle stared in astonishment as he drove by, then waved. Abernathy didn't wave back. On one of these expeditions he had seen a knifing, and now he didn't like to look.

He stopped the car at the curb before his house. The remains of his house. It was charred almost to the ground. The blackened chimney was all that stood over chest high.

He got out of his old Cortina and slowly crossed the lawn, which was marked by black footprints. In the distance a dog barked insistently.

Jill stood in the kitchen, humming to herself and moving black things from here to there. She looked up as Abernathy stopped in the side yard before her. Her eyes twitched from side to side. "You're home," she said cheerily. "How was your day?"

"Jill, let's go out to dinner," Abernathy said.

"But I'm already cooking!"

"I can see that." He stepped over what had been the kitchen wall and took her arm. "Don't worry about that. Let's go anyway."

"My my," Jill said, brushing his face with a sooty hand. "Aren't you romantic this evening."

He stretched his lips wide. "You bet. Come on." He pulled her carefully out of the house and across the yard, and helped her into the Cortina. "Such chivalry," she remarked, eyes darting about in tandem.

Abernathy got in and started the engine. "But Fred," his wife said, "what about Jeff and Fran?"

Abernathy looked out his window. "They've got a babysitter," he finally said.

Jill frowned, nodded, sat back in her seat. Her broad face was smudged. "Ah," she said, "I do so like to dine out."

"Yes," Abernathy said, and yawned. He felt drowsy. "Oh no," he said. "No!" He bit his lip, pinched the back of the hand on the wheel. Yawned again. "No!" he cried. Jill jerked against her door in surprise. He swerved to avoid hitting an Oriental woman sitting in the middle of the road. "I must get to the lab," he shouted. He pulled down the Cortina's sun visor, took a pen from his coat pocket and scrawled *To The Lab*. Jill was staring at him. "It wasn't my fault," she whispered.

He drove them onto the freeway. All thirty lanes were clear, and he put his foot down on the accelerator. "To the lab," he sang, "to the lab, to the lab." A flying police vehicle landed on the highway ahead of them, folded its wings and sped off. Abernathy tried to follow it, but the freeway turned and narrowed, they were back on street level. He shouted with frustration, bit the flesh at the base of his thumb. Jill leaned back against her door, crying. Her eyes looked like small beings, a team trying to jerk its way free. "I couldn't help it," she said. "He loved me, you know. And I loved him."

Abernathy drove on. Some streets were burning. He wanted to go west, needed to go west. The car was behaving oddly. They were on a tree-lined avenue, out where there were few houses. A giant Boeing 747 lay across the road, its wings slewed forward. A high tunnel had been cut through it so traffic could pass. A cop with whistle and white gloves waved them through.

On the dashboard an emergency light blinked. *To The Lab*. Abernathy sobbed convulsively. "I don't know how!"

Jill, his sister, sat up straight. "Turn left," she said quietly. Abernathy threw the directional switch and their car rerouted itself onto the track that veered left. They came to other splits in the track, and each time Jill told him which way to go. The rear-view mirror bloomed with smoke.

Then he woke up. Winston was swabbing his arm with a wad of cotton, wiping off a droplet of blood.

"Amphetamines and pain," Winston whispered.

They were in the lab. About a dozen lab techs, postdocs, and grad students were in there at their countertops, working with great speed.

"How's Jill?" Abernathy said.

"Fine, fine. She's sleeping right now. Listen, Fred. I've found a way to keep us awake for longer periods of time. Amphetamines and pain. Regular injections of benzedrine, plus a sharp burst of pain every hour or so, administered in whatever way you find most convenient. Metabolism stays too high for the mind to slip into the dreamwalking. I tried it and stayed fully awake and alert for six hours. Now we're all using the method."

Abernathy watched the lab techs dash about. "I can tell." He could feel his heart's rapid emphatic thumping.

"Well let's get to it," Winston said intently. "Let's make use of this time."

Abernathy stood. Winston called a little meeting. Feeling the gazes fixed on him, Abernathy collected his thoughts. "The mind consists of electrochemical action. Since we're all suffering the effects of this, it seems to me we can ignore the chemical and concentrate on the electrical. If the ambient fields have changed . . . Anyone know how many gauss the magnetic field is now? Or what the cosmic ray count is?"

They stared at him.

"We can tune in to the space station's monitor," he said. "And do the rest here."

So he worked, and they worked with him. Every hour a grinning Winston came around with hypodermics in hand, singing "Speed, speed, spee-ud!" He convinced Abernathy to let droplets of hydrochloric acid fall on the inside of his forearm.

It kept Abernathy awake better than it did the others. For a whole day, then two, he worked without pause, eating crackers and drinking water as he worked, giving himself the injections when Winston wasn't there.

After the first few hours his assistants began slipping back into dreamwalking, despite the injections and acid splashings. Assignments he gave were never completed. One of his techs presented him with a successful experiment: the two rats, grafted together at the leg. Vainly Abernathy tried to pummel the man back to wakefulness.

In the end he did all the work himself. It took days. As his techs collapsed or wandered off he shifted from counter to counter, squinting sand-filled eyes to read oscilloscope and computer screen. He had never felt so exhausted in his life. It was like taking tests in a subject he didn't understand, in which he was severely retarded.

Still he kept working. The EEGs showed oscillation between wakefulness and REM sleep, in a pattern he had never seen. And there were correlations between the EEGs and fluctuations in the magnetic field.

Some of the men's flickering eyes were open, and they sat on the floors talking to each other or to him. Once he had to calm Winston, who was on the floor weeping and saying "We'll never stop dreaming, Fred, we'll never stop." Abernathy gave him an injection, but it didn't have any effect.

He kept working. He sat at a crowded table at his high school reunion, and found he could work anyway. He gave himself an injection whenever he remembered. He got very, very tired.

Eventually he felt he understood as much as he was going to. Everyone else was lying in the cot room with Jill, or was slumped on the floors. Eyes and eyelids were twitching.

"We move through space filled with dust and gas and fields of force. Now all the constants have changed. The read-outs from the space station show that, show signs of a strong electromagnetic field we've apparently moved into. More dust, cosmic rays, gravitational flux. Perhaps it's the shockwave of a supernova, something nearby that we're just seeing now. Anyone looked up into the sky lately? Anyway. Something. The altered field has thrown the electrical patterns of our brains into something like what we call the REM state. Our brains rebel and struggle towards consciousness as much as they can, but this field forces them back. So we oscillate." He laughed weakly, and crawled up onto one of the countertops to get some sleep.

He woke and brushed the dust off his lab coat, which had served him as a blanket. The dirt road he had been sleeping on was empty. He walked. It was cloudy, and nearly dark.

He passed a small group of shacks, built in a tropical style with open walls and palm thatch roofs. They were empty. Dark light filled the sky.

Then he was at the sea's edge. Before him extended a low promontory, composed of thousands of wooden chairs, all crushed and piled together. At the point of the promontory there was a human figure, seated in a big chair that still had seat and back and one arm.

Abernathy stepped out carefully, onto slats and lathed cylinders of wood, from a chair arm to the plywood bottom of a chair seat. Around him the gray ocean was strangely calm; glassy swells rose and fell over the slick wood at waterline without a sound. Insubstantial clouds of fog, the lowest parts of a solid cloud cover, floated slowly onshore. The air was salty and wet. Abernathy shivered, stepped down to the next fragment of weathered gray wood.

The seated man turned to look at him. It was Winston. "Fred," he called, loud in the silence of the dawn. Abernathy approached him, picked up a chair back, placed it carefully, sat.

"How are you?" Winston said.

Abernathy nodded. "Okay." Down close to the water he could hear the small slaps and sucking of the sea's rise and fall. The swells looked a bit larger, and he could see thin smoky mist rising from them as they approached the shore.

"Winston," he croaked, and cleared his throat. "What's happened?"

"We're dreaming."

"But what does that mean?"

Winston laughed wildly. "Emergent stage one sleep, transitional sleep, rapid sleep, rhombencephalic sleep, pontine sleep, activated sleep, paradoxical sleep." He grinned ironically. "No one knows what it is."

"But all those studies."

"Yes, all those studies. And how I used to believe in them, how I used to work for them, all those sorry guesses ranging from the ridiculous to the absurd, we dream to organize experience into memory, to stimulate the senses in the dark, to prepare for the future, to give our depth perception exercise for God's sake! I mean we don't know, do we Fred. We don't know what dreaming is, we don't know what sleep is, you only have to think about it a bit to realize we didn't know what consciousness itself was, what it meant to be awake. Did we ever really know? We lived, we slept, we dreamed, and all three equal mysteries. Now that we're doing all three at once, is the mystery any deeper?"

Abernathy picked at the grain in the wood of a chair leg. "A lot of the time I feel normal," he said. "It's just that strange things keep happening."

"Your EEGs display an unusual pattern," Winston said, mimicking a scientific tone. "More alpha and beta waves than the rest of us. As if you're struggling hard to wake up."

"Yes. That's what it feels like."

They sat in silence for a time, watching swells lap at the wet chairs. The tide was falling. Offshore, near the limit of visibility, Abernathy saw a large cabin cruiser drifting in the current.

"So tell me what you've found," Winston said.

Abernathy described the data transmitted from the space station, then his own experiments.

Winston nodded. "So we're stuck here for good."

"Unless we pass through this field. Or—I've gotten an idea for a device you could wear around your head, that might restore the old field."

"A solution seen in a dream?"

"Yes."

Winston laughed. "I used to believe in our rationality, Fred. Dreams as some sort of electrochemical manifestation of the nervous system, random activity, how reasonable it all sounded! Give the depth perception exercise! God, how small-minded it all was. Why shouldn't we have believed that dreams were great travels, to the future, to other universes, to a world more real than our own! They felt that way sometimes, in that last second before waking, as if we lived in a world so charged with meaning that it might burst . . . And now here we are. We're here, Fred, this is the moment and our only moment, no matter how we name it. *We're here.* From idea to symbol, perhaps. People will adapt. That's one of our talents."

"I don't like it," Abernathy said. "I never liked my dreams."

Winston merely laughed at him. "They say consciousness itself was a leap like this one, people were ambling around like dogs and then one day, maybe because the earth moved through the shockwave of some distant explosion, sure, one day one of them straightened up and looked around surprised, and said *'I am'.*"

"That would be a surprise," Abernathy said.

"And this time everyone woke up one morning still dreaming, and looked around and said *'What AM I?'* " Winston laughed. "Yes, we're stuck here. But I can adapt." He pointed. "Look, that boat out there is sinking."

They watched several people aboard the craft struggle to get a rubber raft over the side. After many dunkings they got it in the water and everyone inside it. Then they rowed away, offshore into the mist.

"I'm afraid," Abernathy said.

Then he woke up. He was back in the lab. It was in worse shape than ever. A couple of countertops had been swept clean to make room for chessboards, and several techs were playing blindfolded, arguing over which board was which.

He went to Winston's offices to get more benzedrine. There was no more. He grabbed one of his postdocs and said "How long have I been asleep?" The man's eyes twitched, and he sang his reply: "Sixteen men on a dead man's chest, yo ho ho and a bottle of rum." Abernathy went to the cot room. Jill was there, naked except for light blue underwear, smoking a cigarette. One of the grad students was brushing her nipples with a feather. "Oh hi, Fred," she said, looking him straight in the eye. "Where have you been?"

"Talking to Winston," he said with difficulty. "Have you seen him?"

"Yes! I don't know when, though . . ."

He started to work alone again. No one wanted to help. He cleared a small room off the main lab, and dragged in the equipment he needed. He locked three large boxes of crackers in a cabinet, and tried to lock himself in his room whenever he felt drowsy. Once he spent six weeks in China, then he woke up. Sometimes he woke out in his old Cortina, hugging the steering wheel like his only friend. All his friends were lost. Each time he went back and started working again. He could stay awake for hours at a time. He got lots done. The magnets were working well, he was getting the fields he wanted. The device for placing the field around the head—an odd-looking wire helmet—was practicable.

He was tired. It hurt to blink. Every time he felt drowsy he applied more acid to his arm. It was covered with burns, but none of them hurt anymore. When he woke he felt as if he hadn't slept for days. Twice his grad students helped out, and he was grateful for that. Winston came by occasionally, but only laughed at him. He was too tired, everything he did was clumsy. He got on the lab phone once and tried to call his parents; all the lines were busy. The radio was filled with static, except for a station that played nothing but episodes of "The Lone Ranger." He went back to work. He ate crackers and worked. He worked and worked.

Late one afternoon he went out onto the lab's cafeteria terrace to take a break. The sun was low, and a chill breeze blew. He could see the air, filled with amber light, and he breathed it in violently. Below him the city smoked, and the wind blew, and he knew that he was alive, that he was aware he was alive, and that something important was pushing into the world, suffusing things . . .

Jill walked onto the terrace, still wearing nothing but the blue underwear. She stepped on the balls of her feet, smiled oddly. Abernathy could see goose-pimples sweep across her skin like cat's paws over water, and the power of her presence—distant, female, mysterious—filled him with fear.

They stood several feet apart and looked down at the city, where their house had been. The area was burning.

Jill gestured at it. "It's too bad we only had the courage to live our lives fully in dreams."

"I thought we were doing okay," Abernathy said. "I thought we engaged it the best we could, every waking moment."

She stared at him, again with the knowing smile. "You did think that, didn't you."

"Yes," he said fiercely, "I did. I did."

He went inside to work it off.

Then he woke up. He was in the mountains, in the high cirque again. He was higher now and could see two more lakes, tiny granite pools, above the cobalt-and-aquamarine one. He was climbing shattered granite, getting near the pass. Lichen mottled the rocks. The wind dried the sweat on his face, cooled him. It was quiet and still, so still, so quiet . . .

"Wake up!"

It was Winston. Abernathy was in his little room (high ranges in the distance, the dusty green of forests below), wedged in a corner. He got up, went to the crackers cabinet, pumped himself full of the benzedrine he had found in some syringes on the floor. (Snow and lichen.)

He went into the main lab and broke the fire alarm. That got everyone's attention. It took him a couple of minutes to stop the alarm. When he did his ears were ringing.

"The device is ready to try," he said to the group. There were about twenty of them. Some were as neat as if they were off to church, others were tattered and dirty. Jill stood to one side.

Winston crashed to the front of the group. "What's ready?" he shouted.

"The device to stop us dreaming," Abernathy said weakly. "It's ready to try."

Winston said slowly, "Well, let's try it then, okay, Fred?"

Abernathy carried helmets and equipment out of his room and into the lab. He arranged the transmitters and powered the magnets and the field generators. When it was all ready he stood up and wiped his brow.

"Is this it?" Winston asked. Abernathy nodded. Winston picked up one of the wire helmets.

"Well I don't like it!" he said, and struck the helmet against the wall.

Abernathy's mouth dropped open. One of the techs gave a shove to his electromagnets, and in a sudden fury Abernathy picked up a bat of wood and hit the man. Some of his assistants leaped to his aid, the rest pressed in and pulled at his equipment, tearing it down. A tremendous fight erupted. Abernathy swung his slab of wood with abandon, feeling great satisfaction each time it struck. There was blood in the air. His machines were being destroyed. Jill picked up one of the helmets and threw it at him, screaming *"It's your fault, it's your fault!"* He knocked down a man near his magnets and had swung the slab back to kill him when suddenly he saw a bright glint in Winston's hand; it was a surgical knife, and with a swing like a sidearm pitcher's Winston slammed the knife into Abernathy's diaphragm, burying it. Abernathy staggered back, tried to draw in a breath and found that he could, he was all right, he hadn't been stabbed. He turned and ran.

He dashed onto the terrace, closely pursued by Winston and Jill and the others, who tripped and fell even as he did. The patio was much higher than it used to be, far above the city, which burned and smoked. There was a long wide stairway descending into the heart of the city. Abernathy could hear screams, it was night and windy, he couldn't see any stars, he was at the edge of the terrace, he turned and the group was right behind him, faces twisted with fury. "No!" he cried, and then they rushed him, and he swung the wood slab and swung it and swung it, and turned to run down the stairs and then without knowing how he had done it he tripped and fell head over heels down the rocky staircase, falling falling falling.

Then he woke up. He was falling.

"A History of the Twentieth Century, with Illustrations"

"*If truth is not to be found on the shelves of the British Museum, where, I asked myself, picking up a notebook and a pencil, is truth?*"

—VIRGINIA WOOLF

Daily doses of bright light markedly improve the mood of people suffering from depression, so every day at eight in the evening Frank Churchill went to the clinic on Park Avenue, and sat for three hours in a room illuminated with sixteen hundred watts of white light. This was not exactly like having the sun in the room, but it was bright, about the same as if sixteen bare lightbulbs hung from the ceiling. In this case the bulbs were probably long tubes, and they were hidden behind a sheet of white plastic, so it was the whole ceiling that glowed.

He sat at a table and doodled with a purple pen on a pad of pink paper. And then it was eleven and he was out on the windy streets, blinking as traffic lights swam in the gloom. He walked home to a hotel room in the west Eighties. He would return to the clinic at five the next morning for a predawn treatment, but now it was time to sleep. He looked forward to that. He'd been on the treatment for three weeks, and he was tired. Though the treatment did seem to be working—as far as he could tell; improvement was supposed to average twenty percent a week, and he wasn't sure what that would feel like.

In his room the answering machine was blinking. There was a message from his agent, asking him to call immediately. It was now nearly midnight, but he pushbuttoned the number and his agent answered on the first ring.

"You have DSPS," Frank said to him.

"What? What?"

"Delayed sleep phase syndrome. I know how to get rid of it."

"Frank! Look, Frank, I've got a good offer for you."

"Do you have a lot of lights on?"

"What? Oh, yeah, say, how's that going?"

"I'm probably sixty percent better."

"Good, good. Keep at it. Listen, I've got something should help you a hundred percent. A publisher in London wants you to go over there and write a book on the twentieth century."

"What kind of book?"

"Your usual thing, Frank, but this time putting together the big picture. Reflecting on all the rest of your books, so to speak. They want to bring it out in time for the turn of the century, and go oversize, use lots of illustrations, big print run—"

"A coffee table book?"

"People'll want it on their coffee tables, sure, but it's not—"

"I don't want to write a coffee table book."

"Frank—"

"What do they want, ten thousand words?"

"They want thirty thousand words, Frank. And they'll pay a hundred thousand pound advance."

That gave him pause.

"Why so much?"

"They're new to publishing, they come from computers and this is the kind of numbers they're used to. It's a different scale."

"That's for sure. I still don't want to do it."

"Frank, come on, you're the one for this! The only successor to Barbara Tuchman!" That was a blurb found on paperback editions of his work. "They want you in particular—I mean, Churchill on the twentieth century, ha ha. It's a natural."

"I don't want to do it."

"Come on, Frank. You could use the money, I thought you were having trouble with the payments—"

"Yeah yeah." Time for a different tack. "I'll think it over."

"They're in a hurry, Frank."

"I thought you said turn of the century!"

"I did, but there's going to be a lot of this kind of book then, and they want to beat the rush. Set the standard and then keep it in print for a few years. It'll be great."

"It'll be remaindered within a year. Remaindered before it even comes out, if I know coffee table books."

His agent sighed. "Come on, Frank. You can use the money. As for the book, it'll be as good as you make it, right? You've been working on this stuff your whole career, and here's your chance to sum up. And you've got a lot of readers, people will listen to you." Concern made him shrill: "Don't let what's happened get you so down that you miss an opportunity like this! Work is the best cure for depression anyway. And this is your chance to influence how we think about what's happened!"

"With a coffee table book?"

"God damn it, don't think of it that way!"

"How should I think of it."

His agent took a deep breath, let it out, spoke very slowly. "Think of it as a hundred thousand pounds, Frank."

His agent did not understand.

Nevertheless, the next morning as he sat under the bright white ceiling, doodling with a green pen on yellow paper, he decided to go to England. He didn't want to sit in that room anymore; it scared him, because he suspected it might not be working. He was not sixty percent better. And he didn't want to shift to drug therapy. They had found nothing wrong with his brain, no physical problems at all, and though that meant little, it did make him resistant to the idea of drugs. He had his reasons and he wanted his feelings!

The light room technician thought that this attitude was a good sign in itself. "Your serotonin level is normal, right? So it's not that bad. Besides London's a lot farther north than New York, so you'll pick up the light you lose here. And if you need more you can always head north again, right?"

He called Charles and Rya Dowland to ask if he could stay with them. It turned out they were leaving for Florida the next day, but they invited him to stay anyway; they liked having their flat occupied while they were gone. Frank had done that before, he still had the key on his key-ring. "Thanks," he said. It would be better this way, actually. He didn't feel like talking.

So he packed his backpack, including camping gear with the clothes, and the next morning flew to London. It was strange how one traveled these days: he got into a moving chamber outside his hotel, then shifted from one chamber to the next for several hours, only stepping outdoors again when he emerged from the Camden tube station, some hundred yards from Charles and Rya's flat.

The ghost of his old pleasure brushed him as he crossed Camden High Street and walked by the cinema, listening to London's voices. This had been his method for years: come to London, stay with Charles and Rya until he found digs, do his research and writing at the British Museum, visit the used bookstores at Charing Cross, spend the evenings at Charles and Rya's, watching TV and talking. It had been that way for four books, over the course of twenty years.

The flat was located above a butcher shop. Every wall in it was covered with stuffed bookshelves, and there were shelves nailed up over the toilet, the bath, and the head of the guest bed. In the unlikely event of an earthquake the guest would be buried in a hundred histories of London.

Frank threw his pack on the guest bed and went past the English poets downstairs. The living room was nearly filled by a table stacked with papers and books. The side street below was an open-air produce market, and he could hear the voices of the vendors as they packed up for the day. The sun hadn't set, though it was past nine; these late May days were already long. It was almost like still being in therapy.

He went downstairs and bought vegetables and rice, then went back up and cooked them. The kitchen windows were the color of sunset, and the little flat glowed, evoking its owners so strongly that it was almost as if they were there. Suddenly he wished they were.

After eating he turned on the CD player and put on some Handel. He opened the living room drapes and settled into Charles's armchair, a glass of Bulgarian wine in his hand, an open notebook on his knee. He watched salmon light leak out of the clouds to the north, and tried to think about the causes of the First World War.

In the morning he woke to the dull *thump thump thump* of frozen slabs of meat being rendered by an axe. He went downstairs and ate cereal while leafing through the *Guardian,* then took the tube to Tottenham Court Road and walked to the British Museum.

Because of *The Belle Epoque* he had already done his research on the pre-war period, but writing in the British Library was a ritual he didn't want to break; it made him part of a tradition, back to Marx and beyond. He showed his still-valid reader's ticket to a librarian and then found an empty seat in his usual row; in fact he had written much of *Entre Deux Guerres* in that very carrel, under the frontal lobes of the great skull dome. He opened a notebook and stared at the page. Slowly he wrote, *1900 to 1914.* Then he stared at the page.

His earlier book had tended to focus on the sumptuous excesses of the pre-war European ruling class, as a young and clearly leftist reviewer in the *Guardian* had rather sharply pointed out. To the extent that he had delved into the causes of the Great War, he had subscribed to the usual theory; that it had been the result of rising nationalism, diplomatic brinksmanship, and several deceptive precedents in the previous two decades. The Spanish-American War, the Russo-Japanese War, and the two Balkan wars had all remained localized and non-catastrophic; and there had been several "incidents," the Moroccan affair and the like, that had brought the two great alliances to the brink, but not toppled them over. So when Austria-Hungary made impossible demands to Serbia after the assassination of Ferdinand, no one could have known that the situation would domino into the trenches and their slaughter.

History as accident. Well, no doubt there was a lot of truth in that. But now he found himself thinking of the crowds in the streets of all the major cities, cheering the news of the war's outbreak; of the disappearance of pacifism, which had seemed such a force; of, in short, the apparently unanimous support for war among the prosperous citizens of the European powers. Support for a war that had no real reason to be!

There was something irreducibly mysterious about that, and this time he decided he would admit it, and discuss it. That would require a consideration of the preceding century, the *Pax Europeana;* which in fact had been a century of bloody subjugation, the high point of imperialism, with most of the world falling to the great powers. These powers had prospered at the expense of their colonies, who had suffered in abject misery. Then the powers had spent their profits building weapons, and used the weapons on each other, and destroyed themselves. There was something weirdly just about that development, as when a mass murderer finally turns the gun on himself. Punishment, an end to guilt, an end to pain. Could that really explain it? While staying in Washington with his dying father, Frank had visited the Lincoln Memorial, and there on the right hand wall had been Lincoln's Second Inaugural Address, carved in capital letters with the commas omitted, an oddity which somehow added to the speech's Biblical massiveness, as when it spoke of the ongoing war: "YET IF GOD WILLS THAT IT CONTINUE UNTIL ALL THE WEALTH PILED BY THE BONDSMAN'S TWO HUNDRED AND FIFTY YEARS OF UNREQUITED TOIL SHALL BE SUNK AND UNTIL EVERY DROP OF BLOOD DRAWN WITH THE LASH SHALL BE PAID BY ANOTHER DRAWN WITH THE SWORD AS WAS SAID THREE THOUSAND YEARS AGO SO STILL IT MUST BE SAID 'THE JUDGMENTS OF THE LORD ARE TRUE AND RIGHTEOUS ALTOGETHER.' "

A frightening thought, from that dark part of Lincoln that was never far from the surface. But as a theory of the Great War's origin it still struck him as inadequate. It was possible to believe it of the kings and presidents, the generals and diplomats, the imperial officers around the world; they had known what they were doing, and so might have been impelled by unconscious guilt to mass suicide. But the common citizen at home, ecstatic in the streets at the outbreak of general war? That seemed more likely to be just another manifestation of the hatred of the other. All my problems are your fault! He and Andrea had said that to each other a lot. Everyone did.

And yet . . . it still seemed to him that the causes were eluding him, as they had everyone else. Perhaps it was a simple pleasure in destruction. What is the primal response to an edifice? Knock it down. What is the primal response to a stranger? Attack him.

But he was losing his drift, falling away into the metaphysics of "human nature." That would be a constant problem in an essay of this length. And whatever the causes, there stood the year 1914, irreducible, inexplicable, unchangeable. "AND THE WAR CAME."

In his previous books he had never written about the wars. He was among those who believed that real history occurred in peacetime, and that in war you might as well roll dice or skip ahead to the peace treaty. For anyone but a military historian, what was interesting would begin again only when the war ended.

Now he wasn't so sure. Current views of the Belle Epoque were distorted because one only saw it through the lens of the war that ended it; which meant that the Great War was somehow more powerful than the Belle Epoque, or at least more powerful than he had thought. It seemed he would have to write about it, this time, to make sense of the century. And so he would have to research it.

He walked up to the central catalogue tables. The room darkened as the sun went behind clouds, and he felt a chill.

For a long time the numbers alone staggered him. To overwhelm trench defenses, artillery bombardments of the most astonishing size were brought to bear: on the Somme the British put a gun every twenty yards along a fourteen-mile front, and fired a million and a half shells. In April 1917 the French fired six million shells. The Germans' Big Bertha shot shells seventy-five miles high, essentially into space. Verdun was a "battle" that lasted ten months, and killed almost a million men.

The British section of the front was ninety miles long. Every day of the war, about seven thousand men along that front were killed or wounded—not in any battle in particular, but just as the result of incidental sniper fire or bombardment. It was called "wastage."

Frank stopped reading, his mind suddenly filled with the image of the Vietnam Memorial. He had visited it right after leaving the Lincoln Memorial, and the sight of all those names engraved on the black granite plates had powerfully affected him. For a moment it had seemed possible to imagine all those people, a little white line for each.

But at the end of every month or two of the Great War, the British had had a whole Vietnam Memorial's worth of dead. Every month or two, for fifty-one months.

He filled out book request slips and gave them to the librarians in the central ring of desks, then picked up the books he had requested the day before, and took them back to his carrel. He skimmed the books and took notes, mostly writing down figures and statistics. British factories produced two hundred and fifty million shells. The major battles all killed a half million or more. About ten million men died on the field of battle, ten million more by revolution, disease, and starvation.

Occasionally he would stop reading and try to write; but he never got far. Once he wrote several pages on the economy of the war. The organization of agriculture and business, especially in Germany under Rathenau and England under Lloyd George, reminded him very strongly of the postmodern economy now running things. One could trace the roots of late capitalism to Great War innovations found in Rathenau's *Kriegsrohstoffabteilung* (the "War Raw Stuff Department"), or in his *Zentral Einkaufs-Gesellschaft*. All business had been organized to fight the enemy; but when the war was over and the enemy vanquished, the organization remained. People continued to sacrifice the fruits of their work, but now they did it for the corporations that had taken the wartime governments' positions in the system.

So much of the twentieth century, there already in the Great War. And then the Armistice was signed, at eleven A.M. on November 11th, 1918. That morning at the front the two sides exchanged bombardments as usual, so that by eleven A.M. many people had died.

That evening Frank hurried home, just beating a thundershower. The air was as dark as smoky glass.

* * *

And the war never ended.

This idea, that the two world wars were actually one, was not original to him. Winston Churchill said it at the time, as did the Nazi Alfred Rosenburg. They saw the twenties and thirties as an interregnum, a pause to regroup in the middle of a two-part conflict. The eye of a hurricane.

Nine o'clock one morning and Frank was still at the Dowlands', lingering over cereal and paging through the *Guardian,* and then through his notebooks. Every morning he seemed to get a later start, and although it was May, the days didn't seem to be getting any longer. Rather the reverse.

There were arguments against the view that it was a single war. The twenties did not seem very ominous, at least after the Treaty of Locarno in 1925: Germany had survived its financial collapse, and everywhere economic recovery seemed strong. But the thirties showed the real state of things: the depression, the new democracies falling to fascism, the brutal Spanish Civil War; the starvation of the kulaks; the terrible sense of fatality in the air. The sense of slipping on a slope, falling helplessly back into war.

But this time it was different. *Total War.* German military strategists had coined the phrase in the 1890s, while analyzing Sherman's campaign in Georgia. And they felt they were waging total war when they torpedoed neutral ships in 1915. But they were wrong; the Great War was not total war. In 1914 the rumor that German soldiers had killed eight Belgian nuns was enough to shock all civilization, and later when the *Lusitania* was sunk, objections were so fierce that the Germans agreed to leave passenger ships alone. This could only happen in a world where people still held the notion that in war armies fought armies and soldiers killed soldiers, while civilians suffered privation and perhaps got killed accidentally, but were never deliberately targeted. This was how European wars had been fought for centuries: diplomacy by other means.

In 1939, this changed. Perhaps it changed only because the capability for total war had emerged from the technological base, in the form of mass long-range aerial bombardment. Perhaps on the other hand it was a matter of learning the lessons of the Great War, digesting its implications. Stalin's murder of the kulaks, for instance: five million Ukrainian peasants, killed because Stalin wanted to collectivize agriculture. Food was deliberately shipped out of that breadbasket region, emergency supplies withheld, hidden stockpiles destroyed; and several thousand villages disappeared as all their occupants starved. This was total war.

Every morning Frank leafed around in the big catalogue volumes, as if he might find some other twentieth century. He filled out his slips, picked up the books requested the previous day, took them back to his carrel. He spent more time reading than writing. The days were cloudy, and it was dim under the great dome. His notes were getting scrambled. He had stopped working in chronological order, and kept returning compulsively to the Great War, even though the front wave of his reading was well into World War Two.

Twenty million had died in the first war, fifty million in the second. Civilian deaths made the bulk of the difference. Near the end of the war, thousands of bombs were dropped on cities in the hope of starting firestorms, in which the atmosphere itself was in effect ignited, as in Dresden, Berlin, Tokyo. Civilians were the target now, and strategic bombing made them easy to hit. Hiroshima and Nagasaki were in that sense a kind of exclamation point, at the end of a sentence which the war had been saying all along: we will kill your families at home. War is war, as Sherman said; if you want peace, surrender. ! And they did.

After two bombs. Nagasaki was bombed three days after Hiroshima, before the Japanese had time to understand the damage and respond. Dropping the bomb on Hiroshima was endlessly debated in the literature, but Frank found few who even attempted a defense of Nagasaki. Truman and his advisors did it, people said, to a) show Stalin they had more than one bomb, and b) show Stalin that they would use the bomb even as a threat or warning only, as Nagasaki demonstrated. A Vietnam Memorial's worth of civilians in an instantaneous flash, just so Stalin would take Truman seriously. Which he did.

When the crew of the *Enola Gay* landed, they celebrated with a barbeque.

* * *

In the evenings Frank sat in the Dowland flat in silence. He did not read, but watched the evening summer light leak out of the sky to the north. The days were getting shorter. He needed the therapy, he could feel it. More light! Someone had said that on their death-bed—Newton, Galileo, Spinoza, someone like that. No doubt they had been depressed at the time.

He missed Charles and Rya. He would feel better, he was sure, if he had them there to talk with. That was the thing about friends, after all: they lasted and you could talk. That was the definition of friendship.

But Charles and Rya were in Florida. And in the dusk he saw that the walls of books in the flat functioned like lead lining in a radioactive environment, all those recorded thoughts forming a kind of shield against poisonous reality. The best shield available, perhaps. But now it was failing, at least for him; the books appeared to be nothing more than their spines.

And then one evening in a premature blue sunset it seemed that the whole flat had gone transparent, and that he was sitting in an armchair, suspended over a vast and shadowy city.

The Holocaust, like Hiroshima and Nagasaki, had precedents. Russians with Ukrainians, Turks with Armenians, white settlers with native Americans. But the mechanized efficiency of the Germans' murder of the Jews was something new and horrible. There was a book in his stack on the designers of the death camps, the architects, engineers, builders. Were these functionaries less or more obscene than the mad doctors, the sadistic guards? He couldn't decide.

And then there was the sheer number of them, the six million. It was hard to comprehend it. He read that there was a library in Jerusalem where they had taken on the task of recording all they could find about every one of the six million. Walking up Charing Cross Road that afternoon he thought of that and stopped short. All those names in one library, another transparent room, another memorial. For a second he caught a glimpse of how many people that was, a whole London's worth. Then it faded and he was left on a street corner, looking both ways to make sure he didn't get run over.

As he continued walking he tried to calculate how many Vietnam Memorials it would take to list the six million. Roughly two per hundred thousand; thus twenty per million. So, one hundred and twenty. Count them one by one, step by step.

He took to hanging out through the evenings in pubs. The Wellington was as good as any, and was frequented occasionally by some acquaintances he had met through Charles and Rya. He sat with them and listened to them talk, but often he found himself distracted by his day's reading. So the conversations tumbled along without him, and the Brits, slightly more tolerant than Americans of eccentricity, did not make him feel unwelcome.

The pubs were noisy and filled with light. Scores of people moved about in them, talking, smoking, drinking. A different kind of lead-lined room. He didn't drink beer, and so at first remained sober; but then he discovered the hard cider that pubs carried. He liked it and drank it like the others drank their beer, and got quite drunk. After that he sometimes became very talkative, telling the rest things about the twentieth century that they already knew, and they would nod and contribute some other bit of information, to be polite, then change the subject back to whatever they had been discussing before, gently and without snubbing him.

But most of the time when he drank he only got more remote from their talk, which jumped about faster than he could follow. And each morning after, he would wake late and slow, head pounding, the day already there and a lot of the morning light missed in sleep. Depressives were not supposed to drink at all. So finally he quit going to the Wellington, and instead ate at the pubs closest to the Dowlands'. One was called The Halfway House, the other World's End, a poor choice as far as names were concerned, but he ate at World's End anyway, and afterwards would sit at a corner table and nurse a whisky and stare at page after page of notes, chewing the end of a pen to plastic shrapnel.

The Fighting Never Stopped, as one book's title put it. But the atomic bomb meant that the second half of the century looked different than the first. Some, Americans for the most part, called it the *Pax Ameri-*

cana. But most called it the Cold War, 1945-1989. And not that cold, either. Under the umbrella of the superpower stalemate local conflicts flared everywhere, wars which compared to the two big ones looked small; but there had been over a hundred of them all told, killing about 350,000 people a year, for a total of around fifteen million, some said twenty; it was hard to count. Most occurred in the big ten: the two Vietnam wars, the two Indo-Pakistan wars, the Korean war, the Algerian war, the civil war in Sudan, the massacres in Indonesia in 1965, the Biafran war, and the Iran-Iraq war. Then another ten million civilians had been starved by deliberate military action; so that the total for the period was about the equal of the Great War itself. Though it had taken ten times as long to compile. Improvement of a sort.

And thus perhaps the rise of atrocity war, as if the horror of individualized murders could compensate for the lack of sheer number. And maybe it could; because now his research consisted of a succession of accounts and color photos of rape, dismemberment, torture—bodies of individual people, in their own clothes, scattered on the ground in pools of blood. Vietnamese villages, erupting in napalm. Cambodia, Uganda, Tibet—Tibet was genocide again, paced to escape the world's notice, a few villages destroyed every year in a process called *thamzing,* or reeducation: the villages seized by the Chinese and the villagers killed by a variety of methods, "burying alive, hanging, beheading, disemboweling, scalding, crucifixion, quartering, stoning, small children forced to shoot their parents; pregnant women given forced abortions, the fetuses piled in mounds on the village squares."

Meanwhile power on the planet continued to shift into fewer hands. The Second World War had been the only thing to successfully end the Depression, a fact leaders remembered; so the economic consolidation begun in the First War continued through the Second War and the Cold War, yoking the whole world into a war economy.

At first 1989 had looked like a break away from that. But now, just seven years later, the Cold War losers all looked like Germany in 1922, their money worthless, their shelves empty, their democracies crumbling to juntas. Except this time the juntas had corporate sponsors; multinational banks ran the old Soviet bloc just as they did the Third World, with "austerity measures" enforced in the name of "the free market," meaning half the world went to sleep hungry every night to pay off debts to millionaires. While temperatures still rose, populations still soared, "local conflicts" still burned in twenty different places.

One morning Frank lingered over cereal, reluctant to leave the flat. He opened the *Guardian* and read that the year's defense budgets worldwide would total around a trillion dollars. "More light," he said, swallowing hard. It was a dark, rainy day. He could feel his pupils enlarging, making the effort. The days were surely getting shorter, even though it was May; and the air was getting darker, as if London's Victorian fogs had returned, coal smoke in the fabric of reality.

He flipped the page and started an article on the conflict in Sri Lanka. Singhalese and Tamils had been fighting for a generation now, and some time in the previous week, a husband and wife had emerged from their house in the morning to find the heads of their six sons arranged on their lawn. He threw the paper aside and walked through soot down the streets.

He got to the British Museum on automatic pilot. Waiting for him at the top of the stack was a book containing estimates of total war deaths for the century. About a hundred million people.

He found himself on the dark streets of London again, thinking of numbers. All day he walked, unable to gather his thoughts. And that night as he fell asleep the calculations returned, in a dream or a hypnogogic vision: it would take two thousand Vietnam Memorials to list the century's war dead. From above he saw himself walking the Mall in Washington, D.C., and the whole park from the Capitol to the Lincoln Memorial was dotted with the black Vs of Vietnam Memorials, as if a flock of giant stealth birds had landed on it. All night he walked past black wing walls, moving west toward the white tomb on the river.

The next day the first book on the stack concerned the war between China and Japan, 1931–1945. Like most of Asian history this war was poorly remembered in the West, but it had been huge. The whole Korean nation became in effect a slave labor camp in the Japanese war effort, and the Japanese concentration camps in Manchuria had killed as many Chinese as the Germans had killed Jews. These deaths included thousands in the style of Mengele and the Nazi doctors, caused by "scientific" medical torture. Japanese experimenters had for instance performed transfusions in which they drained Chinese prisoners of their blood and replaced it with horses' blood, to see how long the prisoners would live. Survival rates varied from twenty minutes to six hours, with the subjects in agony throughout.

Frank closed that book and put it down. He picked the next one out of the gloom and peered at it. A heavy old thing, bound in dark green leather, with a dull gold pattern inlaid on the spine and boards. *A History of the Nineteenth Century, with Illustrations*—the latter tinted photos, their colors faded and dim. Published in 1902 by George Newnes Ltd; last century's equivalent of his own project, apparently. Curiosity about that had caused him to request the title. He opened it and thumbed through, and on the last page the text caught his eye: "I believe that Man is good. I believe that we stand at the dawn of a century that will be more peaceful and prosperous than any in history."

He put down the book and left the British Museum. In a red phone box he located the nearest car rental agency, an Avis outlet near Westminster. He took the Tube and walked to this agency, and there he rented a blue Ford Sierra station wagon. The steering wheel was on the right, of course. Frank had never driven in Great Britain before, and he sat behind the wheel trying to hide his uneasiness from the agent. The clutch, brake, and gas pedal were left-to-right as usual, thank God. And the gear shift was arranged the same, though one did have to operate it with the left hand.

Awkwardly he shoved the gearshift into first and drove out of the garage, turning left and driving down the left side of the street. It was weird. But the oddity of sitting on the right insured that he wouldn't forget the necessity of driving on the left. He pulled to the curb and perused the Avis street map of London, plotted a course, got back in traffic, and drove to Camden High Street. He parked below the Dowlands' and went upstairs and packed, then took his backpack down to the car. He returned to leave a note: *Gone to the land of the midnight sun.* Then he went down to the car and drove north, onto the highways and out of London.

It was a wet day, and low full clouds brushed over the land, dropping here a black broom of rain, there a Blakean shaft of sunlight. The hills were green, and the fields yellow or brown or lighter green. At first there were a lot of hills, a lot of fields. Then the highway swung by Birmingham and Manchester, and he drove by fields of rowhouses, line after line after line of them, on narrow treeless streets—all orderly and neat, and yet still among the bleakest human landscapes he had ever seen. Streets like trenches. Certainly the world was being overrun. Population densities must be near the levels set in those experiments on rats which had caused the rats to go insane. It was as good an explanation as any. Mostly males affected, in both cases: territorial hunters, bred to kill for food, now trapped in little boxes. They had gone mad. "I believe that Man is this or that," the Edwardian author had written, and why not; it couldn't be denied that it was mostly men's doing. The planning, the diplomacy, the fighting, the raping, the killing.

The obvious thing to do was to give the running of the world over to women. There was Thatcher in the Falklands and Indira Gandhi in Bangladesh, it was true; but still it would be worth trying, it could hardly get worse! And given the maternal instinct, it would probably be better. Give every first lady her husband's job. Perhaps every woman her man's job. Let the men care for the children, for five thousand years or fifty thousand, one for every year of murderous patriarchy.

North of Manchester he passed giant radio towers, and something that looked like nuclear reactor stacks. Fighter jets zoomed overhead. The twentieth century. Why hadn't that Edwardian author been able to see it coming? Perhaps the future was simply unimaginable, then and always. Or perhaps things hadn't looked so bad in 1902. The Edwardian, looking forward in a time of prosperity, saw more of the same; instead there had followed a century of horrors. Now one looked forward from a time of horrors; so that by analogy, what was implied for the next century was grim beyond measure. And with the new technologies of destruction, practically anything was possible: chemical warfare, nuclear terrorism, biological holocaust; victims killed by nano-assassins flying through them, or by viruses in their drinking supply, or by a particular ringing of their telephone; or reduced to zombies by drugs or brain implants, torture or nerve gas; or simply dispatched with bullets, or starved; hi tech, low tech, the methods were endless. And the motivations would be stronger than ever; with populations rising and resources depleted, people were going to be fighting not to rule, but to survive. Some little country threatened with defeat could unleash an epidemic against its rival and accidentally kill off a continent, or everyone, it was entirely possible. The twenty-first century might make the twentieth look like nothing at all.

He would come to after reveries like that and realize that twenty or thirty or even sixty miles had passed without him seeing a thing of the outside world. Automatic pilot, on roads that were reversed! He tried to concentrate.

He was somewhere above Carlisle. The map showed two possible routes to Edinburgh: one left the highway just below Glasgow, while a smaller road left sooner and was much more direct. He chose the direct route and took an exit into a roundabout and onto the A702, a two-lane road heading northeast. Its black asphalt was wet with rain, and the clouds rushing overhead were dark. After several miles he passed a sign that said "Scenic Route," which suggested he had chosen the wrong road, but he was unwilling to backtrack. It was probably as fast to go this way by now, just more work: frequent roundabouts, villages with traffic lights, and narrow stretches where the road was hemmed by hedges or walls. Sunset was near, he had been driving for hours; he was tired, and when black trucks rushed at him out of the spray and shadows it looked like they were going to collide with him head-on. It became an effort to stay to the left rather than the right where his instincts shrieked he should be. Right and left had to be reversed on that level, but kept the same at foot level—reversed concerning which hand went on the gearshift, but not reversed for what the gearshift did—and it all began to blur and mix, until finally a huge lorry rushed head first at him and he veered left, but hit the gas rather than the brakes. At the unexpected lurch forward he swerved farther left to be safe, and that ran his left wheels off the asphalt and into a muddy gutter, causing the car to bounce back onto the road. He hit the brakes hard and the lorry roared by his ear. The car skidded over the wet asphalt to a halt.

He pulled over and turned on the emergency blinker. As he got out of the car he saw that the driver's side mirror was gone. There was nothing there but a rectangular depression in the metal, four rivet holes slightly flared to the rear, and one larger hole for the mirror adjustment mechanism, missing as well.

He went to the other side of the car to remind himself what the Sierra's side mirrors looked like. A solid metal and plastic mounting. He walked a hundred yards back down the road, looking through the dusk for the missing one, but he couldn't find it anywhere. The mirror was gone.

Outside Edinburgh he stopped and called Alec, a friend from years past.

"What? Frank Churchill? Hello! You're here? Come on by, then."

Frank followed his directions into the city center, past the train station to a neighborhood of narrow streets. Reversed parallel parking was almost too much for him; it took four tries to get the car next to the curb. The Sierra bumped over paving stones to a halt. He killed the engine and got out of the car, but his whole body continued to vibrate, a big tuning fork humming in the twilight. Shops threw their illumination over passing cars. Butcher, baker, Indian deli.

Alec lived on the third floor. "Come in, man, come in." He looked harried. "I thought you were in America! What brings you here?"

"I don't know."

Alec glanced sharply at him, then led him into the flat's kitchen and living area. The window had a view across rooftops to the castle. Alec stood in the kitchen, uncharacteristically silent. Frank put down his backpack and walked over to look out at the castle, feeling awkward. In the old days he and Andrea had trained up several times to visit Alec and Suzanne, a primatologist. At that time those two had lived in a huge three-storied flat in the New Town, and when Frank and

Andrea had arrived the four of them would stay up late into the night, drinking brandy and talking in a high-ceilinged Georgian living room. During one stay they had all driven into the Highlands, and another time Frank and Andrea had stayed through a festival week, the four attending as many plays as they could. But now Suzanne and Alec had gone their ways, and Frank and Andrea were divorced, and Alec lived in a different flat; and that whole life had disappeared.

"Did I come at a bad time?"

"No, actually." A clatter of dishes as Alec worked at the sink. "I'm off to dinner with some friends, you'll join us—you haven't eaten?"

"No. I won't be—"

"No. You've met Peg and Rog before, I think. And we can use the distraction, I'm sure. We've all been to a funeral this morning. Friends of ours, their kid died. Crib death, you know."

"Jesus. You mean it just. . . ."

"Sudden infant death syndrome, yeah. Dropped him off at day care and he went off during his nap. Five months old."

"Jesus."

"Yeah." Alec went to the kitchen table and filled a glass from a bottle of Laphroaig. "Want a whisky?"

"Yes, please."

Alec poured another glass, drank his down. "I suppose the idea these days is that a proper funeral helps the parents deal with it. So Tom and Elyse came in carrying the coffin, and it was about this big." He held his hands a foot apart.

"No."

"Yeah. Never seen anything like it."

They drank in silence.

The restaurant was a fashionably bohemian seafood place, set above a pub. There Frank and Alec joined Peg and Rog, another couple, and a woman named Karen. All animal behaviorists, and all headed out to Africa in the next couple of weeks—Rog and Peg to Tanzania, the rest to Rwanda. Despite their morning's event the talk was quick, spirited, wide-ranging; Frank drank wine and listened as they discussed African politics, the problems of filming primates, rock music. Only once did the subject of the funeral come up, and then they shook their heads; there wasn't much to say. Stiff upper lip.

Frank said, "I suppose it's better it happened now than when the kid was three or four."

They stared at him. "Oh no," Peg said. "I don't think so."

Acutely aware that he had said something stupid, Frank tried to recover: "I mean, you know, they've more time to. . . ." He shook his head, foundering.

"It's rather comparing absolutes, isn't it," Rog said gently.

"True," he said. "It is." And he drank his wine. He wanted to go on: True, he wanted to say, any death is an absolute disaster, even that of an infant too young to know what was happening; but what if you had spent your life raising six such children and then went out one morning and found their heads on your lawn? Isn't the one more absolute than the other? He was drunk, his head hurt, his body still vibrated with the day's drive, and the shock of the brush with the lorry; and it seemed likely that the dyslexia of exhaustion had invaded all his thinking, including his moral sense, making everything backward. So he clamped his teeth together and concentrated on the wine, his fork humming in his hand, his glass chattering against his teeth. The room was dark.

Afterwards Alec stopped at the door to his building and shook his head. "Not ready for that yet," he said. "Let's try Preservation Hall, it's your kind of thing on Wednesday nights. Traditional jazz."

Frank and Andrea had been fans of traditional jazz. "Any good?"

"Good enough for tonight, eh?"

The pub was within walking distance, down a wide cobblestone promenade called the Grassmarket, then up Victoria Street. At the door of the pub they were stopped; there was a cover charge, the usual band had been replaced by a buffet dinner and concert, featuring several different bands. Proceeds to go to the family of a Glasgow musician, recently killed in a car crash. "Jesus Christ," Frank exclaimed, feeling like a curse. He turned to go.

"Might as well try it," Alec said, and pulled out his wallet. "I'll pay."

"But we've already eaten."

Alec ignored him and gave the man twenty pounds. "Come on."

Inside, a very large pub was jammed with people, and an enormous buffet table stacked with meats, breads, salads, seafood dishes. They got drinks from the bar and sat at the end of a crowded picnic table. It was noisy, the Scots accents so thick that Frank understood less than half of what he heard. A succession of local acts took the stage: the traditional jazz band that usually played, a stand-up comedian, a singer of Forties' music hall songs, a country-western group. Alec and Frank took turns going to the bar to get refills. Frank watched the bands and the crowd. All ages and types were represented. Each band said something about the late musician, who apparently had been well-known, a young rocker and quite a hellion from the sound of it. Crashed driving home drunk after a gig, and no one a bit surprised.

About midnight an obese young man seated at their table, who had been stealing food from all the plates around him, rose whalelike and surged to the stage. People cheered as he joined the band setting up. He picked up a guitar, leaned into the mike, and proceeded to rip into a selection of r&b and early rock and roll. He and his band were the best group yet, and the pub went wild. Most of the crowd got to their feet and danced in place. Next to Frank a young punk had to lean over the table to answer a gray-haired lady's questions about how he kept his hair spiked. A Celtic wake, Frank thought, and downed his cider and howled with the rest as the fat man started up Chuck Berry's "Rock And Roll Music."

So he was feeling no pain when the band finished its last encore and he and Alec staggered off into the night, and made their way home. But it had gotten a lot colder while they were inside, and the streets were dark and empty. Preservation Hall was no more than a small wooden box of light, buried in a cold stone city. Frank looked back in its direction and saw that a streetlight reflected off the black cobblestones of the Grassmarket in such a way that there were thousands of brief white squiggles underfoot, looking like names engraved on black granite, as if the whole surface of the earth were paved by a single memorial.

The next day he drove north again, across the Forth Bridge and then west along the shores of a loch to Fort William, and north from there through the Highlands. Above Ullapool steep ridges burst like fins out of boggy treeless hillsides. There was water everywhere, from puddles to lochs, with the Atlantic itself visible from most high points. Out to sea the tall islands of the Inner Hebrides were just visible.

He continued north. He had his sleeping bag and foam pad with him, and so he parked in a scenic overlook, and cooked soup on his Bluet stove, and slept in the back of the car. He woke with the dawn and drove north. He talked to nobody.

Eventually he reached the northwest tip of Scotland and was forced to turn east, on a road bordering the North Sea. Early that evening he arrived in Scrabster, at the northeast tip of Scotland. He drove to the docks, and found that a ferry was scheduled to leave for the Orkney Islands the next day at noon. He decided to take it.

There was no secluded place to park, so he took a room in a hotel. He had dinner in the restaurant next door, fresh shrimp in mayonnaise with chips, and went to his room and slept. At six the next morning the ancient crone who ran the hotel knocked on his door and told him an unscheduled ferry was leaving in forty minutes: did he want to go? He said he did. He got up and dressed, then felt too exhausted to continue. He decided to take the regular ferry after all, took off his clothes and returned to bed. Then he realized that exhausted or not, he wasn't going to be able to fall back asleep. Cursing, almost crying, he got up and put his clothes back on. Downstairs the old woman had fried bacon and made him two thick bacon sandwiches, as he was going to miss her regular breakfast. He ate the sandwiches sitting in the Sierra, waiting to get the car into the ferry. Once in the hold he locked the car and went up to the warm stuffy passenger cabin, and lay on padded vinyl seating and fell back asleep.

He woke when they docked in Stromness. For a moment he didn't remember getting on the ferry, and he couldn't understand why he wasn't in his hotel bed in Scrabster. He stared through salt-stained windows at fishing boats, amazed, and then it came to him. He was in the Orkneys.

Driving along the southern coast of the main island, he found that his mental image of the Orkneys had been entirely wrong. He had expected an extension of the Highlands; instead it was like eastern

Scotland, low, rounded, and green. Most of it was cultivated or used for pasture. Green fields, fences, farmhouses. He was a bit disappointed.

Then in the island's big town of Kirkwall he drove past a Gothic cathedral—a very little Gothic cathedral, a kind of pocket cathedral. Frank had never seen anything like it. He stopped and got out to have a look. Cathedral of St. Magnus, begun in 1137. So early, and this far north! No wonder it was so small. Building it would have required craftsmen from the continent, shipped up here to a rude fishing village of drywall and turf roofs; a strange influx it must have been, a kind of cultural revolution. The finished building must have stood out like something from another planet.

But as he walked around the bishop's palace next door, and then a little museum, he learned that it might not have been such a shock for Kirkwall after all. In those days the Orkneys had been a crossroads of a sort, where Norse and Scots and English and Irish had met, infusing an indigenous culture that went right back to the Stone Age. The fields and pastures he had driven by had been worked, some of them, for five thousand years!

And such faces walking the streets, so intent and vivid. His image of the local culture had been as wrong as his image of the land. He had thought he would find decrepit fishing villages, dwindling to nothing as people moved south to the cities. But it wasn't like that in Kirkwall, where teenagers roamed in self-absorbed talky gangs, and restaurants open to the street were packed for lunch. In the bookstores he found big sections on local topics: nature guides, archaeological guides, histories, sea tales, novels. Several writers, obviously popular, had as their entire subject the islands. To the locals, he realized, the Orkneys were the center of the world.

He bought a guidebook and drove north, up the east coast of Mainland to the Broch of Gurness, a ruined fort and village that had been occupied from the time of Christ to the Norse era. The broch itself was a round stone tower about twenty feet tall. Its wall was at least ten feet thick, and was made of flat slabs, stacked so carefully that you couldn't have stuck a dime in the cracks. The walls in the surrounding village were much thinner; if attacked, the villagers would have retired into the broch. Frank nodded at the explanatory sentence in the guidebook, reminded that the twentieth century had had no monopoly on atrocities. Some had happened right here, no doubt. Unless the broch had functioned as a deterrent.

Gurness overlooked a narrow channel between Mainland and the smaller island of Rousay. Looking out at the channel, Frank noticed white ripples in its blue water; waves and foam were pouring past. It was a tidal race, apparently, and at the moment the entire contents of the channel were rushing north, as fast as any river he had ever seen.

Following suggestions in the guidebook, he drove across the island to the neolithic site of Brodgar, Stenness, and Maes Howe. Brodgar and Stenness were two rings of standing stones; Maes Howe was a nearby chambered tomb.

The Ring of Brodgar was a big one, three hundred and forty feet across. Over half of the original sixty stones were still standing, each one a block of roughly dressed sandstone, weathered over the millennia into shapes of great individuality and charisma, like Rodin figures. Following the arc they made, he watched the sunlight break on them. It was beautiful.

Stenness was less impressive, as there were only four stones left, each tremendously tall. It roused more curiosity than awe: how had they stood those monsters on end? No one knew for sure.

From the road, Maes Howe was just a conical grass mound. To see the inside he had to wait for a guided tour, happily scheduled to start in fifteen minutes.

He was still the only person waiting when a short stout woman drove up in a pickup truck. She was about twenty-five, and wore Levi's and a red windbreaker. She greeted him and unlocked a gate in the fence surrounding the mound, then led him up a gravel path to the entrance on the southwest slope. There they had to get on their knees and crawl, down a tunnel three feet high and some thirty feet long. Midwinter sunsets shone directly down this entryway, the woman looked over her shoulder to tell him. Her Levi's were new.

The main chamber of the tomb was quite tall. "Wow," he said, standing up and looking around.

"It's big isn't it," the guide said. She told him about it in a casual way. The walls were made of the ubiquitous sandstone slabs, with some monster monoliths bracketing the entryway. And something unexpected: a group of Norse sailors had broken into the tomb in the twelfth century (four thousand years after the tomb's construction!) and taken shelter in it through a three-day storm. This was known because they had passed the time carving runes on the walls, which told their story. The woman pointed to lines and translated: "Happy is he who finds the great treasure.' And over here: 'Ingrid is the most beautiful woman in the world.'"

"You're kidding."

"That's what it says. And look here, you'll see they did some drawing as well."

She pointed out three graceful line figures, cut presumably with axe blades: a walrus, a narwhale, and a dragon. He had seen all three in the shops of Kirkwall, reproduced in silver for earrings and pendants. "They're beautiful," he said.

"A good eye, that Viking."

He looked at them for a long time, then walked around the chamber to look at the runes again. It was a suggestive alphabet, harsh and angular. The guide seemed in no hurry, she answered his questions at length. She was a guide in the summer, and sewed sweaters and quilts in the winter. Yes, the winters were dark. But not very cold. Average temperature around thirty.

"That warm?"

"Aye it's the Gulf Stream you see. It's why Britain is so warm, and Norway too for that matter."

Britain so warm. "I see," he said carefully.

Back outside he stood and blinked in the strong afternoon light. He had just emerged from a five-thousand-year-old tomb. Down by the loch the standing stones were visible, both rings. Ingrid is the most beautiful woman in the world. He looked at Brodgar, a circle of black dots next to a silver sheen of water. It was a memorial too, although what it was supposed to make its viewers remember was no longer clear. A great chief; the death of one year, birth of the next; the planets, moon and sun in their courses. Or something else, something simpler. *Here we are.*

*   *   *

It was still midafternoon judging by the sun, so he was surprised
to look at his watch and see it was six o'clock. Amazing. It was going
to be just like his therapy! Only better because outdoors, in the
sunlight and the wind. Spend summer in the Orkneys, winter in the
Falklands, which were said to be very similar. . . . He drove back to
Kirkwall and had dinner in a hotel restaurant. The waitress was tall,
attractive, about forty. She asked him where he was from, and he
asked her when it would get busy (July), what the population of
Kirkwall was (about ten thousand, she guessed) and what she did in
the winter (accounting). He had broiled scallops and a glass of white
wine. Afterward he sat in the Sierra and looked at his map. He wanted
to sleep in the car, but hadn't yet seen a good place to park for the
night.

The northwest tip of Mainland looked promising, so he drove
across the middle of the island again, passing Stenness and Brodgar
once more. The stones of Brodgar stood silhouetted against a western sky banded orange and pink and white and red.

At the very northwest tip of the island, the Point of Buckquoy,
there was a small parking lot, empty this late in the evening. Perfect.
Extending west from the point was a tidal causeway, now covered by
the sea; a few hundred yards across the water was a small island called
the Brough of Birsay, a flat loaf of sandstone tilted up to the west,
so that one could see the whole grass top of it. There were ruins and
a museum at the near end, a small lighthouse on the west point.
Clearly something to check out the next day.

South of the point, the western shore of the island curved back in
a broad, open bay. Behind its beach stood the well-preserved ruins
of a sixteenth century palace. The bay ended in a tall sea cliff called
Marwick Head, which had a tower on its top that looked like another
broch, but was, he discovered in his guidebook, the Kitchener Memorial. Offshore in 1916 the *HMS Hampshire* had hit a mine and sunk,
and six hundred men, including Kitchener, had drowned.

Odd, to see that. A couple of weeks ago (it felt like years) he had
read that when the German front lines had been informed of Kitchener's death, they had started ringing bells and banging pots and pans

in celebration; the noisemaking had spread up and down the German trenches, from the Belgian coast to the Swiss frontier.

He spread out his sleeping bag and foam pad in the back of the station wagon, and lay down. He had a candle for reading, but he did not want to read. The sound of the waves was loud. There was still a bit of light in the air, these northern summer twilights were really long. The sun had seemed to slide off to the right rather than descend, and suddenly he understood what it would be like to be above the Arctic Circle in midsummer: the sun would just keep sliding off to the right until it brushed the northern horizon, and then it would slide up again into the sky. He needed to live in Ultima Thule.

The car rocked slightly on a gust of wind. It had been windy all day; apparently it was windy all the time here, the main reason the islands were treeless. He lay back and looked at the roof of the car. A car made a good tent: flat floor, no leaks. . . . As he fell asleep he thought, it was a party a mile wide and a thousand miles long.

He woke at dawn, which came just before five A.M. His shadow and the car's shadow were flung out toward the brough, which was an island still, as the tidal bar was covered again. Exposed for only two hours each side of low tide, apparently.

He ate breakfast by the car, and then rather than wait for the causeway to clear he drove south, around the Bay of Birsay and behind Marwick Head, to the Bay of Skaill. It was a quiet morning, he had the one-lane track to himself. It cut through green pastures. Smoke rose from farmhouse chimneys and flattened out to the east. The farmhouses were white, with slate roofs and two white chimneys, one at each end of the house. Ruins of farmhouses built to the same design stood nearby, or in back pastures.

He came to another parking lot, containing five or six cars. A path had been cut through tall grass just behind the bay beach, and he followed it south. It ran nearly a mile around the curve of the bay, past a big nineteenth century manor house, apparently still occupied. Near the south point of the bay stretched a low concrete seawall and a small modern building, and some interruptions in the turf above the beach. Holes, it looked like. The pace of his walk picked up. A few people were bunched around a man in a tweed coat. Another guide?

Yes. It was Skara Brae.

The holes in the ground were the missing roofs of Stone Age houses buried in the sand; their floors were about twelve feet below the turf. The interior walls were made of the same slab as everything else on the island, stacked with the same precision. Stone hearths, stone bedframes, stone dressers: because of the islands' lack of wood, the guide was saying, and the ready availability of the slabs, most of the houses' furniture had been made of stone. And so it had endured.

Stacks of slabs held up longer ones, making shelves in standard college student bricks-and-boards style. Cupboards were inset in the walls. There was a kind of stone kitchen cabinet, with mortar and pestle beneath. It was instantly obvious what everything was for; everything looked deeply familiar.

Narrow passageways ran between houses. These too had been covered; apparently driftwood or whale rib beams had supported turf roofs over the entire village, so that during bad storms they need never go out. The first mall, Frank thought. The driftwood had included pieces of spruce, which had to have come from North America. The Gulf Stream again.

Frank stood at the back of a group of seven, listening to the guide as he looked down into the homes. The guide was bearded, stocky, fiftyish. Like the Maes Howe guide he was good at his work, wandering about with no obvious plan, sharing what he knew without memorized speeches. The village had been occupied for about six hundred years, beginning around 3000 B.C. Brodgar and Maes Howe had been built during those years, so probably people from here had helped in their construction. The bay had likely been a fresh-water lagoon at that time, with a beach separating it from the sea. Population about fifty or sixty. A heavy dependence on cattle and sheep, with lots of seafood as well. Sand filled in the homes when the village was abandoned, and turf grew over it. In 1850 a big storm tore the turf off and exposed the homes, completely intact except for the roofs. . . .

Water seepage had rounded away every edge, so that each slab looked sculpted, and caught at the light. Each house a luminous work of art. And five thousand years old, yet *so* familiar: the same needs, the same thinking, the same solutions. . . . A shudder ran through him, and he noticed that he was literally slack-jawed. He closed his mouth and almost laughed aloud. Open-mouthed astonishment could be so natural sometimes, so physical, unconscious, genuine.

When the other tourists left, he continued to wander around. The guide, sensing another enthusiast, joined him.

"It's like the Flintstones," Frank said, and laughed.

"The what?"

"You expect to see stone TVs and the like."

"Oh aye. It's very contemporary, isn't it."

"It's marvelous."

Frank walked from house to house, and the guide followed, and they talked. "Why is this one called the chief's house?"

"It's just a guess, actually. Everything in it is a bit bigger and better, that's all. In our world a chief would have it."

Frank nodded. "Do you live out here?"

"Aye." The guide pointed at the little building beyond the site. He had owned a hotel in Kirkwall, but sold it; Kirkwall had been too hectic for him. He had gotten the job here and moved out, and was very happy with it. He was getting a degree in archaeology by correspondence. The more he learned, the more amazed he was to be here; it was one of the most important archaeological sites in the world, after all. There wasn't a better one. No need to imagine furnishings and implements, "and to see so clearly how much they thought like we do."

Exactly. "Why did they leave, in the end?"

"No one knows."

"Ah."

They walked on.

"No sign of a fight, anyway."

"Good."

The guide asked Frank where he was staying, and Frank told him about the Sierra.

"I see!" the man said. "Well, if you need the use of a bathroom, there's one here at the back of the building. For a shave, perhaps. You look like you haven't had the chance in a while."

Frank rubbed a hand over his stubble, blushing. In fact he hadn't thought of shaving since well before leaving London. "Thanks," he said. "Maybe I'll take you up on that."

They talked about the ruins a while longer, and then the guide walked out to the seawall, and let Frank wander in peace.

He looked down in the rooms, which still glowed as if lit from within. Six hundred years of long summer days, long winter nights. Perhaps they had set sail for the Falklands. Five thousand years ago.

He called good-bye to the guide, who waved. On the way back to the car park he stopped once to look back. Under a carpet of cloud the wind was thrashing the tall beach grass, every waving stalk distinct, the clouds' underside visibly scalloped; and all of it touched with a silvery edge of light.

He ate lunch in Stromness, down by the docks, watching the fishing boats ride at anchor. A very practical-looking fleet, of metal and rubber and bright plastic buoys. In the afternoon he drove the Sierra around Scapa Flow and over a bridge at the east channel, the one Winston had ordered blocked with sunken ships. The smaller island to the south was covered with green fields and white farmhouses.

Late in the afternoon he drove slowly back to the Point of Buckquoy, stopping for a look in the nearby ruins of the sixteenth century earl's palace. Boys were playing soccer in the roofless main room.

The tide was out, revealing a concrete walkway set on a split bed of wet brown sandstone. He parked and walked over in the face of a stiff wind, onto the Brough of Birsay.

Viking ruins began immediately, as erosion had dropped part of the old settlement into the sea. He climbed steps into a tight network of knee-high walls. Compared to Skara Brae, it was a big town. In the middle of all the low foundations rose the shoulder-high walls of a church. Twelfth century, ambitious Romanesque design: and yet only fifty feet long, and twenty wide! Now this was a pocket cathedral. It had had a monastery connected to it, however; and some of the men who worshipped in it had traveled to Rome, Moscow, Newfoundland.

Picts had lived here before that; a few of their ruins lay below the Norse. Apparently they had left before the Norse arrived, though the record wasn't clear. What was clear was that people had been living here for a long, long time.

After a leisurely exploration of the site Frank walked west, up the slope of the island. It was only a few hundred yards to the lighthouse on the cliff, a modern white building with a short fat tower.

Beyond it was the edge of the island. He walked toward it and emerged from the wind shelter the island provided; a torrent of gusts almost knocked him back. He reached the edge and looked down.

At last something that looked like he thought it would! It was a long way to the water, perhaps a hundred and fifty feet. The cliff was breaking off in great stacks, which stood free and tilted out precariously, as if they were going to fall at any moment. Great stone cliffs, with the sun glaring directly out from them, and the surf crashing to smithereens on the rocks below: it was so obviously, grandiloquently the End of Europe that he had to laugh. A place made to cast oneself from. End the pain and fear, do a Hart Crane off the stern of Europe . . . except this looked like the bow, actually. The bow of a very big ship, crashing westward through the waves; yes, he could feel it in the soles of his feet. And foundering, he could feel that too, the shudders, the rolls, the last sluggish list. So jumping overboard would be redundant at best. The end would come, one way or another. Leaning out against the gale, feeling like a Pict or Viking, he knew he stood at the end—end of a continent, end of a century; end of a culture.

And yet there was a boat, coming around Marwick Head from the south, a little fishing tub from Stromness, rolling horribly in the swell. Heading northwest, out to—out to where? There were no more islands out there, not until Iceland anyway, or Greenland, Spitsbergen . . . where was it going at this time of day, near sunset and the west wind tearing in?

He stared at the trawler for a long time, rapt at the sight, until it was nothing but a black dot near the horizon. Whitecaps covered the sea, and the wind was still rising, gusting really hard. Gulls skated around on the blasts, landing on the cliffs below. The sun was very near the water, sliding off to the north, the boat no more than flotsam: and then he remembered the causeway and the tide.

He ran down the island and his heart leaped when he saw the concrete walkway washed by white water, surging up from the right. Stuck here, forced to break into the museum or huddle in a corner of the church . . . but no; the concrete stood clear again. If he ran—

He pounded down the steps and ran over the rough concrete. There were scores of parallel sandstone ridges still exposed to the left, but the right side was submerged already, and as he ran a broken wave rolled up onto the walkway and drenched him to the knees, filling his shoes with seawater and scaring him much more than was reasonable. He ran on cursing.

Onto the rocks and up five steps. At his car he stopped, gasping for breath. He got in the passenger side and took off his boots, socks, and pants. Put on dry pants, socks, and running shoes.

He got back out of the car.

The wind was now a constant gale, ripping over the car and the point and the ocean all around. It was going to be tough to cook dinner on his stove; the car made a poor windbreak, wind rushing under it right at stove level.

He got out the foam pad, and propped it with his boots against the lee side of the car. The pad and the car's bulk gave him just enough wind shelter to keep the little Bluet's gas flame alive. He sat on the asphalt behind the stove, watching the flames and the sea. The wind was tremendous, the Bay of Birsay riven by whitecaps, more white than blue. The car rocked on its shock absorbers. The sun had finally slid sideways into the sea, but clearly it was going to be a long blue dusk.

When the water was boiling he poured in a dried Knorr's soup and stirred it, put it back on the flame for a few more minutes, then killed the flame and ate, spooning split pea soup straight from the steaming pot into his mouth. Soup, bit of cheese, bit of salami, red wine from a tin cup, more soup. It was absurdly satisfying to make a meal in these conditions: the wind was in a fury!

When he was done eating he opened the car door and put away his dinner gear, then got out his windbreaker and rain pants and put them on. He walked around the carpark, and then up and down the low cliffy edges of the point of Buckquoy, watching the North Atlantic get torn by a full force gale. People had done this for thousands of years. The rich twilight blue looked like it would last forever.

Eventually he went to the car and got his notebooks. He returned to the very tip of the point, feeling the wind like slaps on the ear. He sat with his legs hanging over the drop, the ocean on three sides of him, the wind pouring across him, left to right. The horizon was a line where purest blue met bluest black. He kicked his heels against the rock. He could see just well enough to tell which pages in the notebooks had writing on them; he tore these from the wire spirals, and bunched them into balls and threw them away. They flew off to the right and disappeared immediately in the murk and whitecaps. When he had disposed of all the pages he had written on he cleared the long torn shreds of paper out of the wire rings, and tossed them after the rest.

It was getting cold, and the wind was a constant kinetic assault. He went back to the car and sat in the passenger seat. His notebooks lay on the driver's seat. The western horizon was a deep blue, now. Must be eleven at least.

After a time he lit the candle and set it on the dash. The car was still rocking in the wind, and the candle flame danced and trembled on its wick. All the black shadows in the car shivered too, synchronized perfectly with the flame.

He picked up a notebook and opened it. There were a few pages left between damp cardboard covers. He found a pen in his daypack. He rested his hand on the page, the pen in position to write, its tip in the quivering shadow of his hand. He wrote, "I believe that man is good. I believe we stand at the dawn of a century that will be more peaceful and prosperous than any in history." Outside it was dark, and the wind howled.

Remaking History

"The point is *not* to make an exact replica of the Teheran embassy compound." Exasperated, Ivan Venutshenko grabbed his hair in one hand and pulled up, which gave him a faintly Oriental look. "It's the *spirit* of the place that we want to invoke here."

"This has the spirit of our storage warehouse, if you ask me."

"This *is* our storage warehouse, John. We make all our movies here."

"But I thought you said we were going to correct all the lies of the first movie," John Rand said to their director. "I thought you said *Escape From Teheran* was a dumb TV docudrama, only worth remembering because of De Niro's performance as Colonel Jackson. We're going to get the true story on film at last, you said."

Ivan sighed. "That's right, John. Admirable memory. But what you must understand is that when making a film, *true* doesn't mean an absolute fidelity to the real."

"I'll bet that's just what the director of the docudrama said."

Ivan hissed, which he did often while directing their films, to show that he was letting off steam, and avoiding an explosion. "Don't be obstructionist, John. We're not doing anything like that hackwork, and you know it. Lunar gravity alone makes it impossible for us to make a completely realist film. We are working in a world of dream, in a surrealist intensification of what really happened. Besides, we're doing these movies for our own entertainment up here! Remake bad historical films! Have a good time!"

"Sure, Ivan. Sure. Except the ones *you've* directed have been getting some great reviews downside. They're saying you're the new Eisenstein and these little remakes are the best thing to hit the screen since *Kane.* So now the pressure is on and it's not just a game anymore, right?"

"Wrong!" Ivan karate-chopped the air. "I refuse to believe that. When we stop having fun doing this"—nearly shouting—"I quit!"

"Sure, Sergei."

"Don't call me that!"

"Okay, Orson."

"JOHN!"

"But that's *my* name. If I call you that we'll all get confused."

Melina Gourtsianis, their female lead, came to Ivan's rescue. "Come on, John, you'll give him a heart attack, and besides it's late. Let's get on with it."

Ivan calmed down, ran his hands through his hair. He loved doing his maddened director routine, and John loved maddening him. As they disagreed about nearly everything, they made a perfect team. "Fine," Ivan said. "Okay. We've got the set ready, and it may not be an *exact* replica of the compound—" fierce glare at John—"but it's good enough.

"Now, let's go through it one more time. It's night in Teheran. This whole quarter of the city has been gassed with a paralyzing nerve gas, but there's no way of telling when the Revolutionary Guards might come barreling in from somewhere else with gas masks or whatever, and you can't be sure some of them haven't been protected from the gas in sealed rooms. Any moment they might jump out firing. Your helicopters are hovering just overhead, so it's tremendously noisy. There's a blackout in the compound, but searchlights from other parts of the city are beginning to pin the choppers. They've been breaking like cheap toys all the way in, so now there are only five left, and you have no assurances that they will continue to work, especially since twice that number have already broken. You're all wearing gas masks and moving through the rooms of the compound, trying to find and move all fifty-three of the hostages—it's dark and most of the hostages are knocked out like the guards, but some of the rooms were well-sealed, and naturally these hostages are shouting for help. For a while—and this is the effect I want to emphasize more than any other—for a while, things inside are absolutely chaotic. No one can find Colonel Jackson, no one knows how many of the hostages are recovered and how many are still in the embassy, it's dark, it's noisy, there are shots in the distance. I want an effect like the scene at the end of *The Lady from Shanghai,* when they're in the carnival's house of mirrors shooting at each other. Multiplied by ten. Total chaos."

"Now hold on just a second here," John said, exaggerating his Texas accent, which came and went according to his convenience. "I like the chaos bit, and the allusion to Welles, but let's get back to this issue of the facts. Colonel Jackson was the hero of this whole thing! He was the one that decided to go on with all them helicopters busting out in the desert, and he was the one that found Annette Bellows in the embassy to lead them around, and all in all he was on top of every minute of it. That's why they gave him all them medals!"

Ivan glared. "What part are you playing, John?"

"Why, Colonel Jackson." John drew himself up. "Natch."

"However." Ivan tapped the side of his head, to indicate thought. "You don't just want to do a bad imitation of the De Niro performance, do you? You want to do a new interpretation, don't you? Besides, it seems to me a foolish idea to try an imitation of De Niro."

"I like the idea, myself," John said. "Show him how."

Ivan waved him away. "You got all you know about this affair from that stupid TV movie, just like everyone else. I, however, have been reading the accounts of the hostages and the Marines on those helicopters, and the truth is that Colonel Jackson's best moment was out there in the desert, when he decided to go on with the mission even though only five helicopters were still functioning. That was his peak of glory, his moment of heroism. And you did a perfectly adequate job of conveying that when we filmed the scene. We could see every little gear in there, grinding away." He tapped his skull.

"De Niro would have been proud," Melina said.

John pursed his lips and nodded. "We need great men like that. Without them history would be dead. It'd be nothing but a bunch of broken-down helicopters out in a desert somewhere."

"A trenchant image of history," Ivan said. "Too bad Shelley got to it first. Meanwhile, the truth is that after making the decision to go on with the raid, Colonel Jackson appeared, in the words of his subordinates, somewhat stunned. When they landed on the embassy roof he led the first unit in, and when they got lost inside, the whole force was effectively without leadership for most of the crucial first half-hour. All the accounts of this period describe it as the utmost chaos, saved only when Sergeant Payton—*not* Colonel Jackson; the TV movie lied about that—when Payton found Ms. Bellows, and she led them to all the hostage rooms they hadn't found."

"All right, all right." John frowned. "So I'm supposed to be kind of spaced out in this scene."

"Don't go for too deep an analysis, John, you might strain something. But essentially you have it. Having committed the force to the raid, even though you're vastly undermanned because of the damned helicopters breaking down, you're a bit frozen by the risk of it. Got that?"

"Yeah. But I don't believe it. Jackson was a hero."

"Fine, a hero, lots of medals. Roomfuls of medals. If he pinned them on he'd look like the bride after the dollar dance. He'd collapse under their weight. But now let's try showing what really happened."

"All right." John drew himself up. "I'm ready."

The shooting of the scene was the part they all enjoyed the most; this was the heart of the activity, the reason they kept making movies to occupy their free hours at Luna Three. Ivan and John and Melina and Pierre-Paul, the theoreticians who traded directing chores from project to project, always blocked the scenes very loosely, allowing a lot of room for improvisation. Thus scenes like this one, which were supposed to be chaotic, were played out with a manic gusto. They were good at chaos.

And so for nearly a half-hour they rushed about the interior of their Teheran embassy compound—the base storage warehouse, with its immense rows of boxes arranged behind white panels of plywood to resemble the compound's buildings and their interiors. Their shouts were nearly drowned by the clatter of recorded helicopters, while intermittent lights flashed in the darkness. Cutouts representing the helicopters were pasted to the clear dome overhead, silhouetted against the unearthly brilliance of the stars—these last had become a trademark of Luna Three Productions, as their frequent night scenes always had these unbelievably bright stars overhead, part of the films' dreamlike effect.

The actors playing Marines bounded about the compound in their gas masks, looking like aliens descended to ravage a planet; the actors playing hostages and Revolutionary Guards lay scattered on the floor, except for a few in protected rooms, who fought or cried for help. John and Pierre-Paul and the rest hunted the compound for Melina, playing Annette Bellows. For a while it looked as if John would get to her first, thus repeating the falsehood of the De Niro film. But eventually Pierre-Paul, playing Sergeant Payton, located her room, and he and his small unit rushed about after the clear-headed Bellows, who, as she wrote later, had spent most of her months in captivity planning what she should do if this moment ever came. They located the remaining comatose hostages and lugged them quickly to the plywood helicopter on the compound roof. The sound of shots punctuated the helicopters' roar. They leaped through the helicopter's door, shafts of white light stabbing the air like Islamic swords.

That was it; the flight away would be filmed in their little helicopter interior. Ivan turned off the helicopter noise, shouted "Cut!" into a megaphone. Then he shut down all the strategically placed minicams, which had been recording every minute of it.

"What bothers me about your movies, Ivan," John said, "is that you always take away the hero. Always!"

They were standing in the shallow end of the base pool, cooling off while they watched the day's rushes on a screen filling one wall of the natatorium. Many of the screens showed much the same result: darkness, flickering light, alien shapes moving in the elongated dance-like way that audiences on Earth found so surreal, so mesmerizing. There was little indication of the pulsing rhythms and wrenching suspense that Ivan's editing would create from this material. But the actors were happy, seeing arresting images of desperation, of risk, of heroism in the face of a numbingly loud confusion.

Ivan was not as pleased. "Shit!" he said. "We're going to have to do it again."

"Looks okay to me," John remarked. "Son of Film Noir Returns From the Grave. But really, Ivan, you've got to do something about this prejudice against heroes. I saw *Escape From Teheran* when I was a kid, and it was an inspiration to me. It was one of the big reasons I got into engineering."

Pierre-Paul objected. "John, just how did seeing a commando film get you interested in engineering?"

"Well," John replied, frowning, "I thought I'd design a better helicopter, I guess." He ignored his friends' laughter. "I was pretty shocked at how unreliable they were. But the way old De Niro continued on to Teheran! The way he extricated all the hostages and got them back safely, even with the choppers dropping like flies. It was great! We need heroes, and history tells the story of the few people who had what it takes to be one. But you're always downplaying them."

"The Great Man Theory of History," Pierre-Paul said scornfully.

"Sure!" John admitted. "Great Woman too, of course," nodding quickly at the frowning Melina. "It's the great leaders who make the difference. They're special people, and there aren't many of them. But if you believe Ivan's films, there aren't any at all."

With a snort of disgust, Ivan took his attention from the rushes. "Hell, we are going to have to do that scene again. As for my theory of history, John, you both have it and you don't. As far as I understand you." He cocked his head and looked at his friend attentively. On the set they both played their parts to the teeth: Ivan the tormented, temperamental director, gnashing his teeth and ordering people about; John the stubborn, temperamental star, questioning everything and insisting on his preeminence. Mostly this was role-playing, part of the game, part of what made their hobby entertaining to them. Off the set the roles largely disappeared, except to make a point, or have some fun. Ivan was the base's head of computer operations, while John was an engineer involved in the Mars voyage; they were good friends, and their arguments had done much to shape

Ivan's ideas for his revisionist historical films, which were certainly the ones from their little troupe making the biggest splash downside—though John claimed this was because of the suspenseful plots and the weird low-gee imagery, not because of what they were saying about history. *"Do* I understand you?" Ivan asked curiously.

"Well," John said, "take the one you did last time, about the woman who saved John Lennon's life. Now that was a perfect example of heroic action, as the 1982 docudrama made clear. There she was, standing right next to a man who had pulled out a damn big gun, and quicker than he could pull the trigger she put a foot in his crotch and a fist in his ear. But in your remake, all we concentrated on was how she had just started the karate class that taught her the moves, and how her husband encouraged her to take the class, and how that cabbie stopped for her even though she was going the other direction, and how that other cabbie told her that Lennon had just walked into his apartment lobby, and all that. You made it seem like it was just a coincidence!"

Ivan took a mouthful of pool water and spurted it at the spangled dome, looking like a fountain statue. "It took a lot of coincidences to get Margaret Arvis into the Dakota lobby at the right time," he told John. "But some of them weren't coincidences—they were little acts of generosity or kindness or consideration, that put her where she could do what she did. I didn't take the heroism away. I just spread it around to all the places it belonged."

John grimaced, drew himself up into his star persona. "I suppose this is some damn Commie notion of mass social movements, sweeping history along in a consensus direction."

"No, no," Ivan said. "I always concentrate on individuals. What I'm saying is that all our individual actions add up to history, to the big visible acts of our so-called 'leaders.' You know what I mean; you hear people saying all the time that things are better now because John Lennon was such a moral force, traveling everywhere, Nobel Peace Prize, secular pope, the conscience of the world or whatnot."

"Well, he *was* the conscience of the world!"

"Sure, sure, he wrote great songs. And he got a lot of antagonists to talk. But without Margaret Arvis he would have been killed at age forty. And without Margaret Arvis's husband, and her karate instruc-

tor, and a couple cabbies in New York, and so on, she wouldn't have
been there to save his life. So we all become part of it, see? The
people who say it was all because of Lennon, or Carter, or Gorbachev—they're putting on a few people what we *all* did."

John shook his head, scattering water everywhere. "Very sophisticated, I'm sure! But in fact it was precisely Lennon and Carter and
Gorbachev who made huge differences, all by themselves. Carter
started the big swing toward human rights. Palestine, the new Latin
America, the American Indian nations—none of those would have
existed without him."

"In fact," Melina added, glancing mischievously at Pierre-Paul, "if
I understand the Margaret Arvis movie correctly, if she hadn't been
going to see Carter thank his New York campaign workers for the
1980 victory, she wouldn't have been in the neighborhood of the
Dakota, and so she wouldn't have had the chance to save Lennon's
life."

John rose up like a whale breaching. "So it's Carter we have to
thank for that, too! As for Gorbachev, well, I don't have to tell you
what all he did. That was a hundred-eighty degree turnaround for you
Russkies, and no one can say it would have happened without him."

"Well—he was an important leader, I agree."

"Sure was! And Carter was just as crucial. Their years were the
turning point, when the world started to crawl out from under the
shadow of World War Two. And that was their doing. There just
aren't many people who could've done it. Most of us don't have it
in us."

Ivan shook his head. "Carter wouldn't have been able to do what
he did unless Colonel Ernest Jackson had saved the rescue mission
to Teheran, by deciding to go on."

"So Jackson is a hero too!"

"But then Jackson wouldn't have been a hero if the officer back
in the Pentagon hadn't decided at the last minute to send sixteen
helicopters instead of eight."

"And," Melina pointed out quickly, "if Annette Bellows hadn't
spent most of a year daydreaming about what she would do in a
rescue attempt, so that she knew blindfolded where every other

hostage was being kept. They would have left about half the hostages behind without her, and Carter wouldn't have looked so good."

"Plus they needed Sergeant Payton to find Bellows," Ivan added.

"Well shit!" John yelled defensively, which was his retort in any tight spot. He changed tack. "I ain't so sure that Carter's reelection hinged on those hostages anyway. He was running against a flake, I can't remember the guy's name, but he was some kind of idiot."

"So?" Melina said. "Since when has that made any difference?"

With a roar John dove at her, making a big splash. She was much faster than he was, however, and she evaded him easily as he chased her around the pool; it looked like a whale chasing a dolphin. He was reduced to splashing at her from a distance, and the debate quickly degenerated into a big splash fight, as it often did.

"Oh well," John declared, giving up the attack and floating in the shallow end. "I love watching Melina swim the butterfly. In this gravity it becomes a godlike act. Those muscular arms, that sinuous dolphin motion . . ."

Pierre-Paul snorted. "You just like the way the butterfly puts her bottom above water so often."

"No way! Women are just more hydrodynamic than men, don't you think?"

"Not the way you like them."

"Godlike. Gods and goddesses."

"You look a bit godlike yourself," Melina told him. "Bacchus, for instance."

"Hey." John waved her off, jabbed a finger at the screens. "I note that all this mucho sophisticated European theorizing has been sunk. Took a bit of Texas logic, is all."

"Only Texas logic could do it," Pierre-Paul said.

"Right. You admit my point. In the end it's the great leaders who have to act, the rare ones, no matter if we ordinary folks help them into power."

"When you revise your proposition like that," Ivan said, "you turn it into mine. Leaders are important, but they are leaders because we made them leaders. They are a collective phenomenon. They are expressions of us."

"Now wait just a minute! You're going over the line again! You're talking like heroic leaders are a dime a dozen, but if that were true it wouldn't matter if Carter had lost in 1980, or if Lennon had been killed by that guy. But look at history, man! Look what happened when we did lose great leaders! Lincoln was shot; did they come up with another leader comparable to him? No way! Same with Gandhi, and the Kennedys, and King, and Sadat, and Olof Palme. When those folks were killed their countries suffered the lack of them, because they were special."

"They *were* special," Ivan agreed, "and obviously it was a bad thing they were killed. And no doubt there was a short-term change for the worse. But they're not irreplaceable, because they're human beings just like us. None of them, except maybe Lincoln or Gandhi, was any kind of genius or saint. It's only afterward we think of them that way, because we want heroes so much. But we're the heroes. All of us put them in place. And there are a lot of capable, brilliant people out there to replace the loss of them, so that in the long run we recover."

"The *real* long run," John said darkly. "A hundred years or more, for the South without Lincoln. They just aren't that common. The long run proves it."

"Speaking of the long run," Pierre-Paul said, "is anyone getting hungry?"

They all were. The rushes were over, and Ivan had dismissed them as unusable. They climbed out of the pool and walked toward the changing room, discussing restaurants. There were a considerable number of them in the station, and new ones were opening every week. "I just tried the new Hungarian restaurant," Melina said. "The food was good, but we had trouble, when the meal was over, finding someone to give us the check!"

"I thought you said it was a Hungarian restaurant," John said.

They threw him back in the pool.

The second time they ran through the rescue scene in the compound, Ivan had repositioned most of the minicams, and many of the lights; his instructions to the actors remained the same. But once inside the hallways of the set, John Rand couldn't help hurrying in the general direction of Annette Bellows's room.

All right, he thought. Maybe Colonel Jackson had been a bit hasty to rush into the compound in search of hostages, leaving the group without a commander. But his heart had been in the right place, and the truth was, he had found a lot of the hostages without any help from Bellows at all. It was easy; they were scattered in ones and twos on the floor of almost every room he and his commandos entered, and stretched out along with the guards in the rooms and in the halls, paralyzed by the nerve gas. Damn good idea, that nerve gas. Guards and hostages, tough parts to play, no doubt, as they were getting kicked pretty frequently by commandos running by. He hustled his crew into room after room, then sent them off with hostages draped over their shoulders, pretending to stagger down the halls, banging into walls—*really* tough part to play, hostage—and clutching at gas masks and such; great images for the minicams, no doubt about it.

When all his commandos had been sent back, he ran around a corner in what he believed to be the direction of Annette Bellows's room. Over the racket of the helicopters, and the occasional round of automatic fire, he thought he could make out Melina's voice, shouting hoarsely. So Pierre-Paul hadn't gotten to her yet. Good. Now he could find her and be the one to follow her around rescuing the more obscurely housed hostages, just as De Niro had in the docudrama. It would give Ivan fits, but they could argue it out afterward. No way of telling what had really happened in that compound twenty years before, after all; and it made a better *story* his way.

Their set was only one story tall, which was one of the things that John had objected to; the compound in Teheran had been four stories high, and getting up stairs had been part of the hassle. But Ivan was going to play with the images and shoot a few stair scenes later on, to achieve the effect of multiple floors. Fine, it meant he had only to struggle around a couple of narrow corners, jumping comatose Revolutionary Guards, looking fierce for the minicams wherever they were. It was really loud this time around; *really* loud.

Then one of the walls fell over on him, the plywood pinning him to the ground, the boxes behind it tumbling down and filling the hallway. "Hey!" he cried out, shocked. This wasn't the way it had happened. What was going on? The noise of the helicopters cut off abruptly, replaced by a series of crashes, a whooshing sound. That sound put a fine electric thrill down his spine; he had heard it before, in training routines. Air leaving the chamber. The dome must have been breached.

He heaved up against the plywood. Stuck. Flattening himself as much as possible he slithered forward, under the plywood and out into a small space among fallen boxes. Hard to tell where the hallway had been, and it was pitch-dark. There wouldn't be too much time left. He thought of his little gas mask, then cursed; it wasn't connected to a real oxygen supply. That's what comes from using fake props! he thought angrily. A gas mask with nothing attached to it. Open to the air, which was departing rapidly. Not much time.

He found room among the boxes to stand, and he was about to run over them to the door leading out of the warehouse—assuming the whole station hadn't been breached—when he remembered Melina. Stuck in her embassy room down the hall, wouldn't she still be there? Hell. He groped along in the dark, hearing shouts in the distance. He saw lights, too. Good. He was holding his breath, for what felt like minutes at a time, thought it was probably less than thirty seconds. Every time he sucked in a new breath he expected it to be the freezing vacuum, but the supply of rushing, cold—very cold—air continued to fill him. Emergency supply pouring out into the breach, actually a technique he had helped develop himself. Seemed to be working, at least for the moment.

He heard a muffled cry to one side, began to pull at the boxes before him. Squeak in the gloom, ah-ha, there she was. Not fully conscious. Legs wet, probably blood, uh-oh. He pulled hard at boxes, lifted her up. Adrenaline and lunar gravity made him feel like Superman with that part of things, but there didn't seem to be anywhere near as much air as before, and what was left was damned cold. Hurt to breathe. And harder than hell to balance as he hopped over objects with Melina in his arms. Feeling faint, he climbed over a row of boxes and staggered toward a distant light. A sheet of plywood smacked his shin and he cried out, then fell over. "Hey," he said. The air was gone.

When he came to he was lying in a bed in the station hospital. "Great," he muttered. "Whole station wasn't blown up."

His friends laughed, relieved to hear him speak. The whole film crew was in there, it seemed. Ivan, standing next to the bed, said, "It's okay."

"What the hell happened?"

"A small meteor, apparently. Hit out in our sector, in the shuttle landing chambers, ironically. But it wrecked our storage space as well, as you no doubt noticed."

John nodded painfully. "So it finally happened."

"Yes." This was one of the great uncontrollable dangers of the lunar stations; meteors small and large were still crashing down onto the moon's airless surface, by the thousands every year. Odds were poor that any one would hit something as small as the surface parts of their station, but coming down in such numbers. . . . In the long run they were reduced to a safety status somewhat equivalent to that of mountain climbers. Rockfall could always get you.

"Melina?" John said, jerking up in his bed.

"Over here," Melina called. She was a few beds down, and had one leg in a cast. "I'm fine, John." She got out of bed to prove it, and came over to kiss his cheek. "Thanks for the rescue!"

John snorted. "What rescue?"

They laughed again at him. Pierre-Paul pointed a forefinger at him. "There are heroes everywhere, even among the lowest of us. Now you have to admit Ivan's argument."

"The hell I do."

"You're a hero," Ivan said to him, grinning. "Just an ordinary man, so to speak. Not one of the great leaders at all. But by saving Melina, you've changed history."

"Not unless she becomes president," John said, and laughed. "Hey Melina! Go out and run for office! Or save some promising song-writer or something."

Ivan just shook his head. "Why are you so stubborn? It's not so bad if I'm right, John. Think about it. If I am right, then we aren't just sitting around waiting for leaders to guide us." A big grin lit his face. "We become the masters of our fate, we make our own deci-sions and act on them—we choose our leaders, and instruct them by consensus, so that we can take history any direction we please! Just as you did in the warehouse."

John lay back in his bed and was silent. Around him his friends grinned; one of them was bringing up a big papier-mâché medal, which vaguely resembled the one the Wizard of Oz pins to the Cowardly Lion. "Ah hell," John said.

"When the expedition reaches Mars, they'll have to name something after you," Melina said.

John thought about it for a while. He took the big medal, held it limply. His friends watched him, waiting for him to speak.

"Well, I still say it's bullshit," he told Ivan. "But if there is any truth to what you say, it's just the good old spirit of the Alamo you're talking about, anyway. We've been doing it like that in Texas for years."

They laughed at him.

He rose up from the bed again, swung the medal at them furiously. "I swear it's true! Besides, it's all Robert De Niro's fault, anyway! I was *imitating* the real heroes, don't you see? I was crawling around in there all dazed, and then I saw De Niro's face when he was playing Colonel Jackson in the Teheran embassy, and I said to myself, well hell, what would he have done in this here situation? And that's just what I did."

Vinland the Dream

Abstract. It was sunset at L'Anse aux Meadows. The water of the bay was still, the boggy beach was dark in the shadows. Flat arms of land pointed to flat islands offshore; beyond these a taller island stood like a loaf of stone in the sea, catching the last of the day's light. A stream gurgled gently as it cut through the beach bog. Above the bog, on a narrow grassy terrace, one could just make out a pattern of low mounds, all that remained of sod walls. Next to them were three or four sod buildings, and beyond the buildings, a number of tents.

A group of people—archeologists, graduate students, volunteer laborers, visitors—moved together onto a rocky ridge overlooking the site. Some of them worked at starting a campfire in a ring of blackened stones; others began to unpack bags of food, and cases of beer. Far across the water lay the dark bulk of Labrador. Kindling caught and their fire burned, a spark of yellow in the dusk's gloom.

Hot dogs and beer, around a campfire by the sea; and yet it was strangely quiet. Voices were subdued. The people on the hill glanced down often at the site, where the head of their dig, a lanky man in his early fifties, was giving a brief tour to their distinguished guest. The distinguished guest did not appear pleased.

* * *

Introduction. The head of the dig, an archeology professor from McGill University, was looking at the distinguished guest with the expression he wore when confronted by an aggressive undergraduate. The distinguished guest, Canada's Minister of Culture, was asking question after question. As she did, the professor took her to look for herself, at the forge, and the slag pit, and the little midden beside Building E. New trenches were cut across the mounds and depressions, perfect rectangular cuts in the black peat; they could tell the minister nothing of what they had revealed. But she had insisted on seeing them, and now she was asking questions that got right to the point, although they could have been asked and answered just as well in Ottawa. Yes, the professor explained, the fuel for the forge was wood charcoal, the temperature had gotten to around twelve hundred degrees Celsius, the process was direct reduction of bog ore, obtaining about one kilogram of iron for every five kilograms of slag. All was as it was in other Norse forges— except that the limonites in the bog ore had now been precisely identified by spectroscopic analysis; and that analysis had revealed that the bog iron smelted here had come from northern Quebec, near Chicoutimi. The Norse explorers, who had supposedly smelted the bog ore, could not have obtained it.

There was a similar situation in the midden; rust migrated in peat at a known rate, and so it could be determined that the many iron rivets in the midden had only been there a hundred and forty years, plus or minus fifty.

"So," the minister said, in English with a Francophone lilt. "You have proved your case, it appears?"

The professor nodded wordlessly. The minister watched him, and he couldn't help feeling that despite the nature of the news he was giving her, she was somewhat amused. By him? By his scientific terminology? By his obvious (and growing) depression? He couldn't tell.

The minister raised her eyebrows. "L'Anse aux Meadows, a hoax. Parcs Canada will not like it at all."

"No one will like it," the professor croaked.

"No," the minister said, looking at him. "I suppose not. Particularly as this is part of a larger pattern, yes?"

The professor did not reply.

"The entire concept of Vinland," she said. "A hoax!"

The professor nodded glumly.

"I would not have believed it possible."

"No," the professor said. "But—" He waved a hand at the low mounds around them—"So it appears." He shrugged. "The story has always rested on a very small body of evidence. Three sagas, this site, a few references in Scandinavian records, a few coins, a few cairns . . ." He shook his head. "Not much." He picked up a chunk of dried peat from the ground, crumbled it in his fingers.

Suddenly the minister laughed at him, then put her hand to his upper arm. Her fingers were warm. "You must remember it is not your fault."

He smiled wanly. "I suppose not." He liked the look on her face; sympathetic as well as amused. She was about his age, perhaps a bit older. An attractive and sophisticated Quebecois. "I need a drink," he confessed.

"There's beer on the hill."

"Something stronger. I have a bottle of cognac I haven't opened yet . . ."

"Let's get it and take it up there with us."

Experimental Methods. The graduate students and volunteer laborers were gathered around the fire, and the smell of roasting hot dogs filled the air. It was nearly eleven, the sun a half-hour gone, and the last light of the summer dusk slowly leaked from the sky. The fire burned like a beacon. Beer had been flowing freely, and the party was beginning to get a little more boisterous.

The minister and the professor stood near the fire, drinking cognac out of plastic cups.

"How did you come to suspect the story of Vinland?" the minister asked as they watched the students cook hot dogs.

A couple of the volunteer laborers, who had paid good money to spend their summer digging trenches in a bog, heard the question and moved closer.

The professor shrugged. "I can't quite remember." He tried to laugh. "Here I am an archeologist, and I can't remember my own past."

The minister nodded as if that made sense. "I suppose it was a long time ago?"

"Yes." He concentrated. "Now what was it. Someone was following up the story of the Vinland map, to try and figure out who had done it. The map showed up in a bookstore in New Haven in the 1950s—as you may know?"

"No," the minister said. "I hardly know a thing about Vinland, I assure you. Just the basics that anyone in my position would have to know."

"Well, there was a map found in the 1950s called the Vinland map, and it was shown to be a hoax soon after its discovery. But when this investigator traced the map's history, she found that the book it had been in was accounted for all the way back to the 1820s, map and all. It meant the hoaxer had lived longer ago than I had expected." He refilled his cup of cognac, then the minister's. "There were a lot of Viking hoaxes in the nineteenth century, but this one was so early. It surprised me. It's generally thought that the whole phenomenon was stimulated by a book that a Danish scholar published in 1837, containing translations of the Vinland sagas and related material. The book was very popular among the Scandinavian settlers in America, and after that, you know . . . a kind of twisted patriotism, or the response of an ethnic group that had been made fun of too often . . . So we got the Kensington stone, the halberds, the mooring holes, the coins. But if a hoax predated *Antiquitates Americanae* . . . it made me wonder."

"If the book itself were somehow involved?"

"Exactly," the professor said, regarding the minister with pleasure. "I wondered if the book might not incorporate, or have been inspired by, hoaxed material. Then one day I was reading a description of the field work here, and it occurred to me that this site was a bit too pristine. As if it had been built but never lived in. Best estimates for its occupation were as low as one summer, because they couldn't find any trash middens to speak of, or graves."

"It could have been occupied very briefly," the minister pointed out.

"Yes, I know. That's what I thought at the time. But then I heard from a colleague in Bergen that the *Gronlendinga Saga* was apparently a forgery, at least in the parts referring to the discovery of Vinland. Pages had been inserted that dated back to the 1820s. And after that, I had a doubt that wouldn't go away."

"But there are more Vinland stories than that one, yes?"

"Yes. There are three main sources. The *Gronlendinga Saga, The Saga of Erik the Red,* and the part of *The Hauksbók* that tells about Thorfinn Karlsefni's expedition. But with one of those questioned, I began to doubt them all. And the story itself. Everything having to do with the idea of Vinland."

"Is that when you went to Bergen?" a graduate student asked.

The professor nodded. He drained his plastic cup, felt the alcohol rushing through him. "I joined Nielsen there and we went over *Erik the Red* and *The Hauksbók,* and damned if the pages in those concerning Vinland weren't forgeries too. The ink gave it away—not its composition, which was about right, but merely how long it had been on that paper. Which was thirteenth century paper, I might add! The forger had done a super job. But the sagas had been tampered with sometime in the early nineteenth century."

"But those are masterpieces of world literature," a volunteer laborer exclaimed, round-eyed; the ads for volunteer labor had not included a description of the primary investigator's hypothesis.

"I know," the professor said irritably, and shrugged.

He saw a chunk of peat on the ground, picked it up and threw it on the blaze. After a bit it flared up.

"It's like watching dirt burn," he said absently, staring into the flames.

Discussion. The burnt garbage smell of peat wafted downwind, and offshore the calm water of the bay was riffled by the same gentle breeze. The minister warmed her hands at the blaze for a moment, then gestured at the bay. "It's hard to believe they were never here at all."

"I know," the professor said. "It looks like a Viking site, I'll give him that."

"Him," the minister repeated.

"I know, I know. This whole thing forces you to imagine a man in the eighteen twenties and thirties, traveling all over—Norway, Iceland, Canada, New England, Rome, Stockholm, Denmark, Greenland. . . . Crisscrossing the North Atlantic, to bury all these signs." He shook his head. "It's incredible."

He retrieved the cognac bottle and refilled. He was, he had to admit, beginning to feel drunk. "And so many parts of the hoax were well hidden! You can't assume we've found them all. This place had two butternuts buried in the midden, and butternuts only grow down below the St. Lawrence, so who's to say they aren't clues, indicating another site down there? That's where grapevines actually grow, which would justify the name Vinland. I tell you, the more I know about this hoaxer, the more certain I am that other sites exist. The tower in Newport, Rhode Island, for instance—the hoaxer didn't build that, because it's been around since the seventeenth century—but a little work out there at night, in the early nineteenth century . . . I bet if it were excavated completely, you'd find a few Norse artifacts."

"Buried in all the right places," the minister said.

"Exactly." The professor nodded. "And up the coast of Labrador, at Cape Porcupine where the sagas say they repaired a ship. There too. Stuff scattered everywhere, left to be discovered or not."

The minister waved her plastic cup. "But surely this site must have been his masterpiece. He couldn't have done too many as extensive as this."

"I shouldn't think so." The professor drank deeply, smacked his numbed lips. "Maybe one more like this, down in New Brunswick. That's my guess. But this was surely one of his biggest projects."

"It was a time for that kind of thing," the volunteer laborer offered. "Atlantis, Mu, Lemuria. . . ."

The minister nodded. "It fulfills a certain desire."

"Theosophy, most of that," the professor muttered. "This was different."

The volunteer wandered off. The professor and the minister looked into the fire for a while.

"You are *sure?*" the minister asked.

The professor nodded. "Trace elements show the ore came from upper Quebec. Chemical changes in the peat weren't right. And nuclear resonance dating methods show that the bronze pin they found hadn't been buried long enough. Little things like that. Nothing obvious. He was amazingly meticulous, he really thought it out. But the nature of things tripped him up. Nothing more than that."

"But the effort!" the minister said. "This is what I find hard to believe. Surely it must have been more than one man! Burying these objects, building the walls—surely he would have been noticed!"

The professor stopped another swallow, nodded at her as he choked once or twice. A broad wave of the hand, a gasping recovery of breath:

"Fishing village, kilometer north of here. Boarding house in the early nineteenth century. A crew of ten rented rooms in the summer of 1842. Bills paid by a Mr. Carlsson."

The minister raised her eyebrows. "Ah."

One of the graduate students got out a guitar and began to play. The other students and the volunteers gathered around her.

"So," the minister said, "Mr. Carlsson. Does he show up elsewhere?"

"There was a Professor Ohman in Bergen. A Dr. Bergen in Reykjavik. In the right years, studying the sagas. I presume they were all him, but I don't know for sure."

"What do you know about him?"

"Nothing. No one paid much attention to him. I've got him on a couple transatlantic crossings, I think, but he used aliases, so I've probably missed most of them. A Scandinavian-American, apparently Norwegian by birth. Someone with some money—someone with patriotic feelings of some kind—someone with a grudge against a university—who knows? All I have are a few signatures, of aliases at that. A flowery handwriting. Nothing more. That's the most remarkable thing about him! You see, most hoaxers leave clues to their identities, because a part of them wants to be caught. So their cleverness can be admired, or the ones who fell for it embarrassed, or whatever. But this guy didn't want to be discovered. And in those days, if you wanted to stay off the record. . . ." He shook his head.

"A man of mystery."

"Yeah. But I don't know how to find out anything more about him."

The professor's face was glum in the firelight as he reflected on this. He polished off another cup of cognac. The minister watched him drink, then said kindly, "There is nothing to be done about it, really. That is the nature of the past."

"I know."

Conclusions. They threw the last big logs on the fire, and flames roared up, yellow licks breaking free among the stars. The professor felt numb all over, his heart was cold, the firelit faces were smeary primitive masks, dancing in the light. The songs were harsh and raucous, he couldn't understand the words. The wind was chilling, and the hot skin of his arms and neck goosepimpled uncomfortably. He felt sick with alcohol, and knew it would be a while before his body could overmaster it.

The minister led him away from the fire, then up the rocky ridge. Getting him away from the students and laborers, no doubt, so he wouldn't embarrass himself. Starlight illuminated the heather and broken granite under their feet. He stumbled. He tried to explain to her what it meant, to be an archeologist whose most important work was the discovery that a bit of their past was a falsehood.

"It's like a mosaic," he said, drunkenly trying to follow the fugitive thought. "A puzzle with most of the pieces gone. A tapestry. And if you pull a thread out . . . it's ruined. So little lasts! We need every bit we can find!"

She seemed to understand. In her student days, she told him, she had waitressed at a café in Montreal. Years later she had gone down the street to have a look, just for nostalgia's sake. The café was gone. The street was completely different. And she couldn't remember the names of any of the people she had worked with. "This was my own past, not all that many years ago!"

The professor nodded. Cognac was rushing through his veins, and as he looked at the minister, so beautiful in the starlight, she seemed to him a kind of muse, a spirit sent to comfort him, or frighten him, he couldn't tell which. Clio, he thought. The muse of history. Someone he could talk to.

She laughed softly. "Sometimes it seems our lives are much longer than we usually think. So that we live through incarnations, and looking back later we have nothing but. . . ." She waved a hand.

"Bronze pins," the professor said. "Iron rivets."

"Yes." She looked at him. Her eyes were bright in the starlight. "We need an archeology for our own lives."

Acknowledgments. Later he walked her back to the fire, now reduced to banked red coals. She put her hand to his upper arm as they walked, steadying herself, and he felt in the touch some kind of portent; but couldn't understand it. He had drunk so much! Why be so upset about it, why? It was his job to find the truth; having found it, he should be happy! Why had no one told him what he would feel?

The minister said good-night. She was off to bed; she suggested he do likewise. Her look was compassionate, her voice firm.

When she was gone he hunted down the bottle of cognac, and drank the rest of it. The fire was dying, the students and workers scattered—in the tents, or out in the night, in couples.

He walked by himself back down to the site.

Low mounds, of walls that had never been. Beyond the actual site were rounded buildings, models built by the park service, to show tourists what the "real" buildings had looked like. When Vikings had camped on the edge of the new world. Repairing their boats. Finding food. Fighting among themselves, mad with epic jealousies. Fighting the dangerous Indians. Getting killed, and then driven away from this land, so much lusher than Greenland.

A creak in the brush and he jumped, startled. It would have been like that: death in the night, creeping up on you—he turned with a jerk, and every starlit shadow bounced with hidden skraelings, their bows drawn taut, their arrows aimed at his heart. He quivered, hunched over.

But no. It hadn't been like that. Not at all. Instead, a man with spectacles and a bag full of old junk, directing some unemployed sailors as they dug. Nondescript, taciturn, nameless; one night he would have wandered back there into the forest, perhaps fallen or had a heart attack—become a skeleton wearing leathers and sword-belt, with spectacles over the skull's eyesockets, the anachronism that gave him away at last. . . . The professor staggered over the low mounds toward the trees, intent on finding that inadvertent grave. . . .

But no. It wouldn't be there. The taciturn figure hadn't been like that. He would have been far away when he died, nothing to show what he had spent years of his life doing. A man in a hospital for the poor, the bronze pin in his pocket overlooked by the doctor, stolen by an undertaker's assistant. An anonymous figure, to the grave and beyond. The creator of Vinland. Never to be found.

The professor looked around, confused and sick. There was a waist-high rock, a glacial erratic. He sat on it. Put his head on his hands. Really quite unprofessional. All those books he had read as a child. What would the minister think! Grant money. No reason to feel so bad!

At that latitude midsummer nights are short, and the party had lasted late. The sky to the east was already gray. He could see down onto the site, and its long sod roofs. On the beach, a trio of long narrow high-ended ships. Small figures in furs emerged from the longhouses and went down to the water, and he walked among them and heard their speech, a sort of dialect of Norwegian that he could mostly understand. They would leave that day, it was time to load the ships. They were going to take everything with them, they didn't plan to return. Too many skraelings in the forest, too many quick arrow deaths. He walked among them, helping them load stores. Then a little man in a black coat scurried behind the forge, and he roared and took off after him, scooping up a rock on the way, ready to deal out a skraeling death to that black intruder.

The minister woke him with a touch of her hand. He almost fell off the rock. He shook his head; he was still drunk. The hangover wouldn't begin for a couple more hours, though the sun was already up.

"I should have known all along," he said to her angrily. "They were stretched to the limit in Greenland, and the climate was worsening. It was amazing they got that far. Vinland"—he waved a hand at the site—"was just some dreamer's story."

Regarding him calmly, the minister said, "I am not sure it matters."

He looked up at her. "What do you mean?"

"History is made of stories people tell. And fictions, dreams, hoaxes—they also are made of stories people tell. True or false, it's the stories that matter to us. Certain qualities in the stories themselves make them true or false."

He shook his head. "Some things really happened in the past. And some things didn't."

"But how can you know for sure which is which? You can't go back and see for yourself. Maybe Vinland was the invention of this mysterious stranger of yours; maybe the Vikings came here after all, and landed somewhere else. Either way it can never be anything more than a story to us."

"But . . ." He swallowed. "Surely it matters whether it is a true story or not!"

She paced before him. "A friend of mine once told me something he had read in a book," she said. "It was by a man who sailed the Red Sea, long ago. He told of a servant boy on one of the dhows, who could not remember ever having been cared for. The boy had become a sailor at age three—before that, he had been a beach-comber." She stopped pacing and looked at the beach below them. "Often I imagined that little boy's life. Surviving alone on a beach, at that age—it astonished me. It made me . . . happy."

She turned to look at him. "But later I told this story to an expert in child development, and he just shook his head. 'It probably wasn't true,' he said. Not a lie, exactly, but a. . . .'"

"A stretcher," the professor suggested.

"A stretcher, exactly. He supposed that the boy had been some-what older, or had had some help. You know."

The professor nodded.

"But in the end," the minister said, "I found this judgment did not matter to me. In my mind I still saw that toddler, searching the tidepools for his daily food. And so for me the story lives. And that is all that matters. We judge all the stories from history like that—we value them according to how much they spur our imaginations."

The professor stared at her. He rubbed his jaw, looked around. Things had the sharp-edged clarity they sometimes get after a sleep-ness night, as if glowing with internal light. He said, "Someone with opinions like yours probably shouldn't have the job that you do."

"I didn't know I had them," the minister said. "I only just came upon them in the last couple hours, thinking about it."

The professor was surprised. "You didn't sleep?"

She shook her head. "Who could sleep on a night like this?"

"My feeling exactly!" He almost smiled. "So. A *nuit blanche,* you call it?"

"Yes," she said. "A *nuit blanche* for two." And she looked down at him with that amused glance of hers, as if . . . as if she understood him.

She extended her arms toward him, grasped his hands, helped pull him to his feet. They began to walk back toward the tents, across the site of L'Anse aux Meadows. The grass was wet with dew, and very green.

"I still think," he said as they walked together, "that we want more than stories from the past. We want something not easily found— something, in fact, that the past doesn't have. Something secret, some secret meaning . . . something that will give our lives a kind of sense."

She slipped a hand under his arm. "We want the Atlantis of childhood. But, failing that. . . ." She laughed and kicked at a clump of grass; a spray of dew flashed ahead of them, containing, for just one moment, a bright little rainbow.

Rainbow Bridge

When I was fifteen years old I visited the Navaho reservation north of Flagstaff, Arizona, to help the Indians celebrate the Fourth of July. Even before I arrived I thought that was kind of a strange thing to do. But something much stranger than that happened to me out there, before I left; something so strange that I have never been able to forget even the slightest detail of it, from that day to this.

On arrival late one Sunday afternoon I got out of my cousin Luke's blue VW, followed by my young brother David. My great-aunt Miriam, a tall gray-haired woman in a cotton print dress, greeted us with a sweet girlish smile, holding our hands in hers. I walked around the car to stretch my legs and survey the grounds.

As it happened our arrival coincided with the onset of a summer storm. Overhead clouds like great dark lobes of marble filled the western sky. The setting sun leaked under the edge of this front, and glazed everything with a harsh orange glare. We stood on a broad, high, bare tableland; the horizon was an immense distance away. The blacktop road merged with the dark land to east and west, one shadow ribbon among many.

Small at the center of all this space, Inscription House Mission stood before us: a church, a house, and some rough outbuildings, all whitewashed, all glowing now in the fan of stormlight, the walls' whites tinged the color of the earth, and striped with solid black shadows, but intensely bright in the surrounding gloom, like lamps at dusk. Before these sun-colored walls my cousin's car, a brilliant metallic blue even in ordinary light, gleamed like the shell of a glittering scarab, a visitor from another world.

We carried our bags into my great-aunt's house just as muddy dark splotches began starring the dusty earth around us. As we entered the house I looked back, and under the gray sheets of the squall I saw a figure, standing on a bare rise to the north, near the horizon. Silhouetted, solitary, somehow more heraldic than real, it raised both arms as if to encourage the coming downpour. My first Indian, I thought, and wondered if I had seen a sort of raindance. I closed the door.

"That guy out there'll get wet," I said wisely.

"Who's that?" Luke asked, surprised.

"That Indian, out there under the storm."

He shook his head. "No one out there, far as I saw."

I opened the door again and looked out. There was nothing under the squall, no one out there on that whole broad plateau. And nowhere to hide. "What . . . ?" A gust of wind pushed at the door, as if something was trying to get in; I shivered.

That was the start of it.

While the rain drummed on the shingles of Aunt Miriam's house the four of us talked; I didn't mention again the figure I had seen. Aunt Miriam served us powdered milk. It was the first time I had drunk it, and I didn't like the taste. "It tastes funny," I said, surprised.

Aunt Miriam smiled. "It's all we've got out here."

"You get used to it," Luke said with a laugh.

The rain stopped after about half an hour, and as it was Sunday we walked over to the church to join the evening service. Yellow light from the church windows streaked the puddles in the yard, under a low black sky. The church's interior was one medium-sized room, filled with Navahos sitting in folding chairs. There were about forty of them, in rows facing a narrow lectern and a piano at the front of the room. I was surprised to see so many people; I hadn't thought very many Indians would be Christian. David and I sat in chairs set against the side wall, near the front.

An older Navaho man spoke to them in Navaho from the lectern; while he did I looked through a Bible and hymnal that had been on my chair. I saw that the Navaho language had an incredible frequency of vowels; there were words like *aanapalaooaa, liineaupoonaa, kreeaiioo* . . . it reminded me of an infant's babbling.

When the old man was done they sang hymns, Aunt Miriam accompanying them on the piano. They used the old tunes of Luther, Wesley, and Watt, but had translated the lyrics, and with all those vowels, and a wild warble in the women's voices, the familiar hymns—"A Mighty Fortress Is Our God," "Onward Christian Soldiers"—were transformed, made utterly strange, unlike any music I had ever heard. Their beauty took me by surprise, and my cheeks flushed as I listened. Up at the front Aunt Miriam sang along, an expression of pure bliss on her upraised face. She had played the flute in the Chicago Symphony, I recalled; but that could never have made her look as she did now.

While they sang these weird hymns I stared at their faces. I was a bookish youth, and I had lived all my life in a southern California suburb, a white middle-class town that couldn't have been more homogeneous if it had been legislated that way. The truth was, in my entire life I had never seen faces like these before me: dark-skinned, sun-wrinkled, hawk-nosed, heavy-lidded, life-battered faces, each the map of a world, each framed and made beautiful by sleek straight black hair, and jewelry of silver and turquoise . . . extraordinary faces: visions out of my book lore, but real. Suddenly I experienced a convulsive blush, as with the music but stronger—because I realized, right then and there, that it went beyond mere stories in books: the world was real. *The world was real.* Man, I thought, not understanding what I felt—these are really Indians!

The next morning I went outside early to walk around a bit.

The great plateau of the Navaho reservation stands over six thousand feet above sea level; I suppose that is part of the reason everything looked different to me that morning. The sky was a dark, pure blue, and in this blue the feathering of a cirrus cloud was a startling white. The cool air was hard and clear, like a glass that sharpened vision. The rainstorm had washed the land, and the earth was dark red, or the color of wet sand. Sagebrush and an occasional pine tree were scattered across the land. The sage was a shifting silvery color, like olive leaves, a shade that fit the earth tones; but the pines appeared to burst with green, as if more color had been pumped into them than they could actually hold: every pine needle poked the air, distinct in itself, dark with greenness flowing outward. I walked over to one of these pines, a juniper, I thought, feeling that I was swimming in color: red earth, green trees, blacktop road, white clouds, cobalt sky. . . .

I had been collecting the small, tight green cones of my tree for several minutes—just for something to do—when I looked up and saw that an Indian was watching me from no more than ten feet away. I jumped back, frightened; I hadn't heard him approach.

He was about my height, and somewhere in his forties or fifties, I guessed; it was hard to tell. He wore old blue jeans, a plaid cotton shirt, and a cowboy hat. His face was like those of the people in church the night before (though I hadn't seen his there): broad, impassive, masklike. "Hello!" I said nervously, afraid that I was stealing his pine cones or something.

"Hello." And he stared at me, calmly. Finally, after a long pause: "Do you like pine cones?"

"Well . . . sure! I mean they're . . . interesting!"

He looked at me. Later I became painfully familiar with that look. . . .

My nervousness increased. Finally, to break the silence, I said, "Do you live around here?"

"North some." He gestured briefly at the road. After that, silence again. He didn't seem to mind, but I was getting more uncomfortable by the second.

Perhaps he saw this. He cocked his head, watching me. "Do you play basketball?"

"Yeah!" I said, surprised. I told him about my ninth-grade team. He nodded without expression. "Come on."

I followed him back toward the mission, confused and uncertain. Then we rounded one of the rough outbuildings, and I saw that the far end of the yard was a big basketball court. A group of Navaho men and boys were crowded under one basket, milling around in a tussle for the ball.

The man stopped beside me. "It's twenty-one. You can play if you want."

So he and I joined the game. Everyone struggled for rebounds, and when you got one the whole group was your opponent; if you managed to score anyway, you went to the free throw line and shot till you missed. Points were scored as in regular basketball, and the first person to reach twenty-one won.

It was a wild game, a free-for-all really, and I dashed around the outskirts of it somewhat at a loss. The court's surface was wet dirt sprinkled with loose gravel; not the most level of surfaces. A skinny tree trunk held up a backboard that was not quite square to the court, and the basket itself seemed unusually high, say eleven feet; perhaps it only looked that way because the backboard was so small. All in all it was not what I was used to, and when a rebound came my way I lost it dribbling. Frustrated, I got into the crowd and was elbowed and pushed with the rest of the boys as we scrambled around the men for loose balls. Impossible to hold on with six or seven hands slapping the ball; discouraged, I moved back outside, and was mostly watching when my new acquaintance took a rebound and drove into the crowd. When he was blocked off he fired a pass back over one shoulder, right at me. I got my hands up just in time to catch it, had an open moment, shot; incredibly, the ball caromed off the backboard and through the net.

At the free throw line looking up, I knew that I would miss. Even back home I couldn't make free throws, and here the basket looked twice as far away. I only hoped I would avoid an air ball.

No such luck. The ball missed everything by two feet. Involuntarily I cried out: "Aaaa!" The men and boys laughed, but in a friendly way; I had amused them by expressing aloud what everyone felt when they missed. I laughed, too, and felt more at ease. Then some men arrived and there were enough to start a real game; the boys were kicked off the court. My Indian walked over to his team without even a glance in my direction, as if he had forgotten my existence.

*   *   *

I sat and watched the game, and Luke joined me. "They like basketball," I said.

He cracked up. "That's right. In fact they love basketball. Basketball and pickup trucks—those are the white man's things that the Navaho have really taken to." He laughed again. "These men— they've all got kids enough that the kids can take care of the sheep during the day. Dad can come down here and play ball with his friends, for an hour or two anyway. They play almost every day."

I pointed out my acquaintance and asked who he was.

"That's Paul. Why do you ask?"

"He brought me over here and got me in the twenty-one game."

Luke smiled. "He's a good man. He's the one I'm trying to get to hike with us to Rainbow Bridge, after the Fourth. A good man." He frowned, tossed a few pieces of gravel back onto the court. "Paul's got a son about your age. But he moved to Flagstaff."

"That's good, isn't it?" Get out there in the modern world . . .

Luke shook his head. "Alcohol's illegal on the reservation, see. It's just too much of a problem for them. So people who are . . . who want alcohol, they generally move down to Flagstaff. And then they're in trouble, because they can get it so easily."

"But he's only my age, you said!"

"That's right."

I didn't understand. He wasn't even old enough to *buy* alcohol. . . .

"Come on," Luke said, standing. "Let's go find your brother and go for a ride. I've got to go to the trading post."

Luke was one of those people whose internal dynamo is pitched several thousand r.p.m. higher than anyone else's. This was his vacation, he was just visiting Aunt Miriam (his great-aunt too, from a different direction), but every day he had a long list of things to do, and he hustled around doing them until everyone with him dropped from exhaustion. Loading pickups with supplies, giving people rides up dirt tracks into the back country, building houses or fences, hunting for lost sheep: it was all great fun to him. I would have thought that Luke would be resented for all this help, but it wasn't so. In fact he had a real knack for pleasing the Navaho, for drawing them out. That afternoon, for instance, three times we passed solitary

Navaho men walking down the road toward the trading post, some six miles away. Each time Luke stopped by them, even though after the first got in the VW was full. "Want a ride? Where you going?" And they all got in, so that after the third one David and I were crushed into a corner of the backseat. The men were forbidding in their silence, and apparently Luke didn't know any of them; it made me nervous. But Luke laughed at the crowding, and started asking them questions, where do you live, how many sheep have you got, how many kids, do you go to that VISTA place, aren't those folks strange (they grinned), did you get caught out in that storm yesterday . . . and by the time we got to the trading post the Navaho were talking away, both to Luke and among themselves, but always in English so we would be included, and they all took up his offer to load the VW and drive back to their homes (how are *we* going to fit in, I wanted to say), and while we were stuffing the Beetle with heavy boxes something Luke said struck them funny, I'm not sure what, and their stoic faces tilted up at the sky and broke into a million laugh lines as they cackled away. Luke just grinned, having a great time as usual. I envied him that ease, that skill.

That night at Aunt Miriam's we had mutton and bread. I had noticed the Navaho ate the same thing, every meal: bread and coffee for breakfast, mutton, bread and coffee for lunch, and mutton, bread, and coffee for dinner. "Boy," I said, "these Navaho must sure like mutton, bread, and coffee!"

From the strain in my aunt's beautiful smile I knew I had said something stupid, but I didn't know what. Over the next few bites I worked it out. "They don't have anything else?"

My aunt shook her head, the smile gone.

"They have some canned stuff," Luke said. "But mutton, bread, and coffee, those are the staples."

I continued eating, and imagined having the meal before me, every day; it tasted different, somehow.

The Fourth of July came. In the cool morning Paul came by in his pickup. Luke introduced him to David and me; he nodded, smiling a little smile at me. We drove out to a gravel pit in a dry streambed, took giant shovels and filled the bed of the truck with gravel. Then we drove back to the mission and shoveled the gravel onto the basketball court.

A fresh coat for the big day. As I spread gravel evenly over the long court I puzzled over the idea of Indians celebrating the Fourth of July. Shouldn't they hate this day, shouldn't they be lighting bonfires and burning flags, or maybe the stray white man or two?

Apparently they didn't feel that way about it. Family after family drove up in pickup trucks. The women set big hampers of food on the picnic tables flanking the yard. They roasted big sides of sheep over fires set in brick pits; fragrant white plumes of smoke rose into the sunny blue sky. The Navaho chatted cheerfully with the large group of white missionaries there for the day. The food was set out beside paper plates, and we filed past and loaded up: mutton, bread, and coffee—and also chili, watermelon, and Cokes. A real celebration. There must have been a hundred people there, maybe two hundred. I wandered around eating and watching, enjoying myself.

Only when the missionaries imposed a sequence of games on the group did the Navaho show the slightest sign that all was not perfect on that day. As these games began they withdrew into themselves, and went along with it all impassively. A missionary friend of my aunt's called me over to him. "Come here, we need you for this one!" I was into it before I understood what the game was; when I did, I groaned. The game was this: one of the missionaries stood with his back to a group of us, and threw wrapped pieces of candy over his head in our direction, and then we scrambled to pick up as many pieces as we could.

I couldn't believe it. No wonder all the kids around me were between five and ten years old, no wonder all the Navaho boys my age had refused to join, and were now standing in the circle of observers, watching me. So *undignified* . . . Then the man threw the candy, and I gritted my teeth and went after some; damned if I could get my hands on a single piece. Those little kids were *serious* about this game, and they were fast as squirrels, and the bits of candy all disappeared almost before they hit the ground. Near the end of the ordeal I straightened up, after managing to wrestle a piece of toffee out of the clenched fist of a six-year-old, and saw the stares of all the boys my age. I felt myself flush scarlet with humiliation. And there was Paul, too, on the edge of the group, watching without expression. He said something in Navaho, and the crowd dispersed; the kids left to tally their prizes; there was no one left for the missionary to inflict the game on. Paul walked off, and I stared after him gratefully, wondering what he could have said.

Immediately I was called by the missionaries into a volleyball game, with the boys my own age. Ah-ha, I thought; I'll get back some lost face, here. I had played quite a bit of volleyball at home, and I jumped about making hits as often as I could. Once I got an opportunity to spike the ball over the low net, and showing off a bit I leaped up and hit it hard. It bounced off across the yard, a clean point for our side. Then I saw the way all the other boys were looking at me, faces impassive but perfectly contemptuous, and I understood in a flash that they played the game differently here; it was like that beach paddle game, where you try to keep the ball in play for as long as possible. Humiliated again, I got my brother to take my place, and left the game. And I saw that once more Paul had been watching, from some distance away, standing there with his arms folded across his chest. I gritted my teeth unhappily.

Then it was time for the basketball game, and all the Navaho men perked up. Here was a real game, a proper way to celebrate the holiday.

They started the game before two in the afternoon, and it didn't end till after five, and the entire game was played in the most manic fast-break style I had ever seen. After a shot or rebound was made, everyone broke for the other basket, gravel spraying, the ball passed as if shot from cannons: a pass or two, a quick shot gunned, a tussle for the rebound, and off they flew the other way. Back and forth without letup, all afternoon long. I sat on the end of one bench, openmouthed at the pace of this wonderful game, and hid from the missionaries. I tried to forget the humiliations they had just caused me, but they kept coming back to mind.

Then about an hour into the game Paul jogged by and said, "Want to play?"

I jumped up and took the place of one of Paul's teammates. I was the only white man out there, and I felt keenly the eyes of the game's audience. My team seemed most comfortable ignoring me, but Paul passed me the ball once or twice, and I managed to dribble and pass it off without mishap. Once I took it and drove for the basket, then passed it out to Paul, just as he had to me in the game of twenty-one: he caught it without a hitch and pumped it through for two.

Like the rest of the men, Paul was an incorrigible gunner. He would take passes on a little rise near half-court, and fire two-handed shots straight for the sky. The ball flew two or three times as high as the basket, it seemed, then swooped down and practically ripped the net off the hoop. No fooling with the backboard for Paul. If he missed and the ball hit the rim, it made an iron crash like the hoop was breaking off, and bounced so far out or up that the rebounders were confused. But I would say he hit about sixty percent of these bombs, and many of the other men were almost as accurate. It made for a high-scoring game; although to tell the truth, I don't think they were keeping score.

I played for about twenty minutes, and left the game so beat I could hardly walk. After some rest and a couple of Cokes I recovered, and I chatted with Luke and David and Aunt Miriam while we watched the rest of the game. "These guys could beat any team in the NBA!" I said, excited. Luke grinned and added, "If it weren't for the fact that the tallest one out there is five eleven." I laughed; I was pleased; the earlier embarrassments were forgotten. The Fourth of July was turning out all right after all.

Only late that night, in bed, did it occur to me whose doing that had been.

A day or two later Luke and I drove north to Paul's home, to fix the date of our hike to Rainbow Bridge, "the biggest natural arch in the world!"—also to make sure Paul would come. Luke was a little vague about it: "Well, Paul's got a lot of responsibilities, we have to see if he's still free. . . ." Up a bumpy dirt track, rocky and pink in the surrounding tans, into the wash of a flat-bottomed canyon, past tall delicate white-barked trees, their broad green leaves translucent in the sunlight. . . .

Tucked up against the canyon wall were fences, Paul's pickup, a low oval hut. We stopped in the yard and got out. Red chickens scattered before us. There were five-gallon plastic jugs lined against one wall of the hut, which seemed *woven,* sort of: wood and wicker and perhaps *mud,* in a complex pattern. The place was quite clearly *handmade.*

Luke knocked on the wooden door and was called in: I stood in the doorway and stared into the gloom, uncertain about following. Paul was getting up from an old stuffed armchair; some others sat around a table, near a fat black stove. Paul greeted us politely, shook both our hands—because we were visiting his home, I guessed. Luke said something and they all laughed. The two men talked, and the eyes around the stove watched me. The interior walls were hung with boldly patterned rugs, earth tones cut by bright white zigzags. There were some sort of masks in the corner, it looked like. Paul and Luke were busy talking and I backed out the door, confused and uncomfortable under the gaze of Paul's family.

Penned against the little house by the fences were sheep—or goats, actually. Goats. They looked dirty, and had an awful smell. The whole place was so shabby, so small. . . . Poverty, I thought: this is what poverty looks like. Maybe I would have gone to Flagstaff too. . . .

Luke ducked out. "We're all set," he said. "He wants to take off tomorrow. Some folks on the Hopi reservation need his help in a few days, so the sooner the better for the trip."

On the drive back I had a hard time collecting myself. Luke noticed; he said, "That's a *hogan* they live in, the traditional Navaho home. You're lucky to have seen one."

I couldn't help myself: "But it was so small! And . . . dirty!"

"Not dirty. They're actually quite clean. Small, true. But it's easier to heat them that way."

"But this is the desert!" We were sweating even with the windows down.

"Yes, but in the winter it snows. Blizzards like you can't believe. Hot in the summer and cold in the winter, that's the high desert for you. It's hard to make housing that will keep you comfortable in both extremes, especially without electricity. A lot of Paul's friends are building new houses, regular framing and walls of stuccoed plasterboard. . . . They look like the houses down in Flagstaff, you probably would think they were nicer, but they freeze in the winter, and bake in the summer, and fall apart in ten years. The hogans are actually better homes."

This was interesting, and I found it comforting to an extent; but the sight of the hogan, home of the man I had thought powerful and influential—so small, dark, *primitive*—had shocked me, and that shock was more powerful than Luke's calm reasoning.

The next morning Luke woke us in the dark, and while the sky bent from indigo to the rich velvet sky blue of predawn, we drove north. David slept on the backseat, and I watched the headlight beams light the asphalt road against the dusty blond shadows of the land. Paul followed us in his truck. We drove uphill, and the low gnarled pine trees, scattered here and there like black boulders, proliferated until we drove through a kind of rocky low forest.

We parked in a gravel lot next to the Navaho Mountain Trading Post, a single wooden building, closed. The lot was empty except for us. Luke was pleased: "We'll have the whole trail to ourselves, I bet." In the morning chill we ate apples, and their cidery smell mixed with the piney odor of the trees.

Paul and Luke had packs, and David and I carried our cotton sleeping bags in rolls strapped to our shoulders. We started walking on the trail, a level white swath through the thick network of trees.

The trees shifted from black to green. The sun rose to our right, and shadows jumped down the slope to the west. Above us the east rugged sandstone ramparts alternated with steep pine-filled ravines; Navaho Mountain, Luke told us, was above and beyond the cliffs we could see. The trees were scattered everywhere now, for as far as we could see. "Piñon pines," Luke said. "Biggest stand of piñon pines in the whole world."

The broad trail was marked every mile by a metal pole, cemented in the dirt and painted bright red. Milestones, I thought. Luke laughed at them. It was fifteen miles to Rainbow Bridge.

The trail turned left, down to the west. The land began to fall away so rapidly that the trail switchbacked; here the tableland fell down into the canyons surrounding the Colorado River. We could see a long way down to the west, over tawny ridges, knobs, shadowed canyon walls. We passed milepole number five.

The trail brought us around the head of a deep canyon that snaked out to the west. "Look down there!" Luke said, pointing. "There's the trail in the canyon bottom, see it?"

There it was, far below, a white line across tan rocks. Between us and it was an immense slope like the inside of a bowl, all jumbled by stratification and erosion. "How will we get down there?" David asked.

I had been wondering that myself; I couldn't see the trail anywhere on the canyon walls. Luke started walking again, to the right rather than down. "The north side is less steep, the trail goes down there." We traversed most of a mile around the head of the canyon, then left the trees and descended the wall by following hundreds of wide switchbacks in the trail. It was fun swinging around each hairpin turn, changing directions and views as we dropped deeper and deeper into the rocky canyon world. . . .

More than an hour later we reached the canyon floor. The perspective was different down there; the broad prospect we had enjoyed up on the forested mountainside plateau was gone, and now our view was confined to the walls of the canyon we were in. Above, white-blue sky. The canyon was a deep flat-bottomed river gorge, and the trail followed the shallow pebbly stream at the bottom. Green reeds, silvery shrubs, and small cottonwoods banked this meager stream. "Cliff Canyon," Luke told us. "We'll stay in this one for a long time."

We followed the stream in its descent, milepole after milepole. I sang "Onward, Christian Soldiers" to myself as a marching song, and discovered that if I took one step for every quarter note, the hymn took me exactly one hundred steps. This seemed to me clever planning on the part of the composer. I counted steps from one red pole to the next; 1,962 steps for a mile. Four more steps and I would have hit the year. I tried to step just a little bit smaller.

We stopped and had lunch at the pool where Cliff Canyon met Redbud Pass gorge. The surface of the pool had a perfect blue sheen to it, while under it polished pebbles gleamed pink and chocolate; and the two colors, satin blue and mottled pebblestone, coexisted without mixing, both completely filling the same surface. I stared at the impossible sight, entranced.

We made the abrupt right turn and hiked up Redbud Pass gorge, and it was unexpectedly tiring to go uphill at even that slight angle. But we came to a section of the canyon that was so narrow that we had to twist to get through some parts; for almost a mile we could touch both walls at once, and they rose straight up on each side for over four hundred feet, Luke said. The sky was no more than a blue ribbon atop these endless rock walls. It was such an extraordinary thing that we were all excited: Luke sang, "Fat man's misereee!" and David and I laughed helplessly as we slipped along. We forgot we were tired, and hiked heads up until our necks hurt. Paul, bringing up the rear, had a big smile on his face: white teeth, brown skin in a million laugh lines: wild hawk face, enjoying the canyon once again, enjoying our first-time amazement.

The gorge of the pass opened up into Redbud Creek Canyon; we took a left turn and started down again. This canyon's stream made many big twists and turns, and the canyon walls S'ed with it, exposing hundreds of fluted sandstone columns, balancing boulders, smooth overhung curves, knobs like elephant heads.

I was getting a little too tired to really enjoy them, however, and poor David was beginning to drag indeed, when the canyon took a big oxbow bend to the left, and there in the outside wall of this bend was a bulge, a narrow horseshoe-shaped extension of the canyon into the cliffside. The cliff surrounding this bulge was a tall, curved, overhanging wall of rust-colored sandstone; the floor of it was flat, and just higher than the canyon floor proper. Underneath the great curving overhang was a stand of big old trees, a pool fed by a cold spring, several old picnic tables, a brick fireplace with a blackened grill on top, a stack of firewood, and scattered about, six old bed-stands, stripped to metal.

"Here's camp!" Luke said, seeing our confused looks.

"But what about Rainbow Bridge?" I asked.

"It's just a little way down the canyon. Let's leave our stuff here and go have a look."

Rainbow Bridge was less than a quarter mile away; we could see it for most of the walk there. A broad arch of sandstone, it began not up atop the canyon walls as I had expected, but down at their bases, to left and right as we approached. The canyon opened up quite a bit here, so the bridge was very wide, and it rose perhaps sixty feet over us. It was flat-sided, rounded on top and bottom, streaked with brown watermarks, and sure enough, it had a broad rainbow shape to it.

Though it was no later than five or six it was gloomy down in the canyon, the sun long gone and only shining on the very tops of the walls. The light tans and and yellows of the sandstone around us were now brown, black, blood red. I stared up at the arch. Compared to the Golden Gate Bridge, for instance, it wasn't very big. And all day I had been walking under the most fantastic contortions of sandstone that wind and water could carve . . . compared to that mad sculpture, the bridge was pretty basic stuff. But it *was* unusual; and pretty big; and when you considered that it had just *happened* out here, accidental-like . . . and the way it loomed in the too-bright strip of evening sky, dark as stone—a stone rainbow, the reverse of an ordinary rainbow: slab-sided, massive, permanent . . .

Luke walked around it in a fever of energy, snapping pictures with his little camera. "I wish the light was better," he said. "We won't get much on film." Paul was sitting on a rock, watching him with his eyelids crinkled, amused. "This will probably be the last chance I get to photograph it in its natural state."

"What's that?" I said.

"The lake. You remember? This canyon leads down to the Colorado River, about three or four miles away. But it's Lake Powell now, you know, because of the Glen Canyon Dam. And the lake is still rising. This canyon is flooding, and they say you'll be able to boat right under the bridge in a couple of years."

"You're kidding!"

"Nope. This'll be water, right here where we stand. It might even flood the whole bridge, although they say it won't." Luke was matter-of-fact about it; that was just the way it was, nothing to get upset over, not when there was nothing to be done.

I glanced over at Paul. No expression on his face, none at all. The Navaho mask . . . he was looking up at the streaked sides of the arch. I walked under it again, on solid ground, and stared up at it. Massive rust band against the sky . . . it looked different, somehow.

* * *

That evening, as night fell and the stars appeared in the arc of sky standing over the cliffs, we started a fire in the brick fireplace and cooked hot dogs for dinner. The flames cast a warm, flickering yellow on the overhanging back wall. This smooth sweeping curve echoed our voices, and the crackling wood, and the low gurgle of the water leaving the spring's pool; it amplified the *whoo* of the wind flowing down-canyon.

We devoured the hot dogs, ate three or four apiece. Afterwards I walked around the camp a little. The big old trees had crumpled gray-green bark, gnarled branches, leaves as smooth and prickly-edged as holly leaves. The bare metal bedsteads gave the place the look of a ruin: giant cathedral, roof fallen in, trees growing up out of the floor, altar a fireplace, beds dragged in. . . . The wind hooted and the sharp-edged leaves clattered, and feeling spooked I returned to the others.

After we had laid out our sleeping bags and gotten into them, I still felt . . . strange. I had chosen to sleep on one of the picnic tables, and was under one of the trees. Between the black leaves the stars appeared and disappeared, pricking at my sight, creating a sense of constant movement that was not necessarily in the leaves. There were a lot of little noises, echoing off the overhang. I had seldom if ever slept outdoors before, and it felt . . . exposed, somehow. Someone could just sneak right up on you! They could sneak up and murder all of us down here, and no one would know! Well, that was silly. But stuck so deep in this deep canyon, with the vault of the sky so far above the tree-filled black horseshoe bend, and the wind whistling over the rock, the world seemed a vast place: vast, dark, windy. . . . I lay there for a long time before falling asleep.

I woke in the middle of the night, having to pee. Something in me resisted getting up: fear of the open darkness, clutching at me. But I had to go and I slid out of my sleeping bag and stepped off the picnic bench, walked down toward the bridge, out of the camp.

Once out from under the trees a great map of stars sheltered me. In their brilliance I recognized not a single constellation. It seemed the moon might be rising, or else the starlight was brighter here than I was used to; the canyon walls caught enough illumination to reveal some of their hieroglyphics of erosion. It was chill but not cold; I walked down the trail to take a brief look at the bridge in this strange light.

A man stood directly beneath the bridge, both arms raised to the sky. Paul . . . I recognized the gesture as that made by the solitary figure I had seen greeting the storm on the evening we had arrived—the figure that had disappeared!—and I understood that that had been Paul out there. He was some sort of . . . I didn't know what.

He turned around, aware of being watched, and saw me. Reluctantly I walked down the trail and joined him.

"You're up late," I said.

"So are you."

We stood there. As my eyes adjusted further to the dark—as the moon, perhaps, rose further in the blocked-off sky to the east—I could see his face better: crags of weathered flesh, shadowed fissures deeply scored; it looked like the sandstone around us. Water sounds, small but distinct, played between us; wind sounds, soft but large, soughed over us, as if the canyon were an immense flute that someone was breathing through. . . . By moving my head a little I could make stars wink in and out of existence, there at the black edges of the arch.

"How can they flood this place?" I said quietly.

Paul shrugged. "Build a dam . . ."

"Oh, I know. I know. But . . . can't you stop it?"

He shook his head.

"I wish you could. . . ."

"It doesn't matter." I was about to protest that it did, when he raised a hand and held it out between us. A narrow silver ring blinked starlight, there on his little finger. "The bridge is like the ring. Your people come to see it, on foot like you have, and soon by boat. Many people. But while the ring takes the attention like that, the rest of the hand—the rest of the body—it's all left alone."

"You mean the reservation."

"All the land here, all the canyons. This ring is precious, but it isn't the body. There are hundreds of canyons out here—canyons and mesas, mountains, rivers without an end to them. Arches, yes. To have all the attention on this bridge, all the visitors . . . it's not such a bad thing."

"I see. I understand."

"Places only we know about are let be . . . cliff dwellings."

"Like the Inscription House ruin?" I said.

"Yes, like that. Only hidden. Never found, you see. Lost forever, perhaps. Let be forever."

Then we were silent, listening to the great flute channel the wind. I thought of Rainbow Bridge as a giant stone ring, buried just a bit more than halfway into the earth. The light in the canyon grew ever stronger, though the sky to the east remained a pure black, the stars there wavering intensely in the shiver of the atmosphere.

"Do you think your son will ever come back?" I said.

He glanced at me, surprised. The wet surface of his eyes reflected tiny pinpoint stars. " . . . Yes," he said finally. "But when he does"— tapping his head with a finger—"a part of him will be dead."

My head felt as if he had tapped me, just over the ear. Quickened—

I woke from the dream with a start. It was dark, stars blinked in the black mesh of branches over me. The stiff, sharp-edged leaves clicked against each other. The dream hesitated on the leaf edge of oblivion—slipped back into my memory, intact. I thought about it.

I did have to pee. I got out of the sleeping bag, stepped off the picnic table, walked around the tree.

When I was done I rounded the tree and almost ran into him. "Ah!" I leaped back, tripped, almost fell.

"Hey," Paul said softly, helping me get to my feet. "It's just me." He let go of me, looked at me. In the dark I couldn't read his expression; I could barely see it. "Still me." He walked past me, toward his bedroll.

When I got back in my sleeping bag my heart was still thumping, as loud in my ears as snapped fingers. *Still me* . . . The side of my head tingled. I looked up at the patternless smeary white stars, sure it would take me hours to fall asleep again; but I don't recall staying awake for even so much as a minute.

*   *   *

The next morning we ate a breakfast of crackers and oranges, rolled our bags and packed our gear, poured water on the ashes of the fire, and took off. It was a warm morning, the cliff-rimmed patch of sky a clear pale blue. Paul didn't mention our encounter of the previous night; in fact he said hardly a word during breakfast, and led the way up the canyon without looking back. Luke, David and I followed.

It didn't take long to discover that hiking back up out of the canyons was harder than descending into them. Yesterday I hadn't even noticed how continuous the descent was; now every step up spoke to me. And at some 1,962 steps per mile ... for fifteen miles ... I couldn't finish the multiplication in my head, but I knew it was a lot of walking.

We had a short respite, going down the Redbud Pass gorge, and the narrow section was still wonderful; but once in Cliff Canyon it was uphill for good. The sun burst over the south wall of the canyon, and the day got hot. Frequently we stopped to drink. We stayed in the same order: Paul, me, David, Luke. I started to sing "Onward, Christian Soldiers," but looking at Paul's back before me I felt stupid doing it, and I stopped.

David was the first to give out; he sat down by a pool and rolled onto his back. I was kind of proud of him: he had walked until he dropped, without a single word of complaint. A tough kid, my little brother.

We sat by the pool and considered it. David, nearly asleep where he lay, was clearly played out. Luke, unworried and cheerful, filled David's water cup at the pool. "Why don't you two go on ahead," he said to Paul and me. "You can take Paul's truck back to the mission, and that way Aunt Miriam won't worry about us. I'll come up with David either late tonight, or tomorrow morning."

Paul and I nodded, and after a short rest the two of us started off.

After about an hour of hiking behind Paul, watching Cliff Canyon broaden and open up, I saw the canyon's head. Before us stood a curved slope just as steep as the walls to right and left. This was where the trail had that long sequence of switchbacks, ascending the left wall, reaching the tableland above, and then skirting the canyon's rim up there, to a patch of piñon over on the top of the right wall. I could even see where the trail went, up among those tiny trees; it was so *far* above. I couldn't believe how far above it was; surely we hadn't come down from there!

Later I learned that the trailhead is three thousand feet higher than Rainbow Bridge; and a full fifteen hundred of those vertical feet are climbed right there, on the headwall of Cliff Canyon. At the time, it looked even taller than that. And the worst part of it, as far as I was concerned, was that the trail took such a gigantic detour to the left! It effectively doubled the distance we had to go to reach that patch of piñon pine on the top of the right wall. And all those dumb switchbacks, adding distance too. . . . I couldn't believe it.

I was tired, I wanted an easier way. "Listen," I said to Paul, "couldn't we just head straight up the right slope to where the trail goes through those trees? It isn't much steeper than the trail side, and we'd get it over with that much faster."

Paul shook his head. "The trail's the best way."

But I had convinced myself, and stubbornly I argued to convince him. "You can see the whole slope from here to there—just dirt—no brush to walk through—nothing to it! It's just like a stairway all the way up! And then we wouldn't have to go way off the wrong way!" On and on I went.

Paul watched me without expression. No agreement with my points; no irritation that I would debate the best route with him; just an impassive gaze, staring at me. That look, becoming familiar: did it hide a laugh?

Finally, after I had repeated my points many times, he looked away, off into the distance. "You go that way, then. I'll take the trail, and meet you up in those trees."

"All right," I said, happy to have my way. I thought it was an excellent plan. "I'll see you up there."

He turned and trudged up the dusty white trail.

It's hard for me now to believe that I could have been that stupid. To think a cross-country route would be easier than trail; to argue with a Navaho about the best way to get from one point to another, in Navaho country; to ignore Paul's judgment, and go off on my own . . . incredible. But I was fifteen, and I was tired, and I wanted an easier way. I wished one into existence, and took off.

I started up the slope. The footing was good, and I made good progress. I imagined greeting Paul at the top when he finally appeared by way of the trail. I glanced over at the other side of the canyon to see how far he had gotten, but the trail followed a crease that was probably the streambed when it rained enough, and there was a bulge in the wall between my slope and that crease, so he was out of sight. I could still see the trees at the top, however; and after a short rest I pressed on.

The canyonside I ascended was sandstone. No doubt it had been formed as successive layers of some primordial beach, eons ago; in any case it was horizontally stratified, and this meant I climbed something very like an ancient staircase, weathered now almost out of existence. Stone ledges protruded from the angled slope of grainy dirt, giving me a few inches of flat surface to step up on. On the dirt itself it was harder; the angle stretched my Achilles tendons, and there was a slight tendency to slip back that had to be resisted.

It was hot, and there was no wind. The sun blazed overhead so that a big quadrant of sky was too white to look at. I had to wipe sweat from my eyebrows to keep it from getting in my eyes and stinging. Once the dirt beneath my shoe gave way, and I went down to one knee, and got up with my sweaty hands all dirty.

Time passed. I began to zigzag a little to decrease the angle of the slope, and give my Achilles tendons a break. I was still low in the canyon. Looking up, I could no longer see all the way to the top; steep points in the slope along the way intervened, and became my temporary skyline. Luckily, the configuration of the slope itself kept me on course: I was climbing a sort of rounded ridge, and if I deviated too far to left or right, the angle of the slope became quite a bit steeper. So I was following the edge of an indistinct buttress (though I didn't know that), and thus I had a clear route.

Onward and upward. I began taking a rest every hundred steps. I had already come to the conclusion that the trail would have been easier: you could step flat on the trail, and you didn't slide backward half the time, and you didn't have to figure out which way to go every step of the way. I felt foolish, as one always does at the halfway station between innocence and experience. Blake missed that category: *Songs of Foolishness.*

The terracing of sandstone ledges began to get more distinct, and larger in scale. Instead of stairs, they were waist or chest high, as if they were stairs for giants, with vertical sections to them that were steeper than I was used to. So each ledge had to be climbed, or else I had to zigzag a route up the various dry gullies that broke through these ledges. It was hard work. Looking up I could usually only see a hundred feet or so at a time, and the view never changed; it kept on like that no matter how long I went between rests. The day got hotter.

I had no hat. I had no water. I had no food. I had no map, or compass (though they wouldn't have done me any good if I had had them). In fact, I had nothing but a cotton sleeping bag hanging from my shoulders, and its straps were really cutting into my arms. I couldn't see my destination anymore, but judging by the canyon below, and the great wall across from me, I still had a long, long way to go. And the way kept getting harder.

Slowly but surely, fear began to seep into me. What if I lost my way, and somehow missed the exact knot of piñon pines that marked where the trail was? It would be impossible to find the trail without that landmark. And then what if I couldn't go on without water, and couldn't find any? Or—I slipped hard and banged my knee on a ledge, which made me cry out with fear—what if I hurt myself so badly I couldn't walk? This slope was so immense, no one would ever find me on it.

I shoved these fears away and climbed on a bit faster, spurred by their presence, pushing in around the edges of conscious thought. But soon enough the surge of adrenaline they had caused was used up, by a hard scramble up a dry streambed. As I got more and more tired it became impossible to hold the fears out of my thoughts, and they came pouring back in. My head ached, in a tight band across the temples. My tongue was a thick, dry thing clogging my mouth; it tasted of dust, and I couldn't work up a bit of saliva. My breaths were like ragged sobs.

The sun had shifted far to the west, and the rocks threw shadows off to the left. The light had that ominous, dark brilliance that sometimes comes late in the day after a cloudless noon, with the lengthening shadows and a mare's tail or two of cloud in the sky. Above me the slope appeared to steepen, into a genuine staircase shape of horizontal, vertical, horizontal, but on a giant's scale, the little cliffs of the verticals now ten feet tall.

The time came when panic overwhelmed me. Not in a single rush, but in a growing crescendo of fear, that pushed, and pushed, and finally became *panic,* that flood of fear-beyond-fear, fear pushed up into another plane . . . how to describe it? All my senses were heightened, though their input seemed malignant: I could feel tiny puffs of breeze chilling my sweat-soaked back, could see every individual pebble and sand grain, for as far as the canyons extended . . . I could feel my breathing, all my muscles, my blood washing about in me, pumping hard through the heart. I knew that I could die, astonishing knowledge for a fifteen-year-old. But I also knew that I still lived, and could act. Panic-stricken, in a sort of exuberance of fear, I climbed again, ignoring the complaints of my muscles and the niceties of the best route, scrambling hard where I had to, moving resolutely upward, attacking the obstacles furiously . . . I suppose I had never been quite as alive as in those moments, ever in my life.

In fact I suppose that all my subsequent interest in the extremities of physical endurance, in the exploration of the bleak and harsh parts of the globe—the poles, the high mountains, the deserts—was born in those moments, when I felt the reality of such extremity myself. Ever afterwards I would know what it felt like to be pressed to the edge, I would remember the strange surge into that other world of panic spring . . . and the memory of it creates a certain (is it morbid?) fascination. . . .

Unfortunately, purest panic cannot last very long, and when it washed out of me, step by weary step, I pressed on in dull misery. As I forced myself up I wondered what Paul would think when I died and never showed up.

His face, hawklike under the gleaming black hair, popped into sight over a ledge above me. "Paul!" I cried. "Here!"

He saw me and grinned. "Glad to see you!"

"You're glad to see *me!* Wow—" I laughed tearfully. "I was hoping you'd look for me. I've been sort of lost down here. . . ."

"There's still a way to go. Here, come up this way, up this crack."

I followed his directions, almost giggling with relief. "Oh, man," I said, remembering the last hour. "Oh, man!" I reached the ledge he was on and stood next to him. We looked at each other. Maybe this time there was the slightest expression on his face: a raised pair of eyebrows. Well, boy?

I shrugged sheepishly, looked down: "How long did you wait for me?"

"An hour or so."

"It—it was harder than it looked."

"That's almost always true, around here. Get far enough away and you can't see ledges like this at all—they just look like water streaks."

"That's right! Why from below it looked like a smooth walk all the way."

He didn't reply. We stood there. "I think I can go on now," I said.

He nodded. We started climbing the slope; I followed him, put my feet in his footprints, which saved me some sliding. Up and up, step after step. He stopped often so we could rest.

I was lucky he had come down to look for me, because the slope of the wall, like the inside of a bowl, got steeper as we approached the top. The vertical sections were now sometimes twelve or fifteen feet tall, while the flat ledges narrowed to little sitting platforms. . . . Time after time Paul found breaks in these faces, footholds, dry streambeds, routes of one sort or another, so that using hands to pull ourselves, we could make our way up.

"Man, how did you get *down* here?" I asked during one rest.

"Same way we're going up—that's how I know the way. It's a lot easier seeing the way down. Harder to actually do it, but if you're patient it's not bad."

On and up. We came to one cliff about fifteen or eighteen feet high—trouble. The only way up that didn't force a long detour was a sequence of knobs and notches that had to be climbed like a ladder. Paul climbed it and showed me the holds. I took a deep breath and started up after him; his head poked over the top as he watched me.

I was almost to him when my right foot slipped out of its niche.

The other foot went too, and I was falling when he grabbed me by the wrist. One hand, clamped on my wrist, holding me up; I couldn't get a purchase on the sandstone I was knocking against. My hand caught his wrist, so we were twice linked.

"Be still." I looked up; his neck muscles bulged out, his mouth was pursed. "I pull you up to here, you grab the ledge with your other hand. Then get a knee over. Ready?"

"Yeah," I gasped. I felt his hand crush my wrist as he prepared for the pull, and then I was scraped up the sandstone, and scrabbling for a handhold on the ledge, pulling up, left knee up and over, like high jumping—and I was on the ledge, face in the gritty dirt. Paul was sprawled back on the ground, still holding on to my wrist. He sat up, smiling a small smile.

"You okay?"

I nodded breathlessly, looking at the white finger marks on my wrist. I didn't want to start crying, so I didn't say anything.

"We'll find a better way up any others like that. Come on."

I staggered up and followed him. True to his word, we were able to climb gullies to make it up every vertical slab. I was thankful; by this point I was past any extra efforts. It was hard just to walk.

Then the slope tilted back, got easier. We snaked up a little gully that was like a miniature of the canyons below. And we came out of the top of it into trees—piñon pines, on flat sandy ground. The top. And there, just by the first trees, threading its way among them, was the trail, a wide whitish trough.

"Oh, good," I said.

Paul stopped in the trail and we rested. He saw the look on my face and said, "Cross-country can be hard."

I nodded mutely.

"The hard way can teach you a thing or two, though. Here. You lead. Set whatever pace you're comfortable with. We still have a way to go."

It was true, but I didn't care. We were on the trail. I walked along it zombielike. It was amazing how easy it was to walk on a trail; no decisions to make at all, no terrible stretch of foot and Achilles tendon . . . wonderful thing, trail. How long had I been off it? Four hours, five? It seemed much longer than that, but the sun still shone, there was a good deal of daylight left; it couldn't have been more than five hours. What a lot of living to fit into such a small span! What a lot of appreciation for trail, to have gained in only five hours!

I was hiking along the trail through the pines, and half thinking thoughts such as these, when I rounded a corner and saw Paul lying there ahead of me, sacked out asleep under a tree, his cowboy hat shading his face.

I jerked to a stop, spun around. No Paul following me on the trail. I had heard his steps behind me just a moment before.

I turned again, confused. The Paul under the tree heard me, tipped up his cowboy hat, saw me. He sat up, calm and slow. "You made it," he said.

I felt the skin on my back crawl. I began to tremble, and for a second light-headedness washed through me, almost made me sick. My vision returned with scores of crawling clear tubes in it. "How—how long have you been here?"

He shrugged. "An hour or so. You get lost?"

I shook my head. "You didn't . . ." I couldn't finish.

He stood, put on his pack, came over and looked at me. He cocked his head curiously . . . something in his look, there . . . not complicity, but perhaps an acknowledgment that I had a right to be confused. . . .

"Here," he said. "Want me to take that sleeping bag?"

"You won't m—You won't mind?" Because my shoulders were aching fiercely under the straps.

He smiled a little—just exactly the smile he had had on his face after he pulled me up the cliff. My wrist tingled with the memory of that crushing grip, and when he touched my arm to slip the sleeping bag off, I almost cried out. I sat down right on the spot, trembling all over, my skin rippling in great shivers of nervous shock, of fear. Rippling fields of goose bumps . . . "But I . . ." But I was too frightened of him to be able to ask him anything. I looked back the way I had come, thinking he might still appear; yet here he was before me, taking off his pack, tying my sleeping bag to the top of it. . . .

He got it secured, put the pack back on. He looked at me, concerned. "It's okay."

I wiped the tears from my face. Nodded, looking down, ashamed.

It was emphatically not okay. But there was nothing for it but to stand, to follow him down the trail.

He stepped in front of me, caught my ashamed gaze, reached out and touched my arm with a single finger. "It's okay, now." Something in his voice, his eyes—as if he knew everything that had happened. . . .

My shivering stopped, I nodded meekly. "Okay. Let's go."

But all the way back I thought of it. The trailhead was a long way across the tableland, and it was a miserable hike, through the long shadows of the last part of the day, sky already darkening with the sun still up, a lenticular cloud over Navaho Mountain glowing the color of the canyons, every little wave of it a perfectly drawn French curve. . . . Cruelly, the Park Service had set the red mileposts farther and farther apart the closer to the trailhead you came; I hadn't noticed on the way in. I tried counting steps one to the next and lost count in the first hundred.

Maybe he had gone down to get me, then as we hiked up the trail, had snuck ahead through the trees to lie down and give me a surprise. Only he couldn't have: the trail cut through a sort of notch there, with thick forest on each side. From the time I last saw the Paul behind me until the first moment I saw the Paul under the tree, only a couple of minutes had elapsed. There just wasn't time for such a maneuver. No . . . I began to shiver again. Each time I forced myself to truly confront the memory of what had happened, I was racked with electric shivers running up and down my back, then all over me, and the spasm shook my head violently, as if my spine were a branch and my head a fruit, orange or apple or pear, that someone was trying to bring down. . . .

In a garish desert sunset we reached the trading post, the parking lot. The trading post was open, and we went in. While Paul spoke in Navaho I went to the big cooler in the corner, one of those refrigerated metal trunks that stands waist high. I flipped the top hatch open and pulled out a Nehi Grape drink; pulled off the flip top and drank it down in two long swallows. I can still remember perfectly the strange carbonated grape flavor of that drink. When I was done I got out another can and drank it too.

Paul drove us home through the dusk, his pickup's big headlight beams bouncing about in tandem as we hit potholes in the asphalt. I was too tired to think much, but once the sight of Paul lying there under that tree, hat over his face, flashed before me, and the goose bumps rippled over me again, like the wind shooting cat's paws over the surface of a lake. My whole nervous system resonated with fear, I once again felt his hand clamped on my wrist, my knees scraping the sandstone, feet free in the air, searching for purchase. . . . I've never had a better demonstration of how completely our skins are linked to our minds. Then the fit passed, and I slumped in the seat again, sweating, watching the headlight beams lance the darkness.

Maybe I had gone crazy. Yeah, that was it: I had gone crazy and hallucinated Paul's presence with me on that canyonside. And I must have hallucinated that fall, too, because if I really had fallen it was certain no hallucination was going to catch me and pull me up. Sure. The whole thing, just a frightened sunstruck dream.

The only trouble was, I knew that it hadn't been. Oh, I know, you can say if you went crazy then you were crazy, and you couldn't tell what was real and what wasn't. But that isn't the way it works, not in the real world. I mean, that's the sad thing about insane people; almost all of them know perfectly well that something is seriously wrong with them; that's what makes them so scared, so depressed. They know.

And I knew, I *knew*, that I had not hallucinated that slip and fall, or the hand on my wrist. It was all a seamless whole, from the start up the slope to the finish in the trees, and no anxious half-hour—not even a half-hour of panic—could have made me so crazy that my senses could have been fooled that badly. Later, when the memory faded some, I could doubt that point; but there in the truck with Paul, my wrist still aching, the whole memory of it still in my body, I was certain of it.

Finally we were back at the mission. Aunt Miriam came out to greet us, and we told her about Luke and David. Paul said he'd go back up the next day to make sure they got out all right; he glanced at me as he said it. And he smiled as he said good night, that small smile I had seen before. . . . For a second I saw in his eyes a clear acknowledgment of what had happened. And I understood: Paul was an Indian sorcerer, he could be in two places at once. But then he was gone, and I wasn't so sure.

I found that my skin could ripple with goose bumps even immersed in the hot water of my aunt's old bathtub; all I had to do was remember that look, that smile, the moment on the cliff face, seeing Paul under that piñon. . . . Despite my exhaustion, I slept very poorly that night; I kept jerking awake as I slipped off the face . . . and it would all come pouring in again, until I moaned at the bright fresh fear of it. Would it never ease, this fear?

The next day about noon Luke and David drove up in Luke's VW, laughing over great adventures of their own: Luke had carried David part of the way, they had slept in the trail, Luke had hiked to the trading post and back in the middle of the night, to make sure no one was waiting and worrying. . . . These adventures sounded quite mundane to me. Luke had already heard some of what had happened to me from Paul, and he laughed at my silence, thinking I was only embarrassed at ignoring Paul's advice and taking off cross-country. I imagine I didn't show much of a sense of humor about it.

The day after that it was time to leave. Luke was going to drive us all the way to Phoenix to catch a plane, and then come all the way back; he was looking forward to the drive.

We were out front saying our good-byes to Aunt Miriam when Paul drove up in his truck. Only later did it occur to me that he had come specifically to say good-bye to us. To me. Only later did I recall we were driving through Flagstaff, only later did I put it together, that for Paul I was . . . I don't know what, exactly.

He got out, walked over. Same jeans, same shirt . . . He smiled at David and me, shook our hands. I recognized the grip, recognized it exactly. He looked me in the eye, nodded once, solemnly, as if to confirm my thought: *it happened.* He tapped the side of his head with his finger. "That was a good hike," he said to me. "Remember."

We got into the VW. As we drove off, Paul and Miriam stood side by side, waving—Paul looking right at me, nowhere else—and the two of them had identical expressions on their faces, that expression you see in the faces of your older relatives, as you wave good-bye to them after an infrequent, too-short visit; they're fond of you, they love you, they look at you with an honesty only the old have, thinking this *will I see that one again before I die?*

Remember. Many years have passed since that happened; my great-aunt Miriam died in 1973, and as it turned out I never did see her again. And I never heard another word of my friend Paul, from that time to this.

But I've thought about him, oh believe me I have: and every single time I have brought myself to think honestly about it, to remember it truly and admit to myself that such an impossible thing happened to me, my skin has reacted with its fearful shivered rippling; just a ghost of the original fear in its power to shake me, but still most definitely there, a cold, uncanny contact with . . . something *other*. Even writing this account, here in a quiet room halfway around the world, nineteen years away, I have felt that shiver—once, in fact, as strongly as any since the first time: the room disappeared, and I was back there in those pines, Paul lying there . . .

Naturally I have attempted, many times, to explain to myself what happened that afternoon. I have read of the Indian shamans of the Southwest with more than the usual interest, and recalling the masks and jugs I glimpsed so briefly at Paul's hogan, I suspect he could have been one. The Navaho are a pretty secular people, but Paul had business with the Hopi, unusual for a Navaho; and you don't get any stranger than the Hopi. And the Navaho treated Paul differently, too, he had a sort of power over them. . . . People are skeptical of Castaneda, and I suppose they should be—I probably would be too—but sometimes when I was reading those books, that shaman spoke right to me, through a face I knew. . . . Yes, it could be I was befriended by a shaman, and shown a little of the world beyond.

And of course the idea has returned to me, often, that I hallucinated Paul's presence, in my fear and need calling up his image to get me up the last, most difficult part of the climb. Sure. It's the explanation that makes the most sense, the one I believe in myself most often. But . . . a hallucinated figure, an imagined conversation, those are one thing; a hallucinated cliff face, an imagined fall? For me, somehow, those are in a different category; and I have never been able to believe that I was that completely disconnected from reality.

Because that *hand on my wrist!* My God, how to tell it? I was hanging there in space, falling, and that hand on my wrist *pulled me up*. It pulled me up to safety, to the life I have lived since then. . . . And I *felt* it.

So. In the end, I always have to let it be. Something strange happened to me, out there in the desert; I don't know what.

But lately, when I think about it, I always see the look that was on Paul's face as we drove away from the mission, and out of his life. And I see him trying to jump the giant gap between our lives, to teach me a little, mostly with looks; I see him letting me hike off on my own; I feel that hand on my wrist, pulling me up. . . . And now when I remember that impossible moment, I have been filled with some sort of huge, cloudy feeling—call it grace: my spirit has soared at the thought of it, flying like a shaman over the surface of this world, exhilarated and intensely happy. Either way it was a gift, you see; a gift from Paul, or from the world. Because consider it: if Paul was a shaman, and out of his feeling for me sent his spirit down that canyon wall to help me up, while the rest of him slumbered there in the sun under a piñon pine—then human beings have mysterious powers that we poor civilized rational people are unaware of, and we are much greater than we know. But if, on the other hand, I imagined Paul's presence there above me, if only I was there to clasp myself as I fell, so that I pulled myself up that cliff, by the power of my mind, and by the strength of my desire to live—then we are free indeed.

Muir on Shasta

"Your goodness must have an edge to it," Emerson had said to him, as if a single week's acquaintanceship in euphoric Yosemite could reveal any of the edges in a man. Still it had been valuable advice, for Muir's edges lay buried under sunny meadows and brook babble, and it could be that the old philosopher had only meant to say You should let your edges show, or It is all right to have edges. A valuable lesson indeed.

Shasta was an Emersonian mountain, it occurred to Muir as he sat on its summit pinnacle. In its youth it had leaped toward heaven, rising ten thousand feet above the surrounding plains; now it was ancient, glacier-cloaked, its broad peak rounded and craterless, its creative fires banked. And yet there were still sharp outcroppings of lava on the ridges, and enough fire rising from the depths to boil a muddy spring near the summit; and there was in the end the massive snowy fact of the mountain itself, isolate, powerful, brooding, god-like. Emerson had been just like that.

Muir hefted a brass barometer. He and an acquaintance, Jerome Bixby, had ascended Shasta that morning to take readings, although really the readings were no more than an excuse to climb the mountain and have a look around. From the peak, one saw mountains everywhere—the Coast Range, the Siskiyous, the Trinity Alps, the northern Sierra, snowy flat-topped Lassen—mountains to every point of the compass, a wild tangle of ridges and peaks.

As he sat and watched, clouds rose out of the valleys and over the ridges, until everything except Shasta was submerged. He stood on a snow island in an ocean of cloud. To the west a thunderhead billowed up, its bright lobes as solid as marble. He gazed at it with a connoisseur's eye, feeling the wind yank his beard, feeling it rake through the weave of his coat, rapt with his usual peak exaltation—

But there was Bixby, plodding across the white summit plain, looking like a black ant. He had been waiting below the ultimate peak, but now he huffed up the small remnant of the crater wall that was the mountain's highest point, and once at Muir's side said, "We should go down—a storm is coming!"

"One more reading," Muir said, irritated. He didn't care about the reading, but he didn't want to descend.

So they stayed on the peak, and the wind freshened, and then the clear air overhead was suddenly marred by streams of mist like carded wool. Just as he completed the last reading they were enveloped in cloud, and the wind grew stronger; and as he followed Bixby down the knob and onto the summit plain, six-faceted hailstones clattered onto the tortured red rock, and thumped into the packed snow, and onto their backs.

Then as they forced their way west, past the hissing fumaroles of the hot spring and over big chunks of black lava, snow began to fall in waves so thick that at times they were unable to see even their own feet. Blasts of wind slapped them on the ear, snow crystals stung their faces, and it got so cold so fast that Muir became curious, and stopped to read his thermometer; the temperature had dropped twenty-two degrees in ten minutes, and was now below zero.

Lightning flicked, dim in the clouds, and thunder began to bang around them, in explosions so violent that they vibrated one's whole body. "Wow!" Muir shouted, inaudible in the barrage. He was grinning. The truth was, he loved storms in the mountains. He had been in them so many times that he was confident no storm could harm him, if he continued to walk in it; the heat engendered by exertion was always enough to counter even the wildest assaults. And so he struggled on through the crashing, howling vortex of snow and wind and thunder, head down, thrusting forward as if wrestling some herculean elder brother, whooping at the storm's high drama and spectacle, its brute strength and godlike grandeur—laughing at its sheer excess—

But he had entirely forgotten to think of Bixby. Who, in fact, had fallen behind, and was out of sight. Muir crouched in the shelter of a giant lava block that marked the route along their ridge, and waited. After a while Bixby appeared out of the snow, and one look made it clear that he was not having the same sort of fun that Muir was.

The two men huddled together in the lee of the block. Weird light illuminated them in flashes, and it was almost too noisy to hold a conversation. "We can't go on!" Bixby shouted.

"What?" Muir said, astonished.

"We can't go on!"

"But we must! We have no choice!"

"We'll be killed!"

"No, no—we'll stay on the ridge, I know the way!"

"It's too exposed!"

This was the very reason that they must take the ridge. The slopes to either side would be swept by avalanches, and even if they escaped these, they would be likely to wander onto a glacier. The ridge, on the other hand, would be blown clear of snow, providing a rocky road down to safety. It would be windy, but no wind could blow a man from a rock; if gusts threatened to do so, one could always lie flat till they were over.

Irritably he tried to explain this, but Bixby would have none of it. He just shook his head and shouted again, "We can't go down!" He looked the same as always, face calm, his shouts in a reasonable tone of voice; but there was a stubbornness in him, and when Muir shouted, "I memorized the way down the ridge," he stared at Muir as if confronted with a madman. And the thunder crashed, and the hurtling air roared across the ridge, catching on a million jagged lava teeth and shrieking, keening, howling, drowning out mere human voices.

"We must go down!" Muir shouted again. "We have no choice!"

"We can't go down! It's impossible! We'll be killed!"

"It's stopping will kill us!" Muir replied, getting angry. Stupid man, did he think this block's feeble shelter would be enough to protect them? "We have no choice!" he repeated.

Bixby shook his head. For an instance he looked like Muir's father, insisting on a point of Bible doctrine. "I won't go on!"

"We must go on!"

"I won't go on!"

And that was that. There is a stubbornness in fear that will balk at even the most perfect logic. Muir tugged furiously at his beard. "What do you propose to do!" he shouted.

Bixby wiped the snow from his face and looked around, blinking cowlike. "The fumaroles are warm," he said.

"The fumaroles are *boiling!*" Muir shouted. Anger spiked through him, he wanted to grab the man by the coat and shake his courage back into him. "Superheated poison gas!"

But Bixby was trudging back toward the fumaroles, hunched into the wind, staggering as gusts shoved him from side to side.

"Fool!" Muir cried, and cursed him roundly.

He stayed by the block, searching the clouds for a break that he could use as argument to convince Bixby to continue. But none came; the storm raged on; and suddenly he realized that his anger at Bixby was a transitive expression of his own fear. He could not leave his companion behind; and so now they were both in very great danger.

The fumaroles near the peak were among the last small vestiges of Shasta's volcanic glory. Superheated gases rose through cracks in the long throat, and emerged in a small depression on the western side of the summit, where they heated a mixture of snowmelt, volcanic ash, and sand, creating a patch of boiling black mud.

Muir approached it. In the storm's cold air the patch steamed heavily, making it look like the clouds were pouring out of the mountain as well as rushing over it: an eerie sight. Bixby was already crouched at the mud's edge. Muir stomped to his side.

Bixby looked up. "This will keep us safe from frost!"

"Oh yes, safe from frost!" Muir said sarcastically. "But how will we keep from scalding ourselves? And how will we protect our lungs from the acid gases? And how will we get off the mountain once we soak our clothes? Storm or clear, we'll freeze on our way down! We'll have to stay until morning, and who knows what kind of day it will be!"

Bixby shivered miserably.

Muir held his breath, let out a long sigh. There was nothing for it. They were there. He crouched and looked over the roiling snow-rimmed pit. Wind whipped any warmth coming off the mud directly away; their zone of safety was about a quarter of an acre in extent, but only an eighth of an inch thick. Scylla and Charybdis, embracing.

Muir sighed again and tromped into the mud, sinking immediately to his knees and feeling the heat burn his legs. Jetting bubbles of gas made the mud look like molten lava. But on the windward side of the pool they would probably be safe from the gas. As long as the wind held steady. And it seemed it would; it roared out of the west, cutting through clothing; they couldn't stand in it long. Growling, Muir finished sitting in the shallows of the pool. Hot water seeped out of the mud into his pants, then his shirt and coat. He lay back, his head against the windward snowbank, his body outstretched in the mud. Spindrift ran across his face. His nose, which had no feeling to it, still conveyed to him the stench of sulphur. The warmth of the mud burned his skin, but he had to admit it was a relief from the fierce wind. A laugh burst from him like gas from the mud; then a jet of rising bubbles scalded his back and he yelped, rolled hastily to the side. He elbowed a snow and mud poultice over the hot spot, dizzy with the carbonic stink. Now he was covered with mud, his coat and trousers completely soaked. Bixby was the same. Standing up would have turned them into ice statues of themselves. They were committed.

It was necessary to shift position frequently, to immerse an exposed limb, or expose a boiled one. The passage of time was marked by pain. The storm continued unabated, and the two men lay isolated by the shrieking wind, so that each might have been there alone except that occasionally Muir would raise his head and cry out, and Bixby would shout something back, and both would subside into solitude again. Snow fell so thickly that they breathed it. It settled on the exposed parts of them, and packed to a rime so hard that they crackled when they shifted.

The sun had apparently set, and it was dark. Muir could see nothing but blackness. At times the mud seemed blacker than the sky; then the sky would seem blacker than the mud. As black as the world had been during his episode of blindness, so many years before. He saw the file leaping into his eye, the aqueous humor draining into his hand, the swift darkening in his sight on the wounded side, and then, that night as he lay trembling in a strange bed, the relentless darkening on the other. Until he was left in total darkness. That fear had been the worst of his life; this was nothing to it, a natural darkness, a storm in its fury to be watched and loved. I will lift up mine eyes unto the hills, and *see*. He had been blind for three weeks, three full weeks of doctor's assurances and secret terror; and when his sight had returned he had walked out of his life and never returned, never looked back, tossing away the destiny that his father and country had thought proper for him, farming, inventing machinery, all that; he abandoned all that and gave himself to the wilderness. So that, properly speaking, it was in fact a blessing to be here boiling in a volcano's caldera with a blizzard thick about his ears. Part of nature's bounty—

Groans from Bixby broke his thought. He saw the lump of the man, rolling to escape a fumarole, struggling to keep from sinking. In some places the mud was viscid clay, in others black tea, whistling in its pot. Lumps of something, perhaps soaked pumice, floated under the surface, and he tried arranging a bed of the lumps under him to protect him from rising gas jets, but they kept slipping away. The wind still howled, but the clouds were thinning; the snow blowing across their bodies must have been spindrift, for he saw a star. If you can see one star, press on! as the saying had it. But not tonight.

Soon the clouds scudded off east, and starlight bathed the scene. The familiar patterns sparked the night sky, drawing around him all the other nights he had lain out in the world. The eye is a flower that sees the stars. If they had continued their descent, they would now be down on the snow slopes, where starlight would have made darkness visible, and guided them home. Instead, soaked as they were, and with a mile of wind-ripped ridge to negotiate, they were going to have to spend the night. But he said nothing. It was done. And his fault really, for staying on the peak so long. Besides, the sight of the stars brought it to him that whatever the discomfort, they were likely to survive; so it did not signify. He had spent many a cold night on a mountain. It could even be said that the boiling mud made this night less miserable than some, though—the skin of his back suddenly flaring—none other had been so purely painful. Still, he was used to pain, accustomed to it. He had grown up with it, working a hardscrabble farm for his father, a mean, small-minded man, a lesson in how not to be a Christian, all those days spent studying the Bible while his boys worked to get his bread, and then beating them with switch, belt—

His leg was on fire. He pulled his knee up into the icy wind, and for an instant smelled the gas. Once his father had set him to digging wells, and seventy feet down seeping gas had overwhelmed him, he had swooned and had only just come to, only just dragged himself far enough up the rope ladder to breathe good air, and live. He lifted his head and shouted at Bixby. "Still there, Jerome?"

A croak. Something about the cold. Still there. Muir settled back into the mud. Forget that whole world, that whole life, the way it could make his stomach knot. Look at the stars. The eye is a flower that sees the stars, immersed in primal cold and heat. His left foot squelched in its boot, propped on the snowbank. Wiggle the toes against wet leather, make sure they were still there. No. They were cold past feeling, only a certain vague numbness; while his right foot burned, scalded so that he nearly shouted, and certainly groaned. Leg yanked up; the wind wrapped the wet trouser to his leg and froze his thigh, while the foot still throbbed with the pain of the burn.

"Are you suffering much?" Bixby called.

"Yes!" Fool, what did he think? "Frozen and burned! But never mind, it won't kill us!" As long as they weren't overcome by gas. A jet of bubbles pushed at his backbone, he rolled and shoved mud over the scalding spot, hitting at it furiously with a fist gone numb with frostbite.

Each hour was a year. The stars were in the same places they had been when they first became visible; so not many years could have passed. Concentrating on the stars near the horizon, he tried to see them creep west. That one, nearly occluded by a low wall of lava: focus on it, watch it, watch it, watch it . . . had it moved? No. Time had stopped. They had continued the descent, perhaps, and died in the attempt, and now they lay in some well-bottom hell of his father's stripe, or in a circle of Dante's inferno, in which heat and cold mingled without moderating the other, creating a pain unfamiliar to those in the simpler circles. He could hear their moans—

Ah, that star was occluded. Half an hour had jumped past all at once. As if time were a matter of instantaneous jumps, from one eternal moment to the next—which in fact it often seemed to him to be, as during those sunny warm afternoons when he would lie in a Sierra meadow by a chuckling stream and watch the clouds, dreaming of nothing, until with a jerk he would return to the meadow and the shadows would be stretching twice as long as before, over perfectly sculpted patches of meadow grass, the larks singing "wé-ero, spé-ero, wé-eo, wé-erlo, wé-it."

Drifting in and out. A call to Bixby got a feeble response. Still alive if nothing else. A bubble burst, splashed hot mud over his face, and he spluttered and wiped his nose clear. He couldn't feel his left arm, or make it move; he wasn't sure when that had happened. That was his windward side, so presumably it was benumbed in the onslaught of air. He tried to dip the arm further under the mud, to bury it. Not a process one would want to carry too far, descending limb by limb into black muck. Now the arm seemed to be burning; was that a fumarole bubbling up? No. In fact he had accidentally plunged the arm into the snowbank; his right hand confirmed it. But how the skin burned!

Then a gas bubble lifted his knee, and the back of his leg felt like glacier melt had been poured over it; it ached with cold, the knee joint creaked with it! He groaned. Cold now scalded and heat froze, and he didn't know which was which!

Perhaps it didn't matter. Caught between cold reason and hot passion, ignorant flesh always paid the price. One could never tell which was which. Outrageous pain! Better to leave all that behind.

A solution occurred to him. He stood up. He looked back down and saw his body lying there, stretched out in the mud, mostly submerged. A sponge, soaked in immortality. A mass of eternal atoms, bound together in just that particular way, to witness the beauty of the universe.

Yes: he stood there gazing down at his boiled and frozen body. Somewhat bemused, he tried a few steps; circled the mud patch; then took off across the windswept snow, toward an exposed rock outcropping. There was a building there, a small square cabin, white in the starlight. As he approached he saw that its walls were made of pure white quartz. Its door and windows were edged with quartz crystals. The door and the roof were made of slate, all dotted with lichen. The windows were thin smooth sheets of water.

He opened the door and walked in. The table was a slab of glacier-polished granite. The benches around it were fallen logs. The bed was made of spruce boughs. The carpet was green moss.

It was his home. He sat on one of the logs, and put his hand on the table. His hand sank into the granite. His body sank into the log, and then into the moss, and then into the quartz.

He felt himself dissolving out into the great mass of the mountain, tumbling slowly down through the rock. He had melted into Shasta. The mountain mumbled in his ear "I am." With a puff of its cheeks it blew him aloft, threw his atoms out into the sky. They tumbled off on the wind and dispersed to every point of the compass, then fell and steeped into the fabric of the land, one atom in every rock, in every grain of sand and soil, like gas in mud, or water in sponge, until his body and California were contiguous, united, one. Only his vision remained separate, his precious sight, the landscape's consciousness soaring like a hawk over the long sand beaches, the great valley, the primeval sequoias, the range of light—but the mountains were different—blinding glaciers covered all but the highest peaks, fingered down through the hills, and cut Yosemite's walls. Then they retreated, dried up and ran away.

He tumbled, soared west. It was night, now, and below lay the bay like a sparkling black map, the black water criss-crossed with bridges of light, the surrounding hills dotted with millions of white points like stars, defining towers, roadways, docks, arenas, monuments; a bay-circling city, impossibly beautiful. But so many people! It had to be thousands of years in the future, as glaciers were thousands of years in the past. He was soaring through time, out of the knife-edge present, back to glaciers and forward to supercities, perhaps ten thousand years each way. An eyeblink in the life of stones, and the Sierra would stand throughout; but chewed at by the future city as much as by the ancient glaciers, perhaps. Sheep cropped meadows to dust in a single summer; and the shepherds were worse. And if so many came to live by the bay. . . .

Curious, fearful, he tilted in his flight, soared east over the great valley, through the gold-choked foothills, up among the peaks. He rose in a gyre and stared down at starlit granite. There a valley had been drowned, a shocking sight. Wheel, turn, soar, take heart: for all was dark. Not a light to be seen, the whole length of the range. The backbone of California, gleaming in moonlight.

This much beauty would always be in danger, there was no avoiding that. Its animals must defend it. All its animals. He soared over the highest peaks, and then looked back; a full moon bathed the great eastern escarpment with white light. Death Valley burned, Whitney froze—

His ankle was in a fumarole, his head in the muddy snowbank. He shifted, saw that the wheel of stars had turned nearly a quarter turn. He took several long deep breaths. His vision cleared with the cold air, he returned to the moment and his bed in the mud. He could feel his lungs and his mind; beyond that, he and the mountain still seemed one undifferentiated mass, which he felt only in a distant, seismic way. But now he knew where he was. For a while he had soared on a great wind through time; but now he was just John again, flat on his back, and numb with cold.

Still, he remembered the vision perfectly. That was quite a voyage great Shasta had sent him on! Perhaps visions like that were why the Indians worshipped it.

As for what he had seen . . . well, the habitable zone was never thick. Caught between the past and future, we squirm in a dangerous eighth of an inch. Perhaps it was like that always. The atmosphere, for instance, was frighteningly thin; hike for a day and you could ascend the larger part of it, as when climbing Shasta itself. The landscape was tightly wrapped in a thin skin of gas.

And the earth itself rolled in a thin temperate sphere around the sun, a zone of heat that neither boiled the seas nor allowed them to freeze solid; that shell might only be a few feet thick, or an eighth of an inch, who knew? It was a miracle the earth rolled within that sphere! Delicate, precious dewdrop of a world, hung in the light with the nicest precision, like every dewdrop in every morning's spider-web. . . .

The wheel of stars had turned again. Bixby was shifting, muttering as in a dream. The sky in the east was the black nearest blue. And then the blue nearest black. Light seeped into the world as if vision were a new faculty, a sense born instant by instant, to creatures formerly blind. The stars began to slip away; he watched a dim one grow fainter and then wink out of visibility, a strange moment. The eyes are flowers that see the stars.

Bixby croaked something about leaving. But they were on the western side of the peak, and it would be hours before the sun appeared. Meanwhile it was cold beyond movement. When they shifted their coats crackled as if made of thin glass.

The sky, though cloudless, was a dull and frosty blue. He could see nothing of the earth but their mud patch, and the snow and lava bordering it. He still felt part of the mountain, with no discernable break between his skin and the mud. As the morning light blossomed it seemed to fill him, pouring through his eyes and down into the rock; he felt himself a conduit in a vast interconnected totality, an organism pulsing with its own universal breath. The heat at his core caught and burned, so that he was warm enough to melt his coat's sheath of ice; that was heat displaced from the volcano, which was heat displaced from the sun; which was heat displaced from the heart of the Milky Way; which was heat displaced from the heart of the universe, from that original heart's diastolic expansion. No dualism was significant in the face of this essential unity: he was an atom of God's great body, and he knew it. The landscape and his mind were two expressions of the same miracle.

On the lonely peak of a nearly extinct volcano, two black specks of consciousness observed the morning light.

*　　*　　*

The time came at last to try a descent. Imagination over reason, action over contemplation; thus he had always believed, and never more than now! It was time to think two thoughts down the mountain.

Spindrift sparked overhead like chips of mica, and then the sun cracked the mountaintop. They stood like golems new-made of clay, ice shattering from their chests, mud sluicing off their backs. They slapped their arms together and the world burned in their fingertips. Nature was the greatest teacher, for those who listened; and Muir had learned long ago that there was a reserve of energy at the end of any long period of suffering. It was something mountaineers often had the chance to discover.

They staggered crazy-legged over the long ridge. They reached the snow slopes and descended more rapidly, swimming through drifts, glissading at the top of little avalanches, falling on their faces; but all downward, and so of use, their weakness only speeding the descent.

Then the clean smell of pinesap cut through the sulphur stench in their hair, and they were at treeline. Bixby sat against a tree and rested, while Muir went on, in search of their host Sisson. Godlike he strode through a meadow, its wildflowers exploding in his sight, dot after dot of pure drenched color. And then he saw Sisson's horses through the trees, and smelled his coffee on the fire. Smoke rose through slanting sunbeams. He was home; and now he was home.

Glacier

"This is Stella," Mrs. Goldberg said. She opened the cardboard box and a gray cat leaped out and streaked under the corner table.

"That's where we'll put her blanket," Alex's mother said.

Alex got down on hands and knees to look. Stella was a skinny old cat; her fur was an odd mix of silver, black, and pinkish tan. Yellow eyes. Part tortoise-shell, Mom had said. The color of the fur over her eyes made it appear her brow was permanently furrowed. Her ears were laid flat.

"Remember she's kind of scared of boys," Mrs. Goldberg said.

"I know." Alex sat back on his heels. Stella hissed. "I was just looking." He knew the cat's whole story. She had been a stray that began visiting the Goldbergs' balcony to eat their dog's food, then—as far as anyone could tell—to hang out with the dog. Remus, a stiff-legged ancient thing, seemed happy to have the company, and after a while the two animals were inseparable. The cat had learned how to behave by watching Remus, and so it would go for a walk, come when you called it, shake hands and so on. Then Remus died, and now the Goldbergs had to move. Mom had offered to take Stella in, and though Father sighed heavily when she told him about it, he hadn't refused.

Mrs. Goldberg sat on the worn carpet beside Alex, and leaned forward so she could see under the table. Her face was puffy. "It's okay, Stell-bell," she said. "It's okay."

The cat stared at Mrs. Goldberg with an expression that said *You've got to be kidding.* Alex grinned to see such skepticism.

Mrs. Goldberg reached under the table; the cat squeaked in protest as it was pulled out, then lay in Mrs. Goldberg's lap quivering like a rabbit. The two women talked about other things. Then Mrs. Goldberg put Stella in Alex's mother's lap. There were scars on its ears and head. It breathed fast. Finally it calmed under Mom's hands. "Maybe we should feed her something," Mom said. She knew how distressed animals could get in this situation: they themselves had left behind their dog Pongo, when they moved from Toronto to Boston. Alex and she had been the ones to take Pongo to the Wallaces; the dog had howled as they left, and walking away Mom had cried. Now she told Alex to get some chicken out of the fridge and put it in a bowl for Stella. He put the bowl on the couch next to the cat, who sniffed at it disdainfully and refused to look at it. Only after much calming would it nibble at the meat, nose drawn high over one sharp eyetooth. Mom talked to Mrs. Goldberg, who watched Stella eat. When the cat was done it hopped off Mom's lap and walked up and down the couch. But it wouldn't let Alex near; it crouched as he approached, and with a desperate look dashed back under the table. "Oh Stella!" Mrs. Goldberg laughed. "It'll take her a while to get used to you," she said to Alex, and sniffed. Alex shrugged.

Outside the wind ripped at the treetops sticking above the buildings. Alex walked up Chester Street to Brighton Avenue and turned left, hurrying to counteract the cold. Soon he reached the river and could walk the path on top of the embankment. Down in its trough the river's edges were crusted with ice, but midstream was still free, the silty gray water riffled by white. He passed the construction site for the dam and came to the moraine, a long mound of dirt, rocks, lumber, and junk. He climbed it with big steps, and stood looking at the glacier.

The glacier was immense, like a range of white hills rolling in from the west and north. The Charles poured from the bottom of it and roiled through a cut in the terminal moraine; the glacier's snout loomed so large that the river looked small, like a gutter after a storm. Bright white iceberg chunks had toppled off the face of the snout, leaving fresh blue scars and clogging the river below.

Alex walked the edge of the moraine until he was above the glacier's side. To his left was the razed zone, torn streets and fresh dirt and cellars open to the sky; beyond it Allston and Brighton, still bustling with city life. Under him, the sharp-edged mound of dirt and debris. To his right, the wilderness of ice and rock. Looking straight ahead it was hard to believe that the two halves of the view came from the same world. Neat. He descended the moraine's steep loose inside slope carefully, following a path of his own.

The meeting of glacier and moraine was a curious juncture. In some places the moraine had been undercut and had spilled across the ice in wide fans; you couldn't be sure if the dirt was solid or if it concealed crevasses. In other places melting had created a gap, so that a thick cake of ice stood over empty air, and dripped into gray pools below. Once Alex had seen a car in one of these low wet caves, stripped of its paint and squashed flat.

In still other places, however, the ice sloped down and overlay the moraine's gravel in a perfect ramp, as if fitted by carpenters. Alex walked the trough between dirt and ice until he reached one of these areas, then took a big step onto the curved white surface. He felt the usual quiver of excitement: he was on the glacier.

It was steep on the rounded side slope, but the ice was embedded with thousands of chunks of gravel. Each pebble, heated by the sun, had sunk into a little pocket of its own, and was then frozen into position in the night; this process had been repeated until most chunks were about three-quarters buried. Thus the glacier had a peculiarly pocked, rocky surface, which gripped the torn soles of Alex's shoes. A non-slip surface. No slope on the glacier was too steep for him. Crunch, crunch, crunch: tiny arabesques of ice collapsed under his feet with every step. He could change the glacier, he was part of its action. Part of it.

Where the side slope leveled out the first big crevasses appeared. These deep blue fissures were dangerous, and Alex stepped between two of them and up a narrow ramp very carefully. He picked up a fist-sized rock, tossed it in the bigger crack. *Clunk clunk . . . splash.* He shivered and walked on, ritual satisfied. He knew from these throws that at the bottom of the glacier there were pockets of air, pools of water, streams running down to form the Charles . . . a deadly subglacial world. No one who fell into it would ever escape. It made the surface ice glow with a magical danger, an internal light.

Up on the glacier proper he could walk more easily. Crunch crunch crunch, over an undulating broken debris-covered plain. Ice for miles on miles. Looking back toward the city he saw the Hancock and Prudential towers to the right, the lower MIT towers to the left, poking up at low scudding clouds. The wind was strong here and he pulled his jacket hood's drawstring tighter. Muffled hoot of wind, a million tricklings. There were little creeks running in channels cut into the ice: it was almost like an ordinary landscape, streams running in ravines over a broad rocky meadow. And yet everything was different. The streams ran into crevasses or potholes and instantly disappeared, for instance. It was wonderfully strange to look down such a rounded hole: the ice was very blue and you could see the air bubbles in it, air from some year long ago.

Broken seracs exposed fresh ice to the sun. Scores of big erratic boulders dotted the glacier, some the size of houses. He made his way from one to the next, using them as cover. There were gangs of boys from Cambridge who occasionally came up here, and they were dangerous. It was important to see them before he was seen.

A mile or more onto the glacier, ice had flowed around one big boulder, leaving a curving wall some ten feet high—another example of the glacier's whimsy, one of hundreds of odd surface formations. Alex had wedged some stray boards into the gap between rock and ice, making a seat that was tucked out of the west wind. Flat rocks made a fine floor, and in the corner he had even made a little fireplace. Every fire he lit sank the hearth of flat stones a bit deeper into the otherwise impervious ice.

This time he didn't have enough kindling, though, so he sat on his bench, hands deep in pockets, and looked back at the city. He could see for miles. Wind whistled over the boulder. Scattered shafts of sunlight broke against ice. Mostly shadowed, the jumbled expanse was faintly pink. This was because of an algae that lived on nothing but ice and dust. Pink; the blue of the seracs; gray ice; patches of white, marking snow or sunlight. In the distance dark clouds scraped the top of the blue Hancock building, making it look like a distant serac. Alex leaned back against his plank wall, whistling one of the songs of the Pirate King.

Everyone agreed the cat was crazy. Her veneer of civilization was thin, and at any loud noise—the phone's ring, the door slamming—she would jump as if shot, then stop in mid-flight as she recalled that this particular noise entailed no danger; then lick down her fur, pretending she had never jumped in the first place. A flayed sensibility.

She was also very wary about proximity to people; this despite the fact that she had learned to love being petted. So she would often get in moods where she would approach one of them and give an exploratory, half-purring mew; then, if you responded to the invitation and crouched to pet her, she would sidle just out of arm's reach, repeating the invitation but retreating with each shift you made, until she either let you get within petting distance—just—or decided it wasn't worth the risk, and scampered away. Father laughed at this intense ambivalence. "Stella, you're too stupid to live, aren't you," he said in a teasing voice.

"Charles," Mom said.

"It's the best example of approach avoidance behavior I've ever seen," Father said. Intrigued by the challenge, he would sit on the floor, back against the couch and legs stretched ahead of him, and put Stella on his thighs. She would either endure his stroking until it ended, when she could jump away without impediment—or relax, and purr. She had a rasping loud purr, it reminded Alex of a chainsaw heard across the glacier. "Bug brain," Father would say to her. "Button head."

After a few weeks, as August turned to September and the leaves began to wither and fall, Stella started to lap sit voluntarily—but always in Mom's lap. "She likes the warmth," Mom said.

"It's cold on the floor," Father agreed, and played with the cat's scarred ears. "But why do you always sit on Helen's lap, huhn, Stell? I'm the one who started you on that." Eventually the cat would step onto his lap as well, and stretch out as if it was something she had always done. Father laughed at her.

Stella never rested on Alex's lap voluntarily, but would sometimes stay if he put her there and stroked her slowly for a long time. On the other hand she was just as likely to look back at him, go cross-eyed with horror and leap desperately away, leaving claw marks in his thighs. "She's so weird," he complained to Mom after one of these abrupt departures.

"It's true," Mom said with her low laugh. "But you have to remember that Stella was probably an abused kitty."

"How can you abuse a stray?"

"I'm sure there are ways. And maybe she was abused at home, and ran away."

"Who would do that?"

"Some people would."

Alex recalled the gangs on the glacier, and knew it was true. He tried to imagine what it would be like to be at their mercy, all the time. After that he thought he understood her permanent frown of deep concentration and distrust, as she sat staring at him. "It's just me, Stell-bells."

Thus when the cat followed him up onto the roof, and seemed to enjoy hanging out there with him, he was pleased. Their apartment was on the top floor, and they could take the pantry stairs and use the roof as a porch. It was a flat expanse of graveled tarpaper, a terrible imitation of the glacier's non-slip surface, but it was nice on dry days to go up there and look around, toss pebbles onto other roofs, see if the glacier was visible, and so on. Once Stella pounced at a piece of string trailing from his pants, and next time he brought up a length of Father's yarn. He was astonished and delighted when Stella responded by attacking the windblown yarn enthusiastically, biting it, clawing it, wrestling it from her back when Alex twirled it around her, and generally behaving in a very kittenish way. Perhaps she had never played as a kitten, Alex thought, so that it was all coming out now that she felt safe. But the play always ended abruptly; she would come to herself in mid-bite or bat, straighten up, and look around with a forbidding expression, as if to say *What is this yarn doing draped over me?*—then lick her fur and pretend the preceding minutes hadn't happened. It made Alex laugh.

Although the glacier had overrun many towns to the west and north, Watertown and Newton most recently, there was surprisingly little evidence of that in the moraines, or in the ice. It was almost all natural: rock and dirt and wood. Perhaps the wood had come from houses, perhaps some of the gravel had once been concrete, but you couldn't tell that now. Just dirt and rock and splinters, with an occasional chunk of plastic or metal thrown in. Apparently the over-run towns had been plowed under on the spot, or moved. Mostly it looked like the glacier had just left the White Mountains.

Father and Gary Jung had once talked about the latest plan from MIT. The enormous dam they were building downstream, between Allston and Cambridge, was to hold the glacier back. They were going to heat the concrete of the inner surface of the dam, and melt the ice as it advanced. It would become a kind of frozen reservoir. The meltwater would pour through a set of turbines before becoming the Charles, and the electricity generated by these turbines would help to heat the dam. Very neat.

The ice of the glacier, when you got right down to look at it, was clear for an inch or less, cracked and bubble-filled; then it turned a milky white. You could see the transition. Where the ice had been sheared vertically, however—on the side of a serac, or down in a crevasse—the clear part extended in many inches. You could see air bubbles deep inside, as if it were badly made glass. And this ice was distinctly blue. Alex didn't understand why there should be that difference, between the white ice lying flat and the blue ice cut vertically. But there it was.

Up in New Hampshire they had tried slowing the glacier—or at least stopping the abrupt "Alaskan slides"—by setting steel rods vertically in concrete, and laying the concrete in the glacier's path. Later they had hacked out one of these installations, and found the rods bent in perfect ninety degree angles, pressed into the scored concrete.

The ice would flow right over the dam.

* * *

One day Alex was walking by Father's study when Father called out. "Alexander! Take a look at this."

Alex entered the dark book-lined room. Its window overlooked the weed-filled space between buildings, and green light slanted onto Father's desk. "Here, stand beside me and look in my coffee cup. You can see the reflection of the Morgelis' window flowers on the coffee."

"Oh yeah! Neat."

"It gave me a shock! I looked down and there were these white and pink flowers in my cup, bobbing against a wall in a breeze, all of it tinted sepia as if it were an old-fashioned photo. It took me a while to see where it was coming from, what was being reflected." He laughed. "Through a looking glass."

Alex's father had light brown eyes, and fair wispy hair brushed back from a receding hairline. Mom called him handsome, and Alex agreed: tall, thin, graceful, delicate, distinguished. His father was a great man. Now he smiled in a way Alex didn't understand, looking into his coffee cup.

Mom had friends at the street market on Memorial Drive, and she had arranged work for Alex there. Three afternoons a week he walked over the Charles to the riverside street and helped the fishmongers gut fish, the vegetable sellers strip and clean the vegetables. He also helped set up stalls and take them down, and he swept and hosed the street afterwards. He was popular because of his energy and his willingness to get his hands wet in raw weather. The sleeves of his down jacket were permanently discolored from the frequent soakings—the dark blue almost a brown—a fact that distressed his mom. But he could handle the cold better than the adults; his hands would get a splotchy bluish white and he would put them to the red cheeks of the women and they would jump and say My *God*, Alex, how can you stand it?

This afternoon was blustery and dark but without rain, and it was enlivened by an attempted theft in the pasta stands, and by the appearance of a very mangy, very fast stray dog. This dog pounced on the pile of fishheads and entrails and disappeared with his mouth stuffed, trailing slick white-and-red guts. Everyone who saw it laughed. There weren't many stray dogs left these days, it was a pleasure to see one.

An hour past sunset he was done cleaning up and on his way home, hands in his pockets, stomach full, a five dollar bill clutched in one hand. He showed his pass to the National Guardsman and walked out onto Weeks Bridge. In the middle he stopped and leaned over the railing, into the wind. Below the water churned, milky with glacial silt. The sky still held a lot of light. Low curving bands of black cloud swept in from the northwest, like great ribs of slate. Above these bands the white sky was leached away by dusk. Raw wind whistled over his hood. Light water rushing below, dark clouds rushing above . . . he breathed the wind deep into him, felt himself expand until he filled everything he could see.

That night his parents' friends were gathering at their apartment for their bi-weekly party. Some of them would read stories and poems and essays and broadsides they had written, and then they would argue about them; and after that they would drink and eat whatever they had brought, and argue some more. Alex enjoyed it. But tonight when he got home Mom was rushing between computer and kitchen and muttering curses as she hit command keys or the hot water faucet, and the moment she saw him she said, "Oh Alex I'm glad you're here, could you please run down to the laundry and do just one load for me? The Talbots are staying over tonight and there aren't any clean sheets and I don't have anything to wear tomorrow either—thanks, you're a dear." And he was back out the door with a full laundry bag hung over his shoulder and the box of soap in the other hand, stomping grumpily past a little man in a black coat, reading a newspaper on the stoop of 19 Chester.

Down to Brighton, take a right, downstairs into the brightly lit basement laundromat. He threw laundry and soap and quarters into their places, turned the machine on and sat on top of it. Glumly he watched the other people in there, sitting on the washers and dryers. The vibrations put a lot of them to sleep. Others stared dully at the wall. Back in his apartment the guests would be arriving, taking off their overcoats, slapping arms over chests and talking as fast as they could. David and Sara and John from next door, Ira and Gary and

Ilene from across the street, the Talbots, Kathryn Grimm, and Michael Wu from Father's university, Ron from the hospital. They would settle down in the living room, on couches and chairs and floor, and talk and talk. Alex liked Kathryn especially, she could talk twice as fast as anyone else, and she called everyone darling and laughed and chattered so fast that everyone was caught up in the rhythm of it. Or David with his jokes, or Jay Talbot and his friendly questions. Or Gary Jung, the way he would sit in his corner like a bear, drinking beer and challenging everything that everyone read. "Why abstraction, why this distortion from the real? How does it help us, how does it speak to us? We should forget the abstract!" Father and Ira called him a vulgar Marxist, but he didn't mind. "You might as well be Plekhanov, Gary!" "Thank you very much!" he would say with a sharp grin, rubbing his unshaven jowls. And someone else would read. Mary Talbot once read a fairy tale about the Thing under the glacier; Alex had *loved* it. Once they even got Michael Wu to bring his violin along, and he hmm'd and hawed and pulled at the skin of his neck and refused and said he wasn't good enough, and then shaking like a leaf he played a melody that stilled them all. And Stella! She hated these parties, she spent them crouched deep in her refuge, ready for any kind of atrocity.

And here he was sitting on a washer in the laundromat.

When the laundry was dry he bundled it into the bag, then hurried around the corner and down Chester Street. Inside the glass door of Number 21 he glanced back out, and noticed that the man who had been reading the paper on the stoop next door was still sitting there. Odd. It was cold to be sitting outdoors.

Upstairs the readings had ended and the group was scattered through the apartment, most of them in the kitchen, as Mom had lit the stovetop burners and turned the gas up high. The blue flames roared airily under their chatter, making the kitchen bright and warm. "Wonderful the way white gas burns so clean." "And then they found the poor thing's head and intestines in the alley—it had been butchered right on the spot."

"Alex, you're back! Thanks for doing that. Here, get something to eat."

Everyone greeted him and went back to their conversations. "Gary you are so *conservative,*" Kathryn cried, hands held out over the stove. "It's not conservative at all," Gary replied. "It's a radical goal and I guess it's so radical that I have to keep reminding you it exists. Art should be used to *change* things."

"Isn't that a distortion from the real?"

Alex wandered down the narrow hall to his parents' room, which overlooked Chester Street. Father was there, saying to Ilene, "It's one of the only streets left with trees. It really seems residential, and here we are three blocks from Comm Ave. Hi, Alex."

"Hi, Alex. It's like a little bit of Brookline made it over to Allston."

"Exactly."

Alex stood in the bay window and looked down, licking the last of the carrot cake off his fingers. The man was still down there.

"Let's close off these rooms and save the heat. Alex, you coming?"

He sat on the floor in the living room. Father and Gary and David were starting a game of hearts, and they invited him to be the fourth. He nodded happily. Looking under the corner table he saw yellow eyes, blinking back at him; Stella, a frown of the deepest disapproval on her flat face. Alex laughed. "I knew you'd be there! It's okay, Stella. It's okay."

They left in a group, as usual, stamping their boots and diving deep into coats and scarves and gloves and exclaiming at the cold of the stairwell. Gary gave Mom a brief hug. "Only warm spot left in Boston," he said, and opened the glass door. The rest followed him out, and Alex joined them. The man in the black coat was just turning right onto Brighton Avenue, toward the university and downtown.

Sometimes clouds took on just the mottled gray of the glacier, low dark points stippling a lighter gray surface as cold showers draped down. At these times he felt he stood between two planes of some larger structure, two halves: icy tongue, icy roof of mouth. . . .

He stood under such a sky, throwing stones. His target was an erratic some forty yards away. He hit the boulder with most of his throws. A rock that big was an easy target. A bottle was better. He had brought one with him, and he set it up behind the erratic, on a waist-high rock. He walked back to a point where the bottle was hidden by the erratic. Using flat rocks he sent spinners out in a trajectory that brought them curving in from the side, so that it was possible to hit the concealed target. This was very important for the rock fights that he occasionally got involved in; usually he was outnumbered, and to hold his own he relied on his curves and his accuracy in general, and on a large number of ammunition caches hidden here and there. In one area crowded with boulders and crevasses he could sometimes create the impression of two throwers.

Absorbed in the exercise of bringing curves around the right side of the boulder—the hard side for him—he relaxed his vigilance, and when he heard a shout he jumped around to look. A rock whizzed by his left ear.

He dropped to the ice and crawled behind a boulder. Ambushed! He ran back into his knot of boulders and dashed a layer of snow away from one of his big caches, then with hands and pockets full looked carefully over a knobby chunk of cement, in the direction the stone had come from.

No movement. He recalled the stone whizzing by, the brief sight of it and the *zip* it made in passing. That had been close! If that had hit him! He shivered to think of it, it made his stomach shrink.

A bit of almost frozen rain pattered down. Not a shadow anywhere. On overcast days like this one it seemed things were lit from below, by the white bulk of the glacier. Like plastic over a weak neon light. Brittle huge blob of plastic, shifting and groaning and once in a while cracking like a gunshot, or grumbling like distant thunder. Alive. And Alex was its ally, its representative among men. He shifted from rock to rock, saw movement and froze. Two boys in green down jackets, laughing as they ran off the ice and over the lateral moraine, into what was left of Watertown. Just a potshot, then. Alex cursed them, relaxed.

He went back to throwing at the hidden bottle. Occasionally he recalled the stone flying by his head, and threw a little harder. Elegant curves of flight as the flat rocks bit the air and cut down and in. Finally one rock spun out into space and turned down sharply. Perfect slider. Its disappearance behind the erratic was followed by a tinkling crash. "Yeah!" Alex exclaimed, and ran to look. Icy glass on glassy ice.

Then, as he was leaving the glacier, boys jumped over the moraine shouting "Canadian!" and "There he is!" and "Get him!" This was more a chase than a serious ambush, but there were a lot of them and after emptying hands and pockets Alex was off running. He flew over the crunchy irregular surface, splashing meltwater, jumping narrow crevasses and surface rills. Then a wide crevasse blocked his way, and to start his jump he leaped onto a big flat rock; the rock gave under his foot and lurched down the ice into the crevasse.

Alex turned in and fell, bringing shoe-tips, knees, elbows and hands onto the rough surface. This arrested his fall, though it hurt. The crevasse was just under his feet. He scrambled up, ran panting along the crevasse until it narrowed, leaped over it. Then up the moraine and down into the narrow abandoned streets of west Allston.

Striding home, still breathing hard, he looked at his hands and saw that the last two fingernails on his right hand had been ripped away from the flesh; both were still there, but blood seeped from under them. He hissed and sucked on them, which hurt. The blood tasted like blood.

If he had fallen into the crevasse, following the loose rock down . . . if that stone had hit him in the face . . . he could feel his heart, thumping against his sternum. Alive.

Turning onto Chester Street he saw the man in the black coat, leaning against the florid maple across the street from their building. Watching them still! Though the man didn't appear to notice Alex, he did heft a bag and start walking in the other direction. Quickly Alex picked a rock out of the gutter and threw it at the man as hard as he could, spraying drops of blood onto the sidewalk. The rock flew over the man's head like a bullet, just missing him. The man ducked and scurried around the corner onto Comm Ave.

Father was upset about something. "They did the same thing to Gary and Michael and Kathryn, and their classes are even smaller than mine! I don't know what they're going to do. I don't know what *we're* going to do."

"We might be able to attract larger classes next semester," Mom said. She was upset too. Alex stood in the hall, slowly hanging up his jacket.

"But what about now? And what about later?" Father's voice was strained, almost cracking.

"We're making enough for now, that's the important thing. As for later—well, at least we know now rather than five years down the road."

Father was silent at the implications of this. "First Vancouver, then Toronto, now here—"

"Don't worry about all of it at once, Charles."

"How can I help it!" Father strode into his study and closed the door, not noticing Alex around the corner. Alex sucked his fingers. Stella poked her head cautiously out of his bedroom.

"Hi Stell-bell," he said quietly. From the living room came the plastic clatter of Mom's typing. He walked down the long hallway, past the silent study to the living room. She was hitting the keys hard, staring at the screen, mouth tight.

"What happened?" Alex said.

She looked up. "Hi, Alex. Well—your father got bad news from the university."

"Did he not get tenure again?"

"No, no, it's not a question of that."

"But now he doesn't even have the chance?"

She glanced at him sharply, then back at the screen, where her work was blinking. "I suppose that's right. The department has shifted all the new faculty over to extension, so they're hired by the semester, and paid by the class. It means you need a lot of students. . . ."

"Will we move again?"

"I don't know," she said curtly, exasperated with him for bringing it up. She punched the command key. "But we'll really have to save money, now. Everything you make at the market is important."

Alex nodded. He didn't mention the little man in the black coat, feeling obscurely afraid. Mentioning the man would somehow make him significant—Mom and Father would get angry, or frightened—something like that. By not telling them he could protect them from it, handle it on his own, so they could concentrate on other problems.

Besides, the two matters couldn't be connected, could they? Being watched; losing jobs. Perhaps they could. In which case there was nothing his parents could do about it anyway. Better to save them that anger, that fear.

He would make sure his throws hit the man next time.

Storms rolled in and the red and yellow leaves were ripped off the trees. Alex kicked through piles of them stacked on the sidewalks. He never saw the little man. He put up flyers for his father, who became even more distracted and remote. He brought home vegetables from work, tucked under his down jacket, and Mom cooked them without asking if he had bought them. She did the wash in the kitchen sink and dried it on lines in the back space between buildings, standing knee deep in leaves and weeds. Sometimes it took three days for clothes to dry back there; often they froze on the line.

While hanging clothes or taking them down she would let Stella join her. The cat regarded each shifting leaf with dire suspicion, then after a few exploratory leaps and bats would do battle with all of them, rolling about in a frenzy.

One time Mom was carrying a basket of dry laundry up the pantry stairs when a stray dog rounded the corner and made a dash for Stella, who was still outside. Mom ran back down shouting, and the dog fled; but Stella had disappeared. Mom called Alex down from his studies in a distraught voice, and they searched the back of the building and all the adjacent backyards for nearly an hour, but the cat was nowhere to be found. Mom was really upset. It was only after they had quit and returned upstairs that they heard her, miaowing far above them. She had climbed the big oak tree. "Oh *smart* Stella," Mom cried, a wild note in her voice. They called her name out the kitchen window, and the desperate miaows redoubled.

Up on the roof they could just see her, perched high in the almost bare branches of the big tree. "I'll get her," Alex said. "Cats can't climb down." He started climbing. It was difficult: the branches were close-knit, and they swayed in the wind. And as he got closer the cat climbed higher. "No, Stella, don't do that! Come here!" Stella stared at him, clamped to her branch of the moment, cross-eyed with fear.

Below them Mom said over and over, "Stella, it's okay—it's okay, Stella." Stella didn't believe her.

Finally Alex reached her, near the tree's top. Now here was a problem: he needed his hands to climb down, but it seemed likely he would also need them to hold the terrified cat. "Come here, Stella." He put a hand on her flank; she flinched. Her side pulsed with her rapid breathing. She hissed faintly. He had to maneuver up a step, onto a very questionable branch; his face was inches from her. She stared at him without a trace of recognition. He pried her off her branch, lifted her. If she cared to claw him now she could really tear him up. Instead she clung to his shoulder and chest, all her claws dug through his clothes, quivering under his left arm and hand.

Laboriously he descended, using only the one hand. Stella began miaowing fiercely, and struggling a bit. Finally he met Mom, who had climbed the tree quite a ways. Stella was getting more upset. "Hand her to me." Alex detached her from his chest paw by paw, balanced, held the cat down with both hands. Again it was a tricky moment; if Stella went berserk they would all be in trouble. But she fell onto Mom's chest and collapsed, a catatonic ball of fur.

Back in the apartment she dashed for her blanket under the table. Mom enticed her out with food, but she was very jumpy and she wouldn't allow Alex anywhere near her; she ran away if he even entered the room. "Back to square one, I see," Mom commented.

"It's not fair! I'm the one that saved her!"

"She'll get over it." Mom laughed, clearly relieved. "Maybe it'll take some time, but she will. Ha! This is clear proof that cats are smart enough to be crazy. Irrational, neurotic—just like a person." They laughed, and Stella glared at them balefully. "Yes you are, aren't you! You'll come around again."

Often when Alex got home in the early evenings his father was striding back and forth in the kitchen talking loudly, angrily, fearfully, while Mom tried to reassure him. "They're doing the same thing to us they did to Rick Stone! But why!" When Alex closed the front door the conversation would stop. Once when he walked tentatively down the quiet hallway to the kitchen he found them standing there, arms around each other, Father's head in Mom's short hair.

Father raised his head, disengaged, went to his study. On his way he said, "Alex, I need your help."

"Sure."

Alex stood in the study and watched without understanding as his father took books from his shelves and put them in the big laundry bag. He threw the first few in like dirty clothes, then sighed and thumped in the rest in a businesslike fashion, not looking at them.

"There's a used book store in Cambridge, on Mass Ave. Antonio's."

"Sure, I know the one." They had been there together a few times.

"I want you to take these over there and sell them to Tony for me," Father said, looking at the empty shelves. "Will you do that for me?"

"Sure." Alex picked up the bag, shocked that it had come to this. Father's books! He couldn't meet his father's eye. "I'll do that right now," he said uncertainly, and hefted the bag over one shoulder. In the hallway Mom approached and put a hand on his shoulder—her silent thanks—then went into the study.

Alex hiked east toward the university, crossed the Charles River on the great iron bridge. The wind howled in the superstructure. On the Cambridge side, after showing his pass, he put the heavy bag on the ground and inspected its contents. Ever since the infamous incident of the spilled hot chocolate, Father's books had been off-limits to him; now a good twenty of them were there in the bag to be touched, opened, riffled through. Many in this bunch were in foreign languages, especially Greek and Russian, with their alien alphabets. Could people really read such marks? Well, Father did. It must be possible.

When he had inspected all the books he chose two in English— *The Odyssey* and *The Colossus of Maroussi*—and put those in his down jacket pockets. He could take them to the glacier and read them, then sell them later to Antonio's—perhaps in the next bag of books. There were many more bagfuls in Father's study.

A little snow stuck to the glacier now, filling the pocks and making bright patches on the north side of every boulder, every serac. Some of the narrower crevasses were filled with it—bright white lines on the jumbled gray. When the whole surface was white the crevasses would be invisible, and the glacier too dangerous to walk on. Now the only danger was leaving obvious footprints for trackers. Walking up the rubble lines would solve that. These lines of rubble fascinated Alex. It looked just as if bulldozers had clanked up here and shoved the majority of the stones and junk into straight lines down the big central tongue of the glacier. But in fact they were natural features. Father had attempted to explain on one of the walks they had taken up here. "The ice is moving, and it moves faster in the middle than on the outer edges, just like a stream. So rocks on the surface tend to slide over time, down into lines in the middle."

"Why are there two lines, then?"

Father shrugged, looking into the blue-green depths of a crevasse. "We really shouldn't be up here, you know that?"

Now Alex stopped to inspect a tire caught in the rubble line. Truck tire, tread worn right to the steel belting. It would burn, but with too much smoke. There were several interesting objects in this neat row of rock and sand: plastic jugs, a doll, a lampbase, a telephone.

His shelter was undisturbed. He pulled the two books from his pockets and set them on the bench, propping them with rock bookends.

He circled the boulder, had a look around. The sky today was a low smooth pearl gray sheet, ruffled by a set of delicate waves pasted to it. The indirect light brought out all the colors: the pink of the remarkable snow algae, the blue of the seracs, the various shades of rock, the occasional bright spot of junk, the many white patches of snow. A million dots of color under the pewter sheet of cloud.

Three creaks, a crack, a long shuddering rumble. Sleepy, muscular, the great beast had moved. Alex walked across its back to his bench, sat. On the far lateral moraine some gravel slid down. Puffs of brown dust in the air.

He read his books. *The Odyssey* was strange but interesting. Father had told him some of the story before. *The Colossus of Maroussi* was long-winded but funny—it reminded Alex of his uncle, who could turn the smallest incident into an hour's comic monologue. What he could have made of Stella's flight up the tree! Alex laughed to think of it. But his uncle was in jail.

He sat on his bench and read, stopped occasionally to look around.

When the hand holding the book got cold, he changed hands and put the cold one in a pocket of his down jacket. When both hands were blue he hid the books in rocks under his bench and went home.

There were more bags of books to be sold at Antonio's and other shops in Cambridge. Each time Alex rotated out a few that looked interesting, and replaced them with the ones on the glacier. He daydreamed of saving all the books and earning the money some other way—then presenting his father with the lost library, at some future undefined but appropriate moment.

Eventually Stella forgave him for rescuing her. She came to enjoy chasing a piece of yarn up and down their long narrow hallway, skidding around the corner by the study. It reminded them of a game they had played with Pongo, who would chase anything, and they laughed at her, especially when she jerked to a halt and licked her fur fastidiously, as if she had never been carousing. "You can't fool us, Stell! We *remember!*"

Mom sold most of her music collection, except for her favorites. Once Alex went out to the glacier with the *Concerto de Aranjuez* coursing through him—Mom had had it on in the apartment while she worked. He hummed the big theme of the second movement as he crunched over the ice: clearly it was the theme of the glacier, the glacier's song. How had a blind composer managed to capture the windy sweep of it, the spaciousness? Perhaps such things could be heard as well as seen. The wind said it, whistling over the ice. It was a terrifically dark day, windy, snowing in gusts. He could walk right up the middle of the great tongue, between the rubble lines; no one else would be up there today. Da-da-da . . . da da da da da da, da-da-da. . . . Hands in pockets, chin on chest, he trudged into the wind humming, feeling like the whole world was right there around him. It was too cold to stay in his shelter for more than a minute.

Father went off on trips, exploring possibilities. One morning Alex woke to the sound of *The Pirates of Penzance*. This was one of their favorites, Mom played it all the time while working and on Saturday mornings, so that they knew all the lyrics by heart and often sang along. Alex especially loved the Pirate King, and could mimic all his intonations.

He dressed and walked down to the kitchen. Mom stood by the stove with her back to him, singing along. It was a sunny morning and their big kitchen windows faced east; the light poured in on the sink and the dishes and the white stove and the linoleum and the plants in the window and Stella, sitting contentedly on the window sill listening.

His mom was tall and broad-shouldered. Every year she cut her hair shorter; now it was just a cap of tight brown curls, with a somewhat longer patch down the nape of her neck. That would go soon, Alex thought, and then her hair would be as short as it could be. She was lost in the song, one slim hand on the white stove top, looking out the window. She had a low, rich, thrilling voice, like a real singer's only prettier. She was singing along with the song that Mabel sings after she finds out that Frederick won't be able to leave the pirates until 1940.

When it was over Alex entered the kitchen, went to the pantry. "That's a short one," he said.

"Yes, they had to make it short," Mom said. "There's nothing funny about that one."

One night while Father was gone on one of his trips, Mom had to go over to Ilene and Ira and Gary's apartment: Gary had been arrested, and Ilene and Ira needed help. Alex and Stella were left alone.

Stella wandered the silent apartment miaowing. "I *know*, Stella," Alex said in exasperation. "They're *gone*. They'll be back tomorrow." The cat paid no attention to him.

He went into Father's study. Tonight he'd be able to read something in relative warmth. It would only be necessary to be *very careful*.

The bookshelves were empty. Alex stood before them, mouth open. He had no idea they had sold that many of them. There were a couple left on Father's desk, but he didn't want to move them. They appeared to be dictionaries anyway. "It's all Greek to me."

He went back to the living room and got out the yarn bag, tried to interest Stella in a game. She wouldn't play. She wouldn't sit on his lap. She wouldn't stop miaowing. "Stella, shut up!" She scampered away and kept crying. Vexed, he got out the jar of catnip and spread some on the linoleum in the kitchen. Stella came running to sniff at it, then roll in it. Afterwards she played with the yarn wildly, until it caught around her tail and she froze, staring at him in a drugged paranoia. Then she dashed to her refuge and refused to come out. Finally Alex put on *The Pirates of Penzance* and listened to it for a while. After that he was sleepy.

They got a good lawyer for Gary, Mom said. Everyone was hopeful. Then a couple of weeks later Father got a new job; he called them from work to tell them about it.

"Where is it?" Alex asked Mom when she was off the phone.

"In Kansas."

"So we will be moving."

"Yes," Mom said. "Another move."

"Will there be glaciers there too?"

"I think so. In the hills. Not as big as ours here, maybe. But there are glaciers everywhere."

He walked onto the ice one last time. There was a thin crust of snow on the tops of everything. A fantastically jumbled field of snow. It was a clear day, the sky a very pale blue, the white expanse of the glacier painfully bright. A few cirrus clouds made sickles high in the west. The snow was melting a bit and there were water droplets all over, with little sparks of colored light in each drip. The sounds of water melting were everywhere, drips, gurgles, splashes. The intensity of light was stunning, like a blow to the brain, right through the eyes. It pulsed.

The crevasse in front of his shelter had widened, and the boards of his bench had fallen. The wall of ice turning around the boulder was splintered, and shards of bright ice lay over the planks.

The glacier was moving. The glacier was alive. No heated dam would stop it. He felt its presence, huge and supple under him, seeping into him like the cold through his wet shoes, filling him up. He blinked, nearly blinded by the light breaking everywhere on it, a surgical glare that made every snow-capped rock stand out like the color red on a slide transparency. The white light. In the distance the ice cracked hollowly, moving somewhere. Everything moved: the ice, the wind, the clouds, the sun, the planet. All of it rolling around.

As they packed up their possessions Alex could hear them in the next room. "We can't," Father said. "You know we can't. They won't let us."

When they were done the apartment looked odd. Bare walls, bare wood floors. It looked smaller. Alex walked the length of it: his parents' room overlooking Chester Street; his room; his father's study; the living room; the kitchen with its fine morning light. The pantry. Stella wandered the place miaowing. Her blanket was still in its corner, but without the table it looked moth-eaten, fur-coated, ineffectual. Alex picked her up and went through the pantry, up the back stairs to the roof.

Snow had drifted into the corners. Alex walked in circles, looking at the city. Stella sat on her paws by the stairwell shed, watching him, her fur ruffled by the wind.

Around the shed snow had melted, then froze again. Little puddles of ice ran in flat curves across the the pebbled tar paper. Alex crouched to inspect them, tapping one speculatively with a fingernail. He stood up and looked west, but buildings and bare treetops obscured the view.

Stella fought to stay out of the box, and once in it she cried miserably.

Father was already in Kansas, starting the new job. Alex and Mom and Stella had been staying in the living room of Michael Wu's place while Mom finished her work; now she was done, it was moving day, they were off to the train. But first they had to take Stella to the Talbots'.

Alex carried the box and followed Mom as they walked across the Commons and down Comm Ave. He could feel the cat shifting over her blanket, scrabbling at the cardboard against his chest. Mom walked fast, a bit ahead of him. At Kenmore they turned south.

When they got to the Talbots', Mom took the box. She looked at him. "Why don't you stay down here," she said.

"Okay."

She rang the bell and went in with the buzzer, holding the box under one arm.

Alex sat on the steps of the walk-up. There were little ones in the corner: flat fingers of ice, spilling away from the cracks.

Mom came out the door. Her face was pale, she was biting her lip. They took off walking at a fast pace. Suddenly Mom said, "Oh, Alex, she was *so scared,*" and sat down on another stoop and put her head on her knees.

Alex sat beside her, his shoulder touching hers. Don't say anything, don't put arm around shoulders or anything. He had learned this from Father. Just sit there, be there. Alex sat there like the glacier, shifting a little. Alive. The white light.

After a while she stood. "Let's go," she said.

They walked up Comm Ave. toward the train station. "She'll be all right with the Talbots," Alex said. "She already likes Jay."

"I know." Mom sniffed, tossed her head in the wind. "She's getting to be a pretty adaptable cat." They walked on in silence. She put an arm over his shoulders. "I wonder how Pongo is doing." She took a deep breath. Overhead clouds tumbled like chunks of broken ice.

A Sensitive Dependence on Initial Conditions

The covering law model of historical explanation states that an event is explained if it can be logically deduced from a set of initial conditions, and a set of general historical laws. These sets are the *explanans,* and the event is the *explanandum.* The general laws are applied to the initial conditions, and the explanandum is shown to be the inevitable result. An explanation, in this model, has the same structure as a prediction.

On the morning of August 6th, 1945, Colonel Paul Tibbetts and his crew flew the *Enola Gay* from Tinian Island to Hiroshima, and dropped an atomic bomb on the city. Approximately a hundred thousand people died. Three days later, another crew dropped a bomb on the outskirts of Nagasaki. Approximately seventy thousand people died. The Japanese surrendered.

President Harry Truman, in consultation with his advisors, decided to drop the bombs. Why did he make these decisions? Because the Japanese had fiercely defended many islands in the South Pacific, and the cost of conquering them had been high. Kamikaze attacks had sunk many American ships, and it was said that the Japanese would stage a gigantic kamikaze defense of the home islands. Estimated American casualties resulting from an invasion of the home islands ranged as high as a million men.

These were the conditions. General laws? Leaders want to end wars as quickly as possible, with a minimum of bloodshed. They also like to frighten potential postwar enemies. With the war in Europe ended, the Soviet Army stood ready to go wherever Stalin ordered it. No one could be sure where Stalin might want to go. An end to the Japanese war that frightened him would not be a bad thing.

But there were more conditions. The Japanese were defenseless in the air and at sea. American planes could bomb the home islands at will, and a total naval blockade of Japan was entirely possible. The Japanese civilian population was already starving; a blockade, combined with bombing of military sites, could very well have forced the Japanese leaders to surrender without an invasion.

But Truman and his advisors decided to drop the bombs. A complete explanation of the decision, omitted here due to considerations of length, would have to include an examination of the biographies of Truman, his advisors, the builders of the bomb, and the leaders of Japan and the Soviet Union; as well as a detailed analysis of the situation in Japan in 1945, and of American intelligence concerning that situation.

President Truman was re-elected in 1948, in an upset victory over Thomas Dewey. Two years later the United States went to war in Korea, to keep that country from being overrun by Communists supported by the Soviet Union and China. It was only one of many major wars in the second half of the twentieth century; there were over sixty, and although none of them were nuclear, approximately fifty million people were killed.

Heisenberg's uncertainty principle says that we cannot simultaneously determine both the velocity and the position of a particle. This not a function of human perception, but a basic property of the universe. Thus it will never be possible to achieve a deterministic prediction of the movement of all particles throughout spacetime. Quantum mechanics, which replaced classical mechanics as the best description of these events, can only predict the probabilities among a number of possible outcomes.

The covering law model of historical explanation asserts that there is no logical difference between historical explanation and scientific explanation. But the model's understanding of scientific explanation is based on classical mechanics. In quantum reality, the covering law model breaks down.

The sufficient conditions model of historical explanation is a modification of the covering law model; it states that if one can describe a set of initial conditions that are sufficient (but not necessary) for the the event to occur, then the event can be said to be explained. Deduction from general law is not part of this model, which is descriptive rather than prescriptive, and "seeks only to achieve an acceptable degree of coherent narrative."

In July of 1945, Colonel Tibbetts was ordered to demonstrate his crew's ability to deliver an atomic weapon, by flying a test mission in the western Pacific. During the takeoff Tibbetts shut down both propellors on the right wing, to show that if this occurred during an armed takeoff, he would still be able to control the plane. The strain of this maneuver, however, caused the inboard left engine to fail, and in the emergency return to Tinian the *Enola Gay* crashed, killing everyone aboard.

A replacement crew was chosen from Tibbetts' squadron, and was sent to bomb Hiroshima on August 9th, 1945. During the run over Hiroshima the bombardier, Captain Frank January, deliberately delayed the release of the bomb, so that it missed Hiroshima by some ten miles. Another mission later that week encountered cloud cover, and missed Kokura by accident. January was court-martialed and executed for disobeying orders in battle. The Japanese, having seen the explosions and evaluated the explosion sites, surrendered.

January decided to miss the target because: he had a visionary dream in which he saw the results of the bombing; he had not been in combat for over a year; he was convinced the war was over; he had been in London during the Blitz; he disliked his plane's pilot; he hated Paul Tibbetts; he was a loner, older than his fellow squadron members; he had read the Hornblower stories in the *Saturday Evening Post;* he once saw a truck crash into a car, and watched the truck driver in the aftermath; he was burned on the arm by stove oil when a child; he had an imagination.

The inboard left engine on the *Enola Gay* failed because a worker at the Wright manufacturing plant had failed to keep his welding torch flame on a weld for the required twenty seconds. He stopped three seconds too soon. He stopped three seconds too soon because he was tired. He was tired because the previous night he had stayed up late, drinking with friends.

In 1948, President Truman lost to Thomas Dewey in a close election that was slightly influenced by a political group called the January Society. The Korean conflict was settled by negotiation, and in February of 1956 a treaty was signed in Geneva, banning the use and manufacture of nuclear weapons.

Light behaves like either wave or particle, depending on how it is observed. The famous two-slit experiment, in which interference in wave patterns causes light shining through two slits in a partition to hit a screen in a pattern of light and dark bars, is a good example of this. Even when photons are sent at the slits one at a time, the pattern of light and dark bars still appears, implying that the single quantum of light is passing through both slits at the same time, creating an interference pattern with itself.

History is an interference pattern, says the covering law model. The conditions are particles; the laws are waves.

The necessary conditions model states that historical explanation requires merely identifying the kind of historical event being explained, and then locating among its initial conditions some that seem necessary for the event to take place. No general laws of history can help; one can only locate more necessary conditions. As William Dray writes in *Laws and Explanation in History,* an explanandum is explained when we "can trace the course of events by which it came about."

Tibbets and his crew died in a training flight crash, and the *Lucky Strike* was sent in The *Enola Gay*'s its place. The bombardier, Captain Frank January, after much frantic thought on the flight there, performed just as Tibbets' bombardier would have, and dropped the bomb over the T-shaped Aioi Bridge in Hiroshima. Approximately a hundred thousand people died. Three days later Nagasaki was bombed. The Japanese surrendered. Truman was re-elected. The Korean War led to the Cold War, the assassination of Kennedy on November 22nd, 1963, the Vietnam War, the collapse of the Soviet bloc in the fall of 1989. Replacing one crew with another made no larger difference.

Richard Feynman's notion of a "sum over histories" proposes that a particle does not move from point A to point B by a single path, as in classical mechanics, but rather by every possible path within the wave. Two numbers describe these possible paths, one describing the size of the wave, the other the path's position in the crest-to-trough cycle. When Pauli's exclusion principle, which states that two particles cannot occupy the same position at the same velocity within the mathematical limits of the uncertainty principle, is applied to the sum over histories, it indicates that some possible paths cause interference patterns, and cancel each other out; other paths are phased in a reinforcing way, which makes their occurrence more probable.

Perhaps history has its own sum over histories, so that all possible histories resemble ours. Perhaps every possible bombardier chooses Hiroshima.

The weak covering law model attempts to rescue the notion of general historical laws by relaxing their rigor, to the point where one can no longer deduce the explanandum from the explanans alone; the laws become not laws but tendencies, which help historians by providing "guiding threads" between events and their initial conditions. Thus the uncertainty principle is acknowledged, and the covering law model brought into the twentieth century.

But can any historical model explain the twentieth century? Tibbetts crashed, the *Lucky Strike* flew to Hiroshima, and Captain January chose to spare the city. He was executed, the war ended, Dewey won the 1948 election; the Korean conflict was resolved by negotiation; and nuclear weapons were banned by treaty in February of 1956.

But go on. In November of 1956, conflict broke out in the Middle East between Egypt and Israel, and Britain and France quickly entered the conflict to protect their interests in the Suez Canal. President Dewey, soon to be replaced by President-elect Dwight Eisenhower, asked Britain and France to quit the conflict; his request was ignored. The war spread through the Middle East. In December the Soviet Army invaded West Germany. The United States declared war on the Soviet Union. China launched assaults in Indochina, and the Third World War was under way. Both the United States and the Soviet Union quickly assembled a number of atomic bombs, and in the first week of 1957, Jerusalem, Berlin, Bonn, Paris, London, Warsaw, Leningrad, Prague, Budapest, Beirut, Amman, Cairo, Moscow, Vladivostok, Tokyo, Peking, Los Angeles, Washington, D.C., and Princeton, New Jersey (hit by a bomb targeted for New York) were destroyed. Loss of life in that week and the year following was estimated at a hundred million people.

At normal energies, the strong nuclear force has a property called confinement, which binds quarks tightly together. At the high energies achieved in particle accelerators, however, the strong nuclear force becomes much weaker, allowing quarks and gluons to jet away almost like free particles. This property of dispersion at high energies is called "asymptotic freedom."

History is a particle accelerator. Energies are not always normal. We live in a condition of asymptotic freedom, and every history is possible. Each bombardier has to choose.

In *The Open Society and Its Enemies* Karl Popper writes: "If two armies are equally well-led and well-armed, and one has an enormous numerical superiority, the other will never win." Popper made this proposition to demonstrate that any historical law with broad explanatory power would become so general as to be trivial. For the school of thought that agrees with him, there can be no covering laws.

In June of 1945, seven of the scientists who had worked on the Manhattan Project submitted a document called the Franck Report to the Scientific Panel of the Interim Committee, which was overseeing the progress of the bomb. The Franck Report called for a demonstration of the bomb before observers from many countries, including Japan. The Scientific Panel decided this was a possible option and passed the Report on to the Committee, which passed it on to the White House. "The Buck Stops Here." Truman read the Report and decided to invite James Franck, Leo Szilard, Niels Bohr, and Albert Einstein to the White House to discuss the issue. Final consultations included Oppenheimer, Secretary of War Stimson, and the military head of the Manhattan Project, General Leslie Groves. After a week's intense debate Truman instructed Stimson to contact the Japanese leadership and arrange a demonstration drop, to be made on one of the uninhabited islands in the Izu Shichito archipelago, south of Tokyo Bay. An atomic bomb was exploded on Udone Shima on August 24th, 1945; the mushroom cloud was visible from Tokyo. Films of the explosion were shown to Emperor Hirohito. The Emperor instructed his government to surrender, which it did on August 31st, one day before Truman had declared he was going to begin bombing Japanese cities.

Truman won the election of 1948. In 1950 north Korean troops invaded the south, until a series of six so-called Shima blasts, each closer to the north's advance forces, stopped them at the 38th parallel. In 1952 Adlai Stevenson became president, and appointed Leo Szilard the first presidential science advisor. In 1953 Stalin died, and in 1956 Szilard was sent to Moscow for a consulation with Khrushchev. This meeting led to the founding of the International Peace Brigade, which sent internationally integrated teams of young people to work in underdeveloped countries and in countries still recovering from World War Two. In 1960 John Kennedy was elected president, and he was succeeded in 1968 by his brother Robert. In 1976, in the wake of scandals in the administration, Richard Nixon was elected. At this point in time the postwar period is usually considered to have ended. The century itself came to a close without any further large wars. Though there had been a number of local conflicts, the existence of nuclear weapons had ended war as practiced in the first half of the century. In the second half, only about five million people died in war.

The great man theory considers particles; historical materialism considers waves. The wave/particle duality, confirmed many times by experiment, assures us that neither theory can be the complete truth. Neither theory will serve as the covering law.

The defenders of the covering law model reply to its various critiques by stating that it is irrelevant whether historians actually use the model or not; the fact remains that they *should*. If they do not, then an event like "the bottle fell off the table" could be explained by either "the cat's tail brushed it," or "the cat looked at it cross-eyed," and there would be no basis for choosing between the two explanations. Historical explanation is not just a matter of the practice of historians, but of the nature of reality. And in reality, physical events are constrained by general laws—or if they are not laws, they are at least extraordinarily detailed descriptions of the links between an event and those that follow it, allowing predictions that, if not deterministically exact, are still accurate enough to give us enormous power over physical reality. That, for anyone but followers of David Hume, serves as law enough. And humans, as part of the stuff of the universe, are subject to the same physical laws that control all the rest of it. So it makes sense to seek a science of history, and to try to formulate some general historical laws.

What would these general laws look like? Some examples:

• If two armies are equally well-led and well-armed, and one has an enormous numerical superiority, the other will never win.

• A privileged group will never relinquish privilege voluntarily.

• Empires rise, flourish, fall and are replaced, in a cyclical pattern.

• A nation's fortunes depend on its success in war.

• A society's culture is determined by its economic system.

• Belief systems exist to disguise inequality.

• Lastly, unparalleled in both elegance and power, subsuming many of the examples listed above: power corrupts.

So there do seem to be some quite powerful laws of historical explanation. But consider another:

• For want of a nail, the battle was lost.

For instance: on July 29th, 1945, a nomad in Kirgiz walked out of his yurt and stepped on a butterfly. For lack of the butterfly flapping its wings, the wind in the area blew slightly less. A low pressure front therefore moved over east China more slowly than it would have. And so on August 6th, when the *Enola Gay* flew over Hiroshima, it was covered by ninety percent cloud cover, instead of fifty percent. Colonel Tibbetts flew to the secondary target, Nagasaki; it was also covered. The *Enola Gay* had little fuel left, but its crew was able to fly over Kokura on the way back to Tinian, and taking advantage of a break in the clouds, they dropped the bomb there. Ninety thousand people died in Kokura. The *Enola Gay* landed at Tinian with so little fuel left in its tanks that what remained "wouldn't have filled a cigarette lighter." On August 9th a second mission tried Hiroshima again, but the clouds were still there, and the mission eventually dropped the bomb on the less heavily clouded secondary target, Nagasaki, missing the city center and killing only twenty thousand people. The Japanese surrendered a week later.

On August 11th, 1945, a child named Ai Matsui was born in Hiroshima. In 1960 she began to speak in local meetings on many topics, including Hiroshima's special position in the world. Its citizens had escaped annihilation, she said, as if protected by some covering angel (or law); they had a responsibility to the dead of Kokura and Nagasaki, to represent them in the world of the living, to change the world for the good. The Hiroshima Peace Party quickly grew to become the dominant political movement in Hiroshima, and then, in revulsion at the violence of the 1960s in Vietnam and elsewhere, all over Japan. In the 1970s the party became a worldwide movement, gaining the enthusiastic support of ex-President Kennedy, and President Babbitt. Young people from every country joined it as if experiencing a religious conversion. In 1983 Japan began its Asian Assistance League. One of its health care programs saved the life of a young woman in India, sick with malaria. The next year she had a child, a woman destined to become India's greatest leader. In 1987, the nation of Palestine raised its flag over the West Bank and parts of Jordan and Lebanon; a generation of camp children moved into homes. A child was born in Galilee. In 1990 Japan started its African Assistance League. The Hiroshima Peace Party had a billion members.

And so on; so that by July 29th, 2045, no human on Earth was the same as those who would have lived if the nomad in Kirgiz had not stepped on the butterfly a century before.

This phenomenon is known as the butterfly effect, and it is a serious problem for all other models of historical explanation; meaning trouble for you and for me. The scientific term for it is "sensitive dependence on initial conditions." It is an aspect of chaos theory first studied by the meteorologist Edward Lorenz, who, while running computer simulations of weather patterns, discovered that the slightest change in the initial conditions of the simulation would quickly lead to completely different weather.

*　*　*

So the strong covering law model said that historical explanation should equal the rigor of scientific explanation. Then its defenders, bringing the model into the quantum world, conceded that predictions can never be anything but probabilistic at best. The explanandum was no longer deducible from the explanans; one could only suggest probabilities.

Now chaos theory has added new problems. And yet consider: Captain Frank January chose to miss Hiroshima. Ten years later, nuclear weapons were universally banned. Eleven years later, local conflicts in the Middle East erupted into general war, and nuclear weapons were quickly reassembled and used. For it is not easy to forget knowledge, once it is learned; symmetry T, which says that physical laws are the same no matter which way the time arrow is pointed, does not actually exist in nature. There is no going back.

And so by 1990, in this particular world, the bombed cities were rebuilt. The Western industrial nations were rich, the southern developing nations were poor. Multinational corporations ruled the world's economy. The Soviet bloc was falling apart. Gigantic sums of money were spent on armaments. By the year 2056, there was very little to distinguish this world from the one in which January had dropped the bomb, in which Tibbetts had bombed Hiroshima, in which Tibbetts had made a demonstration, in which Tibbetts bombed Kokura.

Perhaps a sum over histories had bunched the probabilities. Is this likely? We don't know. We are particles, moving in a wave. The wave breaks. No math can predict which bubbles will appear where. But there is a sum over histories. Chaotic systems fall into patterns, following the pull of strange attractors. Linear chaotic figures look completely non-repetitive, but slice them into Poincaré sections and they reveal the simplest kinds of patterns. There is a tide, and we float in it; perhaps it is the flux of the cosmos itself; swim this way or that, the tide still carries us to the same destination. Perhaps.

So the covering law model is amended yet again. Explanations still require laws, but there are not laws for every event. The task of historical explanation becomes the act of making distinctions, between those parts of an event that can be explained by laws, and those that cannot. The component events that combine to create an explanandum are analyzed each in turn, and the historian then concentrates on the explicable components.

Paul Tibbetts flies toward Hiroshima. The nomad steps out of his yurt.

Lyapunov exponents are numbers that measure the conflicting effects of stretching, contracting, and folding in the phase space of an attractor. They set the topological parameters of unpredictability. An exponent greater than zero means stretching, so that each alternative history moves farther and farther apart as time passes. An exponent smaller than zero means contraction, so that alternatives tend to come back together. When the exponent equals zero, a periodic orbit results.

What is history's Lyapunov exponent? This is the law that no one can know.

Frank January flies toward Hiroshima. The nomad stops in his yurt.

It is said that the historian's task requires an imaginative reconstruction of the thinking of people who acted in the past, and of the circumstances in which they acted. "An explanation is said to be successful when the historian gets the sense of reliving the past which he is trying to explain."

You are flying toward Hiroshima. You are the bombardier. You have been given the assignment two days before. You know what the bomb will do. You do not know what you will do. You have to decide.

There are a hundred billion neurons in the brain. Some of the neurons have as many as eighty thousand synaptic endings. During thought, neurotransmitter chemicals flow across the synaptic clefts between one neuron's synaptic knobs and another's dendritic spines, reversing a slight electric charge, which passes on a signal. The passage of a signal often leaves changes in the synapses and dendrites along the way, forever altering the structure of the brain. This plasticity makes memory and learning possible. Brains are always growing; intensely in the first five years, then steadily thereafter.

At the moment of choice, then, signals fly through a neural network that has been shaped over a lifetime into a particular and unique structure. Some signals are conscious, other are not. According to Roger Penrose, during the process of decision quantum effects in the brain take over, allowing a great number of parallel and simultaneous computations to take place; the number could be extraordinarily large, 10^{21} or more. Only at the intrusion of the "observation," that is to say a decision, do the parallel computations resolve back into a single conscious thought.

And in the act of deciding, the mind attempts the work of the historian: breaking the potential events down into their component parts, enumerating conditions, seeking covering laws that will allow a prediction of what will follow from the variety of possible choices. Alternative futures branch like dendrites away from the present moment, shifting chaotically, pulled this way and that by attractors dimly perceived. Probable outcomes emerge from those less likely.

And then, in the myriad clefts of the quantum mind, a mystery: the choice is made. We have to choose, that is life in time. Some powerful selection process, perhaps aesthetic, perhaps moral, perhaps practical (survival of the thinker), shoves to consciousness those plans that seem safest, or most right, or most beautiful, we do not know; and the choice is made. And at the moment of this observation the great majority of alternatives disappear without trace, leaving us in our asymptotic freedom to act, uncertainly, in time's assymetrical flow.

There are few covering laws. Initial conditions are never fully known. The butterfly may be on the wing, it may be crushed underfoot. You are flying toward Hiroshima.

Down and Out in the Year 2000

It was going to be hot again. Summer in Washington, D.C.—Lee Robinson woke and rolled on his mattress, broke into a sweat. That kind of a day. He got up and kneeled over the other mattress in the small room. Debra shifted as he shaded her from the sun angling in the open window. The corners of her mouth were caked white and her forehead was still hot and dry, but her breathing was regular and she appeared to be sleeping well. Quietly Lee slipped on his jeans and walked down the hall to the bathroom. Locked. He waited; Ramon came out wet and groggy. "Morning, Robbie." Into the bathroom, where he hung his pants on the hook and did his morning ritual. One bloodshot eye, staring back at him from the splinter of mirror still in the frame. The dirt around the toilet base. The shower curtain blotched with black fungus, as if it had a fatal disease. That kind of morning.

Out of the shower he dried off with his jeans and started to sweat again. Back in his room Debra was still sleeping. Worried, he watched her for a while, then filled his pockets and went into the hall to put on sneakers and tank top. Debra slept light these days, and the strangest things would rouse her. He jogged down the four flights of stairs to the street, and sweating freely stepped out into the steamy air.

* * *

He walked down 16th Street, with its curious alternation of condo fortresses and abandoned buildings, to the Mall. There, big khaki tanks dominated the broad field of dirt and trash and tents and the odd patch of grass. Most of the protesters were still asleep in their scattered tent villages, but there was an active crowd around the Washington Monument, and Lee walked on over, ignoring the soldiers by the tanks.

The crowd surrounded a slingshot as tall as a man, made of a forked tree branch. Inner tubes formed the sling, and the base was buried in the ground. Excited protesters placed balloons filled with red paint into the sling, and fired them up at the monument. If a balloon hit above the red that already covered the tower, splashing clean white—a rare event, as the monument was pure red up a good third of it—the protesters cheered crazily. Lee watched them as they danced around the sling after a successful shot. He approached some of the calmer seated spectators.

"Want to buy a joint?"

"How much?"

"Five dollars."

"Too much, man! You must be kidding! How about a dollar?"

Lee walked on.

"Hey, wait! One joint, then. Five dollars . . . shit."

"Going rate, man."

The protester pushed long blond hair out of his eyes and pulled a five from a thick clip of bills. Lee got the battered Marlboro box from his pocket and took the smallest joint from it. "Here you go. Have fun. Why don't you fire one of them paint bombs at those tanks, huh?"

The kids on the ground laughed. "We will when you get them stoned!"

He walked on. Only five joints left. It took him less than an hour to sell them. That meant thirty dollars, but that was it. Nothing left to sell. As he left the Mall he looked back at the monument; under its wash of paint it looked like a bone sticking out of raw flesh.

* * *

Anxious about coming to the end of his supply, Lee hoofed it up to Dupont Circle and sat on the perimeter bench in the shade of one of the big trees, footsore and hot. In the muggy air it was hard to catch his breath. He ran the water from the drinking fountain over his hands until someone got in line for a drink. He crossed the circle, giving a wide berth to a bunch of lawyers in long-sleeved shirts and loosened ties, lunching on wine and cheese under the watchful eye of their bodyguard. On the other side of the park Delmont Briggs sat by his cup, almost asleep, his sign propped on his lap. The wasted man. Delmont's sign—and a little side business—provided him with just enough money to get by on the street. The sign, a battered square of cardboard, said PLEASE HELP—HUNGRY. People still looked through Delmont like he wasn't there, but every once in a while it got to somebody. Lee shook his head distastefully at the idea.

"Delmont, you know any weed I can buy? I need a finger baggie for twenty."

"Not so easy to do, Robbie." Delmont hemmed and hawed and they dickered for a while, then he sent Lee over to Jim Johnson, who made the sale under a cheery exchange of the day's news, over by the chess tables. After that Lee bought a pack of cigarettes in a liquor store, and went up to the little triangular park between 17th, S, and New Hampshire, where no police or strangers ever came. They called it Fish Park for the incongruous cement whale sitting by one of the trash cans. He sat down on the long broken bench, among his acquaintances who were hanging out there, and fended them off while he carefully emptied the Marlboros, cut some tobacco into the weed, and refilled the cigarette papers with the new mix. With their ends twisted he had a dozen more joints. They smoked one and he sold two more for a dollar each before he got out of the park.

But he was still anxious, and since it was the hottest part of the day and few people were about, he decided to visit his plants. He knew it would be at least a week till harvest, but he wanted to see them. Anyway it was about watering day.

East between 16th and 15th he hit no-man's-land. The mixed neighborhood of fortress apartments and burned-out hulks gave way to a block or two of entirely abandoned buildings. Here the police had been at work, and looters had finished the job. The buildings were battered and burnt out, their ground floors blasted wide open, some of them collapsed entirely, into heaps of rubble. No one walked the broken sidewalk; sirens a few blocks off, and the distant hum of traffic, were the only signs that the whole city wasn't just like this. Little jumps in the corner of his eye were no more than that; nothing there when he looked directly. The first time, Lee had found walking down the abandoned street nerve-racking; now he was reassured by the silence, the stillness, the no-man's-land smell of torn asphalt and wet charcoal, the wavering streetscape empty under a sour milk sky.

His first building was a corner brownstone, blackened on the street sides, all its windows and doors gone, but otherwise sound. He walked past it without stopping, turned and surveyed the neighborhood. No movement anywhere. He stepped up the steps and through the doorway, being careful to make no footprints in the mud behind the doorjamb. Another glance outside, then up the broken stairs to the second floor. The second floor was a jumble of beams and busted furniture, and Lee waited a minute to let his sight adjust to the gloom. The staircase to the third floor had collapsed, which was the reason he had chosen this building: no easy way up. But he had a route worked out, and with a leap he grabbed a beam hanging from the stairwell and hoisted himself onto it. Some crawling up the beam and he could swing onto the third floor, and from there a careful walk up gapped stairs brought him to the fourth floor.

The room surrounding the stairwell was dim, and he had jammed the door to the next room, so that he had to crawl through a hole in the wall to get through. Then he was there.

Sweating profusely, he blinked in the sudden sunlight, and stepped to his plants, all lined out in plastic pots on the far wall. Eleven medium-sized female marijuana plants, their splayed green leaves drooping for lack of water. He took the rain funnel from one of the gallon jugs and watered the plants. The buds were just longer than his thumbnail; if he could wait another week or two at least, they would be the size of his thumb or more, and worth fifty bucks apiece. He twisted off some water leaves and put them in a baggie.

He found a patch of shade and sat with the plants for a while, watched them soak up the water. Wonderful green they had, lighter than most leaves in D.C. Little red threads in the buds. The white sky lowered over the big break in the roof, huffing little gasps of muggy air onto them all.

His next spot was several blocks north, on the roof of a burned-out hulk that had no interior floors left. Access was by way of a tree growing next to the wall. Climbing it was a challenge, but he had a route here he took, and he liked the way leaves concealed him even from passersby directly beneath him once he got above the lowest branches.

The plants here were younger—in fact one had sprouted seeds since he last saw them, and he pulled the plant out and put it in the baggie. After watering them and adjusting the aluminum foil rain funnels on the jug tops, he climbed down the tree and walked back down 14th.

He stopped to rest in Charlie's Baseball Club. Charlie sponsored a city team with the profits from his bar, and old members of the team welcomed Lee, who hadn't been by in a while. Lee had played left field and batted fifth a year or two before, until his job with the park service had been cut. After that he had had to pawn his glove and cleats, and he had missed Charlie's minimal membership charge three seasons running, and so he had quit. And then it had been too painful to go by the club, and drink with the guys and look at all the trophies on the wall, a couple of which he had helped to win. But on this day he enjoyed the fan blowing, and the dark, and the fries that Charlie and Fisher shared with him.

Break over, he went to the spot closest to home, where the new plants were struggling through the soil, on the top floor of an empty stone husk on 16th and Caroline. The first floor was a drinking place for derelicts, and old Thunderbird and whiskey bottles, half still in bags, littered the dark room, which smelled of alcohol, urine, and rotting wood. All the better: few people would be foolish enough to enter such an obviously dangerous hole. And the stairs were as near gone as made no difference. He climbed over the holes to the second floor, turned and climbed to the third.

The baby plants were fine, bursting out of the soil and up to the sun, the two leaves covered by four, up into four again. . . . He watered them and headed home.

On the way he stopped at the little market that the Vietnamese family ran, and bought three cans of soup, a box of crackers and some Coke. "Twenty-two oh five tonight, Robbie," old Huang said with a four-toothed grin.

The neighbors were out on the sidewalk, the women sitting on the stoop, the men kicking a soccer ball about aimlessly as they watched Sam sand down an old table, the kids running around. Too hot to stay inside this evening, although it wasn't much better on the street. Lee helloed through them and walked up the flights of stairs slowly, feeling the day's travels in his feet and legs.

In his room Debra was awake, and sitting up against her pillows. "I'm hungry, Lee." She looked hot, bored; he shuddered to think of her day.

"That's a good sign, that means you're feeling better. I've got some soup here should be real good for you." He touched her cheek, smiling.

"It's too hot for soup."

"Yeah, that's true, but we'll let it cool down after it cooks, it'll still taste good." He sat on the floor and turned on the hot plate, poured water from the plastic jug into the pot, opened the can of soup, mixed it in. While they were spooning it out Rochelle Jackson knocked on the door and came in.

"Feeling better, I see." Rochelle had been a nurse before her hospital closed, and Lee had enlisted her help when Debra fell sick. "We'll have to take your temperature later."

Lee wolfed down crackers while he watched Rochelle fuss over Debra. Eventually she took a temperature and Lee walked her out.

"It's still pretty high, Lee."

"What's she *got?*" he asked, as he always did. Frustration . . .

"I don't know any more than yesterday. Some kind of flu I guess."

"Would a flu hang on this long?"

"Some of them do. Just keep her sleeping and drinking as much as you can, and feed her when she's hungry.—Don't be scared, Lee."

"I can't help it! I'm afraid she'll get sicker. . . . And there ain't nothing I can do!"

"Yeah, I know. Just keep her fed. You're doing just what I would do."

After cleaning up he left Debra to sleep and went back down to the street, to join the men on the picnic tables and benches in the park tucked into the intersection. This was the "living room" on summer evenings, and all the regulars were there in their usual spots, sitting on tables or bench backs. "Hey there, Robbie! What's happening?"

"Not much, not much. No man, don't kick that soccer ball at me, I can't kick no soccer ball tonight."

"You been walking the streets, hey?"

"How else we going to find her to bring her home to you."

"Hey lookee here, Ghost is bringing out his TV."

"It's Tuesday night at the movies, y'all!" Ghost called out as he approached and plunked a little hologram TV and a Honda generator on the picnic table. They laughed and watched Ghost's pale skin glow in the dusk as he hooked the system up.

"Where'd you get this one, Ghost? You been sniffing around the funeral parlors again?"

"You bet I have!" Ghost grinned. "This one's picture is all fucked up, but it still works—I think—"

He turned the set on and blurry three-dee figures swam into shape in a cube above the box—all in dark shades of blue.

"Man, we *must* have the blues tonight," Ramon remarked. "Look at that!"

"They all look like Ghost," said Lee.

"Hey, it works, don't it?" Ghost said. Hoots of derision. "And dig the sound! The sound works—"

"Turn it up then."

"It's up all the way."

"What's this?" Lee laughed. "We got to watch frozen midgets whispering, is that it, Ghost? What do midgets say on a cold night?"

"Who the fuck is this?" said Ramon.

Johnnie said, "That be Sam Spade, the greatest computer spy in the world."

"How come he live in that shack, then?" Ramon asked.

"That's to show it's a tough scuffle making it as a computer spy, real tough."

"How come he got four million dollars worth of computers right there in the shack, then?" Ramon asked, and the others commenced giggling, Lee loudest of all. Johnnie and Ramon could be killers sometimes. A bottle of rum started around, and Steve broke in to bounce the soccer ball on the TV, smashing the blue figures repeatedly.

"Watch out now, Sam about to go plug his brains in to try and find out who he is."

"And then he gonna be told of some stolen *wetware* he got to find."

"I got some wetware myself, only I call it a shirt."

Steve dropped the ball and kicked it against the side of the picnic table, and a few of the watchers joined in a game of pepper. Some men in a stopped van shouted a conversation with the guys on the corner. Those watching the show leaned forward. "Where's he gonna go?" said Ramon. "Hong Kong? Monaco? He gonna take the bus on over to Monaco?"

Johnnie shook his head. "Rio, man. Fucking Rio de Janeiro."

Sure enough, Sam was off to Rio. Ghost choked out an objection: "Johnnie—ha!—you must have seen this one before."

Johnnie shook his head, though he winked at Lee. "No man, that's just where all the good stolen wetware ends up."

A series of commercials interrupted their fun: deodorant, burglar-killers, cars. The men in the van drove off. Then the show was back, in Rio, and Johnnie said, "He's about to meet a slinky Afro-Asian spy."

When Sam was approached by a beautiful black Asian woman the men couldn't stand it. "Y'all *have* seen this one before!" Ghost cried.

Johnnie sputtered over the bottle, struggled to swallow. "No way! Experience counts, man, that's all."

"And Johnnie has watched one hell of a lot of Sam Spade," Ramon added.

Lee said, "I wonder why they're always Afro-Asian."

Steve burst in, laughed. "So they can fuck all of us at once, man!" He dribbled on the image, changed the channel. "*—army command in*

Los Angeles reports that the rioting killed at least—" He punched the channel again. "What else we got here—man!—what's *this?"*

"Cyborgs Versus Androids," Johnnie said after a quick glance at the blue shadows. "Lots of fighting."

"Yeah!" Steve exclaimed. Distracted, some of the watchers wandered off. "I'm a cyborg myself, see, I got these false teeth!"

"Shit."

Lee went for a walk around the block with Ramon, who was feeling good. "Sometimes I feel so good, Robbie! So strong! I walk around this city and I say, the city is falling apart, it can't last much longer like this. And here I am like some kind of animal, you know, living day to day by my wits and figuring out all the little ways to get by . . . you know there are people living up in Rock Creek Park like Indians or something, hunting and fishing and all. And it's just the same in here, you know. The buildings don't make it no different. Just hunting and scrapping to get by, and man I feel so *alive—"* He waved the rum bottle at the sky.

Lee sighed. "Yeah." Still, Ramon was one of the biggest fences in the area. It was really a steady job. For the rest . . . They finished their walk, and Lee went back up to his room. Debra was sleeping fitfully. He went to the bathroom, soaked his shirt in the sink, wrung it out. In the room it was stifling, and not even a waft of a breeze came in the window. Lying on his mattress sweating, figuring out how long he could make their money last, it took him a long time to fall asleep.

The next day he returned to Charlie's Baseball Club to see if Charlie could give him any piecework, as he had one or two times in the past. But Charlie only said no, very shortly, and he and everyone else in the bar looked at him oddly, so that Lee felt uncomfortable enough to leave without a drink. After that he returned to the Mall, where the protesters were facing the troops ranked in front of the Capitol, dancing and jeering and throwing stuff. With all the police out it took him a good part of the afternoon to sell all the joints left, and when he had he had walked back up 17th Street feeling tired and worried. Perhaps another purchase from Delmont could string them along a few more days. . . .

At 17th and Q a tall skinny kid ran out into the street and tried to open the door of a car stopped for a red light. But it was a protected car despite its cheap look, and the kid shrieked as the handle shocked him. He was still stuck by the hand to it when the car roared off, so that he was launched through the air and rolled over the asphalt. Cars drove on by. A crowd gathered around the bleeding kid. Lee walked on, his jaw clenched. At least the kid would live. He had seen bodyguards gun thieves down in the street, kill them dead and walk away.

Passing Fish Park he saw a man sitting on a corner bench looking around. The guy was white, young; his hair was blond and short, he wore wire-rimmed glasses, his clothes were casual but new, like the protesters' down on the Mall. He had money. Lee snarled as the sharp-faced stranger approached him.

"What you doing here?"

"Sitting!" The man was startled, nervous. "Just sitting in a park!"

"This ain't no *park*, man. This is our front yard. You see any front yard to these apartment buildings here? No. This here is our front yard, and we don't like people just coming into it and sitting down anywhere!"

The man stood and walked away, looked back once, his expression angry and frightened. The other man sitting on the park benches looked at Lee curiously.

Two days later he was nearly out of money. He walked over to Connecticut Avenue, where his old friend Victor played harmonica for coins, when he couldn't find other work. Today he was there, belting out "Amazing Grace." He cut it off when he saw Lee. "Robbie! What's happening?"

"Not much. You?"

Victor gestured at his empty hat, on the sidewalk before him. "You see it. Don't even have seed coin for the cap, man."

"So you ain't been getting any gardening work lately?"

"No, no. Not lately. I do all right here, though. People still pay for music, man, some of them. Music's the angle." He looked at Lee, face twisted up against the sun. They had worked together for the park service, in times past. Every morning through the summers they had gone out and run the truck down the streets, stopping at every tree to hoist each other up in slings. The one hoisted had to stand out from truck or branches like an acrobat, moving around to cut off every branch below twelve feet, and it took careful handling of the chain saw to avoid chopping into legs and such. Those were good times. But now the park service was gone, and Victor gazed at Lee with a stoic squint, sitting behind an empty hat.

"Do you ever look up at the trees anymore, Robbie?"

"Not much."

"I do. They're growing wild, man! Growing like fucking weeds! Every summer they go like crazy. Pretty soon people are gonna have to drive their cars through the branches. The streets'll be tunnels. And with half the buildings in this area falling down . . . I like the idea that the forest is taking this city back again. Running over it like kudzu, till maybe it just be forest again at last."

That evening Lee and Debra ate tortillas and refries, purchased with the last of their money. Debra had a restless night, and her temperature stayed high. Rochelle's forehead wrinkled as she watched her.

Lee decided he would have to harvest a couple of the biggest plants prematurely. He could dry them over the hot plate and be in business by the following day.

The next afternoon he walked east into no-man's-land, right at twilight. Big thunderheads loomed to the east, lit by the sun, but it had not rained that day and the muggy heat was like an invisible blanket, choking each breath with moisture. Lee came to his abandoned building, looked around. Again the complete stillness of an empty city. He recalled Ramon's tales of the people who lived forever in the no-man's-land, channeling rain into basement pools, growing vegetables in empty lots, and existing entirely on their own with no need for money. . . .

He entered the building, ascended the stairs, climbed the beam, struggled sweating up to the fourth floor and through the hole into his room.

The plants were gone.

"Wha . . ." He kneeled, feeling like he had been punched in the stomach. The plastic pots were knocked over, and fans of soil lay spread over the old wood flooring.

Sick with anxiety he hurried downstairs and jogged north to his second hideaway. Sweat spilled into his eyes and they stung fiercely. He lost his breath and had to walk. Climbing the tree was a struggle.

The second crop was gone too.

Now he was stunned, shocked almost beyond thought. Someone must have followed him. . . . It was nearly dark, and the mottled sky lowered over him, empty but somehow, now, watchful. He descended the tree and ran south again, catching his breath in a sort of sobbing. It was dark by the time he reached 16th and Caroline, and he made his way up the busted stairs using a cigarette for illumination. Once on the fourth floor the lighter revealed broken pots, dirt strewn everywhere, the young plants gone. That small they hadn't been worth anything. Even the aluminum foil rain funnels on his plastic jugs had been ripped up and thrown around.

He sat down, soaking wet with sweat, and leaned back against the scored, moldy wall. Leaned his head back and looked up at the orange-white clouds, lit by the city.

After a while he stumbled downstairs to the first floor and stood on the filthy concrete, among the shadows and the discarded bottles. He went and picked up a whiskey bottle, sniffed it. Going from bottle to bottle he poured whatever drops remained in them into the whiskey bottle. When he was done he had a finger or so of liquor, which he downed in one long pull. He coughed. Threw the bottle against the wall. Picked up each bottle and threw it against the wall. Then he went outside and sat on the curb, and watched the traffic pass by.

He decided that some of his old teammates from Charlie's Baseball Club must have followed him around and discovered his spots, which would explain why they had looked at him so funny the other day. He went over to check it out immediately. But when he got there he found the place closed, shut down, a big new padlock on the door.

"What happened?" he asked one of the men hanging out on the corner, someone from this year's team.

"They busted Charlie this morning. Got him for selling speed, first thing this morning. Now the club be gone for good, and the team too."

When he got back to the apartment building it was late, after midnight. He went to Rochelle's door and tapped lightly.

"Who is it?"

"Lee." Rochelle opened the door and looked out. Lee explained what had happened. "Can I borrow a can of soup for Debra for tonight? I'll get it back to you."

"Okay. But I want one back soon, you hear?"

Back in his room Debra was awake. "Where you been, Lee?" she asked weakly. "I was worried about you."

He sat down at the hot plate, exhausted.

"I'm hungry."

"That's a good sign. Some cream of mushroom soup, coming right up." He began to cook, feeling dizzy and sick. When Debra finished eating he had to force the remaining soup down him.

Clearly, he realized, someone he knew had ripped him off—one of his neighbors, or a park acquaintance. They must have guessed his source of weed, then followed him as he made his rounds. Someone he knew. One of his friends.

Early the next day he fished a newspaper out of a trashcan and looked through the short column of want ads for dishwashing work and the like. There was a busboy job at the Dupont Hotel and he walked over and asked about it. The man turned him away after a single look: "Sorry, man, we looking for people who can walk out into the restaurant, you know." Staring in one of the big silvered windows as he walked up New Hampshire, Lee saw what the man saw: his hair was spiked out everywhere as if he would be a Rasta in five or ten years, his clothes were torn and dirty, his eyes wild. . . . With a deep stab of fear he realized he was too poor to be able to get any job—beyond the point where he could turn it around.

He walked the shimmery black streets, checking phone booths for change. He walked down to M Street and over to 12th, stopping in at all the grills and little Asian restaurants, he went up to Pill Park and tried to get some of his old buddies to front him, he kept looking in pay phones and puzzling through blown scraps of newspaper, desperately hoping that one of them might list a job for him . . . and with each footsore step the fear spiked up in him like the pain lancing up his legs, until it soared into a thoughtless panic. Around noon he got so shaky and sick-feeling he had to stop, and despite his fear he slept flat on his back in Dupont Circle park through the hottest hours of the day.

In the late afternoon he picked it up again, wandering almost aimlessly. He stuck his fingers in every phone booth for blocks around, but other fingers had been there before his. The change boxes of the old farecard machines in the Metro would have yielded more, but with the subway system closed, all those holes into the earth were gated off, and slowly filling with trash. Nothing but big trash pits.

Back at Dupont Circle he tried a pay phone coin return and got a dime. "Yeah," he said aloud; that got him over a dollar. He looked up and saw that a man had stopped to watch him: one of the fucking lawyers, in loosened tie and long-sleeved shirt and slacks and leather shoes, staring at him open-mouthed as his group and its bodyguard crossed the street. Lee held up the coin between thumb and forefinger and glared at the man, trying to impress on him the reality of a dime.

He stopped at the Vietnamese market. "Huang, can I buy some soup from you and pay you tomorrow?"

The old man shook his head sadly. "I can't do that, Robbie. I do that even once, and—" he wiggled his hands—"the whole house come down. You know that."

"Yeah. Listen, what can I get for—" He pulled the day's change from his pocket and counted it again. "A dollar ten."

Huang shrugged. "Candy bar? No?" He studied Lee. "Potatoes. Here, two potatoes from the back. Dollar ten."

"I didn't think you had any potatoes."

"Keep them for family, you see. But I sell these to you."

"Thanks, Huang." Lee took the potatoes and left. There was a trash dumpster behind the store; he considered it, opened it, looked in. There was a half-eaten hot dog—but the stench overwhelmed him, and he remembered the poisonous taste of the discarded liquor he had punished himself with. He let the lid of the dumpster slam down and went home.

After the potatoes were boiled and mashed and Debra was fed, he went to the bathroom and showered until someone hammered on the door. Back in his room he still felt hot, and he had trouble catching his breath. Debra rolled from side to side, moaning. Sometimes he was sure she was getting sicker, and at the thought his fear spiked up and through him again; he got so scared he couldn't breathe at all. . . .

"I'm hungry, Lee. Can't I have nothing more to eat?"

"Tomorrow, Deb, tomorrow. We ain't got nothing now."

She fell into an uneasy sleep. Lee sat on his mattress and stared out the window. White-orange clouds sat overhead, unmoving. He felt a bit dizzy, even feverish, as if he was coming down with whatever Debra had. He remembered how poor he had felt even back when he had had his crops to sell, when each month ended with such a desperate push to make rent. But now . . . He sat and watched the shadowy figure of Debra, the walls, the hotplate and utensils in the corner, the clouds out the window. Nothing changed. It was only an hour or two before dawn when he fell asleep, still sitting against the wall.

Next day he battled fever to seek out potato money from the pay phones and the gutters, but he only had thirty-five cents when he had to quit. He drank as much water as he could hold, slept in the park, and then went to see Victor.

"Vic, let me borrow your harmonica tonight."

Victor's face squinted with distress. "I can't, Robbie. I need it myself. You know—" pleading with him to understand.

"I know," Lee said, staring off into space. He tried to think. The two friends looked at each other.

"Hey, man, you can use my kazoo."

"What?"

"Yeah, man, I got a good kazoo here, I mean a big metal one with a good buzz to it. It sounds kind of like a harmonica, and it's easier to play it. You just hum notes." Lee tried it. "No, hum, man. Hum in it."

Lee tried again, and the kazoo buzzed a long crazy note.

"See? Hum a tune, now."

Lee hummed around for a bit.

"And then you can practice on my harmonica till you get good on it, and get your own. You ain't going to make anything with a harmonica till you can play it, anyway."

"But this—" Lee said, looking at the kazoo.

Victor shrugged. "Worth a try."

Lee nodded. "Yeah." He clapped Victor on the shoulder, squeezed it. Pointed at Victor's sign, which said *Help a musician!* "You think that helps?"

Victor shrugged. "Yeah."

"Okay. I'm going to get far enough away so's I don't cut into your business."

"You do that. Come back and tell me how you do."

"I will."

So Lee walked south to Connecticut and M, where the sidewalks were wide and there were lots of banks and restaurants. It was just after sunset, the heat as oppressive as at midday. He had a piece of cardboard taken from a trashcan, and now he tore it straight, took his ballpoint from his pocket and copied Delmont's message. PLEASE HELP—HUNGRY. He had always admired its economy, how it cut right to the main point.

But when he got to what appeared to be a good corner, he couldn't make himself sit down. He stood there, started to leave, returned. He pounded his fist against his thigh, stared about wildly, walked to the curb and sat on it to think things over.

Finally he stepped to a bank pillar mid-sidewalk and leaned back against it. He put the sign against the pillar face-out, and put his old baseball cap upside-down on the ground in front of him. Put his thirty-five cents in it as seed money. He took the kazoo from his pocket, fingered it. "Goddamn it," he said at the sidewalk between clenched teeth. "If you're going to make me live this way, you're going to have to pay for it." And he started to play.

He blew so hard that the kazoo squealed, and his face puffed up till it hurt. "Columbia, the Gem of the Ocean," blasted into all the passing faces, louder and louder—

When he had blown his fury out he stopped to consider it. He wasn't going to make any money that way. The loose-ties and the career women in dresses and running shoes were staring at him and moving out toward the curb as they passed, huddling closer together in their little flocks as their bodyguards got between him and them. No money in that.

He took a deep breath, started again. "Swing Low, Sweet Chariot." It really was like singing. And what a song. How you could put your heart into that one, your whole body. Just like singing.

One of the flocks had paused off to the side; they had a red light to wait for. It was as he had observed with Delmont: the lawyers looked right through beggars, they didn't want to think about them. He played louder, and one young man glanced over briefly. Sharp face, wire-rims—with a start Lee recognized the man as the one he had harassed out of Fish Park a couple days before. The guy wouldn't look at Lee directly, and so he didn't recognize him back. Maybe he wouldn't have anyway. But he was hearing the kazoo. He turned to his companions, student types gathered to the lawyer flock for the temporary protection of the bodyguard. He said something to them—"I love street music," or something like that—and took a dollar from his pocket. He hurried over and put the folded bill in Lee's baseball cap, without looking up at Lee. The *Walk* light came on, they all scurried away. Lee played on.

That night after feeding Debra her potato, and eating two himself, he washed the pot in the bathroom sink, and then took a can of mushroom soup up to Rochelle, who gave him a big smile.

Walking down the stairs he beeped the kazoo, listening to the stairwell's echoes. Ramon passed him and grinned. "Just call you Robinson Caruso," he said, and cackled.

"Yeah."

Lee returned to his room. He and Debra talked for a while, and then she fell into a half-sleep, and fretted as if in a dream.

"No, that's all right," Lee said softly. He was sitting on his mattress, leaning back against the wall. The cardboard sign was face down on the floor. The kazoo was in his mouth, and it half buzzed with his words. "We'll be all right. I'll get some seeds from Delmont, and take the pots to new hideouts, better ones." It occurred to him that rent would be due in a couple of weeks; he banished the thought. "Maybe start some gardens in no-man's-land. And I'll practice on Vic's harmonica, and buy one from the pawn shop later." He took the kazoo from his mouth, stared at it. "It's strange what will make money."

He kneeled at the window, stuck his head out, hummed through the kazoo. Tune after tune buzzed the still, hot air. From the floor below Ramon stuck his head out his window to object: "Hey, Robinson Caruso! Ha! Ha! Shut the fuck up, I'm trying to sleep!" But Lee only played quieter. "Columbia, the Gem of the Ocean"—

Our Town

I found my friend Desmond Kean at the northeast corner of the penthouse viewing terrace, assembling a telescope with which to look at the world below. He took a metal cylinder holding a lens and screwed it into the side of the telescope, then put his eye to the lens, the picture of concentrated absorption. How often I had found him like this in recent months! It made me shiver a little; this new obsession of his, so much more intense than the handmade clocks, or the stuffed birds, or the geometric proofs, seemed to me a serious malady.

Clearing my throat did nothing to get his attention, so I ventured to say, "Desmond, you're wanted inside."

"Look at this," he replied. "Just look at it!" He stepped back, and I put my eye to his device.

I have never understood how looking through two pieces of curved glass can bring close distant sights; doesn't the same amount of light hit the first lens as would hit a plain circle of glass? And if so, what then could possibly be done to that amount of light within two lenses, to make it reveal so much more? Mystified, I looked down at the lush greenery of Tunisia. There in the shimmery circle of glass was a jumble of wood and thatch in a rice paddy, pale browns on light green. "Amazing," I said.

I directed the telescope to the north. On certain days, as Desmond once explained to me, when the temperature gradients layer the atmosphere in the right way, light is curved through the air (and tell me how that works!) so that one can see farther over the horizon than usual. This was one of those strange days, and in the lens wavered a black dot, resting on top of a silver pin that stuck up over the horizon. The black dot was Rome, the silver pin was the top of the graceful spire that holds the Eternal City aloft. My heart leaped to know that I gazed from Carthage to Rome.

"It's beautiful," I said.

"No, no," Desmond exclaimed angrily. "Look down! Look what's below!"

I did as he directed, even leaning a tiny bit over the railing to do so. Our new Carthage has a spire of its own, one every bit the equal of Rome's, or that of any other of the great cities of the world. The spire seemed to the naked eye a silver rope, a thread, a strand of gossamer. But through the telescope I saw the massy base of the spire, a concrete block like an immense blind fortress.

"Stunning," I said.

"No!" He seized the spyglass from me. "Look at the people camped there on the base! Look what they're doing!"

I looked through the glass where he had aimed it. Smoky fires, huts of cardboard, ribs perfectly delineated under taut brown skin . . .

"See," Desmond hissed. "There where the bonfires are set. They keep the fires going for days, then pour water on the concrete. To crack it, do you see?"

I saw, there in the curved glass surface; it was just as he had said.

"At that pace it will take them ten thousand years," Desmond said bitterly.

I stood back from the railing. "Please, Desmond. The world has gotten itself into a sorry state, and it's very distressing, but what can any one person do?"

He took the telescope, looked through it again. For a while I thought he wouldn't answer. But then he said, "I. . . . I'm not so sure, friend Roarick. It's a good question, isn't it. But I feel that someone with knowledge, with expertise, could make a bit of a difference. Heal the sick, or . . . give advice about agricultural practices. I've been studying up on that pretty hard. They're wrecking their soil. Or . . . or just put one more shoulder to the wheel! Add one more hand to tend that fire! . . . I don't know. I don't know! Do we ever know, until we act?"

"But Desmond," I said. "Do you mean down there?"

He looked up at me. "Of course."

I shivered again. Up at our altitude the air stays pretty chill all the time, even in the sun. "Come back inside, Desmond," I said, feeling sorry for him. These obsessions. . . . "The exhibition is about to open, and if you're not there for it Cleo will press for the full set of sanctions."

"Now there's something to fear," he said nastily.

"Come on inside. Don't give Cleo the chance. You can return here another day."

With a grimace he put the telescope in the big duffel bag, picked it up and followed me in.

Inside the glass wall, jacaranda trees showered the giant curved greenhouse-gallery with purple flowers. All the tableaux of the exhibit were still covered by saffron sheets, but soon after we entered the sheets were raised, all at once. The human form was revealed in all its variety and beauty, frozen in place yet still pulsing with life. I noted a man loping, a pair of women fighting, a diver launched in air, four drunks playing cards, a couple stopped forever at orgasm. I felt the familiar opening-night quiver of excitement, caused partly by the force fields of the tableaux as they kept the living ectogenes stopped in place, but mostly by rapture, by a physical response to art and natural beauty. "At first glance it seems a good year," I said. "I already see three or four pieces of merit."

"Obscene travesties," said Desmond.

"Now, now, it isn't as bad as all that. Some imitation of last year, yes, but no more than usual."

We walked down the hall to see how my entry had been placed. Like Desmond, before he quit sculpting, I was chiefly interested in finding and isolating moments of dance that revealed, by themselves, all the grace of the whole act. This year I had stopped a pair of ballet dancers at the end of a pas de deux, the ballerina just off the base of the display as her partner firmly but delicately returned her to the boards. How long I had worked with the breeders, to get ectogenes with these lean dancers' bodies! How many hours I had spent, programming their unconscious education, and training and choreographing them in their brief waking hours! And then at the end, how very often I had had them dance on the tableau base, and stopped them in the force field, before I caught them in the exact moment that I had envisioned! Yes, I had spent a great deal of time in my sculpting chamber, this year; and now my statue stood before us like the epitome of all that is graceful in the human spirit. —At a proper angle to the viewers, I was pleased to see, and under tolerable lighting, too. On the two faces were expressions that said that for these two, nothing existed but dance; and in this case it was almost literally true. Yes, it was satisfactory.

Desmond only shook his head. "No, Roarick. You don't understand. We can't keep doing this—"

"Desmond!" cried Cleo, flowing through the crowd of sculptors and their guests. Her smile was wide, her eyes bright with malice. "Come see my latest, dear absent one!"

Wordlessly Desmond followed her, his face so blank of expression that all his thoughts showed clear. A whole crew followed us discreetly, for Desmond and Cleo's antipathy was legendary. How it had started none remembered, although some said they had once been lovers. If so, it was before I knew them. Others said Desmond hated Cleo for her success in the sculpture competitions, and some of the more sharp-tongued gossips said that this envy explained Desmond's new, morbid interest in the world below—sour grapes, you know. But Desmond had always been interested in things no one else cared about—rediscovering little scientific truths and the like—and to me it was clear that his fascination was simply the result of his temperament, and of what his telescope had newly revealed to him. No, his and Cleo's was a more fundamental hatred, a clash of contrary natures.

Now Desmond stared at Cleo's new statue. It is undeniable that Cleo is a superb artist, especially in facial expressions, those utterly complex projections of unique emotional states; and this work displayed her usual brilliance in that most difficult medium. It was a solo piece: a red-haired young woman looked back over one shoulder with an expression of intense vulnerability and confusion, pierced by a sharp melancholy. It was exquisite.

The sight of this sculpture snapped some final restraint in Desmond Kean; I saw it happen. His eyes filled with pity and disgust; his lip curled, and he said loudly, "How did you do it, Cleo? What did you do to her in your little bubble world to get that expression out of her?"

Now, this was a question one simply didn't ask. Each artist's arcology was his or her own sovereign ground, a physical projection of the artist's creative unconscious, an entirely private cosmos. What one did to one's material there was one's own business.

But the truth was no one had forgotten the unfortunate Arthur Magister, who had exhibited increasingly peculiar and morbid statues over a period of years, ending with one of a maiden who had had on her face such an expression that no one could bear to look at it. Though the rule of privacy was maintained, there were of course questions muttered; but no one would ever have found out the answers, if Arthur had not blown up himself and his arcology, revealing in the wreckage, among other things, a number of unpleasantly dismembered ectogenes.

So it was a sensitive issue; and when Desmond asked Cleo his brazen question, with its dark implication, she blanched, then reddened with anger. Disdainfully (though I sensed she was afraid, too) she refused to reply. Desmond stared fiercely at us all; were he an ectogene, I would have stopped him at just that instant.

"Little gods," he snarled, and left the room.

That would cost him, in reputation if not in actual sanctions. But the rest of us forgot his distemper, relieved that we could now begin the exhibit's opening reception in earnest. Down at the drink tables champagne corks were already bringing down a fresh shower of jacaranda blooms.

It was just a few hours later, when the reception was a riotous party, that I heard the news, passed from group to group instantly, that someone had broken the locks on the tableaux (this was supposed to be impossible) and turned their force fields off, letting most of the statues free. And it was while we rushed to the far end of the greenhouse-gallery, around the great curve of the perimeter of the penthouse, that I heard that Desmond Kean had been seen, leaving the gallery with Cleo's red-headed ectogene.

Utter scandal. This would cost Desmond more than money; they would exile him to some tedious sector of the city, to scrub walls with robots or teach children or the like: they would make him pay in time. And Cleo! I groaned; he would never live to see the end of her wrath.

Well, a friend can only do so much, but while the rest were rounding up and pacifying the disoriented ectogenes (which included, alas, my two dancers, who were huddled in each other's arms) I went in search of Desmond, to warn him that he had been seen. I knew his haunts well, having shared most of them, and I hurried to them through the uncrowded, vaguely Parisian boulevards of the penthouse's northern quarter.

My first try was the broken planetaria near the baths; I opened the door with the key we had quietly reproduced years before. An indiscretion!—for Desmond and the young ectogene were making love on the dais in the middle of the chamber, Desmond on his back, the woman straddling him, arced as if all the energy of the great spire were flowing up into her . . . he was breaking all the taboos this night. Immediately I shut the door, but given the situation saw fit to pound loudly on it. "Desmond! It's Roarick! They saw you with the girl, you've got to leave!"

Silence. What to do in such a situation? I had no precedent. After a good thirty seconds had passed I opened the door again. No Desmond, no girl.

I, however, was one of those who with Desmond had first discovered the other exit from the planetaria, and I hurried to the central ball of optical fibers which even he could not fix, and pulled up the trap door beside it. Down the stairs and along the passageway, into one of the penthouse's other infrastructures I ran.

I will not detail my long search, nor my desperate and ludicrous attempts to evade rival search parties. Despite my knowledge of Desmond's ways and my anxious thoroughness, I did not find him until I thought of the place that should have occurred to me first. I returned to the northeast corner of the viewing terrace, right there outside the glass wall of the greenhouse-gallery, where (as it was now dusk) if the artists inside could have seen through their own reflections, they would have looked right at him.

He and the redhead were standing next to Desmond's telescope, their elbows on the railing as they looked over the edge side by side. Desmond had his duffel bag at his feet. Something in their stance kept me from emerging from the shadows. They looked as though they had just finished the most casual and intimate of conversations—a talk about trivial, inessential things, the kind of talk lovers have together after years of companionship. Such calmness, such resignation . . . I could only look, at what seemed to me then an unbreakable, eternal tableau.

Desmond sighed and turned to look at her. He took a red curl of her hair between his fingers, watched the gold in it gleam in a band across the middle of the curl. "There are three kinds of red hair," he said sadly. "Red black, red brown, and red gold. And the greatest of these is. . . ."

"Black," said the girl.

"Gold," said Desmond. He fingered the curl. . . .

The woman pointed. "What's all that down there?"

Dusky world below, long since in night: vast dark Africa, the foliage like black fur, sparking with the sooty flares of a thousand bonfires, little pricks of light like yellow stars. "That's the world," Desmond said, voice tightened to a burr. "I suppose you don't know a thing about it. Around those fires down there are people. They are slaves, they live lives even worse than yours, almost."

But his words didn't appear to touch the woman. She turned away, and lifted an empty glass left on the railing. On her face was an expression so . . . lost—a sudden echo of her expression as statue—that I shivered in the cold wind. She didn't have the slightest idea what was going on.

"Damn," she said. "I wish I'd remembered to bring another drink."

A conversation from another world, resumed here. I saw Desmond Kean's face then, and I know that I did right to interrupt at that moment. "Desmond!" I rushed forward and grasped his arm. "There's no time, you really must get to one of our private rooms and hide! You don't want to find out what sort of sentence they might hand down for this sort of thing!"

A long moment: I shudder to think of the tableau we three made. The world is a cruel sculptor.

"All right," Desmond said at last. "Here, Roarick, take her and get her out of here." He bent over to fumble in his bag. "They'll put her down after all this if they catch her."

"But—but where should I go?" I stammered.

"You know this city as well as I! Try the gallery's service elevator, and get on the underfloor—you know," he insisted, and yet he was about to give me further directions when the far greenhouse door burst open and a whole mob poured out. We were forced to run for it; I took the woman by the hand and sprinted for the closer greenhouse door. The last I saw of Desmond Kean, he was climbing over the railing. *My God*, I thought, *he's going to kill himself!*—but then I saw the purposefully rectangular package strapped to his back.

A Transect

—*for Thabo Moeti*

After he had secured a window seat in the Amtrak coach, he set his dark brown leather briefcase in his lap and unlocked it. *Clunk. Clunk.* He liked the way the gold-plated hasps snapped open. About fifty times more power in the springs than was necessary. Sign of a well-tooled briefcase: big, heavy, powerful. Expensive. Something for clients to note with approval. Part of their confidence in him.

Riffling through his account files was depressing. Nothing in there but bad news. No one was buying fine paper in quantity these days; he had to bust a gut just to stay even. Northeast Section Marketing and Sales Vice President, forever and ever amen. He sighed; at times like this he felt utterly stuck. No chance of advancement whatsoever. Stuck at forty-five thousand a year for good, and with wife and kids throwing it away faster than he could make it. Lucky his credit was good, he could spend his future right up to his death and beyond, no doubt. Ah, the end of a long, hard trip: he needed a drink.

The train came out of its hole and he looked into the industrial yards of Montreal. Beyond them was the city center where he had spent the day selling. Sun setting behind it. Funny how much Canada looked like the States (he always thought that). He let his files accordion back into the briefcase and pulled out his copy of the day's *Wall Street Journal.* Up and down the train car, other copies of the same paper were blooming over the plush maroon seats, covering the businessmen behind them. A young punk wearing earphones sat in the aisle seat beside him, cramping his reading. Faint whispers of percussive music joined the rustling of newspapers in the strangely hushed car.

Nothing in the day's *Journal* was of interest. He folded it and put it in his lap. They were out of the industrial district, in the trees between suburbs. Too late in the fall: the half-bare trees looked bedraggled, the leaf-matted ground wet and boggy. He folded his suit jacket over twice and used it as a pillow against the inner window. It would have to be dry-cleaned anyway; he had spilled a few drops of Burgundy on it at lunch, right on the top of the right cuff, where clients would see it when he signed things.

"*Hei broer!* Watch out where you going when you walking backwards like that! Here, you need a hand with those?"

"Thanks, I got them." He heaved up on the straps tied around his two boxes and pulled them past the old man down the center of the train. The benches on both sides were crowded with migrant workers going home, jammed together hip to hip. Their boxes and bags were stacked on the wooden floor, leaving him just enough room to maneuver to the end of the car. There, because it was the last car on the train, he could set his two boxes in the middle of the aisle and sit on them, as several other men had already done. He greeted them with a lift of his chin.

"Where you from, *broer?*"

"Mzimhlophe Hostels. I did my eleven months there—now I going home. Home to Kwa-Xhosa."

"Home," said a thin colored man bitterly. "Just how is Kwa-Xhosa Bantustan your home?"

"My folks is there," he said with a shrug.

"Your folks is there because the government moved them there," the man said. "Me, my home is Robben Island. It been my home nine years, and all because of one night's A.N.C. meeting at my house.

They gave me two and a half years for taking subscriptions, one and a half years for meeting, and five years for distributing pamphlets. All the same night!" He laughed harshly. "Now I'm out, and they ban me! Clearly I must be meeting a whole bunch of Communists in those nine years, for they ban me the moment I out! Ban me to Kwa-Xhosa, where I never been in my whole life, where I can never see my family, for five long years."

The others laughed their sympathy. "That too bad, Pieter!" "You got to watch all those bad phone calls you make from the island, man!"

The conversation focused on the newcomer. "What your name?" "Norman."

"What did you in Soweto?"

"Bricklayer," Norman said.

The train jerked twice and they rolled out of Park Station.

"That against the law, you know," Pieter said. "If they pay attention to their own law, you could not have that job. *Nie kaffir* bricklayers, *nie!*"—this with the heavy Afrikaaner tone. The men laughed. Several in the car turned on transistor radios, and the hard rhythms clashed. The train cleared the outskirts of Johannesburg and clattered through the outlying townships.

Norman looked out the window and saw three women sitting on a step, leaning in on each other in a stupor. Empty bottles. Blank faces under the streetlight. He recognized in the slump of their shoulders that moment of exhaustion and peace, and felt his own shoulders relax with it. He was on his way home.

The train swayed as it took a sharp turn. One last view of Montreal. He put his suit jacket on the chair arm and pulled a Sherman cigarette from the box in his briefcase. The punk next to him appeared to be asleep, although faint music still whispered from his earphones. He lit the Sherman with the gold lighter his boss had given him, and felt a certain uneasiness leave him, breath by breath. Hard to sleep on a train. Another station stop. The people in his car were mostly commuters. Briefcases, cuff links, polished shoes. The *swish-swish* of nyloned legs rubbing together; his head shifted so he could see the tight dress between the two seat backs in front of him. She sat two seats ahead. A man with a cough sat behind him. Muted voices came from the car behind theirs, until a door hissed shut.

When the Sherman was finished, he took a last look at the night lights of Montreal. The company's awards dinner had been in Montreal, just a month earlier, in the fashionable district downtown. He had expected to win the regional sales award for the year, because things were tough everywhere and he did have some big regular clientele. He took his wife along. All that backslapping and joking about the awards at the cocktail party before, as if no one cared about them, as if they were bowling trophies or something—when everyone knew they were a strong indicator of what the upper echelon thought of your prospects. So that in that sense they represented thousands of dollars—careers, even. So that looking around the room there was a part of him that hated all his colleagues, his competitors. Even more so afterwards, when he had to do like all the rest and go up to congratulate the winner, George Dulak, head of the Midwestern Section (which in itself was an advantage): beaming winner surrounded by envious admirers, shiny gold pen set cradled in one hand. . . . Finally he had gone away to get a drink. It was just like management to make the work a contest like this, to get them all at each other's throats. Competition more productive than teamwork: the American way!

"On Robben Island," Pieter said, "the *agter-nyer* is the one the warden uses to control the rest—he the guard inside, and gets the little extras you know, tobacco and such. But our *agter-nyer* was not a bad man, he help to get us food sometimes. And one night we was entertaining one another, Solly, he acting out the various guards and the wardens—all without one word, you see, but just watching him we knew exactly who he mean. And we giggling and brushing—we never clapped, you see, for fear of the guards' attentions, so to applaud we rubbed our hands together like so." They heard nothing of Pieter's prison applause over the talk and the radios. "And we in such a state we never in the world hear the guard coming, but for the *agter-nyer* sitting on the cement at the door watching for them. He been standing watch for us all those nights, and never let us know till he had to." He laughed. "A good man!"

"I been living in a prison, too, these last eleven months," Norman said suddenly, surprising them all, including himself. "A prison called the Mzimhlophe Hostels."

Most of them had been living around Soweto in the men's dormitories that house the migrant laborers from the bantustans, and some said, "We hear that, *broer!*" But Pieter quickly disagreed—"nothing's prison but prison, man"—and continued telling stories of Robben Island. Norman was not listening to Pieter anymore, however; he was back in the hostels, looking over row after row of low gray brick dorms, their chimneys jutting out of asbestos roofs into the sky. One morning after a Friday night's drinking, he had gotten up and stumbled out of the dorm to the toilets in the next building—in the door, past the cement troughs for washing dishes and clothes, to the open toilet basins, there to retch miserably. As he returned to his dorm, he felt so sick he was sure he would die before his eleven months' stint of work in Soweto was up. That certainty gave him new eyes as he entered the dorm and crossed the dusty concrete floor, past the low concrete slabs on metal struts that were their tables, past the benches also made of concrete slabs to the sleeping cubicles, where men slept on the doorlike lids of the brick trunks that held all their possessions. In the gloom it seemed they slept on coffins. Beyond in the kitchen cubicle, men were still playing guitars connected to little amplifiers, and the low electric twangs were the only signs that the men sitting around the small stove were still awake, still alive—a single candle on the slab beside them, shadows everywhere in the dim air, drying shirts hung overhead—and bitterly he thought, what a place to die in.

Perhaps he would get a drink. The restaurant car was only two ahead, and he was thirsty and needed to wash down some aspirin. He needed a drink. He stood and managed to step over the sleeping punk; debated taking the briefcase with him, but after all it was locked and no one was going anywhere anyway. Hopefully by his presence the punk would guard it.

Down the car. His balance was shaky; something wrong with him this night. He should have gotten a sleeper. Too much pride in his endurance as a traveler. Out of the soundproofed compartment and into the cold, jouncing passageway between cars. Here you could believe the train was really moving. Back into the hush of the next car. Only half the overhead lights were still on here, and most of the occupants were asleep. Some read or listened to earphones. Half their heads were shaved or tinted green or purple, it seemed. Craziness. His daughter, only fourteen years old, had brought one of those home once. He hadn't known how to express his disgust; he left it to Vicki, tried to forget about it.

There was a line at the little bar in the restaurant car. The two black bartenders went at the work casually, chatting to each other about vacationing in Jamaica, just as if there weren't a line. When one of them asked him what he wanted, he curtly ordered a gin and tonic and a foil bag of nuts, but his disapproval didn't seem to register. He sipped the gin and tonic—a weak one—to give himself some room for jiggling while he walked, then saw that the woman in the tight dress was sitting at one of the little tables. He sat at another and watched her as he drank. Not actually very good-looking. When he finished the drink, it felt like a million miles separated him from everyone else there. He stood and returned to his seat. Should have gotten a sleeper. Something wrong with him, some kind of tension somehow . . . had to avoid that kind of thing, or it was back to the Tagamet for him.

Back in his seat he stared through his reflection in the window at the world outside. Clanking red lights at railroad crossings, time after time. A sleeping town, even the neon off. Loading docks, laundromat, Village Video Rental. You saw a lot of those video places these days, even in the little backwoods towns. "Movies in the privacy of your own home!" and then it was gone. The drink began to go to his head, and the repeated hoot of the train's horn—so distant, so muted—was like the cry of some mournful beast, lulling him toward sleep and then calling him back, time after time.

The beauty of the Witwatersrand took his breath away. He had forgotten that such open, clean land existed in South Africa, and at the sight of it something in his chest hurt. White clouds sprawled across a cobalt sky, and there in the yellowwoods and Camdeboo stinkwoods dotting the sere grass of the veldt flew loeris, doves, hoepoe, and drongos, with small white hawks circling far above. Wild gardenia growing by the tracks. It affected all the men similarly, and they threw open the windows and laughed and shouted at the sky, aware suddenly that they really were going home. They danced in the aisle to the fast mbaqanga beat and sang American spirituals. "Swing Low, Sweet Chariot," accompanied by a fifteen-year-old boy playing harmonica for all he was worth—it was grand.

Then the train pulled into Vereeninging Station. Still in a celebratory mood, the men stuck their heads out the train window and shouted for the platform hawkers. "Dresses and aprons for your loved ones at only five rand, *broers!*" "Not a chance, *suster*, you bore me with your dresses, let that *bierman* through to us." They bought dumpies of beer at an extortionate price, and downed most of them before the train rattled off again. Then through the outskirts of town: corrugated iron, donkeys, pigs, children, Indian corner groceries, pawpaw trees, women with washtubs, prickly pears, and scraps of paper everywhere, all over the hard-packed earth of the streets. "Oh, how I hate this town, the most hateful town in the world to me," one man cried. "My wife got off the train at this station and I never saw her again up to this very day." The men whooped their sympathy. "Wasn't that Georgina the hippo left you, man?" "She found you were undermining her interest with that girl in Joburg, didn't she? You lucky you didn't see snake's butt that day instead!" And the man laughed "hee, hee, hee," as he shook his head to deny them.

The man in the seat behind him could not stop coughing. A couple minutes' labored breathing, the strained efforts to control it—then *kar! karugh! urrkhkraugh!* He couldn't believe it. Next time, he thought, I'll drive. To hell with this. His throat was beginning to tickle a little, right there below his Adam's apple, and briefly he glanced over his shoulder in irritation. Old pasty-faced man with dark rings under his eyes, in a shabby gray suit. Italian-looking. Incredibly inconsiderate of him to travel sick and infect everyone else on the train. He really was coming down with it! He swallowed over and over. There was only a single light on in the car—some insomniac businessman reading *In Search of Excellence,* still looking fresh and unruffled at 2 A.M. Yeah, you'll win the award, he thought angrily, and me, I'll just catch a cold. And all because of the luck of seating availability. He hated being sick. You couldn't possibly make a good impression with a cold. Sales out of the question. Might as well stay at home and watch Vicki take care of things. More coughs; it was enough to make him envy the sleeping punk his earphones. Although that would still be no protection for his throat.

Abruptly he stood and took a walk toward the restaurant car. It was closed for the night. Back between cars, in the cold passageway, he noticed that the train was moving very slowly. He looked through the thick little window in the passageway door. They were over water; Lake Champlain, he guessed. The railroad bridge was so old and rickety that the train had to cross at about ten miles an hour. Looking down he couldn't even see the bridge, it was so narrow. White mist lay over the water, swirling eerily under the half-moon. He shivered convulsively: something *odd* about this night, the hush too quiet, the distances too great . . . he must be getting ill. Or . . . something. For the last few years he had gotten his life into such a groove, such a routine of day to day activities, each day resembling its predecessor from the week before, Mondays all alike, Fridays all alike, Saturdays . . . that he had found himself with time on his hands. It seemed he could live his life on a sort of automatic pilot, leaving him all sorts of time to just . . . think. Like he really never had before. And once or twice in this new thinking he had wondered what it (*it* being his life, the world, everything) was all about. No great answer had jumped immediately to mind; often he was left with just this sort of uneasy feeling. Out there, was that another train? No, just mist. A lake of white cotton. . . .

Nothing for it but to return to his seat. As the night progressed he fell in and out of a half-sleep that resembled a trance. Several times they stopped at stations briefly, and once he woke completely when the police boarded to check everyone's passbooks. Two big white security police, making an old black ticket taker do most of the work. The migrants dug through their possessions for their reference books. Tins, boxes, old water drums bound with straps, all heavily loaded with basic groceries to help out the families on the bantustans. Norman's boxes were full of sugar, salt, and tea, all packed under his extra shirt and pants. His passbook was in the spare shirt's pocket; he pulled it out and bent the corners back down. All his stamps were in order, and he gave the ticket taker the book without looking up. Out the window Cape fig trees shaded the tiny veldt station, flanking the tracks like a hedge. Signs marked the entrances to the station house: BLANKES. NIE-BLANKES.

One of the security police took Pieter's passbook from the ticket taker's hand and inspected it closely. Suddenly no one in the car was talking. The radios babbled in Zulu and Xhosa. Then the policeman showed it to his companion and laughed. "*Robben vir Kwa-Xhosa! Die lewe is swaar né, Pieter!*"

"*Ja, my baas,*" Pieter said, looking at the floor of the corridor. "Life is hard, all right."

"Listen to me, *seuntjie,*" the policeman said, and gave Pieter a little lecture: more God, *volk* and trek, as someone said when they were gone. Pieter resolutely stared at the floor. When the policeman finished, Pieter looked up at him, the hatred clear in his eyes. "My stamps are good, *ja baas?*"

"*Ja, seuntjie,*" the big man said easily, and tossed Pieter his passbook. The two police led the ticket taker out of the car, laughing over something, the pass check already forgotten. "Cape town whores are best." "Moering kaffirs will kill you in bed, though!"

Then they were gone, and everyone started breathing properly again. Only now could they be sure that all the passbooks were really in order; often they were not, and so one didn't discuss the matter. There had been a good chance someone on the car would be dragged off to jail. But they were all legal this time, and the talk began again. "They stick him on the tenth floor by the open window, you know, but he refuse the jump and so he in jail and his kids is starving with hungry—"

"—you ever try sharing a bed with such a hippo? You got to sleep like a flea, ready to jump quick. And the fatter she got the worse her temper! Man I kissed Mother Earth daily living with her. Ha! Ha! She ransack me good sometime—"

"—ja, and if you get out, it's to the labor bureau like me, to sell yourself off to the coal mines of Witbank a thousand miles from home. We had a bad one at our labor bureau—he says, which of you boys wants a job, and of course we all jumping up and down like dogs, pick me *baas,* pick me, and he pick one after another to tell them no, they not good enough. Then he pick me and look through my workbook, won't your wife sleep around while you gone, boy, I bet she sleep with me for giving you this job, until he tire of the game and give me the joy of eleven months work away from my folks."

"And that better still than prison," Pieter took it up; but Norman turned from Pieter's bitter comedies and looked out the window. Train noising out of the station with hard jerks, as if the engine were yanking on it. An old man sitting in the dirt by a wheelbarrow stacked with baskets; too late in the day to sell anymore, but still he sat, in that twilight moment. . . . SLEGS BLANKES.

He got up to go to the bathroom, feeling distant, disoriented. Stepping over the punk was getting easy—the kid was slumped lower every time. Once again, trouble with balance. Something wrong. Everything too hushed, almost silent. Like cotton in his ears. Everything a great distance away.

The bathroom at the front of the car was occupied. He turned and went to the car behind, the last one of the train. Maneuvered through all the tight turns and heavy narrow doors between cars, found an empty bathroom. For the disabled, but he used it anyway. Not *exclusively* for the disabled, right? Down the iron toilet he could see the track ties flashing beneath the train. When he was done he looked at himself in the cracked coppery mirror: hair mussed, face stubbly, some odd disquiet in his eyes . . .

The beer wanted out of him, and he stood up to use the lavatory at the end of the next car up. By now the travelers were drowsy with beer and fatigue, and he had to step over men sleeping in the aisles. Somehow they sprawled in a way that always left footing just where it was needed. Outside in the dusk the hillocks bordering the Orange River were etched against a moonless blue sky. Igqili River, he said to himself, mother of my country Azania. He stepped through the doorway into the connecting corridor, over the shifting joints of the iron floor. The joints squealed loudly and looking down at them he almost ran into the man coming his way. A white, from one of the first-class cars: confused, he said, "Sorry, *baas.*"

The black kid muttered something under his breath, so sullenly that he was suddenly afraid he might be mugged right there between the two cars. The wheels rolling over the track were loud, no one would hear him: "Sorry about that," he said hastily, feeling dizzy, and yielded to the right. The train jerked and they bumped together hard;

the black man reached out a hand to hold him steady, then withdrew as if shocked, his frightened eyes round and white in the gloom. Their gazes met and held.

The look.

Dark brown iris, the whites a bit yellowed; pale blue iris, the whites a bit bloodshot. And the pupils identical round black holes, the windows of the soul, through which one can fall, spinning dizzily, to land cut, confused, stunned, in a new place; and all with a look—

... He wasn't sure how long the kid's feral stare had held him still, when he jerked free and pulled himself, staggering slightly, away. The doors were heavy and had to be pulled into the walls to right and left. Back in his car the hush seemed more pronounced than ever. Unsteadily he stepped back over the sleeping punk, feeling utterly shaken. The plush maroon velvet of his seat arm. Silvery ashtray, sliding in and out of the arm. Long brown cigarette butts wasted inside. Looking around: such incredible, excessive luxury—and this was just a train! He stared. . . .

The migrants swayed with the train like luggage as he made his way in some confusion back to his boxes. Smell of sweat, beer, the hot veldt night. He ended his *dwaal* on his boxes and looked at his companions. Their clothes were frayed and dirty. Their shoes were broken and full of holes. They slept, or slumped in stupors of non-thought; and suddenly it seemed he could read what pain had chiseled in each worn face. The boy still hummed thoughtfully into his harmonica—bleak falling chords—

Finally they slid into the labyrinth of Penn Station. Darkness, trains passing by, their lit windows making them look like submarines. Then track lights everywhere. The punk woke and stood up. Everyone standing, stretching. He put his coat on in the aisle, feeling its smooth texture. The sick man was struggling to get his suitcase off the overhead racks, and awkwardly he helped him get it down. A haggard smile for thanks; he nodded quickly, embarrassed. A press of people (he held his briefcase close by his side), and he was out of the train, onto the long, crowded platform. Up a set of stairs, turn and follow everyone else to the next set. Up again. Into the light and glare of Penn Station's big central waiting area, with the businessmen and the students and the cops and the cleaning men and the bums. And then suddenly his wife was upon him, with a quick hug and kiss. Strong scent of perfume. She laughed at his exhaustion and held his arm as they made their way up to the street, chattering over something or other and pleased that she had found a legal spot to park their car. She drove, and he sat back in the deep seat and looked at the bright dashboard, at her: glossy cap of blonde hair, blush on her cheeks like two bruises, upper eyelids blue, purple, lashes spiky black. He thought: she's mine. This is mine. I'm safe. At a red light she glanced over at him and laughed again, lips dark red, teeth perfectly white, and quick leaned over to steady themselves as the old train clattered up the grade and out of the hills. Night passed, dawn arrived, they were in Kwa-Xhosa now and it was as if S.A. Railways had been a time machine, taking them a century into the past overnight. Women they passed wore white turbans and led donkeys on dirt paths. On the plains before the blue mountains on the horizon were villages of circular thatched rondewels, whitewashed under the thatch and around the doors. Finally the train clanked into e'Ncgobo, past some men on donkeys and around the last curve to the small wooden building and platform that served as the train station. As the train rolled in, all the men stuck their heads out the windows on the right to look; but under the harsh morning light they saw that the station platform stood deserted, white splintered dusty planks utterly empty in the sun. Not a single soul was there to greet them. *And Thabo said to me, "So many had gone and come back, and so many had gone and never come back again, that no one waited anymore."*

The Lunatics

for Terry Carr

They were very near the center of the moon, Jakob told them. He was the newest member of the bullpen, but already their leader.

"How do you know?" Solly challenged him. It was stifling, the hot air thick with the reek of their sweat, and a pungent stink from the waste bucket in the corner. In the pure black, under the blanket of the rock's basalt silence, their shifting and snuffling loomed large, defined the size of the pen. "I suppose you see it with your third eye."

Jakob had a laugh as big as his hands. He was a big man, never a doubt of that. "Of course not, Solly. The third eye is for seeing in the black. It's a natural sense just like the others. It takes all the data from the rest of the senses, and processes them into a visual image transmitted by the third optic nerve, which runs from the forehead to the sight centers at the back of the brain. But you can only focus it by an act of the will—same as with all the other senses. It's not magic. We just never needed it till now."

"So how do you know?"

"It's a problem in spherical geometry, and I solved it. Oliver and

490

I solved it. This big vein of blue runs right down into the core, I believe, down into the moon's molten heart where we can never go. But we'll follow it as far as we can. Note how light we're getting. There's less gravity near the center of things."

"I feel heavier than ever."

"You are heavy, Solly. Heavy with disbelief."

"Where's Freeman?" Hester said in her crow's rasp.

No one replied.

Oliver stirred uneasily over the rough basalt of the pen's floor. First Naomi, then mute Elijah, now Freeman. Somewhere out in the shafts and caverns, tunnels and corridors—somewhere in the dark maze of mines, people were disappearing. Their pen was emptying, it seemed. And the other pens?

"Free at last," Jakob murmured.

"There's something out there," Hester said, fear edging her harsh voice, so that it scraped Oliver's nerves like the screech of an ore car's wheels over a too-sharp bend in the tracks. "Something out there!"

The rumor had spread through the bullpens already, whispered mouth to ear or in huddled groups of bodies. There were thousands of shafts bored through the rock, hundreds of chambers and caverns. Lots of these were closed off, but many more were left open, and there was room to hide—miles and miles of it. First some of their cows had disappeared. Now it was people too. And Oliver had heard a miner jabbering at the low edge of hysteria, about a giant foreman gone mad after an accident took both his arms at the shoulder—the arms had been replaced by prostheses, and the foreman had escaped into the black, where he preyed on miners off by themselves, ripping them up, feeding on them—

They all heard the steely squeak of a car's wheel. Up the mother shaft, past cross tunnel Forty; had to be foremen at this time of shift. Would the car turn at the fork to their concourse? Their hypersensitive ears focused on the distant sound; no one breathed. The wheels squeaked, turned their way. Oliver, who was already shivering, began to shake hard.

The car stopped before their pen. The door opened, all in darkness. Not a sound from the quaking miners.

Fierce white light blasted them and they cried out, leaped back against the cage bars vainly. Blinded, Oliver cringed at the clawing of a foreman's hands, searching under his shirt and pants. Through pupils like pinholes he glimpsed brief black-and-white snapshots of gaunt bodies undergoing similar searches, then blows. Shouts, cries of pain, smack of flesh on flesh, an electric buzzing. Shaving their heads, could it be that time again already? He was struck in the stomach, choked around the neck. Hester's long wiry brown arms, wrapped around her head. Scalp burned, *buzzz*, all chopped up. Thrown to the rock.

"Where's the twelfth?" In the foremen's staccato language.

No one answered.

The foremen left, light receding with them until it was black again, the pure dense black that was their own. Except now it was swimming with bright red bars, washing around in painful tears. Oliver's third eye opened a little, which calmed him, because it was still a new experience; he could make out his companions, dim redblack shapes in the black, huddled over themselves, gasping.

Jakob moved among them, checking for hurts, comforting. He cupped Oliver's forehead and Oliver said, "It's seeing already."

"Good work." On his knees Jakob clumped to their shit bucket, took off the lid, reached in. He pulled something out. Oliver marveled at how clearly he was able to see all this. Before, floating blobs of color had drifted in the black; but he had always assumed they were afterimages, or hallucinations. Only with Jakob's instruction had he been able to perceive the patterns they made, the vision that they constituted. It was an act of will. That was the key.

Now, as Jakob cleaned the object with his urine and spit, Oliver found that the eye in his forehead saw even more, in sharp blood etchings. Jakob held the lump overhead, and it seemed it was a little lamp, pouring light over them in a wavelength they had always been able to see, but had never needed before. By its faint ghostly radiance the whole pen was made clear, a structure etched in blood, redblack on black. "Promethium," Jakob breathed. The miners crowded around him, faces lifted to it. Solly had a little pug nose, and squinched his face terribly in the effort to focus. Hester had a face to go with her voice, stark bones under skin scored with lines. "The most precious element. On Earth our masters rule by it. All their civilization is based on it, on the movement inside it, electrons escaping their shells and crashing into neutrons, giving off heat and more blue as well. So they condemn us to a life of pulling it out of the moon for them."

He chipped at the chunk with a thumbnail. They all knew precisely its clayey texture, its heaviness, the dull silvery gray of it, which pulsed green under some lasers, blue under others. Jakob gave each of them a sliver of it. "Take it between two molars and crush hard. Then swallow."

"It's poison, isn't it?" said Solly.

"After years and years." The big laugh, filling the black. "We don't have years and years, you know that. And in the short run it helps your vision in the black. It strengthens the will."

Oliver put the soft heavy sliver between his teeth, chomped down, felt the metallic jolt, swallowed. It throbbed in him. He could see the others' faces, the mesh of the pen walls, the pens farther down the concourse, the robot tracks—all in the lightless black.

"Promethium is the moon's living substance," Jakob said quietly. "We walk in the nerves of the moon, tearing them out under the lash of the foremen. The shafts are a map of where the neurons used to be. As they drag the moon's mind out by its roots, to take it back to Earth and use it for their own enrichment, the lunar consciousness fills us and we become its mind ourselves, to save it from extinction."

They joined hands: Solly, Hester, Jakob and Oliver. The surge of energy passed through them, leaving a sweet afterglow.

Then they lay down on their rock bed, and Jakob told them tales of his home, of the Pacific dockyards, of the cliffs and wind and waves, and the way the sun's light lay on it all. Of the jazz in the bars, and how trumpet and clarinet could cross each other. "How do you remember?" Solly asked plaintively. "They turned me blank."

Jakob laughed hard. "I fell on my mother's knitting needles when I was a boy, and one went right up my nose. Chopped the hippocampus in two. So all my life my brain has been storing what memories it can somewhere else. They burned a dead part of me, and left the living memory intact."

"Did it hurt?" Hester croaked.

"The needles? You bet. A flash like the foremen's prods, right there in the center of me. I suppose the moon feels the same pain, when we mine her. But I'm grateful now, because it opened my third eye right at that moment. Ever since then I've seen with it. And down here, without our third eye it's nothing but the black."

Oliver nodded, remembering.

"And something out there," croaked Hester.

Next shift start Oliver was keyed by a foreman, then made his way through the dark to the end of the long, slender vein of blue he was working. Oliver was a tall youth, and some of the shaft was low; no time had been wasted smoothing out the vein's irregular shape. He had to crawl between the narrow tracks bolted to the rocky uneven floor, scraping through some gaps as if working through a great twisted intestine.

At the shaft head he turned on the robot, a long low-slung metal box on wheels. He activated the laser drill, which faintly lit the exposed surface of the blue, blinding him for some time. When he regained a certain visual equilibrium—mostly by ignoring the weird illumination of the drill beam—he typed instructions into the robot, and went to work drilling into the face, then guiding the robot's scoop and hoist to the broken pieces of blue. When the big chunks were in the ore cars behind the robot, he jackhammered loose any fragments of the ore that adhered to the basalt walls, and added them to the cars before sending them off.

This vein was tapering down, becoming a mere tendril in the lunar body, and there was less and less room to work in. Soon the robot would be too big for the shaft, and they would have to bore through basalt; they would follow the tendril to its very end, hoping for a bole or a fan.

At first Oliver didn't much mind the shift's work. But IR-directed cameras on the robot surveyed him as well as the shaft face, and occasional shocks from its prod reminded him to keep hustling. And in the heat and bad air, as he grew ever more famished, it soon enough became the usual desperate, painful struggle to keep to the required pace.

Time disappeared into that zone of endless agony that was the latter part of a shift. Then he heard the distant klaxon of shift's end, echoing down the shaft like a cry in a dream. He turned the key in the robot and was plunged into noiseless black, the pure absolute of Nonbeing. Too tired to try opening his third eye, Oliver started back up the shaft by feel, following the last ore car of the shift. It rolled quickly ahead of him and was gone.

In the new silence distant mechanical noises were like creaks in the rock. He measured out the shift's work, having marked its beginning on the shaft floor: eighty-nine lengths of his body. Average.

It took a long time to get back to the junction with the shaft above his. Here there was a confluence of veins and the room opened out, into an odd chamber some seven feet high, but wider than Oliver could determine in every direction. When he snapped his fingers there was no rebound at all. The usual light at the far end of the low chamber was absent. Feeling sandwiched between two endless rough planes of rock, Oliver experienced a sudden claustrophobia; there was a whole world overhead, he was buried alive. . . . He crouched and every few steps tapped one rail with his ankle, navigating blindly, a hand held forward to discover any dips in the ceiling.

He was somewhere in the middle of this space when he heard a noise behind him. He froze. Air pushed at his face. It was completely dark, completely silent. The noise squeaked behind him again: a sound like a fingernail, brushed along the banded metal of piano wire. It ran right up his spine, and he felt the hair on his forearms pull away from the dried sweat and stick straight out. He was holding his breath. Very slow footsteps were placed softly behind him, perhaps forty feet away . . . an airy snuffle, like a big nostril sniffing. For the footsteps to be so spaced out it would have to be. . . .

Oliver loosened his joints, held one arm out and the other forward, tiptoed away from the rail, at right angles to it, for twelve feathery steps. In the lunar gravity he felt he might even float. Then he sank to his knees, breathed through his nose as slowly as he could stand to. His heart knocked at the back of his throat, he was sure it was louder than his breath by far. Over that noise and the roar of blood in his ears he concentrated his hearing to the utmost pitch. Now he could hear the faint sounds of ore cars and perhaps miners and foremen, far down the tunnel that led from the far side of this chamber back to the pens. Even as faint as they were, they obscured further his chances of hearing whatever it was in the cavern with him. The footsteps had stopped. Then came another metallic *scrick* over the rail, heard against a light sniff. Oliver cowered, held his arms hard against his sides, knowing he smelled of sweat and fear. Far down the distant shaft a foreman spoke sharply. If he could reach that voice. . . . He resisted the urge to run for it, feeling sure somehow that whatever was in there with him was fast.

Another *scrick*. Oliver cringed, trying to reduce his echo profile. There was a chip of rock under his hand. He fingered it, hand shaking. His forehead throbbed and he understood it was his third eye, straining to pierce the black silence and *see*. . . .

A shape with pillar-thick legs, all in blocks of redblack. It was some sort of. . . .

Scrick. Sniff. It was turning his way. A flick of the wrist, the chip of rock skittered, hitting ceiling and then floor, back in the direction he had come from.

Very slow soft footsteps, as if the legs were somehow . . . they were coming in his direction.

He straightened and reached above him, hands scrabbling over the rough basalt. He felt a deep groove in the rock, and next to it a vertical hole. He jammed a hand in the hole, made a fist; put the fingers of the other hand along the side of the groove, and pulled himself up. The toes of his boot fit the groove, and he flattened up against the ceiling. In the lunar gravity he could stay there forever. Holding his breath.

Step . . . step . . . snuffle, fairly near the floor, which had given him the idea for this move. He couldn't turn to look. He felt something scrape the hip pocket of his pants and thought he was dead, but fear kept him frozen; and the sounds moved off into the distance of the vast chamber, without a pause.

He dropped to the ground and bolted doubled over for the far tunnel, which loomed before him redblack in the black, exuding air and faint noise. He plunged right in it, feeling one wall nick a knuckle. He took the sharp right he knew was there and threw himself down to the intersection of floor and wall. Footsteps padded by him, apparently running on the rails.

When he couldn't hold his breath any longer he breathed. Three or four minutes passed and he couldn't bear to stay still. He hurried to the intersection, turned left and slunk to the bullpen. At the checkpoint the monitor's horn squawked and a foreman blasted him with a searchlight, pawed him roughly. "Hey!" The foreman held a big chunk of blue, taken from Oliver's hip pocket. What was this? "Sorry boss," Oliver said jerkily, trying to see it properly, remembering the thing brushing him as it passed under. "Must've fallen in." He ignored the foreman's curse and blow, and fell into the pen tearful with the pain of the light, with relief at being back among the others. Every muscle in him was shaking.

But Hester never came back from that shift.

Sometime later the foremen came back into their bullpen, wielding the lights and the prods to line them up against one mesh wall. Through pinprick pupils Oliver saw just the grossest slabs of shapes, all grainy black-and-gray: Jakob was a big stout man, with a short black beard under the shaved head, and eyes that popped out, glittering even in Oliver's silhouette world.

"Miners are disappearing from your pen," the foreman said, in the miners' language. His voice was like the quartz they tunneled through occasionally: hard, and sparkly with cracks and stresses, as if it might break at any moment into a laugh or a scream.

No one answered.

Finally Jakob said, "We know."

The foreman stood before him. "They started disappearing when you arrived."

Jakob shrugged. "Not what I hear."

The foreman's searchlight was right on Jakob's face, which stood out brilliantly, as if two of the searchlights were pointed at each other. Oliver's third eye suddenly opened and gave the face substance: brown skin, heavy brows, scarred scalp. Not at all the white cutout blazing from the black shadows. "You'd better be careful, miner."

Loudly enough to be heard from neighboring pens, Jakob said, "Not my fault if something out there is eating us, boss."

The foreman struck him. Lights bounced and they all dropped to the floor for protection, presenting their backs to the boots. Rain of blows, pain of blows. Still, several pens had to have heard him.

Foremen gone. White blindness returned to black blindness, to the death velvet of their pure darkness. For a long time they lay in their own private worlds, hugging the warm rock of the floor, feeling the bruises blush. Then Jakob crawled around and squatted by each of them, placing his hands on their foreheads. "Oh yeah," he would say. "You're okay. Wake up now. Look around you." And in the after-black they stretched and stretched, quivering like dogs on a scent. The bulks in the black, the shapes they made as they moved and groaned . . . yes, it came to Oliver again, and he rubbed his face and looked around, eyes shut to help him see. "I ran into it on the way back in," he said.

They all went still. He told them what had happened.

"The blue in your pocket?"

They considered his story in silence. No one understood it.

No one spoke of Hester. Oliver found he couldn't. She had been his friend. To live without that gaunt crow's voice. . . .

Sometime later the side door slid up, and they hurried into the barn to eat. The chickens squawked as they took the eggs, the cows mooed as they milked them. The stove plates turned the slightest bit lumi-nous—redblack, again—and by their light his three eyes saw all. Solly cracked and fried eggs. Oliver went to work on his vats of cheese, pulled out a round of it that was ready. Jakob sat at the rear of one cow and laughed as it turned to butt his knee. *Splish splish! Splish splish!* When he was done he picked up the cow and put it down in front of its hay, where it chomped happily. Animal stink of them all, the many fine smells of food cutting through it. Jakob laughed at his cow, which butted his knee again as if objecting to the ridicule. "Little pig of a cow, little piglet. Mexican cows. They bred for this size, you know. On Earth the ordinary cow is as tall as Oliver, and about as big as this whole pen."

They laughed at the idea, not believing him. The buzzer cut them off, and the meal was over. Back into their pen, to lay their bodies down.

Still no talk of Hester, and Oliver found his skin crawling again as he recalled his encounter with whatever it was that sniffed through the mines. Jakob came over and asked him about it, sounding puzzled. Then he handed Oliver a rock. "Imagine this is a perfect sphere, like a baseball."

"Baseball?"

"Like a ball bearing, perfectly round and smooth you know."

Ah yes. Spherical geometry again. Trigonometry too. Oliver groaned, resisting the work. Then Jakob got him interested despite himself, in the intricacy of it all, the way it all fell together in a complex but comprehensible pattern. Sine and cosine, so clear! And the clearer it got the more he could see: the mesh of the bullpen, the network of shafts and tunnels and caverns piercing the jumbled fabric of the moon's body . . . all clear lines of redblack on black, like the metal of the stove plate as it just came visible, and all from Jakob's clear, patiently fingered, perfectly balanced equations. He could see through rock.

"Good work," Jakob said when Oliver got tired. They lay there among the others, shifting around to find hollows for their hips.

Silence of the off-shift. Muffled clanks downshaft, floor trembling at a detonation miles of rock away; ears popped as air smashed into the dead end of their tunnel, compressed to something nearly liquid for just an instant. Must have been a Boesman. Ringing silence again.

"So what is it, Jakob?" Solly asked when they could hear each other again.

"It's an element," Jakob said sleepily. "A strange kind of element, nothing else like it. Promethium. Number 61 on the periodic table. A rare earth, a lanthanide, an inner transition metal. We're finding it in veins of an ore called monazite, and in pure grains and nuggets scattered in the ore."

Impatient, almost pleading: "But what makes it so special?"

For a long time Jakob didn't answer. They could hear him thinking. Then he said, "Atoms have a nucleus, made of protons and neutrons bound together. Around this nucleus shells of electrons spin, and each shell is either full or trying to get full, to balance with the number of protons—to balance the positive and negative charges. An atom is like a human heart, you see.

"Now promethium is radioactive, which means it's out of balance, and parts of it are breaking free. But promethium never reaches its balance, because it radiates in a manner that increases its instability rather than the reverse. Promethium atoms release energy in the form of positrons, flying free when neutrons are hit by electrons. But during that impact more neutrons appear in the nucleus. Seems they're coming from nowhere. So each atom of the blue is a power loop in itself, giving off energy perpetually. Some people say that they're little white holes, every single atom of them. Burning forever at nine hundred and forty curies per gram. Bringing energy into our universe from somewhere else. Little gateways."

Solly's sigh filled the black, expressing incomprehension for all of them. "So it's poisonous?"

"It's dangerous, sure, because the positrons breaking away from it fly right through flesh like ours. Mostly they never touch a thing in us, because that's how close to phantoms we are—mostly blood, which is almost light. That's why we can see each other so well. But sometimes a beta particle will hit something small on its way through. Could mean nothing or it could kill you on the spot. Eventually it'll get us all."

Oliver fell asleep dreaming of threads of light like concentrations of the foremen's fierce flashes, passing right through him. Shifts passed in their timeless round. They ached when they woke on the warm basalt floor, they ached when they finished the long work shifts. They were hungry and often injured. None of them could say how long they had been there. None of them could say how old they were. Sometimes they lived without light other than the robots' lasers and the stove plates. Sometimes the foremen visited with their scorching lighthouse beams every off-shift, shouting questions and beating them. Apparently cows were disappearing, cylinders of air and oxygen, supplies of all sorts. None of it mattered to Oliver but the spherical geometry. He knew where he was, he could see it. The three-dimensional map in his head grew more extensive every shift. But everything else was fading away. . . .

"So it's the most powerful substance in the world," Solly said. "But why us? Why are we here?"

"You don't know?" Jakob said.

"They blanked us, remember? All that's gone."

But because of Jakob, they knew what was up there: the domed palaces on the lunar surface, the fantastic luxuries of Earth . . . when he spoke of it, in fact, a lot of Earth came back to them, and they babbled and chattered at the unexpected upwellings. Memories that deep couldn't be blanked without killing, Jakob said. And so they prevailed after all, in a way.

But there was much that had been burnt forever. And so Jakob sighed. "Yeah yeah, I remember. I just thought—well. We're here for different reasons. Some were criminals. Some complained."

"Like Hester!" They laughed.

"Yeah, I suppose that's what got her here. But a lot of us were just in the wrong place at the wrong time. Wrong politics or skin or whatever. Wrong look on your face."

"That was me, I bet," Solly said, and the others laughed at him. "Well I got a funny face, I know I do! I can feel it."

Jakob was silent for a long time. "What about you?" Oliver asked.

More silence. The rumble of a distant detonation, like muted thunder.

"I wish I knew. But I'm like you in that. I don't remember the actual arrest. They must have hit me on the head. Given me a concussion. I must have said something against the mines, I guess. And the wrong people heard me."

"Bad luck."

"Yeah. Bad luck."

More shifts passed. Oliver rigged a timepiece with two rocks, a length of detonation cord and a set of pulleys, and confirmed over time what he had come to suspect; the work shifts were getting longer. It was more and more difficult to get all the way through one, harder to stay awake for the meals and the geometry lessons during the off-shifts. The foremen came every off-shift now, blasting in with their searchlights and shouts and kicks, leaving in a swirl of after-images and pain. Solly went out one shift cursing them under his breath, and never came back. Disappeared. The foremen beat them for it and Oliver shouted with rage. "It's not our fault! There's something out there, I saw it! It's killing us!"

Then next shift his little tendril of a vein bloomed, he couldn't find any rock around the blue: a big bole. He would have to tell the foremen, start working in a crew. He dismantled his clock.

On the way back he heard the footsteps again, shuffling along slowly behind him. This time he was at the entrance to the last tunnel, the pens close behind him. He turned to stare into the darkness with his third eye, willing himself to see the thing. Whoosh of air, a sniff, a footfall on the rail. . . . Far across the thin wedge of air a beam of light flashed, making a long narrow cone of white talc. Steel tracks gleamed where the wheels of the car burnished them. Pupils shrinking like a snail's antennae, he stared back at the footsteps, saw nothing. Then, just barely, two points of red: retinas, reflecting the distant lance of light. They blinked. He bolted and ran again, reached the foremen at the checkpoint in seconds. They blinded him as he panted, passed him through and into the bullpen.

After the meal on that shift Oliver lay trembling on the floor of the bullpen and told Jakob about it. "I'm scared, Jakob. Solly, Hester, Freeman, Mute Lije, Naomi—they're all gone. Everyone I know here is gone but us."

"Free at last," Jakob said shortly. "Here, let's do your problems for tonight."

"I don't care about them."

"You have to care about them. Nothing matters unless you do. That blue is the mind of the moon being torn away, and the moon knows it. If we learn what the network says in its shapes, then the moon knows that too, and we're suffered to live."

"Not if that thing finds us!"

"You don't know. Anyway nothing to be done about it. Come on, let's do the lesson. We need it."

So they worked on equations in the dark. Both were distracted and the work went slowly; they fell asleep in the middle of it, right there on their faces.

Shifts passed. Oliver pulled a muscle in his back, and excavating the bole he had found was an agony of discomfort. When the bole was cleared it left a space like the interior of an egg, ivory and black and quite smooth, punctuated only by the bluish spots of other tendrils of monazite extending away through the basalt. They left a catwalk across the central space, with decks cut into the rock on each side, and ramps leading to each of the veins of blue; and began drilling on their own again, one man and robot team to each vein. At each shift's end Oliver rushed to get to the egg-chamber at the same time as all the others, so that he could return the rest of the way to the bullpen in a crowd. This worked well until one shift came to an end with the hoist chock-full of the ore. It took him some time to dump it into the ore car and shut down.

So he had to cross the catwalk alone, and he would be alone all the way back to the pens. Surely it was past time to move the pens closer to the shaft heads! He didn't want to do this. . . .

Halfway across the catwalk he heard a faint noise ahead of him. *Scrick; scriiiiiick.* He jerked to a stop, held the rail hard. Couldn't reach the ceiling here. Back stabbing its protest, he started to climb over the railing. He could hang from the underside.

He was right on the top of the railing when he was seized up by a number of strong cold hands. He opened his mouth to scream and his mouth was filled with wet clay. The blue. His head was held steady and his ears filled with the same stuff, so that the sounds of his own terrified sharp nasal exhalations were suddenly cut off. Promethium; it would kill him. It hurt his back to struggle on. He was being carried horizontally, ankles whipped, arms tied against his body. Then plugs of the clay were shoved up his nose and in the middle of a final paroxysm of resistance his mind fell away into the black.

The lowest whisper in the world said, "Oliver Pen Twelve." He heard the voice with his stomach. He was astonished to be alive.

"You will never be given anything again. Do you accept the charge?"

He struggled to nod. I never wanted anything! he tried to say. I only wanted a life like anyone else.

"You will have to fight for every scrap of food, every swallow of water, every breath of air. Do you accept the charge?"

I accept the charge. I welcome it.

"In the eternal night you will steal from the foremen, kill the foremen, oppose their work in every way. Do you accept the charge?"

I welcome it.

"You will live free in the mind of the moon. Will you take up this charge?"

He sat up. His mouth was clear, filled only with the sharp electric aftertaste of the blue. He saw the shapes around him: there were five of them, five people there. And suddenly he understood. Joy ballooned in him and he said, "I will. Oh, I will!"

A light appeared. Accustomed as he was either to no light or to intense blasts of it, Oliver at first didn't comprehend. He thought his third eye was rapidly gaining power. As perhaps it was. But there was also a laser drill from one of the A robots, shot at low power through a cylindrical ceramic electronic element, in a way that made the cylinder glow yellow. Blind like a fish, open-mouthed, weak eyes gaping and watering floods, he saw around him Solly, Hester, Freeman, mute Elijah, Naomi. "Yes," he said, and tried to embrace them all at once. "Oh, yes."

They were in one of the long-abandoned caverns, a flat-bottomed bole with only three tendrils extending away from it. The chamber was filled with objects Oliver was more used to identifying by feel or sound or smell: pens of cows and hens, a stack of air cylinders and suits, three ore cars, two B robots, an A robot, a pile of tracks and miscellaneous gear. He walked through it all slowly, Hester at his side. She was gaunt as ever, her skin as dark as the shadows; it sucked up the weak light from the ceramic tube and gave it back only in little points and lines. "Why didn't you tell me?"

"It was the same for all of us. This is the way."

"And Naomi?"

"The same for her too; but when she agreed to it, she found herself alone."

Then it was Jakob, he thought suddenly. "Where's Jakob?"

Rasped: "He's coming, we think."

Oliver nodded, thought about it. "Was it you, then, following me those times? Why didn't you speak?"

"That wasn't us," Hester said when he explained what had happened. She cawed a laugh. "That was something else, still out there. . . ."

Then Jakob stood before them, making them both jump. They shouted and the others all came running, pressed into a mass together. Jakob laughed. "All here now," he said. "Turn that light off. We don't need it."

And they didn't. Laser shut down, ceramic cooled, they could still see: they could see right into each other, red shapes in the black, radiating joy. Everything in the little chamber was quite distinct, quite *visible.*

"We are the mind of the moon."

Without shifts to mark the passage of time Oliver found he could not judge it at all. They worked hard, and they were constantly on the move: always up, through level after level of the mine. "Like shells of the atom, and we're that particle, busted loose and on its way out." They ate when they were famished, slept when they had to. Most of the time they worked, either bringing down shafts behind them, or dismantling depots and stealing everything Jakob designated theirs. A few times they ambushed gangs of foremen, killing them with laser cutters and stripping them of valuables; but on Jakob's orders they avoided contact with foremen when they could. He wanted only material. After a long time—twenty sleeps at least—they had six ore cars of it, all trailing an A robot up long-abandoned and empty shafts, where they had to lay the track ahead of them and pull it out behind, as fast as they could move. Among other items Jakob had an insatiable hunger for explosives; he couldn't get enough of them.

It got harder to avoid the foremen, who were now heavily armed, and on their guard. Perhaps even searching for them, it was hard to tell. But they searched with their lighthouse beams on full power, to stay out of ambush: it was easy to see them at a distance, draw them off, lose them in dead ends, detonate mines under them. All the while the little band moved up, rising by infinitely long detours toward the front side of the moon. The rock around them cooled. The air circulated more strongly, until it was a constant wind. Through the seismometers they could hear from far below the rumbling of cars, heavy machinery, detonations. "Oh they're after us all right," Jakob said. "They're running scared."

He was happy with the booty they had accumulated, which included a great number of cylinders of compressed air and pure oxygen. Also vacuum suits for all of them, and a lot more explosives, including ten Boesmans, which were much too big for any ordinary mining. "We're getting close," Jakob said as they ate and drank, then tended the cows and hens. As they lay down to sleep by the cars he would talk to them about their work. Each of them had various jobs: mute Elijah was in charge of their supplies, Solly of the robot, Hester of the seismography. Naomi and Freeman were learning demolition, and were in some undefined sense Jakob's lieutenants. Oliver kept working at his navigation. They had found charts of the tunnel systems in their area, and Oliver was memorizing them, so that he would know at each moment exactly where they were. He found he could do it remarkably well; each time they ventured on he knew where the forks would come, where they would lead. Always upward.

But the pursuit was getting hotter. It seemed there were foremen everywhere, patrolling the shafts in search of them. "Soon they'll mine some passages and try to drive us into them," Jakob said. "It's about time we left."

"Left?" Oliver repeated.

"Left the system. Struck out on our own."

"Dig our own tunnel," Naomi said happily.

"Yes."

"To where?" Hester croaked.

Then they were rocked by an explosion that almost broke their eardrums, and the air rushed away. The rock around them trembled, creaked, groaned, cracked, and down the tunnel the ceiling collapsed, shoving dust toward them in a roaring *whoosh!* "A Boesman!" Solly cried.

Jakob laughed out loud. They were all scrambling into their vacuum suits as fast as they could. "Time to leave!" he cried, maneuvering their A robot against the side of the chamber. He put one of their Boesmans against the wall and set the timer. "Okay," he said over the suit's intercom. "Now we got to mine like we never mined before. To the surface!"

The first task was to get far enough away from the Boesman that they wouldn't be killed when it went off. They were now drilling a narrow tunnel and moving the loosened rock behind them to fill up the hole as they passed through it; this loose fill would fly like bullets down a rifle barrel when the Boesman went off. So they made three abrupt turns at acute angles to stop the fill's movement, and then drilled away from the area as fast as they could. Naomi and Jakob were confident that the explosion of the Boesman would shatter the surrounding rock to such an extent that it would never be possible for anyone to locate the starting point for their tunnel.

"Hopefully they'll think we did ourselves in," Naomi said, "either on purpose or by accident." Oliver enjoyed hearing her light laugh, her clear voice that was so pure and musical compared to Hester's croaking. He had never known Naomi well before, but now he admired her grace and power, her pulsing energy; she worked harder than Jakob, even. Harder than any of them.

A few shifts into their new life Naomi checked the detonator timer she kept on a cord around her neck. "It should be going off soon. Someone go try and keep the cows and chickens calmed down." But Solly had just reached the cows' pen when the Boesman went off. They were all sledgehammered by the blast, which was louder than a mere explosion, something more basic and fundamental: the violent smash of a whole world shutting the door on them. Deafened, bruised, they staggered up and checked each other for serious injuries, then pacified the cows, whose terrified moos they felt in their hands rather than actually heard. The structural integrity of their tunnel seemed okay; they were in an old flow of the mantle's convection current, now cooled to stasis, and it was plastic enough to take such a blast without shattering. Perfect miners' rock, protecting them like a mother. They lifted up the cows and set them upright on the bottom of the ore car that had been made into the barn. Freeman hurried back down the tunnel to see how the rear of it looked. When he came back their hearing was returning, and through the ringing that would persist for several shifts he shouted, "It's walled off good! Fused!"

So they were in a little tunnel of their own. They fell together in a clump, hugging each other and shouting. "Free at last!" Jakob roared, booming out a laugh louder than anything Oliver had ever heard from him. Then they settled down to the task of turning on an air cylinder and recycler, and regulating their gas exchange.

They soon settled into a routine that moved their tunnel forward as quickly and quietly as possible. One of them operated the robot, digging as narrow a shaft as they could possibly work in. This person used only laser drills unless confronted with extremely hard rock, when it was judged worth the risk to set off small explosions, timed by seismometer to follow closely other detonations back in the mines; Jakob and Naomi hoped that the complex interior of the moon would prevent any listeners from noticing that their explosion was anything more than an echo of the mining blast.

Three of them dealt with the rock freed by the robot's drilling, moving it from the front of the tunnel to its rear, and at intervals pulling up the cars' tracks and bringing them forward. The placement of the loose rock was a serious matter, because if it displaced much more volume than it had at the front of the tunnel, they would eventually fill in all the open space they had; this was the classic problem of the "creeping worm" tunnel. It was necessary to pack the blocks into the space at the rear with an absolute minimum of gaps, in exactly the way they had been cut, like pieces of a puzzle; they all got very good at the craft of this, losing only a few inches of open space in every mile they dug. This work was the hardest both physically and mentally, and each shift of it left Oliver more tired than he had ever been while mining. Because the truth was all of them were working at full speed, and for the middle team it meant almost running, back and forth, back and forth, back and forth. . . . Their little bit of open tunnel was only some sixty yards long, but after a while on the midshift it seemed like five hundred.

The three people not working on the rock tended the air and the livestock, ate, helped out with large blocks and the like, and snatched some sleep. They rotated one at a time through the three stations, and worked one shift (timed by detonator timer) at each post. It made for a routine so mesmerizing in its exhaustiveness that Oliver found it very hard to do his calculations of their position in his shift off. "You've got to keep at it," Jakob told him as he ran back from the robot to help the calculating. "It's not just anywhere we want to come up, but right under the domed city of Selene, next to the rocket rails. To do that we'll need some good navigation. We get that and we'll come up right in the middle of the masters who have gotten rich from selling the blue to Earth, and that will be a very gratifying thing I assure you."

So Oliver would work on it until he slept. Actually it was relatively easy; he knew where they had been in the moon when they struck out on their own, and Jakob had given him the surface coordinates for Selene: so it was just a matter of dead reckoning.

It was even possible to calculate their average speed, and therefore when they could expect to reach the surface. That could be checked against the rate of depletion of their fixed resources—air, water lost in the recycler, and food for the livestock. It took a few shifts of consultation with mute Elijah to determine all the factors reliably, and after that it was a simple matter of arithmetic.

When Oliver and Elijah completed these calculations they called Jakob over and explained what they had done.

"Good work," Jakob said. "I should have thought of that."

"But look," Oliver said, "we've got enough air and water, and the robot's power pack is ten times what we'll need—same with explosives—it's only food is a problem. I don't know if we've got enough hay for the cows."

Jakob nodded as he looked over Oliver's shoulder and examined their figures. "We'll have to kill and eat the cows one by one. That'll feed us and cut down on the amount of hay we need, at the same time."

"Eat the cows?" Oliver was stunned.

"Sure! They're meat! People on Earth eat them all the time!"

"Well. . . ." Oliver was doubtful, but under the lash of Hester's bitter laughter he didn't say any more.

Still, Jakob and Freeman and Naomi decided it would be best if they stepped up the pace a little bit, to provide them with more of a margin for error. They shifted two people to the shaft face and supplemented the robot's continuous drilling with hand drill work around the sides of the tunnel, and ate on the run while moving blocks to the back, and slept as little as they could. They were making miles on every shift.

The rock they wormed through began to change in character. The hard, dark, unbroken basalt gave way to lighter rock that was sometimes dangerously fractured. "Anorthosite," Jakob said. "We're reaching the crust." After that every shift brought them through a new zone of rock. Once they tunneled through great layers of calcium feldspar striped with basalt intrusions, so that it looked like badly made brick. Another time they blasted their way through a wall of jaspar as hard as steel. Only once did they pass through a vein of the blue; when they did it occurred to Oliver that his whole conception of the moon's composition had been warped by their mining. He had thought the moon was bursting with promethium, but as they dug across the narrow vein he realized it was uncommon, a loose net of threads in the great lunar body.

As they left the vein behind, Solly picked up a piece of the ore and stared at it curiously, lower eyes shut, face contorted as he struggled to focus his third eye. Suddenly he dashed the chunk to the ground, turned and marched to the head of their tunnel, attacked it with a drill. "I've given my whole life to the blue," he said, voice thick. "And what is it but a Goddamned rock."

Jakob laughed shortly. They tunneled on, away from the precious metal that now represented to them only a softer material to dig through. "Pick up the pace!" Jakob cried, slapping Solly on the back and leaping over the blocks beside the robot. "This rock has melted and melted again, changing over eons to the stones we see. Metamorphosis," he chanted, stretching the word out, lingering on the syllable *mor* until the word became a kind of song. "Meta*mor*phosis. Meta-*mor*-pho-sis." Naomi and Hester took up the chant, and mute Elijah tapped his drill against the robot in double time. Jakob chanted over it. "Soon we will come to the city of the masters, the domes of Xanadu with their glass and fruit and steaming pools, and their vases and sports and their fine aged wines. And then there will be a—"

"Meta*mor*phosis."

And they tunneled ever faster.

Sitting in the sleeping car, chewing on a cheese, Oliver regarded the bulk of Jakob lying beside him. Jakob breathed deeply, very tired, almost asleep. "How do you know about the domes?" Oliver asked him softly. "How do you know all the things that you know?"

"Don't know," Jakob muttered. "Everyone knows. Less they burn your brain. Put you in a hole to live out your life. I don't know much, boy. Make most of it up. Love of a moon. Whatever we need. . . ." And he slept.

* * *

They came up through a layer of marble—white marble all laced with quartz, so that it gleamed and sparkled in their lightless sight, and made them feel as though they dug through stone made of their cows' good milk, mixed with water like diamonds. This went on for a long time, until it filled them up and they became intoxicated with its smooth muscly texture, with the sparks of light lazing out of it. "I remember once we went to see a jazz band," Jakob said to all of them. Puffing as he ran the white rock along the cars to the rear, stacked it ever so carefully. "It was in Richmond among all the docks and refineries and giant oil tanks and we were so drunk we kept getting lost. But finally we found it—huh!—and it was just this broken-down trumpeter and a back line. He played sitting in a chair and you could just see in his face that his life had been a tough scuffle. His hat covered his whole household. And trumpet is a young man's instrument, too, it tears your lip to tatters. So we sat down to drink not expecting a thing, and they started up the last song of a set. 'Bucket's Got a Hole in It.' Four bar blues, as simple as a song can get."

"Meta*mor*phosis," rasped Hester.

"Yeah! Like that. And this trumpeter started to play it. And they went through it over and over and over. Huh! They must have done it a hundred times. Two hundred times. And sure enough this trumpeter was playing low and half the time in his hat, using all the tricks a broken-down trumpeter uses to save his lip, to hide the fact that it went west thirty years before. But after a while that didn't matter, because he was playing. He was playing! Everything he had learned in all his life, all the music and all the sorry rest of it, all that was jammed into the poor old 'Bucket' and by God it was mind over matter time, because that old song began to *roll*." And still on the run he broke into it:

"Oh the buck-et's
got a hole in it—

Yeah the buck-et's
got a hole in it—

Say the buck-et's got a hole in it—

Can't buy

no beer!"

And over again. Oliver, Solly, Freeman, Hester, Naomi—they couldn't help laughing. What Jakob came up with out of his unburnt past! Mute Elijah banged a car wall happily, then squeezed the udder of a cow between one verse and the next— "Can't buy no beer!— *Moo!*"

They all joined in, breathing or singing it. It fit the pace of their work perfectly: fast but not too fast, regular, repetitive, simple, endless. All the syllables got the same length, a bit syncopated, except "hole," which was stretched out, and "can't buy no beer," which was high and all stretched out, stretched into a great shout of triumph, which was crazy since what it was saying was bad news, or should have been. But the song made it a cry of joy, and every time it rolled around they sang it louder, more stretched out. Jakob scatted up and down and around the tune, and Hester found all kinds of higher harmonics in a voice like a saw cutting steel, and the old tune rocked over and over and over and over and over and over and over and over and over and over, in a great passacaglia, in the crucible where all poverty is wrenched to delight: the blues. Meta*mor*phosis. They sang it continuously for two shifts running, until they were all completely hypnotized by it; and then frequently, for long spells, for the rest of their time together.

It was sheer bad luck that they broke into a shaft from below, and that the shaft was filled with armed foremen; and worse luck that Jakob was working the robot, so that he was the first to leap out firing his hand drill like a weapon, and the only one to get struck by return fire before Naomi threw a knotchopper past him and blew the foremen to shreds. They got him on a car and rolled the robot back and pulled up the track and cut off in a new direction, leaving another Boesman behind to destroy evidence of their passing.

So they were all racing around with the blood and stuff still covering them and the cows mooing in distress and Jakob breathing through clenched teeth in double time, and only Hester and Oliver could sit in the car with him and try to tend him, ripping away the pants from a leg that was all cut up. Hester took a hand drill to cauterize the wounds that were bleeding hard, but Jakob shook his head at her, neck muscles bulging out. "Got the big artery inside of the thigh," he said through his teeth.

Hester hissed. "Come here," she croaked at Solly and the rest. "Stop that and come here!"

They were in a mass of broken quartz, the fractured clear crystals all pink with oxidation. The robot continued drilling away, the air cylinder hissed, the cows mooed. Jakob's breathing was harsh and somehow all of them were also breathing in the same way, irregularly, too fast; so that as his breathing slowed and calmed, theirs did too. He was lying back in the sleeping car, on a bed of hay, staring up at the fractured sparkling quartz ceiling of their tunnel, as if he could see far into it. "All these different kinds of rock," he said, his voice filled with wonder and pain. "You see, the moon itself was the world, once upon a time, and the Earth its moon; but there was an impact, and everything changed."

They cut a small side passage in the quartz and left Jakob there, so that when they filled in their tunnel as they moved on he was left behind, in his own deep crypt. And from then on the moon for them was only his big tomb, rolling through space till the sun itself died, as he had said it someday would.

Oliver got them back on a course, feeling radically uncertain of his navigational calculations now that Jakob was not there to nod over his shoulder to approve them. Dully he gave Naomi and Freeman the coordinates for Selene. "But what will we do when we get there?" Jakob had never actually made that clear. Find the leaders of the city, demand justice for the miners? Kill them? Get to the rockets of the great magnetic rail accelerators, and hijack one to Earth? Try to slip unnoticed into the populace?

"You leave that to us," Naomi said. "Just get us there." And he saw a light in Naomi's and Freeman's eyes that hadn't been there before. It reminded him of the thing that had chased him in the dark, the thing that even Jakob hadn't been able to explain; it frightened him.

So he set the course and they tunneled on as fast as they ever had. They never sang and they rarely talked; they threw themselves at the rock, hurt themselves in the effort, returned to attack it more fiercely than before. When he could not stave off sleep Oliver lay down on

Jakob's dried blood, and bitterness filled him like a block of the anorthosite they wrestled with.

They were running out of hay. They killed a cow, ate its roasted flesh. The water recycler's filters were clogging, and their water smelled of urine. Hester listened to the seismometer as often as she could now, and she thought they were being pursued. But she also thought they were approaching Selene's underside.

Naomi laughed, but it wasn't like her old laugh. "You got us there, Oliver. Good work."

Oliver bit back a cry.

"Is it big?" Solly asked.

Hester shook her head. "Doesn't sound like it. Maybe twice the diameter of the Great Bole, not more."

"Good," Freeman said, looking at Naomi.

"But what will we do?" Oliver said.

Hester and Naomi and Freeman and Solly all turned to look at him, eyes blazing like twelve chunks of pure promethium. "We've got eight Boesmans left," Freeman said in a low voice. "All the rest of the explosives add up to a couple more. I'm going to set them just right. It'll be my best work ever, my masterpiece. And we'll blow Selene right off into space."

It took them ten shifts to get all the Boesmans placed to Freeman's and Naomi's satisfaction, and then another three to get far enough down and to one side to be protected from the shock of the blast, which luckily for them was directly upward against something that would give, and therefore would have less recoil.

Finally they were set, and they sat in the sleeping car in a circle of six, around the pile of components that sat under the master detonator. For a long time they just sat there cross-legged, breathing slowly and staring at it. Staring at each other, in the dark, in perfect redblack clarity. Then Naomi put both arms out, placed her hands carefully on the detonator's button. Mute Elijah put his hands on hers—then Freeman, Hester, Solly, finally Oliver—just in the order that Jakob had taken them. Oliver hesitated, feeling the flesh and bone under his hands, the warmth of his companions. He felt they should say something but he didn't know what it was.

"Seven," Hester croaked suddenly.

"Six," Freeman said.

Elijah blew air through his teeth, hard.

"Four," said Naomi.

"Three!" Solly cried.

"Two," Oliver said.

And they all waited a beat, swallowing hard, waiting for the moon and the man in the moon to speak to them. Then they pressed down on the button. They smashed at it with their fists, hit it so violently they scarcely felt the shock of the explosion.

They had put on vacuum suits and were breathing pure oxygen as they came up the last tunnel, clearing it of rubble. A great number of other shafts were revealed as they moved into the huge conical cavity left by the Boesmans; tunnels snaked away from the cavity in all directions, so that they had sudden long vistas of blasted tubes extending off into the depths of the moon they had come out of. And at the top of the cavity, struggling over its broken edge, over the rounded wall of a new crater. . . .

It was black. It was not like rock. Spread across it was a spill of white points, some bright, some so faint that they disappeared into the black if you looked straight at them. There were thousands of these white points, scattered over a black dome that was not a dome. . . . And there in the middle, almost directly overhead: a blue and white ball. Big, bright, blue, distant, rounded; half of it bright as a foreman's flash, the other half just a shadow. . . . It was clearly round, a big ball in the . . . sky. In the sky.

Wordlessly they stood on the great pile of rubble ringing the edge of their hole. Half buried in the broken anorthosite were shards of clear plastic, steel struts, patches of green glass, fragments of metal, an arm, broken branches, a bit of orange ceramic. Heads back to stare at the ball in the sky, at the astonishing fact of the void, they scarcely noticed these things.

A long time passed, and none of them moved except to look around. Past the jumble of dark trash that had mostly been thrown off in a single direction, the surface of the moon was an immense expanse of white hills, as strange and glorious as the stars above. The size of it all! Oliver had never dreamed that everything could be so big.

"The blue must be promethium," Solly said, pointing up at the Earth. "They've covered the whole Earth with the blue we mined."

Their mouths hung open as they stared at it. "How far away is it?" Freeman asked. No one answered.

"There they all are," Solly said. He laughed harshly. "I wish I could blow up the Earth too!"

He walked in circles on the rubble of the crater's rim. The rocket rails, Oliver thought suddenly, must have been in the direction Freeman had sent the debris. Bad luck. The final upward sweep of them poked up out of the dark dirt and glass. Solly pointed at them. His voice was loud in Oliver's ears, it strained the intercom: "Too bad we can't fly to the Earth, and blow it up too! I wish we could!"

And mute Elijah took a few steps, leaped off the mound into the sky, took a swipe with one hand at the blue ball. They laughed at him. "Almost got it, didn't you!" Freeman and Solly tried themselves, and then they all did: taking quick runs, leaping, flying slowly up through space, for five or six or seven seconds, making a grab at the sky overhead, floating back down as if in a dream, to land in a tumble, and try it again. . . . It felt wonderful to hang up there at the top of the leap, free in the vacuum, free of gravity and everything else, for just that instant.

After a while they sat down on the new crater's rim, covered with white dust and black dirt. Oliver sat on the very edge of the crater, legs over the edge, so that he could see back down into their sublunar world, at the same time that he looked up into the sky. Three eyes were not enough to judge such immensities. His heart pounded, he felt too intoxicated to move anymore. Tired, drunk. The intercom rasped with the sounds of their breathing, which slowly calmed, fell into a rhythm together. Hester buzzed one phrase of "Bucket" and they laughed softly. They lay back on the rubble, all but Oliver, and stared up into the dizzy reaches of the universe, the velvet black of infinity. Oliver sat with elbows on knees, watched the white hills glowing under the black sky. They were lit by earthlight—earthlight and starlight. The white mountains on the horizon were as sharp-edged as the shards of dome glass sticking out of the rock. And all the time the Earth looked down at him. It was all too fantastic to believe. He drank it in like oxygen, felt it filling him up, expanding in his chest.

"What do you think they'll do with us when they get here?" Solly asked.

"Kill us," Hester croaked.

"Or put us back to work," Naomi added.

Oliver laughed. Whatever happened, it was impossible in that moment to care. For above them a milky spill of stars lay thrown across the infinite black sky, lighting a million better worlds; while just over their heads the Earth glowed like a fine blue lamp; and under their feet rolled the white hills of the happy moon, holed like a great cheese.

Zürich

When we were getting ready to leave Zürich I decided to try to leave our apartment as clean as it had been when we moved into it two years before. An employee of the Federal Institute of Technology, owners of the building, would be coming by to inspect the place, and these inspections were legendary among the foreign residents living in the building: they were tough. I wanted to be the first *Ausländer* to make an impression on the inspector.

Certainly this wasn't going to be easy; the apartment's walls were white, the tables were white, the bookcases and wardrobes and bedtables and dressers and bedframes were white. The sheets and towels and dishes were white. In short practically every surface in the place was white, except for the floors, which were a fine blond hardwood. But I was getting good at cleaning the apartment, and having lived in Switzerland for two years, I had a general idea what to expect from the inspection. I knew the standard that would be applied. My soul rose to the challenge, and defiantly I swore that I was going to leave the place *immaculate*.

Soon I realized how difficult this was going to be. Every scuff from a muddy shoe, every drip of coffee, every sweaty palm, every exhalation of breath had left its mark. Lisa and I had lived here in our marvelous domestic chaos, and the damage proved it. We had put up pictures and there were holes in the walls. We had never dusted under the beds. The previous tenant had gotten away with things, having moved out in a hurry. It was going to be difficult.

Immediately it was obvious to me that the oven was going to be the crux of the problem. You see, once we went over to some American friends to have a home-like barbeque, and the grill was out on the balcony up on the fifth floor in the town of Dübendorf, looking out at all the other apartment blocks, the fine smell of barbequed chicken and hamburger spiralling out into the humid summer sky—when there was the howl of sirens below, and a whole fleet of fire engines docked and scores of firemen leaped out—all to combat our barbeque. One of the neighbors had called the police to report a fire on our balcony. We explained to the firemen and they nodded, staring coldly at the clouds of thick smoke filling the sky, and suddenly it seemed to us all that a barbeque was a very messy thing indeed.

So I never bought a grill for the balcony of our apartment. Instead I broiled our teriyaki shish-kebob in the oven, and it tasted all right. We use a fine teriyaki sauce, my mother got the recipe out of a magazine years ago; but it calls for brown sugar, and this was the source of the problem. When heated, the liquefied brown sugar caramelizes, as Lisa and her chemist colleagues are wont to say; and so on every interior surface of the oven there were little brown dots that refused to come off. They laughed at Easy Off, they laughed at Johnson and Johnson's Force. I began to understand that caramelization is a process somewhat like ceramic bonding. I needed a laser, and only had steel wool. So I began to rub.

It was a race between the flesh of my fingertips and the brown ceramic dots; which would the steel wool remove first? Flesh, of course; but it grows back, while the dots didn't. Only the miracle of regeneration allowed me to win this titanic battle. Over the course of the next two days (and imagine spending fifteen hours staring into a two-foot cube!) I muscled off every single dot, hour by hour become more and more enraged at the stubbornness of my foe.

Eventually the victory was mine; the oven was clean, a sparkling box of gray-black metal. It would pass the inspection. I stalked through the apartment in an ecstasy of rage, promising similar treatment for every other surface in the place.

I attacked the rest of the kitchen. Food had suffused into every nook and cranny, it was true; but none of it had caramelized. Stains disappeared with a single wipe, I was Mr. Clean, my soul was pure and my hands all-powerful. I put Beethoven on the stereo, those parts of his work that represent the mad blind energy of the universe: the *Grosse Fugue,* the second movement of the Ninth, the finale of the Seventh, and of the *Hammerklavier.* I was another manifestation of this mad blind energy, cleaning in a dance, propelled also by the complex and frenetic music of Charlie Parker, of Yes, "Salt Peanuts" and "Perpetual Change." And soon enough the kitchen gleamed like a factory display model. It would pass the inspection.

The other rooms offered feeble resistance. Dust, what was it to me now? "I am the mad blind energy of the universe, I vacuum under the beds!" Cleaning lint from the vacuum I sliced the very tip of my right forefinger off, and for a while it was hard not to get blood on the walls. But that was the most resistance these rooms could offer. Soon they shone with a burnished glow.

Now, inspired, I decided to get *really* thorough. It was time for details. I had been going to leave the floors alone, as they appeared clean enough to pass; but now with everything else so clean I noticed that there were little dark marks around the doorways, little dips in the grain of the wood where dirt had managed to insinuate itself. I bought some wood polish and went to work on the floors, and when I was done it was like walking on ice.

I dusted off the tops of the bookcases, up near the ceiling. I put spackle in the nail holes in the walls. When I was done the walls were all smooth, but it seemed to me that I could see a little discoloration where the spackle had gone. A few moments' pacing and inspiration struck: I got some typewriter White-Out from our boxes, and used it as touch-up paint. It really worked well. Nicks in doorways, a place where the wall was scraped by a chair back; typewriter White-Out, perfect.

In the evenings during this week of cleaning frenzy, I sat with friends, drinking and feeling my hands throb. One night I overheard by chance an Israeli friend tell a story about a Swiss friend of hers who had unscrewed the frames on her double-paned windows, to clean the inside surfaces. I shot up in my chair, mouth hanging open; I had noticed dust on the inner sides of our double-paned windows that very afternoon, and figured it was something I wouldn't be able to do anything about. It never would have occurred to me to unscrew the frames! But the Swiss know about these things. The next day I got out a screwdriver, and unscrewed and polished until my wrists were liked cooked spaghetti. And the windows sparkled from all four surfaces. They would pass the inspection.

On the morning of Inspection Day I walked through the big rooms of the apartment, with their tan leather chairs and couches, and the white walls and bookcases, and the sun streamed in and I stood there transfixed as if in the dream of a cognac advertisement, in air like mineral water.

Glancing at the long mirror in the foyer something caught my eye; I frowned; I walked up to it, feeling uneasy as I often do around mirrors, and looked at it closely. Sure enough, some dust. I had forgotten to clean the mirror. As I went to work on it I marvelled: you can see the difference between a dusty mirror and a clean one, even when—staring at the paper towel in my hand—there is only enough dust to make a thin short line, like a faint pencil mark. So little dust, distributed over such a large surface—and yet we still can see it. The eye is that powerful. If we can see that, I thought, why not ourselves? Why not everything?

So I strode around the cognac advertisement in a state of rapture; until I remembered the sheets, down in the washing machine. All would have been well, if not for the sheets. All through the week I had been washing those sheets, downstairs in the basement. Red plastic laundry basket filled with linen: we had seven bottom sheets, seven pillow cases, seven big duvet cases. The duvets were fine, as white as cotton. But the bottom sheets, the pillow cases. . . . Well. They were yellowed. Stained. Alarming evidence of our bodies, our physical existence: oils, fluids, minuscule scraps of us rubbed into the cloth like butter, ineradicably.

Certainly, I thought, the Swiss must have methods for dealing with evidence as serious as this. So I had gone out and bought bleaches. Recalling the bleach ads from back home, I trustfully assumed that the stained linen would emerge from one trip through the wash gleaming like lightning. But it wasn't so. Wash after wash did nothing to change their color. I went out and bought a different kind of bleach, then another. Two powders, one liquid. I upped the doses on each of them. Nothing worked.

And now it was the morning of Inspection Day, and I had recalled the sheets in the basement, and my rapture was shattered. I hurried down stairs, walked down the long concrete underground hallway to the laundry room. I saw that the building would stand for a thousand years. It would resist ten megatons. The washing machine was trilingual and as big as a truck. I brought it online, gave it its pre-run check-off for the final attempt, set my array of bleaches on top of the machine. It was the fourteenth time I had run things through this week, and I had the procedure streamlined; but this time I stopped to think. I looked at the three different kinds of bleach on top of the dryer, and I had an idea. I took the largest cap and turned it open end up, then poured in liquid bleach until the cup was half full. Then I poured in some of both of the powders.

Synergy, right? Singing a little tune in praise of the mysterious force of synergy, I took the pencil from the sign-in book and stirred the mix in the cap vigorously. It began to bubble a little, then to foam.

Only at that point did I remember my wife, the chemist, yelling at me for mixing two cleansers together in an attempt to get a bathtub clean. "If you had mixed ammonia and Ajax it would have made chloramine gas and killed you!" she had said. "*Never* mix stuff like that together!"

So I left the cap of bleaches on the dryer and ran out of the room. From the concrete hall I stared back in, sniffing carefully. Glancing down I noticed the pencil, still clenched in my hand; and the bottom half of it, the part that had stirred the bleaches, was as white as a stick of chalk. "Ho!" I exclaimed, and retreated farther up the hall. Synergy can be a powerful thing.

After some thought, and a closer inspection of the pencil, which now had a pure white eraser, I returned to the washroom. The air seemed okay. I was committed at this point, I had to meet the Swiss challenge. So I tipped the capful of bleaches carefully into the plastic opening on top of the washer, and I stuffed our yellowy bottom sheets and pillow cases inside, and I closed up the washer and punched the buttons for the hottest water available, ninety degrees centrigrade. Walking back upstairs I noticed that the very tip of my left forefinger had a white patch on it. Back in the apartment I found it wouldn't wash off. "Bleached my flesh!" I exclaimed. "That stuff is finally working the way it's supposed to."

An hour later I returned to the washroom apprehensively, hoping that the sheets had not been eaten to shreds or the like. On the contrary; when I opened the washer door there was a glare as if several camera flashes had gone off right in my face, just like in the ads; and there were the sheets, as white as new snow.

I hooted for glee, and stuffed them in the dryer. And by the time the Inspector rang the bell below, they were dried and ironed and folded and neatly stacked in the linen drawers of the bedroom wardrobe, looking like great hunks of Ivory soap.

I hummed cheerfully as I let the Inspector in. He was a young man, perhaps younger than myself. His English was excellent. He was apologetic, defensive; it was a boring task for both of us, he said, but necessary. No problem, I replied, and showed him around the place. He nodded, frowning slightly. "I must count the various items in the kitchen," he said, brandishing an inventory.

That took a long time. When he was done he shook his head disapprovingly. "There are four glasses missing, and one spoon, and the top off the tea kettle."

"That's right," I said happily. "We broke the glasses and lost the spoon, and I think we broke the tea kettle, though I can't remember." These things didn't matter, they didn't have to do with the essential challenge, which concerned not number but order; not quantity, but quality; not inventory, but cleanliness.

And the Inspector understood this too; after listening to my admission, he shook his head seriously and said, "Fine, fine; however, what about *this?*" And with a satisfied look he reached up into the the back of the top shelf of the broom closet, and held out before me a short stack of grimy kitchen towels.

In that moment I understood that the Inspector wanted dirtiness, in the same way that a policeman wants crime; it's the only thing that can make the job interesting. I stared at the kitchen towels, which I had completely forgotten. "What about them?" I said. "We never used those, I forgot they were up there." I shrugged. "The previous tenant must have done that to them."

He stared at me disbelievingly. "How did you dry your dishes?"

"We stood them in the drainer and let them dry on their own."

He shook his head, not believing that anyone would rely on such a method. I recalled the Swiss friend of ours who dried her bathtub with a towel after showering. I shrugged stubbornly; the Inspector shook his head stubbornly. He turned to look in the broom closet again, to see if there were any other forgotten treasures. Without forethought I quickly reached behind him and touched the stained kitchen towels with my bleached forefinger.

They turned white.

When the young inspector was done searching the broom closet, I said casually, "But they're not that bad, are they?" He looked at the kitchen towels and his eyebrows shot up. He regarded me suspiciously; I just shrugged, and left the kitchen. "Are you about done?" I asked. "I have to go downtown."

He prepared to leave. "We will have to see about the missing glasses," he said, voice heavy with dissatisfaction.

"And the spoon," I said. "And the tea kettle top."

He left.

I danced through the sparkling air of the empty apartment. My work was done, I had passed the inspection, my soul was pure, I was in a state of grace. Weak sunlight lanced between low clouds, and out on the balcony the air was frigid. I put on my down jacket to go into the city center, to see my Zürich one last time.

Down the old overgrown steps and through the wintry garden of the ETH, past the big building housing the Chinese graduate students. Down the steep walkway to Voltastrasse, past the Japanese fire maple and the interior design store. I touched one red rose and was not particularly surprised to see it turn white. My whole fingertip looked like paraffin now.

Down at the Voltastrasse tram stop, in the wind. Across the street the haunted house stood, a pinkish wreck with big cracks in its walls; Lisa and I had always marvelled at it, there was nothing even remotely as derelict as it anywhere in Zürich. It was an anomaly, an exile like we were, and we loved it. "I'll never touch you," I said to it.

A Number Six tram hummed down the hill from Kirche Fluntern and squealed to a halt before me. You have to touch a button to get the doors to open, so I did that and the whole tram car turned white. Usually they are blue, but there are a few trams painted different colors to advertise the city museums, and there are some painted white to advertise the Oriental museum in Rietliberg, so I assumed that this car would now be taken for one of those; and I climbed aboard.

We slid off down the hill toward Platte, ETH and Central. I sat in the back of the tram and watched the Swiss in front of me, getting on and off. Many of them were old. None of them ever sat in seats beside each other until all the seats had been filled by single parties. If single seats were vacated at a stop, people sitting next to strangers in double seats would get up and move to the single seat. No one talked, though they did look at each other a little. Mostly they looked out the windows. The windows were clean. These trams on the Number Six line had been built in 1952, but they were still in factory perfect condition; they had passed the inspection.

Looking down, I suddenly noticed that each pair of shoes on the tram was flawless. Then I noticed that each head of hair was perfectly coifed. Even the two punks on the tram had their hair perfectly done, in their own style. Shoes and hair, I thought, these will reveal the wealth of a nation. These extremes reveal the soul.

At the ETH stop a Latin American man got on the tram. He was dressed in a colorful serape, and thin black cotton pants, and he looked miserably cold. He was carrying an odd thing that looked like a bow; it was painted crudely, in many colors, and there was a small painted gourd attached to it, where you would hold the bow if it were meant to shoot arrows. The man had long lanky black hair that fell loosely over his shoulders and down the back of the serape, and his face was big and broad-cheeked; he looked like a *mestizo,* or perhaps a purebred Indian from Bolivia or Peru or Ecuador. There were quite a few of them living in Zürich, Lisa and I often saw groups of them on Bahnhofstrasse, playing music for change. Pan pipes, guitars, drums, gourds filled with beans: street music performed right through the winter, with the players and audience alike shivering in the snowy air.

When the tram started to move again, this Latino walked to the front of the car and turned around to face us all. He said something loudly in Spanish, and then began to play the bow and gourd instrument, plucking it rapidly. Moving one thumb up and down the metal bowstring changed the pitch of the sound, which reverberated in the gourd, making a kind of loud twang. The resulting sound was awful: loud, unmelodic, impossible to ignore.

The Swiss stared resentfully at this intrusion. This was not done; I had never seen it before, and neither had the others aboard, it was clear. And the sound of the primitive instrument was so insistent, so weird. The disapproval in the car was as palpable as the sound, the two vibrations battling each other in tense air.

The tram stopped at Haldenegg, and several people got off, more than would usually; clearly some were just escaping the musician, and would get on the next tram to come along. Newcomers, unpleasantly surprised, stared at the man as he twanged away. The tram doors closed and we moved off again, down the hill to Central. The captive audience stared at the musician, as belligerent as cows eyeing a passing car.

Then he broke into song. It was one of those Bolivian or Peruvian hill ballads, a sad tale dramatically told, and the man sang it over the twanging of his absurd instrument in a hoarse wild voice, expressing all the anguish of the exile, lost in a cold land. What a voice the man had! Suddenly the ridiculous twanging made sense, it all fell together; this voice in a foreign langauge cut through all the barriers and spoke to us, to each and every person on the tram. That kind of singing is impossible to ignore or deny—we knew exactly what he was feeling, and so for that moment we were a little community. And all without understanding a word. What power the voice has to express what really matters! People shifted in their seats, they sat up, they watched the singer intently, they smiled. When he walked up and down the tram, holding out a black felt hat, they dug deep in their pockets and purses and dropped change in, smiling at him and saying things in Swiss German, or even in High German so he might perhaps understand. When the doors hissed open at Central, they were surprised; no one aboard had noticed our arrival.

The Swiss! I had to laugh. So closed in, so generous. . . .

Then as each person touched the white parts of my white tram, they went white themselves. Chairback or railing or overhead support, it didn't matter; they touched the tram and left it as white as porcelain figures of themselves. And no one at Central paid any attention.

As we left the tram together, I touched the musician on the shoulder, in a sort of greeting, or an experiment. He only looked at me, eyes black as obsidian; and it seemed to me that the vivid colored thread sewn riotously into his serape actually grew more brilliant, more intensely colorful: little rainbow crosshatchings, scarlet and saffron and green and violet and pink and sky blue, glowing in crude brown woolen cloth. Without a glance back the musician walked off into the Niederdorf, Zürich's medieval town.

I crossed the bridge looking down at the white swans in the gray Limmat, feeling the wind rush through me, buoyant with the memory of his music and my apartment's purity. I walked down Bahnhofstrasse seeing it all again, seeing it fully for the first time in a long while and the last time in who knew how long, perhaps forever, and my heart filled and I said "Ah handsome Züri my town, my town, I too am one of your exiled sons," and I caressed the granite blocks of the stolid elegant buildings and they turned white as wedding cakes under my hand, with a keening sound like violins taped and played backwards. When would I ever see it again like this, with its low pearl gray sky rushing overhead in the cold wind, with the Alps at the end of the Zürichsee standing up like cardboard cutout mountains, steeper than mountains could ever be? I touched the tram tracks and they turned to white gold, in a wide street of glazed sugar. And I walked down this white street looking in the sparkling window displays of the rich merchants, the jewelry and clothing and watches all perfect and gleaming, and, as I traced my fingers over the window glass, as white as white opals.

In among the narrow alleyways of the medieval town I wandered, touching every massive building until it seemed I walked in a silent world of milk and baking soda, saying good-bye with every touch. To consciously be doing something you loved, for the last time! Past St. Peter's church which was already alabaster before I touched it, past Fraumünster and across the river to Grossmünster with its painfully spare interior, like a tall empty warehouse made entirely of white marble. . . . Then back across the river again, on a paper bridge. And looking down the gray Limmat I saw that much of Zürich had turned white, bleached by my touch.

I came to the lakefront at Burkliplatz, touched the steps and suddenly the fine little park and the boat docks gleamed like soap carvings. The beautiful statue of Ganymede and the eagle looked like they had been molded out of white ceramic, and in Ganymede's outstretched arms it seemed to me a whole world was being embraced, a rushing world of gray sky and gray water where everything passed by so fast that you never got the chance to hold it, to touch it, to make it yours. Can't we keep anything? These years of our life, we were happy, we were here, and now it was all white and clean and still, turning to marble under the touch of my hand. So that in the pure rapture of final things I walked down the white concrete ramp to the lapping lake water and crouched down and touched it; and before me I saw the whole long lake go still and turn white, as if it were an immense tub of white chocolate; and in the distance the magnificent Alps were white; and overhead the rushing clouds pulsed white and glowed like spun glass. I turned around and saw that the city's transformation was complete: it was a still and silent Zürich of snow and white marble, white chocolate, white ceramic, milk, salt, cream.

But from a distant street I could still hear that twanging.